THE HA

GOD

and

THE RAPE OF
THE ROSE

THE HAWTHORN GODDESS

and

THE RAPE OF THE ROSE

———— ✳ ————

Two Novels by

GLYN HUGHES

Chatto & Windus
LONDON

Published in 1992 by
Chatto & Windus Ltd
20 Vauxhall Bridge Road
London SW1V 2SA

The Hawthorn Goddess first published by
Chatto & Windus 1984
The Rape of the Rose first published by
Chatto & Windus 1987

The definition on p. 3 of *The Rape of the Rose*
is from *The Shorter Oxford English Dictionary* and is
reproduced by permission of Oxford University Press.

A CIP catalogue record for this book is
available from the British Library.

ISBN 0 7011 4011 9

Printed in Great Britain by
Redwood Press Ltd, Melksham, Wiltshire

THE HAWTHORN
GODDESS

Forget this rotten world; And unto thee
Let thine owne times as an old storie bee...

Look upward; that's towards her, whose happy state
We now lament not, but congratulate.
Shee, to whom all this world was but a stage,
Where all sat harkning how her youthfull age
Should be emploi'd, because in all shee did,
Some Figure of the Golden times was hid.
Who could not lacke, what ere this world could give,
Because shee was the forme, that made it live;
Nor could complaine, that this world was unfit
To be staid in, than when shee was in it;...

Shee, shee is gone; shee is gone; when thou knowest this,
What fragmentary rubbidge this world is
Thou knowest, and that it is not worth a thought;
He honors it too much that thinkes it nought...

from *The Second Anniversarie*
Of The Progresse Of The Soule

JOHN DONNE

JOHN DONNE

(1)

Through the passageways of Lady Well a mob of weavers and other
artisans, of women, children and youths, chanted at Anne Wylde,
throwing stones at her, chasing the seventeen-year-old girl (called 'the
'Awthorn Maiden') from the enclosure where she had been scything
oats for her father, a stonemason. All her pursuers looked the same.
Their common emotion and purpose transfigured them with an identical mask. It was as if looking at Anne Wylde turned them to stone.
Whilst their shouting was like the banging of hammers hitting stone:

'GOD made MAN! MAN made MONEY!
GOD made BEES, the BEES made HONEY!
GOD made the DEVIL, THE DEVIL MADE SIN –
GOD MADE A HOLE TO PUT THE DEVIL IN!'

they shouted. And,

''Awthorn, 'awthorn, burn in t'fire!'

Anne was a tall, dark, untamed, careless, *conspicuous* girl with mud
on her from scrambling about the Yorkshire hills. Her form was lean
and beautiful, her eyes exceptionally dark, her nose was sharp: all her
features were pointed, expressing her menacing (for so they thought
of it) curiosity. She was considered 'careless', because she adored
things to which other females did not lend their attention. She showed
an unwomanly love of learning, and with it an unbecoming quickness
in answering back. Partly, this was why they chased her. Her cotton
apron was smirched and frayed, she had lost her cap and her un-
combed hair writhed in thick black snakes which were described as
'intolerable'. For about her appearance she did not care, not in the
usual way. (Sometimes she dressed her hair with flowers – trefoil, and
the unlucky may.) She loved wild animals, flowers and birds, especially the skylarks, whose songs warmed gaps in the skies on spring

days. From early childhood she had nursed lame creatures. With little splints, with drips of milk, or by holding them to the warmth of her breast (the sort of attention that most of her female neighbours only gave to the pigs and calves upon which their livelihoods depended) she succeeded in bringing them back to health. She shared with all that was hunted a readiness to bolt, even when still and safe. And yet, though the child had all her life been such an animal at bay, she did not whine or show fear. On the contrary she was often annoyingly casual when reprimanded. Today, for instance (knowing that her long legs gave her an easy advantage), she found time to observe a butterfly's beauty, and then to insult her breathless persecutors with a long, contemptuous stare.

'Get out, you witch! You sinner! My uncle's cow ran dry because of you!' shouted Amos Culpin, a thin weaver embittered by the death of his wife and baby. He flushed when Anne Wylde stared at him.

'Our dog went blind last winter!' Joshua Binns, also a woollen piece-maker (married to a fair lady, but having a dark one in his heart), complained to Dick Whitely.

Whitely was the constable, the innkeeper, the owner of the slaughterhouse, an (unlicensed) preacher, and the chairman of the Society For Prosecuting Felons. He let Methodists meet in his rooms so that through preaching to them himself he could sell ale, and he was nicknamed 'Dick Almighty' - 'sin-catcher, thief-catcher, innkeeper and doctor'. A man usually of many words who at the moment could not answer, for he was overweight and had been running. His narrow, worldly-experienced lips were quivering and frothing in the largest, roundest, reddest face in Lady Well, upon it the tallest hat, bright yellow. All that was worldly was settled in beefy weight on him, and the keys of the town lockup dangled and rang from his belt. One further reason why they could not catch Anne Wylde was because no one dared to step in front of him in the chase, even though he was the slowest, windiest runner in Lady Well.

He was also a widower; and, despite his worldly windiness, his little eyes, like Binns's, like Culpin's, expressed his instinctive tender desire for the woman of his soul and imaginings; for a goddess who lurked hidden within himself, and who in reality directed his life - his foolishness and creativity, his secret ambitions as well as his public ones, his 'accidents' as well as his choices. This yearning for an inner

2

woman, as in all the other pursuers, was mixed with hatred and fear.

'I took Wylde's mad daughter t'other night!' Amos Culpin intended to whisper, but it came out loud and boastful, and he rolled his tongue with a hungry expression over his lips.

'Has she a large mole with hairs upon her stomach?' Dick Almighty panted. (But with that steady interrogating look in his eye that came when he was about to catch a rogue.)

'That she has! I saw it clear.'

'Well, thou'rt lying, for Stott took her and says she is as fair as a new mushroom!'

''Tis Stott who lies! Jabez'd never get near her, he's afraid of his own shadow!'

Jabez Stott, a carpenter's apprentice, timidly changed his mind at fear of being convicted of an untruth by Dick Almighty. 'She did have a mole, an ugly lump like th'old mound upon Raven's Hill,' he said, and bashfully struggled to appear manly.

But to Anne it seemed that there was not one *man* amongst them: not one similar to the Apollo of her imagining, whose kindly face was flown direct out of the sun, and was of shining brass, like the nameplate on a clothier's pew.

'Mole or not, she can read like a parson! There's no chance of Grace with 'er in Lady Well, and so we are inflicted with such curses as seditious nocturnal assemblies of paupers and other cheaters of innkeeper and King,' sin-catcher Whitely said, spluttering over each s.

Esther Kershaw (who almost dared to step in front of the constable) threw a stone. As always, she wore an apron stained with three drops of blood; this was because, having said that times would not mend until the 'Wylde witch' had been driven from Lady Well, she had received in her lap the drops of Christ's life-fluid which had dripped from the roof of the church. She had screamed like an owl, alarmed in the dark-time forest that was her soul. The people rushed to her, examining aghast the splotches of fresh crimson spreading upon her white apron. Then they searched Esther's nose and teeth, but found nothing except scraps of grain from her bread, shreds of greens, and oats which she had been nibbling and casting before the painting of Saint Uncumber which was on the wall of the nave. As the stains had

3

not come from her orifices, they were forced to believe that, for having abused Anne Wylde, and for telling everyone that the mason's daughter was truly the witch out of the may-tree, Esther was blessed with the sight of the shadow of Christ amongst the roof-beams.

'She should be excavated from the church!' Esther's voice was high and sharp. 'The church should excavate and whip 'er!'

'Go fuck your sheep!' the virgin yelled and set off running again, her lengthy stride making a distinctive clatter that brought others to their doors.

'You hear 'er, Amos Culprit! Dick 'Itely!' Esther shouted, 'The loud young witch should be stocked, lest she pollute all our souls on our certain road to Heaven!'

Lady Well, in the eighteenth century of *Our Lord's* reign upon earth, was populated by weavers, tradesmen and artisans, a solemn party of whom at the time of the Reformation had filled in the Well (that miraculous shrine – 'Our Mother Mary's ever-flowing womb in the ground', as the last Catholic encumbent had described it – that cured everything, warts, civil-war, childlessness and disease) and cut down the nearby hawthorn. They had thanked God afterwards, 'declaring his counsel' in a meadow, and (their diarist recorded) 'gone quietly home', there to deliberate and, upon concluding their meditations, build a commemorative workhouse. People had now forgotten the site of the Well and the tree, whilst they settled down content with their lot in the century to which they were called to live; as if to show it, they proudly had the mason, John Wylde carve the date and their initials over their lintels.

Though prosperous, the town was haunted by this loss, or by some other. The inhabitants seemed in mourning (though they did not know what for). From time to time they guiltily took consolation in some victim such as Anne Wylde; in music and dancing on the few remaining saints' days; in legitimate inns, or, if they were both poorer and more radical, in 'hush-houses', as they were called, where were brewed sedition, as well as untaxed liquor – both of these being the despair of Dick Almighty.

Lady Well had originally been made of wood in a forest clearing. Now that the hilltops had been cleared and burnt, the forest creatures vanquished and wealth manufactured, it had a heart of the local stone

4

(which was dark and gritty, but a brilliant gold if you split it open) and a crushing ravel of stone intestines in which the wind fluted and there was not a blade of grass; instead, there were those many reminders to fear God, carved over doorways, and taught also by man's experience of the fickle market.

A stone landed at Anne's feet and she put out her tongue. Swaying on her long legs, she sang a rude song, then ran again. She fled by the shops of wool-combers, carpenters, loom-repairers and other artisans. She went by the workhouse where sixty silent children, dressed in uniform gowns and under the eye of a taskmaster, were spinning coarse wool (at threepence a pound) and where the old quiet paupers were labouring in the orchard. (It was the silence of the poor that had always frightened Anne.) She passed the apothecary, who was loquaciously filling his *magic rubbing bottles*; water from the spring in his kitchen was tinctured with laudanum and with his own mysterious brown extract of herbs. 'Use it on your chest night and morning, miss! Or – madam! – take a spoonful upon judicious occasions to cure piles, rheumatic fever, or any other pains, and to excite your husband's venery. Yes, madam! – it brings children to the childless and Grace to the Godless, wi' a golden vision!' he shouted. Anne passed women who had their doors open (it being a fine day), and were spinning on their doorsteps, complaining that the huge furnaces in the wool-combers' shops caused fires; or they were discussing, more wisely than apothecaries and physicians, cures for the men and children in their hands; and now were wondering (seeing Anne Wylde flying by) when the mason's mad daughter might be subdued sufficiently to deserve being made party to female secrets.

(Men and boys were often shy of walking past. So they suffered the greater embarrassment of being laughed at; some developed a lifelong fear of women from the experience. It was assumed at the men's inns that the talk was of babies, of secret dyes for cloth, and of magic for the fidelity and potency of husbands. Yet they must endure this freemasonry of women; for spinning encouraged it, and they could not do without spun thread.)

Anne, careless, dodged by a string of packhorses, bandy-legged under rolls of cloth and waiting to labour over the hills. She went by the dilapidated church's north wall, that the witches and beggars haunted. She passed troughs overflowing with rapid glittering water, and up steep alleys that led her above the roofs to look down upon slopes of stone tiles, golden or bright green with moss, and across the deep gorges brimming with trees that surrounded Lady Well. From this height she could fling her glance across much of Yorkshire.

In its menace it was unique among landscapes. It inspired murder and madness. Sheer hillsides – a sense of the rough stone even underneath the green slopes – rose into cliffs with wind-and-rain warped rocks leaning over them that at will took on the forms of various monsters: at dawn, they were huge heads, and by evening they had turned into birds or lizards. (Or so it seemed, at least to those who had taken the apothecary's laudanum or had been drinking liquors brewed in hush-houses.)

Amongst those who now watched Anne, one was on the side of caution, thinking that something must be done to prevent the persecution; a second believed in innocence, saying, 'The Devil takes care of his own!'; a third had moral anxieties, and was for reporting to the Reverend Doubtfire; whilst a fourth was tortured by nostalgia for his own youthful pleasure in chasing witches, beggars, preachers, itinerant soldiers and other outcasts.

'There's nothing to surprise us 'bout folks wanting to hunt after her!' an old woman, spinning on her doorstep, told her grandaughter. The woman spoke with a rhythm picked up from her wheel upon which the yarn was hissing and humming. 'She is descended from Lady Sybil who changed herself into a white doe that slept under a hawthorn bush – she wished t'escape her vile suitor, Lord William, and be free for ever to roam the crags and moors. But another witch told him to go hunting on All-Hallow's Eve, and he surprised the white doe. Lord William and his dogs they chased all day upon them hills and did not catch the fair beast, until at evening they were joined by a strange hound, his witch's familiar – that soon had the animal by the throat! Lord William he attached an enchanted leash and brought the deer home and confined her in a tower where in the night during a thunderstorm she was changed back to the Lady Sybil, so he was able to lead her to altar and had many children by her, from whom the Wyldes come. It is because she is descended from a doe that she has such long legs and is always running.

'They say that after a few years Lady Sybil used to go frolicking wild on the moors again in the shape of a white cat, until a miller caught her and cut off her paw. Next morning Her Ladyship would not leave her bed. Then the miller came to the castle door with a hand which was shown to be Lady Sybil's by its fairness and the diamond rings upon it. Though it was re-joined to its proper body by magic, there was always a red ring around her wrist. Prevented from racing wild upon the hills, she pined away and died, leaving her children orphans. 'Tis a sad story.'

'Doesn't Anne Wylde want to go to Jesus?' The little granddaughter, light-haired as thistledown, stared unbelievingly at the flying 'witch', and merely breathed her words, hardly daring to disturb the air with such heresy. 'Parson Doubtfire tells us allus to pray to die and prepare for't in our sad life by being modest. Grandma, why hasn't Parson teached Anne Wylde to be modest?'

The grandmother, being asked such dangerous questions, reached for a *magic rubbing bottle*, a spoonful of which sent children to sleep.

Meanwhile Anne heard the voices of Culpin, Binns, Stott, Dick Almighty, Esther Kershaw and others coming closer, chanting with a loud heavy rhythm, as if they were a new sect of dissenters determined to dominate the town with their hymn.

'GOD MADE THE DEVIL, THE DEVIL MADE SIN,
  GOD MADE A HOLE TO PUT THE DEVIL IN!'

So off Anne set again, cursing upon her neighbours' disgusting offspring – two-headed babies, or sons with toads' legs, – that she had heard talked about amongst woolcombers, carters and soldiers returned from the wars, or amongst the tribes expelled from their distant homes because parks were being built there, and who now camped amongst moors or marshes.

Going through the shadow on the north side of the church, and then under the east window, Anne came out by the school. A fiddler and 'vagabond' known as 'Dick O'Lovely', whom Dick Almighty could never imprison or move on as he was so popular, was calmly trying a melody, tuning his strings, then plucking the air again. Because of his 'profane' tunes the Reverend Joseph Doubtfire had come out to glare from the school portal, though Dick did not seem to see him.

The Parson was a tall man with a long face and a hooked, lecherous nose. With his hands gripped tightly together, he clutched his groin as if he feared that his bag of seeds might fly away or roll to the ground. Because the fiddler smiled in a kindly way in Anne's direction, and as she smiled back, Doubtfire glared at her also.

He had first noticed Anne Wylde when she was fourteen and they had chosen her as Queen of the May. How all winter they had waited for this day! The thorn trees, so long gnarled and black that they looked as though they could never live again, in a week or two had their cragginess swallowed first in bright green, then in the consuming globe of creamy flowers. The young people had gone at midnight to the brink of the woods to light fires, and had played, touching Anne, decorating her with flowers that looked blue in the moon. When the sun rose and painted in daylight colours her cascades and wreaths of hawthorn, she still hadn't given in to them. So they attached long ribbons and led her like a captive spirit into Lady Well, where she wept a trail of petals and the warmed, wilting may-blooms gave off a strong, female smell. It was now affirmed that, like her mother, she would become pregnant with the Devil, or by a hare, goat or moorland beast. They brought her to Doubtfire expecting he would bridle, purge and put her in the stocks, or have her dressed in a white shift to confess before the congregation.

What was she truly like, 'this monster, this infant Gorgon, this Eve, this witch-terror-scourge, this curse and punishment for our sins, this profane polluted Graceless being' whom he had been led to expect? Before him had stood but a sensitive girl-child, who had a tendency to bolt, her long too-sensuous animal-legs aquiver. With her 'intolerable' locks of black hair, her suitably named *wild* look, her stance improperly proud for a female, and her unmaidenly cleverness, he could not think of her as *beautiful*, but she was definitely affecting and striking. And, though she was as certainly wicked as any other child of Eve, she was a child still – who dreamed of maypoles and of apples coated in sugar, no doubt; and yet one conspicuous and loud, who did rant too much for a woman, for her 'father' was a dissenter (a curse of this Realm!) who had taught her to read, and she in consequence lapped up knowledge as a starved mare gobbles oats. Captivated by her appearance and her cleverness, Doubtfire had been unable to punish her.

Releasing one hand, he now beckoned her. As her footsteps passed by, Dick O'Lovely played her on her way. She entered under the great porch of the school, where was carved a sun, flames writhing out of it, at its centre a round, grinning male face with underneath in weighty letters:

Rich'd Horsfall Facit. A:D: 1660. FEARE GOD

Anne was afraid, all right – both of God and also because the grammar school was a boys' empire which she had never entered before. (The domain of the Yorkshire woollen-traders' God and that of the boys' grammar school where she had been taught not to trespass being the same thing in Anne Wylde's mind.) But 'God made a hole to put the Devil in!' still pierced the alleyways.

Doubtfire addressed her with vanity and confidence: as one who knows that his opinions are well thought-out and cogent, but does not recognise how prosaic they are. 'You are too Conspicuous, Anne Wylde! Woman's flesh is the house of the Devil and must Submit to Godly men or be flogged, lest she Pollute us!' (The Parson naturally spoke with capital letters.) 'It has always been my own daily care to Crucify the lusts of the Flesh, to cut off and cast away Sins as dear to me as my right hand or eye. I have desired to be a Mourner in Zion, and to grieve for the Abominations of the place in which I dwell.'

Anne's mouth was silently open with amazement, like a simple girl's, and she was for a moment stilled.

The cheeks of the willowy, truculent priest were purple and twitching; he'd been at the brandy. Disappointed that the young witch did not answer him back, Doubtfire led her into the very interior of the forbidden building, as if he intended to instruct her further.

The boys had left an odour of leather, sweat and dust. She saw a chart of the Greek alphabet, maps of the Holy Lands, sculptured mementi mori as in church, and frightening steel engravings of exemplary deaths or martyrdoms, and also of the ruins of Italy and Hellas. There were some stinking relics of anatomical investigations into birds, animals and even humans – the Vicar's pastime. Windows showed the green summer paps of the hills, which seemed so far away, and the stocks, which were horribly close.

Doubtfire made her sit down. Her legs sprawled carelessly and the priest stared, just as other men did. How could she be resisted? – long thighs shifting eloquently beneath her grimed apron and gown, suggesting therefore also smirched behaviour, and treacherous too for a man of Doubtfire's years. Those things which wasteful youth took for granted excited with a sad useless longing a man who felt that his lusts were ugly (even had he been capable of fulfilling them) and who preached to the young that they should pray for death to come.

With drunken stumbles he closed the shutters (although the pursuers had melted away before the Vicar). '"Man that is born of woman hath a short Life full of trouble! He is born unto Trouble as the sparks fly upwards".' Whilst he misquoted his Bible he nervously played with a child's skull: pale, almost transparent, as fragile as a bird's egg, it had been washed out of its grave on a steep and stony hillside in a rainstorm. He sheared away from his thoughts, and asked, 'Is the mason at home ... have you spoken together?'

Anne nodded, and her response made him still more apprehensive – she did not understand why.

'Reading Deists and French philosophers, is he? There are such nonconforming Devils amongst us today...'

'No, for my father often foolishly forgets his proper hopes and ambitions. He is all the time now thinking of a new kind of building, to be filled wi' spinners – not paupers, but with women coming daily from the cottages. He says that in future times the weavers'll be weaving by steam. Sometimes he reads his books at night and I hear him through my sleep raking the fire, sir.'

Evidently the mason and his daughter had not talked together, and the Parson was relieved, whilst Anne felt that some secret was being kept from her.

'I am surprised that with your sins you enjoy any sleep, Anne Wylde!'

She laughed, and Doubtfire frowned as he closed another shutter: there were six of them. Before the last one he lit a candle, and inspected the wick closely, as if the poor woman who peeled rushes for candles for a living had not done her work correctly. 'Fire is so admirable a Servant but so Terrible a master! Pestilence, sword and famine do not make such outrageous Havoc. Some day you will be going as a servant, you ought therefore to be warned of the accidents which happen by Fire. Chimneys too long unswept ... great blazes in the Fireplace ... a candle brought into a hay-loft. Where the floor is grown spongy with age, a spark may fall on it. In going to bed use a short candle and a large flat candlestick, taking care to have an extinguisher. These observances regard as thy Duty to God and thy neighbour.' There was an excited gleam like a small candle-flame in Doubtfire's eye.

Anne stared thoughtfully, and not listening. Her expression had changed from that of a young woman who enticed him to that of a small child; changes typical of maidens, he thought, as a sky in spring switches between clear sky and cloud. She then asked a question which had been on her mind for a long while, whilst she baked bread alone in her father's kitchen, scythed oats or, equally alone, roamed the moors, the cliffs and the enclosures: 'Mr Doubtfire, do angels eat in Heaven?'

This was too trivial a question for a Theologian to answer. Doubtfire instead replied, 'I, too, am weighed down by Sin. Oh, I have indescribable thoughts! If you are persecuted, console yourself with how much more tormenting it is to wait until the Fires of Purgatory to be purged. We all are such terrible sinners in Lady Well, in this horrible violent district, this terrible exile from Eden, awaiting the awful Judgment!'

Doubtfire came up to the schoolmaster's desk. Impulsively, as if to do it before wiser thoughts pursued, he snatched up the birch. His hands trembling, his eyes tearful, he approached Anne in a cloud of brandied breath. She saw a pitiful, broken, pleading, sin-wrecked man. 'Oh, Anne Wylde! I am able to beat the schoolboys for their acts of Wickedness, but who is to Birch me to make me clean and whole? Oh what Sorry sons of fallen Adam we are, in need of Correction!'

His second thoughts winging near, Doubtfire hurriedly turned his back, raised his cassock and leant over his schoolmaster's whipping bench. His reddened face between his toes, he waved the bundle of birch twigs impatiently; for Anne was grasping neither his meaning nor the birches. But at last, with a child's wondering and accepting expression, she took hold of the implement, gingerly, as if it was a poker out of the fire. Doubtfire's lips dribbled, and his upside down, staring bulging eyes were like those of a calf in the slaughteryard. She cautiously tickled the naked bottom. 'Harder! Oh Anne, I have so many Sins!' Then Anne made up her mind and blindly laid it on, purging, if not him, at least herself of what she had suffered in Lady Well. She was a practical girl, with firm hands and strong limbs, and used to work.

Doubtfire groaned, 'No! ... No! ... Oh for pity!' so Anne paused, aghast at the livid red bottom streaked by her birches.

'Go on!' Doubtfire hissed. 'Don't stop now!'

Anne swung her birch twigs again, just as she was commanded. Seeing that it didn't seem to be doing the Vicar any harm, she started to enjoy it. He began to writhe and yell, with sudden fear of the pain which he himself had willed. He rolled off the bench, putting his hand out to stop her, and she obeyed. The horrible priest was now grovelling at her feet. 'Anne, oh Anne, such a weight of Sins lie upon us poor mortals! Now I feel cleansed pure and whole.'

During Anne's childhood men had once or twice stopped her in passageways and shown her their parts, yet she had not been as disgusted as she was at this moment. 'If 'tis true that it is as difficult for a rich man to enter Heaven as f'ra camel to pass through the eye of a needle, how can a bishop be admitted?' she asked. 'Do you want this punishment because if you are not treated as a beggar you are too rich to enter Heaven?'

'Yes! Yes!' Appealing eyes were turned up to her. For he was not yet satisfied. He was not at peace. She thought of King Nebuchadnezzar, condemned to crawl amongst stones and eat grass.

'I don't believe you,' Anne declared. She moved away and, with confidence now, began to unfasten shutters. She hung up the birch. Doubtfire, returning from darkness and fantasy, fastened his clothes, feeling the weals beginning to smart and swell.

'Mr Doubtfire, how can women ever go to Heaven when they are cursed because they betrayed and deceived Adam?'

'They can be forgiven in life by honestly coming to God and Jesus, conscious of their sin against man and purging themselves through submissiveness to father and husband.' He stroked himself tenderly under his gown.

'When we go to Heaven, Mr Doubtfire, do we stay the same sex as on earth ... as men and women?'

'We remain men and women, yes.'

'Then what does God do to satisfy our desires which, you tell us often, are so wrong in His sight?'

'Shame on you for speaking of them! In Hell we suffer our Lusts and are Degraded, but in Heaven we do not have Them.'

'Are we then so old there? I would like to stay young in Heaven.'

What impertinent, foolish questions the child does ask! Doubtfire thought.

'We are ageless,' he added, crossly. 'You mustn't tell anyone about This, you know. God will never forgive you.' She paused, uncertainly. He waited also; he had finished with her. 'You may go now.'

Anne walked out through the alleyways, carefully as a hare comes into the evening dew. But all her enemies had disappeared and she returned safely to her father's house.

Anne's home was a comfortable solid building which had a handsome porch of carved pillars. The lintel was carved in the form of a heavy, sensual lip, and the door within echoed this same design. Above was a date-stone: FEARE GOD 1700.

Its master, the mason John Wylde, was, like the house, a large secure man, of substantial philosophy and dreams; a person who did indeed need over his entrance a reminder that there was One mightier and more secure than himself. He was a rationalist, and God's world seemed to him nothing but a huge stone ball like the ones that he carved for gateposts and gable-ends. He regularly journeyed around all England, staying with groups of artisans who disputed the Bible and about Greek philosophers, 'substituting Reason for superstition', as they put it. He also had visitors, which made him seem strange (like his daughter) to his neighbours. Radical dissenters or 'lunatics' came; working men whose philosophies were driven into the mad, twisted channels of *enthusiasm* through lack of any ordinary conventions of society to express their ideas. Scottish, even French, philosophers, whom John Wylde had met in Edinburgh, called on him. Also, other ambitious masons. Some had set themselves up as architects, or planners of estates and gardens, and their books and diagrams of parks laid out on the classical pattern, or of lavish interiors, inspired Anne Wylde, by the way, with exotic dreams of luxury – of palaces, gilded beds, silk clothes, blackamoor servants, and libraries of books that had gold and leather bindings – a life utterly unimaginable in bleak Lady Well.

Nowadays, John Wylde enjoyed more time for dreaming. For he had half abandoned the sheds where with his apprentices and journeymen he carved traditional heart-shaped dripstones for windows, or figures for door lintels and corbels. He had also ceased his wandering. Instead he would sit poring over charts, calculating the strengths of beams and floorboards, the spans of arches and the means of lifting the stones for a great manufactory that would surely make a fortune for his patron, Nicholas Horsfall, and himself. But at this clerkish unfamiliar work his eyes grew tired (though the Vicar had presented him, in return for his 'amiable repairs' to the church, with a pair of spectacles), and he would slip back in his chair and dream. He thought of God, the Great Craftsman, fondling in his hands the stone ball of the world; and as he turned it daily, the light crept over one side and the shadow in the opposite direction slipped along the other; a wave passed around it, of men waking up to the dawn, whilst another went along the far side of those going to their sleep.

This vision had been amazing John Wylde when the Vicar disturbed him, earlier in this day. The mason did not think that Joseph Doubtfire was much of a man: he was one of those victims of Nature who fill their lives with unnecessary misfortune. Moreover, Wylde liked to synthesise his thoughts; whereas the Parson's interest was in analysis. (Like Death itself, thought Wylde, which breaks down bodies, plants and all the seasons.) So John, instead of offering serious matters, bantered with the Vicar.

'What sort of winter will we poor sinners be enjoying, Mr Doubtfire?'

'It is, like all else, in God's hands.'

John Wylde glanced at the Parson's elongated, twitching, 'useless' fingers, stained and pale with the formalin he used for preserving 'specimens'. Fingers which, if a stone was placed in them, would surely drop it; and Wylde trusted that God's hands were not like those. The mason, holding *his* world of charts and calculations in his own firm grasp, looked outside carefully and slowly. Then, with his superior knowledge of the seasons and of all practical things, he put the Vicar in his place. 'Nay, we'll not be getting any weather yet! I don't know when, though ... I thought maybe God would tell you what he has in mind for us poor artisans.'

Wylde was easy with and respectful of all, even a generally unloved Parson, so his mocking and contempt were gentle compared with what Doubtfire suffered from other dissenters: some threw mud at him, let dogs into his church or carved lewd symbols upon it, and stamped their boots through his sermons. Certain nonconforming children even burnt little images of him on secret bonfires.

'It does not seem to me that *you* have to fear the winter's Savagery,' the Parson answered.

'Horsfall has it in mind to put the spinners all under one roof in what he calls a *manufactory*. Whilst they are in their cottages, the master cannot rely upon them to deliver their yarn and has to go in search of it himself.'

'And you think that the women will come to your "manufactory" every day, just as if they are resident Paupers? Surely they will not suffer the Indignity willingly!'

'Many are quite poor and lonely enough long before they reach the stage of dependency upon the Parish. If they are paid a small wage, they will think that better than falling to the state of imprisoned paupers, yet doing the same work. Or so our Captain Horsfall reasons, after talking with some great "economists" and "improvers". Such men are exerting a great influence on the proprietors of estates all over England, I am told. Well, it is at least a shelter.' Wylde paused. 'But as soon as we escape Nature's anger, it seems that we have to face the scorn of men.'

'You are thinking now of your daughter? The reason is, you have given her too much Scope for a woman's upbringing. How can she follow the instructions of Saint Paul after such a rearing? "Wives, submit unto your Husbands, as unto the Lord. For the Husband is the head of the wife, even as Christ is the head of the Church: and He is the Saviour of the body." Since you have Polluted her meek nature with so much freedom, you have made it impossible for her to be a good wife and servant. So those who perceive her to be Wilful chase her through the streets.'

'She's all right! "There's nothing wrong with right folk," as we say – her nature is kindly. And they are guilty men who pursue her, treating her as they feel they deserve to be treated themselves. For such is our human nature.'

Nonetheless, insight was no answer to a practical problem. So John Wylde listened to the Vicar's proposal of a way to 'remove' Anne, and now he was ready to face her with it when she came home.

Anne slipped oftenest through a back gate into the mason's yard,

15

because there she found men who loved her – the old stone-cutters and dressers who when she was small had put her tenderly upon their knees whilst they took their cheese and ale squatting against the wall, and had told her, for instance, about the Great White Cow, who succoured everyone upon the moors, and about her 'ancestor' Lady Sybil.

At its centre the yard was golden-white with dust, and around the perimeter were damp sheds. The stones were a purple-black colour, except where they had been cut to show the bright gold. Many had the beginnings of carvings: dragons, fawns, interlacings, and column-flutings.

The place now echoed with the sharp, dry, regularly repeated sound of a chisel striking stone, like the call of a harsh exotic bird in a thicket: two apprentices were squaring up a block for a 'Grecian' column, such as was called for by gentlemen these days. The lads were laughing at it, thinking it feeble work compared with the bold rough stuff they were used to. Next, they turned to sniggering at Anne Wylde.

Anne went into the kitchen. The scrubbed stone floor, the broad and thick single board of the table with two wooden platters upon it, washed; a clean pot hung over dead embers in the fireplace, and around it a tidy hearth. There was no house-servant. Anne did the work herself, and fed the mason's journeymen and apprentices. She had been brought up as an only girl, indeed as the only woman in the house, resourceful and learning what she knew of domestic economy from aunts and neighbouring women.

She burst into her father's parlour in her usual 'excessive' fashion: like a calf that has been let loose over a moor and, dazed and amazed by the breadth and wonder of the world, has found itself again baffled in the gloom of its barn. So suddenly entering it, the room gave her an impression of brown stillness, as of peaty water lying upon a moor. The oak panels, the clock with its carefully oiled machinery ticking and snoring, the books and charts, and above her father's head the large brown painting of that group of seven frighteningly-still and patient men, standing in Puritan clothes and hats, who had filled in the Well; their rigid arms all pointing to one spot like a grave of new earth before them on the ground, and behind them a bonfire made of the famous Lady Well hawthorn tree. (A curious picture, given – like the spectacles – to Wylde by the Parson in return for what he had done for the fabric of the church.)

John Wylde loved his only, motherless daughter; who fussed over him, making him camomile tea, pestering old women for herbal medicines more effective than the apothecary's 'rubbing bottle', trying different diets for him, worrying when he lingered in stone-yards and quarries through the cold and wet. ('Thou'll not find a husband by spending yourself on your father!' had remarked the foolish old hags and the wise-women – who in any case doubted Wylde's paternity.) John had transferred to Anne the love he had felt for his wife, who had died in giving birth. Following closely on the death of his own mother, this was a blow that seemed to destroy everything feminine in the world. It was as if for him Nature herself had died. The air was no longer pure and sweet, nor the grass, trees and earth. So he compensated by smiling upon Anne, whilst she grew up running free everywhere – a girl who did not lower her eyes nor keep silent because men were speaking; yet still he gave her everything that she wanted.

But at sight of her with bits of thistle and grass in her hair he placed himself imperiously before the fire. In a manner typical of him when deliberating he raised both hands to waist level, held them the span of a building-stone apart, spread his thick fingers as if balancing some heavy thing and put his words together carefully, quietly. He could have been building a cathedral.

'And where's the sickle thou's been cutting oats with?' he demanded.

She had forgotten all about that when they chased her from the enclosure and now could not remember against which bank, stone or tuft of grass she had left it. Whilst Anne was careless with such things, to John Wylde all tools were precious objects, to be nursed and coddled as a mother with a baby. More than anything else, her neglect of this put him in a rage.

'It'll be rusted and useless when thou finds it,' he said at last.

She dared not answer. She merely stooped her shoulders more, for she was taller even than her father, and at the moment this seemed improper.

'It'll need taking and grinding. 'Appen you've already broken the edge off it by catching it on stones, in your usual fashion.'

He was silent, waiting for the retort that might excuse the release of his anger. But she did not answer.

'And I've no time to do it!'

Silence, still, from Anne.

'All our neighbours are orderly, obeying God's commands, but thou goes about like a savage beast! However, Doubtfire came today, offering to arrange for you to be civilised at Makings where he said they'd be able to make a good servant of you.' (So that was what the Parson had been hiding from her!) ' "To get her out of the way of folks throwing stones and calling her a witch?" I asked him. "You know what they did to Alison Wooler, tied to the tail of a cart," he answered me. It seems that Benjamin Greave wants to build a big family vault in the church. Our local clothier, though his father was nothing, plans to stop being a maker of rough kersey woollens for soldiers and hospitals, and to become foppish, weaving worsteds – callimancoes and shalloons for lining ladies' dresses. He says that is the "future". He thinks that making cloth for the gentry will turn him into a gentleman, and so our Parson believes he has influence over him. "I must be grateful that you take such an interest in my maid," I answered him – with sarcasm in my response. "I think you favour her because she was the youngest hereabouts to learn her catechism!" "She does catch on to things fast," he said. But I told him, "I taught her to read and write for more than to pay lip-service to folk." '

The mason spoke quickly to prevent his unruly daughter interrupting him. But now, at last, Anne herself broke out angrily. 'Doubtfire's getting rid of me because he's feared of me! You're all feared!'

'Making Hall is a grand place,' John Wylde said, trembling. ' 'Tis a grand sight, like the Parthenon was of old to the peasants of Greece.'

The mason normally hid his deepest feelings, as if to show them would attract an evil demon. But all afternoon he had balanced his desire to have Anne with him, against what her fate might be if she remained in Lady Well, and now his pain at the thought of losing her twitched in his face.

Anne felt as though she had been suddenly dropped into a hole. What could she imagine at Makings? Surroundings of elegant mirrors and gilt, a stream of visitors from far away, foods such as she could hardly think of; but her pride humbled, like a nun's.

Her expression, so distant from him, neither assenting nor disagreeing, made her father exclaim impatiently, 'Sometimes I think you are not my daughter!'

From then on, events seemed to belong to Anne's past the moment they were born. Everyone behaved differently towards her. When she went to the apothecary's or the grocer's, the women would usually stop their gossiping. Anne was annoyed only because they did not obtain their goods on first entering the shop, thus saving her having to wait through silence whilst half a dozen or so obtained their purchases. Now, however, the shopkeeper immediately said, 'What may we do to help you, Miss Wylde?' and this was even worse than having to wait, for she was being even more deliberately shunned and hastily got rid of.

When she passed the Vicar in the street he blushed and looked elsewhere. Out of embarrassment, he whom she had beaten might become angry with someone, or make excuses to rush away; whilst Anne grinned back, direct and fearless, making him cower.

But he could not avoid her eyes in his church of Saint Mary the Virgin.

John Wylde used to please himself which churches he visited and took his daughter to. (Or even whether he would go at all, for often they stayed at home and read their Bible to one another.) Though loyal to the tiny chapel of his own sect, sometimes Wylde liked to taste a new theology. Every Saturday evening and Sunday morning father and daughter bantered over which place to visit. The weather often decided the matter: if it was fine they enjoyed crossing the moors together, to startle some remote hideout of a rare sect where the mason indulged his greatest joy: friendly dispute with clever strangers. When the weather was wet they showed their faces at the parish church – the place where as a child John had first marvelled at sculpture. (Or what battered remains there were of saints, devils, gargoyles and kings.) On these next Sundays, though it was fine and warm, Anne wanted to stay in Lady Well to tease the Vicar.

As usual, she got her way with her father. She sat, her expression innocent of any intention to disconcert, demure with her hands folded upon her prayer book and with flower-like calm, even though the people tittered around her. Above and behind on the balcony were the Greaveses and their flock of servants, with Captain Horsfall, his mother and some of their servants. Enjoying ample space there, they were also hidden in the high-pews that were their own gift to the church, so that they could sleep undetected. Not even Dick Almighty – much as it offended his dignity – was allowed up there, so close to Heaven. The humble congregation, in smelly kersey-woollens, crowded into the earth- and damp-smelling nave, whilst Almighty, being a churchwarden, stamped up and down the aisles, ringing his keys and banging his staff as if he was Saint Peter himself, clouting round the ears those who were not sufficiently bent in prayer, kicking out the curs and mongrels: why, he even interrupted sermon and anthems for these important duties. Because of Almighty's edict, those such as Dick O'Lovely, who paid no rates or taxes, must miss God's words altogether and stay in the churchyard. (Where however Dick often played his own tunes, that were wilder and more thrilling than hymns, in order to collect pennies from the thankfully departing congregation.)

Anne felt glad to see her persecutors bowed, even though she knew that it was their stooping to them that gave fire to the Parson's sermons. She, like her father (who had first pointed out the beauties of the church to her – so unlike other fathers, who took them for granted), loved the atmosphere of the building: a wrecked and rustling forest of dark columns, numinous shadows and mysteries, throwing her into a vertiginous spin when she peered into the roof at the carved angels with rubbed-out faces and damaged limbs. Sunday after Sunday the child had sat here, like other children and their parents trying not to be noticed by Dick Almighty; wondering what her female fate would be, and why, and whether she would be able to bear it, with Christ and Saint Paul as her masters; or whether she would be different from others. At the age of thirteen, on the verge of menstruation, she first became aware that a female's whole world was one of shadows and mystery: of muttered secrets, of careful calculation when to be silent and when to affect a temper, of devices to manipulate menfolk without their realising it – even of magic potions (slipped into the men's oatmeal porridge or beer) to make them active or sleepy, quarrelsome or passive, according to a woman's devices. She saw that men, though they never admitted it, were afraid of women, who had such secret control of what went into their mouths and their homes.

So, in thoughtful dreamy hours in the church, Anne swung and kicked her legs, scared of how fast they were growing, wondering if she were turning into a monster, just as they said she was; week by week getting used to being shunned, sometimes scared by her fate, sometimes silently arrogant, sometimes screaming and raging about it.

The church was drilled with shafts of coloured light. The window-glasses, which were left undamaged from the old days – red for warriors, blue for saints and yellow for Heaven – were a view not into Lady Well but into another world, where Anne's imagination loved to wander and wonder. The statues (many of which had the wrong heads, because after the Puritan soldiers had gone through, lopping them off at the necks, pious people had crept in to place the heads back again, often on the wrong trunks). The paintings, with their pale colours faded or scratched off the walls. Saint Uncumber, patron saint of unfortunate women, depicted crucified upside down so that her long red hair fell from her tormented body like a river of blood; a scattering of oats on the floor below, placed secretly by unhappy wives to bring true their prayers to be rid of their husbands. A picture of the scourging of Christ. Jesus did not look like a man being whipped – except for his beard, he was more like a dreaming virgin girl. Perhaps Christ enjoyed the scourging! Anne, elected, with irony, to be God's agent, His punisher of sin, now asked herself if she had done her birching properly and for assistance she looked at the pictures of the expert scourgers on the walls; but they, like herself, didn't seem really to mean it.

Sunday was the most important day of the week for everyone in Lady Well. It was when they came down from lonely places on the hills and could gossip with their neighbours. It was when they heard what had been aired far away in newspapers and what had occurred in parliament (so long as Doubtfire was disposed to tell them about it). It was when the young people met, showing off whatever fine clothes they had. Here one could rest, once one had developed the trick – for Almighty's benefit – of seeming at the same time to have an ear cocked to the psalms, anthems and sermons. It was when one could daydream.

And so, whilst Doubtfire preached about Mary Magdalene, the 'natural woman' humbled to the feet of Christ, Anne's mind drifted into a blasphemous fantasy: in this, it was not the Parson, but Christ Himself whom she had whipped.

Anne tried to depart secretly from Lady Well. On the eve of Lammas Day she sorted her belongings (her mother's clothes, her Culpeper's Herbal, a Bible, a copy of Homer translated by Mr Pope, so full of exotic beings) and before dawn her father took them on his mason's cart to Making Hall, leaving her for a short while alone at home, where she prepared a table-load of baking to leave behind.

Many claimed later that they had heard during the previous night the eerie whistling known as 'Gabriel Ratchers'. (Amos Culpin said it was like the sound of a piece of timber hurled through the air, whilst another described it as the yelping of a pack of dogs.) Joshua Binns saw two stars fighting. But at the time, nobody especially remarked about Anne Wylde, who had with such great pride maintained her apparent indifference to her destiny.

After her father returned from Makings, Anne hesitated over kissing him goodbye – unsure whether or not she had been taught that it would be unseemly. She decided that it was bound to be another sin upon her head, and she walked off, alone, unhampered, along the route already followed by her belongings.

It was close to the end of a fine August morning when most had abandoned their looms and spinning wheels to make hay or go hunting for rabbits or hares. Those who watched might have thought that she, too, was taking a stroll to the enclosures and the hills. Yet she was washed, combed, dressed in her best gown of sky-blue wool with a bright white apron, and with tears dampening her eyes because of that missed embrace.

The Vicar, though some had begged him to cut the first corn, was poised in the schoolroom. He cast one quick glance through the window before turning back to reprove his tittering pupils. A dunce turned out for misbehaviour, who lingered in the doorway with a fool's cap on his head, stared lustily and he momentarily turned cheerful. Housewives, washing clothes at a spring, cackled after her.

Dick O'Lovely, alone and playing his fiddle outside a hush-house (the drinkers paid him to do this; if he stopped it was a signal that Dick Almighty or some other busybody was approaching) paused, though only for a second until he recognised her footsteps, and blew her a friendly kiss. He looked hungry, she noticed – even though it was summertime.

In the small stone-walled fields cramped around Lady Well – their bright grass like emeralds mounted within the dark moorland – weavers stretching their cloth, and women rolling hay, laughed and shouted, sure that now their milk would not turn sour, nor their pups be born blind, nor their rabbits devour their young; that the harvests would not be storm-beaten and that future winters would not kill the poor.

At one point a group of villagers, some grinning but most silently trying to hide their fear, gathered to watch her passing. They showed the usual embarrassment caused by the sight of a tall woman and she decided to scare them by running forwards, waving her arms and cursing. 'I'll pick thee out ... oh, yes! You who are mean from the generous, and the kind-hearted from the cruel!' she shrieked. Unbelievably, these hard weavers and farmers shuffled quietly and guiltily before the girl, who appeared to be driving them before her like a flock of hens. They gathered sullenly, and in truth frightened, in an enclosure corner to watch her pass – this alien spirit who had been born amongst them for their sins – and only when she was out of hearing did they fall to muttering again.

Meanwhile, with joy Anne leapt into sunlight beyond the last house. She saw the quiet hills and valleys draped around and below her: grey soft lips pursing upwards out of the dense woodlands. The smells had changed, from oily woollens and urined passages to hayfields and flowers, and some lane-banks were already scented with ripening blackberries.

Rooks rose off a plateau. Reaching the edge, they played with the breeze that scattered them over the skies. Their wings were shot with glossy blue, purple and green, like coal or iron settling and cooling out of the furnace of Creation. At other turns, the birds became an insubstantial colourless glitter; they were transformed to mere air, or water. Time and again they flew into the wind, full of pleasure.

A flock of larks twisted and skimmed over the slopes, their backs gleaming like fragments of glass, as if some brightness up there had been shattered and pieces of mirror were cascading, enjoying their descendings. All this turning of light wings inspired Anne with freedom, with an impulse to be also scattered in bright pieces about the Heavens.

(Anne Wylde's pleasure in the birds and flowers was unusual in being unpossessive. Others liked blossoms because they anticipated the fruit to be eaten, or they thought of decoration to their persons or houses that would impress their friends; hearing a lark sing they wished to cage it. But Anne hardly wanted to touch them – except just sometimes, she would bring a jar of modest wild flowers indoors, but not to make an effect on anyone, and she would occasionally put a blossom behind her ear.)

For several miles she followed a track along the spine of the hill. It overlooked two sun-filled valleys on either side glittering with streams and throwing up a warm smell of drying hay. The moors were smouldering purple with heather blossom from which Anne some- times disturbed a thunder of bees. The countryside was busy, with gangs of men and women building enclosure walls and extensions to farms which were prospering with the trade in woollens; with travellers also happy at the sunshine; weavers leading their bowed packhorses, merchants, carters with their vehicles laden with wool and a drover bringing a flock of sheep. Scared of the eyes of these people, Anne used her shawl to flatten out her beautiful breasts. Meanwhile she stepped forwards with a simple desire to make her life happy.

A seven-mile clamber upon the hills was no effort to the long-legged girl. She burst over the brink of another valley, out of which these tradesmen climbed in their continuous ant-like file. Unlike the rock- strewn gorges that dropped away from Lady Well, this place was broad, shallow and fertile, the trees cleared, the land cultivated and enclosed, with the menacing moorland held back. It was evenly scat- tered with weavers' cottages, neat and as carefully placed to avoid touching one another as nonconformists ranged in a chapel; sur- rounded with ruffs of enclosures and linked in a web of small streams. The higher up the hillsides were these walled green oases, the more they were threatened by vast sombre areas of surrounding moorland. The lower part of the dale narrowed and steepened abruptly where all the spouts of water funnelled into one that rushed through water- falls and was banked with the dense trees of Blood Wood. From the foot of the wood, Anne could hear the mechanical banging of hammers in the fulling mill at Lower Laithes, which belonged to Benjamin Greave.

At the head of this valley, which he virtually owned (as well as controlling the livelihoods of his tenants) stood his home, Making Hall, where he had first use of the water oozing out of the hills above. Everywhere in sight was prosperous and it was clear that Makings was the reason; for all the roads led to or from it, as sheep-tracks over a field radiate from the place where the sheep are fed. Benjamin Greave's clothing trade kept two hundred weavers in employment and a thousand women spinning for them in this valley, the next one and the one after that. It promoted a quarry industry, also carting, loom-repairing, carpentry and land-clearing. Children were found work (fitting the wires into the wool-combs) as soon as they could walk, whilst old women were engaged to their days' ends in brewing dyes. Anne could see the industrious weavers, their women and children, carrying on ponies or on their own backs their pieces of woven cloth to Making Hall. Others were returning with wool advanced by Benjamin Greave, whilst yet more were journeying to and from the fulling mill.

Anne walked down the slope, crossed the stream by a stone bridge (worn like an old tooth after a lifetime's chewing by the traffic that had passed over it) and she climbed the steep hill to Making Hall, hanging above her like a fortress. It had been built during Civil War days, when despite burnings and destruction the clothiers sensed a better time for tradesmen coming with Oliver Cromwell. Three huge broad barns stood around it, and there was a clutter of well-made outbuildings. The walls of the enclosures here were more grand than anything that could have been built by an ordinary farmer and were heavily capped with semi-circular stones, the gateposts thick, proud, and carved in a herringbone pattern, with globes on the tops of them.

Anne entered beneath a great archway into a crowded paved yard ringing with the noises of hooves, iron cartwheels and shouts, whilst over it hung a pungent smell of dyes, wet wool, yarns and fleeces. Weavers who had brought their 'pieces' (but who today would rather be scything their hay) were grumbling about having to take so much trouble making the fine worsteds that Benjamin Greave wanted now, when for centuries they had got by through weaving rough kersey-cloth. A couple of wool-combers had left the furnace-side in their overheated outhouse, just to come out and argue (as travelling combers notoriously would); they were also flirting with the weavers' wives and daughters, a small crowd of whom had gathered around the door waiting to take home the combed wool and spin it. The aloof Anne Wylde was a gift to them as they looked for sport on a summer's day. Noting the fine blue shalloon wool of her dress, and the laundered white of her apron, it seemed to them that though she entered as a servant yet she was not of that class – perhaps she was some rich daughter playing at being a simple girl!

They laughed whilst Anne climbed a flight of stone stairs to a kitchen, the door of which had been left open for the summer air to dry up the damp. She entered a room that was larger and loftier even than Lady Well church, with sun and firelight glittering on pewter and brass, high passageways leading off it, and many female servants busy. Mechanical contraptions – gears and pulleys – turned meat against the huge fireplace, before which some expensive, young-man's linen underwear was drying. Rows of kitchen implements shone against the walls, and a large clock was placed in an important position. There were pies being baked, smoke curling around the shelves, cats hissing and screeching over bones, a girl spreading a mop over the flagstones, and other maids arguing and gossiping.

But the first thing that Anne noticed properly was that here she did not need to stoop. Secondly she observed that the kitchen had been built over a well and she thought, with relief, that on dark rainy nights she would no longer have to cross a yard to get water.

(2)

Making Hall, everywhere apart from the kitchen, was a male house, and its dark rooms and passageways creaked like a ship under the weight of their transactions. The place smelled of tobacco, alcohol, snuff, ledgers and money. The talk was of money, trade, weather and the woollen industries of foreign countries. If God was mentioned he seemed but another prosperous clothier, His interest being in trade and His Heaven being a great 'piece-hall' where the finest materials were bought and sold. The visitors were male also: throughout the summer there was a stream of bankers, clerks and merchants from Holland, Russia or Spain. They came after difficult journeys and expected to be given splendid dinners eaten with silver implements and served by liveried lackeys. Much of the wealth of the countryside was gobbled into the maw of Making Hall. Whole flocks of sheep and geese were swallowed; carts laden with pots of honey; trout, salmon and pike; strawberries coddled to ripen in early summer; and presents from abroad sent ahead of the visitors.

But Benjamin Greave offered soups, oatcakes, boiled nettles and roughly-hacked sides of beef or mutton, to be eaten out of wooden platters at one end of a huge oak table, with the servants at the other; who were dressed in the same modest but good kersey-woollens (hidden under aprons of leather or cotton) as their masters; and who simply rose with their mouths full of their own food to bring further dishes. There was no elegance, and the house was without privacy. Foreign merchants, the Greave family, their servants, artisans and workmen, were thrown together promiscuously for eating, sleeping, conversation and entertainment.

One day a visitor – coming for the first time and badly (that is, foppishly) dressed for this part of the country – raised his white lace cuffs to save them from being touched by an ill-shaped, heavy lump of coarse bread and inquired, disdainfully, 'What ... is ... that?'

'A cake!' Benjamin Greave shouted back, dragging the 'a' so that it sounded like the bleat of a sheep. His visitor did not understand, so, 'An oat c-a-a-a-y-k' the clothier repeated, loud, impatient and grumpy. (He knew that what the man wanted was his cloth, which was the best in the world.) 'It's what we eat!'

Pause, and only the sound of the stranger swelling his chest. Greave thought his customer a fool and the customer considered Benjamin an animal. (In other words: this was a quite usual meeting between the clothier and the purchasers of his cloth.)

'The Duke of Buckingham' (the visitor pronounced it 'Back-ingham') 'deigning to call upon an inn at Marlborough, required the utmost decorum, all the servants to be in his own livery, though it was but an overnight stay. And he paid the bill.'

'Then the man had more money than sense!' Greave was small but made up for it by barking in a dry, commanding voice, like a dissenting preacher who behaves always as if he is in the pulpit: to shout was his normal voice, even for intimacies. 'He couldn't have worked hard for what he had. It would have been better for him to spend time thinking on Eternity. Or at least on a thought for 'ow we poor folk have to manage in t'North.'

So, without feeling (except for fine woollens), Benjamin Greave shovelled into his mouth oatcakes, blood puddings, stewed nettles, choice dandelions from the garden, or oranges from Italy. All vanished untasted through those thin pale voracious lips, as into the mouth of a pike.

The spectacle distracted his son Oliver, a man of twenty-four compelled to live here because he was a widower and had a sickly daughter to care for. He would, by holding a strawberry delicately in his mouth for a moment and melting the cream off with his tongue, try to show that life was not intended for the greedy swallowing of everything in sight.

'I've bought Upper Spout this week!' Benjamin Greave yelled at his son. (Ignoring his sensitive feelings, as usual.) 'I told 'em it was poisoned water up there and they believed me! They're fools and gobslutches at Spout, and one of them – though he's nowt but a weaver like the rest of us – has, so I believe, been reading a book. Novels and political philosophy'll be the ruin of us. Anyway, I was telling you 'bout the water. There's sulphur in t'spring! It's the best cure there is in these parts, they tell me. We'll have ladies coming from all over to take their baths in it, and we'll be rich as dukes afore we die! There's no more than one or two gaps in our possessions at that end of the valley now. I plan to shift the cottagers by building them better places up the moor over a pump, so they can wash their cloth without going out of doors. That should please them! Give them more time for reading seditious volumes, though!'

Possessions became merely acres written into deeds, whilst gifts were locked in cupboards by the housekeeper. Though so much silver, plate, linen and lace was never used but only regularly counted, though so many rooms were permanently fastened and those that were open lacking the continuous change that a mistress brings, with fresh flowers, pictures, new curtains, or a shifting around of the furniture, yet it was not that the two widowers who were its masters had such mean temperaments. It was because for them both the place was the shell of past lives. It was a dried-up womb without female blood pulsing through it – leathery and colourless.

Oliver Greave had from childhood been open-hearted, restless, desiring and inquisitive. He was fond of drawing; he learnt the fiddle, had written songs and verses from an early age. But his composing came to a pause when his father sent him to the grammar school (to learn just sufficient spelling and arithmetic to save him from being cheated by lawyers) and where the Reverend Doubtfire fought with birch and lexicon to impose dead Latin Grammar upon the chaotic stream of Anglo-Saxon that tumbled through the mouths of tradesmen's sons. Doubtfire taught that only the classical languages were perfect and that Oliver's native tongue was a midden, a muck-heap, of polluted heathen speech. Whilst it had always seemed to Oliver that the people of his own background had a lot to express, in their bitter, comical, abbreviated fashion, now he learnt that he had come out of a silence with, so far as elegant modes of expression were concerned, 'no more language than grunts in a farmyard', just like those of their own animals, and shouts across the moor. In their speech, 'Greece' meant *stairs*, an ant was a 'pissmole', a 'bandyhewitt' was the word for any man's *canine companion* or *fidus Achates*, 'beleakins' or 'farrantly dame' was the complimentary diminutive address for a lady, 'off-cumbling' was a stranger or indeed anything strange, 'laikin' was both to laze or to write poetry; and a 'basting' was the beating that a 'gobslutch', or dunce, got (or rather, *received*) for laikin instead of struggling with the off-cumbling language under the tutelage of his ecclesiastical vocabularian, orthoepist and orthographer, the Reverend Doubtfire.

Though Oliver at first got hottering mad with it, he struggled until in the end he fell in love with Hellas, and instead of laikin with old men, gobslutches and fiddlers, he spent time mooning over Thucydides or the ancient myths, gazing at and drawing maps of the classical lands or dreamily playing in puddles by the stream where he constructed archipelagos modelled on the Isles of Greece.

One day, some 'demon' (so Benjamin Greave put it) inspired an ingratiating customer to give the boy a copy of Pausanias's guide to ancient Hellas. Through its engravings, pernickety as an old spinster's needlework, Oliver entered that dry brilliant land of sun-bleached temples upon headlands overlooking the glittering sea – his Eden of ineffable wisdom and proportion. Now the Yorkshire hills began to close him in, and he ached at the thought of the huge distance that separated him from Greece. He imagined that the local dark rocks were white Greek ones, and that the mist sometimes flooding the valley was Homer's sea ... 'wine-dark' though it was not, but the colour and texture of phlegm.

Whilst his son for hour after hour with his lexicon fenced his native speech and poetry in Latin Grammar, Benjamin Greave enclosed moor and marsh with stone walls and hedges of hawthorn; or he discussed with parsons and Methodists ways of disciplining and encompassing the barbaric natures of weavers. All were occupied, one way or another, with enclosures. With prisons for language, land and people.

Yet the similar crucifixions of the souls of father and son did not bring them together. Oliver's new words and languages which could not be used in 'normal' conversations lay between them, like icy plains without the warmth to fertilise spring growth.

When Oliver was thirteen and finding his half-literate father unbearable, Benjamin apprenticed him to Joshua Binns, a manufacturer successful enough to pay a subscription to *The Society For Prosecuting Felons*, and who possessed six looms – Benjamin thought the lad had better learn of the sweat, noise and dust out of which fortunes are made, even though he'd never need to practise weaving. (Oliver

Greave had received his Christian name in honour of Oliver Cromwell – the father of modern trade, and especially of opportunities for English clothiers.) So both at home and in his apprenticeship, Oliver overheard trade, and the work of its Industrious God, often discussed. He slowly realised how this man's world of woollens, and all other trade also, depended upon an empire supported by battlefields and slaves; by forests burned and ploughed, or savage tribes exterminated; and it repelled him. Yet repulsion made him listen harder, and come close to inspect it (as he had once sniffed at the leather bindings in Doubtfire's library). He was further disgusted. Then he ran off, into woods, fields, moors, or to scribbling in the back rooms of inns. A shy, gentle, uncertain boy, who was sometimes full of fun and some-times tongue-tied.

Binns was soon declaring that the lad was the worst apprentice ever to have come his way, wasting hours writing those verses imitative of Pope, Dryden, Milton and Horace. All that saved Oliver from beatings and fines was the position of his father, with whom Binns sought an advantage and (whilst the great clothier looked with contempt over the rough kersey-cloths that satisfied Binn's ambition) lied to him, 'Why yes, Mr Greave, your son will make an excellent weaver!' During the rest of the time it was curses and threats – the truth being that Oliver was not only feckless himself, but his fiddle, dreams, wild talk and escapades influenced the other apprentices; he flung open a magical door in a dark prison for them.

They were, in fact, locked in a dormitory. Oliver found how to break out. Taking his violin he led the way to moorland inns where they spent the nights singing, dancing and, occasionally, fighting: though Oliver when sober had a quiet nature, yet if someone angered him when he was drunk he might well hit out viciously or throw bottles at the walls. Sometimes Oliver was still playing as he led over the moors at dawn; an eerie sound and sight in the grey-green twilight. During the day, Oliver's weariness exasperated the master. The lad's aristocratic distaste for weaving, and for all manufacture, expressed in scornful satires, jokes and couplets, also set Joshua Binns against him. Moreover, the mistress, Binn's dissatisfied wife, a large kind-hearted beauty who fed the apprentices beyond the weaver's generosity, further annoyed her husband by siding with Oliver because he was a good-looking entertaining boy who treated her gallantly and watchfully (as no doubt a poet behaved towards his muse).

At last Benjamin Greave understood what was going on. After their quarrel, Oliver one night crept finally out of his master's house. (Mistress Binns from then on would not speak to her useless husband, whose love-making was like the bundling into her of a goosedown pillow – though she rejected him less for this than for his more important impotence, his meanness.) Meanwhile the remaining apprentices, feeling sadly abandoned by the rich spirit who had dwelled amongst them, were bullied into becoming commonplace weavers.

For seven years, whilst the melons of Mistress Binns's full bosom heaved sorrowfully through those same silent nights in which Benjamin Greave tossed and turned in anxiety for the future of the turd-piles of his wealth, no one knew where Oliver had gone.

Oliver Greave had always felt (perhaps he was born with the feeling) that he was in the wrong place at the wrong time, in the wrong age and the wrong class, doing the wrong thing, with a destiny he could not escape, never satisfied, but driven by a secret nature not expressed; a conflict which made him think that if he was indoors he should be outside, or if he was enjoying the open air that he should be toiling in his study. Now he was maddened into searching for he-did-not-know-what over the moors. Occasionally Benjamin Greave received a letter (one so poetical and metaphorical that it made no reason or sense to him) from an inn, but Oliver would disappear before a messenger could be sent there. Occasionally he was briefly glimpsed in Lady Well, where he called for laudanum or a *rubbing bottle* to ease a toothache; finding also that it eased the deeper ache in his heart.

He left across the hills a legacy of village schools set up in barns and unused sheds to earn money by teaching children to write, fiddle, scan verses and long for a dream Hellas. Also a trail of infants fathered to console maidens for the loss of 'their' poet, after Oliver had grown tired of his occupations and of them. There was something about women that he could not face. Though he felt weak and humble before them, yet he did not believe that it was right to express it, and instead he set off across the wastes again. He was avoiding himself, and therefore found that he yearned for something though he did not know what it was. When he heard hedge-preachers talk of vanished Edens, he felt that he understood what they meant.

But he did not comprehend why, when duties beckoned or even when things that he loved called, he would *flee*, for months or, as he was now doing, for several years. The more compellingly he felt himself addressed by his obligations, the more dilatory he was in obeying. He had not yet met anyone else who had this wayward characteristic, and he was confused and grieved by it. It was as if he was nursing himself in that womb of removed silence where poetry is nurtured, and to which both duty and happiness can be a threat. He was seeking that state in which a question might be raised from a mysterious source, the struggle to answer which is the stuff of poetry: one was as it were the warp, to the weft of the other.

Yet because he was such good value if in a laughing humour, and stayed capable of creating music and fun at those remote morose inns in return for his nights' lodging, they put up with him when he was so despondent that no kind word – no word at all – could be dragged out of him.

He was tormented by the struggle to articulate, in the iron mould of classical verse, his own complicated nature; and to bring to 'proper' speech the silence lying under the wounds of his ancestors – of dissenters whose tongues had been torn out, and of farmers' wives who had their bones broken for being 'witches'. Oliver's ambition was to make those who had been dumb for centuries, speak. He stared so deeply into the scars marking the history of his forebears that they turned into flowers: into pentameters and hexameters. The rhyming couplet, the muscular iambics leading majestically to the final syllable – these were life itself for Oliver.

But his workaday habit of exercising with words (or of 'flowery talking' as they called it) irritated tradesmen who were content with limited language – who were more than content, were proud of their narrowness and regarded Oliver's sprinkling of sentences with Latin, Greek, or references to myth and legend, as worse than vanity: they thought he was deliberately trying to offend them. They begrudged him both words and experiences.

Oliver soon felt his natural heritage, especially that of local language, as an impediment to his ascent of Parnassus; whilst his grip high upon the cliffs of Poesy separated him from all below. He could go neither up nor down, and yet must choose whether to soar or to fall.

He fell. When he met Zillah he was brought home at last to settle in marriage at Lower Laithes, a house his glad father built near Makings. It was Zillah's prettiness and her expensive fashions that captivated him. From his marriage onwards Oliver's days were spent in his father's trade, earning to provide for his wife, whilst his muse was in hiding somewhere up on the moors, and his fiddle was secreted in a cupboard because he could not bear its reproach, asking to be played. The engine that drove Oliver's true nature was a desire for wider experience, and greater means of expressing it. (For him, language was synonymous with experience, and using words was the same thing as going to foreign countries.) But now the engine was choked of fuel and his gay character dimmed.

A daughter was born, who was christened 'Betty'. Oliver doted upon her, in a way that is common amongst fathers; he liked to talk of the silkiness of her hair, the blueness of her eyes and so forth, at inns and parties, whilst leaving the practical care of her in the hands of nurses. Soon, Zillah died of a consumption. Oliver returned, in his dispirited state, not to wildness and wandering but to Makings, although also to writing verses; whilst continuing to search for the physical embodiment of that shadowy yet certain figure who always haunted him, seeming to hide behind the twigs of the wood or on the moors: his muse. It was his devotion to the unspoken woman of his imagination that made him appear, in the eyes of others, a flaccid, ineffective and indecisive man: though he was, in fact, merely an absorbed one.

Since childhood he had shown an extreme curiosity about women. He was fascinated by their scents, as of banks of different flowers; by their movements and their mysteries, their haughtiness and humility. But the only women at Makings were servants and these, even the young girls, showed a hard, dry, deliberate, take-it-or-leave-it, blunt manner. Most of these females had been in the one employment for so long that they even menstruated at the same time, as they say long-immured nuns do.

(Oliver had seen them washing their monthly cloths together in the Making stream: the water already arrived a dark brown colour out of the moorland peat, and at certain times it left the Hall the colour of

34

dried blood. Thus enriched, it ran downhill to feed the weavers' starved lands in the lower part of the valley, just as the male Greaveses fed their bellies with trade.)

In this company, Oliver's whole being ached for one whom he had never met. He imagined her so strongly and tantalisingly, that often he was sure she must be lingering behind those bushes, or that he would meet her beyond the next turn in the street.

One day Oliver glimpsed across a yard at Makings a tall dark girl with wild snake-like hair protruding from her cap. She was singing, her skirts tucked up for work so that they added volume to her hips and displayed her ankles. The poet instantly felt his inside turn to water. A cascade of pleasure ran through him, swept everything else away and left him clean. His eyes doted on her movements and the shifts of her dress, his back stiffened, his penis stirred and his ears took in the excitement and unbearable longing for some ancient past, or mystery.

The spontaneous notes seemed to surprise the girl herself as they came into her mouth. She sang as a lark, robin or thrush does in winter sunshine, when it amazes itself with a scrap of exquisite melody – the music opened moist and sensual, as a woman before a man she loves (so the poetical Oliver Greave pictured it), or as a dewy rose before the sun. (Though the tune would have seemed 'impolite' to most of his circle, and the words of the ballad would have shocked members of established and dissenting churches alike.)

His attention stopped her singing and she looked at him.

'However did you come to our establishment?' he asked, apparently mildly, because of the severe self-control he was practising.

As he was one of the masters, Anne Wylde defended herself by adopting vulgar speech and delivering it coarsely. 'I come straight up Swine's Lane, sir, same as everybody else does. I come from Lady Well on Lammas Day.' With a modesty not shown whilst she sang, she sagged her shoulders so as not to embarrass him with her height.

'Swine's Lane? Which is that?' he teased her, amused at her 'rude simplicity'.

'Straight up from th'mill.'

'I have heard it named more poetically "Swaine's Lane".'

She now wore the innocent face that she often used to disguise her

35

cleverness. 'I think we common folk call it "Swine's" because it is so filthy and dirty, sir.'

Though he bantered plainly, as her patron and her master, yet from this moment Oliver was in reality her servant. His attention became as helplessly fixed upon this girl as a prisoner's is on the window of his cell at dawn. It was in an instant revealed to him that every beautiful freedom that gave meaning to life lay through her.

Anne Wylde was never sure whether a new person would turn out to be a friend or a persecutor; whether, or when, he would change from one to the other; and she was always uncertain in discourse whether she was unintentionally offending against a God whom she did not understand. Instead of speaking much, she looked searchingly into a face that stared like a child's in wonder, yet wasn't absorbing the outside world. For an instant his eyes would focus brightly, like an ignited candle, and then would turn inward, snuffed; his lips having for a moment trembled with eagerness for some new thought or opportunity, then become still and unexpectant. He dressed with some vanity, she noticed - silk cravat, bright waistcoat, cutaway jacket of fine bay wool. Following the fashion of republicans and radicals, he did not wear a wig, but his thick hair was carefully dressed for an appearance of wildness. So evidently he did have some show to make to the world. Anne guessed that he had been many times disappointed in converse, which was why his speech was mannered and stiff. She saw that there was something else on his mind, and that it was inexpressible. She decided that he was a gentleman (despite his rude father). A little bit weak, because of the refinement of his feelings, and he could never truly become a tradesman. But it was a weakness she found attractive, just as many girls did: he appeared helpless and in need of women, and was smaller than herself. She entertained for him some of that tenderness that she gave to frail wild creatures. Yet he also had something powerful. He showed both the capacity and the weakness (though Anne did not realise this was what she was looking for) to sacrifice himself for her.

Oliver Greave still took museful ramblings around the countryside - especially when business should have been transacted, or when worldly men called. Nature was for Oliver (as for many sensitive men) wholly feminine; in his case she was also identified or confused with that mental mistress to whom he was devoted. He had always sensed the presence of the goddess of Nature. (Parallel to that vision of the other one: She who especially belonged to himself, the secret one; she whom he was bound to meet one day in the street. Or were they both the same person?) But he had wasted much of his life, for the sake of the conveniences of trade, pretending that She was not there; She had to be ignored, for if She distracted his thoughts, then huge volumes of trade were lost and the whole valley suffered. So her lineaments became as tarnished and faded as those of Saint Uncumber in Lady Well church. Whilst at other times – on his rambles, or when he stared out through a porchway at the moors – the femininity of nature's forms overwhelmed him. For Oliver, She was softly-rounded hills, trees exploding with green, and other pregnant forms. Tempting rustlings, lithe and liquid movements; and the inspirer of exclamations from his inner voice that could only have been duplicated by raptures addressed, if ever he became forgetful of himself through passion, to an actual woman.

So what loneliness he endured on returning to Makings, where his father and acquaintances (Benjamin had none to describe as 'friends') saw Nature as a different kind of female – as man's handmaiden; they measured Her as yards and acres, yields and prices, obstructer or beneficial servant of 'progress'.

One day Oliver watched a young woman removing stones out of his father's enclosure. She was bent under the boulders like a straining ox; a beauty was turned, by a stone, ugly and peasant-like. Oliver was detachedly delighted by her classical profile, her statuesque posture, and for a moment wanted to sketch her or commit her to memory for his verses. But then a second thought came: those with such classical form had lost their appeal before the unconventional appearance of that servant-girl in his father's house, who seemed to be his Nature-Muse Herself.

By such revelations Oliver realised that he was in thrall. For so many years since the death of Zillah there had been in his heart a blank feeling upon the throne of happiness. But Anne Wylde had the effect of a powerful icon in a dim church. She transformed him from an unowned, unwanted wanderer in the wilderness into a worshipper and slave, but one whose dependency brought a happiness and stea-diness that had been unimaginable in his previous freedom. She was hardly a real person to him, since he knew so little of her. And his instinct kept her an inscrutable icon. If he had faced her it would have sent ripples across the mirror-surface of that still pool of idealised womanhood, in which Oliver was in fact staring at himself. But of course he didn't recognise the image. She was the looking-glass which reflected his deepest hidden self; she was that mirror of fairy-tales which answers riddles, if you ask the right ones, and if you can understand the inscrutable answers.

He had glimpsed the one love of his life. He was standing before the open temple, on the walls of which his visions were painted. He did not dare to hope, for surely the girl must have a sweetheart in Lady Well. Yet she had placed a glow over nature, such as he had read of amongst the most modern poets. Encouraged by his reading and by his image of her, for a time Oliver Greave sought no company other than landscape and his own thoughts.

One evening sitting amongst his books and drafts of poems before the fire, smoking his pipe and drinking common ale in a little room where he went to be alone (to the bafflement of his father), Oliver found himself staring at the cupboard where his fiddle had been entombed for so long and he was moved to root it out. It lay under discarded weaving patterns, clay pipes and waistcoats, buried in a black case like a child in a coffin. He raised it lovingly, blew the dust off, and opened it; he had almost forgotten its once-so-familiar pattern of scratches and stains, acquired at many inns and farm kitchens. Delicately he took out the corpse, which was as light as a butterfly, ran his fingers over the mellow brown body, tightened strings, lifted the bow and tried a few notes, tensed the strings again and in rapture played an air.

The housekeeper, Patience Helliwell, using the excuse of serving beer, interrupted to find out what was happening.

'You have come to help renew my devotions at the shrine of Bacchus!' Oliver remarked.

Patience always had a bedraggled, despised look. It was as if someone had recently thrown a bucket of water over her. She was short, dumpy, whiskery, with heavy boots, other mannish clothes, a male manner and a Methodistical accounting memory watchful as the big kitchen clock, ticking with the number of silver spoons and pewter

38

dishes that were locked away. Above all else she disliked fiddle tunes. And she hardly understood a word of her master's 'flowery nonsense' (though accepting it, as appropriate to one of his superior class). So she did not answer him.

'Who is the new servant-girl, Miss Helliwell?' Oliver asked, more severely, but still playing. She looked at him shrewdly, wondering how to get him to tell more than he intended. 'The tall dark-haired girl,' he added.

Patience Helliwell pretended that she couldn't hear because of the 'noise' of the fiddle. Oliver put it down.

'The crazy one with a mad look and a terrible cough?' Patience answered. 'It'll be Mary Ingham, she's from such a poor cot! I've many times had girls who've barked like that. It is the Lord knocking on her chest as on a door and she'll not be absent from Him for long.'

'No, it's not her! The one I saw looked particularly healthy.'

'Are you meaning Jane Oddy? The young widow?'

'Oh no, she can't be a widow! She is as fresh and untouched as an apple coming into ripeness on a branch.'

'Her father a mason? I hope it's not Anne Wylde you're carried away with – a terrible witch. They used to throw stones at her for her sins in Lady Well.'

'This one has a look of complete innocence and beauty . . .'

Patience could not think what had happened to make him so light-hearted and merry. 'Then it cannot be Anne Wylde! Mr Greave, sir, being a poet you do not understand the schemes that young women in need of prospects get up to.'

'Why do they call her, "The Hawthorn Goddess"?'

'That girl is of the Devil's brood and bound most certainly for Hell! We common folk say that every few generations one like her is born out of the sins collected amongst our forefathers – as flies are born out of filth. It is a purging or bloodletting that we must suffer, for one like her to be born. A temptress – she shall like Jezebel be eaten by the dogs. You must pray, pray, pray to the Lord for strength to snatch your eyes off, for she has bewitched you!'

'Ah, Miss Helliwell, I am confined to these moors as Prometheus chained to his rock, torn by the eagles of learning and poetry. What can I do for sport?'

The housekeeper looked puzzled. 'Sir, you are in need of a true wife to care for you ... not Anne Wylde. Look for some Godfearing woman to be a helpmate for Betty and yourself. Turn your mind that way. As we say ... "Only get thy spindle and thy distaff ready, and God will send the flax"!'

(3)

One rainy dark autumn day, when the moorland was blotted out in a mist of seething porridge and when candles were lit indoors, Oliver met Anne Wylde again. She was cleaning a passageway and he could not avoid her, though now his feelings made him nervous. Besides which, his daughter Betty was clinging to her skirts, and the warm association that had developed between these two demanded that the father remark upon it.

He delicately fondled Betty's head. He often found that to touch the hair and skin of infants revived his joy, his sensitivity, his desire – in a word, his belief in the world. After a moment, the child, sensing perhaps an incipient, exclusive conspiracy between the two adults, skipped off into the shadows of Makings, which were so familiar to her, leaving the young clothier and the girl facing one another.

'Do you like it at Makings, Anne Wylde?' Oliver asked at last.

'It's somewhere to be.'

He pulled back his shoulders. 'I hear they were ganging up on you back home.'

Oliver found himself smiling with the open countenance that he had not shown for years. One moment later, these two near-strangers were magically extracting laughter out of each other. It was as if she was drawing glittering water out of an overgrown well.

He was carrying a leather-bound folio in which were mounted duplicates of the sample-sheets given to agents to sell the Greaves' cloth, and, 'Would you like to see our wool patterns?' he asked her.

All about Makings there were little desks for clerks to scribble at. Oliver rested the volume on one of them and lit the candle that waited there. (Clerks were always careful about such things as candles, quills and tidy account books.) The girl came close to his side, her face as waxy as the taper in its wavering light. Her gown (of blue stuff, smelling of dampness; she must have been in the yard), brushed his sleeve. Their faces were close. As he opened the book, she placed her

41

hand upon it and he noticed how large were her palm, fingers and knuckles; and also a curious red line around her wrist, as if she had been wearing a too-tight chain.

Shaking because of her proximity, Oliver forced himself to turn pages and explain patterns in a matter-of-fact way, just as he would to a client.

Meanwhile, Anne's breath was taken away by the beauty of the samples. Gems of brilliant dyes. Strips of glowing red, blue, orange, chrome yellow, deep purple, velvet green. Beyond the window were the familiar tones and colours of the landscape – soft grey-greens and browns melting in the rain. But here, distilled out of its herbs, heather and roots, did she walk through some garden of brilliant flowers? There were strips of 'amens' – woollens embossed with minute suns, flowers, or with geometric designs like formal summer gardens. One page showed a dozen shades of mauves, purples and blues mixed with yellow, like gorse flowers amongst heather on the Yorkshire hillsides. The first pages were of old-fashioned kersey-cloths – strips of plain colour so heavily fulled that they had lost the nature of woven things and had a nap on them like moss. Next were the new callimancoes, delighting with the delicate grain of their threads and so closely woven that this woollen was like silk. Most beautiful of all, there followed the materials worked in small detail with stripes and patterns in many colours; with minute hearts, leaves, flowers and what looked like clumps of trees. Then came pages of tiny samples forming together the rich delicate beauty of a moth's or butterfly's wing. Around these were fine sepia engravings of ships, anchors, mermaids, and of Greek temples, which Oliver had designed.

Affected by Anne's breathless mood, he handled the pages in greater reverence and silence, as if turning a holy book in a monastery. He would never have thought that a volume dedicated to trade could be so transformed merely because of her attention to it. Time was suddenly passing in ecstacy and at great speed. Both wanted to grasp and slow down the minutes, but were also impatient for the next stage of happiness to arrive.

Anne Wylde was overcome. She could not believe that the dour weavers who threw stones at her and went about with clenched teeth and bowed shoulders, the postures of defending themselves from the malevolence of man and weather, could from their shuttered hearts, in their dark stinking noisy cottages, produce such beautiful things. They were like the local stone, the 'millstone grit'; dark and rough outside, but when you broke it open, it was bright gold. And Oliver Greave in her eyes appeared to be the mastermind of a great art.

From dealing with merchants who did not find it in their interest to praise the cloth that they bought, he had forgotten that it could inspire such warmth. He was dazzled and amazed. 'Would you like to look into our barns and warehouses?' he asked.

So there they suddenly were, the two of them, with the rain singing for them in the yard – a soft hum as if a hundred spinners were working. The cobblestones shone, polished by hooves and carts, whilst the wet made the walls dark purple. Further away the weather was rougher. Clouds were torn off the valley rim like ragged fleeces upon a fence. They evaporated, re-formed, and swept away in torn screens, or looking like the underbellies of sheep. To ease their intense feeling, Anne broke into a run. Leading merrily, she splashed in the puddles. Reaching the porch of the barn, they together shook off the rain drops, as two birds on a branch.

They went into the building. It was a vast shadowy cathedral with a cart-road down its centre and ponderous arches letting the light in at either end. The rattle of carts and echoes of voices were muffled in the huge bales of finished cloth, where servants and weavers sifted through the multitude of alleyways. They passed a Dutchman with a clerk, thoughtfully fingering samples. The next gentleman was Russian. Oliver read off the names on the bales, tapping each with pride but otherwise, Anne thought, unfeelingly, having now come back to earth and trade. 'Everlastings. Kerseys. Grograms. Callimancoes. Moreens . . .'

'I can read for myself, Mr Greave! My father taught me.'

'I didn't mean to offend you – I know that you are educated. Why don't you want to make something of yourself? I am surprised that you are not ambitious.'

'In Lady Well they believe there is a Great White Cow upon the moors and that whoever meets her will be fed with an endless fountain of milk. I think that life is too sweet to spoil it with foolish longings, Mr Greave. I am mostly well-off where I am, though I didn't like coming here at first – I suppose it's the same for gentlefolk when they're sent to university?'

43

'I've never been away, though I've travelled about our own hills in a period of my youth when I was . . .' He paused. 'My father thought the grammar school in Lady Well a good enough grounding in the business he supposed I was meant for. But I am glad that I learnt Greek and Latin there, he continued.'

'You don't sound happy about being confined at Makings.'

'Kitchens and passageways packed with artisans and weavers in unwashed stinking kersey-cloths! Evenings with Patience Helliwell conducting a howling meeting for Methodists in the kitchen! Yards and sheds wi' greasy pieces bleached in vats of piss!'

'A place where you cannot move for the gifts that folk send,' laughed Anne.

'Worst of all I lack the privacy for my own thoughts – which my father does not understand at all. What I enjoy about Yorkshire, Anne, is the wind on the hills, the scent of heather in my nostrils, and the crack around the fire at a moorland inn. But I also wish sometimes to travel to the places our cloth goes to. Most of all I would like to go to the cradle of our civilisation, Hellas, where the sunlight shines in endless calm on time-worn monuments and all men are civilised.'

This was a strange way to talk, Anne thought. It was as if she was reading a novel. 'You are a poet, aren't you, Mr Greave?' she suggested.

Oliver realised that she asked this because he was being pompous, with 'flowery talking'. He looked crestfallen, the corners of his mouth turned down, dimpled. But this too charmed her – he could do nothing wrong.

'To what school of verse do you belong?' she asked, to put him at his ease.

'Schools of poetry! So you've heard about them, have you? For real poets there's no such thing, despite what is said by writers on the art. It's only dead ones who are herded into "schools". In real life there's just people like me struggling with the unkind climate of Yorkshire and its even unkinder philistines. The true poets, the real makers, are always alone, they are the victims of the muse to whom they must be sacrificed in love, as Adonis to Venus or Hippolytus to Artemis – these myths are parables of poetic creation! Tim Bobbin says that God nowadays is only on the side of clothiers, and that he curses all true poets.'

44

'Who's Tim Bobbin?'

'My old friend and a true maker, in love with the muse. His real name is John Collier. He's the son of a parson suddenly struck blind as Homer, lost his living and could not send his son to Cambridge, but apprenticed him to weaving, where we first met side-by-side on the hard wooden bench of a loom. His verses are in the Aristophanic vein, satirical-comical by way of analogies to the animal kingdom. His blackbird is a magistrate, his goose a parson. So he must flee about the hills with a pack of angry worthies at his heels. When he is not running before these persecutors, he labours unhappily as a schoolmaster. Tim admires his native speech best, deeming the common language of men and women to be also that of the muse, and so for the use of future poets he has compiled a dictionary of our local words, stating whether their origin is Anglo-Saxon, Belgic, French or Teutonic. I'll tell you properly about him some other time – I hope you don't believe I am being enthusiastic.'

Anne noticed that when Oliver spoke about poetry he became animated, as if a burden had been lifted. 'Say me some of your verses then,' she demanded.

'Now from her chamber Chloe smiling comes
Like summer's empress decked with airy ...'

'Plums!' Anne instantly felt sorry for having made fun.

'... plumes!
The Cyprian goddess whose transporting charms
Calms furious Mars when in her snowy arms ...'

'That's Aphrodite,' Anne remarked. 'My father taught me a lot of things,' she added, for the knowledge possessed by one as humble as herself needed explaining.

'Showed no such beauty when for golden fruit
Juno and Pallas did with her dispute.'

'What admirable verses.'

45

Because of poetry, their conversation had run to an embarrassing halt. 'Why do you make so many kinds of cloth?' Anne asked.

Oliver now spoke dully – as one who has been running a race afterwards walks drearily. 'Father and me, we have to find new ways to keep the weavers occupied and interested lest they desert for the new manufactories. You have seen the new buildings erected along the river? There is a lot of discontent today, father gets very upset about it. He feels sick after dinner and I think he's decided to invest in the Americas. When I was a boy the weavers were very satisfied with what they had. They were forever able to build on to their houses and put in new looms with the money gained from us. But now they send their girls into manufactory sheds, with which the home-workers cannot compete. My father does his best to keep things in the old way, which benefitted every weaver under his care. He keeps trying out new kinds of cloth so as they'll think that something fresh will make them prosperous again. But I do not think he will succeed. I think he'll have to go and profit out of the black folk from Africa. Or invest in a ship bringing sugar from Cuba. Or in the East India Company, who anyway take our cloth . . .'

'Sometimes I lie in bed and try to imagine Africa. All that jungle, and no God. Perhaps the negroes are lucky.'

'But they suffer badly. They need our missionaries.'

'Other folk suffer, too – because of their souls, which black men do not have, the Parson says. It isn't missionaries they need. I think they are luckier than us if they are out of the prying eyes of God. Women don't have souls either, Mr Doubtfire tells us. We are formed to be man's servants, out of Adam's rib. If most men are free, why cannot women be so, too? But I think if we are slaves it is because of our natures, so I could never be turned into one.'

'What seditious talk, Anne Wylde!'

Walking the alleyways amongst funereal shadows and oily smells of wool Anne noticed that the labels on the cloth were enscrolled like tombstones, and that in fact many were called after those in the Greave family who had died. An 'everlasting' bore the name of Oliver's mother, and a 'flowered amen' that of his dead wife Zillah.

'You must be sad for your wife who died so young, Mr Greave?'

Oliver remembered how he had held Zillah whilst she coughed, the bark echoing in her chest like a small animal stirring in a deep box or burrow. His eyes glistened wetly. 'She was but nineteen and we had only two years of married life. And one sickly child.'

'I'm sure that one day you'll not be melancholy.'

'I don't think so. I *always* feel that I am in mourning, yet I do not think it is entirely for Zillah, since I experienced it even before I met her. I have always felt it. I think it has something to do with the age and the place in which we live. As if we have lost something that was there in the past. That is why so many people are melancholic these days. Only last week a carpenter in Lady Well simply walked himself to death upon the moors. He had always been melancholic, and brooded over the literature of the subject – Young's "Night Thoughts" and the rest. A farmer at a lonely cot murdered his wife and children and then he hung himself. Such things are happening all the time in our district. Our housekeeper tells me one can only be happy from "knowledge of sin and redemption" which has to be daily sought for fresh sins, but I don't think such a carry-on would suit me.'

'I haven't noticed that Methodists are so joyful. They have tormented souls. I've seen bands of them about the countryside or preaching by our church wall and coming to the kitchen here. Happy folk leave others alone to enjoy *their* pleasures. But I don't think I could ever not be happy. If I was one of your manufactory spinners or your black slaves I would find ways. Mr Greave, I was told that you too used to be a jolly person, always playing your fiddle. They say in the kitchen that you were performing some sinful airs the other night!' Anne made his face break once more into laughter.

But they were interrupted by Benjamin Greave entering at the far end of the building. He was accompanied by a tall young man in a cavalry officer's uniform which, amongst the subdued colours of the barn lit only by the grey rainy light, was a vision of amazing magnificence: white woollen trousers tucked into polished cavalry boots, sword and spurs glinting, and a cockaded hat exhibiting the white death's-head of the 27th Light Dragoons. The wearer of this costume moved as carefully as a cat so as not to be touched by the oily bales belonging to the clothier. His affected indifference showed that he was used to making an impression. He was indifferent to Old Man Greave, and also to the poet who could not keep from ogling. Anne keenly observed that Captain Horsfall had straight-looking handsome eyes, but a spoilt slack mouth – a contradiction expressing to her that he was used to having others provide for him, and was not aware of difficulties in life. Yet she could not help but be stirred by the magnificent bold sight of this Apollo, all his colours glowing like the sun.

'The greatest benefits and wealth of civilisation come from mutual trade!' Benjamin Greave shouted in his usual hard dry voice, as if his listener was on the far side of a moor.

'But you need us warriors and seamen to give you the advantage in the bargain, my friend.' The officer spoke quietly and was courteous because he wanted a loan from the old fellow.

'Nay, an exchange benefits both sides.'

'Though we give trinkets to an African king in return for all that he has?' The soldier laughed. 'I think we must force such exchanges upon them by keeping them ignorant through our strength of arms, otherwise what will happen to our wealth and our civilisation?'

Benjamin Greave was puzzled by the argument of his travelled and educated acquaintance. He scratched at his small, bony, scampily-haired head. 'However it is, if your fellows command sailors who wear low-priced kerseys I can send them from twelve pence a yard, or the equivalent in blacks from Africa. But I'm bound to tell you I love worsteds best!'

Oliver had heard this type of conversation before, before, before, and how it repelled him! He noticed again with what delicate feeling his father handled pieces of cloth, but was bluntly insensitive to everything else: which Oliver could not comprehend, for he himself followed the Renaissance ideal, that perfection in one thing made for a wholesome perfection in everything else. Yet despite his criticisms, when his father was within hearing Oliver's tone became like his.

'These kerseys are for Christ's Hospital, Miss Wylde. We send t'Amsterdam, Rotterdam, Utrecht, Antwerp and Bremen. Father and I have managed thirty thousand poundsworth of trade this year, all woven in our valley. This is soldiers' cloth for Saint Petersburg. In one year we have sent them a thousand bales. We post the same to France, Prussia, Holland and Spain – there is so much fighting and growth in their armies on the Continent that they go through a deal of cloth, which turns out very good for Yorkshire! We make enough to be spoilt by both sides in their wars; and we don't leave our customers, when they have finished with our woollens, to lie useless on their foreign battlefields, Miss Wylde. You must have noticed the fine grass we grow? We're bringing their bones home to fertilise our enclosures – cartloads over the sea through Hull in exchange for our woollens. Even if peace comes, I think we'll survive the inevitable recession.'

Oliver was no longer true to himself, instead he was hiding behind the opinions of a commonplace tradesman. This inspired not anger, contempt, or impatience in Anne Wylde, but tenderness for him. Yet because Mr Greave had come up, Anne, knowing her place, turned aside. Before her was a bale of fine red material, its rich colour glowing like glass in the church window. She thought of all the young manly chests, like the one of the soldier before her now, that it would cover, then she imagined the cloth spoiled and muddy on a battlefield, and the vision was so ghastly that she could not bear it. She winced so that the captain suggested to the clothier that perhaps she was being overcome by a witch-fit.

As a way to indicate that the girl was not worth much attention, the officer shook and flicked the rain daintily off himself. Dismissing the rain was a metaphor that he expected Anne Wylde to appreciate. Benjamin Greave on the other hand let the water soak down to his feet – in his shaggy clothes he was as indifferent to it as sheep are in a field. Anne Wylde saw all the difference between them expressed in this.

The father put his arm round his son. Oliver cringed away from the gesture, resentful of being spoilt – of his father's blindness towards his failings as well as to his talents.

Benjamin Greave noticed how keenly the tall girl was taking this in and he gave her a glance which made Anne feel as though she had been hated by him all her life. It was not for her, merely. It was for the force that he sensed was poised beyond her: he recognised one of those women who appear before us as messengers out of our own deepest fears.

Was Oliver Greave blind to all this? Blind as poets traditionally are? For he announced, blithely, 'Father, this is Anne Wylde. She is a girl educated well above her present station.'

Benjamin cut his son with a long stare – as when he confronted a competitor, 'eyeball to eyeball'. Then, totally ignoring what had been said, 'Captain 'Orsfall is kind enough to take an interest in our making and to further it through his regimental influence abroad,' he snapped back.

'Father, I'd like you to take notice of Anne Wylde . . .'

Benjamin Greave, seeing there was no way out but to confront the matter, gripped Anne's forearm. (How tightly he gripped things – ledgers, bales, a gate that stood in his way, the arm of a customer, or of a girl he might be about to hurry off to the witch-pond – as if in need of securing his grasp on the world!) 'You must be the madcap then? The one with books in her room? Do you know what they do with such girls, considering them no better than whores? I'd say you'd better burn them before it's you they come and set fire to! Before you preach about destroying wealth and property, you'd best give a thought to how it acts as a cement to the whole neighbourhood. And what will you have to replace it?'

'A six-foot wooden box is all we need in the end, sir.'

'Seven foot, in your case!' the Captain said.

So far Anne had been smiling, her nature stirring in admiration for his figure, but now her expression was wiped clear – she did not like this Horsfall, her father's patron.

'It's also beneficial to have something to leave to your heirs so that wealth might prosper in the future, thou impudent girl,' Greave continued.

'All books are not about destroying wealth. You are confusing me with my father's way of thinking.'

'Then you must be reading novels, that all offend against decency!'

'I must go back to my work, sir.'

Benjamin Greave watched her departure sullenly, Horsfall as if he would have liked to strike her (or something else violent), whilst Oliver was perplexed to see the joy, that had been gently flowering, cut down.

Benjamin Greave said, 'That girl is a spy! She's been seen with you today taking a great interest in our trade designs and patterns. For what reason does a girl speaking Latin better than a parson come here, my fool of a son? I'll send her back to Lady Well! They know what to do with her there and will soon throw her in the pond for being conspicuous.'

'If she leaves, I'll go the same day.'

Oliver flushed.

'You always were a rascal for roaming with women. The worst of 'em could easily make an ass of you! Forget the witch, and come and see the curiosity that Mr Horsfall has brought us from the Grecian Isles.'

Horsfall waved his arm, producing a flash and clatter of the metal variously about his person. 'It's nothing – merely a token of my friendship with our ambassador to Turkey.'

Whilst Benjamin Greave wanted to rush back to the house, Horsfall was aristocratically refusing to be hurried and he lingered, as if thinking of following the servant-girl. It was in fact he who in the first place had suggested to Greave that she be brought here, expecting her clashes with the old Presbyterian clothier to provide amusement. Waiting for Horsfall to catch them up, Benjamin Greave paused in the yard where the rain had now stopped and the weavers with their packhorses and pieces, the women with their yarns, the woolcombers from Somerset, Wiltshire and Norwich, now for Greave's benefit pretended to be busy. When the Captain joined him, the clothier shouted across the surrounding hills, and as if defying Nature Herself, 'Ever since she could walk and shriek, that one's been causing trouble in Lady Well, until I offered to the Vicar to find her a home!' (As usual with ideas, Benjamin Greave had forgotten that he himself was not the inventor.) 'A most generous kind benevolent offer I made, so I consider it; for all the worldly-wise were reminding me't brings misfortune into a home to tak' hawthorn into't. I am not a superstitious man, Mr 'Orsfall, and ours is reckoned to be a reasonable age, yet I find that now I'm doubting, for there might be some truth in their omens. 'Appen we do need charms and safeguards, even in our present state of reason. Captain – yon carving's a fair warning to 'em, depicting t'proper fate of such witches! I'll have it over my porch gable.'

For once Benjamin Greave avoided the kitchen door; though that was his usual entrance, even taking stylish guests that way – his principle being whenever possible to 'kill two birds with one stone', and route his journeys so that he could at the same time supervise his servants. That was the policy that turned a halfpenny into a penny! But not wanting to meet Anne Wylde again, he went through a small side-gate into the walled garden at the front of the house.

They reached the main porch. It was thick-walled and deep, giving the impression of a burrow safe from the weather. Benjamin pushed open the oak door and they were in a passageway lined with dark furniture and gloomy stone. But the scrubbed paved floor was the colour of honey. The sculpture was propped on a sideboard. It was in low relief, fifteen inches high, of sun-bleached and sea-washed marble: a carving that, after long scouring in the elements, seemed never to have been touched by man.

'Perseus slaying the Gorgon Medusa!' the Captain said in that arrogant way of people who have picked up a little knowledge for the purpose of dominating others with it. 'Instead of teeth, the Gorgon women, representing barbarous untamed nature, had the tusks of boars and whoever looked at them was turned to stone. But the handsome Perseus, as brave and clever as he was handsome ...'

'He might have been a Horsfall!' Oliver interrupted.

'... averted his eyes. Afterwards he gave the monster's severed head to the goddess Athene – the patroness of Athens in its golden age of Socrates and Plato. No doubt it signifies that Reason can be born only after such witches have been slain.'

On his galloping horse, Perseus, though 'brave and clever', yet looked over his shoulder frightened of the pursuing women, the Furies, whilst in his right hand he dangled the bleeding female head. The decapitated Gorgon sprawled beneath him – her knees collapsed, her arms and wings plaintively outstretched, blood seeping out of her neck. But this particular Gorgon, who ought according to the Captain's claims to have been grotesque and ugly, was beautiful. She wore a girdle of snakes and her transparent draperies rolled gently over her form as the small waves of a calm sea lap the sand. One artist, at least, had evidently loved her whom he was supposed to have found horrifying!

'It's a crude carving, my friends, probably made by some illiterate local mason such as our own, and much surpassed in elegance and proportion by the products of our present age,' Horsfall opined.

'Perseus looks as furtive as a cut-purse,' Oliver commented. 'As well he might. For the murder of Mother Nature has given birth to monsters of Reason and Progress!'

(4)

to ... the ... winter ... darkening the ...

Winter grew close. Doors and windows were shut tight and the passageways became mouldy. Stone floors, greasy with the damp, were a sombre colour, exhuding a moist chill. The heather was first dusty, then faded and bleached by the autumn rains. In fear of winter, and oppressed by the darkened hills, the weavers grew mutinous or bullied their wives. The memory of summer's business at Makings made the winter desolation seem bleaker. Anne's fellow-servants were bad-tempered. The leaves that drifted into wells, troughs, and against walls, the wet areas that spread over ceilings under damaged roofs, and winds in the open yards that needled you like the Devil's stings, all annoyed them. Plasterers blamed carpenters, dyers cursed fullers, chambermaids blamed kitchenmaids, who threw their slops over the cats. People died in the countryside, in ditches where the frost turned them to stone, in cottages where they had been forgotten, or on moorlands where 'reasonable' men walked overcome with Melancholy.

During the nights Anne Wylde often read her *Iliad*, or in her Bible – loving those sensuous passages that were like a pagan undergrowth to it. '*A bundle of myrrh is my well-beloved unto me: he shall lie all night betwixt my breasts.*' Secret beneath the words, it seemed to her, unreasonable, subdued Nature had once laughed, screamed and sang – before the Prophets put an iron cage about Her, and an iron brank upon Her tongue, as a dangerous witch.

Whilst Anne read and pictured Nature laughing and dancing with her children in Eden, Patience Helliwell and her friends (also desperate, it seemed, about the Expulsion from Paradise) in the kitchen beneath howled and groaned for salvation. Under the hams and salted meats hooked to the ceiling like God's flayed condemned victims hanging in Hell, they cried, they wept, they openly and loudly accounted for their faults (going so far as to enter debit and credit for their sins and their piety, in a ledger first intended to be the clothier's account book). They sang and prayed, even if the good God could

53

not hear above the roar and rattle of the wind at the latch. At other times it had been the odours of cooking that had risen through Anne's floorboards; now it was prayers and hymns, a steam of misery seeping up between the oak planks – high intense beseechings, the most ghastly hymns of the Wesleys:

'Signs in the Heavens see,
And hear the Speaking Rod;
Sinner, the Judgment points to Thee,
Prepare to meet thy GOD!

Terrible GOD! and true,
Thy justice we confess,
Thy sorest Plagues are all *our* due,
We own our Wickedness,
Worthy of Death and Hell ...'

and:

'Constrained by the Stroke of thy Rod
I pour out a Penitent Prayer:
Ah! do not abhor my sad Moan,
Extorted, alas! by Distress,
But hear, and with Pity look down,
And send me an Answer of Peace.'

One day Anne suddenly thought: these are cries to a *mother*, not to a father! They express the feelings of a whipped child in terror of being cut off from female care, burying himself in his mother's lap!

They were, literally, the howls of those poor little boys, John and Charles Wesley, who had been beaten so savagely by their mother Susanna. *These* had become the harrowed wails of clothiers, farmers and tradesmen who felt guilty of an offence against the green moorland world. Who were also thrilled by their own guilty natures:

'A deep Revolter I,
And ever to my Vomit turn ...'

In another part of the house, Benjamin Greave (who tolerated the Methodists because their orderly principles were useful for disciplining the weavers but who himself clung to the Presbyterians, the 'Old

54

Dissent'), schemed over the wars and revolutions of the Continent – butcheries, iconoclasms which he could hardly imagine – thinking of where he could next sell worsteds.

(The news of each crisis was hastened to him from the stagecoach by the Vicar, who always wished to consult with Lady Well's prominent gentlemen over whether or not it was advisable to announce these matters to the general populace in church. Doubtfire, also, sometimes overheard the crying in the kitchen – and wondered whether, after all, there might be some Righteousness spoken by these Methodists with their songs about *the speaking rod, the stroke of Thy rod*, and *the scourge's o'erflow*.)

Or Greave fussed over his tomb – that flock of marble angels intended to block the nave of Saint Mary the Virgin.

Whatever the clothier might have to offer in the form of an erection in the nave and passageways to the Virgin, as he grew older he was losing his potency with his own household. Despite his threats, Anne Wylde was still at Makings. For she had proved a good and careful servant, surprising her colleagues (who had expected little of her) with her knowledge of how to brew and bake, milk cattle and churn, tend poultry; how to prepare cheeses and take care of winter provisions; also (so that her hands should not be idle in the evenings) she had learnt to spin, to card, and the secrets of dyeing, from her aunts. Because she now had a protector in the young Master Greave, she was becoming a happy young woman, and her look was less savage.

Yet she was different from the other women, for she saw into their fates. Having got free of squalid cottages, it was only to spend years in another's house, hoping for marriages that would make them mistresses and also slaves again of just such grimy cots as they had in the first place escaped from.

Here, in this house that was without a mistress, where all the women were servants, she especially noticed how men could work with broad and easy gestures – handling large sums of money, travelling, making decisions, moving stone and wood easily, quartering the land and enclosing the hills with brute strength and physical command over nature. But women's labour was tight and cramped. From earliest childhood, females made thousands of tiny stitches upon a few square inches of 'sampler'; and small fingers remained necessary to do most of their tasks in life. The cut of their clothes confined them to small and ritual movements. In the production of wool their main work was in spinning, dyeing or otherwise preparing the material which their menfolk, the weavers, finished and sold – so that males alone held power and control. The women listened to men, and obeyed. If in some – perhaps many – instances they ruled in bed, this was kept secret and not referred to even between the couple themselves during the day. And if a woman held subtle command between the sheets, the land outside the window always lay passive to the men, ready for them to do what they wanted to Her, though it was a scouring, a burning, a poisoning and robbing for profit.

Anne often found it difficult to talk to the women; whilst men could hardly be addressed at all with any intimate conversation, without it being compromising. She was always glad to be sent out of the kitchen, say to feed the poultry and dogs in the yards. She felt more at home with the amazing abilities and agilities of animals. She watched a cat strip the discarded remains of a fish and discover a complete meal out of it: ravenous, yet still delicate, and nicely poised, the animal would leave a complete, neat skeleton behind. The beauty of its movement thrilled her to the point of tears. Whilst if Anne threw the remains of a meal over a wall, then a crow, with incredible eyesight, would fly from half a mile away to eat it, pecking carefully, gobbling the bits, and turning its head watchfully, in one alert stance and movement that was in contrast to the muffled and lazy apprehensions of humans.

As an alternative to Methodist meetings to cheer some of the winter evenings, a barrel of ale would be opened in the kitchen. Then music was made, out of coarse voices; violins and clarinets; the rattle of dry bones, the vibration of stretched skins, or plucked catgut, or breath in a trembling reed. Oliver described Hellas, and played his fiddle, often joining in a duet with Dick O'Lovely, or some other. Oliver from his wandering days had a network of 'rascally' acquaintances, whom he knew from their hours – or days, or even weeks – of relaxation at remote inns, where they lived passionately for their music or song. Apparent ne'er-do-wells, who lived as scavenging cats do and on the watch-out for Dick Almighty; who thieved and cheated unblushingly over taxes and tithes; they were in fact, in their souls, true artists, giving dedicated labour to their music. They knew how much they were hated in some quarters, being considered as 'barbarians'. Yet 'the young master' welcomed them to the Makings kitchen, and so there at least no one asked them where they had slept the previous night, or who with, and they played their music with joy, until later they melted back into the moorland landscape.

Oliver performing was a man possessed. His passion made his instrument physically part of himself – as impossible to imagine them being parted as to take away an arm or a leg. He would close his eyes tight and his foot went tap, tap to the melody – cascades of music filling the great stone room where smoke and the fumes of ale hung in rosy firelit clouds below the ceiling, and where the furniture was pushed aside to make way for dancing. How he adored drawing his bow across the strings, from the first bars that tested the acoustic of the room – a thrill like that of plunging into a pool and sensing the water – to the last that sighed confidently away through some improvisation of his own. In this circle of rascals and musicians, he, too, was loved and admired as he could never hope to be through his father's business.

Anne took glass after glass of gin. This, and the music, and the knowledge that the artist who produced so much of it – who was the admired golden centre of this company – had sworn himself her sweetheart, inspired her dance. Dance was her element, as the swallow possesses the air or the trout commands the stream. 'Look! Look at Anne Wylde!' She became isolated on the floor. Oliver's tunes made her feel that she was weeping deep inside herself. Yet in this mood melancholy was so mixed with joy that it was indistinguishable from it. Her stomach seemed to fill with air, rise and float through her throat.

Meanwhile the poet-musician showed only a stone-blind face, his feelings turned in to his music, captured and captivating. Everyone would then be reminded that Anne and Oliver were a couple – whatever Anne did it brought envy, admiration and spite. And everyone took notice of her.

One night Anne first met Mr Tim Bobbin. Oliver, in a burst of energy which new love had given him for prosecuting his life, had rescued Tim from his schoolmastering to do the Greaves' ledgers, 'because he wrote the best copperplate in the district', he told his father. Tim, though no more fond of being a clerk than of acting as schoolteacher, yet recognised a sinecure in idleness (or thought he recognised one: he forgot that he would have to reckon with Benjamin Greave) that would be fruitful for his poetry and for his favoured companionships.

Anne saw a small man with bright little eyes and a sensual mouth flowering in a pale face above double chins. Not a handsome face, but a beautiful one because of the happy and adaptable temperament that shone out of it. With great impertinence amongst traders and clothiers, he wore a revolutionary's blue woollen 'cap of liberty'. He was a serious clown, and to express the latter aspect, his breeches were made out of the leather of his old mare, 'to immortalise her by making her the second skin of a poet'.

He put his arm around Anne, but she slipped out of his grasp.

'You are studying to be a clothier, sir?' she asked.

With the arm that had been rejected he made a gesture to express his hatred of such interests. 'I am averse to learning anything of worldly use, I prefer my savage liberty!' He swayed, glass in the other hand, and his extravagant words were delivered in a high-pitched voice. His mere presence brought merriment. 'My greatest living fault is what th'old Greeks called "hubris",' he squeaked, tipping some of his drink on to the floor. 'I gave up being king of the birch when I found I had nothing of the mundane sort to impart. One day a fond parent discovered me asleep on my bench, even the brawling of the infants unable to wake my slumbers. (Though I could have flogged them, as the Parson does ... "God is love!" Wham! Wham!) "What does thou teach the little ones, my good man?" quoth my visitor. "Nothing, sir." "Nothing! Why *nothing*?" "Because I know nothing myself," answers I. "Same as Socrates, who thought he was the wisest man on earth, because he knew that he knew nothing."'

Anne laughed, unmaidenly-loud and suddenly. Then she noticed that Tim was not shocked by it. It surprised her, for most men were.

'But you have no family to care for?'

Froth dropped excitedly from Tim's lips. 'An unhappy wife and some brats to fetch into Benjamin Greave's kingdom when I have found them a cottage!'

'There are plenty of cots in the Greaves' domain. Why did you marry her if it was to make her unhappy?' She easily fell into teasing him – many women did.

As Anne Wylde would not dance with him, the clerk manfully

puffed clouds of smoke out of his pipe – imagining that this added to his dimensions, although the disproportion in size between pipe and himself made him seem even smaller.

'That's a question I have often asked myself. Why make one woman unhappy when I could make many women happy?' Tim answered, pretending extreme thoughtfulness now. 'One day whilst we were courting we saw a maid driving two swine to market. "Those are very pretty, clean pigs!" my Mary remarks. "Then," says I, "we'll each purchase one and the first to draw out of the promise to wed shall forfeit a porker to the other." Mary grew so fond of her porcine companion that she married me rather than lose it. Don't look so fretful, Miss Wylde! We soon got through the fortune she brought into our partnership, and then we were happier, for it tamed my *savage liberty* and I had to seek employment, which kept me at home for a while.'

'Say her some of your poems, Tim,' Oliver encouraged.

Tim set himself up grandly. He held his hands out like a priest, made scything gestures to count the rhythm, and rolled his eyes around the ceiling. The fact that so many in the crowded Makings kitchen were noisy with drink and were ignoring him did not put him off his recitation.

'Some write to show their wits and parts,
Some show you Whig, some Tory hearts,
Some flatter knaves, some fops, some fools,
And some are Mister Greave's tools!'

His dramatic rendering or (more accurately) squealing of his verses arrested many of the drunks. They listened to him with mouths agape in amazement at the very existence of poetry.

Anne saw that Oliver adored Tim, as the only committed maker whom he knew. But she did not like to think she was walking out with a man who did not believe himself to be the best one in the world. So she sought distraction from, as she thought of it, Oliver encouraging her to play fickle with his own friend. And there was Betty, Oliver's daughter who – small and sickly though she was and used to scurrying pale as a lost bewildered ferret about the passage-ways, cared for by the housekeeper or whoever would take charge of her – had come into the arena of music and conversation where she

59

struggled to imitate Anne Wylde's dancing. It was obvious how much the child admired Anne. Laughing, Anne took the hands of the girl and led her through steps that were an erratic caricature of her own.

Afterwards Betty sank back into her weird, watchful silence, her expression turned both inward and outward at one and the same time, and with a curious adult patience. It was as if she had already rushed quickly into maturity because she knew that her life would be a short one; and yet still she was unable to comprehend these people, these adults, who had lived already for such a long while.

On the following mornings Miss Helliwell would return to where she had been expelled by the gaiety. With a hymn on her lips; resentments and loathing on her teeth; *clunk, clunk, clunk*, on her stumpy legs, and a rattle of keys, her first task was to turn sore-heads out of doors. Sulky apprentices and other rascals who had sat through drunkenness to become sober again, and then in blind stupidity swallowed more drink until they collapsed, were woken roughly from corners and trestles and thrust out to face cruel daylight, rain, wind or shine, over their own vomit which they had forgotten having left on the doorstep. 'That was a good night!' they assured one another, reeling and unable to bear the too energetic stirrings of moorland air and light. For them, it would be too bright even on the gloomiest winter day. Meanwhile the kitchen was scoured and aired, whilst guilty eyes were ducked from those who had Methodistically taken themselves early to bed.

'You affect conviviality as happily as if you had thrown a jug of water on a fire,' Tim Bobbin told Patience Helliwell. His waving hands and arms seemed to threaten the housekeeper. He was addicted to making extravagant gestures with his limbs.

She ruffled and puffed like an aggravated sparrow with the wind in its feathers. 'I am one that walks the right road to redemption! Oh what a weight of sin lies on those poor mortals that at night do so much to scourge themselves for i'the morning!'

Thinking of those in need of the *scourge's o'erflow*, she would fix especially on Anne Wylde. The housekeeper would look the girl up and down as if she was an animal in a pen at a fair. Anne realised that Patience's dislike could easily transform into its opposite; she was as one who has been spurned, rather than one who hates. She would shift unpleasantly close to Anne and seem tongue-tied, then move off briskly with pursed lips. Brush close again. Rustle her keys as if they opened the gates of Heaven.

'There is none without hope!' Patience whispered softly one day. 'I've witnessed as many as twelve wicked sinners awakened all in one day by the preacher Elkanah Beanland at a crossroads. This is a time of miracles in Yorkshire – eight of them were redeemed, and not one backslider later amongst them! You could join us still, if you've a mind. What a victory 'twould be for the Lord! There is still time to escape the eternal fires. Just imagine them eternal fires, suffocating, flaming, choking thee, burning for ever and evermore again and through Eternity always!' As she gloated, her eyes had a moist shine, like those of someone in sickness.

Patience was driven crazy by Anne's ignoring of her, so on the next occasion she spoke not apocalyptically, but bitterly. 'You hope that your ways will turn a few heads, believing that men never understand what goes on in the hearts of maidens, thinking them as pure as snow. But the Lord has his surprises in store for you, Hawthorn Maiden!' Her voice rose bitter and high, to an edge of terror like an animal trapped. 'The Lord, I am bound to tell thee, *will* visit with the scourge, whips and rods of His judgment! There was a foolish woman fro' Lady Well scoffed recently at a preacher who was giving out the Words of Light on the river bank. A week – no, I lie, a fortnight – later she was wringing her mop at that same spot when the Good Lord sucked her into th'waters and drowned her. Took her straight t'Ell – she was found in Huddersfield. Drifted down t'river and caught on a bush. Another thing! There was an ungodly parson delivered a sermon against us Methodists and was overcome wi't'plague . . .'

The rebuffed housekeeper revived Benjamin Greave's desire to get the servant girl out of his son's sight. With the master-clothier's approval, Patience set Anne the most unpleasant work, in the cellars and remote rooms, or sent her on errands in the fiercest weather so that she might catch pneumonia, come near death, and realise how little time there was to repent and save her soul.

Despite her good works, Patience was troubled and guilty, even in her bedchamber, by the questioning judging presence of the Lord. Sometimes He took on the outlines of a black bull, looming out of the darkness, setting up a great pounding as if about to stampede. At other times He was formed like a raven; or the dark bird's-wings were, in her dreams, His spread-eagled cloak as He scoured a thousand devils out of the corners of Makings just as she herself did for spiders. Sometimes she even felt His beard tickling her between the sheets.

One windy night she lay questioning whether a noise was her visiting God, or a rat, or a loose board banging in a draught; and though she dozed off once or twice, she soon awoke, more nervous than before. Was a thief prowling? Terrified, grasping her prayer book, Patience raised the household. Servants with pistols, carving-knives, meat skewers and half-rusted swords rushed to the landing outside her room. There had not been time to light enough candles, and many others were blown out in the draughts, so her panicking defenders fell over one another. Those who fancied that they had deep manly voices shouted fearfully at the ceiling. But one of them had to dare the rafters and to avoid being chosen most busied themselves comforting Patience, who broke down under the unaccustomed attention, stuttering and wailing as if (Tim Bobbin said) the Devil already had her by the toe.

Tim was the only one to brave the roof. He felt in need of some opportunity to display his virtue; for Benjamin Greave had been complaining about his fecklessness, had been quarrelling with Oliver about the 'clerk', and though Tim didn't 'give a pig's whistle' for the old clothier, it pained him to compromise the young one who was his friend and patron. So in virtuous gallant defence of the housekeeper he crept, balancing on the ceiling joists, crouching beneath the filthy slates, dodging sharp gusts of wind that threatened to blow out his light; knowing how easily he could miss his foot-hold, break a rotten timber and fall through a ceiling; startling rats and mice, and truly scared.

At last, 'Your thief and demon's nothing but a chimney-flap blown in the windy!' he shouted and he came thundering down.

A group of menservants, to cover their shame, now claimed that he had tackled the disturbance wrongly and that they themselves knew better and braver solutions which the poet's rashness had prevented their executing; whilst the maids converted Tim Bobbin into a hero and giggled as they led him away to wash off the soot.

'I who have never dreamed of robbers nor slept with a door closed in my life, come t'a rich man's house and have to be raised up to crawl in the rafters like a bat, for fear of a chimney-flap!' Tim shrieked. 'You all tremble with an ague fit. Do you think the Devil with his cloven-footed squadrons is after you? You can keep your wealth, if it brings such fears!' he spluttered through gobfuls of cold water. 'I've seen enough to satisfy me that he who has a bare living and can sleep soundly at nights with his door open is the only happy man. I've had enough of you! I've spoilt my best hat wi' taking it off, sticking it under my arm to bow and cringe to piece-makers! My neck's grown crooked and my chin turned into my shoulder with obsequious humility! From the worries of being a clerk I can carry large quartos in the breast of the jacket I could hardly button a few months back. I'll be off to retrieve my savage liberty!'

Tim was one who dealt in poetic, not in mundane truth; in other words, so far as merchants were concerned he was a liar. But in matters of change and movement he meant what he said. Also, his account books were in a muddle. Tim left Makings as thoughtlessly and unpreparedly as he had arrived. But it was to the envy of Oliver, who had found in Tim the only other person with the same feckless and unreasonable instinct as his own for wandering.

Oliver sometimes, on mornings of fine weather, could also get away, though only to travel the cottages seeing what progress was made with spinning and weaving. He was then offered, here a jug of ale, there an artisan's views on poetry, on rational philosophy, on Calvinistic predestination or on the easier more-magical redemption offered by Messrs Wesley. But on most days, with cold compresses over his forehead, inside which buzzed regrets and resolutions, Oliver designed labels for woollen goods: surrounding 'Amens. 28sh. per yard', and 'Bays. 18sh. per yard', with wreathed Ionic columns and lewd drawings of the love of Adonis for Venus, or he laboured over correspondence to persuade merchants to take his father's worsteds. Both the clerk to the governors of Christ's Hospital in London, and the factor who supplied soldiers' cloth to the Empress Catherine of Russia, could not understand why the clothier was so little interested in their requests for rough woollens, instead wanting them to bring shalloons to the attention of their clients. Oliver hardly cared what types of cloth were sold nor whether it was suitable for paupers or for ladies.

But his father was always at his elbow, insisting that the only way to 'defeat' the clothiers of Somerset and Gloucestershire, and 'raise-up' a Yorkshire industry, was to make finer and yet even finer woollens.

So Oliver wrote: '*If you would be pleased to accept our calliman-coes you will benefit from the best making in England.*' Then he added a more persuasive afterthought: '*I also trust you will find to your satisfaction these sides of pork from our own native hills.*'

His mind wandered constantly, but settled longest on the subject of Anne Wylde. In the idle drift of his thoughts, he often considered what a dismal place Makings must be for such as her. For that was how he himself found it to be.

And that, obviously, was how it appeared to his daughter Betty. Oliver was sad that, being a widower, he could do so little for her.

Betty drifted amongst the temples of wool bales, the dark tombs and ziggurats of its piles, as detached as her father was from the woollen industry – sitting and swinging her legs here, dashing along that warehouse alley, darting between a surprised Dutchman's legs, then peeping out scared but interested from some burrow made of kerseys and callimancoes. She was like a kitten, or like a scrap of winged seed that had blown in and was puffed hither and thither, having nothing to do with this place and possessing nowhere to take root. When she was bored with the barns, she played with the fowls and the dogs in the yards.

But always eventually she had to join Patience Helliwell, who was responsible for her.

'All this will be hers someday!' Patience remarked to Oliver – disapproving, envious, but putting on the measured air of one who is wise and sagacious. 'Well then, she must be brought up to her responsibility.'

'How?' Oliver asked in surprise. For he had never thought about the subject of educating a daughter, and no one else had ever suggested that it was of importance.

'So as to devote 'er wealth to good works and not bad ones, she must 'ave a clear knowledge of the dark world of sin that surrounds us. She must learn to fear God, for only 'E can save us. The spectacle of *funerals* is most instructive to children. She should be taken to one, instructed in the awful fear of death, and then to make the lesson stick brought home, whipped and locked in a cellar to meditate on our earthly lot.'

'I will have no such thing done to my lovely daughter! It is preposterous!'

Patience touched his arm, and let her fingers linger there. 'Maybe it sounds harsh to your ears, but trust me it is the only way. "Spare the rod and spoil the child", Mr Greave. 'Twas done to me and it did no harm, as you can see. 'Twas the method by which Mr Wesley himself was brought up and it made him a saint. One of our own brethren is to be buried next week, Mr Greave. It should be an instructive occasion ...'

'Miss Helliwell!' Oliver interrupted – but could then think of no reasonable arguments against her monstrous suggestion. So, 'Where is Anne Wylde?' he asked, to change the subject.

'She is cleaning a cellar.'

He grasped the opportunity for diversionary anger. 'Such a Venus, such an Aphrodite, set to clean cellars! I will not have it, Miss Helliwell!' He threw down his quill so that it splattered on his letter. 'I think you are in league with my father to keep the fair maiden from me! I say I will not suffer it! This is the last straw! Like Mr Bobbin I am sick of heart, and I'll be off to Athens tomorrow ...'

That evening he went to Anne's room. She was snipping her hair. Her scissors slipped so that she cut her neck, and he rushed to mop it with his handkerchief.

'I cut myself because you came upon me! They say we women are to blame for our troubles, and that we mutilate ourselves, seeking suffering.' Oliver lingered with the handkerchief. 'I have been waiting for you, Oliver.' There were tears in her eyes.

Her tenderness released his hands. He began lightly, touching her knuckles, her wrist encircled by the strange red line that never faded, then up her arm, across the back of her shoulders, lingering with delicate fingering at the pit of her neck, feeling the flesh thrill; whilst with the other hand he held her waist. This first occasion that he came really close to her, he with relief discovered that her breath was fragrant and he tried to kiss her. He fingered her breasts, and he ached for those white fluttering doves.

Anne was used to hard graspings or fumblings, and no one had ever fondled her so delicately. She had never imagined that a man who was hardly touching her at all, his fingers doing little more than rest and flutter upon her skin like a butterfly, could melt her thus.

But she also had her reasons for not trusting men. From what practice with other women had he learnt to do this? she thought. The acquirement must have involved many deserted maidens. So when his hands played near her breasts, 'Ah no, sir!' she said.

'Anne, do you know what a passionate creature you are?'

'Do not touch me like that.' As she moved his hand, she felt something harder pressing into her below. 'Do not do that,' – although she was absorbed and lost in desire for him to do just *that*.

Over his shoulder, she caught the eyes of Patience Helliwell in the passageway. Anne put two hands on Oliver's chest so that he turned to see what alarmed her. Patience after glaring for a moment, her hands grasped together – not as if making a prayer, but tight and trembling as if pulping something, flower or insect, beyond recognition between them – disappeared into the shadows.

The housekeeper felt that just by showing her presence she had issued sufficient warning. What she had actually achieved was to bind the lovers together in the common purpose of having to do something about the housekeeper; and, far from being parted, they found they had now reached that state of closeness in which they did not need to speak, for a touch and a meeting-of-eyes would communicate enough.

Patience Helliwell returned after Oliver left. Full of jealousy she stroked Anne's hair. Anne could see no way of escape. Patience smiled sweetly. 'Attractive young servant girls are soon tempted – especially when they think themselves intended to be more than servants. But thou's bound only for eternal fires along yonder road. Why do you never seek redemption along with the rest of us at our joyful hour? Those who were at Upper Spout, 'til Master Greave opened sulphur springs have joined recently, not cast down by the loss of their home but secure o' their reward in Heaven. Elkanah Beanland has preached, wi' fire in his voice. Richard Whitely a time or two has delivered eloquent sermons telling of the deceit o' scamps and wicked travellers. Binns has called upon us, and Amos Culpin, and others you'll know from Lady Well. You stay aloof from the right-thinking folk, with your fine ways, when you could be so happy with us! There are all classes visit. Many of the most rejected of mankind come in to hear the Good Book and the sermons sent to us by Mr Wesley and others.'

'The scourings of the countryside enter because the room is warm! You can sing and shriek and write your "rules for conduct" in your ledger like weavers' clerks, but it'll never make me believe that is the way to Heaven!'

'Oh, there can be such Heaven for us poor sinners and I am one who is already 'cquainted with the taste of it!'

Patience was swooning. With desperate roughness she took hold of the girl's hand and forced it to stroke her own thigh. Then she abruptly raised her dress and thrust Anne's fingers into her opening, although it was quite dry. The girl sprang away so quickly that for once she forgot to stoop and caught her head on the low ceiling. Patience withdrew into herself. But she was shaking, like a cat that has been rudely swept out of doors.

'And what does thou think Mr Greave will make of your evil tempting of his son? You're a servant still and nothing'll turn thee into anything else, Miss. Be glad of the Lord's will, if you would escape the Everlasting Fire!'

The housekeeper moved to the far side of the room, turned her back (which was shaking violently, a frightening sight in its lack of self-control), opened her legs and desperately fingered; forgetting Anne Wylde, she was lost in a dream of her own.

Snow tumbled over the hills. A sharp wind followed and raised it in clouds of white smoke above the walls, laying drifts upon the road-ways. The West Country was quite cut off, and so was Norwich, they learnt, before Yorkshire too was isolated in an ocean of silent pillows. Even the goods and presents already sent away would arrive late and damaged from having stood on snowbound wharfs at Hull.

The more Benjamin Greave's imprisonment and damaged trade became unbearable, the more he attributed it to a bewitching of his household by Anne Wylde, was sure that she brought nothing but ill-luck and must be got rid of. All the weavers if they could get together through the snowdrifts had stories to tell about Anne. Through alcoholic fumes in the early hours of the morning her shape or her spirit loomed out of the smoky shadows of dozens of hush-houses and inns.

Oliver was distracted by her. When she walked out of a room, it was for the poet as if darkness descended. When *she* was not there was when he felt a prisoner. He was immured in his room simply because there was nowhere he wished to go; all freedom was taken from him because there was nothing he wished to do without her. In a house in which he had access to all the keys, he paced his room as a prisoner does, trying to think of some way out of his dilemma, or of some diversion from his desire, and wondering (because, after all, he was no young fool in love for the first time!) whether she was with equal impatience thinking of him. Was this the true 'happiness' of love – this mixture of the sweet and the sour so intermixed that you could not tell which was which?

Meanwhile the thought of Anne Wylde's 'spells' upon his son and indeed over the whole valley preyed upon Benjamin Greave's mind whilst he was in his barns, brooding amongst the stranded and growing mountins of cloth. The snow, which like his cloth was piled up uselessly everywhere, and the frost, which seized the springs, the milk in the jugs so that they cracked, and even the piss in the chamberpots, was, he decided, the curse laid by this evil pagan spirit who had been born in the hotbed of a community's sins. After days of sulky temper, he came out with his thoughts to Oliver.

'I'm deeply troubled! If that girl gets into our family she'll go through my fortune like a knife through butter. And thou'd never be able to maintain thy superiority. It'd be silks and fine dresses and trips to London to choose them and a king's ransom spent in candles for her balls every winter!'

'If Anne Wylde leaves, I'll go with her.'

Benjamin realised that he could not prevent this if it arose. Yet even the mildest threat from his son gave the clothier a desperate fear of being abandoned – an apprehension that he kept to himself as much as he could. He swung his arm at Oliver, who stepped back, trembling at his temptation to strike his father.

'Now look how she has set father against son as well as servant against master!' Benjamin shouted, frightened of the loneliness he saw looming. 'I tell you I'll not have her here! And I forbid you to see her!'

Nonetheless the lovers did meet. In the frozen garden a single rose managed to flower. Nobody noticed it but Anne, who intended to pluck it for Oliver when the petals opened in perfection. She fluttered with anxiety lest they became frostbitten and black. Each morning and evening she strode out, stooped in the snow on which frost

68

glittered, and she cupped the fragile crimson in her hands, blowing gently upon it until she grew stiff with cold. The petals seemed each morning gratefully to open a little more, and each evening to close gladly upon her own warmth that she had sacrificed for them.

She hoped she was unobserved. But Horsfall (who was always hanging around Makings) saw her. 'Look, my friend,' he confidingly told Oliver, 'I'll find some way to keep the Old Man busy whilst you go out to your sweetheart.'

Oliver, torn between love for Anne and for his father, was glad of the ruse. It succeeded. As the couple met, snow whitened the northern flank of the house, whilst trees were as thick with frost as they had been with leaves all summer, and it looked like a white, bridal blossoming. Everything about the lovers, even their speech, was frozen; they were mute with the silence of a couple newly meeting who believe any converse too mundane a vehicle for their mutual gifts of love.

Oliver wanted to lead Anne towards a stone belevedere (one which had been built by her own father; though his buildings were so common about the countryside that she never took notice of them), and she, not wishing him to detect her business with the rose, let him take her there. 'Anne, before I met you I lived like someone sickening. I saw no reason to climb out of my bed. I could sleep until noon and yet still be tired. I saw no purpose in any conversation. In my father's business. In poetry, even. I remembered that beauty does exist, but I could not feel it ... perhaps such memories, such numbness, is Hell itself? All my comforts meant nothing to me. I was trapped here, yet without the strength to move. And now because of you all the light and beauty has flooded back into the world! How can I explain it? I am in love with you. I am your heart's slave.' As they sat on the frosted bench, his *own* heart was thumping with fear and excitement at the consequences of her accepting his love.

Anne had previously been wooed with stones and catcalls, so she yearned for such tenderness as he had shown her; such spiritual and artistic refinement, as was the cause of Oliver's weakness. Now this 'weakness' shone at her with sun-like Apollonian radiance.

'You say that you are my "heart's slave", but I want you to be independent, as you deserve to be, free as the sun and the air.'

'It is a poetical figure of speech.' He flushed. 'I am quite free.'

'But you are not free of your father. He keeps you confined when your desire is to travel.'

'I told you that I would leave Makings if you were forced to!'

'I would want you to leave for you own desires, not because of mine. Poor Oliver, you are not free, because you understand so little of the cruel results of human frailty. We poor folk and servants see much more. We have to, to survive.'

'You are like some ancient priestess from whom flows a fount of sensibility!'

'Tim Bobbin said I am a Celtic Queen who should be decked in jewels and flowers. Why cannot I be just a *woman*? In truth I am no wiser than many a washerwoman. It seems there are as many clever washerwomen as there are parsons, who should listen to what is said in kitchens before they write their sermons.'

Her apparent lack of sympathy with his sentiments was so equably expressed that it was unnerving. For the first time ever, Oliver felt cut by the razors of her cool quick answers. As the Reverend Doubtfire, as his own father, as *her* own father, and many others so reasonably opined: her cleverness degraded male dignity and superiority. At this moment he thought that he understood why they stoned her. Yet when he looked into her face, he realised he was staring into a mirror: his muse. This woman was her own self. He felt helpless.

'No one is like you – I would like to lay my fortune at your feet,' he answered, weakly.

'And I have always wished merely to be left alone.'

They could talk, talk, talk about love for ever. But it was becoming unbearingly cold. The rooks, that scavenged daily in Greave's well-manured enclosures where the dung-straw now lay upon the snow in golden tresses, were returning to their roosts and were speckled across the last strands of the sunset. Darkness and frost would fall tonight as sudden as an executioner's axe; as the trap of the notorious guillotine in the nearby town of Halifax. They walked back through the bare and frozen rose-garden whilst the lamps and candles were lit in the mansion and they could hear from beyond a wall the clatter of hooves and wheels as workmen prepared to return home.

'Oh, Oliver, though I feel so much for you yet I cannot give myself in-to the care of someone so foolishly trusting. In Horsfall, for instance...'

'He is helping us to meet now! It seems that suddenly no one can see any innocence – even you, who are yourself full of innocence. My father suspects you, you suspect Horsfall, though he tells us that he is our friend!'

'A man like that never does anything that's not to his own advantage. I don't know what there can be in it for him to bring us together, but his desiring it is no good omen. Look. I want to show you something.'

She raced him back to the garden, plucked the rose and pressed it, a token of her body, to his breast.

When Anne looked at flowers, it was as if *they* gazed even more intensely at her, he noticed. Staring flowers seemed to undress her. Birds and animals were the same; they peered, fascinated, straight into her. From the way she held the rose, Oliver realised that for Anne Wylde every plant and creature, wind and water, rock, hill and valley, had a living spirit. It was a pagan sense with which she had been born and she was not aware of it. If her attention was fixed, even upon a mere glass of water or a half-frozen rose, her nature responded appreciative of the living, separate being. She loved, but left alone. There was no division into demons and the children of God for Anne. The Universe was a harmony to her.

Restless in her bed, Anne overheard the Methodists beneath. '*Oh God Thy Righteousness we own,/ Judgment is at the house begun/ With humblest Awe thy Rod we bear,/ And guilty in Thy Sight appear!*' blistered the floor. '*Our Sin and Wickedness we own,/ And deeply for Acceptance groan!*' cut through the passages and stairways, out over the hills to join the harsh, stony calls of starving rooks and winter-thrushes.

Anne could not sleep for it. She huddled herself into a shawl to hurry through the damp stone passageways, where in some places icicles and sheets of ice hung upon the walls, and she went downstairs. The kitchen door was open and no one saw her enter the crowded room, with most backs turned to her. They were packed even upon the long table, which an hour or two ago Anne had scrubbed, and were holding on to one another like shipwrecked people clinging to a storm-tossed raft. At the far end of the room the faces ran with sweat for there a huge fire licked the black cavern of the chimney. To Anne, it looked like the gate of Hell. To Patience Helliwell, it offered the same symbol. That was why, smiling upwards with nervous self-satisfaction next to the visiting preacher, and twitching her fingers around her keys to Heaven, Hell and Benjamin Greave's knives, forks and pewter, she stood before it: because all, whether sweat-tormented at the front of the room or frozen white at the back of it, were turned towards this reminder of th'eternal furnace, and its infernal machinery for roasting souls or sides of bacon. Betty crouched there too, hesitantly afraid to warm her toes at the 'fires of Hell'.

When they became aware of Anne, it was as when she used to walk into the apothecary's at Lady Well and the women were gossiping; there was a silence, and a feeling that nothing further would be prosecuted until she had left. Only Betty ran to her, relying upon finding warmth and comfort in the folds of Anne Wylde's gown.

But Patience had been preparing for such a moment as this, and she struck up the hymn that she had saved for it. She conducted by holding a large kitchen-knife in her hand. Anne noticed how fiercely this 'humble and meek' woman clutched the handle, and how viciously glittered the blade which, Patience insisted, must always be razor-sharp. Her congregation – the servants dried up from a lifetime's service to the clothier, the shuffling wanderers out of the countryside defeated of all hope except for a last sad reflective anchorage in God the Father (as interpreted by this kitchen-evangelist), and those tradesmen who saw advantages in Methodist doctrines of regularity and sobriety, or perhaps thought it worthwhile to use any means to get inside Benjamin Greave's house – whilst seeming to ignore Anne Wylde and avoid her sensual eyes, yet they wailed more loudly for her benefit. They howled in the pitiful way of beasts who have seen that their life's journey is but to the slaughterhouse, and who find perverse consolation in their own helplessness:

'Abandoned to the Fury's will,
I prove her utmost power,
And twice ten thousand deaths I feel,
Yet live to suffer more!

With me the ghastly spectre walks
In every secret shade,
In all her horrid forms she stalks
Around my sleepless bed

My poor despairing soul she racks
With agonising smart,
Her whip of knotted vipers shakes,
And tears my bleeding heart!

My soul shrinks back – but oh! to whom
Or whither shall I run?
Will God, the just, reverse my doom,
And hear my latest groan?'

Their bowed, guilty shiftiness! Their spiritual ledgers, their clasped brown books of horrid verses – verbal enclosures similar to those stone ones that imprisoned the moors, to those hedges that gripped the pastures, and that kept out life, light and the wild creatures of moor and woodland!

Anne with her hands clasped over her ears tore away from the surprised, hurt Betty and ran from the room, hunted again, this time not with stones, but with hymns. These tore like Patience Helliwell's knives when they rended the flesh of hares, rooks, salmon, sheep, cattle and pigeons. Along the passageways, not knowing which ones she was following, Anne fled shrieking. Often she ran through darkness, yet some spirit seemed to save her from collisions. Back and forth, on different levels of the house, shrieking.

The Methodists paused in silent awe and horror listening to this ghost, this banshee. Anne's pained scream travelled, louder, softer, louder, softer. It was like a trapped bird's cry: a lark baffled in a cage of hymns.

At last, the preacher calmly said, 'She is a mad woman that must be confined in irons. Makings and our useful countryside must be purged, must be rid, must be saved from her – praised be the Lord!'

'Confine the witch! Lock her up! Lock 'er in Bedlam! Praisèd be the Lord!' the other Methodists exclaimed. And then (with more vigour than they had shown all evening) they chanted:

'GOD MADE THE DEVIL, THE DEVIL MADE SIN,
GOD MADE A HOLE TO PUT THE DEVIL IN!'

Whilst Betty, stinging from Anne's apparent abandonment of her, raised her thin voice mercilessly with the rest of them.

(5)

Escaping before it was Dick Almighty who came jangling chains and keys to remove and confine her, Anne returned to Lady Well in April. On her walk there she saw a clothier's barn that had burned down. It was a recent event, for it had melted a bright green patch out of the snow, and there was still a smell of wet ashes. The stone roof-tiles had broken and fallen, except for one or two perilously hanging over the edges of walls and clinging to the charred timbers that poked into the sky. Poor children, women and discharged soldiers making their way across the country – winter starvelings – were picking amongst the ruins, risking their lives under tons of collapsing masonry in the hope of finding rags or some corn. Half a mile further on Anne came across a once-fine building erected by John Wylde, and now also burned to the ground. These destructions were the only changes in Lady Well, although she naturally expected the rest of the world to be as much transformed as she herself had been in the past eight months.

She was menstruating and the blood was uncomfortable, making her irritable. The stone-upon-stone of the town oppressed her once again; stone underfoot, stone portals framing God, the sky, and the greening moors. Even the familiar tap, tap, tap growing steadily louder as she approached the mason's yard did not seem a welcoming sound any more, bowed as she was by her sense of failure, feeling wearied and cold because of her menstruation. But as she came up the pathway, sadness was at last overborne by a glow from her father's house, where she noticed that the snow had disappeared off the roof because of the warmth within. Yet, on entering under its low ceilings, she was forced once more to stoop.

Her father had been reading Lavater's *Aphorisms on Man*. He did not expect her and had received little news; only sometimes a passing weaver or workman had brought a message. When he glanced up and saw his daughter, he could not speak. Something, that could not be contained within Reason (though to the mason this was 'God's great-est attribute'), overwhelmed him. His spectacles grotesquely enlarged his eyes and their welling tears, until with shaking hands he put his lenses on the table. 'I was just thinking of you,' he said (but he was always thinking about her), and he flushed, with (Anne sensed with alarm) what might have been an incapacity of the heart. He was of those middle years when a person who leads a tiring worrying life seems on certain days to grow old suddenly, and Anne was stabbed with compassion for his helplessness, large as he was.

John Wylde felt for his daughter something akin to a mother's love, so purified was it by self-sacrifice. He led her gently into the parlour where his charts and treatises were, scattered just as when she had left.

'Father, you should not be alone. I ought to be here taking care of you.'

'But I've got me a servant woman!'

'At last!'

'At last, as you say. She's a poor thing, who'd not otherwise have survived the winter. Martha!'

Anne heard a shuffling in the passageway. It did not seem to be a person walking on two feet, but was more like an animal brushing against things. There entered a small crippled woman apparently about forty years of age. One side of her hip sagged uselessly. Her face was pale, blotchy, stupid. Even so it expressed loving tenderness and she looked at John Wylde adoring him.

'Martha, this is my daughter, Anne.'

'Please t'meet you, Ma'am.' As the cripple attempted a curtsey, it looked as though her bones would collapse into jelly. It made Anne feel sick and she turned away.

'That's all right, Martha, you lay out oatcakes and soup and we'll join you presently.'

After she had left, Wylde explained, 'As a baby she was dropped at the door of the hospital and when she was nine they put her out to service for seven years. The mistress beat her and broke her bones so she was little use to man or beast. They would have killed her and when they wanted to be rid it was only kindness to take her in. You know I do not like to have servants about the house. But this is a good one. She is still only fourteen years of age and there is no one more willing.'

75

Anne suffered a jealous pang, seeing the willingness with which her father brought a stranger into his family (though according to gossip she was herself adopted). 'A thing like that cannot care for you! Th'ospital can take her back and I will stay here!' Anne shouted angrily.

Wylde looked startled. Then he understood. 'Something's happened at Making Hall. The truth shows through no matter what pleasant lies you send ahead of you to soothe me.'

She was silent for a while. Then she said quietly, 'I saw two buildings burned down on my way here, Father.'

'We have discontented weavers or some of that sort, "having a mind to bring revolution by setting things afire", so Dick Almighty says. "Folk i' moorland taverns and hush-houses who drink untaxed brews, sell stolen game, and enjoy night-long suppers of their poachings over which they discuss elections, poetry, Reason, or the downfall of the innkeeper and the King," that is the way he puts it. "Subscribers to penny libraries." I believe Dick thinks that I'm one of them. This week he's hunted out the Rhodes family that once lived at Upper Spout, who have been hiding books i'Greek and seditious pamphlets in a coffin that was supposed to be awaiting the passing of a sick grandfather.'

'I've not heard anyone but our housekeeper at Makings and the Vicar talk of fire. I remember he wanted an artist to depict the flames of Hell eternal upon the church walls but the wardens wouldn't have such "Popery". Nor could they understand why our Parson was so interested in such depictions, for he had always shown hatred of art and graven images before.'

'Doubtfire used to think so much of you and now he can't say a good word! He tells folk that you've bewitched them at Benjamin Greave's and are spreading sedition there. "You know what your lass is like," he says. "They'll be after her for a witch there, too. They'll be looking to her as the cause o't'fires and will be setting *her* upon a blaze".'

Anne in shame pressed and rubbed her fists into her eyes. 'The housekeeper didn't like me because she's a Methodist and she gave me the worst work to do! Old Man Greave thought I was after his fortune. I cannot go back. Father, I have been so unhappy – but for one person, a fair good man, I have been made so unhappy! You know how you may sink to such depths of misery that you become too weak to alter it and appear to choose to continue in your state, in spite of yourself you go on, confusing those around you? That's how I was.'

When his daughter was upset, it evaporated John Wylde's temper. 'Well, perhaps there's no need for you to return. We'll think of something. These are not the Dark Ages, for we now know that all problems can be resolved through Reason. I've been reading some of our greatest philosophers this winter, to pass the time on. The Universe, I've discovered, is but a great rational instrument like a clock in which, once set in motion by God, one thing brings about another. As in a mill or a manufactory, after the raw wool is fed in it continues through due process, all hands obedient to Reason and playing their part. We have but to accumulate enough knowledge in order to set everything right. God is our mill-master. Abundant Nature is as it were the handmaiden of Man, serving him with materials to exploit; whilst Reason is the manufactory through which he puts it, turning it into goods for his ease and prosperity. It's proven that every single thing is caused by another. So now we can sit peacefully by the fireside and trace all your misfortunes to one original cause, or to one misuse of the clockwork of knowledge – so I've learnt from the doctors – and correct it. Come now, go and tell Martha to serve oatcakes and we'll settle down and adjust your nature to the facts.'

'I don't think you can understand everything from philosophers.'

Her father grew impatient. He restored his spectacles and spoke more emphatically. 'God's universe is such a marvellous balanced instrument that if so much as one thing or person is out of step, the whole is by that degree, be it ever so small, upset, just as with an unreliable servant in a manufactory. I have always tried to teach you, believing that it is everyone's birthright, but it seems the result has only been for you to show too much independence for your female station! A woman that is wise as well as clever should ever struggle to be modest – a lesson you have never taken to heart, though you have learnt so much else. Be taught that, and I'm sure all else will follow, when you are less conspicuous.'

John Wylde angrily left the room, returning himself with the food. They ate in silence. Then the father read aloud from Lavater's *Aphorisms*. ' "Forwardness nips affection in the bud." And here's another

77

wise saying for you to think on, now. "If you mean to be loved, give more than what is asked, but no more than is wanted." Your main fault, Anne, from which all your troubles spring, is excess.'

'It is the world that is mean and timid.'

'So you blame the world now!'

'I am very unhappy.' She played clumsily with her hair that tumbled stiffly about her head like thorns. 'I think I will go to bed.'

'We'll bring your things home tomorrow. The day after we will go to church with Martha. I have a bacon joint for dinner and we can wash it down with ... with something that Dick Almighty knows nothing about.'

'You will not want me in church. I am unclean.'

'Oh.' He smiled, with tears pricking his eyes. 'Well, then – here's a last thought from Lavater. "Whom smiles and tears make equally lovely, all hearts may court".'

She laughed again – her father and his philosophers talked such nonsense. Once more comforted by this familiar house and the memories of soothings received in it, she climbed the oak stair, the very dimensions of it making her happy. The big carefully oiled clock ticking in the passageway. And the shape of the hill outside her bedroom which seemed to her like a crouching hare, gladdened her, lying under stars in the snowy dusk.

She stripped, and as Martha had thoughtfully put a bowl of water ready in her room, Anne spent some time cleaning up her blood.

It led her to staring at this desirable body of hers. In the candlelight it was long and snake-like, smeared at the top of her thighs. She twisted this way and that, watching fascinated as different bones projected. She squeezed her freckles, counted them, traced the pattern of a scar, then she pulled at her mouth and eyes. She rearranged her hair. Put two hands under her breasts and tried how they looked when she lifted them. Examined that opening amongst the bushes where in a fountain of blood the Devil was supposed to dwell. She pictured him, with his little ram's horns and impish eyes, peeping out of the well of blood.

She stopped caressing herself when the feeling of something uncanny outside made her look through the window. The tradesmen and artisans mostly went to bed at seven, to save the expense of candles, and even the Constable did not find it necessary to make any

78

rounds; instead he attracted the rascals to listen to his 'sermons' in his public house. Yet there was Doubtfire, presumably on his way to visit someone who was sick. His eyes glittered impishly in the light that he carried. Realising that he was seen he vanished amongst the walls.

When Anne came down the next morning Martha was babbling about another clothier's house that had been fired. It pleased her greatly and she was chuckling to herself as she served oatcakes.

The burned house belonged to the family of Esther Kershaw who like a Papist kept a holy relic in her bedroom – the apron stained with blood which had dripped on her from the church roof during one of Doubtfire's services and which she believed was the blood of Christ. (If it was not, then what else was it?) Esther was the only one to escape the flames, clutching this garment, and now was to live without father, husband, children or home. 'All my years living faithful in Holy Monotony gone to waste!' she had cried. 'We grow a rose in a garden only for our menfolk to pluck it, and soon as 'tis plucked, then all is gone...!' She was half mad, walking up and down Lady Well shrieking this, tearing at her hair and her apron, and claiming that it was the Reverend Doubtfire who had set the fire in revenge for her making a holy image. Esther said that henceforth she would wander the moors wearing the apron as a 'sign' and would go only amongst poor people, there to look for the true Christ whom she did not find through the Lady Well Vicar.

'Esther is I suppose slandering our Parson because he will not raise an appeal in church for her relief – she being something of a Papist,' John Wylde said.

'Everything that Esther says is not foolish, Father.'

John Wylde took no further interest in Martha's and Anne's talk of Doubtfire and magical spots of blood. His face was shut. Anne now cared only about her father's expression. She felt guilty at remembering how irritable and selfish she had been, and at not having inquired about *his* affairs, and she thought he was sulking because of this.

Yet as so often she said the wrong thing. 'You cannot consider a person as being like nothing more than a spinning machine – or even a shed full of machines. Our natures are not so mechanical and we do not accumulate understanding like money added to a store, for often

79

one thing that we think we know conflicts with another ...'

'Doubtfire watched you display yourself at your window last night!' John Wylde burst out. 'When they went to tell him about the new fire he thought it a small matter compared with what he had seen of "The Lady Well whore", as he called my daughter!' Quivering, breathing heavily, he was removing his belt. 'No wonder they call you "whore"!'

'That's not reasonable, Father ...'

'To Hell with reason! All of Lady Well is looking to find fault with my daughter! Almighty's *Felon Society* has met to discuss ways of apprehending the fire-raiser and even there the Vicar had to tell 'em that their time'd be better spent rooting out witches and sinful women. Yet still you taunt them with your wickedness! I'm thinking that folk are right and thou'rt truly a demon from the Old Religion sent to plague us. Something bred like a gadfly out of the manure of our sins. Oh, what a daughter! I've always been too gentle with you, thou's done untold harm to my business, and folk are laughing at me. The Constable will be coming to *us* before long!' Wylde was swinging his belt, one end wrapped around his thick wrist. 'It seems that rough timber must have many blows to hew it even and fit for the Lord's building!'

'No!' Anne screamed. Or rather, a scream possessed her – a sound not human but intense as the cry of a vixen or a peacock: all her being was consumed in that yell.

John Wylde, who had been unnerved by this unearthly howl once or twice before, shouted, 'Thou'rt no daughter of mine!' and, afraid of what he heard both from himself and from Anne, he chased her down the path. Then, so that no one would witness his tears, he returned indoors.

As Anne fled, housewives cackled, artisans whistled and shouted, and the young ones again threw stones, thinking that the old days of baiting their scapegoat had returned. ''Awthorn! 'Awthorn! Burn in t'fire!' they shouted, and the familiar:

'God made the Devil! The Devil made sin!
God made a hole to put the Devil in!'

Hurtling through the flowerless stony narrow streets, where the hard echoes cruelly mocked her flight, Anne recalled the many occasions when she had escaped. But this time she had even deserted her father's house.

Beyond town she kept on running, through an air tainted with last night's ashes, and she made for the moors, where there were no people. She was already on Black Hill before she remembered that there lived her Aunt Pity, with whom she could take shelter.

It was said of Pity that she was so old, she had been around at the time of the earliest Christians. One thing at least could be truly said of her: she offered comfort and healing, not only to her neighbours, but even to vagabonds, wandering soldiers, gypsies, and other travellers with cut feet who called on her. So Anne ceased to rush or sweat and she peacefully climbed the slopes looking lovingly about her. Most of the snow had vanished in the morning sun. The urgings of grass or buds could be felt and primroses were straightening after the burden of snow. Moisture necklaced the plants with pearls, and upon them light trembled, whilst dappling further hillsides with broad sheets that were flowing with shadows. Tentative robins and thrushes were singing to test the coming spring. She saw a wren. Bright tongues of water licked out of so many enclosures and banks, it seemed that all the hills and valleys floated upon it: as if everywhere underneath was the one substance, breaking out with a voice cheerful as the bird-song.

Meanwhile the road was growing stonier and there were more, larger patches of snow. On Black Hill she could look across other hills stretching silver and dark grey for miles. The moor was animated with a scattering of boulders shaped by wind and rain into forms seeming full of dormant life. There were vast purple-dark pregnant stomachs balanced on slender stalks. Rocks like old molar teeth, or like tiny virgin breasts popped up out of the grass. You could imagine anything. The stones were alive, and changing constantly, as she walked by, from one form into another. Here there was no grass, only withered rushes, their tips capturing the gold given by the sun so that there seemed to be swarms of dancing sun-spots around her feet. The hilltops and slopes, too, leaped about under the delicate touches of light. It shifted from one peak to another, brightening them momentarily with the special yellow-green of the Pennines, set against blue watery pools of shadow in the valleys.

The moortops were governed by a different god from the valleys.

Everything on the hills belonged to infinite light. In the distance, rock and moor, such heavy things, dissolved into the milk of the hazy sky. As intoxicated with height and space as a skylark, one wanted never to descend. The few people living here showed reluctance to come down into the towns and hamlets, even though they might starve because of it. From isolation, they experienced different lives; they were harsher, according to the philosophy at each solitary farmstead developed in response to the God of bleak weather, sky and dark stones. Without realising it, they dressed differently. They experienced different dreams. Their speech grew clipped and brutal. Everything was thinner – their bodies, expectations, purses, poultry and cattle.

After Anne Wylde disappeared, she was talked about even more than when she had been present. Travellers returned to Holland and Spain with tales of a giant gorgon who haunted the English moors and had adopted the shape of a maidservant in a clothier's household, in order to destroy him. According to various accounts Anne had three, four or five breasts which poured forth honey under a full moon and she went about dressed in a girdle of snakes, like the figure of the Medusa which Captain Horsfall had given Benjamin Greave to put over his door. Or they said that Anne was a form of that wandering White Cow which still gave milk even after being sucked by a regiment of men. It was hard to believe that the maiden Anne Wylde of Lady Well, a mason's daughter, had ever actually existed.

Benjamin Greave was impatient of these superstitions. He agreed that the girl was a witch, and that in his youth she would not have been tolerated; but foolish laws had come in for the defence of such. However, the form that her witchcraft took was not worth his bothering his head about. He was too old and wise. He was too busy. Not wanting to travel south so often to buy wool, nor to trust factors, he was experimenting with keeping his own sheep. Modern improvements in the management of grassland indicated that even Yorkshire's sour hilltops could be grazed if the land was cleared, an enterprising visitor had told Greave; and the clothier joked back that maybe one of the useless hawthorn trees that he was destroying was the vanished devil, Anne Wylde, so he'd rid Yorkshire finally of her and deserve to be knighted for't. If the old heather was burnt, it would leave a layer of fertilising ash. When he had been setting fire, the district hung under drifting smoke. The Making's food, bedding and clothes were tainted, and the people, already with lungs full of wool-dust, coughed through work and sleep. Greave's whole life had become a dream of selling worsteds to the Empress of Russia, of burning useless heather and hawthorn from the moors and of planting straight lines of cuttings from the old wild chaotic hawthorn trees to make enclosure hedges.

Gobbling up the hills and valleys, shovelling food rudely into his maw untasted in the smoky kitchen, he saw Oliver's distaste, his unhappiness and restlessness without Anne whom he could not trace, and he challenged it.

'What's th' matter? Thou's like someone that's lost sixpence. Thou wants a dose o' th' apothecary's rubbing bottle to raise thy spirits.'

This produced no answer, so Benjamin tried another tack. 'You think the Devil-woman might make a good wife for you – if you can find her! But I fear she's been spirited away, to save us. I'd not let such a one in sight of my pattern books! A young girl is filled with love as a cistern with water, she wants only somewhere to empty it. And then it is impossible to stop her, as when a dam is breached. Also, having such a strong purpose makes her blind to her lover's defects – though he's as big an ass as you!'

Meanwhile the clothier chewed noisily, like a horse, upon a turnip. It was the earliest one, plucked from his garden: he had a fondness for roots. Also, so as not to 'waste time' whilst he was eating, he fingered a small sample of weaving that had been brought to him. Turning it and turning it, like a Catholic with a rosary, he was perfectly self-absorbed.

Oliver burst out, 'Do not preach to me! If you will not be just to Miss Wylde. I will leave this house. I'll go to London . . .'

Benjamin studiously nipped off the tail and removed a few green leaves that were sprouting from his turnip. 'Aye, I'm told you've only to know 'ow to hold a knife and fork for them to make a great man of you down yonder. Even thou should be able to manage that!'

'I'll tak' myself to Greece. Or to Russia. I'll mak' worsted for 'em there. I have heard that the Empress's court gives encouragement to strangers who wish to settle at Astracan, for the convenience of the woollen manufacture of Persia.'

Bits of turnip spluttered from the exasperated clothier's mouth. Then, anxious for his samples of beautiful cloth, he shook the scraps off it. 'Thou's forever restless to get by thyself somewhere! When a child you were always hiding in rabbits' or foxes' holes and by t'streams, instead of ganging to school with other children, though you risked a whipping for it. Never satisfied with us all working and living together, man and beast, to be prosperous and happy in *this* life. Thou'lt find the grave private enough . . .'

'I'll settle again at Lower Laithes, where I was with Zillah.'

'Wylde's girl'll not make a wife for you! She's about as domesticated as Genghis Khan!'

'She is experienced and skilled at every branch of domestic economy.'

'*When* thou can keep her at home!' Benjamin paused. 'She'll have no dowry, neither.'

'John Wylde is a successful man.'

'He won't be if he keeps on reading them books.'

When Benjamin Greave mentioned 'bewks', as he called them, it meant he had thrown his final argument – if the contentious subject was guilty of reading, there was no need to say more. (Especially if the reader was a female.) The word 'bewks' fell like a tombstone on a villain's corpse.

So Oliver said no more. Yet he had made up his mind. Through clouds of smoke rolling off the hilltops, hearing the tormented screeching of larks above their burnt nests, Oliver rode down through the oak trees, and the grey glacial boulders the size of houses, into the pit of the gorge below Lady Well. There John Wylde was erecting a big new spinning-building for Captain Horsfall. Along the river – a place which no one had been interested in before, except to chase wild duck or snipe through the marshes, or to graze oxen on meadows dry only for a few months in the summer – it was as if a new world had to be built overnight: though it was impossible to tell what sort of world it would be, there was such confusion. From high up Oliver saw a row of bonfires and black smoke where they were burning waste wood. When he came close he found oily putrefactions out of wool or timber, and the chemicals or oils used by engineers and carpenters, coiling in the water where until a year ago he had watched the grey muscular shadows of salmon nosing upstream and the trout, flicking into the currents, or bubbling peacefully from the depths. Barges carrying Russian pine were tied up under the sites for several long stone sheds, Horsfall's being the largest. Carts laden with fittings of iron and gleaming brass stood by.

Dick Almighty was standing there with gold to invest, and a greedy anxious look as he tried to speak to busy engineers or to the impatient bankers who had rolled up in their carriages. He flattered them by telling them what they already knew only too well: that they were *important Gentlemen*. As a reward for being this, Sin-Catcher Almighty offered to enrol them in to *The Society For Prosecuting Felons*, which was short of members (subscription a guinea per year). They answered him that they were from Leeds, 'an important universal city': a clear suggestion that they were not interested in a parish-pump constable. Almighty was apoplectic at being spoken to in this way, for such a thing had never happened before. Nonetheless he must control himself before such distinguished people. They off-handedly told him to 'see what he could for himself'; in fact nobody, not even the workmen, had time to bother with him.

Almighty could make out clearly only two things that were quite novel. Firstly, the delivery of pine for building. He had never seen anything but oak used before. Secondly, they were digging a canal that headed direct to the hills.

'So our river is to be as straight as the path to God!' he smartly exclaimed, to the only man he could at last find with the time and the will to listen to a fool. 'You cannot take water up a mountain! 'Tis against the will of Lord!'

He received the coyest of smiles.

'Sure you can, if you make a hole to put it into,' the Irish labourer answered.

They were going to dig a tunnel, which would destroy for ever the separation of Yorkshire from Lancashire! This alteration of God's ordered universe at a single stroke was the product of Horsfall's genius; he had sold the land for the waterway at a cheap price in return for other advantages from the bankers. (Another slight to Almighty; for the Captain had declared nothing, neither to him nor anybody else, about his plans.)

At sheds in which spinning machines were already installed were lines of women and girls seeking employment. They were a desperate

85

kind to seek such work – drifters from other counties, turned from their homes because a gentleman desired a park there or was improving the land – and some attempted to be saucy because Oliver was one of the masters.

Oliver found John Wylde raising a huge flagstone, weighing several tons, for a machine-bed. Several men with pulleys had it balanced in mid-air. There was a confusion of noise all around – carts struggling through mud, saws and masons' hammers – but this circle was silent and tense as if concentrating on a ritual. Some of the labourers twitched with nervousness, afraid to move under the vast stone swaying precariously above their heads. Others, used to brutal work and boasting of their roughness, acted rashly. John Wylde calculated the whole action. With the same accuracy that he applied to stones, he balanced the temperaments of his workmen, anticipating characteristic reactions, and with a slight movement of eye or hand encouraging or restraining them. For half an hour Oliver watched the machine-bed inch its way ten feet across the sky, to rest one end on a wall and the other on a pine beam. By which time Oliver appreciated, for the first time, the delicate skills of these workmen compelled through every hour of labour to trust one another.

When the flagstone was safe, the slackened ropes sagged as if they were as glad to relax as were the workmen; two of whom sang bawdy songs (one brought out a fiddle), whilst the third took Plato's *Republic* from his pocket.

John Wylde smiled, not especially with pleasure at seeing Oliver Greave, but at the neatness of the operation. 'We use pine instead of oak for the spinning sheds because it is more supple and therefore does not have to be of such thickness,' the mason said. 'It does not matter that pine is not so enduring. Perhaps our manufactories will not be wanted for ever.'

Oliver seemed uninterested.

'The skills of my labourers would amaze many a gentleman,' Wylde offered next. 'Jeremiah Rhodes there can understand ten languages, yet until the age of twenty he could hardly read or write. He used to live at Upper Spout, but ever since your father told 'em it was poisonous to drink from the spring there – and they believed him, being ignorant, though Mr Greave, pardon my saying so, has made good use of the water – he has stayed up every night teaching himself.

86

Before that, he was satisfied to let Methodists preach at him. Though I suppose they have given him orderly habits.'

Oliver was not surprised by that either: he had met this type of fellow many times at Library-Subscription Clubs, Rhymesters' Clubs and Debating Societies.

John Wylde knew, of course, what Oliver Greave really wanted. The mason, following his usual manner with visitors, was simply keeping the conversation going in the hope of obtaining in return something instructive or entertaining from the clothier. But he saw that he was not going to get it, for the young man was distracted. At last, Wylde gave up the attempt. 'She's left home. Gone over the moors,' he said.

Wylde was reluctant to add more where he could be overheard: Dick Almighty and Doubtfire had already been to him, investigating a 'curse' upon the clothiers consisting of more fires, mysterious swelling in a child's body, a 'plague of sinfulness' with fiddlers playing night and day, and a woman whose mouth filled with blood whenever she spoke of the Devil. He led Oliver to one side and whispered, 'My wife had a sister lived in a cottage beyond Black Hill. She's another queer witch, maybe she's gone there. Anne follows her own rules, though. It wouldn't do any good for me to seek her out.'

Oliver ascended Black Hill, over the bouldered moor into thick smoke, hurrying and yet frightened of his horse breaking an ankle amongst ashes, tangled heather and stones. He saw his father's blazing hawthorns, which as they darkened to charred wood bled a reddish-yellow sap like blood. And as if to warn him (though of what he could not think) larks screamed from the advancing fire, and then returned arching over it to find that nothing was left of their nests.

When the smoke cleared Oliver saw a line of cottages circling below him where water burst out of rocks and rushes. Following the course of a stream he descended into a valley that had a different spirit; one out of Benjamin Greave's reach, unenclosed except by its majestic circle of hills, and with no 'useful' packhorse-route into it; unburnt, undrained, with bright patches of bog-flowers and freely blossoming hawthorn. Each cottage here gave forth a different, peaceful domestic smell. From over there it was of pigs, here of oily wefts, and in another place of horses. The odours rose to choke a calm afternoon, with the silver light melting the silk of distant hills, so that moor and light became sometimes one, and at other times indistinctly separate. Oliver tried to pinpoint the likely home of an eccentric spinster. But at one there were children. At another a weaver moved amongst rows of cloth spread out-of-doors on his tenter frames. A third had a horse nearby, whilst at a fourth, a man was digging drains.

Oliver approached a derelict-looking house that might be the home of a witch. But it held nothing except sheep. So he turned along the track linking the cottages. In the next, two or three looms were clattering. The father came to his door: a gaunt man, brusque and cheerful but not good at giving directions because he got lost in his memories of each place.

'You'll see up yonder a bridge!' he bawled, as if he was delivering a command. 'Just go over and thou'll find a rowan tree, for my Uncle Matt planted it. He had a home there, but it's tumbled now. There's still fruit bushes that he grew in yonder wild place. They seemed to find time for much more in the old days, didn't they! Then thou goes to the right – no, is it left? – up by a spout of water. "Foul Syke", its name. Or better still, stay this side of the bridge, though then thou'll miss where Uncle Matt lived. I wish I could go with you to see the old place again and show you the way! But you know what they say?' He nodded over his shoulder to the noisy looms. 'On Monday and Tuesday the loom chants, "Plenty of time! Plenty of time!" But on Thursday and Friday, it's "Thou's a day too late! Thou's a day too late!" So I'll have to be finishing my piece or time'll be catching up on me. Good day to you now!'

Oliver turned the corner of the hill, saw a flourishing rowan-tree and a tumbled cottage, followed the energetic little stream along Foul Syke, and reached the open space of a north-facing slope where hardly anyone wished to live. It was called, indeed, 'the Dark Side'. However, there was one dreary cottage. Its grounds were walled off, and a sign pointed into a bog: MERCHANTS WOOLMEN WORLDLY FOLK THIS WAY. Other crude boards declared: BLESST BE HE THAT TURNETH TO THE LORD, and CONSIDER THEE DOOM.

There came out an old man who Oliver recognised as one who went about preaching and who sometimes came to Makings. At first the man was fierce and hostile, just as he usually was when he visited the clothier's mansion. Then, because they were in the open air, the two of them fell into that relaxed understanding of those who recognise in one another that they both enjoy wandering the hills.

'Elkanah Beanland, I can't pass on my way through that miry trough!'

Elkanah's flesh was a tangle of veins standing out on the sunken scarred skin and of tendons that threatened to tie themselves into knots, as he shouted, apparently irate, 'Then thou shouldn't be one wi' the worldly folk! Let this be thy journey's end. Come in and pray with me. Aren't thou Oliver Greave, a poet and student, as they tell me, of the classics, that recommend sodomy and incest shamelessly to all?'

'Elkanah!'

'They write about nothing else! Follow that path and thou'lt end in antinomian piss-mires worse than any I can lay before ye! I've seen poets before and what Devil's piss-mires they fall into!'

'Mr Beanland, I'm looking for the cottage of a woman named Pity.'

'Another sinner! But a good one.' The 'preacher' mellowed his voice now. In fact he whispered, awestruck. 'She's up there. Well thou can take a short way through my garden if thou's a mind, Master Greave. And if thou wishes to arrive in Heaven wi' dry feet, carry this text in thy heart...'

Rejecting the text but thankfully accepting the dry way (to Pity's, not to Heaven) Oliver climbed the garden wall and pressed on through the cold shadow covering the moorside.

Just when he was becoming desperate he stumbled on to the sight of a cottage chimney-stack rising out of a crack in the moor like a hand drowning in Hades. From the lip he saw below a waterfall thundering through rowans, hawthorns and alders, and a garden where, in this place lit by only a few hours of sunlight each day, grew fruit trees, roses and other flowers, and the earth was freshly planted with seeds. Hens wandered and a cow was tethered near the water. As Oliver brushed down the hillside, even at this early time of the year he raised the scents of herbs and he imagined how perfumed this spot must be in late summer. It seemed both the entrance to a scented flowery paradise, and also to the dark secret underworld.

Before he reached the gate a fierce black dog leaped on its chain, as though to throttle itself. Its yellow eyes gleamed with malevolence, hair bristled on its neck and it gnashed its mouth of slavering teeth in frustration. Whilst Oliver hesitated, an old woman came out with a bucket and calmed the dog. She was so bent that her chin was close to her stomach, and yet she seemed very strong as she ducked her container in the waterfall.

'What a delightful place!' Oliver shouted. 'You must practise witch-craft to make so much grow here!'

The woman looked sideways at him and shaded her eyes, even though there was hardly any light. The little that Oliver could detect of her features was remarkable: weathered brick red, but without a wrinkle, it was a maiden's skin preserved within a mane of grey hair. Her voice was weak, but because of its authority one realised that it had once been forceful.

'I cannot see you, my dear! The sky hurts my eyes. Though it's a long time since I stared it in the face, it seems never tired of punishing me! I've never got on too kindly with the sun; th'old brass-face and I are ancient enemies. By the sound of your voice I'd say you was from Makings. Oh, yes, I'd recognise a Greave's voice anywhere. You will have come to find Anne Wylde, I suppose? The Vicar tolls a bell and all must come to church, a woman calls differently and men come hurrying to her ... She escaped from your clutches! But she's just inside. You can go right in, my dog won't touch you now and no one's unwelcome here.'

Easily carrying the filled bucket, the old woman hobbled down the path to her cottage door whilst she talked, her dim eyes meanwhile taking in a hazy view of the ground, snails, dirt, grass, weeds and spring plants sliding beneath her. 'I've planted dandelions there as'll be ready soon. How was the comfrey up the hillside?'

'I didn't notice, Madam.'

'You come right past it! Eh well, we don't all see what's under our noses.'

Aunt Pity stayed outside, tending her plants whilst Oliver entered. Indoors there was the hiss and flash of several cats. He noticed bunches of primroses and other spring flowers in jugs, a pungent smell of vegetation brewing and a large vat of dye. Aunt Pity, like many unmarried women and widows, made her living by colouring cloth. They used roots and herbs but kept their recipes secret, and Aunt Pity's speciality was that particular soldier's red for which Benjamin Greave and other clothiers had to come to her.

Anne was wearing a red gown, a white apron and a cap that could not control her hair. She was singing. The words glided bouyantly on an invisible current of air – a river of words delighting in its lightness. Seeing Oliver she became silent. And after such a long break, Oliver was too shy to touch, even to speak to his beloved.

'It is my birthday in April,' Anne said. 'That is why Pity fills our cottage with flowers.'

Oliver told her, nervously and bluntly, 'I have left my father's house and taken Lower Laithes and I need a housekeeper. Your father could live with us, as he grows weaker in the flesh. I will give you an interest in my affairs. Anne, I love you ...' He spoke of love so pitifully: as if it was as much a sickness as a joy, and as if he anticipated as much pain as pleasure from it.

For a few moments the heart of the hunted virgin drummed and fluttered, like a small bird cupped in warm hands, at the thought of being held by this gentle man. Then the alternative idea that had already kept her so often distant grew uppermost. She feared that he might begin to neglect her as soon as he was satisfied.

'I am happiest collecting herbs and whinberries with my Aunt, who has noone to look after her,' she said.

'You cannot live up here isolated in this bleak place! Your beauty was intended for palaces.'

Anne interrupted him. 'Aunt Pity came here when her sweetheart died in the wars. They said to her, too, that she could never make a life up in this place, and without a man. But you see she has done quite well out of brewing dyes.'

Pity came in then, kittens and hens around her skirts. She had an intimate consciousness of each one of them, the grey, the tabby, the speckled moult, even whilst she gave her attention elsewhere. When she turned to Oliver, she spoke with that certainty of being listened to which women who have been beautiful retain throughout their lives. 'Aye, but we have little choice in this world except to be as men wish it!' she said.

(6)

Lower Laithes, built as a home for Oliver and Zillah but according to Oliver's taste, was symmetrical and spacious in a classical style, with an extravagance of Corinthian pillars, pediments, statues and mottoes in Greek. Benjamin Greave always said that there were too many 'private' rooms for it to be a happy home, and that they were too high for anything except for a bird to fly in. Nobody had wanted to live there since Oliver and his wife. This was mainly because, the crafty father having planned that his son should at least overlook his fulling mill, the big wooden hammers clattered in hearing all day long and the stream roared nearby, tumbling over waterfalls and dams made by Benjamin Greave's engineers; who schemed and suffered sleepless nights to make Nature do what she did not intend. The place was usually wrapped in a damp woodland twilight and the tracks were muddy from daily traffic to Makings.

A week after Oliver had called upon Anne, inhabitants of Lady Well heard an eerie whistling, and Joshua Binns saw a pack of black hounds flying in the sunset. Or they claimed that they did: and this was, they said, because it was when Anne Wylde went down to Lower Laithes.

She walked lightly and smiling, with her usual challenging expression. The spring day and the sunlight were still. Patches of the moor were bright green with fresh whinberry leaves and the watery places floated crowfoot flowers. The smell of juices leaked out of the grass that was cut in the enclosures. Across budding trees cut a sharp edge of shadow, out of which mossy trunks rose in lit tapers and spread into delicate cobwebs of branches. Everywhere, in wood, field and moor, was a green reflected light.

Anne strolled around the unloved forgotten mansion, peering through dusty windows at bare boards and frozen-looking furniture. She wondered what curtains would best suit. Before long (remembering those volumes of engravings that architects and masons had

92

brought since her earliest childhood into her father's house) Anne had in her mind carpeted, refurnished, altered the withdrawing room and peopled everywhere with a flutter of servants. The rank lawns and overgrown gardens – patterns marked out with low hedges of yew and boxwood – were at present unfashionably formal, so she 'planted' spreading trees (forgetting that they would take fifty years to achieve the proportions of her imagination). Peacocks on the lawns . . .

Nearby, engineers were tampering with the dykes, weirs and watercourses. They were experimenting to find out whether, by storing water in reservoirs at higher contours, its natural force could be submitted to machinery. Acquisitively they glanced up to scrutinise the invisible wind and wonder how that too could profit them. Thereby they caught glimpses of the strange young woman in the overgrown garden. One went to Makings, and said (in a blunt, challenging but humorous typically Yorkshire manner), 'Trouble's turned up again yonder, Mr Greave!' Whereupon Oliver rushed downhill to find it.

He surprised Anne as she paced back and forth tyrannising the desolation. Being withdrawn, her features appeared disdainful. But he knew by her air of possession of his house that he had won her. When she had focused upon him, she smiled, shivered slightly and then frowned, as if intimating that he ought to do something for her protection or comfort. So he lifted the shawl that had half-slipped from her and, boiling with desire, put it as slowly as he dared around her shoulder.

'It would take the women a week of scrubbing before you could move in here,' Anne said, coolly ignoring his manifest longing. She slowly plucked a forget-me-not, tumbled it in her fingers, and led him around the building. 'You must arrange for my things to be sent from Makings, for I am never going *there* again. Pay me what wages you like, but let me in charge and I promise you, you will be pleased. But you must not come here again for one whole month.'

They had followed the gravel walks around the house and had come to the front. A crack in one of the pillars of the colonnade, in which weeds and flowers grew, appeared ludicrous. That something so monumental should so soon prove vulnerable to time and the energies of an ordinary English spring! The whole classical façade was crumbling and the green light emphasised the moss on the building. Set into the pediment was a flaking inscription in Greek.

Oliver translated, ' "Know Thyself." It was a saying of Socrates, the Greek philosopher.'

'I can read that too!' Anne replied indignantly. 'I have met a lot of men who think that they can "know themselves", because the ones who visit my father always talk about it. Socrates must have been such a person as them.'

To find servants for Lower Laithes, Anne made her way to the camp of 'hardy ruffians', as everyone called them, in Blood Wood. For if she employed Lady Well people, she would be bringing her tormentors into her home, thus inciting envy; also, because their need was less, they probably would not work as hard as strangers.

The air was suffocating with the smell of the bluebells that had now reached their fullest blossom and lay like drifts of thick mist. Whitethroats and other warblers, robins and thrushes were singing, though faintly, because the end-of-May, summer-drowsiness was overcoming them. The first thing that Oliver had done for his house-keeper was to purchase the finest clothes that he could for her, and she wore a full and heavy walking dress of brilliant red wool – officers' cloth, the best that the weavers could make. She had delicate shoes, brought from London.

She found her way to the camp by the music. For in their savage tongues, Irish, Scottish, Welsh and Cornish, the outcasts sang laments for their homelands; melodies that rang mysteriously through this rocky northern woodland. Some of them had been wandering for years. Several children had been born on the unenclosed watery heaths, amongst treacherous rushes, alder swamps and willows. They had perhaps not left such places until they were in their teens, when upon bursting out of the brown and trackless wastes they had been amazed by the sight of bright green manured grass weeded to make fine and even pastures, and enclosed in squares of hedgerow or wall. A sight as amazing to them as would have been sudden glimpses of magnificent palaces of the Orient. Yet nothing had surprised them like the sight of this fabulous fine lady seeking them out.

Fiddles and flutes were silenced at her coming and the smutty derelicts rushed to hide what they had been cooking. Yet from a close look at Anne's weather-darkened skin and large hands, they saw that, despite her fine clothes, she was nothing special. When she asked for those who might be her servants, they answered her sarcastically, 'No one in this clearing is fit to dwell in fine houses, Ma'am, as you can see well enough.' (Meaning: 'Who are you to be wanting servants, and not dwelling yourself amongst brooks and stores?') 'Some of us unfortunates has spent th'ole winter in the countryside, *Ma'am!*' one added.

But when they realised that the lady meant what she said, the staring people behaved as if a load of beef or apples had fallen from a cart in front of them. They crowded around her, one or two horribly close to her face, or on their knees plucking at her gown, and some of the girls thrusting forward starved babies. Anne had come here disdainfully, thinking only of her own fine home. Now she could hardly speak, witnessing such misery.

'Madam, my husband came home to me drunk and threw our baby on to the fire. That was in Somerset. Then because I was angry and distressed it annoyed him and he did trample over my throat and breast until my crying brought a neighbour. Today he lies in the low jail in Bristol, though the lawyers say that it was my fault for opposing him, and now there is no one to care for us!'

(How do men come to describe the God who created this world as good and wise? He is neither! Anne thought and she felt ashamed of her fine clothes.)

'Madam, a farmer's son got me with child! The other women where I was servant whispered and searched my breast and found milk, so I confessed then and was given a licence to marry. My husband told me I would make a fine widow after he had gone. That is all he said to me, "Thou'll make a fine widow when I am gone!" On our wedding night he hanged himself in his father's barn. Oh Madam, what have I done to deserve such a sad hand of God? Give me work, please give me work!'

Anne could not cope with such unhappiness. Could not be expected to.

'Why is that one saying nothing?' Anne pointed at a lank-haired girl who sat sorrowful and bewildered by the fire. She was wearing camblett (a rain-proof worsted not made in the north), so Anne recognised another stranger.

'Bridie is from Ireland, where the soldiers burned down her village because it did not beautify an Englishman's estate. 'Twas not "picturesque" he told them. Some went west to the bare white rocks of Connaught – "To Hell or Connaught" as Cromwell said, for there was nothing to choose between the two – but Bridie drifted east to Liverpool. I do not think she knew which direction she was walking in. She does not speak a word of English and is too ignorant and stupid, like a beast, to learn.'

'I'll take her! You tell her what I want.'

'But she is pig-Irish, can't do nothing, Miss!'

It seemed that no one who had themselves anything to hope for would help the girl, because she was Irish. Then a huge uncomplaining woman, badly-scarred from the pox, gently led her over. The kind woman knew enough Gaelic to explain what was wanted, and the wretch was transformed. Her face took on a tranced look: it had the phosphorescence of those who have received an epiphany, or found themselves "redeemed" by a crossroads preacher. At last her lips quivered into speech.

'She says she don't expect to be paid, she'll be happy to work just for her food.'

The big kind woman who said this had once been amongst the merriest at fairs, wakes and saints'-days, until love and happiness led to the pox. Now the hair was almost gone from her head, and her face was marked as if with fire. Yet she was not ugly; and though she was large, she was not cumbersome; for her inner spirit vitalised her features. Perhaps because of embarrassment caused by her scorched appearance, she had a trick of not talking directly to one; she spoke as if addressing an invisible person at one's side, and would half turn away, laughing. The effect however was not of furtiveness, but as if she feared that her jokes might not be understood, except by some other, invisible, friendly company that she kept. 'As they write over the pillory in th'ospital, Ma'am, "Better to work than to suffer thus",' she remarked in her curious, sideways fashion.

Seeing that she wore a wedding ring, Anne asked the whereabouts of her husband.

'I'm Mary Pickles, Ma'am, and my husband was unjustly imprisoned. I know it was unjust and tried to prove it. When I could get no hearing from the lawyers, I seed no point in living, though we had a

fine house and some acres with a pig and a cow, and I gave them up
t'abide in the woods by the sun and the moon.'

'You gave up what you had because of love?'

''Twas for lack of justice, mostly. That wore me out, that did, for
I saw no purpose in life any more.' She turned her cindered features
appealingly to Anne Wylde – begging, not for work, not for money or
bread, but for understanding. 'Yet it is only love that justifies us, I
believe. And the only one to have seen and told us that is the Jesus
who is so hard to find in the church. I have been turned away too
often not to know that!'

'I'll take you also,' Anne said.

A man who by his grand diction, his purple skin and swollen nose
Anne took to be a hedge-preacher or a renegade parson too drunk to
preach, then shouted, 'Mary Pickles drowned her baby in the river
to save it from getting the pox from its mother! Madam, you are choosing the most Godless sinners, outcasts from Grace, doomed to Hell,
who will pollute the souls of your household on their journey thither!'

'The only outcast I will not employ is a God-fearing Methodist!'
Anne answered, to almost everyone's laughter.

When gossip had spread that Anne Wylde – Anne Wylde! – was
'mistress' of Lower Laithes and taking on any rascal as servant, Amos
Culpin came to her.

Though once he had been energetic enough to throw stones at Lady
Well's scapegoat, now his doubts and sufferings had left him weary.
It tired him of life to think that everyone was born of a filthy act which
made us no fitter than animals to enter Heaven. He was amazed that
men still dared to pray. Our sexual organs were our curse, for they
prompted continual anxieties and, helplessly in the Devil's hands
because of them, our eyes were directed away from God. Culpin's
jolly maypole had turned into a cross upon which the Christ of his
virtue was hung. His single consolation was the thought that the
worst misfortunes proved that God did look into our foul hearts,
sufficient at least to want to punish us, and so this was proof of His
care. Such trials were our only hope of being purged. Culpin had at
one stage turned to nonconforming sects, but these unsettled him
further. Some believed in the abandonment of morality, saying they
were born 'the Elect' and therefore would be saved no matter what

they did; or they thought that sin was the very road to freedom, before the world was destroyed tomorrow. Other groups of 'worshippers' were merely seeking a cover for radicalism and sedition, and they even sheltered atheists amongst their number. Then there were the 'magical Methodists' (as some called them); vulgar believers in miracles, revelations, manifest spirits, and mysterious vengeances.

These groups were all over Yorkshire. It was as if an ant-heap had spewed upon the hills. (A spawning of Hell or Paradise? Only time would tell which.) Amos, confused, on some days felt that there were now only a few untidy remnants of faith left in him; whilst other moments were full of the terror of God. His worldly affairs reflected the erratic state of his soul. He was notorious for being unable to keep any employment for long. So now he came humbly to Anne Wylde, who smiled at her victory, and made him her footman.

Next, Anne's inquiries for a personal maid brought her to one Jack Loveless, a widower, who needed to be rid of his 'hungry' daughter, whom he could not feed. He lived in a stone shack perched on a ledge on the edge of the moor and overhung with rocks. It took an afternoon's scramble to reach it. A richer artisan would have chosen a more sheltered spot but Loveless, in order to benefit from the nearby spring, had also to accept a magnificent spectacle of the valley and the maelstrom that often raged out of it. The cottage was backed against the hill out of which water seeped, or streamed, over the stone floor. The shelf of land was a wet, spongy green so brilliant that the eye could pick it out from far away. It was sufficient to feed a few hens, grow some oats, and keep alive an undernourished pony.

It was evening but Jack Loveless was still working the loom that filled the single downstairs room. The cupboards shook. The cottage was like a small ship with a huge engine in it. On the hearth squatted a small child setting wire teeth into pieces of leather used for 'carding' the wool. Michael Loveless spent all the hours of daylight thus and, frustrated of companions, adventure, play and the variety of the open air, he was muttering or laughing to himself. 'Jack o't'Crows,' he tittered. Like all children, he had been taught to distract boredom by naming the wires after people whom he knew, but Michael's self-absorption and self-made fun was slightly mad. He stared hungrily at the lady. 'I know someone who ate meat last Quarter Day, Ma'am,' he said, wistfully. Meanwhile his thirteen-year-old sister, Jenny, was bleaching the grease out of newly woven cloth by trampling it barefoot in a large shallow stone sink set into the floor, which contained the urine of the family and their pony.

The amazing product of this dreary industry was a stretch of blue weaving glowing upon the loom. 'They say that freedom glows brightest in prisons! That is blue wool for the French to make their "caps of liberty" from, God bless 'em,' the weaver explained.

Without removing her riding habit in the damp cottage, Anne went to the fire and warmed each delicately booted foot in turn. The child continued to set his wires, from which there was no release until he fell asleep over his work. Jenny Loveless had stopped trampling cloth, but she stayed in the sink, turned to stone by the sight of Anne Wylde who had risen out of the valley.

Jack Loveless proudly looked over his woven piece. This luminous stretch of colour, dyed-in-the-wool from roots of local herbs for the sake of *Liberty*, was the sublimation of all his sufferings.

But, though his loom had stopped working, its hammering continued in his head, and would do so all night even whilst he was singing, shouting and talking sedition at a hush-house, or whilst lying in his narrow box-bed; banging, although increasingly faint, until its noise was resumed at the hard wooden bench at dawn.

Jack was a small shrivelled man, crippled in his thigh and leg, and he had a closed expression; though, as Anne knew, such as he often have the deepest tales to tell when they have been prised open. So Anne remarked suggestively, 'If we fine ladies knew what was needed to manufacture our woollen dresses, I wonder how we should think of them?'

'You have furs also, for which another kind of animal other than a weaver has died in traps,' he answered drily.

'Where do you find all those beautiful colours and rich patterns?'

Loveless took a clay pipe from his pocket, stuffed it with tobacco from a tin over his fireplace, and lit it with many puffs before answering. 'I sometimes look at the church windows and take my designs from the bright glass. If there is a God, that is where He shines – in the pictures of the artists – for it is not in the homes of poor people, where parson and t'Bible and all our "lords and masters" tell us to find Christ and virtue. I've seen enough poverty to know. Designing cloth has been my undoing.' He ended his sentence bluntly, as was his manner, and he stared unflinchingly, to show he was unwilling to explain more unless she asked for it.

'How so, Mr Loveless?'

'Going too far with it. I made black "amens", with embossed patterns of yew and laurel leaves, for widows' cloth in Spain – the soldiers cause a lot of mourning there. I wove striped callimancoes for elegant ladies. Throwing away designs that didn't suit, wasting time whilst my children were hungry and my old wife coughing blood under a heap of blankets – it was ceasing to flow from one opening and now it came out of another! But when I took my work to Mr Greave, who aims to make the finest pieces in England, he'd say: "That's a grand cloth, Loveless, grand, but I'd be ruined if I made it." "Why so, Mr Greave?" I'd ask – tho' my own politeness stuck in my teeth. "It's *too* good and even in St Petersburg or down London they would not pay the price." Now *I'm* paying the cost, with my dear wife passed on and me living in this hut. I have heard tell that in Oliver Cromwell's day we were promised something better.'

'I think that what you weavers make is the most beautiful art and shouldn't be rewarded with poverty.' Poverty made Anne shudder with repulsion; she saw here a lesson in what her own fate would be if she lacked control of her destiny. 'But at least I can give you something in advance for the services of your daughter,' she offered.

'I'd be glad o' summat. But you are doing me a turn just in taking her away from here. Though we conceive 'em with pleasure enough and so are bound, by God! to take care of 'em, yet girls are nothing but a curse to us from birth until they marry. Are you not, Jenny?'

The maid did not answer. Obviously she was used to not answering. Anne ordered her to go and wash her feet in the spring, then she left two sovereigns with Jack Loveless and led Jenny away.

At Lower Laithes the girl entered a state where everything was different, yet she did not show surprise. There were large rooms, statues, paintings, and formal gardens. There were clocks. Although Jenny could not herself tell the time, yet she recognised that others did so, for they gave her orders by them. Also they rose from and returned to bed according to the numbers on the dial, instead of by when the pony stood up and shook himself in the enclosure, or when the raven settled upon the cliffs. She accepted all these, and other, changes in her life. She was too numbed to respond. The maid had a born slave's temperament. Contentment characterised her as she performed whatever task was set in front of her, and she never questioned it. She doted on her mistress, who knew so much about life and human nature. Only sometimes, when she was tired, Jenny would simply stare at the sky. It was for all the world as if a thought, a desire, even an ambition, was leaving its glittering track across her dark mind, and arousing the still waters of her eyes to look upwards for Heaven and God.

In her heart, where no one had ever looked, Jenny carried the image of a master, and this fantasy filled up those inscrutable, silent moments. He was not a small, dry, worried, embittered man like her father, but someone large, confident, powerful, certain of his position in the world, indeed in the whole universe, and expressing himself with large spacious gestures, with grand language and easy humour.

When Anne had peopled Lower Laithes with servants, she was occupied with them – singing around the house, keeping everyone cheerful, knowing her business as one who has herself scrubbed floors, and discovering that, even though she was of the same class, yet she was one whom servants liked to obey.

Because it looked as though the house might at last become as fashionably splendid as it was originally intended to be, the foppish servile tradesmen flocked around. Dealers in silk, damask and velveteens. Cabinet-makers with samples of mahogany or other new woods brought back by traders and explorers in Africa and the East, and with drawings of temples, Greek, Egyptian, Assyrian, which they proposed to apply to tables and chairs. Artists in plaster who made tinted cornucopias of grapes, chrysanthemums, oranges and the other newly discovered colonial benefits for mankind which Flora, or Mother Nature (a lady after Titian or Tintoretto with a swelling bust and fair hair swept from a broad brow like the wife of the weaver Joshua Binns), poured out of her capacious horn-of-plenty. Thanks be to the Lord who was giving us so much of India, Africa and the Americas! One artist wished to depict the personification of tea. He painted a nubile black woman rising from a steaming brew. Hairdressers visited Lower Laithes. Peruke-makers. Shoe- and stocking-makers. Traders with pictures of nature (or, at least, with *landscapes*) in the style of Gainsborough. (Those park walls, those deer, those golden oaks, were clearly *owned* by someone, which was why the limners were able to sell their paintings; and the artists expected to depict the Greaves' domain in the same style, for what else would a clothier desire? But Anne Wylde would have nothing to do with it.) They all came to scoop up Oliver's money, as mice gather round a tear in a sack of corn. They forgot that Anne was a 'witch'. It was no business of theirs, they now said (so long as they could conspire to cheat her), and they replied to questions with the invariable complaint of the worldly: 'What can I do? I have to live!' Three such tradesmen would secretly agree for two of them to ask an exorbitant price, so that the third could offer an apparently cheap tender. Smilingly offering credit, they anticipated turning Lower Laithes into a showplace of the new and unnecessary things that the whole of Lady Well, following a fashion set by the richest family, would have to purchase to replace their sound tables and chairs or the dowries already collected for their daughters.

Anne's father, loathing these parasites, stayed away. Whilst people he despised collected money that might have been his, he continued to build a manufactory for Horsfall. There was little understanding now between father and daughter.

Anne still held off Oliver's advances, fearing that if she gave in he would despise her and so treat her just as other men had done. Secretly it tortured her. Often when alone in bed, and imagining what that strange experience of copulation might be, she found herself damp for him. It further tormented her that he did not realise the degree to which abstinence was deepening her love, or at least her desire. Instead he of course thought that her feeling for him was weak.

To compensate him, she struggled to be a 'muse', even though she did not know what one was. She imagined herself one of those expensive plaster figures that craftsmen now hauled up to the Lower Laithes ceiling – all breeze-blown drapery, bottoms and breasts. At other times she realised that 'muse' was a gentleman's word for a poor girl's giving her life in order to make Oliver happy. Beneath her thoughts and actions was this simple ideal of a tormented village girl: that domestic luxury would make possible all other beautiful things, especially Oliver's poetry.

On the day when Oliver had arrived at Lower Laithes, holding Betty by the hand, he had been made speechless. The door was opened by the lugubrious 'unemployable' ex-weaver Amos Culpin, dressed in a livery of wig, blue frock coat, yellow stockings, and with a black 'solitaire' ribbon around his neck. He was now capable, apparently, of holding himself erect. The old carved black oak of the house had been replaced with walnut, mahogany and rosewood, decorated with inlay *à la mode*. A huge ill-featured woman with the pox was scrubbing the floor of the hall, on the ceiling of which buxomly cavorted all nine of the muses freshly painted *trompe l'œil* in colours of rosy flesh.

Oliver had then been ceremoniously conducted into the presence of Anne Wylde, his housekeeper (the scrubbing-woman, seemingly devoid of Reason, laughing crookedly after him). Dumbfounded, he looked this way and that, his mouth opening and shutting but speechless, and his movements indecisive.

After a few days this first and (when Oliver had reflected upon it) delightful surprise settled into an uneasy, constant feeling of truancy. It was a mood largely fed by Benjamin Greave, who found a hundred ways to express his disapproval of Anne Wylde, and his hope that his son's infatuation would not be serious, but only a temporary flight from reality. When in a jovial humour, the clothier addressed his son jokingly with new epithets, as 'sinner', 'malefactor', or 'condemned', so repetitively that it set Oliver's teeth on edge (was the old clothier, alone at Making Hall, falling fast under the spell of Patience Helliwell?). But if there was a hitch in his trading – a consignment of woollens delayed by storms, or some credit-notes proving too long in arriving – he argumentatively took it out on his son. So eventually Oliver refused to listen.

Introspection, also, was soon haunting Lower Laithes. The couple found a great deal of time, whilst sitting together for sweet long hours in quiet rooms, for studying one another in that different way that couples discover when they live together, and after other energies have spent themselves. (Such as the effort to overcome a fear that this liaison might be a mistake; and the making of practical arrangements for their career.) Oliver observed Anne as previously he had never done. He even noticed fresh things about, for example, her hands. Of course he had seen before that she was left-handed and he knew that in childhood she had been beaten for it. But he had not realised how practical that hand was for everyday life – as distinct from the right, which she used for caressing.

She would caress him, and expect him to stroke her, for hours on end. She closed her eyes and he felt the softening of her body, melting in waves – a sea of wax. Yet as the point was reached when he was sure he could approach her, she would stiffen and prevent it. He never understood to what extent this will of hers tortured her; this suspicion taught her by her experience of the threatening male. He merely saw that she flushed. She coloured partly with the violence of sudden frustration, though caused by herself, and partly with invented anger. As excuse she would pretend some alarm, and stiffen like a fawn in the grass.

Anne was waiting every day for Oliver to settle to writing poems. She believed that this would satisfy the desire which she was refusing to fulfil. With all her sensual longing hidden behind it, she laid out his ink, quills, lexicon, paper, pipes, tobacco, and placed his chair temptingly before his desk; all other services were available by tugging a bell-rope. And she waited.

But Oliver was used to penning his verses at inns, in briefly held schoolmaster's lodgings, or out of doors, and it took him a long time to settle amongst these grand surroundings. Around him it was too quiet, the very furniture menacing him with its silence. Or contrarily there was too much noise of squabbling servants coming from the kitchen. His fine clothes, worn to impress Anne, impeded him. Lace cuffs got tangled with his pen, tight trousers made it uncomfortable to sit, whilst his shoes pinched. Though it was his own home, he was more constrained here than he had been at Makings. And whilst the only place he would have felt free to play his fiddle was the kitchen, there it seemed improper, for his relationship to Miss Wylde was an embarrassment to him before the servants.

At last, amongst plush damasks, velveteens, silks, carpets, silver, china and mahogany, he got down to his verses. He hewed the marble block of poetry:

'When bright Apollo's flaming car had run
The southern course, and in our climes begun
To perfect blossoms and the budding flowers,
To paint the fields, and form the shady bowers...'

But his verses, like his surroundings, were a texture of rich furnishings within a crumbling classical edifice. (And 'perfect' didn't scan!) He could not push his lines forward. His mind was elsewhere, straying to the bosky embodiment of *tea* upon the ceiling, or to the bosoms of the plaster muses who roared across the ceiling like spirited English ladies engaged in a fox-hunt. He daydreamed of sitting with Tim Bobbin before the fire in some secret and convivial moorland inn (or wherever that ariel-spirit had now disappeared to), smoking a long clay pipe, his feet on the hob, and a scrap of paper on his knee to scribble down whatever was dictated by a flesh-and-blood muse, who was whichever lady brought jugs of ale to his elbow. Recalling his past years of wandering, when adventure and health had mounted to blossom out of his fiddle or his pages of verse, and progress marked every day, he could hardly believe with what zest and undoubting purpose he had lived, although he was then but a poor traveller about the hills. Nor could he disentangle 'the messy skein of time' that had left him, despite Ann Wylde, feeling bereft. What was it about himself, that – though he grasped the opportunities before him, and he had no *reason* to be dissatisfied with his tremendous good fortune – yet a demon of unhappiness, a constant cloudy shadow, would not go away? He longed and longed for Anne and was in various moods of torment because of this. But she was not the total cause. Was it some unrecognised part of himself that was unsatisfied?

Ironically it was Anne Wylde, his Nature Muse, who unwittingly drove him into anxieties about trade. He found himself repeating the mistaken pattern of his life with Zillah; for all this luxury had to be paid for, and because of quarrels with his father, mostly about Anne, his livelihood grew insecure.

Whilst Oliver was writing, Anne would often move restlessly around the room, picking up and putting down various things, wanting to stay near but knowing that she upset his concentration. He had no conception of what tides and cross-currents were racing through her mind. She would be longing to 'give in' to him – sometimes keeping her legs stiff to control her moistening, to make it possible for her to remain upright, whilst she imagined what it might be like. Next she forced herself to believe that the best use anyway for his energies was for them to go unadulterated into the permanent mould of his poems. The verse that he might write became her substitute for the man. She thought of all his gentle, warm character being poured into them, and this way she loved him possibly more than she could ever feel physically for an erratic living human.

When Oliver looked up, he saw only her inscrutable eyes staring at him.

'Poor Oliver! You wouldn't have these troubles if it were not for me,' she said, one day. (Almost Zillah's very words! Oliver reflected.) 'Perhaps they are right to throw stones and call me "witch", though I cannot help myself.'

Typical of his good nature, he did not even think that what she was doing was blaming herself for his sexual discontent. (If he had, he might have suspected her of teasing.) It was his opinion instead that she was worrying over the problems of the woollen industry. This, he thought, was preposterous. 'No! No! No! It is only that the weavers are so discontented,' he answered. 'Inspired by the Republicans in France they want more money than they truly earn from my father. So they do offhand workmanship, which means that our goods are returned. Now poor father is aged and does not have the control of his affairs that he used to.'

Oliver would then be soothing Anne and soon she would in her turn again be consoling him, convincing him of the advantages of life at Lower Laithes. She would move close and kiss his frown. He would kiss her in return, and try to do more. She would resist. Thus Oliver's scruples and doubts would dissolve into a mist of lovers' sentiments – as Anne intended.

Sentimentality, which always bears the promise of fulfilment *later*, was the perfect way of keeping Oliver adoring her: so Anne thought. The two of them caressed, fetched things for one another, fed titbits; until Oliver, with his author's detachment, thought that this spectacle of two people pretending to be one because they believed they were in love was ridiculous, and his frustration then showed itself once more in erratic anger. He felt that old instinct for violence rising in him, and he crushed it.

So love remained everything but consummated. When he was on the edge of impatience Anne kept one step ahead in making him amused or baffled. She always seemed to be changing her mind, and yet to be consistent to something deeper. Her sensibility was, like the spring season, full of surprises but underneath moving into fullness and blossoming. He grew dependent on her ever-resourceful faculty, tried to forget his lust, and doubted any opinion of his own until Anne had confirmed it. Often he did not understand her enigmas. But though he was confused and insecure with an unpredictable muse, he decided to be loyal to her sensibility. And always she was able to keep him afraid of annoying her, and of her despising his simplicity.

Once everything was running well and there was little for her to do, Anne Wylde found a dullness about Lower Laithes. It was without visitors. Despite her new fashionableness and the money spent, 'Society', no different from the more primitive people of Lady Well, shunned her, this time as an upstart. At first they paid some prying calls but these soon fell away. A few invitations were received, though only to the houses of tradesmen employed, or hoping to be employed, at Lower Laithes. Even these were at difficult hours, and the one visited was likely sick with an illness that kept others away. Anne made one spectacular effort to recover: she had an ox roasted out of doors, employing two men to turn it day and night. But no one of importance came to eat it and after a few days it stank, so it was given to the poor who lived, or who squatted in the woods, outside the walls of Lower Laithes. Anne and Oliver were finally too proud to accept this treatment and they became recluses, whilst their coachman grinned as he polished the equipage that was never required to go anywhere. Not only Benjamin Greave, but none of the Makings' servants either, would come near Lower Laithes. Those on their way to the fulling mill shunned the house, with its tall polished windows, its neatness as if it had nothing to do with trade nor any practical business, and its ornaments in the Greek style; it was the home of a witch. No one came to the kitchen door courting the maids. The only visitors were beggars wanting to look around and steal something. The menservants stopped going to the local inns, where the drinkers extracted tales, making grooms, gardeners and kitchen-boys afraid to return and face their mistress. So there was no feeding of stories back into the Lower Laithes kitchen either. The flow of life stopped and there was much brooding over petty obsessions.

Even Oliver was often not nearby. Either business genuinely called him away; or, to hell with the torments of desire! he thought and grasped excuses to be free of the strangling of his muse. Often he did not inform Anne of his comings and goings, assuming his freedom just as he had always done. He relaxed in an illusion, and returning reality only brought him ill-temper. He would come home smelling of alcohol, or sooty with pipe-smoking, and she met him reproachfully. The reproaches turned into quarrels. They became bitter.

Innocently, Anne had thus created loneliness around herself. She was without her father, and Aunt Pity, whilst Oliver had turned into a stranger; and there were no other friends in Anne's life. She missed especially her father as never before – imagining that he would have some wise solution to offer her, just as he had so often in childhood.

One Sunday morning she went to Lady Well to win him. Riding her handsome black gelding (a present from Oliver) she rushed so quickly clear of the wood that her blood raced, whilst the horse sweated in the clear dry summer air. The beast's incalculable temperament was very like her own, and both thrilled with a harmonious desire to get free of the stuffy house and the moist dark trees. For a few moments Anne felt that she never enjoyed with humans such love as was now between herself and this animal.

Enclosures and farmyards were empty of people, who instead shuffled towards parish church or to one of the scattered chapels – Congregationalist, Methodist, Baptist (Calvinist or New-Connexion) and Quaker. Sealed in their separate Sunday tribes, they communicated to those of another group only silent glances of pity, contempt, hatred, fear or incomprehension. What did they share as humans all together of God's great, glossy, open summer day, though it fell so powerfully and equably upon them all? They agreed only on this: that the impatient arrogant woman whom they saw, dressed in 'Jezebel's red silk' and clouding them with dust, was hurrying to Hell itself. They said that she was surely at one with the secret moorland spirits which fled as larks through the blue dome of air, and they cried for her 'justified undoing'. Some even chose to blame her for 'taking her trade to foreign parts' by purchasing genteel silk instead of local wool. Some were also jealous because today was an excellent one for making hay and if they were as bold as she they would be doing what in their hearts they really wished, and be scything grass, or bleaching cloth in the sun.

At Lady Well on marshy ground on the north side of the church Anne found a small crowd making a great noise. She peered over their heads and saw Esther Kershaw digging out heavy spadesful of the clogged wet earth. When they tried to stop her, Esther lifted up her magical apron and waved it in their faces. The charm worked, for even the staunchest Protestant stepped back. Anne guessed that Esther was either burying, or digging up, an unbaptised illegitimate child that had been sneaked into the holy ground – perhaps one belonging to another woman whom she intended to prosecute. But Jabez Stott (less adoringly shy of Anne Wylde, now that he was a journeyman carpenter with his own sweetheart) told Anne that Esther, after a long, long search, had discovered the ancient well and was going to make it flow again. Since her father's house had burned down Esther had, as she promised, wandered the moors in her apron that had been blessed by Jesus. (Some thought, not in search of Christ as she claimed, but to find and tether the Great Mother Cow.) One day at an inn she had heard a drunken old man toasting the servant (who was named Mary) saying 'Here's health to *all* Marys,' and Esther realised that he was a Papist. So she asked him if he knew the whereabouts of St Mary's Well in Lady Well, because she wished 'to look for the image of Christ in its clear water', and he had told her to dig on the north side of the church.

By the time of Anne's arrival, Esther had uncovered a circle of stones on some uncommonly wet ground, within it a tip of old cooking pots, 'superstitious' carvings that had been broken from the church, bits of tiles, and broken crutches. Also some coins. Thereupon the well performed its first miracle, reminding several that the gold belonged to them; for, 'come to think of it', their 'grandparents had thrown them in long ago to buy wishes'. Esther, frantically excited, hoped to reveal the crystal water in time to lead Doubtfire to it, that he might be resurrected by the true image and pure spring of Christ before beginning another drunken sermon. Meanwhile her neighbours, who were in horror thinking that she had turned to that scarlet blood-beast, the Pope, and was trying to satisfy his thirst for magic wells, were throwing all sorts of rubbish at her.

'This should quench thy doubtfire!' Esther screamed. 'Will you stop throwing stones and slutch, all you sinners, for I am no Papist dressed in carnal!' and she flapped her apron. 'I tell you, there are some things that I know. There are some things that I know even though I was never in a school to be learned to read, write and menstruate!' She was up to her knees in mud. It daubed her face, arms and dress, 'like a painted pagan savage', someone said; whilst her limbs jerked with brisk madness like a showman's doll.

'Let the poor woman be!' Anne shouted, so that all listened to her and Esther could at last straighten up.

Anne's cry silenced everyone. That the woman who had stones thrown at her since birth should not be relieved when a different scapegoat was found! 'Anne Wylde! For you to defend me! Here is the second miracle!' Esther's voice was breaking with emotion.

The mason's daughter, sad at this never-ending persecution, moved off to her father's house. What madness and un-reason swarms outside, he was thinking, in his brown sober rooms, though he said nothing. He only, with great patience, *looked*. When Anne met John Wylde's eyes, she thought how rare it was to find orbs as level and unflinching as his. That steady gaze, resting without embarrassment upon its object, could measure a stone or just as accurately weigh up a disputatious parson or philosopher.

Anne found that, during her absence, John Wylde and the fifteen-year-old ancient-child-servant-creature Martha had grown close together. Both had relapsed into taking old persons' diets of dry crusts, oat biscuits and bodiless soups, and to picking bits off one another's plates. Anne saw that Martha had replaced herself in the house, perhaps also in her father's affections, and she felt jealous. Meanwhile the servant girl prattled about the doings of clergymen: one fell asleep in his pulpit after being out hunting since dawn, another insisted on being buried on the north side of the church (reserved for witches, criminals and heretics) because it was in sight of the ale-house, whilst a third composed what Martha called 'jeering verses' and threw them upon a rival, nonconforming, parson's coffin as it was being lowered into the ground ...

Anne interrupted, 'I see that Esther Kershaw thinks that she has discovered our well, father. I saw a great crowd who had no will to abuse me because of their throwing stones and rubbish at her.'

'It is no wonder that the innocent and vulgar of our countryside lapse into superstition, when Joseph Doubtfire is in his pulpit not one Sunday in four, but raking around the countryside in search – he says – of "specimens". When he returns he has nought to show for it but a mutilated badger, or the swollen liver of a dead pauper. He never has a concise thought to offer us, or even a well-constructed phrase. He rarely has a sermon to take into the pulpit. He is most often drunk, and too incensed about the burnings to preach the gospel of Christ. And all the clergymen of our district are seemingly hewn from the same rough quarry!'

'Parson's importuned all t'time to give relief for those that's lost everything i'fires,' Martha said.

'Do you still go to your chapel at Clay Slack?' Anne interrupted again.

'Martha likes to remain faithful to the town church.'

'I did not ask you about our servant!'

Once again Anne's bristling unsubmissive speech scalded his ears. John Wylde looked wearily at her. 'You, my daughter, do not change, though Lady Well becomes the home of pagan beasts and is burnt to the ground.'

''Tis awful, the fires, and there's more and more of these wool-combers opening their shops with furnaces, a danger to us all. 'Tis the new worsteds that ruin us,' Martha said.

When they were about to set off for Clay Slack, Martha put on her bonnet, but Anne firmly sent her to the local church of Saint Mary the Virgin, alone. Anne was determined to have her father to herself. Yet she felt regretful, for she had come to woo him softly and here she was already creating anger, dispute and irritation once again.

John Wylde was not able to step out as briskly as he used to up the hillside. Yet he wanted to walk, savouring the old days. In order to give him time to draw breath and not insult him by it, Anne stopped to pluck bunches of heather, which was just coming into bloom. There was a large purple variety and some with smaller, tighter, white flowers. She chose the more luxuriant purple. The thin stems were tough, bending into supple knots before they would break; but her father (unusually) did not help her. Either he was too weak, or too impatient of her, or both.

'I do not know what our congregation will make of your dressing so immodestly,' he remarked.

'I do not care what they think.'

'It seems that since you became the seeming-mistress at Lower Laithes you do not walk in the ways of Christ as I have shown you.' He pointed to a cottage, standing alone and sheltering against some rocks. 'There is a witch yonder who blasphemes, saying that all females are cursed because of Christ's religion, which is for men. Even if women go to Him daily on their hands and knees. Now her mouth fills with blood whenever she speaks.'

'A tooth is bad in her head.'

'She hath become very wasted and lies in bed ready to die. I think it is her soul that sickens for her wrong-doing and is preparing for Hell eternal. No one will go near her.'

'I believe you are becoming a superstitious Papist yourself, my father. Your mind narrows because you do not travel so much and are staying in Lady Well building manufactories! You used to tell me, "Heaven is but this world when men laugh and are merry. Hell is also this world where they suffer grief and pain." Has all your reason left you? Has all your joy deserted you? What do your books tell you now?'

'My eyes are none too good any more, and I cannot read so many books. But I know that the ways of God are strange.'

The track was solitary, dreary, hot and straight. Wind-warped, weirdly shaped stones peered with foreboding over the skyline high above them; monsters leaning down out of a nightmare. A pair of curlews glided like disinherited spirits after the father and daughter. The birds moved heavily, yet took in a great deal of sky in wide easy sweeps. 'Cur-*lew*! Cur-*lew*!' followed by a gentler noise as of bubbling fountains came from their long scissoring fragile beaks, which Anne could pick out against the light. Upon Raven's Hill a flock of sheep grazed, their mouths making a loud drumming noise upon the turf. And, indeed, it was hollow beneath it; there was a great chamber, its entrance lost, where 'ancient people used to go to talk to their dead'.

Near to this, isolated and huddling next to each other as if for comfort, were two small plain buildings. One was the nonconformists' place of worship, the other the home of the couple who cared for it. The eye could not help but fix upon them in this empty landscape. Near one building were several hens and a pig. The other was fringed with small graves and had KNOWE GOD carved above the entrance in the heavy style of lettering that was now out of fashion (but followed by the mason) and seeming ugly to others' eyes. The doors of both were flung open and women in workaday aprons were carrying oatbread and ale from the cottage into the chapel.

'Well, mason, and what news has thou brought us from afar?' the visitors were genially asked. Amongst smiles and kindnesses, Anne and her father entered. They were confronted by a high wooden rail forming a horizontal passage for men to go to the right and women to the left. The Independents' clothes, of black or white wool or cotton, were tight at the throat, the wrist and the ankles, as if to say, 'Lord, how humbly imprisoned we are within our sin compared with your unbuttoned wrath and bliss about the skies!' The chapel's possessions were similarly confined, being locked in the many dark cupboards. The congregation consisted of weavers and spinners. They treasured cramped little enclosures that they had grasped out of the moor's bosom and had claimed with tight walls. Everything of theirs was brown, black or white, without decoration. The only strong colours were the tints of eggs, butter and hams which the community bartered before worship; the astounding red and green of some apples on a pewter plate; Anne's even more astonishing red clothes, and the purple of her heather.

She twisted her nosegay around the passage-rail. A moment later, one of the women with an angry expression briskly threw it out of the door, as if it was unclean. The hens came running but then stalked away, disappointed, whilst the woman muttered to her friend. She was a tough person, her piety surviving regular beatings from her husband on Sunday afternoons (before he took her to bed) for having attended the chapel, and her voice was hard and spiky.

Anne felt lonely, as if she had stepped under an icy deluge. Even in the Sunday presence of The Lord nothing was more important to these people than the trading of eggs for hams or the affairs of one who had deserted chapel because of a dispute over a pound of wool. Where was their serious discussion of God, the equality of man, the nature of the lost Eden and the future Paradise?

However, they did assume that all people were equal (so long as they had equal things to trade). Even women, though they had to enter at the left hand, yet were allowed to be equivalent intellects with men. And all, men or women, who wished to preach could do so in their turn. No one was more welcome for this than a stranger or one who had been absent for a while. So John Wylde – who shone with happiness in the community – was asked to give a sermon.

Gesturing firmly and still the solid mason even in the pulpit, he began, quoting fluently, and some passages by heart, from the Book of Jeremiah: ' "Say unto the King and to the Queen, humble yourself, sit down. For your principalities will come down, even the crown of your glory! The cities of the south shall be shut up . . . lift up your eyes and behold them that come from the north." '

The congregation had no doubt that this prophesied the supremacy of the northern woollen-traders over sinful, Bacchanalian southerners, especially those in London and Bath, and so they were as pleased to hear these words as the mason was to deliver them. Whilst John Wylde preached in his most careful, solemn voice, the chapel became so silent that, although Anne made no more movement than her breathing, yet a continuous rustling of her silk could be heard. When her father reached the passage, 'For the greatness of thine iniquity are thy skirts discovered, and thy heels made bare . . . Therefore will I discover thy skirts upon thy face, that thy shame may appear,' several turned to look at her, sure that the quotation signified that only *she* was an obstacle to their triumph and prosperity. Meanwhile the mason was squinting short-sightedly and unaware of the effect of his words. 'I have seen thine adulteries and thy neighings, the lewdness of thy whoredom, and thine abominations on the hills and fields . . .' Anne put out her tongue at the congregation, whereupon the staring women withdrew under their black bonnets and the men into coat collars, like retreating snails.

When the service was over and they were eating oatcakes washed down with ale, John Wylde was so bloomingly happy that he noticed nothing of his daughter's gloomy silence. She was wondering: what better things might be done amongst clever people in a chapel, besides praying and trading? She was also unhappy because her errand had been to ask her father to live at Lower Laithes, but now this seemed threatened with bad omens.

They were released at last on to the hot moor, which was brazen with sunshine and colour. The two curlews still swung in great interlocking circles over the barrow, and the people going home from chapel radiated over the sheep-tracks, trying to disperse without drawing attention to themselves, and lost in this huge bright bowl of space.

Between John Wylde and his daughter her question was poised, circling like the curlews in the air. 'Come and live with me,' Anne pleaded, at last.

For some time they marched silently upon the turf and the stones.

'And how is the young master – Oliver Greave?' John Wylde merely answered, slyly.

Anne knew what he meant, and realised from it how gossip about her must have spread. She laughed softly. 'Mr Greave is only happy when he is playing his fiddle and writing poems,' she told him affectionately.

'Are you together as man and wife?'

'No. Come and live with me, Father,' Anne repeated.

'Nay, I shall only be a trouble to you, and thy conscience will not be any happier.'

So Anne returned alone to Lower Laithes. There one servant showing pleasure took her cloak, another her shoes, and she moved through the high rooms feeling liberated after the cramped chapel.

But she found Oliver worrying (as so often these days) over his accounts and poring over wool-patterns. The sheets were covered with mean little figures and calculations: a clear sign of trouble.

'Let me have charge of the pattern books, and I will make you prosper,' Anne said.

'Why? Will you cast a spell?'

'Yes!' She came close. As he stared at her, Oliver awoke to an uncanny realisation. Anne Wylde was *himself*! She was not substance, but reflection. He was looking into a mirror in which his own feminine part was revealed. He was facing his own manifestation, his twin. Knowing each other so well was the reason why they loved deeply, but also why they were so intolerant of one another.

Or was it Anne who was real, and he who was her reflection?

Her wide-spreading gown (which showed off the money he had spent on her) swallowed him and drowned his revelation – or whatever it was. There was a rustling in his ears like a wood full of birds. Some new strong feeling, or instinct, also clothed her, invisibly, like a perfume. Was this *the* moment? Was it?

It had been such a long anxious wait that he was afraid now of being unable to fulfil it: or alternatively that he would 'fulfil' it too soon. He was tired from his worries; often he did not sleep because the screaming of Anne's peacocks woke him at dawn; and he gave in to her beckoning, offering the pattern books – the secrets of his and his father's trade – to her scrutiny and care. She then fell even further upon him and he realised that this afternoon was indeed his chance to take her. He was smothered by her dress, like a sparrow under a hawk.

He surfaced with the intention of leading her, his doppelganger, to his room. But she would not be led, and instead took him to her own place. 'You know I am a virgin,' Anne whispered, as if this explained all her remoteness from him.

His throat was too dry to answer. And it was she who undressed confidently in front of *him*, just as if she was used to men. He drew the curtains (she did not seem to care) and helped with her stays and underclothes – trying to look and yet not to look at her body. As she lifted her dress her arms were twisted behind her back, thus raising her breasts, and she grimaced.

'I cannot undress without my maid,' she complained. She was grasping at the commonplaces of life as if they were posts or rocks that she could cling to in an ocean. He realised that she was trembling.

'You must have managed in the past.'

'I did not need such gowns as these.'

'Need?' Oliver wondered. He himself stripped, producing a tiny pile of brown cloth next to her mountain of silk. The moment was held in a drugged aura and he could not believe it was happening. Because of his erection he felt ashamed to remove his intimate clothes.

She knelt before him. 'I want to see what it looks like before it goes inside me,' she whispered as if a louder voice would have frightened her. He blushed and opened his legs slightly. 'I have only seen a child's before, never an erect one. Except once Amos Culpin showed me his, in a dark passage, but I did not look.'

'Amos Culpin! Him you employ as your servant?'

'What better use for someone who tried to mak' use of me?'

Oliver opened his legs more widely. She touched with one finger delicately. He leant to put his lips in the valley of her breasts. His mouth travelled over the soft hills of her stomach that was white and slender, with the thin bones under the flesh, like the breast of a plucked bird. So they fell together on the floor. She turned over, encouraging him, saying, 'I want you to kiss me all the way up, oh so slowly, as the spring comes with flowers over the moors, so gently!' He moved his lips over her thighs and between her buttocks. 'Your kisses are like petals,' she said. He had never explored such secret places of anyone before. 'Along inside my legs,' she whispered, opening them for his convenience.

His mouth brushed the deep and shaded wood. Her hands reached down for his armpits and drew him up so that his penis, beginning to moisten, could enter her. He did not realise he had broken the hymen until she cried, a sharp sound like a disturbed bird.

Oliver wanted to hold himself for her pleasure and he waited for her thighs to start twitching under him, but they did not do so. He twisted her nipples and she took hold of his hand as if she wanted him to play with her more firmly, which he did. Oliver came, his eyes closed and crushed upon her throat.

He opened them and returned his gaze to hers, which had not left his for a moment. She did not even bother to look down, and she was calm, just as if she had done this before. 'Is that all?' she asked. Oliver did not answer. She was frustrated and angry, and turned her face away from him, with no interest in the blood and semen trickling from her body.

'Tell me about Zillah,' she said. She was crying.

He sat apart, trembling and ashamed of the failure. 'My father trusted and liked her, particularly when she gave birth. It was then that he shared his business with me, thinking that his wealth was now fertile. We Greaves are not gentry stock who are sure of their pedigree and my father's greatest desire in making wealth is to have someone to pass it on to and a memorial. It was a blow when Zillah produced only a daughter.'

'Was there much passion in your marriage?'

With Anne, even whilst she had held herself from him, he had felt immersed in the great bowl of all womanhood. So he had to answer, 'It was not an all-consuming passion. At the time I thought it was, but it was not. For I have learnt since what it is to be consumed. But you must be thinking that I'm saying this only because I'm with you!'

'No. I know you are not wayward and dishonest.'

Then, being unsatisfied, she was off on another train of thought. 'Oliver – there is such poverty, darkness and ignorance in Yorkshire. Couldn't we build them schools which those of any age might attend on Sunday when they have no work to do? They might say a prayer or two at the same time, to please the Parson.'

'What will you have them taught?'

He began to dress.

'Oh, reading and good breeding. They could learn to show me proper respect and be cured of their barbarous custom of throwing stones.'

He was engrossed in his own fulfilment and discovery. He was transformed. It was as if a flock of birds was circling inside the tower of his skull, looking for somewhere to settle. He felt that for so many years he had been living inside a womb, sleepy, like a snake that is casting its skin or a baby waking only for its food. Now he had woken alert, conquering, vigorous, and as if he had been given eyes with which to see in the darkness of our mundane world where vision is so clouded and obliterated. He felt that he had been purged in fire, or in ice. That he had been taken back, back, to the roots of poetry.

Conscience-stricken that he had failed to make her happy, he searched for an excuse. 'You are so strange, Anne Wylde. You do not seem to feel.'

Anne shrugged. 'I have heard that some women pretend to be happy, just for the sake of keeping their husbands.'

'And I have heard that you are of unnatural birth and that you have long legs because you are descended from a deer!' For the first time that he had seen, she looked confused, did unnecessary things with her hands, looked about distractedly. 'Is John Wylde your father? They say not. Culpin says not.'

'I do not know my father. Not in reality.' She paused. 'I do not know who he is.' Pause. 'I do not know him. I do not think I am of this world.' She paused yet again. 'I am from somewhere else, I do not know why I am here, and I do not like it!'

'Tell me who your father is, then.'

'I do not know.' That did not seem helpful, either. So just as confusingly, she added, 'I knew my mother.'

'But she died when you were born!'

Anne looked at him blankly.

'I still know her. Not what she looked like, only what she felt. I cannot explain to you, and you'd better go!' Because he did not move, she suddenly screamed out, '*Leave me alone and go!*'

'I would like to know who your father was,' he repeated, timidly.

A peacock screamed in the gardens.

She smiled. 'You can believe the stories, so long as you do not dare to do as others in the end and throw stones at me for it. My father came and went, and I do not know what he was. Ask Esther Kershaw, perhaps she has met him, for she wanders about as my mother did. John Wylde is a good man ... oh, go away now!'

When he had left, Anne rang for Jenny and told her to bring water.

Jenny Loveless, as she bathed her mistress, watched with dark eyes that showed neither sorrow nor happiness – an expression that it was easy to ignore. If it had occurred to Anne to wonder what the girl thought as she washed away the stains, Anne might have imagined envy. A desire, too obscure to express, for comforts of her own, the privilege of rising late in the mornings, and for a powerful husband to provide these things.

Jenny silently raised the cloud of red silk and stood patiently upon a stool to dress Mr Greave's 'housekeeper'.

The following April Oliver arranged, through one of his father's agents, to collect a black boy from Liverpool as a present for Anne Wylde. The Negro was on the quayside waiting in the charge of a sailor, and clutching a small bundle, plus a Bible. He was smiling, in the way of one who always smiles, but he was bewildered. He had ended up in Liverpool from Africa by way of China, having been exchanged for some perfumes. Next he had been bartered for a horse. He expected only to be used again, and was waiting for a master because that was a law of life.

The boy followed Oliver down the street. He would willingly go anywhere so long as it was in the opposite direction to the clutter of tall masts along the quay: when Oliver for a short distance went that way, the Negro halted, gibbering and stubborn. So Oliver had to cheat him, seeming to turn only inland. At a crowded tavern he gave the boy a meal. The blackamoor scooped with his fingers and Oliver was amused, wondering at this queer creature's indeterminate position half way between animal and man.

Having the boy's confidence now, it was no trouble for Oliver to fix him on top of his carriage. Whilst Oliver read within, they set off across the marshy Lancashire plain. When they crossed a river the slave threw away his Bible, for the charm had done its work of finding him a kind master.

The first lesson the Negro learnt in England was about toll gates and the bad temper into which they threw travellers – although he himself was glad of the pauses because he was shivering and wet on top of the coach, his grin fixed to his face as if it was frozen there.

They stayed overnight in Manchester, where the Negro unfortunately lost his bundle, for Oliver might have learned from its contents something about him. Oliver, wondering how he might find the parcel again, raised his hand to scratch his head and the slave for the first time ceased to grin, cringing because he expected to be beaten. When Oliver quickly lowered his arm, the boy smiled again.

The next morning they climbed over the hills. It was a cold day. Whereas grass, flowers and tree-buds flourished upon the lowlands, the Pennine moors were still bare and dirty-looking with the accumulation of winter. Cold mists swept around the carriage. People who had never seen a black person before poured out to laugh at him, huddled against the mist. 'Put him into the river and set dogs on him!' someone shouted. Nevertheless the Negro, not understanding a word, kept on grinning.

Eventually he was standing, shivering, wet and dazed, in the kitchen at Lower Laithes whilst the servants formed a laughing circle around him. Oliver told them to get rid of the lad's rags, wash him and find better clothes, and he left.

Whilst Jenny went to scour attics and lumber rooms, Mary Pickles undressed him. She touched the boy as delicately as if she feared that he might fall to pieces in her hands. The others stood around watching silently, and wondering whether he was dark all over. They thought Master Oliver meant them to scrub all the black off, so Mary led him by the ear to the well. There she scrubbed harder and harder whilst the floor ran with water and everyone laughed or scolded because the black could not be removed. 'I've seen chimney boys before, but never one like this!' Amos Culpin grumbled. ''Tis a pagan sin to keep such a creature, dark as the Devil, and a mark of God's displeasure with him that he cannot be made clean!' Gardeners and stableboys came in from the yard to see what caused the laughter. The Negro still kept grinning, pleased to bring amusement. He winced only when Mary Pickles worked over-generously at his neck, which was marked and evidently sore. They tried poking to make him tell them why he was so black. The boy simply grinned and danced about in the cold water.

Culpin turned to the scullery girl, Bridie. 'It knows no more civilised English than you do! Try him in your Irish tongue.' At the word 'Irish' Bridie spoke rapidly but ineffectively in Gaelic.

Now Jenny appeared with some oddments of pantaloons and a tunic. The Negro was dressed and Jenny led him away. They were both children of the same age and she took him sympathetically by the hand to where Oliver sat with Anne.

The gift was partly for Anne's birthday. It was also to celebrate the fact that, by withholding himself powerfully, and with a great deal of caressing, Oliver had recently brought this apparently bold but in truth deeply shy creature, Anne Wylde, through to the full happiness and forgetful blindness of love.

How excited he had been that he *could* hold himself steady, feeling her eagerness and anticipation mount, the tension climb in her body, her head thrown this way and that. At the last moment she had wrapped her legs around his waist and pulled upon him tightly. He thought that he had *heard* the spasms in her body, growing louder. As Anne felt the semen spread inside her, she sank into a great peace. Her eyes had opened and, in harmony with her lips, smiled, a smile slow as though certain of itself that it was now to become a permanent expression.

When the lad entered the splendid room he rubbed at his skin and was frightened. Anne clapped her hands. 'You've brought me a slave boy!'

She looked at Oliver nowadays with a different expression. She was calmer, but above all she was more absorbed in him, and this was because ever since the first successful love-making almost every occasion had been happy – and when it wasn't, neither sensed a reason to be distressed about it. Whilst Oliver showed some pride in his love-making.

'A servant, not a slave. We don't do that sort of thing in England,' he replied.

'Your father is investing in them in the Americas.'

'But that isn't Yorkshire! I thought we would teach the lad, quite freely, to stand behind a carriage.'

Anne stroked the boy gently with one finger. 'What a lovely blue-black skin! What shall we call him? Earth! That's a name for a Negro, isn't it?'

Anne knew too well how the people might stone this vulnerable creature if he were set loose, so to protect him she planned to take him to the blacksmith and have riveted around his neck a collar which said, *Earth. Anne Wylde's Negro. Lady Well.* She chose her design from a volume delivered by a merchant: it was engraved with bunches of grapes, and with kneeling blacks offering up globes of the world. On the way to the smith, the Negro, though he did not know English, certainly understood the symbol of slavery which dangled from his mistress's fingers. He draggled hopelessly and helplessly behind, wondering where he could run to in these woods and hills, even if he escaped. Sometimes he refused to go on and hid behind bare trees and bushes, presumably satisfying needs of nature brought on by apprehension.

The blacksmith laughed as his big hands held the boy's head. 'Whatever will our Anne Wylde think to do next! It's just like a monkey. I've never seen anything like it!'

The resigned grin returned to the Negro's face, for he had known collars before and he did not even bother to put his fingers up to feel it. Some day, no doubt, another accident would cast him on a different shore into some other hands. Meanwhile these grey-faced people with their looms and their bandy-legged horses laden with wool were not bad masters and did not torment him, starve him or load him with chains.

Back at Lower Laithes, Anne had ready for him a newly woven blue livery and she wrapped upon his head a pale silk turban, which like his silver collar glittered against his dark skin.

The black boy broke the ice, for because of him curiosity overcame Society. So that the Negro could be inspected, Oliver Greave and Anne Wylde were invited where clothiers, merchants, artisans, schoolmasters and parsons were not usually welcomed – to the Snawdens: a family grand and old enough to know nothing of weaving and coal pits. The event that inspired an invitation was a 'musical evening'. A daughter was to play upon the spinet and a son, come from Oxford ('down' from Oxford, he called it, although everyone else said 'up') would perform various pieces upon the flute, with eloquent introductions.

Anne was not so easily flattered. She realised that whilst the common people attacked with stones, those of a better class abused you with their whims and sarcasms. They flattered and held out enticements but when they had grown tired dropped you back again into that pit of the lowest society, with contempt for your 'presumption'.

Anne and Oliver stalked boldly into the withdrawing room, just as they would have done if they were stepping on to the carpet of turf on a moor. Indeed, the couple always had a breeziness that was not remarkable amongst clothiers and weavers who were always scrambling about moorlands, but which was most conspicuous in a genteel drawing room. There was a stiffening of the faces of the Snawdens and other people who lived almost unseen in the district. (They did not even have to show themselves in church if they did not wish to, for they were rich enough to be safe from Sabbatarians.)

All behaved as if the last thing to excite their curiosity would be the black boy, who followed behind Anne without function other than to be decorative. 'I believe that Negro attendants are commonplace in London,' one said languidly, and at last. 'The practice is now discontinued as being vulgar.'

A lady, with a ship in full sail rouged upon her cheeks, fingered the black youth. 'I trust that he carries no diseases,' her escort warned.

Her alarm painted a sunset behind the sails of her man-o'-war, and she quickly withdrew her exploring fingers.

'Ah, Miss Crabtree!' another gentleman remarked. 'I believe the true position is that *we* are taking the diseases to *them*. Some tribes, I am told, have been quite wiped out after the coming of our sailors.'

'What kinds of diseases?'

'Too delicate to mention!'

'I believe that Miss Wylde is no more than the daughter of a mason!' Anne was allowed to overhear. 'She has such a *healthy* complexion. Quite weathered. Almost as dark as her Negro!'

'It is said that she is not popular with her own class. Quite notorious, in fact.'

'*Conspicuous!*'

'Though she sings trippingly, so I am told.'

Oliver turned aggressively. '*Trippingly*? What's that?'

A friendly hand soothed him. 'The young man is "up from down South", as you vulgarly put it. You should not take notice of our humour, for 'tis only fun.'

Some of the people, in the light of hundreds of candles, did have kind expressions. But it was inexpensive for them to give and they did it thinking it was all they lacked to achieve God's Grace. Others had found out, with pleasure, that riches made it possible to be cruel, and no one dared tell them so to their faces. As could be seen by their attitudes to footmen and maids, they acted without restraint or responsibility to those beneath them; thus they would do to weavers, tradesmen, old soldiers, artisans, lunatics and the poor. This was Anne's first experience of a gathering of her Betters. What a contrast these were to Anne's father and his friends, with their books, their humble desires for knowledge, liberty and expression! She did not enjoy their musical pieces either – realising that one was here not for true delight, but to applaud and feel satisfied with oneself for doing so, touching one's hands together softly.

Horsfall said clearly within her hearing, 'By God, my friends, you would not think her father-in-law was the old clothier with a dry wit and a tight grasp on his purse!'

'Father-in-law, you say? She is married, then?'

The young flautist, who had a polish like marble on his unweathered cheeks, looked gratefully down at his white fingers, for the thought had struck him that God's Grace could suddenly be removed and leave him with hands as coarse as Anne Wylde's. Then he remarked to her, 'Perhaps one could find at Oxford an engraver to immortalise one, so tall and statuesque, with one's Negro?'

He was sufficiently amused by this scandalous beauty-from-the-artisan-class to want to take her away from Oliver Greave and make her fashionable in London, Bath or Oxford. So his mother, sensing the threat of a dangerous liaison, interrupted, savagely and censorious, 'Miss Wylde, I have not seen you at our parish church!' Thus the thought was born in Anne Wylde: And why *not* visit one's parish church with one's Negro?

The next Sunday Oliver and Anne went to Saint Mary's, audaciously to claim a place in the Greaves' pew. They were laughing as they set out, although it offended their servants. On top of their carriage, Earth carried two prayer books on a green velvet cushion.

But when they burst from the Lower Laithes gardens into the changing landscape of burnt moors, cleared woodlands, drained marshes and new enclosures of stone or quickset-hawthorn that hurt Anne so deeply she would often literally close her eyes to it, their laughter ceased. Some wild thorn-trees still lingered, burnt or mutilated by the axe, in the open countryside. Mostly only their trunks remained. Some had grown fiercely contorted, as if registering the pain, or were twisted so tightly that they had burst into splinters: bright yellow jags leaking a bloody sap.

At last opening her eyes to see the destroyed hawthorns that had given up their last cuttings for the hedgerows – there intended not to blossom freely, but to enclose – Anne felt a premonition of ill-luck and disaster. Death of children and cattle, loss of fortune, parting with loved ones, were all foretold by the destruction of May-trees. Anne could not laugh again that day.

She timed her entrance into church to coincide with the beginning of the sermon. She had not been to Saint Mary's for many Sundays and she recognised its atmosphere with fresh surprise. A thousand years of bearing all the crises of Lady Well – births, marriages, sickness and death – had overloaded with weariness this tiny space, this theatre, as the scent of flowers that have passed maturity weighs down and sickens the air. Even the wedges of creamy light (or of multicoloured lights where it fell through the remains of the old glass) that carved the shadows, seemed made of a substance weighty enough to bow down the unexpectant congregation.

Anne alarmed this atmosphere with a daring clatter and squeak of the oak doors of the Greaves' pew, up on the balcony. The Horsfalls and the Snawdens, who had been preparing for a dozy Sunday and to take naps snug and hidden in their great wooden boxes, now peered out hoping to enjoy the first-ever comical incident in Lady Well church. There was a titter from the maids with whom Anne had once worked; whilst Patience Helliwell tightly gripped her prayer-book. Benjamin Greave, who had been daydreaming about the pile he intended to erect in the passageway to the altar of Saint Mary the Virgin ('The columns fro' the Greek, the angels carved by John Wylde so perfect you could hear 'em sing'), awoke to mutter boldly and sourly, 'Pride comes before a fall!'

Doubtfire was struck dumb. But, tipsy (as usual) though he was, he rallied himself to fight back. His lean face reddening above the pulpit, like a plum ripening in a dark orchard (or could it be a roasting soul in Hell?), he gripped the carved oak as if its enduring strength might lend itself to him, whilst he stirred his memory for where to find described in the Bible the *just deserts* of the *most execrable woman*. He also raked the pit of his own soul to discover shadowy female shapes, bringing them forth so that he might hate them. They were there, all right, like snakes in a ravine; ancient lurking vengeful mothers.

(Sometimes, in dreams, daydreams and drunken stupors, they rose, and seemed as beautiful as Anne Wylde. He recognised in himself then longings so deep that he did not know what they were, nor out of what well they had sprung. Desires for a goddess made flesh; for the ancient Mother. But before he could properly recognise her, she would vanish.)

Kings – that was where she was to be found! *Kings. Chapter ...* With fingers stained by the formalin in which he preserved his specimens of 'natural science', he ruffled the pages desperately to find Jezebel. Meanwhile the congregation was waiting. Anne Wylde coughed and sniffed. Ah! Kings 2, not 1. Chapter 9 ...

' "And Elisha the prophet called one of the children of the prophets and said unto him, Gird up thy loins, and take this box of oil in thine hand, and go to Ramoth-gilead! ... And when he came, behold, the captains of the host were sitting; and he said, I have an errand to thee, O captain ... thou shalt smite the house of Ahab thy master, that I may avenge the blood of my servants the prophets, and the blood of all the servants of the Lord, at the hand of *Jezebel* ..." '

Then occurred something quite unknown before in Lady Well. The Parson, in mid-sermon, was interrupted by a woman! (Doubtfire was used to disturbances in his services: but by men, not by women.) That clever female, Anne Wylde, of course, who, questioner though she was, knew her Bible well enough to continue the Vicar's quotation and flaunt him with it. "For the whole house of Ahab shall perish and I will cut off from Ahab him that pisseth against the wall!" she shrieked. There followed laughter and whistling, whilst someone's dog, sneaked into the building, began to yap. Dick Almighty, confined down below in the nave of the church, could do nothing to control disorder amongst his superiors upon the balcony. He could merely grow red, turn his leonine angry head this way and that, and bang his staff.

Doubtfire retorted, viciously, ' "And the dogs shall eat Jezebel ... and there shall be none to bury her!" '

' "And he opened the door, and fled!" ' Anne Wylde continued the quotation, angrily.

This was too much for Doubtfire, and he did, indeed, flee from his church, amidst a chaos of ribaldry and laughter. Even the picture of Saint Uncumber was smirking, it seemed to Anne. As she glanced at the upside-down crucified face, with the miraculous smile upon its lips, the similarity of that gaunt crucified form to her own struck her. Except that Saint Uncumber's hair was red, she was an exact replica of herself. Whilst Anne gasped at this fact (which she had never noticed before), 'Bang! Bang!' went Almighty's staff, with the brass knob and the little eagle glowing on top of it. But he was impotent because Anne Wylde, with the other superior members of the community, had her own way out of the church, down a broad oak staircase and through a special door, that was definitely outside his jurisdiction. She slipped away, for one moment at least something of a heroine amongst her own people.

Before the next Sunday, Anne set afoot rumours that she was going to pay another visit to Lady Well. So people stationed themselves for a good view of her. Although recently they had stoned her, many because of her wealthy connections, and the way that she had defeated Doubtfire, were now just as ready to curtsey and remove their hats.

Anne enjoyed making a spectacle of herself even more because Oliver was embarrassed by this gaunt, uncontrollable, sometimes menacing beauty with whom he had 'thrown in his lot', 'lived over the brush', or 'over the broomstick'.

'You are not God!' he tersely expressed himself at last.

'I haven't forgotten that God is a man!' she answered, primly.

That day, Doubtfire foolishly allowed the words, 'Christ has merely delivered us from mercy into misery,' to slip unguarded from his lips. He had lost control of himself, Anne Wylde had unmanned him.

Though it was an honest and deeply felt speech, one of Doubtfire's few, the congregation thought of it what he might have expected them to think (and did, later, when he had recovered self-control): though no one disagreed about the misery, yet if a clergyman is to tell us it is Christ's fault, then where are people to look for a saviour? So an angry crowd, Anne Wylde laughing amongst them, gathered at the church door, catching the heretical Parson before he ducked into the inn with Dick Almighty, Joshua Binns and the other churchwardens. Anne gaily shouted out her father's words, 'Heaven is only this world where men are merry, Hell is also this world, when they suffer grief and pain!'

'You talk like a damned Dissenter!' Doubtfire roared back, pulling his skirts about his stick-frame as he escaped, with Dick Almighty covering his retreat by waving the oak-and-brass staff of office.

Anne yelled after him, 'Your religion is only for those who have been cast out of paradise, where I still dwell!'

Through the following weeks Doubtfire appeared even less frequently in his pulpit. At the locked church door small groups of unhappy people, many of them old, begged Almighty to turn the key and let them in to pray even though there was no Parson. Or they drifted off to join the Methodists and the Baptists, perhaps never to return to the Established Church. Before what few services he gave, Doubtfire would be until three in the morning staring either into the bottom of a tankard, or through the eye of a microscope, to find the courage to face Anne Wylde's scorn. Finally, he spent almost all of his Sundays slipping across the moors, creating with tinder and flint his own fiery hells out of hay ricks and barns, or collecting 'specimens' –

paupers, or horses that had collapsed under their loads – whilst leaving his parishioners to what pleasures they could invent for themselves.

Jack Loveless's conversation with Anne Wylde had stirred his roots. Grievances rose to 'pollute' (as Doubtfire and others would have expressed it) the stream of thoughts which trickled through his head whilst at his loom. He remembered for instance when a traveller had turned up from South America with a piece of 'traditional Indian weaving' which Jack recognised as one of his own designs that had been taken to the southern hemisphere and copied by the Indians, its source in Yorkshire forgotten.

After his day's work Jack used to limp down to Lady Well and spend until the early hours in seditious talk with wool-combers and wool-croppers, these being the most radical artisans. Giving the password *Ezekiel* at the door (only for the sake of formality, since the guard knew Jack well) he entered a hush-house where illicit whisky, used to wash down a hare poached from Nicholas Horsfall's park, inflamed poetry and republicanism. Loveless soon realised that if his friends did not express themselves to such as Benjamin Greave or find an outlet in a written manifesto, the boil would burst more dangerously. Others already knew what the wool-combers were doing even though they swore one another to secrecy, debated mostly in darkness, and left their meeting-room on tiptoe. There seemed always to be someone to watch them. John Wylde would be up, squinting at a book by candlelight. (Though the mason had been a frequenter of hush-houses himself, in his time.) The Vicar might be slipping through the streets, 'keeping watch'. Or Esther Kershaw would be woken from where she often slept against the north wall of the church.

The wool-combers and croppers instructed Jack to ask Oliver Greave if he would write down their ideas in the form of a pamphlet and give them some money to print it. They argued that firstly Oliver was a poet, secondly that his quarrel with his father must at root have some grievance sympathetic to the wool-combers' cause, and thirdly that his woman, Anne Wylde, belonged to the common people. 'If he does not agree,' said one, 'tell the fellow we'll fire Lower Laithes, wi' his mistress in it.'

Loveless found the poet settled into a corner of an ale house, one of the many he went to in a futile search for Tim Bobbin and for his moorland muse. It was ironic that Anne Wylde, now in full sensuous happiness, and in a home furnished according to the best taste, still did not satisfy him. It was because she herself was not satisfied: he realised that Anne was even now not completely with him, but that part of her lay amongst the wiry moorland grasses. His muse still seemed out of reach. It was as if there was a veil, with on one side of it his elegant *verses* and on the other, *poetry*. The latter, in his imagination was identified with the moorland winds (whose variations he knew so well, from the soft breezes upon flowering heather to the shrill and cutting blasts of January), searching for expression in verse as the breath of a musician finds its true note in the mouth of a flute. But he, it seemed, was not the instrument. Or he was not the musician who was able to bring forth the sweet right air.

His failure to produce poetry angered Anne and even her sensual happiness was adulterated. In some violent arguments, she threw at him the questions that he must answer, the riddle, that he must solve, if he was to become a real poet. One was that of discovering that mysterious, shy wisp, who for a second would stand clearly embodied before him and then would disappear, convincing him only that what he had seen was an illusion: himself. There was also the question of feeding upon older roots, of growing in deeper soil, than what satisfied fashionable verses. It was all too much for Oliver. He took more of the apothecary's *magic rubbing bottle*. His feckless wanderings, seemingly irresponsible because he was obeying the mysterious voice of something he could not see, touch or understand, began again.

So when during his regained 'freedom' he rested the night at a moorland inn, he did not feel disposed to discuss money and materialistic grievances. 'Is it you combers that are setting fire to houses? You'll be hanged!' he briefly answered Loveless.

'We have done nothing so far. But it is not unlikely that the weavers will burn the new manufactories if they remain unsatisfied. In our work we know the necessity of trusting one another and acting as one, and with the strength that comes of it we will overturn – we will overturn every hindrance. We will also claim back our common land, before all England becomes private and enclosed. For then when they want someone to die on foreign battlefields for't, they'll be telling us it is *our* country that we are defending, though we'd be hung for trespass if we dared even to walk upon it, let alone enjoy its fish and game!'

Oliver waved his pot for more ale. 'The weaver and the wool-comber, the mason and the carpenter, are their own aristocracy, showing its virtue in a job done well and with skill. Instead of investing your pride there, you hunt worldly wealth as dogs pursue a hare and the longing you have for yellow dirt transforms you into galley-slaves! You should desire leisure and art more, not money.'

They burst out laughing at this last sentence. So Oliver shouted, 'Afore long you'll give up keeping saint's-days altogether! And when you do have gold you put on the haughtiness of Spanish dons and mix it with the meanness of Dutch merchants!'

'If you wish to discover the true poetic muse in these times, you should look for her amongst our radical causes,' Loveless told him, in a level voice.

One night, shortly after the wool-combers and the croppers had received this rebuff, the spinning mill which John Wylde had built for Captain Horsfall was ignited. Loveless realised that his friends would be blamed for it, unless rumours were killed at birth. Gossipers were already tracing a connection between the public threats to burn Anne Wylde in her own house, and the fate of the mill built by her father. Though it was two o'clock in the morning, and dark but for the flames in the sky, Jack hurried to tell his friends that they must quickly explain themselves to the Vicar and to Benjamin Greave.

A large crowd was already attracted by the fire. Not only the plotting radicals were there, but also many others who in their hearts wanted to see the new manufactories burned down, saw that this was popular, and were therefore ready to assume some credit for it if it was to their advantage. Binns thought it might bring him the renewed love of his wife, and Jabez Stott hoped it would make him a hero amongst the wool-combers. So it took Loveless some time to sift out trustworthy friends, and lead them across the hills. Others, out of curiosity, followed after.

Doubtfire, they discovered, was not at home, so they went to Making Hall. When Greave came into his porch he saw the sky on fire as if with the Apocalypse. It illuminated men with big fists and forearms developed from handling for fourteen hours a day the huge cropping shears that cut the nap off the wool. He saw artisans such as

Jeremiah Rhodes, who could read, and so, Benjamin assumed, could only be poring over Tom Paine and seditious pamphlets, or making some nonsense of their own out of the Bible. This he believed had inspired them now to burn down Makings.

Frightened though Benjamin was, he spoke to them calmly and jovially, his tone one of amazement that they should feel the lack of anything. 'Good evening, sinners! What can I do for you?'

'More payment for our pieces and longer credit.'

Loveless's unequivocal, unaggressive manner made the clothier feel secure. 'Thou'll not get that without working for it!' he answered, and (recalling the preaching he did during his early manhood at the chapel of the Presbyterians), he drew what breath he could in to his tight little chest and launched upon a speech. 'In the old days, men, how much we completed in a day! In the morning cutting grass, threshing corn, walling, or churning milk. Before midday we'd maybe weave six yards, weed a garden or spread dung. Fetch peat home, and still have time to listen to a preacher. That's the attitude with which I built my business, and you must be the same if you wish to succeed. Instead of that you're risking hanging by setting fire to property.'

'We've not burned down no buildings. But we've all worked as hard as you, Mr Greave. Only you're luckier than some, and you've built what you have on our backs,' Loveless answered.

Benjamin was flattered by this implicit celebration of his wealth, and secretly he was glad that the rival mill had been burned. He understood these men, for as a trader and their master he had cared for them like a pastor with his flock. They had pride in their craft, but also an unadventurous ungenerous attitude, simply wanting 'things to stay as they'd always been', though with more prosperity and less interference from 'incomers' and foreigners. So he wooed them gently. 'If thou'lt come along wi' me in weaving new cloths, though it seems strange to you and I cannot offer so much money at present, yet I'll make you in time the most prosperous weavers in England! A little sacrifice from you now will bring in a new age! You often hear folk preach of a new time that is coming. What *is* the "Heaven on earth" that you hear hedge-preachers and Methodists and suchlike talk about? I'll tell you: it is *The Period of Worsted Cloth*! Moreover ... Moreover! ... that its destiny, to prosper or sink in dismal failure, lies in your hands! We already 'ave the Empress of the Russians eating out of our palms, and I'm told she's a bit of a Jacobin like ourselves, believing in the rights o' the people. Think on that! Eh lads, what a prospect, what a destiny, what a future, what an opportunity lies before you! Mak' the new woollens, I tell thee, mak' a little sacrifice for't, and it'll make thee!'

'Mak! Mak! Mak! All you thinks of is new "making"! But it takes so long to weave, is so much trouble, and then you say you cannot pay us so much for it. If it's rivalry from Horsfall keeping the price down, that's settled for you now,' Loveless replied.

'I aren't giving up my children's food for callimancoes and such stuff, Mr Greave. We've been all right so far weaving kerseys. I cannot see *thee* sacrificing so much!' said Jeremiah Rhodes. 'You do whatever you've a mind to do. But, "The exercise of the natural rights of man has no other limits than those which are necessary to secure to every *other* man the free exercise of the same rights." That is what they said at the National Assembly of France.'

'I am, but I am tho'!' Some of them laughed at Benjamin, and he smiled back the stiff smile of one who is actually afraid. 'You're being short-sighted, friends. Where's your ambition? Oh, what a glorious vision, what a future, there lies before us wi' worsteds!'

Jack Loveless's hungry face in the light from the distant burning mill was like a flame itself, escaped to speak out of the fire. 'Citoyen Jeremiah Rhodes is right,' he said, 'Worsteds'll make one man rich for a hundred poor. And that hundred'll be those asked to make the sacrifices now! It's happened before in the King's England and for sure it'll happen again.'

'Nay, friends, how short-sighted you are!'

Benjamin was still genial. Then Jabez Stott mentioned his son and Anne Wylde.

'What about my son?' the clothier snapped. 'He is at liberty to do as he wishes. You say that you believe in Liberty. Anyone who has anything to say about him may step forwards!'

'You know they're keeping a black boy down there in illegal slavery?' Loveless asked.

'I'm told he's an indentured apprentice.'

'With a collar round his neck!'

'What's that to do with weaving pieces? I've always given *you* your dues.'

Joshua Binns answered, 'We cannot possibly live in this valley whilst they are at Lower Laithes. There's no hope of morality with their example. It is sinfulness for which they will burn for ever in Hell's fire.'

'Then let them pursue their Hell-bent course in peace! There are plenty of others have been courting Hell. You do not need to join them.'

Loveless continued, 'We think that the reason you have been unwilling to pay and give us work is because your business is impeded by your son's associating with Miss Wylde. She herself is all right, I wouldn't have no harm done to her. Yet because of her very nature, and where she is from, and the Devil that gave her birth, she interferes with the progress of trade. She is as unlucky as a woman taken on board a ship. No one can work without doing as she wishes, and Oliver Greave is like wax in her hands. So we shall go to Lower Laithes to make him answer for it.'

'He is not there, he has gone south to buy wool. Friends, your hardship is due merely to it taking time for a new fashion to catch on. Now we have to grab the business from them West Country clothiers by making finer woollens than them, and if we do not do so the whole north is doomed. It is fated right on the shores of a sea, of an ocean, of a great tide of prosperity. With our good sense we'll better them, you'll see! But first we have to defeat the machines that threaten us and I can only pay you more if I do not have to fear their competition. Though I would not encourage you to do what is not legal. What is not right within the law.'

'He talks good sense, he's one with us!' Joshua Binns said.

Most of the men now wished to help Benjamin Greave and therefore (they thought) themselves also, by going that night to fire another mill. Binns especially believed that the way to grow into a large-scale manufacturer was keenly to follow Greave's example. Loveless retired with them into the darkness. Whilst Greave returned thankfully and at peace indoors, Jack, sweating with fear, persuaded them that what the clothier really wanted was to get the most troublesome hanged, at the same time to be rid of competing manufactories, and also to redirect animosity from his son at Lower Laithes.

'You know how it is with magical conjuring doctors at a fair?' Loveless said. 'They tell you, "Look at such and such". But if you do, you never discover the trick, for you must search in the opposite direction to what you are told. So it is with the clothing masters. You must go in the opposite way to where they direct you if you would save your lives and liberties.'

Loveless managed to divert them from firing a manufactory. They went instead to Lower Laithes. There, the peacocks screamed like huge cats, and dogs barked through the darkness. The men left pale grey trails across the dew of the lawn; it was as if they had entered a carpeted room wearing muddy boots. Anne looked out of her window. For a moment she indulged the sweet thought that the 'mob' could not reach her any more, and then she returned to bed. Instead of her, Mary Pickles, Jenny Loveless and Amos Culpin went out.

'We are citizens who have come here in defence of our natural liberties,' Jeremiah Rhodes announced.

'You are right to think of freedom from wickedness. Our mistress here lives in savage, mortal sin,' Culpin lugubriously told the weavers.

Jenny Loveless added, 'If she were still in Lady Well they would squeeze her bubbies to see if there is milk in them! That is what they are like in that town. Mistress is sick every morning these days.'

They all looked up to the iron grille in the stable-loft where Earth peered out. At sight of the torchlight, the flames, the intense faces, the cries of exotic birds, and the outlines of woodlands, the slave was transformed with sweet memories of Africa.

'That one takes our bread, too,' Joshua Binns said.

Eyes gleamed in torchlight as they wondered what to do.

It seemed up to Joshua to think of something. 'We could treat her to rough music,' he suggested, disarmingly meek. 'A crowd of honest citizens banging drums and rattling sticks outside the window does a lot towards teaching respect to a shrewish female. When next Lammas Day Fair comes round there'll be opportunity for it. It's but a few months' wait until August.'

They were all silent for a while with horror.

'The light of the morning shames the work of the night,' Mary Pickles sighed, at last, and as if with the weight of a heavy stone in her breast.

Three days later Oliver returned, in a good mood because he had enjoyed a pleasant journey in spring weather. Southern landscapes had suffocated him with what he thought of as 'airless comforts'. The trees were thick, close, over-rich canopies. He was frustrated by lack of distant horizons. Occasionally he would cross through the heather, water, or oak trees of a heath, and burst out of them to see carved out of the distance a gentleman's seat, a park, some neat, hedged, drained, enclosed fields, or a town clustered around its church; though mostly he found himself drowned for mile after mile in leaves. But upon northern hills the spring (arriving late) was a slender, athletic, dancing sprite, rather than a plump spirit. Through clouds, scraps of light daubed the moors, for thrilling seconds only, and then were torn away restlessly to other places. The valleys and slopes were rinsed and wrung in the brisk hands of the rain showers, as a strong weaver rinses and fulls his green making. Oliver loved especially the sound of water gurgling in stone holes hidden under the grasses, and the positive feel of the land's structure beneath his feet. Here you knew what the rock was, because its dark stones in cliffs and jagged piles stuck out through fields and littered the rivers. It felt firm, you saw and sensed under your shoes what sort of land you trod. The elements were restless, the ground was stony, and the marriage of the two expressed the nature of the people and the society dwelling there.

As soon as he tipped Raven's Hill and looked into his native valley he saw anew the scars of burning. Down by the river was a charred manufactory. Speckled around Lady Well were little burnt spots of ruined farms. Close at hand, his father's men were destroying gorse bushes, heather and hawthorn with fire. Smoke seemed a permanent taint in the air. Lady Well is like a battleground, he thought. Oh, when will there be an end to conflagration and trouble? And he knew that the bedrock of it all was the dissatisfaction of the weavers and the ambitions of the clothiers.

'Your mistress Anne is in her withdrawing room, drinking gin,' Mary Pickles told him in the stableyard, in such a tone that he could not decide whether her words were tender or insulting. Certainly they were now too familiar. But he was sorry for the huge, bowed, once-happy woman and he never reprimanded her.

Oliver's southern business had largely been an excuse, understood tacitly by Anne Wylde and himself, to be free of one another for a while. Their arguments had culminated in one when he had *demanded* that she marry him. It was a preposterous thing to say in an argument.

Of course she would not: it was for his gentleness that she loved him, and here he was betraying it with roughness! Once she had feared to give her love in case it led to his despising her; now that was overcome, she was restrained from tumbling into marriage because she thought that once Oliver possessed her he would mistreat and neglect her as wives generally were. Because she could not give him this true reason, she would not answer him at all, which inflamed his anger, and – as sometimes in the old days – he had trembled with incipient violence.

But now, as they had both hoped, their love was refreshed. He could think of little else except being in her presence again, and she wished to be in his. He instantly tumbled into his old feelings about her. He was so happy, he was on the edge of both laughing and weeping at the same moment. He felt it in his stomach, and in his eyes which through sheer joy in life would water and glitter at something beautiful or sad. Oh, why, why, had they ever chosen separation? Some day there would be parting enough! Whenever they were together, unsatisfactory days were turned into good ones merely because they touched one another or kissed in the first rituals of love that reminded them that another full day had circled into happiness again: lips, neck, hair, feet, then the pink rose and the bird nesting in its petals. Thus they embarked upon the long moon-voyage of the night, with whispering, fantasies, scents, touchings, and brief soft landings on the shores of strange dreams. When they turned from one another to sleep, they held hands lightly until tiredness loosed their clasp. On awakening each was conscious vaguely of lightness or darkness first of all, but next, they desired the assurance that the other was still there.

Whatever bad or unpleasant thing the day held for either of them, the other would be there. Sexual joy was not of the night-time only. Oliver was always aware of Anne. Even when she was in another room a constant inner voice would hardly let him get on with his book or his papers, for wondering what she might be doing. The simplest acts that they performed for one another were invested with sensuality. When he laid a shawl around her it became as full with sexuality as was the moist flower between her legs. So the whole day and night were sexual and he was always in a state of mild distraction. If he felt she was unhappy, he took it to be his own fault; and so he became quick to defend himself, bursting out in excessive blame of her, for which later he would hate himself. But for almost the whole time the background of his mind was filled with the happiest thoughts, such as of the way she moved about a room, or what she had said, or would she in a moment move just-so and show her liquid legs? For so many years now, he reflected, he had been bursting with an ecstatic readiness both to laugh and cry at the same moment.

But when they met they did not speak of this. She was drunk. Yet still he saw her love for him shining out and she saw his.

They talked about the insulting manner of the servants, of which Anne made light even though she had begun a habit of avoiding her household, complaining of headaches and tiredness, and staying in her room. The stories overheard amongst servants, to which she was previously aloof, now made her shudder. Noticing this, though at one time they used to grow quiet in the kitchen at her presence, these days they became garrulous.

'Martha Jolley at the Snawdens was washing clothes in an out-house. They saw she was heavy and slow, being with child, 'til she crept from her wash-tub and delivered herself in the garden, buried it and come back to her work. They searched her and found milk so she confessed, and they discovered the babe with earth stopped in its mouth, so she was sent to York and executed!'

''Tis nothing to what I'll tell you! Rebecca Pogson she shared a house with a woman but sent her off for a time. Rebecca was delivered and made it away. The other returning noticed the change in her and told neighbours, who forced a confession. At first she lied that she had thrown it into the brook, so the town was raised to search for it. When they found it not, she said it was in a coal-pit and there they discovered it laid upon a ledge, halfway down, upon a cushion. That mother was committed to die, also. Oh, the unhappy woman!'

The maids had contrived that Anne should overhear such tales as these. Anne knew they were suggesting that she herself would be producing a bastard, would do away with it, be committed to York – for they would see to it! – and executed. Once she fainted and Mary Pickles loosened her throat and carried her to her room.

When Oliver saw Anne's tiredness and sickness (especially in her eyes, which were heavy, moist, and steady with all the sadness she did not speak of, but that at last was weighing her down), he felt that she was not so much ill physically, as faint and listless with her premonitions of unhappiness and disaster. He had the image of an ocean of intuitions within her, formless, continuous, fathomless and uncharted, where he merely stood on the edge, timidly dabbling his feet.

Soon Oliver had to talk to his father about business. The son wanted to share his deepest worries, but he dared to speak only about his purchases of wool. As they both knew, it was going to prove more difficult than ever to get the weavers to make it into worsted cloth, after all the dissension in the valley. So Benjamin Greave after all raised the matter that was closest to Oliver's heart.

'What unsettles the weavers is not the prices we pay them, but your sinful association with Miss Wylde,' Greave said. 'As always she is at the bottom of all misfortune! She ruins our prosperity, and so it'll be until we are rid of her! I'll not have that woman thought a fit garden to grow an heir of mine in, and I hope you're not planting her with any bastards!'

Oliver flushed. 'She would have married me by now if we were not at Lower Laithes, which is too wet, gloomy and unhealthy for her to contemplate the prospect of spending a lifetime there. And the servants wouldn't gossip so maliciously if they were not confined to such a place. No art can refine it nor make it enjoyable or habitable, though we have employed the best craftsmen. You built it only so that I could watch over your fulling mill, and it was no *gift* for it brought on Zillah's ill-health in such a damp bottom of the woods. It is doing the same thing now to Anne Wylde, who is not well from these persecutions, but I will not desert her!'

'So you're ready to marry your housekeeper? What have you had so far with her?'

When Oliver would not answer, Benjamin continued, 'I have t'impart to you the saddest news of my life. But all our miseries have sprung from taking in a witch and the time is come to put an end to it. As you are determined to stick to this madcap who enslaves you, one without morals or decency, and you have become the same, then I will break my association with you. I will cut off my branch of the business and you and Miss Wylde can fend for yourselves. You may go to Hell together!'

'I will not abandon Anne Wylde, not for yours nor any man's worldly interests!'

In this moment it seemed to Oliver that whatever security with his father had existed had finally collapsed beneath him, like a wood-wormed floor.

At Lower Laithes Anne was white and sweating. He loosed her stays. 'I am with child,' she whispered.

He was certain that now she would marry him.

'You do not know Doubtfire as I do, otherwise you would not be so keen on his approval of our lying together,' she answered him this time.

'Anne! My father, his clerks, the servants, and the weavers, are all angry about you. If people see you with child they will not be stopped from setting fire to our house. You need protection.'

'Then let us pretend we are married, to satisfy them.'

'My station is not that of a gypsy nor an outcast! You cannot bear our baby unless we are married!'

'Then I will hide myself at my aunt's.'

He looked as though she had destroyed him. It quite deflated the impatience he had been expressing so far.

'Don't worry, I will not kill your child,' she added.

Her firmness made him weaker. He was overwhelmed by an irony: what his father longed for was an heir, this was the source of his hardness and bitterness, and yet Benjamin Greave was at enmity with the womb that grew it.

Oliver was weeping. Anne struggled to uplift him.

'The whole household would turn on me if I married you and stayed here, Oliver. I am used to stones being thrown at me, ever since birth, but if envious Lady Well saw that I was married to your fortune they would kill us both. They would find their way, for they have always wanted it. The only safe thing is to hide. The world's hurt is not as hard to bear as you think and we are both strong enough.'

He clung so pathetically to her that she had to snatch back her clothes and he fell to the ground. When she escaped he was weeping into clenched fists upon the carpet.

(9)

As Anne left her home, taking only Earth with her, the rain was shuttling across Blood Wood, weaving lines of the pale undersides of leaves across the green. She reached above, into even stronger rain. Mingled with the showers came light thrown about the skies and hills. Scraps of rainbow were thrust out of a cloud and blown away on a ribbon of wind. Sometimes she saw a lark daring a fling, to be tossed aside and plummet back on to the grass.

The Negro from Africa seemed to feel the cold and wet less than herself, who was born here. Expressionlessly he carried her bundle, whilst Anne shuddered and protected herself. Walking lankily, and on the balls of his feet, even his movements made him different to the weavers, who shifted along stolidly: a Yorkshireman put the whole of his foot down at each step, as if asserting his right to the earth and rock, his grip of it, and his defiance of wind or rain's attempt to remove him.

As they climbed, Anne saw how the small valley, that had always been the theatre of her life, lay bosomed in a larger dale, which was in turn nursed by the slopes of a still wider depression, itself lying in yet larger arms – layer upon layer surrounding, and all hidden from those who toiled in Lady Well. How tiny in the scope of the moor were her village, Makings and Lower Laithes. She was amazed to think that these unimportant stony spots on the sweet earth had troubled her so much. She imagined the people twisting through those dark alleys, believing that their neighbours, their property, and the walls shutting them in were all that mattered in the Universe, being blind to the great space surrounding. Anne felt that Lady Well could slip or blow off the hilltop in one puff and it would not make any difference to the eternity of the hills.

Anne and her Negro climbed beyond Upper Spout, where set in the black soggy peat was a small Greek temple made of black stones. It had carved Nereids holding vases out of which tumbled Benjamin

Greave's cold, sulphurous spring. It was a bleak place. No fine ladies had yet come to bathe and the keeper, Israel Merrybent, in his inconvenient but majestically fronted cottage (based upon the Niké temple of the Athens Acropolis, to match the nearby 'Parthenon') spent his time (or so it appeared to his few visitors) reading his Bible.

Beyond these absurd erections were no more buildings good enough even to be termed 'cottages'. Yet still a few people lived in huts made of peat-stacks and reeds: squatters, rush-gatherers, 'moor-edgers', freaks of religion and politics, soldiers and ruffians of every breed. They did not go to church or village much and they had never before seen Anne Wylde with her black boy. So as these two climbed, groups appeared on the skyline. Many of them were drunk. At first the watchers were silent. Then loud cruel laughter followed after Anne and Earth. Behind the laughter and the drunkenness, she sensed the madness and misery of outcasts. A few years ago Anne had not guessed what deep oceans of feeling were brewing their hidden storms under the frozen crusts of most people's characters. Were these too – jeering now – in the secrecy of their homes called upon to navigate such gales as she herself had to weather?

Further on, amongst the mud and stones of Raven's Hill, nothing watched her but the larks struggling to sing against the showers. She descended unseen into the shadow on the far side and slipped – brushing by the scent of thyme, comfrey, mint, so that the smells clung and mingled upon her dress and skin – into her Aunt Pity's narrow tear in the earth where everything was moist and still. She had dropped through a rent in the roof of the Underworld.

The Negro, frightened of the snarling dog with hair raised in barbs on its neck, and of the moist shadowy cleft into which he was being led, looked desperately back at the view. Weavers' cots, clumps of trees, stone enclosures and streams, all standing out unusually brilliantly in a moment of sun, were now disappearing. The world was setting over his horizon. Soon there was left only a patch of light, brittle as glass, and becoming narrower, narrower ... he was drowning ... he would enter the jaws of the beast ...

But the animal recognised Anne and calmly sniffed her hand, so she brought the Negro for a friendly smell at him, too.

He was happier still inside the cottage. Anne and Earth had it in common to be at home with bare floors, crude tables and chairs and the clatter of wooden bowls. Earth (as was usually expected of him) stood by the door but Anne this time took hold of his shoulder and steered him to the hearth.

Aunt Pity glanced at Anne's condition. 'Call upon Saint Felicitas, and hope to be blessed with a boy!' she remarked. The aunt ritualistically poked at the fire and tidied her things. More and more now she fussed over insignificant possessions that were by unnoticed degrees becoming tattered and unusable. The less time she had to live, the more of it she devoted to what would soon be thrown away. She continuously closed doors and curtains. She sat by choice in the shadiest corners, and she liked most often to be quite, quite still. It was as if she was preparing herself for being shut in a clammy grave.

Pity ran her trembling finger greedily over the black skin as though feeling the soundness of a vegetable or fruit. 'Can he chop wood and shovel snow? There might be some more up here yet. I couldn't open my door for three days a month since, and each snowfall I think it'll be the last one I'll see. Elkanah Beanland had to scythe my enclosure for me last year, and he brings me my bits and pieces. He's glad to do anything so long as I'll let him spend an hour now and then reading his Bible at me!'

The two women and the Negro lived off preserves of whinberries or blackberries, on oatcakes, and the trout that Earth caught skilfully, with boyish joy, in his hands. Having almost no English he lived very much either inside his own head, or amongst the moorland spirits, and he enjoyed an illusion that he had escaped – at any rate, he had never before been so happy. There passed for the three of them a short eternity of joy, peaceful and contemplative. Anne discovered that, contrary to what Parson Doubtfire told her, Negroes did have souls. Obviously happier than in his previous pampered and decorative existence, Earth before the women's eyes thickened into a laughing lusty youth, who was gradually picking up the language of his mistress, whilst at other times he gabbled forgetfully in his natural tongue.

Whatever was growing inside Anne began to stir, slide about and thrust out lumps. Slimy and formless it would then retreat into her like some monster sinking back into the deep. It was as if she had caught a slippery fish, a mermaid, or a dolphin. Her womb was a net which had been trawling through an ocean. When, some day, she dragged it finally out, she would find what was pulling at her so far down on the end of a line at the bottom of a dark and heavy sea.

Anne suffered violent pains. It was several months too early and she went to bed horrified at the thought of the dead creature, or the monster, she was about to eject. Witches gave birth to things with eyes in the centres of their foreheads or without mouths. A long while, an eternal moment of horror, passed as she waited for the next spasm – Anne was more conscious of minutes passing than of pain. There was time now for her to weep. She saw, swimming before her tears, this huge fish-shape that her imagination had given birth to. Now it seemed not a beautiful mermaid, such as Oliver was fond of drawing on wool-bales, not a playful dolphin all shyness and delight: it was something cold-bodied, pike-toothed and grinning, with expressionless glassy eyes.

Another spasm came. Anne clutched and rocked her way through it. She was being drawn through strange oceans, past weird creatures, and grappled by terrifying slimy weeds ...

Afterwards she realised how quickly she had ceased to cry, and she was comforted to find that the rapid demands of her body could overcome both agony and sadness. Then a further pain announced itself, surprising her by its fierceness.

She saw coming out of herself a white ghostly sac, like a moon, and half-transparent. Within it was a beautifully formed arm with its tiny fist clenched. This little creature moved.

For a moment she was thrilled by the beauty of what was appearing from that bloody place where the Devil was supposed to dwell.

Then she realised that, born so early, it would be malformed, if it lived at all. It would be something black, horned and foul engendered in the 'womb of darkness' (as Parson Doubtfire called the origin of evil and of ourselves), and a hideous curse upon her and her lover. Before Anne could glimpse whether, inside the veined little moon, it was mouthless or eyeless, she fainted.

As she lay with strings of jelly, blood and wetness emerging pulsing from her, Aunt Pity cut off the mess that was Anne and Oliver's 'child'. Then she gave her attention to the mother.

Coming round, Anne saw that her baby was dead. She closed her eyes again in weariness and at the final numb end of grief. Aunt Pity and the Negro then buried the foetus in the garden. Both women tried to be glad at least that it was a dead thing and not a malformed living one; whilst Anne wanted not to know where its grave was. Yet the vision of that minute fist clenched in its sac, and its little movements, would stay with her for ever.

On the following day Anne suffered a rush of blood that drenched her bedding. More the next day. She still kept on weeping. Weeping. But after several weeks it gradually lessened.

Meanwhile the spring continued steadily upon the moor. Firstly a brightening green appeared at the edges of the stream and its surface was starred with crowfoot flowers. Then the air lightened. The wild birds recognised with delight that their calls and songs were not now crushed by the wind. The curlews returned to Lady Well, enjoying lazy sweeps across calm open skies. They seemed to be pursuing their own mournful cries, as if these were echoes of something they had lost. The larks drilled into the Heavens like dark sparks, melting in rapid flickerings of wings and pulsings of their throats; substance dissolved into energy which finally disappeared in the sun, the song still sprinkling down. Then the lark would drop, body restored to it and its wings folded, except for pauses when it spread and caught itself. It would fall like a pebble, glide before touching grass, and sing another short burst, clearly reluctant to leave the skies. At last it would hop through the grass just as if it hadn't done these things. But then, with crest raised proudly, it would look around as if for applause. Anne regained her strength by watching the larks, as she lay in ecstasies upon banks facing the radiance that stroked her with the sensitive firm fingers of a lover.

August came, burning, breeding hot tempers and rebellion. People smelled always of sweat. They were restless all night with the energies stored up in them out of the heat during the day when they had felt so sleepy. As the moon swelled more and more pregnantly, men and women increasingly roamed through its greater light, drinking, loving, picking fights, looking for release. But neither Dick Almighty's ale and sermons nor the apothecary's rubbing bottle could cure them. The moors wore a silk veil of heat. People every day expected them to catch fire and at night, if they imagined a smell of smoke, they left their beds. Surprisingly the conflagrations did not happen, but everyone was nervous.

The enclosures of wheat, oats and barley turned the colour and texture of cream. When the first was ready Doubtfire was made to take up a position next to Dick O'Lovely, who was playing his violin, and the two led a procession of men and women (who had been drinking for most of the day) out of Lady Well, where his black-gowned arm was forced to an unpractised scything of the corn. The cadaverous Puritan hated doing this, which he condemned as 'Druidic'. He found Dick O'Lovely's company frightening, because he never spoke, (the Parson believed in words). But his parishioners (who had chased him before) could be a frightening tribe also and the Church, as Doubtfire well understood, held a frail truce with their savagery.

Doubtfire was further employed (a group of big-limbed, threatening women and men standing by) to say a prayer over the first sheath, which was then taken (Dick O'Lovely's fiddle still playing) to start a Lammas Day bonfire, after the fair and at the height of what the Parson contemptuously called, 'the Lady Well Saturnalia'. For this, Benjamin Greave provided a pig and an ox to be roasted, Horsfall gave wood from his overgrown estate, Dick Almighty (anticipating revenue from ale) paid for the carting of it, whilst Esther Kershaw, Dick Almighty and Elkanah Beanland all supplied free preaching.

Whilst the afternoon of the 'Saturnalia' wore on, the dust that lay golden on the streets or, having dropped from corn and hay, gilded the enclosures, rose in a parching cloud that needed washing down with ale. No one realised how reckless it was making them – they being eager for the evening, and the bonfire. Elkanah, who had taken up his pitch early under the full sun, yet had few to listen.

John Wylde was one of these few. Since the burning down of Horsfall's mill, in which Wylde's capital had been invested, he had been reduced to labouring, working hard as he had not done since he was a young man. He, who had been sociable and popular most of his life, was now much alone. As his faculties dimmed he was no longer sought out by philosophers and radicals. He was without family and was remote and different from his neighbours, though they respected him. This morning he had been laying a stone floor in a kitchen. He worked with two careless unambitious men, yet what they did was dangerous, so John could not help but give advice. 'Thou's not set above us any longer, John Wylde!' they answered and had then acted more rashly than they needed, to 'show' him. Wylde hated doing anything in which craftsmanship did not count, and yet he was not nowadays fit for heavy labour. His tired body seemed detached from his awake spirit – his soul inhabited a strange dwelling, his limbs would not obey his will, whilst his spirit tried to wriggle free, as one climbs out of a suit of clothes. But today he rested, listening to Elkanah's description of how God had with His own hands once built the world perfectly, though now it had filled up with fools and sinners.

Nearby was an example of it, according to Elkanah. Four strong women were tossing Jabez Stott in a blanket. Each time he rose spread-eagled grasping at the air, the women shrieked:

'Jabez Stott!
What've you got
To make a woman happy?'
'Plenty!'
'Canst rise as high as this then?'
'Aye, and mo-o-o-o-re!'

'Will't stop thy sinful doings and hear the sayings of the Lord?' Elkanah shouted. 'Then we all might be taken back with the words of the old preachers to the time when there was nobbut God, at the beginning of the world, which was a waste of darkness, water, and muddle. And there are some as say it hasn't improved much since!'

'We are resurrecting Jabez for his marriage. Cannot we do it for Jabez to be married after Lammas Day?'

The gypsies who had sold their goods and had spent the money on ale, horses, and trinkets for women, now dozed or copulated on the grass. Or they drank illicit whisky brewed by Israel Merrybent, lonely keeper of the Upper Spout waters which had been quite useless until he turned to using them for brewing. He brought the liquor down to the fair in two ox-bladders, fastened together by a leather thong, slung around his neck and hidden under his coat so that he looked like a grotesque woman. The only other female more ugly was his own wife who walked always five paces behind him. This was as much to keep out of range of his curses as for any other reason, for he continually swore over his shoulder at her. Israel was a poor conversationalist.

His only other addiction besides cursing and whisky making was for reading and rereading but one page of his Bible per day, and even for this little he had a bad memory. But his cheap whisky made him popular.

On this, the musicians got drunk with the dancers and the harvesters. Or with the boys and girls who had come to be hired, whose fortunes were now decided, and whose clothes that were so neat earlier had become ale-splattered and torn. During the late afternoon some girls ran a naked race because Captain Horsfall offered a dress to the winner, and she who might have won, had she not stopped to wipe her lover's stains from her thighs, fought with the victor so that the frock was torn to rags.

The one place where the elusive Tim Bobbin could reliably be found in his uncharted moorland wanderings was at a saint's-day fair, and he turned up at Lady Well. There he set a group of woolcombers' apprentices to creating a name for Dick Almighty's inn. This was an elaborate establishment, as befitted its many-sided owner: there was a slaughterhouse, a preaching-room (for which Almighty, being so powerful a man, did not have to bother applying for a licence), a butcher's shop and cottage, besides the brewhouse, well-house and drinking parlour. As it was said that Almighty Whitely feared neither God, man nor Devil, 'Fear Nought' was suggested for a title. But it was also believed that he had a pact with Satan, so 'The Devil's Friend' was put forward. Finally, inspired by Elkanah preaching about the Creation, Tim got Dick Almighty to accept 'The Adam and Eve' – saying that the original Blissful Pair would have got all they wanted here: meat, preaching or ale – and some painters, for free beer, designed a sign showing our first parents in shameful copulation.

But, as everyone realised, this was mere filling-in of time compared with what came next when the sheath of corn was carted in by some of Lady Well's chief revellers, Joshua Binns prominent in harness. Dick Almighty strutted in front. 'Mak' way all you honest sinners!' he shouted. From time to time he gave his huge belly a friendly slap with his carter's whip, or took off his tall hat and waved it to the ladies, whilst leading the singing of John Barleycorn. He winked and shook his whip as he passed three recruiting sergeants who were drumming up potential soldiers by the church door. It was as if these were the three men from the north who were described in the ballad, come for their victims:

'There were three men came out of the north,
They all did swear and say,
They greatly made a solemn oath,
John Barleycorn should die!'

At this moment, someone said within John Wylde's hearing, 'They've an effigy of Anne Wylde to burn in yonder barn.'

John, his stance fierce as in the old days, swung round to face the man. But the malicious gossiper had slipped into the crowd, who got in the mason's way when he gave pursuit. Meanwhile the rumour had trickled from its bourne and must spread through the flood of people.

'When is it to be burnt?'

'After dark.'

A calm twilight was already settling upon the hills and the sun was a trembling disc reddening more and more as it sank into a haze. The cart led by Dick Almighty creaked up the alleyways leaving, upon the stones, ears of corn which were plucked to wear in hats or button-holes, or stuck in a sweetheart's hair.

John Wylde was the only sober one, as he searched barn after barn. He scrambled over roofs, looking for access to locked places. He passed from group to group, trying to wring reason out of rumour and to save his daughter from such mockery that it would chill the heart of the most rational of men. He spoke to those by Dick Whitely's tavern and around the barrels of ale set up on carts. He went amongst the drunks who were leaning stupidly against walls, rolling in the grass or being sick. Nobody seemed to know in which place the effigy was stored, nor who its makers were, nor who was paying the bill, nor whose straw stuffed the figure, 'Nor whether 'twould take place at all, for it was only a joke and a rumour.'

There was an ugly moment when John Wylde grabbed Joshua Binns around the throat for saying this. Binns's fellow cart-pullers tried to help, for the mason could still be a frightening man. All that saved the weaver was that the cart swayed backwards down the hill, so everyone ran to stop it, and turned upon Wylde for 'spoiling a happy day'.

The corn sheath was stuffed into the unlit bonfire at the moment when the sun disappeared into Raven's Hill. Doubtfire and Benjamin Greave then came out of the Parsonage where they had spent the day away from the populace, and in discussions, over brandy. The tall parson and the small clothier paced about with smiles and patronising words. Then they led, not towards the great tithe barn as John Wylde expected, which was always locked and guarded, but towards a mere cart-shed – which the mason, though he knew intimately every stone building in Lady Well, had overlooked.

Torches were lit, the doors swung back and out of the shadows, on a hay-cart that creaked through the silence, was wheeled the effigy of Anne Wylde. Her red dress was of spoilt soldiers' cloth, her head made from a swede with a candle flickering inside (as Anne's eyes flickered) through the holes that were the shapes of her eyelids, whilst her black curls were of barley-straws dipped in tar.

Yet it was a calm and beautiful figure, for its makers had unintentionally shown their admiration by reproducing her lovely shape. But it began to shake as they wheeled it along. The head slipped sideways like an idiot's and the straw with which the body was stuffed shifted and made it lumpy. It was as if she aged from a young girl to an old woman in her journey from barn to bonfire.

They looked around for Dick O'Lovely to play an accompanying fiddle tune, but he had disappeared. It was amazing that Dick was not there when a fiddle was required. He must have disapproved of what he saw happening.

'Nay, that's not right! That's not right!' Elkanah shouted. But his voice was drowned by a tin whistle eerily played, by a cacophany of drums and bagpipes, and by the accumulated, drink-enflamed, bursting anger of weavers and wool-combers. 'We'd've prosperity in Lady Well without the witch! Burn the sinful witch!' they yelled.

'She has not deserved this! Let her good and respected father protect her,' Almighty pleaded. But (as his experience of being constable, innkeeper, and chairman of this, that and t'other had taught him), beyond a certain point one could not control a 'mob', short of using soldiery and cannon. If one tried, one's own authority was weakened. So he said no more.

They struggled to hold John Wylde back, for despite their lust to see his daughter damned and burning, no one wished to harm the mason, but only to have him removed. ''Twill sour our beer to have poor John around,' they said. So Lady Well's champion wrestler was called up to restrain him as gently as possible.

Meanwhile Doubtfire pointed his long finger to the tip of the unlit bonfire. 'Where the sparks fly upwards, there is man's salvation and destiny!' he declared. 'Not in such worldly Saturnalias as I see today.'

'Salvation is to the north!' Esther Kershaw shrieked back at him. 'For all our moors are mostly to the north, and that is where the Great Sweet Cow roams free, but you all go about mindfolded and you cannot see!'

'And for my part, the road to salvation is southwards, to Greece and Italy!' Tim Bobbin laughed.

'Thou Bobbin Never-Do-Good-Fellow, 'tis in the north!' Esther retorted and flushed.

'Don't thou gesticulate at me!' Tim answered, good-humouredly. 'I'll testicle-ate as much as I wish!'

Tim was so exasperated by this silly discussion that he snatched off his wig and threw it at the Vicar. Doubtfire at the same moment grabbed his own peruke and flung it at the poet because he was so ignorant of the geography of Hell and Heaven.

Seeing this, John Wylde could not help but smile at the stupidity of human dispute and at his own foolishness in bothering about it; and having no one able to understand why there was a *smile* upon his lips, he let himself be led away.

The wrestler was a man whose appearance could be described entirely by his aggressive-looking neck. His solar plexus was not for ruminating over philosophy, his spreading anus was not primarily for manuring God's earth: the first purpose of his whole body was to carry forwards that great neck, which was so thick that it would hardly bend or straighten, but was stuck obstinately at forty-five degrees, like a bull's. Yet his nature was gentle. He had a great love of children, who followed him about Lady Well as he brought out of his pockets small toys, rag dolls and nuts.

'Now, John,' he said calmly, 'Thou's been a good man in thy time – all the old folk say so – but that one yonder's no daughter of thine, is she?' Since no one ever argued with the wrestler, he was as confident as God Himself that everything he said was true and he spoke with that domineering certainty in his voice.

He left John Wylde on the steps of the church.

After Wylde had sat for a while he stood up and discovered his aches. The side of his face stiff from a punch. A deadness in his thigh from a kick. One eye beginning to close. He was like an old stag that can no longer hold its own; he was like his beloved church, with its war-smashed sculptures, its paintings and much of its glass destroyed by a parson who hated art.

Meanwhile dreaded Melancholy, or Reason's shadow, stalked up on him. As usual she came suddenly and unexpectedly. First of all she baited him with rational thoughts and fears for his daughter, or longings for those days when he had travelled and met interesting companions, when his eyesight was clear and his hand steady. But this was only Melancholy's entrance, in her outer dress – as he well knew, for she had opened his door and trespassed on him many times before. Soon she would disrobe and overwhelm him with her naked black self. John would not admit that something existed if it was not accessible to Reason. At most he would dub it 'a dark meditation of the Devil'. Yet this misery for which there was no antidote in rational thoughts was real enough in its effect. It often drove him to walk for miles upon the moors – not as in the past with the joyful purpose of seeking good society, but simply, he found, to *woo* this very Melancholy. And this he did not understand at all. How could he comprehend such an unreasonable thing? It was as if in suffering he copulated with her, in hope that she would give up her secret, and he would learn what he grieved for. But he never found out what it was, unless it be for the lost mother-garden of Paradise.

Saint Mary's Church, being at the highest point in Lady Well, was still catching the last of the sun. One ray speared a window, and scattered the blurred coloured lights of saints (surviving high up out of Doubtfire's reach) to dissolve on the pavement and over the half-cut stones and stacks of timber placed for the Greaves monument. Astonishing colours, like a garden packed with summer flowers, grew over the deathly-white marble angels lying on their backs in the grass, their limbs slack and sensual as if they had capitulated to love, their mouths open as if in an orgasm with death; upon the Greek columns in designs taken from engravings in the best textbooks, and over the stone blocks meant to impress with their vastness. (A monumentality not in keeping with the shrivelled little man who was to be buried under them.) The rest of the church was an enclosed mysterious purple-dark forest where pigeons fluttered and roosted, and John imagined that the sculptures, with their rubbed-out faces and limbs broken through the enviousness of war, religion and politics, had also retired to settle here one evening in the past.

'Call no man happy until he dies.' Aeschylus's words passed through John Wylde's head. For those who had been his friends, indebted to him, and whom he had served well, were now performing magical acts against his daughter.

Meanwhile two strong weavers were standing on the cart to lift 'Anne' on to the crown of the bonfire, which was then lit at the sheath of straw. The flames burst suddenly, driving people back. The fire climbed more slowly up rotten timbers, fetched from old houses, and decayed boughs from Horsfall's park. When it reached Anne's body it spurted quickly again. The lower part burned first, and flames licked at her head which was broken, like a hanged woman's suspended from a gallows, over the fire. The head dropped off and out of the neck sprang snakes of smoke.

'Let's have a look what's under her skirts!'

'Beware anyone that goes near! She's got teeth like razors inside there!' Binns shouted.

Elkanah Beanland felt once again the weight of his sadness at the foolishness and brutality of men that had in the first place turned him into a preacher. 'There's nothing wrong with the lass, she's right enough if you'd let her alone! There's nothing wrong with right folk! She knows more o' God's ways than most of you!' he declared angrily. He packed up his Bible and in disgust walked away rapidly towards the moors.

Joshua Binns whispered to Horsfall, 'That woman was of unnatural birth and so she should not enjoy a natural death. She was born from a hawthorn tree (though some say from a wild white doe) and is a curse to us. Oh yes, 'tis true enough! 'Tis certainly true. I know 'tis true. At six months of age she had to be churched and was brought forth a second time in mockery from under her mother's shift to make it legitimate after she married John Wylde. Oh yes, she was a bastard all right, for she was not John Wylde's daughter. The woman he married had been on to the moor and lay with a goblin that crept out of tree roots, and Wylde only married the woman out of pity!'

'She is definitely conspicuous and loud,' Horsfall very reasonably answered, 'so it is time to pull her down!'

He talked to some mummers. With Horsfall, these left the fairground, just as they were, in their animal disguises. 'You're not off to some nocturnal assembly?' Dick Almighty asked threateningly. He guessed where they were bound, but as it was Captain Horsfall who led he could see no way to stop them.

Rustling their bells and from time to time throwing out scraps of tunes with their flutes and drums, as sleepless birds do on light nights, they climbed Black Hill where moths blundered out of the heather. From the moortop, moonshine flooded the valleys and the spaces reeled about the drunken men. A slender moon stood above, sharp as a polished axe, and smiling. Binns pointed to it: 'When the man can fall out of his boat, it will bring foul weather. That moon is completely upside down – some dreadful thing is foretold,' he said.

'Nonsense, you old fool,' Horsfall answered him. 'Never mind the moon. Just watch where you are setting your feet.'

Here and there the lights of farms floated like luminous fish rising through dark water. A shadowy thing that they took to be a boulder turned out to be a great valley opening up before them. Streams rustled musically amongst the stones at immeasurable distances away or below. What they thought of as a short drop turned out to be one of several hundred feet. Such surprises jolted like explosions inside their drunken heads, and they were sick upon the grass.

They came to Elkanah Beanland's house. His candle flickered in a window as it illuminated a chapter of Revelations which he read over and over again to induce prophetic dreams. Because of the burning of the effigy, and what he feared might follow next, he was praying for Anne Wylde. Hearing noises, he looked out. He saw a fox-man, a Negro with vast antlers, and a huge trout – its mouth open and its large expressionless eye staring at the moon, whilst the silver head tapered into the body of a man. 'Good Lord deliver us!' Elkanah cried with sweat upon his forehead, and he fell to his knees. The 'creatures of the Apocalypse' laughed, banged their horrid drums, shook their wreaths of flowers and bells, and kicked over Elkanah's notices – *Blesst be he that Turneth to the Lord*', '*D'sire Him to forgive thee sins*'. Then they pressed on into another broad swathe of moonlight.

As they came to Aunt Pity's, the dog barked from where he slept curled up against the Negro in the barn. Earth peeped out and saw the creatures on the skyline. He could have loosed the dog, but he thought instead only of defending it, his only trustworthy friend, from the monsters. The fish, the antlered black-man, the fox and the mummers with blackened faces and flowers in their hats, therefore freely circled the cottage, rattling and banging bells and drums, clattering on doors and window panes; the 'rough music' with which Binns had threatened Anne Wylde, a terrible tuneless noise. Tuneless and yet it gathered force into a rhythm, mechanical and pitiless as the march of soldiers, broken with piercing shrieks and with bleats like the noises of wounded animals. It was the rhythmic voices of an ancient terror. It was as if the tortured earth herself cried out.

It stopped, eerily.

'Come out Anne Wylde! We are here to see if you are hiding a bastard!' Horsfall, the fox, shouted.

Joshua Binns, who was the fish, mumbled through huge narrow lips, 'The good women of Lady Well are coming to tear you to pieces!'

As she did not answer them, the 'rough music' began again. The dog was howling and gnashing in the barn, where Earth watched. He longed to protect his mistress. He felt a deep pang when he realised she had been his one protector against a world that would destroy him as unfeelingly as sharks or wild dogs devour whatever strange vulnerable thing falls amongst them. But the habit of slavery prevented him from doing anything. He was a big lad but he stayed frozen in the barn, restraining the frantic dog, and watching in terror through a vent-hole in the wall.

Anne Wylde appeared at her window. The spectators saw a slender outline, craggy like a thorn-branch. 'We have come to squeeze your bubbies and see if you give milk, Anne Wylde!'

Horsfall climbed up, followed by the antlered 'Negro' and the huge trout's head under which two elbows appeared to prop it whilst it watched. The 'Negro' and the 'trout' stayed there, whilst the fox-man entered slowly, saying nothing. He lit Anne's candle. Pulled a dresser across the door.

'Where are your bubbies, Anne Wylde?'

She grabbed a knife and fell back on to the bed as if to dare him to come near the blade. She turned on to her stomach with her legs clutched together, hid her face and bit the pillow. Frustration and anger as well as fear raised the beat of her heart. The fox came close and she turned to slash at him. He caught her wrist and the blow that Anne intended to answer him with glanced sideways, catching her own neck. She cried as the cut began to sting and blood smeared her dress. The fox put his hands heavily upon her breast, but she pushed him away. She glimpsed his smiling face, whilst he dived for her clitoris.

Anne realised it would be less painful if she were moist and she suffered his fingers. When at last he entered her, she struggled to think of something else – anything but her beloved Oliver, in case that thought induced orgasm.

Thankfully, the fox-man soon came. Anne lay still, weeping, partly with gratitude that she had felt no joy, and turned her face into the blood-smeared pillow. The fox threw her nightgown over her.

'I know who you are!' Anne hissed.

As soon as she heard him and his companions descend the ladder, she rushed to the door, pulled the furniture away and shouted to her aunt. With tears and water the two women washed the semen out of her, trying again and again to rid her of every foul drop, whilst the mummers and the animals paraded around the house a few more times. The women washed and washed, though hopeless of ever quite removing the pollution. Neither of them slept that night. After their tormentors disappeared laughing into the moor, Pity built up the fire, then Anne cried and shivered for hours in her arms.

Oliver, one gentle sunny afternoon when he expected his child to have been born, came across the hills. The first trees in Blood Wood were turning yellow; a new glittering beauty shaking amongst the dark monotonous green of late summer. The bleached lank grass of the wood was incandescent, there was a clean yellow light in the sky and the stream, and he had no doubt that the greatest happiness awaited him. At one or two moments, as the breeze stirred the heather or a turn in the ground revealed a view so beautiful that it took away his breath, he felt about to become the instrument of his muse. But when he paused to write, the damned habit of mechanical jingles got in his way. He reached Aunt Pity's cottage wistful, dazed by what he had almost grasped, and longing for a few inspired lines which might be the first true verses of his life. But the words stayed locked in the stone of his breast.

As he heard no crying, he guessed that his heir was asleep in his cot. He expected Anne to have the milky smell of a woman who is feeding a baby, but that was missing too. Yet she seemed more matronly. She moved heavily and the virgin bloom was gone from her cheeks. He anticipated that she would be happy, but she was restless, even bitter. What was it? He went to kiss her, and she would not accept it.

'Are you pale and pining? Lovesick?' she asked, sharply. 'Not eating, in danger of falling into a consumption?'

'Where is my son?' he asked, confused.

'What is my father doing now?' she answered curtly.

'He still will not live at Lower Laithes – I have asked him. It is difficult for him to uphold his honour in present circumstances, and he is erecting enclosure walls on the moors until he recovers better prospects. It's rough work, but they say that his walls are better made than anyone else's and will be standing in a thousand years after all others have fallen. He is building for my father. He spends a lot of time alone these days and is hard to communicate with. But where is my son?'

'It is a daughter.'

'We hoped for a son, but I can love a daughter nearly as well. I want to see her.'

'She is sleeping.'

'I want to see her asleep. What did you feel when you found her at your breast? When Betty was born the first thing I did was to count her fingers and toes. The midwife laughed, telling me that Zillah had done the same thing.'

'It would be best if no one saw it for some time. We must hide it away for a few years here and then show her as a "servant's child" that we have adopted. You suffer so much already for us, I do not want you to have more to bear.'

'I see no reason why I should not see her! God, but this woman has a demon in her!'

'Hush! I am afraid of your feelings! You know that farmers never dare allow the cow to see her calf before taking it away from her.'

As much to give expression to his exasperation, as to search for his child, he paced the cottage, opening doors, going into rooms, and standing several times at the foot of the ladder which led upstairs, but not venturing on it.

'What about baptism? Suppose the dear one should go back as an unchristened pagan and be condemned to Hell for eternity, full of sin?' he asked.

'Hush you, "eternity" is so terrible a word! It can be done later. Your child is healthy and no more than a girl anyway, so why do you fret?'

She was leaving the room, either to get away from him, or for him to follow, he was not sure which. He came after, grudgingly.

'I hate the word "eternity",' she said, 'it makes me think of grave-yards and monuments.'

She led up the ladder to her bedroom. There she enticed him into a gentle fondling of her breasts and then to kissing slowly upwards along her limbs, the way she enjoyed love-making. Just before he was ready to enter, Anne imagined herself a hole in the earth, warm, damp with spring rain; and that he was a farmer about to plant seeds. She felt the cavity become moist. As he touched and sank into her, it seemed to her that she was nothing else but this opening.

Oliver had by now learnt to stir his penis inside her. He would almost remove it, then delicately touch around the mouth of the Paradise Garden, and go inside again, moving from side to side, which drove her mad with joy; try thrusting as deep in as he could; draw back delicately for a few moments, and when he was about to come, crush his mouth between her breasts as if to seek that blindness and obliteration which a second later consumed him. Thereupon she came with him, twisting, bucking against his spasms. She did not know where she had been or for how long, when she returned.

They both also loved the resting in one another's arms afterwards, her legs thrown across his thigh; usually a time when they spoke their deepest thoughts.

It was now dark outside. Oliver had lost his agitation and she walked quietly with him across the garden. They climbed to the ridge where sounds from beyond rose out of the wells of night-time. Bleats and bellowings were scattered over the velvet darkness. They saw lamps moving far away, as if they were distant luminous planets. Near at hand, Aunt Pity was calling her poultry by banging the bottom of a bucket. Then Oliver disappeared, over the bank into the darkness, as if over the lip of the world.

(10)

The following May, Anne Wylde gave birth to a boy. She kept Oliver away with the argument that spies might follow him and discover that he was hiding a bastard. He was not too difficult to persuade, for while Oliver Greave was intensely sociable he had an incompatible love of solitariness and irresponsibility, which he found necessary to cultivate his poetry, and he was ready to grasp a chance of being alone. By midsummer the child was weaned and Anne prepared to leave this pitiful, sometimes helplessly loved and at other times hated creature of Horsfall's, this hopeless baby, in the care of Aunt Pity – buying three sheep to provide milk for him. The Negro filled the draughty chinks in a small shed and made a cradle.

For the last time Anne walked the garden with her child, showing him the midsummer flowers, (or was she showing the flowers, him?); the tall white daisies and the buttercups. She fed and nursed her baby in the shed. When he was asleep she laid him in the cradle, slipped out, barred the door, and sat off with Earth back to Lower Laithes.

Over the hill-crest, and into the Makings valley, she saw that new enclosure walls were drawing an ever-tighter grip. The sight of the burnt stumps of oak, hawthorn, and gorse clutched with premonitions of ill-luck at her throat. It choked her like the smell of burning itself. Around Lower Laithes even Oliver Greave had been persuaded to do some clearing of 'the wastes'. The ugliness of cleared woodlands, the way water lay in pools or mud on the bared earth which later would turn hard and uncooperative as stone, should have been sufficient to show him its unnaturalness, Anne thought.

Her now-ragged dress, apron and cloak smelled of soot and herbs, so she entered her home secretly and tried to disperse her tears by going through her old wardrobe. When she had changed her appearance she noisily and bravely took command again of her kitchen, passageways, larder, brewing-house and cellars.

She saw Oliver before he had spied her. He was arguing weakly with a Dutchman, who was wearing his hat and cloak as if unwilling to stay. 'You do not wish to see what I have been making, Mr Van Broyes?' Oliver pleaded. 'I have an officers' cloth, as smooth as cream ...'

'Forgive me, but I cannot buy from both your father and yourself. Also as the wars are for the time being over, soldiers are returning and therefore the woollen trade suffers. Perhaps I will purchase more happily from you in the future, when the son is not competing with the father. Maybe next spring. In winter my family do not like me to travel so far as Yorkshire. They think I should trade only in Holland where there is no sin!'

Oliver desperately chased after the departing Dutchman, who was waving his hand over his shoulder as one brushes away flies.

Anne meanwhile read a paper on Oliver's desk: 'Your Broad Shalloons having been shown to the Honourable Buying Committee of the United East India Company, I am ordered to acquaint you that they are too loose made and bare, therefore they will not have any at present. And please to send first a sample of any new makings, that the Committee might see your goods do not fall short in quality, as with previous bales.' Another letter read: 'Sir, your woollens have met with so many disputes about the quality and measure that I have now placed orders for next year in other hands. We must confess, that after your fair promises, saying that the face of your shalloons was more like glass than woollens, we little expected to have such complaints about quality and price of several articles ...'

'Anne!' He stood confused, torn between his unsuccessful pleading with the Dutchman, his joy at finding her, and the adulteration of that joy with her annoyance and dissatisfaction at what she had seen in his papers. For his sake she cleared her frown, and reassured him with her touches.

'The clothing trade does not seem to be prospering,' she ventured to say.

'Pooh! They care about nothing but work and trade in this valley!' Oliver tapped his ledger. 'This is their Bible now.'

The account book was indeed in size and proportion like a family Bible, with its light-brown cover of soft highest-quality calf's leather, greasy at the edges from being so much fondled. Anne remembered that it was an identical book which Patience Helliwell used at Makings for the Methodists to debit and credit their sins and good works before God. Anne opened it at the back, glanced at the index of customers, then turned to the front, flipping through until she came to the latest entries, marked by a sheet of blotting paper on which Oliver had made calculations. The early accounts were crowded on the page with many sorts of woollens listed for each customer, and cash totals of one or two thousand pounds per month entered in a minutely careful hand. The later entries were loosely scrawled and for low amounts. Often Oliver had abandoned a page in the hope that starting a new one would change his luck.

Anne saw how sheepish he was about his decline, and to cheer him she began, 'Our son is . . .'

'You told me it was a girl!'

'Oliver! Absence has estranged your memory!' She tried to distract and caress him, but now he would not be touched.

'Heaven knows, I am convinced you told me of a daughter.'

'Why should I lie to you? Oh Oliver, there is nothing to be gained from being quarrelsome! Tell me what you think of Peter for a name? "Upon this rock shall I build . . ." I want him to grow a secure, firm man.'

'I would call him Benjamin Tim.' Oliver was dreamy. 'I want to see my son.'

He was overwhelmed. Thinking of being an example to the boy, Oliver from this moment stood more firm and erect. How would he cultivate that good in Tim which, if it exists in a man, shines only upon others and is unrecognised by himself? Oliver saw ahead moments when, being turned to for help or advice, his own manhood would be tried, and he vowed to respond always with kindness. He reminded himself in all circumstances to behave generously, no matter what he felt at the time, that his acts might be a future example to the child. He imagined Benjamin Tim grown to manhood, sharing a pipe of tobacco or a mug of ale, and able to listen to Oliver's telling-over of his own trials and experiences.

Anne retorted, 'You know that cannot be! Stay patient for a year or two and then you can "adopt" him as your heir.'

Trade declined and superfluous servants were one by one dismissed. Mary Pickles and Bridie left, on the verge of winter, to be swallowed into the countryside. Soon only Amos Culpin, Jenny Loveless and Earth remained.

Culpin was burdened with the power of more responsibilities and honoured with confidences. Cloth-factors, bankers and weavers as well as the craftsmen and traders who had decorated Lower Laithes but were still without payment, and whom Oliver therefore did not wish to receive, were met by Amos, who was relied upon to give 'the soft answer that turneth away wrath'.

Many of these one-time intimates of Oliver, but now of Culpin, agreed with Amos about 'the weight of sin laid upon the English nation', and would meet him secretly to plot how to uproot it from the North Country. A 'hearty religion', they said, 'diverted revolution and rebellion'. Beyond their wages, men must seek God; whereas their present pleasures (in these days 'happily diminishing') of fiddle-playing, singing, and in the music of rattling bones, cows' bladders and the newly fashionable clarinet, brought them no permanent ease but instead engendered even greater dissatisfaction with their masters.

It was Culpin's duty to fetch the weekly mail from the stage-coach. On one occasion he appeared exultantly drunk (though it could not be with alcohol, for he never touched it), as he brought an exceptionally bulky sack to his master. Culpin waited, to see it opened.

'There is a difference betwixt my father and me over money, Culpin!' Oliver remarked. 'I am an artist, so I treat all that I receive as a matter of fate. In any case I am most likely to spend it on what husbands my poetry, and fall into debt. My muse will not allow me to invest it merely to make more money.'

'No, sir.'

Culpin had to remain unsatisfied in his curiosity. For Oliver was never eager to break the seals, and it was three days before he did so this time. He procrastinated and deliberated; took truant-walks with his sweetheart (like all truancies they on the one hand offered the intense delight of stolen time, but on the other they were fundamentally aimless); he called Amos to stoke the fire; opened and closed a volume of Ovid; lit, sucked and relit a pipe; tinkered with a poem he was writing, and stared ten times out of the window, before at last reading his letters.

A refusal of payment from Saint Petersburg because the colours delivered were not identical with the samples. A reluctance to settle an account since bales contained short measure. Another complaining that a shalloon was 'too loosely woven'. A demand note for five shillings for a stone figure of Cupid. Also, in this unusually pregnant Pandora's Box, was a storm of demands from staplers for instant payment for raw wool. Knowing how every clothier's solvency depended upon receipts reaching him from investments sent all over the world, the staplers normally gave ample credit. 'Do unto others as you would have done to yourself' was a Christian precept reciprocated to keep them all out of debtors' prisons; and which also gave a most bloody axe to wield, if turned upon its head. Conspiring to demand immediate settlement of bills was a well-known way to bankrupt an unpopular trader. Especially at the onset of winter, for Oliver could not possibly expect money from beyond the Alps until spring.

His associates had turned into hawks stooping to destroy him. Sober-suited merchants and bankers in Norwich, London, Leeds and Somerset (well-padded men who gave money for almshouses and grammar schools, and who had plaques and statues erected to memorialise their own generosity) had plotted over his fate, using the magic of their credit-notes and bills, as witches conspire with pins over a figure made of wax.

'The Lord brings deliverance to poor sinners in the end,' Culpin softly remarked as he came by Oliver's side, to comfort and to see if the fire needed attendance.

'Ah, Culpin, you're an excellent loyal fellow, but I'm afraid that the troubles besetting us are because the best of the weavers have stayed with my father – as is natural and admirably loyal. What I have left in my cottages are scamps and scoundrels who skimp their work, punishing me because they are discontented and not realising this makes their own position worse. There is no more market for soldiers' woollens, and that's the reason for it – there is a lull in our wars. They must either weave better cloth, for the satisfaction of the fine ladies abroad and in London, or instead indulge their passion for defacing the coinage of the realms and for illicit brewing, to support their domestic economies.'

'Unless the manufactories come,' Amos muttered. Then he announced more loudly, 'We are an ignorant lot, is poor servants, who do not know the ways of business. But if you'll pardon me, the warnings is that they are incensed about Miss Wylde, sir.'

'Nonsense, Culpin, many a man cares for his housekeeper!'

'Yes, sir.'

The woeful Culpin gave great attention to the fire. Then he added, 'It is well-known that ours is one of the disaffected districts of England, sir. It is forever being found necessary to bring soldiers here to quell rebellious subjects. Either the people will be driven by their poverty and their animosity to the government to sinfully clipping bits of gold from coins deposited with them by gentlemen like yourself, sir, and stamping out fake money, or they will purge the district of what, some say, is an evil spirit that dwells amongst us, bred from our collective sin. A Jew that I spoke to – only on behalf of your business – said that in his religion Miss Wylde would be described as being possessed by a "dybuk". He also said it was an "incubus". An evil ghost from the past that lives in a body and makes it do all manner of things that are out of keeping with a life of Grace. Of course, I do not believe such superstitions, but there are many who do.'

Oliver, after he had brooded over this, tried to express his worries for Anne's safety. 'Anne, creditors are closing in on us, they consider our liaison ...'

'Neither the Dutchman nor any others care if we are immoral or not! They all have the same interest – they all "piss in the same pot", as we say – all they think of is to get hold of your father's money, by making him feel compelled to pay your debts. Therefore they must make sure that you have plenty of them.'

'Well, I have ample money owing me. I have only to collect it from abroad, and could try to cross the Continent myself before winter sets in. I suppose the staplers can be persuaded to wait for a while.'

Anne saw that if Oliver left, he might not ever return. It was the very instability of their lives, sometimes happy and sometimes quarrelling, that made her long the more for him to stay with her. 'You could avoid the creditors by making over Lower Laithes and your other possessions to me,' she remarked.

He looked at her sadly. 'Then we will never marry, because if we did so they could claim "your" property as my debt. My son will always be a bastard.'

'You will be able to pay them off soon, and then we can wed.'

'What do I want with it all?' Oliver said impatiently. 'Take it then! You can have Lower Laithes and everything else.'

'But if they find out you have given property away, they will say that you disposed of what is rightfully theirs, to avoid paying your legal bonds. "Sell" them to me, properly.'

So a written agreement was made through a lawyer, stating that Miss Wylde would receive Lower Laithes for the sum of £5 with revenues from cottages and from timber in Blood Wood, 'as recompenses for her care and diligence about my business'.

In what was now Anne's house (and which was growing steadily shabbier, through lack of servants), Oliver despondently consumed his way through wine, port, and small beer. Irresponsibility, his shedding of his possessions upon Anne Wylde, and this new form of his enslavement to her, actually gave him some peace of mind – especially when he saw how boldly and well she could bear it.

It was not his drinking that annoyed Anne so much as his long silences. Sometimes, recognising the disquiet caused in her by his drunken gaze, he said (either looking painfully directly at her, or at other times mysteriously beyond), 'I want to see Benjamin Tim.'

'That would bring unhappiness to us all,' she prevaricated.

In such scenes Anne, being without logical answers, would pretend anger. (The mixture of frustration with pity that she felt at his impotence and shabbiness was usually quite enough to inspire her annoyance.) Tears would then dampen Oliver's eyes. They knew that one of them would have to be the first to leave the room, and they became practised at the game of angry exits.

Oliver's excuse was generally to see about the ale in the cellar. (God bless Mary Pickles who had left such a store of it!) On the way he might stare into Blood Wood for a while, perhaps moved by the music of wind in the boughs, or by their flickering which made it look as though the stars were racing madly about the Heavens. Or maybe he glimpsed the spies who these days were always nearby, (acquaintances of Culpin, go-betweens to Mr Van Broyes), lurking and accosting people in taverns.

He dreamed up schemes to save his fortune. His father's sulphur springs at Upper Spout had not been a success because the climate was too bleak to attract frail ladies. Israel Merrybent's activities behind the Hellenic façades were attracting only seditious radicals and meat-stealers, hence also the attentions of Dick Almighty. It had become a place of ill-repute, though the soldiers who were sent up there never found anything, because their red tunics shone for miles across the moors and their clatter was broadcast ahead of them through the hamlets. Oliver planned to reclaim this little Parthenon, and to heat it with coal dug from the moor. He thought of prospecting for coal in Blood Wood, just as other clothiers, suffering hard times, were doing. Horsfall had told him that young miners could be imported from Scotland and made 'indentured apprentices', so that they had to accept their masters' terms and were as firmly enslaved as Negroes from Africa.

The only practical outcome of Oliver's deliberations was that night after night he took his violin, left Lower Laithes, plunged into the wood and visited a house where an untemperamental woman, who laughed and did not blame him for anything, sold ale or even let him have it on credit. 'You cannot be cheated wi' ale!' Oliver sang out in this tavern. 'Them that buys beef, buys bones; them that buys land, buys stones; them that buys eggs, buys shells; but them that buys ale, buys nowt else!' As night progressed he drank more, sang even more idiotic ditties, took his naps by the fireside, and recalled with nostalgia the days when, like Tim Bobbin, he never worried for a moment where he would lay his head. The journey home became more and more difficult to make. He began to be proud of himself again because he was a daring reckless fellow, Tim Bobbin's second self.

One night after he had gone too far with his boasting, a big quarryman allowed Oliver to overhear him say, 'John Wylde, the mason, has been found dead. Frozen on a heap of stones he'd set aside to build a wall with.'

The group watched, out of the corners of their eyes, Oliver fidgeting with his tankard.

'He died of the Melancholy,' another declared.

'He was the best mason of all in these parts. I used to cut the stone for him. Why, how he could choose it! He knew exactly what would suit, and could measure dimensions at a glance. He just held his hands out, and it'd be right size. They'll be coming to view his work in future days, yet see how he was served in his lifetime!' Their eyes slid even more towards Oliver. They regarded him as people do a man about whom they believe that he follows a different, secret and irrational order when he is alone with his wife, and so cannot be trusted.

'Nobody would go tell his daughter, because she's living like a queen wi' a bankrupt piece-maker who has pretensions, though he can do nothing without his father and is under her heel into the bargain. A "poet", so they say, though no gentleman or parson'll subscribe to his verses – and yet they're too fancy for homely singing either.'

'Yonder fellow's looking sickly!'

Oliver rushed out. The dawn, a sodden red flower dripping upon the hills, refreshed him. As he returned determinedly to Lower Laithes it began to rain in the woods, hammering the boughs like a thousand shuttles banging and making a single melody. Sneaking under the rain came the smell of woodsmoke and he imagined the comfort of the fire. Yet he felt that he was not in a fit state to tell Anne his news. He wavered, looked for an excuse, and found it when he spotted a stranger's horse tied in the yard. So he went away again.

Between the oaks and beeches were misty vistas, speckled with gold. The remaining leaves clustered like yellow lanterns upon the boughs, whilst the rest swirled over the stream and paths. There was a satisfying odour of decomposing leaves. Fungi had recently appeared, livid upon all the rotting places: sickly orange trumpets like pigs' ears, erect pink spotted horns, and grey clustered slimy things that seemed to belong more to the bottom of an ocean. Oliver climbed until the trees changed from oaks to birches and he could look down upon the singed brown tips below. The tiny, metallic autumn leaves of hawthorns pattered around him like showers of gold coins.

He knew that it was all beautiful, even the seasonable rotting things, yet he could not feel it. Was Oliver, also, becoming a victim of Melancholy? (For so many were.) The more he stared, the more he was convinced that beauty had vanished for him. Permanently. Her grave was in the enclosures and the foundations of manufactories. He blinked, and shook his head, as if some quick movement like that would skim off the world's deadening veil. He consoled himself by thinking that the truly lovely had always been haunted, if not by aching sadness, then certainly by nostalgia. As if what was called 'beauty' was in fact a faded ghost, a memory, from the womb. Though he must face the present, with its 'consummate villainy', its 'disgrace and reproach that bowed his face to the earth', yet just like John Wylde (and like many other men in these days, though all entirely unknown to Oliver), his yearning was still for Paradise: for a half-remembered tantalizing mother-land where the world's beauty truly existed.

He reached the moor, where it was cold, wet, lonely and greasy. Oliver walked here to avoid the reproaches of starved weavers living upon the lower slopes: in recent days other mills had been burnt, and more images of Anne Wylde made out of wax, straw and bits of wood, mainly by children or by peddlars, to be sold at fairs. Was he as weak and contemptible as they had suggested in the public house? He himself so often felt that he was only half a person and that he was adrift: his other half was Anne Wylde. Perhaps they tore at one another with hooks because they were grappling to be united. Perhaps the reason that they both acted selfishly was because they felt this lack of being bonded together. Their selfishness was a perverse attachment, for they were doing whatever they could to attract one another. It was like looking into a mirror, and clawing at the reflection.

Amongst the bogs he saw an isolated cottage, known to him by its secret reputation, and which at last put a *practical* idea into his head. When Oliver came close, a loom clattered peacefully in an upstairs room, the children ran out to finger the fine worsted of his coat, and the housewife stood on the doorstep, suckling a young pig at her breast. The animal was satisfied. With its long-lashed bright eyes it peeped out of her blouse without any of those kicks and wriggles natural to a piglet. The woman, having this substitute for the baby of her own that had died, also looked contented. She glanced at Oliver, then stared dreamily beyond him at the patches of dark water glittering amongst the rushes around the cottage. You would not guess that she had just been hurriedly shifting a heavy loom to cover what had been hidden under the stones of the kitchen floor.

Her attention regretfully flicked back to him, as if she had been reminded of a duty. 'What does *thou* want?' she asked, unwelcoming. Her voice grated, her throat having been made coarse by the moorland wind.

'My name is Oliver Greave, I'm from Lower Laithes ...'

'I know that. And I hear that trade with merchants down London or wherever is not what it was.'

But she stepped aside (frightening the pig into making a desperate stab at her), indicating that he might enter the cottage. He walked into a warm smell of new-made oatcakes which were drying upon strings stretched above the fireplace. Yarn hung on a distaff. A peaceful scene, apparently showing that all the family was usefully employed. Yet a child, after stroking Oliver's arm in wonder, pointed her finger at her open mouth, with the habit of begging. Because Oliver pulled nothing out of his pockets, she and the other children returned to their work: this consisted of trampling a freshly-woven piece in animal and human urine, in order to bleach it. The loom did not cease to clatter until the woman shouted up the ladder, 'There's someone 'ere to see thee!' She looked Oliver up and down a few more times, then solemnly added, 'A man.'

Whilst the weaver descended, the woman stared some more at Oliver and then asked bluntly, 'Does something ail thee?' He could not answer.

The weaver, when he appeared, puffed and panted with a great show of weariness. He displayed his dusty hands. 'I didn't know we had a visitor,' he humbly and courteously excused his slowness. 'It's growing over such a dull day, and I'm getting so old that I can hardly see. But I've woven eight yards! Been at it since daylight. If it's fine tomorrow I'll have to be spreading dung on my enclosures instead of going to hear the preacher. 'Tis a terrible hard place this for us to make a living. It never lets us forget we are descendants of Adam, expelled here from th' Garden of Eden for our sins.'

'You look decently prosperous.'

'Looks deceive! If yonder pig does not live to fatten we shall starve this winter. But as thou can see, women are sometimes of use to us! Is there a purpose to your visit?'

'I am suffering financial embarrassments and I have been told that you are coiners. We might help one another.'

The weaver ceased to be humble. 'I must ask you to leave my house, sir.'

'I was sent by Mr Horsfall.'

'I do not know a Mr Horsfall. I'm sorry, sir, I must ask you to go.'

'Do you know Israel Merrybent? – He is in my father's employ.'

'I do not know him either, sir. We are merely poor people struggling to make our honest living up here where the world is so unkind.'

Oliver left, shamefaced, pitying these poor weavers whom he had apparently slandered, and muttering his apologies. But when he was a hundred yards across the moor a different woman came to the door and called him back. It was Bridie! She had learnt much more English here. 'It is all right, sir!' she whined. 'They did not know you were desperate. But perhaps it is now our turn to employ you!' Oliver went back to the cottage.

'What you accuse me of is a hanging offence,' the weaver said. 'For aught I knew, you might have been a customs' man.'

'I quite understand. Look, to ease my unhappy prospects I am eager to take part in your business.'

'You must deposit gold pieces for us to clip, then.'

'But I have no gold. That is why I have come here!'

'I have told you our way of doing trade. You must lend us your own gold pieces for us to clip the corners from and stamp out new ones. Then we will return your money, with interest even though devalued – for those who'll bother weighing it. Or we will invest it quietly for you in our own concerns. We are the bankers for the common people and many of us wish to escape our miseries and buy passages to the Americas. But now you are wasting our time.'

Bridie laughed. 'Can you give the young master work and let him earn his bread with his sweat, as we do? He can drain the wet moor for us and spread dung on the fields whilst you go listening to sermons!'

The weaver's wife doubled up laughing, so that the pig fell out of her bosom and squealed across the floor, chased by the children. 'He's got some fine cloth and boots to keep out the rain! Would you like the job, sir?'

Bridie repulsively rubbed herself against him. 'Come and lie with me and I'll give you a clipped guinea for it!'

'No other whore would *give* you money to go with her,' the housewife mocked.

'I'm so grateful that Mistress Anne took me in out of the cold!'

Oliver pulled away, frightened. He walked backwards towards the door, turned and left as fast as he dared, without indecently running, whilst their laughter rolled after him. He made not towards the open moor by which he had slyly come, but towards the nearby packhorse track – the busy traffic of which was of advantage to the coiners who wanted to transport and take delivery of gold without attracting attention to travellers who elsewhere would be unusual. Though

Oliver was avoiding people, yet this was the quickest way home. His destiny, after all, still awaited him, at Lower Laithes at the foot of the hills exactly where he had left it on departure the previous evening.

(11)

It was a long while before Anne could weep for her father. Then at last, after his funeral, the preparing for which numbed her grief, unexpectedly she was convulsed with such tears as she had never experienced before. Cried so that her chest hurt. When she could produce no more because her voice was broken she kept up a strangled sobbing, trying to save herself from the pain in her chest, throwing her head from side to side, up and down, her capless untidy hair this way and that, in a fit that consumed her whole body. It caused Oliver to fear for her heart, her lungs, and her sanity. But she had to exhaust herself. Then she slept with her head upon Oliver's chest, and he, though with an aching arm under her head, bore it happily.

Searching John Wylde's house before creditors claimed it, Anne found the frail insect-like spectacles through which her father had peered to understand Voltaire, Tom Paine and Socrates. She also had taken to Lower Laithes the large brown painting of seven gentlemen, uniformly Puritan, balefully staring over the filled-in well. As it had frowned over all her childhood and growing up, she had become nostalgic for it.

Anne was not the only unhappy one in Lady Well these days. When she rode out in elegant mourning clothes on her fine black gelding, she witnessed such misery as she had never thought possible in this self-satisfied place. Instead of the prosperous tradesmen of a few years ago, now, after the intervention of a few savage winters, and a peace in Europe, the moorland tracks were full of shuffling weavers and returned soldiers who with no hope of work were turning over the brambles in case there might be a few sour blackberries left untouched. They set traps for rabbits or they stared wistfully into streams that had already been fished bare of trout. Hundreds had left the district and ruined cottages stood about the moor: the main roof-beams sagged, the tiles slipped and let rain in, rotting the floors, freezing in the slates so that when the thaw came the stone split and crumbled.

Israel Merrybent's wife died of cold and hunger. Or was it from that painful lump, solid as a stone, in her chest? No one knew, or cared. Except, yes, Israel, who though he had done nothing but curse her since their courtship was over, was distraught. He took his breast-like bladders of whisky from place to place, hungry, weeping and from habit muttering soothing fragments of his old curses under his breath as if they might summon the ghost of his former 'happiness'.

There was a woman who used graciously every Sunday to give charity to the poor outside the church, and (because her husband was purchasing one loom after another), was cultivating a manner for the time when she hoped to pass by in a carriage; she had now lost her husband in the army and was reduced to scraping dried dung from drovers' highways and from commons, taking it from door to door to sell it for fuel. She spat at Anne's gelding. 'The mighty, too, shall be fallen!' she shouted.

Coal pits were all that flourished, like sulphurous pustules breaking out of the sweet hill's surface. What were they hewing coal for? Anne did not know, but seeing the tips she felt sure there would soon be too much unless there was found some new use for it. Around one place Anne came across a group of unhappy battered people flapping like distressed birds that had lost their chicks. The miner had descended the shaft (which was simply a hole a hundred feet into the ground), and had his breath taken away by fire-damp. As they pulled him back he was too dizzy to hold the rope and he fell again, breaking his bones. He was an old man who had spent his life as a weaver and was now forced to become a collier. His wife, crippled with arthritis and insane with pain, had come out into the confusion of rain and wind on the moortop. There was also his newlywed daughter and her husband; several small children, five years of age upwards, who had just begun to work in the pit; and the son, who descended to make a rescue but was overcome by the fumes of the mine and fell with his father into the water. Apart from the weeping old woman there was an awed, tense silence when Anne arrived. The son-in-law was going down next. He defeated the fumes by telling them to drop him rapidly, and was able to load first the father, then the son into the basket. The casualties looked like messy crushed fruit. Red juice, pumping out of them, swamped their rags and smeared their black flesh. The old collier's wife forgot her suffering and with cramped

174

limbs tried to wash her unconscious husband's forehead in rain and spit.

Anne could not speak. She gave them the one guinea that she had on her. They did not answer. She rode off into the rain, haunted by the sulphurous stench and by a woman's words shouted after her: 'They look like niggers, don't they? But black slaves have an easier life than miners, dressed up in silks wi' powdered wigs. Gentlefolk dress animals to be better than us!'

Anne next went to Lady Well. Some weavers of old-fashioned woollens were arguing in the street with a group of wool-combers (engaged in making the new worsteds). The former said that the furnace in the combers' shop would someday burn Lady Well to the ground, and it would be a judgment on them for changing their methods from using cold teasels. Others talked of the well cleared by Esther Kershaw, which had now performed a third miracle: a family that lived lower down the hill and who used to be sickly from drawing contagious water from a choked spring were now enjoying their first autumn without illness. The rim of the well, which Esther had built up with stones, had become a place where people leaned to gossip, and with idle peaceful gestures improve Esther's masonry. They had rediscovered their old pastime of reading fortunes by watching the water's winged spirit – a tiny fly – flit about the surface. Old people and children spent pleasant hours and days thus. They had begun once more to hang rags (fragments of clothing from sick people) on nearby hawthorns and votively to offer old nails, brooches, horses' shoes and coins to the water-spirit. Doubtfire described them as 'superstitious whimsical persons idling their hours waiting upon a fly as it imbibes the panacean dews'. He had appealed to his bishop for help to restrain the people, or at least for him to pay a visit and overawe them; but His Lordship, forgetful of Christ, replied that Lady Well and its moors was 'no fit place for a gentleman', and had refused. So Parson Doubtfire ill-temperedly smashed more of the church windows, shouting out that 'the brutish inhabitants of Lady Well are not worthy of the Gospel of Jesus Our Saviour.' Bright blue chips of Mary's gown and scraps of Christ's red garment still glittered on the path. Finally he had the temerity to paint out Saint Uncumber, though he feared that the women would throw stones at him for it. He next wanted to remove the cross from the tower, saying it was an 'ornament of superstition and idolatry', and he had ladders already placed; only, he could find no one who would climb them.

Anne found Doubtfire at home, dissecting a corpse. It was that of Dick O'Lovely, who had died of starvation against an enclosure wall, with only his violin for a companion.

'Our most famous local fiddler was blind,' Doubtfire said, 'quite sightless.'

'Him, *blind*?' Anne questioned. 'He could find his way everywhere!'

'I have just Examined his eyes. There could never have been sight in them.'

'I think our Dick O'Lovely saw more than most of us. Especially those responsible for ruining us and bringing such misery upon Yorkshire. Mr Doubtfire, many of those dependant upon Mr Greave are now beggared. Two hundred weavers and a thousand spinsters are suffering.'

Though it was a cold day, Doubtfire sweated with embarrassment before her. 'Ah yes, I have seen much Evidence of it. I was called only yesterday to the Bedside of a Valuable weaver who had Died for lack of food. His wife and children were most Distressing. I was entertained in my scientific Interests by the appearance of the body. When the Grieving widow leant upon the stomach, it ejected air and Appeared to make the Signs of Life.'

Oblique ideas, half-escaping his attention, slithered across the back of Doubtfire's mind. A thought of flesh, which our souls must inhabit as our prison and punishment because we are sinful. Merely thinking of flesh's satisfaction filled Joseph Doubtfire with foul horror, yet there before him was the beautiful Anne Wylde, only an arm's length – and yet also an ocean's space – away. Whilst all around and around and around were the foul grass, flowers, birds, and animals, at their cavortings.

'At least our clothier's satires and the many affecting compositions of his muse must bring you delight,' Doubtfire suggested.

'No so much as you suppose,' Anne answered.

'Why so? Surely he will confer lasting Celebrity upon our great Emporium of the woollen Trade!'

'Because two hundred weavers and a thousand spinsters are starving.'

'Ah! And Oliver Greave's muse is responsible, for because of her he

Skulks in Holes to avoid his debts? Evidently genius is not always accompanied with Prudence in everyday concerns! Let it be a lesson to him to leave the Lord to account for His miseries and not interfere. Oh, but this is a most Sinful spot of a Sinful country, and surely the Lord is known by the Judgment He executes?'

'Mr Doubtfire, could we set up a charitable school for the weavers whilst they are unemployed, for them to study and think about the Bible and be taught economy and given flour for their wives to learn to bake it?'

'*Think* about the Bible? Why should they think on it? 'Tis doctrine that we must all *accept*.'

'To learn it then, if you wish. We could offer them food to encourage them to come, for they would tend to stay away, suspecting our motives.'

'And who would subscribe to it?'

'The Snawdens, the . . .'

'Your servant Amos Culpin has been struck with a strange providence, Anne Wylde. He has cut off his own Members, cast them into a Fire and come to my house seeking comfort, leaving so much Blood that his way may be traced by the cakes of it. "Why have you treated yourself so barbarously?" I asked. He answered "I have had one wife and baby that died long ago, and 'twas more than enough of the joy of flesh to satisfy me." He said that lately he had a vision that he could not be Saved unless he Dismember himself and go on a pilgrimage to Jerusalem. I fear Amos Culpin will meet his Maker under the surgeon's hands, and not in Jerusalem. There is Filthiness of the spirit everywhere to be Cured, before you teach them to bake! Amos confessed to me some antecedent Filthiness that drove him to this Extreme. Thus, the parts that were Abused have Smarted by the hands of the same person, and that is why I say that the Lord is known by His Judgment.'

'God's love is sometimes in *our* hands to discharge as we can.'

'*Woman, are you questioning my Ability to interpret God's will?*' The parson's hand was forgetfully raised against her. Then he remembered himself, and let it fall unaggressively upon his table that was littered with the heart, liver and empty stomach of Dick O'Lovely. Anne left hurriedly, sick of the stench of formalin, analysis and death.

She next went to Makings. There they were crowded into the

kitchen for a special prayer-meeting to 'save the countryside from poverty'. All those who considered themselves The Elect were present.

Benjamin Greave stood on the table and declared, 'The Lord it appears 'as now sent His check upon our walling and improvement of the wastes! But no doubt He has His good reasons for favouring instead th'impulse for "democratic liberties", as some have a mind to call it, and that are bringing ruin to our times, to the Age in which we live! So as we must abide with it . . .'

Dick Almighty impatiently scrambled up next to him, livid with exasperation. For, far from accepting that God intended 'a check upon our walling', he had decided that God's province was Heaven, whilst it was up to himself – with a little aid from other sensible men – to do something about the world in which we lived. He had therefore called a meeting of the Society For Prosecuting Felons to discuss 'the propriety of petitioning the government and the King for funds to employ the deserving but distressed poor of the township known as *Lady Well* in enclosing the waste called "*Raven's Hill*" for the benefit of some Gentlemen of the district'.

Though Dick's great heroic efforts to provide 'honest labour' had not met with success, had in fact (unknown to Dick) stopped a good way short of reaching the ear of the King, yet his eloquence still did not fail him. In his opinion the clothier's speech was far too dry for the times, which required a 'full-blooded, honest rhetoric', especially if it was to reach a royal ear; and this he delivered, shouting over his belly, 'I'll tell thee what, my friends! If the Lord has taken away thy dinner, He has also in His wisdom given thee the brains to think of a way to get it back again! Listen to what happened to me – for 'tis a parable. My dinner was stolen. Yes, *my* dinner was stolen, only the other day.' Dick paused, letting an eloquent and weighty silence impregnate the room. 'Would I hunt the villain (for you know the manner of thief-catcher that I am) to the world's end, have him transported and hung, and tie the noose myself? On this occasion, no. "I was expecting it," I lightly told the assembled company ('twas at my own inn). "For I exchanged words with the Devil himself upon that very subject this morning."'

The kitchen-congregation was astonished.

'How's that, then? It's said that you pretend concern for the poverty o' the weavers.'

'Licking his chops the while, His Awful Majesty, Satan, otherwise known as the Devil, otherwise known as Beelzebub, sagaciously remarks in my own, my very own ear, "Be assured thy meal will be stolen from thee by twelve o'clock!" "Then," I smartly answered him (for I have almost as much experience as the Devil himself in apprehending villains!), "I warrant I'll discover the culprit by four in the afternoon!" "How's that?" asks the King of the Nether Regions – puzzled by my clever devious devices, of course. Whereupon I proceeds to sprinkle deadly poison upon the meat – that the Devil might have his disciple with him more quickly.'

There was laughter. (Laughter at a prayer-meeting!)

'I left the room then for them to think about my words. On returning one hour later, I found, as I expected, my joint replaced.' Almighty smiled upon his audience: such an innocent, confident, unapprehensive smile, unlike an adult's and more typical of a babe who has made the happy discovery of a full breast.

Patience Helliwell sidled close to Anne. 'Women also are allowed to preach amongst us, Miss Wylde. You'd happen enjoy that. Would you like to address us with a few words of prayer for Mercy and Grace?'

'No.'

'Because "the Lord is known by His judgment" – so I was told by our Parson today. I do not see any purpose in praying to Him, if what He wants is what I see in Yorkshire today. Only the practice of love can do anything for it.'

'That is what we are doing – praying for God's love.'

'You do not need to pray. Either you have love in your heart, in which case it will come out of itself, or you have it not. There is no use in praying.'

'If the *old parson* was alive, you'd be whipped i' the stocks for saying less than that.'

Then Benjamin Greave came up, so Patience melted away, feeling sure that *he* would be able to reprove the 'careless witch'.

'I dunna want to see thee in this house!' Benjamin thundered.

'Mr Greave, you must do something for the weavers and spinners under your care.'

'What does thou think we are at today, then? We're praying so hard that I'm in a muck-sweat with it! Ar't'married to my son yet, Whore of Babylon? *Thou'rt* architect of all our troubles! Thou'rt maker of 'em! Go do something yourself – get out of my house! The weavers'd be prosperous and peaceful if it was not for your interference. Get out! Thou'rt a demon! I'll leave nothing to thee nor thy bastard progeny, so there's no call for you to be hanging around Makings! Thou'rt not to be the vessel of *my* heirs! Get out of my house! Get out! Out!'

'All you will achieve is to make your legacy sterile.'

'Are you cursing me now? It was always known thou'rt a conspicuous witch. Jezebel! Get out o' my house! I say, get out o' my house!'

Anne could think of nowhere and no one else to turn to. A few days later, and without saying anything to Oliver, she took three hundred pounds that was intended for his creditors and secretly bought several cartloads of raw wool for those cobwebbed, dusty looms of Lady Well.

When Oliver was summoned to the Bankruptcy Court, Anne Wylde for the first time left her native district. In the lowland city of York she felt as though she had tumbled into a pit devoid of all that she loved; she was stark and alone when removed from Lady Well's moors and heather. Also she suffered a sickening conscience, thinking that this bankruptcy had somehow been brought about by her own unconscious desire for her lover to be sacrificed.

In the Court, Oliver felt strangled and drowned by the brown box in which they placed him, looking up steeply to the bench of three judges. It was hot and still; he could smell the varnish blistering, and hear it pop. Through a tall window, he could see the avenging crowd outside. Israel Merrybent was there with a peddlar's tray of long-legged, black-haired dolls. To entertain children, some of his customers strung up these Anne Wylde figures on toy gallows.

'Your creditors claim that, using Anne Wylde, you have secretly purchased wool with £300 that rightly belongs to themselves,' a judge declared, with all the weightiness that his robes and state gave him.

'It was with her own money spent to save the weavers from starving,' Oliver answered 'This was only after many other schemes for their relief had been raised or tried, and none of them had come to anything. I have seen women in this county gnawing bones that were discarded by a rich man's dogs. Other females, often elderly, hire themselves out like ponies to carry loads of cloth for miles over hills and dales. Even children whose parents can afford to send them to a dame's school subscribe a penny a week to the expenses of their own probable funerals during the next epidemic of typhus fever. To describe Yorkshire today, an author's pen would need to be dipped in gall.'

'A pretty speech! The weavers starve because of Greave's mismanagement of his affairs whilst he is devoted to foolish poetical flights of the imagination: or versifying, to state it plainly. Let him put his business straight first!' one of Oliver's accusers interrupted.

Oliver, born in wealth, had not, until he heard the intensity with which these men spoke, realised how determined the ordinary person is to get money. Nor how vehement this mundane passion can make him in his hatred of art, of radical aims, and of anything in which money is not the prime purpose.

'It is also accused that you have made over possessions and rents to Miss Wylde, in order to impede your creditors,' a judge said.

'They were payments to her because I am in her debt.' Oliver added, 'For her services,' and a titter rustled by.

'As your muse?' his accusor sarcastically suggested.

Oliver nervously picked at a blister of varnish.

One of the creditors shouted, 'It makes no difference that Anne Wylde received payments and rents, for as she is married to Greave, what she has is due to us! He is guilty of concealment!'

'Are you married to Miss Wylde?'

'No, I am not.'

'He married her in secret down London!'

Anne Wylde was brought into court.

'Have you ever been to London town?'

Anne was feeling only homesickness. 'I have never travelled out of my native valley until today, sir. York is a very fine town, full of very fine buildings, and a beauteous river such as I have never seen in ...'

'Are you married to Oliver Greave?' they interrupted her sternly. 'Swear your answer.'

Anne swore that she had entered into no contract other than for her business and housekeeping services. The court admitted that indeed she did not bear herself like a married woman. Lawyers then pushed forward dated inventories and contracts, in penmanship looped and artistic to the point of illegibility, and which after scrutiny (producing a scratching sound like the scurrying of mice), convinced the judges that property had been made over to her before the declaration of Oliver's bankruptcy.

The weakness in her case was the £300 payment for wool. That did not belong to her.

The judges retired. Two of them wished to acquit Oliver, but the third said, 'If we keep him in York Castle for a while, we might discover something from him that will lead us to the coiners with whom he has been dealing. It is not an easy matter to apprehend these criminals, for in the Lady Well district – a region of savage moorland and a still-barbarous people, one unvisited by any reliable clergymen – they have formed what they term a 'Society For The Prosecution of Felons', the aim of which is *not* to give support to our honest soldiery! Its real purpose is to ensure that there are brought to court only those criminals guilty of offences that the local gentlemen wish to prevent – that is, ones against their own property, or concerned with the stealing of cloth, especially from where it is hung out to dry in the open air upon tenter frames. For woollen cloth is the chief love of that district. In other words, Gentlemen, The Society For The Prosecution of Felons exists mostly to safeguard exemption for coining, in which they themselves are involved.'

Oliver's prison smelled of urine, damp and fear-sweat. Amongst the straw, the stained walls, and the monstrous shadows, there was a fierce struggle for food, for a drier corner free of draughts, or for the gaoler's favours. There was continuous coughing, and muttered swearing. Oliver watched one 'sinner' drive himself crazy by masturbating all day on his wet straw, his gaolers and companions having long abandoned him to the Devil. The prisoners had an unforgettable pallor which Oliver could not imagine any amount of sunshine removing. They were resigned, shunning visitors and light as if fearing what these might bring, more than what they suffered already. Oliver was a man of the free air and spacious moorland, and to have the door locked upon him caused him instant fear, panic and pain. He did not dare dwell on the thought of his future days. He did not dare imagine the moors. Yet he was determined that Mr Van Broyes and the other traders would not get the better of him, nor of his father.

Meanwhile Benjamin Greave met his son's creditors. They saw an aged fool with red eyes.

'My son writes telling me not to have dealings with you because you are aiming at destroying me through his trouble,' Benjamin told them, bluntly.

The clothier had so much admired his son for this action, deciding that he was not so attached to a woman's skirts after all, and it made his sorrow doubly hard to bear. Unhappiness had now bent him to look like some poor moor-edge farmer, subject to the whims of weather, trade and sickness, in shabby clothes, and with a grey skin, lined and grimed. When he was a young man this was apparently to have been his lot; strange how fate had brought about, at least, the appearance of it.

'I'll tell ye what I'll do. So long as you keep it secret from him, I'll pay £10,000 to acquit him of his debts.'

Oliver, as soon as he was released, without warning, rushed to Anne. She saw him pale, frail, vulnerable, and too nervous to smile after the time that had separated them. She was overwhelmed once again by her feelings, of protectiveness mixed with admiration for the strong innocence that kept him erect through his troubles in an alien world.

Only later did Oliver visit Makings, sure that justice had prevailed and that it was now in his stars for reconciliation with his father. But Benjamin Greave, because he had heard that Oliver had returned first of all to Anne Wylde, withdrew into his resentments and refused to see his son.

The loving couple remained in peace for some weeks until, one day when Oliver was out, an agent of the creditors called; a lean nasty man with a horrid forcefulness, and old greasy neglected clothes polished by squatting on benches. He peered around Lower Laithes possessively, like a bailiff, and he would not give his name.

Anne said, 'Darkness is descending and I do not nowadays have a boy to accompany you over the moors. Please come to the point, sir.'

The man seemed to think that the last thing he should be expected to do was to explain himself to such as her. After a silence which he intended to be unnerving, he leered at her and replied, 'Let me express myself this way: you should not make such a display with your black gelding, nor with your other possessions, Miss Wylde. For there is a revolution on the Continent that will sweep away all those with despotic pretensions, and I expect that even in this savage corner of England you have heard of it. More likely here than in other districts, in fact. This place is notorious for disaffection.' He paused, then added threateningly, 'I myself like to wear the cap of liberty when I can.'

'Don't let your masters hear of it, then!'

He became more animated. 'But the danger of rebellion seems diverted in this valley! I was expecting distress, and found weavers supplied, even after the heavy judgment against Mr Greave, with wool. I wondered how they have obtained it?'

'Perhaps you would rather find poor people, to be recruits in spinning mills?'

'Manufactories are the agencies of progress and reason, like the revolution in France that will free the passages of capital and trade from royal impediments. You and your black gelding, Miss Wylde, are an interference to the time of plenty that is at hand. Your sort are rotten posts which pretend to stop an ocean, to prevent the future, and if your creditors do not sweep you away, some more bloody hand will do it.'

'I heard this talk from my father years ago, sir.'

'John Wylde has already profited from manufactories!'

'Other men profited, not my father, and so it will be when you have built for my poor weavers. Only the worst and most designing will flourish. They are better off when I care for them in their homes.'

'"My weavers", is it? Then you admit that, whilst you have debts to bear, you are providing wool for them?'

Knowing that he was driving her to the edge of her self-control, he keenly watched her features.

Anne screamed, 'What would you expect of us? To rot in the gaols in which you would so gladly have thrown us?'

'I do not think I need to wait for Mr Greave,' the stranger said, and left.

When Oliver returned, Anne told him, 'A visitor called to talk of revolutions. Your creditors are planning to throw you in prison again.'

'I will go abroad before I will be returned there! Anne, today I met Nicholas Horsfall obstructing my path. No, let me tell you how I felt! I know he is not always trustworthy, but he was such a bold handsome sight – red jacket, white wool trousers, red sash, boots and the skull-and-crossbones on his hat – he made me feel guilty about the face that I myself turn to the world! He talked to me of going abroad. He told me it would be his pleasure to help me into a commission in the 17th Dragoons, as a return for all that my father has done for him. Don't be startled! I shan't accept, but . . .'

'You could not live abroad. You love too much "the wind on the hills, the scent of heather, and the crack around the fire at a moorland inn". That is how you expressed it to me once.'

Oliver shrugged. 'We are always strangers on earth, wherever we are – expelled from Paradise. We are in a foreign land all our lives. It is called "*woman*". We are conceived inside that foreign garden. We spend all our lives as aliens within her, first as mother then as wife, never quite understanding her customs or her language. It does not matter if I live in Yorkshire, Greece or France. Compared with that first fact of existence, I am no more a stranger in one place than I am in another.

'But first I want to see my son.'

Anne would do anything to prevent a meeting between Oliver and the 'by-blow', the bastard, the curse whom he took to be his own child. She would lie to him, she would divert, she would act forgetful, she would pretend anger. Finally, as the weeks went by, she could devise nothing further to frustrate his curiosity and his wish. Together they followed the paths that Anne had often secretly taken.

When Aunt Pity saw Oliver, she without a word took the key of the shed and led the couple to it . . . Anne walking a little behind, so as not to let him see her expression, read her thoughts, or observe her conflict about this creature that was hers and yet not hers; that she saw one moment one way, the next another; this ferrety animal she wished to hate, yet for which love was torn out of her unwillingly in pain-pangs like yet another birth.

The imprisoned child heard visitors arriving, and though only two years of age he drummed on the door, in anguish to be freed of the terror of being alone. But when it opened he was equally frightened of the strangers (including the one who was his own mother) and he dived at Aunt Pity's well-known skirt. Then that seemed insufficient and he scrambled back into the familiar corner of his shed, to his straw, a spinning top, and a crude rocking-horse.

Anne picked the child up, hiding her tearful face by kissing his hair (which struck Oliver as being so unlike his own). When she had given sufficient comfort, she tried to hand the boy to Oliver, whilst still averting her head.

The child struggled free and stood between them, for a moment glaring at his 'father'. Then on tottering but determined legs he made arrow-like for the garden.

Autumn sunlight brought the gold out of everything and before him rose gilded banks of flowers, some erect, some fallen. A red admiral butterfly paused for a moment, its broad crimson wings panting upon a Michaelmas daisy. The face of the tiny infant turned brutal. '*Peter!*' Anne shrieked. For with an expression of ferocious intense evil that Oliver, at least, had never before seen on a human, the child snapped his hands together and crushed the butterfly. Smiling and proud for the first time, he held up his chubby palms smeared with the remains of the red admiral.

'Come and live with me at Lower Laithes, Aunt Pity,' Anne tearfully pleaded.

'Nay, not there, lass,' Pity said. 'I'll not!'

As they returned home, Anne continued to hide her thoughts, and also her face, because she knew that it displayed her pain at the necessities that overwhelmed them. Though they believed themselves to be so close that they were as one body, both lovers had discovered the poignant agony of realising that in extremes there was little help they could give one another. There was nothing Oliver could say. He did not even precisely understand what ailed his beloved.

There was only one comfort he could offer. And so they lay together through the mid-morning, apparently deep in their sweetest love. But Anne was still from time to time turned away from him. Until at last she cast off into forgetfulness, she sailed from mortal life, and then 'Oh . . . oh . . .' she murmured; it turned to wild grunts, and finally she was whirled away. Whilst Oliver entered through that bushy door into that familiar room paved with gold and precious stones, fountains playing, that was like a vision by a saint or a martyr. When it was over, he still kept his eyes closed. Anne saw that he was absorbed in himself, and did not want to come back from wherever he was. When eventually he looked into Anne's eyes he experienced vertigo there, too. As if he was looking down wells of clear water right to the earth's centre. As if they were mirrors of infinite reflection, back ... back ... back...

Afterwards, her mind pacified, or at least her thoughts blanked out for a while, she bore his resting body, his head upon her breast, with more than usual patience, as if she gave particular importance to this moment. From time to time they shifted position, limbs glued with sweat, yet neither wanting to move apart. Neither wanted to admit how fragile was their hold upon one another. Soon they came together again. Each time Oliver penetrated, Anne was whirled into a desire for him to go deeper, deeper. Quite without reason, and out of what well of her being she did not ever understand, the word 'Kill' came upon her lips, as softly as a sparrow landing upon a bough; and she could not help but whisper, *'Kill, kill!'*

She did not know whether it had been a suicidal longing, or too great a desire for life. For life's ultimate challenge, its extreme expression, is to death to overthrow it.

Anne dressed and Oliver watched in quiet contemplation of her movements.

'What are you looking at?' she asked, sharply. As it was obvious, and he felt that he had the right, he did not answer. 'What are you staring at?' she repeated.

He crimsoned. 'Do you think I have no right to look at you, who has caused all my pain?'

Although she thought that his failings were weaknesses, and not wicked, yet Anne at this moment remembered how sometimes she had secretly resented the patience he required of her, wanting her to mother him. She knew he was no Apollo! Also, recalling her father's death, her Aunt Pity's frailty in old age, the loneliness and the obstinacy all about her, and the poverty of the weavers, she felt powerless to help anyone, no matter how much love she gave. She felt a painful hollowness in her breast. 'Do not blame *me* for your downfall,' she answered – bitter words, though she could still feel his semen within her. 'I cannot do anything for you any more. I expect you will go abroad and leave me, in the end.'

Oliver could not bear that look which showed her to be so separate from himself – mentioning his 'downfall' like any greedy trader or magistrate; talking coldly of his 'leaving'. He could hardly imagine that a few moments ago they had been glued together, searching for cooler places upon one another's bodies and yet not able to part.

'And "Hell hath no fury like a woman scorned!"' he answered sarcastically.

'Women become "furies" because if they do not attack, they always are the ones left with the suffering.'

'You have killed the joy between my father and myself,' Oliver said coldly. Immediately, he crimsoned with shame, and had to obliterate it. Also, her unwanted truths caused a desire for violence to rise like sickness choking and tightening his throat.

His first blow fell on her neck. As she went down he shouted, as if his cries would drown the blow, 'All my dear father's hopes and ambitions ruined! Oh, if you had never left Lady Well, never been born, Anne Wylde!'

She lay on the floor, a bloody mess. A dead body, his love.

Oliver flew around the house in a panic. When he recovered slightly he placed a sheet tenderly over her. She looked pathetically young and frail. What was most horrible was that the murder had been such a simple, brief act – like killing a sparrow.

An hour later Oliver left, wearing a suit of thick kersey cloth, with stout shoes and a simple bag, so that he looked like a peddlar, or a merchant of the middling sort. He walked away a few steps. Then ran back towards her. He could not believe that an hour ago Anne was alive – that she had ever been alive. But neither was she yet dead for him. Not really, no not really. He could shake her and she would wake up. Yet he could not bring himself to touch her now. Perhaps she had merely left that body, and she would come in through another door, tomorrow, or the day after that. Yes! *No!* He tried to drive the truth in by banging his fist on his forehead. He wrenched himself away. He stepped a few yards again into the bright cold wintry garden, his life over, yet going on. Anne, oh Anne. Forced himself to tear away. Stumbled, found his feet and went into the wood. He could even now feel the impression of her body as if she was still snuggled sweetly and happily against him: his twin, his own self. He was stamped with that arm flung around his neck whilst she slept, that thigh resting peacefully between his buttocks, her toe against his ankle, her forehead comfortably into his left shoulder as if it had

188

found a socket for itself there. Her body-scents still covered his skin, and he could smell them clearly.

Yet his suffering was for the time being frozen, and lacking pain, except for one moment of agony when he longed, most vividly, to retrieve their past hours. For the sheer sake of remaining upright, he shook that moment away.

Following the river, he forced impressions into his memory and lingered at favourite spots to absorb one last, slow taste of his native hills. He surveyed, too, those manufactories where the women spun, row upon row of them at machines; emblems of the new times that had killed his love, blighted the Greaves' trade, and driven the salmon and trout from the river, which now contained only the reflections of these long, dark palaces in its waters.

Then he pulled himself together to think more positively of the unwanted freedom that lay before him. He realised that he had now only his own lonely self to care for. From then until he reached the stopping-place of the stage coach he walked hastily, with his head down, stubbornly fighting off grief by thinking of his future.

Two days later Anne woke up, with Dick Almighty and the apothecary at one side of her, Earth and Jenny Loveless at the other.

(12)

Nicholas Horsfall's family troubles began when his ancestor, an abbot, was hanged in the porch of his own church for taking part in a pilgrimage, during that earlier century when 'sin' first wore the dress of Catholics. Aghast at the wickedness of men's doings, the Abbot had turned to feminine things: he had become a Marian. But his devotion to 'Our Lady' softened his defences against the worldly, so he was easily trapped, convicted, and executed. His niece, Margaret, in her turn horrified at Catholic Marian suffering, slipped out of danger by marrying the Protestant Horsfall. Then a hen became agent of the family's ruin: because this Horsfall tenanted a farm for which one fowl per annum was paid in extra rent and the Protestant refused to submit to this feudal obligation, whereupon the Lady of The Manor (a vicarious *Lady of The Heavens*) persecuted, or at any rate sued, him (for she received eight hundred hens annually this way). She won her case – for the judges were in her favour and patronage – whilst Horsfall, stubbornly pursuing justice, ended in the debtors' gaol. He tried to escape, so both his legs were fettered. He lay in the mire at the bottom of York Castle for six years, never able to remove his clothes, and eventually they had to be cut from him. All for a hen. Meanwhile his estate fell into ruin. His daughter, called 'Mad Mathilda Horsfall', or 'the Crazy Horsewoman', rescued the family home by presenting its mortgages and bills to her husband as (undeclared before their marriage) her dowry.

The Horsfalls had been Catholic or Protestant, rich or poor, skin-flint or generous, martyrs, heretics or rulers, as the centuries dictated, to an extreme degree. With such aristocratic ancestors, what wonder that Nicholas Horsfall looked down upon Benjamin Greave who had no history but a scramble for a living upon the soaked moors, and for God's Grace in mean nonconforming chapels?

Nicholas Horsfall one winter's day rode out of his dilapidated mansion, with its mortgaged flaking stone, to visit Benjamin Greave.

He wore his cavalry uniform, as if going into battle. His bright red coat looked vivid as freshly shed blood against the snow, which was drifted in the lanes, whilst new flurries that made one dizzy to look at dropped into a silence that swallowed them upon the white banks and altered slopes. The streams were frozen. Nobody who didn't need to showed out of doors, and cottages had their shutters fastened. There was an expression of terror in the eyes of the few who struggled about the countryside, either because hunger forced them to search, or because they were pack-horsing illegal whisky, or gold coins hidden in rolls of cloth. Even the locked shutters on the roadside houses seemed to emphasise the fact that these were outcasts. Fires glowed wherever they gathered to warm themselves – knowing that in this weather no one was likely to chase them from taking wood or, if they could, from finding a rabbit to eat.

Horsfall, wearing his usual contemptuous expression for the world (unless it was one at war), found Benjamin Greave dreading, fearing, and as cowardly as he expected an old man (even a rich one) to be, when left alone in winter.

'A ship went down near Yarmouth with all hands lost, God help all the sufferers!' the old fellow remarked. Greave had now formed the habit of wringing his hands. 'I'm worried if I had some cloth aboard. If so, you may pray the Lord's help for our weavers, for I have no money for them. I've not seen the snow lie up to the eaves like this for seven years! My barns are full of stuff that I cannot get rid of, and I daren't get my folk making more. There'll be some frozen toes and nipped fingers in our cottages this season! The servants cannot get to chapel and church to pray for release, so I have put up with them reading sermons in my own house. You never heard such wailing – I can't imagine who fathered such hymn tunes as they sing today. I don't know where to escape to, what wi't'plagues of business, and manufactories growing up everywhere taking the trade from me. On top of it all I'm worried about that lad of mine, my son. Oh, what a woeful world is this.'

'Oliver has deserted to the Continent to escape his debts. Not a worthy or noble action.'

'He left me to die in the winter like a dog!'

'The worst is, that if you do, your inheritance will then go straight to his woman and her bastard progeny.'

The old man gripped Horsfall's arm tightly. For once in his life he whispered. 'They have such, do you think?'

'It is thought that a son is hidden in some cot on the moors, and for sure the bastard'll emerge later to claim your fortune.'

'Has Oliver married the Wylde woman before he left?'

Horsfall stuffed his pipe with tobacco that he helped himself to from the mantelpiece. 'You must take care of your money!'

Ironic advice, considering the Horsfall's traditionally spendthrift ways, and Benjamin's thriftiness.

'Will thou be trustee of my will, then? I'll send for my lawyer straight as there's a thaw, and make a new one.' Benjamin Greave was still wringing his hands.

'Anything I can do by way of return to you would be very little.' Horsfall's spurs struck sparks from the stones as he moved to light a taper at the fire.

'Would you root out my son and discover whether he says he is married to Miss Wylde? I'll pay you for it.'

'I already know that Oliver has gone to Brussels. It is worthwhile, you know, for a gentleman to employ spies in the times through which we are living. I will gladly follow him. There is no need of recompense, I have enough of those from you already.'

'Ah, if only you were my son! Or if only I had a daughter. What perfection it would be to marry your old family to my humble clothier's fortune. Would you do something for me?'

'Your wish is my command. I am your humble servant in all things.'

'What a winter this is! I've not seen a weaver coming down from the hills for weeks.'

'What can I do for you, old friend?'

Horsfall was impatient to learn 'the worst': one never knew what the 'eccentric old piece-maker' might want.

'The work at Lady Well church has been at a standstill for I don't-know-how-long. Nobody seems to get on wi't, though I leave instructions. They're more interested in reading 'bout Tom Paine, I think, instead o'making worthwhile improvements to their church. Would you see to the design of my monument? No one has more knowledge of what's tasteful in art and tombstones, and I was relying on Oliver for that job. Art and frippery and hanging on to a woman's skirts are the only things he's any talent for. I feared that he'd desert me, afore long!'

'Nothing would give me greater pleasure than to assist in the design of your tomb.'

'You're a good fellow! What do you say that I should do, then, to preserve my fortune?' The old trader's face took on the incandescent trusting look of a child.

'I'd advise you not to leave it direct to your son, but to his daughter Betty and her male children when she has some. It will then stay in your line but be in no danger of diversion to Anne Wylde and her bastards.'

'There's but one fault wi't'plan, Mr 'Orsfall. Betty's a sickly creature. What if she dies before marriage and without issue?'

'Surely she will last that long!'

'I aren't so certain. I haven't seen her for a long while. She is away staying with an aunt since my son disgraced himself.'

'The important thing is to be assured that the inheritance does not pass either to Anne Wylde, or to Oliver's creditors. If Betty dies issueless before the age of twenty-one, then there is no way to cheat a malignant fortune.'

'Oh aye, but there is though! I'll leave my money to thee, Nicholas Horsfall, before I'll let my enemies get hold of it. I always thought that Oliver sharing my business would bind us together in a symbol, for all t'weavers, of the family happiness and prosperity of the whole valley under the fatherhood of trade. But now I see my interest'd be better spent on thee.'

'That is too much! I do not seek payment for what I have done!' Horsfall put his cheerful, youthful arm around the old man's shoulders, and it made Greave feel so protected! 'You have crossed the Rubicon of old age, Benjamin Greave! You are defenceless and in need of looking after.'

'You've been more of a son to me than my own lad and you must have some security in the end as reward for your pains. You would be doing me a service, even then, by helping me "cheat a malignant fortune", as you say. And yet it may not come to that! If my son is in wedlock with Anne Wylde, he might still have legitimate progeny in whom I can invest my immortality.' Benjamin paused, ruminating. 'And thou's made a mistake or two, investing in foolish manufactories. Aye, if only the old could teach the young!'

'If he married her, any children would still be of the blood of Anne Wylde.' Horsfall hurriedly pointed out.

'But how am I to tell if my son and Miss Wylde are wedded or not? If I ask him outright, he's bound to give me a crooked reply.' Benjamin laughed. 'Thou'lt never get a straight answer from someone who's been brought up in our trade.'

'Write a letter for me to deliver, saying that you would be more glad if she were his wife, than anyone else on earth. Then he will tell you, either quite truthfully that he is already married to her, or he will promise to wed her on the instant. No other device could encourage a more spontaneous heartfelt response.'

Benjamin Greave's eyes became damp with admiration. 'No one knows like you Horsfalls how best to defend a family line!'

One dry, sunny day in Brussels Oliver passed a gardener watering a lawn and the sudden smell of wet grass transported him home. Oh, those moist, milky Yorkshire nights, full of the music of water, of streams, rain, and the never-ceasing sound of the wells and springs! The pangs of homesickness were as physical to him as gallstones. Anne Wylde's guilty, incredulous murderer, slinking through the alleyways of a foreign city, was filled with a vision of banks of fox-red grass, of bracken rising in the autumn sunlight, of grey boulders carved by streams into softly-rounded hips and breasts, of the fraternity of the inns, and especially of the friendship of that elusive maker whom he loved, Tim Bobbin.

Everywhere in Oliver's life there was still the spirit of Anne Wylde; she who had never harmed anyone. This way, that, he tore, distracted, and yet looking for distraction. He stared transfixed in an agony of knowing that he could not escape his guilt and loneliness. Should he kill himself?

Oliver Greave spent much of his time composing letters, literary essays and poems. He never sent his epistles, because a critical glance later showed him that they had not expressed his heart. And his work would probably never be published, for where now was his access to gentlemen-subscribers? Still, he wrote. He was trying to give expression to something inside himself that did not seem to love him and his career in the world; at frightened moments, he named it 'conscience'

- a chariot driving him to Hell. Oliver wrote because when not doing so he became a prisoner of himself, of that inescapable person the murderer of Anne Wylde, and he fell into silence. The nearest he came to happiness was in writing.

In efforts to struggle free of the brake upon him, he began many days two or three times. He would return to his bed hoping to frustrate the prospect of another day of failure, and rise to start again, forcing himself to a second breakfast and a further run at those manuscripts, those longings. Such fresh starts and failures played havoc with his night's rest. Working and sleeping in short bursts destroyed his sense of day and night.

Not only was his eating irregular: as he had never been forced to look after himself, but always found that some woman was preparing his meals, his cooking was bad and he swallowed it quickly so as not to have to taste it - thus further ruining his digestion.

However, his poetical digestion was working better in this silence and isolation. His confused thoughts burrowed down into his soul and there restored themselves, becoming articulate. These illuminations would take him by surprise. They hung before him in the air only for a moment, and if he did not write them down instantly, they evaporated. They were like pictures from some ancient Tomb, broken into by grave-robbers, fading quickly in the light. However when he did grasp them, he wrote a new kind of poetry.

All night upon my thigh I've felt her hand
Which rested there, those years ago.
Oh, Heaven is that woman's charms!
No golden apple trees, no
Angel-crowded vistas, you can keep all those,
Whilst I spend eternity in her arms!

Horsfall had to wait for a month before the weather made it possible to travel to find Oliver, and Benjamin Greave was kept on tenterhooks. Twice Nicholas Horsfall received urgent messages to go to Makings. He expected to find the clothier dying. But the first call was merely to consult yet again over the phrasing of his letter, and the second was to remark that the sudden spring weather looked as though it would last; the sodden fields were drying out, the roads had regained their firmness, and a cargo of Russian pine on order since autumn for his mausoleum had arrived, so surely it was possible to reach Brussels? Horsfall laughed off his annoyance and realised that the sooner he crossed the Channel the sooner he'd enjoy peace from 'the boorish old chaw-bacon'.

Oliver's room (when Horsfall found it, through the post office where the poet went daily in futile hope of letters) reeked of dissolute living. It was musty, smelling of tobacco and stale food, and untidy with manuscripts and books. The Captain found it disgusting.

Horsfall first handed over the gold sent by Benjamin Greave. 'It must be a fine thing to be a gentleman abroad!' he laughed. 'You should be more cheerful, enjoying your free hand with the ladies, and no prying faces. What sport *are* you up to these days?'

Oliver, who had phrased so many fine sentences, now could hardly speak, but could only turn crimson. (The Captain was not surprised to find a refugee from justice nervous.) 'We English find Brussels on the whole . . .' he got out, and choked. '. . . Articles of convenience are dear . . . the price of fish . . .'

Then, 'How is Anne Wylde?' he blurted (whilst trying to cover some papers).

'Surely you are not pining for your English mistress amongst all these foreign fruits, my friend? I saw such beauties strolling near the harbour for the sailors to take their pick. I don't want to upset you – but, you know, they say the witch was unfaithful. Don't be angry with me, old fellow! It's only gossip. You remember what we are like for that in Lady Well. It is rumoured that she was enjoyed by a whole gang of sinners one Lammas Day, and that as a result she has a child hidden. A fine infant, too, coming from elegant stock, they say.'

'What happened to Anne Wylde?'

'Do you have some tobacco, old friend?'

Oliver fidgeted around his room until he found tobacco. Horsfall rummaged through his pockets. 'Have you a pipe?'

Oliver rooted in drawers and found a clay pipe. Horsfall packed it and sucked away. 'It is very dry,' he remarked.

'Anne Wylde?'

'Ah! Your father has entrusted me with a letter for you.'

Oliver rushed to break the seal. No, he could not believe what was happening to him . . . oh yes he could . . . he could . . . When, flushed

196

with excitement and confusion, he looked up, he caught Horsfall again taking in the details of the room.

'My father says that he wishes I would marry Anne Wylde, for she would be more agreeable to him than any other woman! Is she alive and well then?'

'This is uncommonly dry tobacco, old friend ... why shouldn't she be?'

'Wait a moment and I will compose a reply!'

Oliver rushed into another room. As he tried to sit down, he knocked over a chair. Once seated, he could not write. He got up, danced about, grabbed the pen again, and cut himself in trying to sharpen it.

Horsfall meanwhile rummaged through Oliver's papers. There were lists of phrases: 'Nobody believes it ... *pas un ne le croit.*' 'My shirt is dirty ... *ma chemise est sale.*' 'I love you with all my heart ... *je vous aime de tout mon coeur.*' And literary utterances, evidently part of a novel. 'Little does he feel the sad variety of pain, the curse attendant upon family and home, who never knew misfortune and is surrounded with pleasure.'

Oliver re-entered. 'Anne Wylde is well, then?'

'Why shouldn't she be, old fellow? Upon my word, you are too excited! At about the time you escaped ... left ... some ruffian knocked her down, and (not for the first time in her life) left her for dead. Oh, it's all right, she recovered! The justices are still searching for the culprit. They have a few clues. But you would not know about that ...'

Oliver grabbed and kissed him.

'In God's name you are too enthusiastic, fellow! It comes from living amongst foreigners. Look, sir ... you must be needing employment.'

'Indeed, sir! It's kind of you to think of that! Though only until I return to England to marry Anne Wylde. For I cannot come straightaway, I must be circumspect ... the justices, you say ...'

'I'd stay where the garden is still fresh, if I was you. She is after all no more than a common girl without ancestry or, I suspect, even dowry. You should think higher of yourself, my friend, and not forget what you will doubtless be heir to one day! Give me your ear, for I have a plan for you, old fellow. I'm profiting from what I've learnt from the old clothiers of our district, for one cannot rub shoulders with them and not gain by it, and though my first manufactory was burnt down by plotters against their King, yet I am still a cloth-factor, in a small way of business, and I'd make it worth your while to extend my interest abroad.'

'I'm sure I can form a most perfect judgment of what foreign people consider to be perfection in English woollen goods. On the other hand, my wish is to return straight to England to marry Miss Wylde.'

'Best be circumspect, old friend.' Horsfall winked. 'You never know what the justices might invent. And I will provide you with the means to stay abroad, whilst you consider the matter.' Horsfall offered his hand and Oliver shook it.

'You are a true friend,' Oliver said.

The poet's visitor departed, leaving him to his frightening excitement, and not knowing what to do with himself; to his plans for returning to England, to the apprehensive hesitations engendered in his mind by Horsfall, and to his exiled scribblings.

Benjamin Greave tore open Oliver's reply even before he had wished Horsfall good day. *'What do you make of that?'* the clothier asked.

The Captain read: 'It always used to be my intention never to marry. Not to be unhappy, or that I thought no woman so deserving, but because I found a single life preferable. That is, until I met Miss Wylde, for since then I have been in entire happy agreement with your presently expressed wishes.'

'I still cannot tell whether the lad is wedded or not!' Benjamin Greave shouted.

Everything these days was unsettled; why, the whole of Europe was 'on fire with revolution'. Or so Benjamin Greave's visitors were always telling him – as a way of explaining the 'difficulties' of selling cloth. All property and inheritance was threatened by seditious traitors; whilst at home in Lady Well the Society For Prosecuting Felons had found it necessary to demonstrate their loyalty to 'the Constitution and the King' by burning publicly an effigy of Tom Paine.

Determined in such times at least to find the truth about his own heirs, Greave rode over to Aunt Pity's cottage. The spring sunshine cheered him; as did the sight of farms, because they were mostly his own property. His tenants had recovered from the winter, he was glad to see. They looked thinner, and it was good for them, he thought, to get rid of a bit of fat. There were fewer of them, and families were better off for being rid of a few dependent old folk. Benjamin set foot on Black Hill. He had not been so far up on the hills since he was a young man, collecting whinberries and courting young ladies. Little had changed since: here a quarry had been cut, there some reprobate or gallow's-bird-in-hiding had thrown up a rough cottage near a watercourse. This constancy was a relief, because he more habitually looked down into the valleys where he was offended by the sight of alteration and new building, nothing but building and more building – manufactories for spinners that were getting as large as palaces.

Dried grasses rustled as he descended to the old woman's cottage. Aunt Pity hobbled out and silenced the dog. To Benjamin Greave, she looked no older than in his youth (and she'd seemed an old woman then), when they used to tease her. But he was glad to see that she was none the worse for it, and nowadays she was left in peace. He remembered how when she lived in Lady Well he and the other children used to visit her with their stomach pains, headaches, bleeding limbs, and she would go into her dark cellar, or out to her garden, for aromatic leaves. Women also came, for private consultation or with complaints about their husbands, so she had become the counsellor and keeper of all the secrets of the town.

'Are your hens laying yet? It must have been a hard winter up here!' he shouted down the hillside, with the condescending jokiness of the persecutor who is hiding his conscience from his victim.

'They lay most of the year round, for me.'

'You must have bewitched them, then! There's truth in the old rumour, after all.'

'I do no more than talk to them because I'm lonely. But never mind my hens. What can I do for you, Benjamin Greave?'

'How do you know who I am, when you can't lift your nose off the ground?'

By now he had reached the door. He walked into the house as if he owned it. (Perhaps he did: he was not sure any more how much property was his. Only lawyers knew things of that kind.) Sharp-eyed, he looked around. He would dearly like to know the secret of her red dye. If he found that out, he might profit from setting up a commercial manufactory. What were those dried-up plants on the table there?

'I can tell folks by their voices ... and their smell. You stink of money and of wool-oil. You always did. You're the same as your son.'

'He's been here then, has he, a time or two?'

'A time or two, as you say. Benjamin Greave, what are you doing to the hawthorn?'

'She has taken *herself* off, I am told, without the necessity of the aid of respectable and devout men. I don't know where she is.'

'Nay, I mean the hawthorns upon the hill. It looks very bleak there now.'

'Ah! We are felling them to make room for improved grazing.'

'It will bring ill-luck on you all.'

'They say it is the hawthorns that bring the bad luck, not the honest men who do away with them, you old witch!'

''Tis the hawthorns that preserve us.'

'That's right! For we use cuttings of the old trees to plant new ones in the form of hedgerows for enclosures. So all things are improved for mankind thereby.'

'You cannot take only what *you* want of the old spirits.'

'You old fright! They say that after the first Christians came you went to the civilisation of the Arabs, together wi' everyone else not fitted to being a monk, and left Christianity in darkness for a thousand years. What does tha' answer to that?'

Pity answered nothing.

'And what brought my son to this desolate place, visiting an old witch?' Benjamin next asked. At last he sat down, rinsing his hands in invisible water, and his eyes still prying for secrets in the dark corners of the cottage. He noticed some apothecary's mixing-bowls and retorts, battered and foolish-looking as the tools of scientific investigation often look when they drift into the kitchens of old women.

'I expect you know.'

'It wouldn't be because he's got a child hidden, would it?'

'Eh, Benjamin Greave, always worrying about what you're leaving behind and who's going to get it – like a dog with its droppings. You get madder and madder:

"As foolish as monkeys
Till twenty or more;
As bold as lions
Till forty and four;
As cunning as foxes
Till three score and ten,
They then become asses,
Or something . . . not men!"

'You know the old rhyme. Whoever has your wealth will only spend it for you as fast as if they've set fire to it, not having worked for it. They'll not consider you!'

'We must all think of what we leave behind, though.'

'We leave the memory of our good deeds. Unless we do bad ones. And they're remembered, just the same.'

'You talk like a parson. I never expected that, for I thought you'd be full of the Devil's words. Has he a son left here or not?'

'Can you see any child?' Aunt Pity poked at the fire. 'Though it's warm outside, it's still cold within until June up here.' As she grumbled, she turned her neck sideways to peer at him, because he was wringing his hands, and peeping around her room. He tried to control himself.

'Maybe you've an infant hidden somewhere. It'd be a terrible fate for the lad if he hasn't been christened.'

'Poor creature!'

Benjamin shouted loudly and angrily, 'I have to learn if I have a grandchild, and whether 'tis a boy or girl, to know where to leave my fortune, you old crow!'

'Poor creature!'

Greave realised that he would not get a better answer. 'Well, if I have no grandson, I know what to do for my heirs!' he shouted and left, hoping that he was leaving in the air a threat menacing enough to prise open Pity's secret. She did follow into the garden. But there she merely sang to her hens.

Benjamin climbed back on to the moor, breathless and annoyed. He trod carelessly. One foot sank into a hollow covered by grass, and his old heart raced from surprise and fright. God help him, there was lying, betrayal, disillusion, disloyalty to th'government and poverty for th'weavers on either hand, whilst even the ground underfoot could not be trusted! What it was to be old and suffer this. If only the Empress of Russia would take more shalloons ...

He sat down on a bank whilst his thumping breast quietened down, and a haze spread across his eyes. As it cleared he saw a viper coiled, small and very neat, upon a stone. It raised its head and slithered, moving daintily as a maiden dressed in her best and going to her first hiring-fair. The glowing yellow underbelly and the dead-leaf back were shifting with eerie silence and smoothness. Benjamin froze, very frightened. The snake raised her delicate striped oval head, sensing with exquisite pleasure and tasting the air with sharp flicks of her tongue. Benjamin knew that he ought to remain still, but he instead panicked and scrambled up the bank. Before he had even raised his arm off the heather, the viper struck, and vanished as if ashamed of what she had done. Benjamin stared at the undignified wriggle disappearing into the heather, as though wishing to call her back, to change her mind and retrieve her poison. Then, seeing his arm already swelling, he sucked and spat but it steadily swelled and became numb.

He rushed to the nearest cottage, which was Elkanah Beanland's. Slithering clumsily in his hurry through mud and stones, Benjamin banged on the door.

'I thought it was robbers coming, Mr Greave! But you're always welcome, man, to sup with me!' Elkanah shouted.

'Find me a horse! I've been bitten by a snake!'

'A snake! You can ride my nag if you like, but the woman yonder's the one to heal you. Go see her, and put your trust in God.'

'I've just come from there, you old fool! You must pray me God's speed to Makings, Elkanah. I cannot go back to Pity's house.'

'Has thou offended her, Mr Greave? Happen the snake was one of her familiars, Mr Greave!'

'Happen so! Stop shouting in my ear! Where's your *horse*, man?'

Elkanah turned his face towards the blank moor, and whistled so that his whole cheek turned blue. An old nag appeared out of a hollow where she had been enjoying the sun. 'Look at her staring at us!' Elkanah shouted. 'She's a tired old girl now, and like me she's none too secure of her legs on *this* earth.' He cupped his hands and yelled, 'Thou'd better hurry up, see! Mr Greave the master's been bitten by a snake!' The mare shook her ears and trotted casually down the slope. 'Come on old lass, you've got the grandest man in this valley to ride on your back, he'll reward you for it, I'm sure . . .'

'I'll give you five pounds if I get home and recover.'

'Nay, I want none of your money, man! Just say a prayer to the Lord for my old horse. Maybe, after all, she'd enjoy being buried decently, something of that sort to send her off. We all want that if we can afford it, don't we, Mr Greave! Let's help you up, Mr Greave! Thou's looking a bit green.'

Benjamin, lopsided and fainting, cantered away on the tired old mare. It seemed to take all afternoon to reach Makings, where he fell into the arms of Patience Helliwell.

(13)

It was a long while before Anne realised that Oliver had left the country. (It was a long time before anyone knew of it.) She did not mind too much that he had struck her, as most men did that to women, but she was resentful of his having run away. Then she forgot it in her longing. During the hazy days of her recovery she would imagine that he was in the next room, or that he must be one of those vague figures at her bedside. She once mistakenly touched Dick Almighty's hand, and realised what she had done when she saw him blush – his round face like a sun setting in water – and felt his desire.

As the autumn advanced, and the woodlands shivered to pieces as if they would never live again, the more she thought: I am recovering, and it is not I that am collapsing, but the world around me.

Although she had rents from the farms, she would not touch them (other than for necessities and to pay the bills of the apothecary) because she felt that they were really Oliver's. She could have had revenues from felling Blood Wood, but she would rather starve than touch the trees. Everyone but Earth and Jenny left Lower Laithes. Whilst Jenny often worried what eventually might become of her, the Negro, who had always been tossed about the world without regard for his wishes, never gave it a thought.

When Anne was well enough to go out, she realised that during her sickness she had travelled rapidly in the direction of old age. Her back had begun to stoop, just like Aunt Pity's, and even if from time to time she remembered to straighten it, yet it soon sank over again. Time however brought no relief from persecution. Children and weavers still shouted after her, 'Jezebel shall be eaten by dogs!' and ''Awthorn, 'awthorn, burn int' fire!'

So she was glad to return to her rooms. Anne's loneliness transformed the appearance of things. Clock, carpet, door, the gowns in her wardrobe, had turned into stubborn strangers full of hostile silence and stillness. She tried to fill the aching freezing space of her mind by staring, staring out, clock, china tea-service or the shoe casing her foot. In her transfixed gaze they retreated, an inch, a yard, and then floated away into mist. She blinked and they snapped back again, leaving her head spinning. She attacked them at last, violently throwing her shoe across the room, and it clattered against the wall. At least it was a sound! But it was like a shriek in a foreign tongue.

She could not think why Oliver did not send a letter to her. Perhaps some tragedy had occurred. But she knew his scrupulousness with language: more likely, she told herself, he was writing and tearing up the pages for lack of some nice poetic phrases. At certain times she visualised him so clearly that she felt sure he must be thinking of her at the same moment – as if his concentration was forcing his image complete across the seas, hills, cities unimaginable to her, and the wide green estates of England, France or wherever he was.

The only love, she knew, that she would ever have. The poor woman would go to her door, sometimes in the night, and stare around pathetically sure that he was approaching out of that blankness muffling her senses – smothering her even on a summer's day, though birds were singing.

Anne sometimes tried to concentrate herself and magic her image to him. The effort tired her and left her with that aching time again, there merely to be filled. She had played the part of a poet's muse for so long that without it she felt no more than an old rag: the muse's dress, tossed aside into a hedge. She was looking more and more like an old witch, too. Her tall frame became gaunt and stooped, her nose hooked, her eyes sunken and sharp.

Her first winter alone arrived. It was a vicious one, and, whilst the young ones frolicked like puppies in the snow, she for the first time suffered that common old-person's meditation that she might not survive this particular season. Gulleys were levelled and outlines thickened with drifts. Objects stood sharp and dark against the sun. Hardly anyone or anything moved, except during the short midday thaw, which was so slight that the melted frost merely hung in still globes and had not time to fall before the cold tightened its grip again. For only an hour each day water trickled out of the drifts. Its runnels wove the fields, then stiffened, and were creased with ice. The ice came into the house, lining the windows, thickening on bowls of standing water, forming a crust on Anne's chamberpot and skimming newly-washed floors. It mocked her, reminding her that she would soon have to leave this place which she could not warm or clean, where she could not pay for servants. The icicles seemed to glitter with grinning faces. The muses tumbling off the ceiling now mocked her – Erato, the naked inspirer of love poetry with her saucy grin, and Melpomene, the darkly-painted lady of tragedy, scowling deeply. 'Know thyself!', carved over the door and growing moss, mocked her. For she did not know where exactly to look for 'herself', only feeling vaguely that it was not in her own breast, but in some unknown foreign place with Oliver.

The true thaw came, but did not change the silence, for it arrived as a moist warm fog, like piles of wool before it is spun. Anne felt even more maddened and imprisoned. She could see nothing, and all she heard was the banging of hammers in the fulling mill. Bang! Bang! The insistent unceasing hammering of trade as if driving nails into nature's coffin.

One Sunday, when no one was at work, Anne told Earth to fetch his spade and hatchet and they went to the fulling mill, finding their way by touch amongst eerily dripping boughs where all was soundless but for the church bell clanging monotonously. (Twenty times, to announce that it was the twentieth day of the month.) The Negro was good at feeling his way. He would go a few yards ahead before he turned, grinning, twirling the spade and hatchet in the air. His look was devilish and frightening, and he was so ragged, with his torn tunic, and only a silver collar to remind of his previous pampered state. But Anne had not allowed fear to rule her life before, and so she advanced boldly. Earth skipped ahead, touching the trees – their moss luminous upon the grey day – until he was almost out of sight, then he waited for her to catch up.

They came to where the stream poured over a weir to drive the hammers of the mill. There was hardly any light in the water and it went over fleshy, grey and thick, like a collier's muscles, and with a sullen pounding at the bottom of the fall before thundering under the building. Anne told Earth to attack the bank of the weir hanging above the wood. The Negro looked horrified. But when Anne began with the hatchet, he laughingly joined her, as if this was the slave-revolt in San Domingo. Earth was tireless, his spade and his muscles one everlasting pendulum.

The sluggish water trickled over the bank. Soon it moved faster, carrying stones and soil tumbling as Earth gladly helped it on its way. It became a cascade, roaring in its escape through the trees, finding a way round the mill, and in at the windows where piles of cloth were waiting for tomorrow to be fulled.

The two conspirators, who could barely understand one another through language, communicated, as they had never done before, with looks directly into one another's faces. Anne held out her arms. They held hands, then danced and skipped round one another on the bank top that was crumbling more and more under the power of the stream. As they returned to Lower Laithes, the Negro chuckled to himself.

On Monday the workmen, finding their wool ruined and no water-power to drive the hammers, at first suspected Loveless and the combers. But Earth's naked footprints were seen leading along the banktop, so men went with dogs to Lower Laithes.

They found the Negro digging in the garden; he was making a stand against the encroachment of weeds, and destroying completely what was now no more than a palimpsest of the ornate borders, in his hope of creating a plot for vegetables. As they gave chase, other men, boys and dogs joined in, leaving their looms thinking that Benjamin Greave, made generous by an unexpected profit, had restored one of the forgotten saints' days. A trumpet and a tin whistle were produced. They were arguing about whether fiddlers and mummers should be called forth, when the Negro ran into a tenter field, ruining the fifteen shilling's worth of drying cloth in which he got tangled and making them forget all else in their fresh anger with him. But when he was cornered, and they had called off the dogs, his captors fell silent: for they had not yet thought what to do with him.

'Let's peg him in the stream, since he has ruined its use for us, and set the dogs on him as they used to wi' beasts – wi' bulls and bears – in grandfather's day!' said Joshua Binns. So two held Earth's arms and pushed him triumphantly through the lanes.

'Yon poor animal's tired, let him be!' an old weaver shouted over a wall.

'Nay, we're having sport as in grandfather's day!' an apprentice answered. And another young man: 'Nay, you'll not be against a bit of sport.' A fresh generation of tormentors was evidently growing up to replace Binns and his friends, who were getting stiff in their limbs.

They took the Negro to a place just above the mill. The water was freezing cold and the weavers could not think how to get into the stream to peg him there. 'Let him go, we've had enough of him now,' one said.

'Are we to be defeated for lack of a bit of invention?' Joshua exclaimed. 'Where's thy spirit? We've always found a way before, we Yorkshire folk!'

To the Negro's waist they tied a rope with two leads, one of which was taken across the stream near a bridge, thus dragging Earth to the middle. Before he could scramble on to the far bank, the other length was used to tether him in mid-current.

The young man's first instinct was to climb on to one of the boulders, and though it was slimy he made progress, fascinating his persecutors with the way in which he gripped with his toes.

Because the water was so cold, the dogs at first merely barked up and down the bank. But eventually one bold rough terrier plunged in and the rest followed. The pack's excitement made the spectators forget the sporting chance they had intended to allow the Negro. Back and forth across the stream, throwing stones, banging drums and blowing trumpets, they built up a competitive frenzy; for the one with the least pity would prove to be the boldest inventor of torments, and so each cultivated pitilessness in himself.

The Negro squatted on a stone, his head tucked into his arms: as a victim he was boring. Whilst the dogs snarled and leaped, he chafed his rope upon the edge of the rock. When he was free he sprang up the far bank, his slender legs working and his ribs beating like a panicking young deer as he disappeared into the trees. The weavers and dogs were too tired to give chase, and no one ever saw Earth again.

For Anne's part in ruining the mill and the wool, Dick Almighty fetched her to the stocks. Considering the sedition, arson and malicious wrecking of manufactories taking place in Yorkshire, it was amazing that he did not make a greater example of her – at least bring her before magistrates, who would remand her to York castle. Lady Well inhabitants might indeed have been delighted by that, enjoying bonfires and fireworks for a week.

As it was, the mild punishment that she received left them wondering who they were more furious with – Anne Wylde or Dick Almighty. There seemed to exist a conspiracy between the victim and the Constable who brought her along the roads. In fact Almighty was actually seen to defend her, as the populace shouted, 'Jezebel's being fetched to the dogs!' and when women, as heartily as men, ripped Anne's petticoat, and plastered mud on her head.

The stocks were in sight of John Wylde's house, which was now inhabited by the Methodist manager of a spinning mill. 'We have seen some changes, you and I, Anne Wylde, but I don't think we've improved things none,' Almighty remarked in a kindly way. His limbs were now almost as stiff as the old oak bars of the stocks, and he panted as he lifted them, replacing them over her with a tenderness that seemed improper coming from a thief-catcher. He might have been a lover placing a coverlet upon his sweetheart.

'It is but the way the weft is shuttled across the warp,' Anne answered, whilst she did what she could do to make herself comfortable.

'I beg your pardon? As always, you talk in riddles and henigmas. You are too clever for us simple people. That is why you have ended up in the stocks.'

Almighty patted his stomach with a gesture of irritation that was familiar to all rogues. He had no patience with mysteries and he punctured those cloudy devils as soon as they were apprehended. But the patting-of-his-stomach was no more than a habit and he did not intend any malice to Anne Wylde by it.

'The warp is what is given in our lives. Call it fate. The weft is what is woven across it by fortune. Every moment – such as this one – is made of the meeting of the two.'

'And how did you come to comprehend the symbols of the first weavers: of Athena, Penelope, Ariadne and Aphrodite?'

'I have had the time for thinking.'

Almighty finished his work and turned the big key in the lock with a gesture of artisan satisfaction which was second nature to him. But afterwards he hesitated, apprehensive of the behaviour of his Lady Well flock during his absence. Though fortunately, because the rain was tearing through the alleys, few people bothered to come out.

'It will not be a long day,' Almighty promised, with a sweetness quite untypical of him. Yes, there was dampness on his eyes. Yet he could think of no further excuse to linger.

Anne, left alone in her soaked rags, with rain running off her matted hair, realised that a stage of her life was finished. She adjusted to becoming just such a beggar and scoundrel of the highways and wastes as she was now shown to be; no more than a poor woman fastened into heavy wooden stocks. Whilst Lady Well looked equally beggared. Before her was the church stripped by a mad parson. Over there was the 'new well', where a few loiterers despite the rain were watching flies, or searching for the blood in the water that would foretell war. In vistas between buildings Anne saw a scattering of burnt farms on the hillsides.

Dick Almighty often returned anxiously to inspect his charge. He excused himself for being solicitous by saying that he was on his way to the apothecary's, whilst the second time he was 'going to meet an informant to illegal brewing'. Both visits, however, followed immediately after shouts and jeers from over-excited spectators. During mid-afternoon Dick released her. He came dragging by the ear a travelling ex-soldier. The Constable told the crowd that the stocks were now needed for this 'villain, scofflaw, miscreant and son of Belial', who, though warned thrice of his offence of lingering in Lady Well, yet had stayed longer than the churchwardens would suffer. Besides, the soldier had a snuff box with the seditious word *Liberty* engraved upon it. This Almighty had pocketed – as evidence. (Incidentally, it was made of silver.) 'Do you not know that in the King's England you can be transported in chains for life and hung after being made to suffer a multitude of torments, for uttering that dread word *Liberty*?' he bellowed at his victim, as much to frighten the folk of Lady Well into giving up any republican objects made of silver and gold that they might possess, as for the soldier's benefit.

Almighty let Anne go, with that same desiring gentle touch that he had shown once at her bedside. Then, in case his sentiment was observed by some malicious observer as sharp-eyed as himself, he compensated for it by threatening the 'sinning pole-cat of a soldier' with a whipping before he left town. Jangling the keys of the stocks and the lock-up, Dick guarded Anne safely out of Lady Well. Yet, uniquely for him, he said nothing all the way. When she had passed quarter of a mile beyond the boundary she turned and saw him watching her. She waved, and he returned it, still solemn and thoughtful.

Almighty that very evening sent around his servant-boy to call together at his inn the most powerful body in Lady Well, the *Society For Prosecuting Felons*. He placed the deeds of the Adam and Eve and of all his other properties on the table, and instructed the company to scrutinise them most carefully. Moreover, he provided them with the first round of ale free of charge. 'Gentlemen,' he announced, 'I have spent too many long, painful, sad years as a widower. I am therefore in immediate want of a real, good, handsome prime wife, and any single woman possessed of attractive charms wishing to better her condition is bound to consider my offer a most advantageous one. For her only duty in addition to the usual affectionate ones, will be to give directions to servants – as I have no children. Now sup your beer, gentlemen, and think on it, before you decide what you shall do.'

After they had lingered awhile to see whether Dick Almighty was offering a second round of free ale and decided that he was not going to do so, Joshua Binns rose and answered, 'I think I speak for the whole company of us when I say that should you, Mr Whitely, meet with a spouse as beautiful as the Goddess Diana, who may bring you children as the vine bringeth forth grapes ...'

'What, at his age?'

'He might get Anne Wylde!' Jabez Stott sniggered.

Binns continued '... Your possessions, real, personal, and funded in a proper bank, as well as in other places that some of us know of, are sufficiently ample for the support o't'same, as appears from th'papers and deeds you have so honestly and in keeping with your genial, upright, God-fearing, righteous, law-abiding character placed afore us.' The weaver cast his shrewd narrow eyes over his confederates. 'I therefore move that we, the Gentlemen of the Society For Prosecuting Felons, print and publish advertisements for Mr Whitely's benefit and that we all contribute to th'expense, as a mark of our esteem for our beloved Constable, innkeeper and sin-catcher ...'

'As amanuensis to the Society I move that I herewith draft it!' interrupted Jabez Stott, who was impatient to exert an influence. 'In fact I've already noted a wording, on a piece of paper.' He paused to receive the agreement and congratulations of the Society. But it was not forthcoming because being Yorkshiremen they wanted to see some substance in the gesture before offering praise. So Jabez continued, 'After Mr Whitely's words, as already expressed to us, it runs thus: "Private personal application is requested to be made and none but such as can give testimonials of a virtuous highly respectable character need apply. Time of application to last until he, Dick Whitely, be suited." How's that? I am used to penning advertisements for my master.' Now that he had got his speech out, Jabez was nervous and baffled.

'Put in that I'll be at home every Monday.' Dick Almighty patted his stomach, this time affably and beamed with satisfaction. He had saved himself perhaps three shillings in expenses for printing and advertisements and he had received the renewal of their acclamations. 'Well, gentlemen,' he wittily, God-fearingly and uprightly concluded, 'I owe no person anything but *love*, and I warrant I'll keep open house the day I am married!'

After her release, Anne planned to move into a cottage. Though poor she still decided not to sell any of the fine things in Lower Laithes, wanting all to remain as Oliver had left it, for when he returned. She took only some fine linen for her bed. Anne and Jenny covered the furniture and fastened the shutters. Paint flaked from the muses, who were still unpaid for. Damp rose up and mildewed the classical legs of escritoires and tables. A small bird had got in through a broken window and died; it was so weightless that a slight draught from an opened door blew it across the floor. Behind the two women, moving through the house, shade lapped the rooms, window by shut window, a tide of darkness, until only a few chinks of light stabbed the bared breast of an antique figure, or a honey-coloured piece of stone.

Anne gave Jenny a guinea, which was all she could afford, and made up the rest of her wages with gifts; a heavy shawl, a bundle containing whinberry and blackberry jam, oatmeal cakes, and a flask of rum. The women, now so equal, parted in the weed-filled garden. Spring was in spate. Birds sang freely, whereas for so many months only their sharp alarm calls had cut the misty silence. Over the hills, the weavers and the wild animals were moving about happily, free of ice and starvation. A soapy froth of bright new green was incandescent upon field, moor and trees, and the dew glittered like church glass.

Anne attempted to embrace Jenny. But even at this tender moment, her servant kept some distance from her. Anne first thought that it was out of respect. Then she realised it was because her breath was no longer sweet.

Anne went to a cottage on the top-side of Blood Wood. Walls fended off the moor and its predatory creatures from her poultry, herbs and vegetables. It was not the poorest type of cot, but it was simple. The ground floor was paved and there were ample passage-ways, a covered well in the kitchen, two bedrooms with floors of oak planks, and on one wall she placed the brown painting of the men who had filled in the well. A thing that she especially liked at this place, in contrast to Lower Laithes, was that the animals and poultry wandered close around it, so their scents mingled with those of herbs and wild flowers.

Jenny instinctively made towards Lady Well, where there were walls to shelter her, and where someone might take her in as a servant. She actually had work in Dick Almighty's Adam and Eve in mind, when she saw pinned on the door a copy of his advertisement. She asked a passing tradesman to read it to her. Circumspectly, Jenny did not rush in. Instead she sat in the graveyard to think up a plan of campaign. When she had considered for a quarter of an hour she went to the apothecary. 'You want a rubbing bottle?' he asked her. No; she risked most of Anne Wylde's guinea on a comb, a little mirror, and some cosmetics. She took these back to the churchyard and propped up the mirror. But what could *she* do to beautify herself? She had never thought of such a thing since she was a child, and at Lower Laithes where mirrors were available she had hardly ever bothered to look into one because it always disheartened her. Nor could she expect to charm a man with her speech.

But she would not need a clever tongue with Mr Whitely, she realised, for he would do all the talking. He was as powerful a man as any woman could wish for, and if she *could* win him, she would be as obedient a wife as any man could want, and his most faithful servant even though he did not ask for that. On the other hand, if it was as Mr Almighty said and she could be more than servant and live like Anne Wylde...! After a while, Jenny plucked up her courage, arranged her shawl as she had often seen Anne do, and went to knock on one of the rear doors of the inn.

Anne soon grew into one of those mysterious women, like her own Aunt Pity, who appear to give all their love to the plants in their garden, and to their hens. By the age of thirty she had turned into an 'old crone'. The skin receded from her bones. Like her Aunt Pity's it had few wrinkles, but as it pulled tight it made her features even sharper. Her eyes seemed brighter, her lips became more prominent, and the movements of her limbs more gaunt. She formed a habit of walking outside her house, even in night or fog, as if in a daze, staring at nothing, not recognising, thinking of no one knew what. She stayed alone, until she found two foxcubs deserted by their mother and, with that tenderness for vulnerable wild creatures that had typified her when she was a child, she raised them as her companions.

Oliver still did not return. Why did he not come back to Yorkshire? At thirty-five when, people thought, she should be ashamed of her desires, Anne was nevertheless longing for her lover's touches.

On better days, as the age of forty approached, she would peep at some old weaver, disturbing him once again with a return of the power she once had over his sleepless nights; and he might smile back, foolish in his years, blush, and talk.

Anne would not go into a manufactory. She would rather work with the gangs of labouring women. (She had no weaver menfolk for whom she could spin.) They gathered stones out of the enclosures. They scared birds. They weeded crops, sacks over their shoulders to absorb the rain. The men who employed Anne looked now not at her beauty, but at her hands to see if she was used to work, and at her shoulders to observe whether she could bear loads. They were no longer shy of her face; instead they stared with indifference or distaste at this old person, afraid that she might call on them for assistance. Anne found no joy in looking at herself, either. But thankfully, month by month her increasingly bowed back made her less able to peer into her mirror, and gave her no encouragement to hang her glass upon a lower nail. She had become like Aunt Pity who had passed away, how long since? – it was after Peter escaped and fled.

Anne was reduced to going to the slaughterhouse gate for blood to make puddings. Around her the flock of poor women (all belonging to Lady Well, all known to her, and many of whom had once served her) squabbled like starlings, with harsh voices and elbows sharp as beaks as they fought to get in when the gates were periodically opened for them to scoop up the blood running from the hanging beasts. The fights amused the butchers, which was why they locked the gates and only opened them for short periods.

Sometimes they would have sport at the expense of one of their apprentices or cattle-boys, by sending him to face the roaring flood of women. One day, these massed, bloody gorgons were laughing at the mincing, timid footsteps of a youth at his first day's work and Anne recognised Michael Loveless. His words when she had gone to collect Jenny, years ago, rang through her mind: '*I know someone who ate meat last Quarter Day.*' The terrified lad inserted his key into the lock and the women mimicked it obscenely.

'That must be the black milk of a witch still on thy lip, for it cannot be a moustache!' Esther Kershaw shouted.

Anne was wracked by her desire to protect him, yet was too weak to do anything. Then a huge old woman, with a scarf hiding her skull and a smile upon her pox-marked face, stepped forward and lifted the boy into the air. It was Mary Pickles. Michael thought that the hungry monster was going to gnaw the flesh off his bones or throw him to the oxen, but soon he realised the tenderness of her touch. As he relaxed, high above the raging females, the savage terrified animals and the rivers of blood, he began to cry, not now from fear but from nostalgia for long-forgotten tender womanhood.

Fortunately the men could not see him, and the women took no notice as they rushed past to the blood. Mary Pickles put the lad down and he ran away.

A few months later he was transported to Van Diemen's land for setting fire to spinning mills.

Anne stayed by the gate, where her eyes met those of Mary Pickles. 'My fine house is no use to me any more,' Anne said, and then (not wanting to talk about the past), 'How do you make your puddings?' When Mary described her method, Anne shook her head. 'Pour your oatmeal into the blood when it is warm,' she told Mary. 'Together with salt, eggs, and cream if you have some, adding marjoram and thyme, and then put beef suet in by the handful.'

Thus the two made friends. Mary was invited to Anne's cottage to collect marjoram, and they talked until the stars were out – the four eyes of the foxes glinting under the sofa. (A place they would not leave until the visitor departed; when, with turns and timid hesitations, they frolicked around their mistress.)

In a few more years, Anne was to be found every afternoon climbing the barrow on Raven's Hill, to stare in the London direction and see if Oliver was coming. She went there so often that the lane came to be called Fox Lane because of her two animals gliding and scurrying through the laneside gorse.

She began this habit after one occasion of extraordinary irrational certainty that her lover was arriving. So she had hurried up the barrow and started southwards, her eyes screwed up (for she could not see well any more) until darkness came.

The next midday, disturbed, she found herself walking several times around her cottage; one moment hesitant and the next feeling compelled to rush to some bush or tree as if Oliver might be behind it, until eventually she felt assured that she *would*, this time, find him from the mound. She stared so keenly into the distance that her eyes ached. Yet if for a moment her glance strayed elsewhere she soon switched her attention guiltily back to the horizon. She might have missed him in that one moment when her glance was absent! Day after day she suffered pangs of hope and disappointment. Sometimes she raced downhill to greet a mere stranger, who decided that she must be the local madwoman.

She could not bear to leave the hill before darkness fell: the lean half-blind old woman with the foxes. Lingering where there was naught but rock, gorse and heather, a wistful look on her face and about her bearing, she frightened and disturbed many a traveller who came upon her by surprise. At all times before her imagination, when at work amongst the stones of the fields or in her bed, was her vision of this one road – the boulders softly eroded like bales of raw wool, the rough herbage, the changing birds and flowers of the seasons, the Clay Slack Chapel over there, and, under her, the barrow where the ancient people also went to meet their dead.

One day on her way to Raven's Hill Anne saw that workmen were taking down Making Hall. They would not talk to an old woman, for they were too busy, or too dusty and wanting to get to an alehouse. But at last a man of her own age was troubled by a memory of something in that tallow-coloured flesh of hers, working upon her frame like the strings of a rickety loom, and he exclaimed, 'Anne Wylde! Well, well! What a dance *you* have led us through your life!'

Anne anxiously pulled at the joints of her fingers, in which she now suffered arthritis. 'That is all over now. Tell me, what is happening to Makings? It is Oliver Greave's property.'

'Nay, lass, it is Horsfall who has bested since the Old Man wove himself to th'far end. You must talk to Horsfall about it.'

The mason's eyes turned inwards, sadly. 'Betty Greave died, Benjamin left her everything, but failing any issue of her body, then all to Horsfall who is building a mansion in the new style, out of the stone. He is a powerful man now is Mr Horsfall, for he has friends in London, and, they say, all over the world. Greave never even got his own tomb made because he left it in the charge of Horsfall, and died sudden. You shouldn't be such a recluse, you should fight and then thou'd know what everyone else knows. Lawyers have done this work, I suppose! As Saint Luke says, "Woe unto ye lawyers, for they mak' only trouble with their wills." There was a man in Lady Well once left nothing but two worn suits to three sons. There has been some cackling in Hell over that legacy, too, I fancy . . .

'Do you want a reminder of the old place?' the mason added. 'Come with me.' He led her through the rubble. 'It's just a carving done by someone in the old days, I thought myself that maybe it was from the hand of old John Wylde.' He put into her hands the sculpture of Perseus slaying Medusa which had once been fixed over the porch.

Anne took the carving to her cottage and placed it over the mantelpiece. The place was full of mementos. Oliver's tobacco tin, still holding a few dusty bits of tobacco just as he had left it; a piece of door-lintel carved by her father; some bits of jewellery that she never wore.

She went outside to prowl and poke thoughtfully around her garden. It was spring and the primroses were breaking forth. As she prodded her fingers in the moist earth, piled it up to keep them comfortable, or removed little grass-plants, she muttered to her flowers, and to her foxes. These two darted and leaped around her, never still. 'Has tha' got fleas, then?' Anne used to say to them, so often that, she reflected, if they had been humans they would have been bored by her. Perhaps it was a good job that she had little human company!

217

Her first sign of a person approaching was when first one, then the other, fox stiffened and vanished into the banks and undergrowth. It was a long while before Anne heard or saw anything. Yet she too felt apprehensive. She had a habit of fearing who might be coming for her, although she had now been left in peace for years.

Jenny was approaching down the road. Anne's one-time maidservant was dressed in fine clothes, though a little bedraggled, and she was a good deal plumper than she used to be. But Jenny was crying. She could say nothing; she merely blubbered and mumbled. All that could be got out of her was that she wanted Anne to accompany her to Lady Well.

The two women, taking short cuts across enclosures, walked there in an hour. Jenny snivelled the whole way and Anne realised it was useless asking questions.

Before the Adam and Eve, Dick Almighty stood upon an empty barrel. Workmen, directed by bailiffs, were removing the inn's contents and piling them into a cart, whilst Dick Almighty harangued a crowd that had gathered. He saw Jenny and Anne at the back of it, but it made no difference to what he had to say, though his confidence was diminished a little.

'Gentlemen!' (There were many ladies present also, but Dick took no account of that.) 'I have made the first mistake of my long life! And I have been ruined by it – by that and by my generous disposition towards our native poor, of which you all have knowledge and have perhaps benefitted. As you all know I took a woman into my house and bed, to be my wife. I gave her love and all else besides, and now I have been ruined by it. For Jenny who seemed so meek and well-suited, turned into a veritable harridan! A strumpet, a Jezebel, a Messalina and Delilah rolled into one, a wanton hetaera, a lascivious wastrel!' His voice rose as he cried over the heads of the crowd, to the hills. 'Whatever possessions she has not forced me to sell to pay for her excesses, she has smashed in her rages! It is as if she has been waiting for *me*, her poor victim, for the whole of her life! I frankly admit that she has ruined me, and so we are both turned out of doors to beg.'

Jenny cried quietly to Anne, 'He struggled for hours upon hours to bring himself up. He used his hands until he was sore, and was puffing and blowing. But no matter how he went at it nor what I did to entice him, Dick Almighty could work up nothing bigger than a baby's finger!'

Anne was about to laugh. But Jenny gave out a loud and tragic cry – the first time in her life that she had ever raised her voice: 'All I ever wanted was a strong and manly husband!'

(14)

Anne Wylde, Mary Pickles, Esther Kershaw, Jenny Loveless and others were working in one of Horsfall's enclosures. They were carrying stones from the field to its outer edge – jagged rocks used only for the foundations of the dressed-stone walls that were now more and more cast like intricate lace over the Yorkshire hillsides. The rough edges cut the women's hands. The gang was paid according to how much they shifted. Fools to themselves, each woman tried to prove that she was the strongest and fastest. Anne, Mary and Jenny – three friends – stayed aloof, which often led to fights with the others. Bitter, foolish battles in which, rather than exchange blows, clothes and hair were torn. Tiredness made their heads reel and clogged their brains. They were absorbed by the work's rhythm, tugging out the boulders and carrying them along the web of tracks.

It was autumn. Silver mists lay, became frayed into long strands, floated upwards, and vanished as the mornings wore on. The woods were shivering to pieces. Dewy blackberries and whinberries were ripening on the banks and hedgerows, hanging close to their mouths, beckoning them as they came to their work. The air glittered with winged and wandering seeds. Sometimes there was a light but threatening frost in the mornings; soon they might, after all, be well advised to search for work in a spinning mill.

Anne looked knowingly at one newly-erected manufactory to which, no matter what happened to her, she would never go. It was Horsfall's. It had lewd statues of naked women in 'the antique style' around its portals, and above them a motto in Latin that few could understand – *Labor Omnia Vincit* (a corruption which had been suggested by Doubtfire of *Amor Omnia Vincit*). On the roof was a clock-tower – a gift making it unnecessary for anyone in Lady Well to own a clock, and also benefiting Horsfall because it reminded everyone that time and duty, especially the duty to arrive at his spinning mill, was of primary importance. At the foot of the tower was the workers' entrance, where was placed a large Bible of which the foreman turned a fresh page every day. The canal in which so many had invested, hoping for a great highway linking Yorkshire with Lancashire, stopped there at the mill. For though Horsfall had encouraged the use of his land for 'the cut', when it reached his own building he unexpectedly refused to allow it to go further; so the only revenue available to the canal company was in transporting coal to Horsfall's, and his products away from it, on the Captain's own terms.

The women saw men in ragged soldiers'-jackets coming over the hilltop. They had scars or dirty bandages, and some were limping or on crutches. To help them face the women they were drunk, and though not hurrying were sufficiently menacing to cause the more alert and suspicious females to keep hold of their stones.

The men lined up by the largest piles on the field's edge, and repeated loudly what they had been saying over and over again for many hours in a hush-house. 'We soldiers have fought for you in France or Spain, and now we need our work back. 'Tis only fair, because you can go to the spinning mill!'

'All guilty rogues should be whipped!' sang out Anne's own son, Peter. Though they did not recognise one another, and he now called himself 'Jonas Pity'. He was tall, like Anne, but neither beautiful nor kind, and a bully. After escaping from the shed he had worked for a farmer, excelling at killing, butchering and being cruel to animals. He was soon drifting about the moors, joining but soon leaving various gangs, and sometimes when he was drunk boasting that he was descended from Benjamin Greave of Making Hall – a rumour that he himself did not believe when he was sober. After falling for the wiles of a recruiting sergeant 'Jonas Pity' discovered that he would pine away with homesickness within a week of being away from Lady Well, whereupon he deserted and returned to the hills that he loved, determined never to leave them again. His deepest philosophy, often quoted by him, was, 'All guilty rogues should be whipped.' He went about mostly with two dogs (descendants of Aunt Pity's), which were so large and fierce that everyone guessed his reason for having them was because he believed he had enemies; these animals were the only ones to which he was kind.

The women appeared to be short of an answer, yet the men were waiting for one. Eventually Esther taunted them, 'Thou's never been a soldier, Jabez Stott, for you couldn't bear the slaughter!' whereupon a stone was thrown at her. Mary Pickles flung one back, and a battle began with the men returning a hail of rocks from the pile that the women had taken a morning to lift painfully out of the enclosure.

'Let 'em lie and we'll pick them up for you!' Jabez shouted. He had been such a fine looking man, a virgin bloom upon his skin, until he followed the army, and now his teeth were broken in a vicious leer.

The women took to their heels. But Anne Wylde stayed. If a stone had struck her head, she would not have minded; but it is such that the stones always avoid. She let the poor laughing soldiers and her unrecognised son's dogs surround her. Then they did not know what to do with her, for she looked so old that she roused only compassion. She walked off slowly leaving them 'triumphant' in the field, herself beyond caring what she would now do for bread.

All the other women, like mice seeking their holes or stores of seeds, had scattered towards what comforts they could hope for, or even half-hopelessly imagine. Mary Pickles went to the Cloth Hall to hire herself for carrying bales on her shoulders across the countryside. Jenny Loveless entered the poorhouse – it was better to be imprisoned than to starve through another winter.

(She would not return home: she had tried that once before. 'The worst of daughters is, they always come back,' Jack Loveless had remarked in his dry, philosophical manner – he did not mean to be cruel. It had been on her mind to retort, 'Michael will for sure not come back, for he has been transported!' But she said nothing. She had shouted out once before in her life, when the bailiffs had removed Dick Almighty's goods, and it had only brought the culminating humiliation to one who, after all, had been kind to her. Although Jenny had not yet even got her bundle over the doorstep, she turned away, and her father was just too slow in expressing his regret. He did not utter another word until she had turned the corner, by which time she had hardened her heart, so that when he chased after her she would not speak to him.)

When Jenny reached the poorhouse she saw husbands and wives being separated in tears and for ever on the doorstep of old age. But she herself was one of the lucky ones. For Jenny met there a man who was adept at breaking or shaping all human laws and regulations: her husband, Dick Almighty! He was so thrilled at their being reunited that his confidence and skill in manipulating worldly affairs magically returned. He not only broke the rule that kept the sexes apart, and slept with her for comfort and warmth that night and subsequently on all others: he also arranged a welcoming dinner.

That very day he wrote a letter to the Society For Prosecuting Felons.

'Sirs! Last night I dreamed that you sent me a small parcel containing plum pudding, apples from what as you know used to be my own orchard, some game fairly paid for and not poached, and two trouts even though these be very rare now in our native streams. For a long time my inflamed and sorry eyes have been a stranger to sleep. I now desire an increase in my growing faith in human kindness by sending a little of the above which will prove that dreams come to pass as they did in former times. Your attention to these broken hints will much oblige your poor afflicted pauper, in truth, Dick Whitely.'

After Jenny had been in the workhouse for a few months, reconciled and happy with her husband whom, she at last realised, she could trust to be her protector, her secret little nest of happiness was brutally destroyed, as callously as the shelters of robins and thrushes are by bird-nesting boys. For the master pressed her into signing indentures to work for five years in a spinning manufactory; and Dick Whitely, with innocent hope and trust in the benevolence of The Coming Age, let her go, thinking her youth more important than the comfort of his own declining years.

After the battle with the soldiers, Esther Kershaw, like an escaped hare, went straight to the moors. As a hare makes its form in the grass, so she had learnt to contrive comfort out of turf-stacks, abandoned, unfinished or burnt buildings, peat-gulleys and the leesides of walls, of flocks of sheep or of cattle. A rain-stained Bible was her companion, and for amusement she read the signs of the wind, sky, flowers, berries and shifting flocks of birds. With these aids she prophesied everything, from a hard winter, or the burning of a mill, to the Second Coming. She instinctively turned every day towards the weak midday sun, to store warmth in her cheeks for the approaching winter, or for energy to survive the Apocalypse. Unlike other travellers she never varied her pace, since she was without appointments. She walked something between slowly and quickly. She was weighed down with all her possessions, either worn or carried upon her back. Esther only bothered to move at all in order to stop her limbs locking together, and to convince herself that her life was not without purpose. Though she set off in a direct line southwards, it would always eventually (sometimes after months) become a circle, usually turning westwards after the sun, thus bringing her back to Lady Well – where she never stayed for very long, being saddened because the Baptists had built a chapel over the well to stop its use by 'pagans'. At first Esther had followed the rivers. But now that manufactories had been built along them, the way was so sulphurous, dangerous and churned with mud, and the watercourses so unfit to drink or to bathe in, that she kept to the moortops for as long as she could find whinberries or trout, and could lay nooses of animal-gut to catch rabbits and hares.

But she survived mainly by being encased in the shell of her preaching, for which people gave her food, shelter or money. She took up her stations at busy cross-roads, holding her Bible open at Revelations – not to read from it, for she knew her texts by heart, but because to have a book in her hands made her feel like an educated preacher rather than a vagrant. She told the weavers and merchants who were hurrying by before winter came on that her husband, too, had like themselves been storing up goods and credit as if for more than his earthly stay; but to what fires had it led him?

With the wooden emphasis of all those certain that they have been Elected or Saved, Esther shouted that *she* was the one who had uncovered the pure springs of Christ, and had encountered the great succouring White Cow, even if only in dreams.

Why did Oliver Greave procrastinate for so many years? Was it simply because of his indecisive nature? Or was his long-damned instinct to follow his wanderlust so strong as to overcome even his love? Oh, how can anything except his muse comprehend a poet's will! Or so Oliver Greave excused himself.

Sometimes he missed boats as if he had actually contrived to do so. At other times he allowed wars and skirmishes to intervene – or imagined that they did. The complications of Horsfall's business caused Oliver to wait, in which period there would develop, as if by malign influence, further difficulties that demanded to be resolved before his return. Sometimes (it must be confessed) a lady delayed him. For he could not live without a female body warm against him, even though it did not offer true love. At such times the ache of Anne Wylde's absence momentarily receded. The act of love linked his hidden and his conscious worlds. Without it Oliver would never have known what strange ambiguous forces lay within him, rushing upwards out of deep pools; his inner being was a theatre for mad, hidden gods, who emerged at his copulations. Also, as he grew older his hair vanished, his stomach sagged and his windiness increased, so he developed scares for his virility and had to prove himself.

For a multiplicity of reasons, without ever trying to correct what he was doing, Oliver allowed women, wars, misunderstood departure times, floods, storms, business, drunken stupors, revolutions, even the guilt of his own impotence in this matter, to cut off his daily-renewed ambitions to return to Yorkshire.

All over Europe he stumbled into revolutions, or the intentions for them. He remembered what Loveless had told him in Yorkshire about finding the true muse for the times in such causes. Yet their energy baffled as well as intrigued him, in his own queer state of doing practically nothing to improve upon his fate. In revolution was there embodied a rational ideal, its hour come round at last? Or, on the contrary, a bursting out of instinct?

He drifted across land and sea finding a fresh delight in travelling without baggage, friends, family, or the encumbrances of loyalties. On many a dusk when he passed by lit windows where families were settling to meals, or to playing cards, or to musical entertainments, and when he was inclined to be sad and sorry for himself as he sought brief shelter under a bush or the lea of a rock, and in a strange place, he fought his mood by reminding himself of the advantages of his state. He enjoyed a necessarily keen sense of the whole world around him, and he was rewarded with an independent, naked, fresh, innocent watchfulness. He realised too that the whole of mankind similarly was discovering a new and naked identity. Everywhere man was breaking out of old enclosures, in politics, in philosophy, in religion; whilst as a poet he happily observed here and there the common man's language being freed into literature (Tim Bobbin's dream). He even saw his own Nature Muse make her entrance into poetry.

Yet, paradoxically, the more keenly Oliver appreciated Nature, the more horribly he was haunted by a feeling that She had departed. He would dash here and there – from bush, to meadow, to the edge of the sea – staring fascinated at some beautiful thing that filled him with *despair*. Beauty was a chimera. If one touched it (as he often did – leaves, fruit or flowers), the loveliness was damaged even by one's own gentle hands. To comprehend beauty was dangerous and frightening. He felt he was at the edge of a terrible ocean in which he might be drowned and torn to pieces.

In this mood he journeyed as far south as Greece, just as he had always longed to do. There he found the real sun, that had for so many years burned and glowed as a dream in his northern belly. Now it was hung in a hot, featureless cage of light. There was a sky of such fierce blue as he had never before experienced, either in pigment or glass; he felt that if he hit it, it would clang like a steel shield.

Oliver Greave, this man of complicated thoughts, appeared amongst the Turks, and the Greeks whom they enslaved, merely as a typical English traveller. In his blue worsted coat and his three-cornered hat he stood back from things with a peculiar mixture of shyness and arrogance, yet doing no harm, not cheating or robbing anyone, and interested mainly in comfortable beds, the times of ships, and in ruins. Hesitating on quaysides or in confusing and brutal markets, and amongst broken temples, he had always Pausanias, his ancient guide to Greece, in his pocket. But time and again he was disappointed. He so rarely found the glittering erections to Demeter or Athena, Zeus or Apollo. Instead he saw perilously collapsing piles being quarried to build mosques, Christian churches and houses. The 'greatest civilisation ever known to man', had been reduced to sterile stones in a land that had now lost its oak groves and its rivers of classical times, and was white and dry as a sun-bleached prehistoric skull: the shelter of vipers, kites and spiders. Whilst the Greeks cared nothing about their ancient past but were, like the rest of Europe, interested in revolution, freedom, and a 'rational' future.

Oliver, even before his beloved monuments, could still feel Anne Wylde all over his skin. So eventually, eventually, he *did* return to Yorkshire along the roads from the south. He now saw his past life, indeed the whole of his own materialistic age, as if it was one of those dreams that are unintelligible in the moment that you awake from them but become steadily clearer in meaning. He felt that he was only waiting for some clarity that was hiding round a corner (as his muse had once seemed to do) to jump out and replace the confusion.

When at last he reached England it seemed so *green* – it was as if nature conspired to create a cheerful harmony for his homecoming. Until he reached his native valleys in the north, and what a foul mess he saw there! Smoke was rising from a chaos of spinning mills and cloth manufactories. The hills were darker. They were glowering like damp cinders, as if spring would never come to them again. When he drank at streams whose waters had delighted him in boyhood, they tasted of soot. *Reason* had not stopped the ruin of nature! Hanging dramatically upon the hillsides above the manufactories were Methodist and Baptist chapels ostentatiously elbowing out of the way the older, smaller, simpler Congregationalist and Quaker places of worship. One was on the site of a cock-pit, one was where an ancient cross had been, another where had grown a thorn tree 'from the time of Christ', whilst several of the Baptists' churches were built over famous springs so as to make sure that never again could these places evoke their ancient mysteries. At the foot of every steep village was a manufactory, houses crowded in its shadow, and at the crown of the streets was a chapel – so that now the community hung between a symbol of earth or work and of God in His sky.

Only the narrow packhorse-road over the moors was the same, busy with traders scurrying to the rear door of Horsfall's new mansion just as they had once hurried to Makings. Their weaving was still piled over the backs of bandy-legged ponies, even though yet vaster quantities of the new trade was transported in large carts, or by canal barge. Here was the clothier's true symbol: a pony crippled with the weight of sin that God had laid upon his back, just as he loaded an animal with wool! This was the price, for all, of prosperity for some.

At dusk Oliver came across a mad scrawny woman preaching at a crossroads, where laughing merchants made wide sweeps to pass her by. 'As birds perched upon a winter tree all face the same way, backs to the wind so's it'll not ruffle their feathers, so you men of this Age flock all in the same direction, wanting not to be ruffled by the unpleasant blasts of Truth!' Esther Kershaw screeched.

Though no one else listened to her, she did think that she had 'pinned her cross' through the heart of the bowed, prematurely aged stranger paused before her; that she had transfigured and transfixed him, just as the Great Preachers did, John Wesley, William Grimshaw of Yorkshire and Saint Paul.

But then he smiled at her, which made her irrationally angry. So she spluttered and abused him with words from *Revelations*. The stranger laughed even more and Esther grew more angry.

'I am Oliver Greave, Esther!' he interrupted.

She stopped in amazement. 'Risen from the dead! And did you find the Original Paradise on your travels?'

Oliver shook his head.

'You were looking in the wrong places,' Esther said. 'You will find the First Garden not in Africa, not in the Americas, not in the South Seas, but only in your own heart, when all is peace there because you are true to yourself. Then you will always take Paradise with you . . .' She paused. 'Oliver Greave, Mistress Anne has been driven off by soldiers . . .' Esther flushed and was silenced by the realisation that she could not possibly tell all, and she did not know where to begin. Then she started to tumble over her words. 'She keeps two foxes and has grown terrible strange. She has a cottage yonder down by the rocks, along the stream course, you'll find it by the fruit trees in the garden . . .'

Oliver would not stay for any more preaching.

Esther watched him depart. She saw in his back, and in the still-cocky way that he swayed his shoulders, just a ghost of the young poet who had delighted the taverns, and been so wayward. It was as if a faint, invisible flame was still burning there.

After she had reflected for a few moments, Esther thought that she had better forewarn Anne. She packed up her Bible and hurried by a short cut across the flank of the moor.

Though the sun had just set, yet miraculously it appeared to be rising again in the east! Esther saw a glorious rosy light flickering upon the landscape. A sunrise such as she had never witnessed before: the whole eastern sky was in beautifully formed crimson and purple feathers, or maybe like tiny sea-shells, rising out of Lady Well. Instantly she saw the 'meaning' of it. This was from the marriage of Christ with the virgin Anne Wylde, which was spreading cascades of blood as described in Revelations!

So it was not after all true, then, the rumour that Oliver and Anne had been in wedlock! – for otherwise there would be no hymen to burst in clouds of blood. But now Greave would be too late to find a bride, for she was married to Heaven!

Esther hurried to Anne's cottage not knowing what amazement to expect.

From his house Doubtfire watched the flames of his burning church, and he waited for the Inevitable. Soon people were running back and forth, outlined against the Fire like wiry black flies squirming in Pain. Miserable, ignorant Creatures! It was as if the Lord held them with Tweezers and was dipping them in the flames of Hell. They had brought out a fire-machine (patented, but imitated and built nevertheless in a workshop opened by Jabez Stott). It was a long wooden box improvised out of a surplus coffin (for its intended occupant had unexpectedly recovered from typhus fever), already lead-lined so that it would hold water and with a force-pump attached, leading to a copper pipe. The six strongest men of the town were furiously working it, the motions of their limbs like tentacles of the ineffective machine. Others were bringing buckets of water from the fortunately proximate well, inside the Baptists' Chapel. Perhaps the well would now save the church?

'What must it be like to wake in Hell?' Doubtfire calmly wondered. Death, he thought, was no more than a preliminary Sleep to it, containing nothing worse than Nightmares. But when the Parson of Lady Well woke in Hell, his Thoughts could not be a sweet gratitude that his Bad Dreams were over. Waking must be so Horrible that one's first Longing would be to retreat into that Nightmare which one had just escaped. And there would be a realisation that this was for Eternity and without return. Also, even in the most Horrible Dream there is no *physical* Pain, unless perhaps a Discomfort of the bed: a cold draught about the head that makes one dream of snow, or thirstiness that puts one in mind of fruit. Hell must have real Pains, Fetters and Cramps, for which dreams do not console. Perhaps the whole skin would be too sore to touch.

By whom? Doubtfire remembered Demons. They would have green faces, and smiles. Their smiles would be the most Unfortunate thing about them. They would be the once-loved ones, Mocking; though Doubtfire thankfully had no person to love him. But one would be

Mocked also because out of reach of what one loved – the scent of bluebells, that tall strange girl Anne Wylde, brandy, or a Congregation swayed.

His once-submissive congregation had now turned into a swarm of enemies shouting, '*Doubtfire!*' against the crashing slates and timbers. The evidence of someone who had caught him with his tinder and flint, and moreover had actually believed the evidence of his eyes, (for years people had surprised the parson near a burning building, but had suspected him of nothing other than of being custodial) had been passed around Lady Well. They gathered near his door, and three of the Society For Prosecuting Felons came forward, one of them being the magistrate, Nicholas Horsfall. They were bound to take him to Bedlam, and yet it was they who were apprehensive, because it was so rare for them to have to arrest one of their own class.

Doubtfire enjoyed letting them batter for a while on his door. At last he let them in. He was calm, as he had not been for many years, even in his own church. They entered his room, still decorated with its skulls, draped urns, books of devotion, mementi-mori, and cruel steel-engravings of martyrdoms. Everything in Doubtfire's religion had to do with death; whilst the scalpels, microscopes and other instruments of his vocation lay amongst the partially dismembered corpses of animals and birds.

The Parson first became truly afraid when he was taken away in a common cart which smelled of manure, the rough wood giving him splinters: and yet also it could be thought of as some kind of pulpit that jerked and rocked him to Hell. 'Why are you not all a-bed! Get back to your wives!' Doubtfire shouted.

The dark outline of the church crumpled. Its walls swelled and it collapsed in flames that scorched his eyes. Its 'vainly coloured glasses' and its 'idolatrous statues' were finally done for! He saw revealed, like the core of a broken fruit, the firelit rose-coloured remnants of Benjamin Greave's unfinished tomb. Also some kind of red sap was bleeding out of the roof-beams, and Doubtfure remembered Esther Kershaw's apron.

'I am in peace,' Doubtfire told his captors. 'I have but to step off my earthly Seat into eternal Hell!'

'No, I will not have Oliver Greave see me as I am now,' Anne told

Esther. 'It is finally too late. He carries the purest picture of me already in his heart.' As Anne collected her things into a bundle, she could not think what she was doing, and she wept. 'I have nothing, and I have created nothing. The only child I gave birth to is from a rape.' She went out of her cottage, leaving no message but the door invitingly open and candles lit inside.

Oliver was hurrying over the dark flickering hillsides. He felt as glorious as Adonis, Hippolytus, or the sun himself, as he came to his loved one, bearing his experiences as his gift brimming in the chalice of his love. On the way he was confronted by an old woman of the roads – one such as he had met all over England, indeed everywhere in Europe, displaced by war, revolution, or by the pastimes and the gardening-tastes of nobles. Women usually selling clothes-pegs, sprigs of heather, or telling fortunes. What experiences must that old crone have suffered, to double her up like that and make her so uncurious about what is to her right hand or her left! he thought. As he scrutinised her he found such an uncanny echo of Anne Wylde that he thought he must be going mad, and that he'd better hurry on quickly to find the real one.

Anne passed him by, dragging her feet into the dusk without looking at him. How could she, her heart would fail.

She went right out of Yorkshire. No remains of her were over found. No long skeleton, its bones as slender as a bird's, in a moorland gulley after the snows. There are no records of her having knocked at the doors of almshouses. She disappeared as dreams do: when Reason awoke, she had gone. You have seen the dew fade. Though some watch it second by second, no one ever sees where the glittering jewels go to.

When Oliver arrived at the cottage's open door he calmly sat outside amongst the flowers lit by the stars and by the strange red sky. He was most intrigued by how Anne had laid out her garden. It was so simple, and so roughly designed, as if after her period at Lower Laithes she had been swept back in spirit to the artisan world of her childhood. He contemplated their future old age, being wise and venerable together, their reduced circumstances having brought wisdom in its train. As he waited, he anticipated Anne's appearance. He would have the advantage and be able to enjoy her expression as it changed when she saw who was sitting there!

Then a realisation that the place was empty crept over him. His fear was quite unreasonable and yet he knew it would prove justified. He got up and went inside, a smile still lingering upon him, then fading. Looking around in the candlelight – at the pathetic sight of her recently washed pots, the table, the old sculpture from Makings propped upon the fireplace, the chair with a cushion still bearing her, *her* imprint – he was possessed by the uncanny but absolute certainty that Anne would never return.

He sat down, weary. He had made up his mind to come back to Yorkshire, but it was not Yorkshire without her. He knew what his life would be now. Sitting in the corners of alehouses, just as in his youth, but without merriment, alone, hoping to meet anyone who had known her. Musing whether her spirit had perhaps entered that owl's cry; staring at the harebells and wondering if it was there; hearing her dashing about the spring sky in the songs of the larks – above all she would be amongst the larks that she had loved so much. Wondering if the soot had come upon the moors because she had fled. She was like a butterfly hatched in a January frost, he thought. Was she someone I dreamed of? *Or is she dreaming me?* he wondered. As a bough broken from a may-tree in the autumn will sometimes give out unseasonable buds that come to nothing, he thought, so Anne Wylde was born into our time in Yorkshire.

THE RAPE
OF THE ROSE

'We have, Sir, this night made one of the greatest discoveries ever made by a House of Commons ... that all our greatness and prosperity, that our superiority over other nations, is owing to 300,000 little girls in Lancashire. We have made the notable discovery, that, if these little girls work two hours less in a day than they do now, it would occasion the ruin of the country; that it would enable other countries to compete with us; and thus make an end to our boasted wealth, and bring us to beggary.'

William Cobbett speaking in Parliament in July 1833 in support of a Bill to reduce the number of hours worked by children in factories to ten.

The Bill was defeated by 238 votes to 93.

As the modern world has shrunk, Cobbett's enslaved Lancashire has removed itself a little further, to be out of sight. It now exists in countries reaching from South America to Africa and the Far East.

The Sick Rose

O Rose, thou art sick!
The invisible worm
That flies in the night,
In the howling storm,

Has found out thy bed
Of crimson joy:
And his dark secret love
Does thy life destroy.

WILLIAM BLAKE
Songs of Experience, 1789–94

To the memory of
MY FATHER
and
FOR JANE
My happiness with her
has made possible
the writing of
The Rape of the Rose.

PART 1

March–April 1812

(1)

March 12th

LUDDITE. 1811. [Said (but without confirmation) to be f. Ned Lud, a lunatic living about 1779, who in a fit of rage smashed up two frames belonging to a Leicestershire 'stockinger'.] A member of an organised band of mechanics and their friends, who (1811–16) went about destroying machinery in the midlands and north of England.
The Shorter Oxford English Dictionary.

Where there is fear, everything is fearful. Mor Laverock Greave, handloom weaver, schoolmaster, scribe to a Luddite band and 'King Ludd's' messenger, returned twelve miles from his mission in Huddersfield to his home in Lady Well, Yorkshire, walking over the hills, looking this way and that. If he had taken the twisting valley roads it would have been twice the distance. Also, he was safer on the hills, where he could see from a great way who was following him. He was not able to run quickly because his lungs were narrow and full of wool-dust, his legs were short and crooked, his knees were bent inwards from being cramped since childhood over a loom. For what he had done, for associating with machine-breakers, for treasonable statements against the King, he might be transported, put on trial for sedition, even hung.

The hills in their ceremonies of moving light were around and above him. The larks for the first time in the year danced free in the air. At least, he thought of them as free. Mor, climbing breathlessly up to Outlane Moor, three miles from Huddersfield, and staring about him, turned his ankle. The pain caused him panic. If he could not walk at all, he would be . . .

He sat down. He had to ease open his old leather coat, releasing the belt, in order to reach his ankle. He massaged it and sat upright again. He removed his hat, to wipe and cool the brim. His dark hair was unusually long for the fashion, and though it was a cold March day, he was damp at the neck. He thought of his youngest child Edwin, his wife Phoebe, his eldest boy Gideon and his home in Lady Well, as if already plunged into penal separation from them.

Staring down the track he saw, caught in a swab of light, a couple of soldiers staggering drunkenly from a public house. There was an old woman, reduced to doing a donkey's work of carrying warps on her back for the weavers. Then there was a more mysterious fellow talking outside a woolcomber's shop, pointing up the hill in Mor's direction; who was that?

Mor had realised that he was an absent-minded insurrectionary, careless in his speech. What a clown, what a fool I am, he thought. He wrote and delivered his Luddite messages on behalf of his comrades, John Tiplady, Arthur Crawshaw and the others, because he was literate and they were not. But foolishly he had left clues to his appearance and character, and testimony to his sedition, in the first cheap pothouse at which he had called, after he had left the Huddersfield hotel where the mill-masters were meeting. Placing his greasy bit of paper sealed with tallow, his message 'to the manufactory owners and gentlemen when they come out of their room', in the hands of the hotel lackey who might well have guessed the contents and called for help, had left Mor with a dried-up mouth and quaking shins. He had not been able to travel a quarter of a mile further without quenching his thirst, resting his limbs and, foolishly, talking to the pothouse servant girl.

This sort of work doesn't suit me at all . . .

He stroked his ankle. It was all right. Relieved, Mor Greave leaned forward and plucked some pendulous flowers that were growing in the bank. They were small, frail and clean, their white suffused with pale green.

Galanthus nivalis, thought the auto-didact, the schoolmaster.

He wreathed some around his hat and hooked others through his lapel. He belted his coat. The leather jerkin was old and scratched, having been left to him, like his cottage, by his foster parent, also a handloom weaver. He set off again, more careful of the stones. He nodded to people and passed the time of day, raising his hat to a maiden returning to her village with milking-stool and can. She thought him a gentleman. It looked to the world as if he had done nothing wrong at all, but his heart was pounding like a steam-driven engine.

Looking over his shoulder and all around from time to time, he climbed still further, reaching the hilltops clear of habitations, with uninterrupted views, here of amateurish militiamen drilling and there of cavalry pinning a notice on a church.

4

Step by step, towards the steel beckoning of moor light, the climb shed from him what was superfluous, human and wicked. Upon the hills he felt, as always, that layers of clothing were being cast off; the cluttering vests of the soul that hampered as well as sheltered him. Larks bulleted out of the grass, upwards, or flung themselves horizontally off the slopes. The sky was alive with them. It was indisputably *their* sky. They paused hanging on vibrating feathers, then folded their wings to drop, unceremoniously, necessarily, and Mor's soul, speeding and gliding with them, grew as free as theirs.

He walked a dozen miles. He clambered over a wall and, plummeting out of the air as the larks did, he landed on a hard road. With relief, he was now in sight of Lady Well.

Looking along this high, gaunt, exposed route between moor above and marsh below, he felt able to take off and glide, westerly into Lancashire, easterly to York, Hull and the sea . . . somewhere away from Yorkshire, away from the pain. In the distance, silver-green valleys fingered their way, following streams and rivers that tumbled from the ridges. The valleys opened like the parted lips of sensual mouths and Mor was tempted to run his fingers along the edges.

The courses of the streams were littered with new manufactories for spinning wool. Many had sprung up where they could hide their secrets some distance from hamlets and villages, but they were now gathering clusters of their own cottages; industrial hamlets that sprouted along the bright streams like dull, leaden fungi.

A slow, heavy waggon, battered and dirtied through travel, was struggling over the rocks and undulations. It was not one of the carts of Mr Horsfall of Lady Well, which would have had 'Paradise Mills' painted in gold along its sides. Its cover was lashed down and it was pulled by four large, tired horses. They trampled the bright yellow celandines that sprinkled the ribbon of grass between the ruts. The iron-rimmed wheels tore the flowers from the bank, leaving others bedraggled and crippled.

The carter, a stranger, looked weary. His cloak shrouded him. His broad-brimmed hat was pulled over his brow, and one eye opened and shut again at one minute intervals. His eye was trapped in a hail-fellow-well-met, shallow wink. He was a giant of a man, who looked out through one eye, like a Cyclops. He had a single vision of the world.

Muffled screams, cries and whimperings came from within the cart and Mor thought that it was full of animals.

'Lady Well? Mr 'Orsfall's man-ure-fact-ory?' the stranger asked.

His voice, roughened from pipe-smoking and the dust of turnpikes, was like the tumbling of gravel. His belly and plum-coloured nose showed that he indulged a great thirst. He was too tired or contemptuous to phrase his question properly. Also, he spoke hopelessly because he had already asked many people and, in this 'surly' part of the world, had either been barely answered, or had been misled so often that he hardly cared any more. In village after village they had thrown stones. They thought that strangers were Government spies, or were here for Napoleon who wanted Yorkshire cloth; for any other reason they could dream up, or for no reason at all. People in the midlands and the north knew that they could only trust their own kind. The carter wanted to be back home in the south. Here the air was still full of knives. It might even snow.

There was a Yorkshire saying: 'Here all and say nowt, sup all and pay nowt, and if thou does out for nowt, do it for thyself' . . . it was the safest defence against such strangers. Mor, who could be most gracious in his speech, and generally was so in his schoolroom, pretended to be an ignorant, boorish villager. He put on a heavy accent.

'Paradise Mills are at t'bottom o't'valley, 'alf a mile's walk down th'ill, master. Thou's wasted thee time coming up 'ere, I'm *sorry* to say.' (As he so much disliked the carter.) 'It must 'ave been a sweat, climbing up 'ere! And thou could 'ave come straight along by the river from the turnpike! But thou'd have to pay a penny toll that way. Mr 'Orsfall makes even 'is own work-folk pay for 'is road. Thou wouldn't want to waste a penny, wouldst thou? Looking at you, I mean . . . I don't mean to be unkind, sir.'

'Godforgi'me, I've been ten days on the road from London!'

'That's a long way to bring us calves and lambs, sir.'

The carter laughed.

'Mr 'Orsfall pays good money for my "calves and lambs", 'cos my "calves and lambs" come from the 'Ackney Workhouse!' He thought this very funny. 'Just you take a look at 'em. But mind they don't bite! Godforgi'me, they're 'ungry beasts and are used to living like rats. Don't you open too much, or Godforgi'me they'll be off across them hills like a pack of Jack-rabbits.'

Mor tentatively unstrung an edge of the covering. There came a smell of sweat, urine and fouled straw. The white face of a child was thrust to the gap. Mor could not at first tell what sex it was for it looked so frightened and demented, its features obliterated by dirt. Similar children, exhausted, stinking, bruised and bleeding from being tumbled about imprisoned in the cart and from fighting each other, crowded to the chink of light. One pissed in Mor's direction, sprinkling him out of the darkness. A second one spat and the gob was as thick as an old man's bronchitis.

A little girl, her thin arm scratched and scabbed, thrust herself forward. Seeing neither food nor freedom, she grabbed at the wild flowers in Mor's hat. She missed, as Mor pulled back, shocked. There was a bright, wild look in her pale eyes, her remarkably pale eyes, that were greedy for beauty and light.

'What's 'at?' she demanded, with the ferocious squeal of a little animal. 'Gi'it me.'

He raised his hat to her, pretending she was a lady, and gave her a flower. He changed his tone, and spoke like a gentleman.

'Snowdrops, miss. In Latin, *Galanthus niv* . . .'

But what use is such knowledge to her?

She vanished with the flower, in case it was quickly taken away.

The carter laughed. The little girl also laughed, though differently, from within the waggon.

Mor, convulsed with nausea, leaned against the cart.

Godforgi'me, thought the carter, Thou'd be sick if thou knew of the two that died and were buried; me bribing a parson, and a magistrate too, so as to do it without death certificates; having to carry gold in my pockets, in these seditious times.

'The mill doesn't need any more children,' Mor told him. 'Our own young ones are already there. If you saw my eldest boy's legs – he can hardly walk at the end of a day's work. The youngest is set to grow the same . . .'

What's he laughing at?

But the carter laughed and winked and said nothing, evidently with something at the back of his mind.

He was intrigued by the flowers in Mor's hat, and other things he could not understand about this Yorkshire working man; such things as the book sticking out of his pocket.

He'd be curious if he knew its title, Mor thought when he followed the carter's glance. It was Paine's *Rights of Man*. All the way from Huddersfield it had prodded Mor in the thigh.

Mor listened to the infants bumping inside the waggon.

When men are without work, and starved, the women and children are put under contract at the mill before the family will be given poor relief, so they have little choice but to be slaves at Horsfalls'. Now he's bringing children from London.

'You see what it is to live in a man's world today,' remarked the carter – as the flowers and the book showed that Mor did not quite belong to a man's world. 'But profit has to be made out of someone. Someone has to suffer, if we are to defeat Bony-Part.'

'Then 'tis a pity, sir, that it must be children . . .' Mor stopped. This is not the kind of man to say such things to.

'Whoa! Whoa!' the carter shouted to the restless horses. 'They are to be apprentices, by order of Parliament, so, Godforgi'me, fasten down that cover now. They'll be off as soon as wink. I nearly lost two of 'em when I exercised 'em through Cromford.'

Mor had heard of Cromford in Derbyshire. That was where Sir Richard Arkwright, one of the richest men in the kingdom but still greedy to make more before he lost his doubtful patents for cotton-spinning machinery, used to employ children of five years of age on day and night shifts. The infants were brought from distant pauper houses so that no one would know or care for them. They were beaten to keep them awake through the twelve or fifteen hour stretches, worked in sight of the mansion where the gentlemen and ladies idled and danced. For such 'industry' as this Arkwright had been awarded a knighthood. His had been the first spinning manufactory in the world, the first to be machine-driven, and also the first to enslave children.

Mor returned the little ones to their darkness and went round to the front of the vehicle; to the plump, well-fed horses stirring their rich brass harness, the carter's pride. On each day of the journey one of the children had been made to polish the brasses.

'You don't need to train anyone as a craft apprentice to work a machine. Women and girls can do it.'

'Are you a politician, sir? I told you, they are to be apprentices, to serve until they are twenty-one in Mr 'Orsfall's public mill.'

The carter did not like to be contradicted. Having thirty children to discipline, he needed to be a man used to having his own way. He had, too, a gun in his pocket. He could afford to be bold.

8

But he turned intimate again. He prided himself on being able to form friendships with strangers.

'They say this is the most seditious corner of England, where King Ludd will finish you off as you lie in your bed. Have you, sir, seen any signs of this "King Ludd"?'

'Oh, every place has its own "King Ludd" in these parts,' Mor answered airily. 'He's everywhere at once and yet no one ever meets 'im. There's so many stories put about. As soon as one is catched and they put it in their newspapers, another appears. Often 'e's in several places at the same time. I know nowt about 'im. It's all foolishness.'

'Is that so?'

The carter lingered over his words, teasing Mor out.

'That is so. That's what they say of 'im, though I know nothing about 'im myself.'

'They speak of a "Lady Ludd", too. Who's she?'

'She is one for upsetting stalls at markets. She's against the prices, so I'm told. I don't know anything about her, either. None o' my business.'

'Well, Mr Perceval, the prime minister in the Parliament, is going to hang them all for it. The Ludds. *Quee* . . .'

The carter made the gesture of a rope tightening around his neck, and laughed.

'They've got a new bill to deal with machine-breakers. Yet I see you've enough soldiers in Yorkshire already to save honest citizens from having their throats cut whilst they lies asleep. I've met regiments and companies of militia coming here along all the roads. Are you expecting French Bony-Part 'imself to land out of an 'ot air balloon? Most of England's expecting an invasion, it seems. I've heard it in every public 'ouse from 'Ackney to Yorkshire.'

Mor longed to get away, to get away from this foulness of humanity.

'We're up to our necks in fear,' he agreed. 'There was a man in Lady Well hid in a chicken shed for a week because 'e was told the French were coming.'

The carter, again, laughed.

'They still don't think they've enough soldiers yet. We've curfews, Watch and Ward patrols,' Mor said. 'They're still raising local re-cruits. Any man who 'as less than three children born in wedlock and is over five feet two inches is liable to be recruited. There's a

9

notice by the church door about it. And I 'ave but two children surviving.'

Once more the carter laughed.

'You'll maybe not reach that height, though?'

He didn't sympathise with Mor's troubles. With mammoth swaying and grumbling of its springs, the vehicle jolted into cumbersome action again, bending the grasses, crushing the flowers, with its load of little boys, and little girls from Hackney bringing their dowries of shifts, stockings, work-frocks, aprons and their two guineas each for prayer books and bedding, two hundred miles for their marriages to Horsfalls' Paradise Mills in the north.

'I'm five foot five!' Mor shouted after it.

The carter laughed.

The little town of Lady Well was no more than a stone huddle on its narrow shelf of stone-walled fields. Here the smallest group of houses was called a 'town', so long as it possessed a church. It clung below further hills, above a steep fall of woods. A cold silver light, opaque behind a linen screen, lay over the huge stones cast along the top edge of the moor. The moor commenced a hundred feet above that ledge of dainty fields, on which the weavers cultivated and caressed a green verdure, kept a pig or a few hens and dried their cloth. The hub of these enclosures was Lady Well itself. It was a cluster of old grey-stone walls, heavy roofs made of thick stone tiles, and stone-paved alleys without trees or grass. It was veiled in its balloon of smoke, like a foetus in a dirty sac.

The sight of the hills with snow clinging to them reminded Mor of the winter past. Yet would that winter of especial starvation be ever forgotten? And the hungry one before it?

Lady Well, like every other village, stark, clear, but impossible to reach across the steep moorlands, had been isolated for months. The snow blew through gaps in walls, a cruel invader, forming knife-edged, glaring drifts like rising prows of marauding Viking ships. The streams were sealed under glittering tapes of ice. The only road cut was down to Paradise Mills in the valley where the stranded woollen pieces filled the warehouses of Messrs Horsfall, father and son. Mor's friend, John Tiplady, the woolcomber, had worked, after he had finished in his shop, with hands frozen on the chisel, to carve for Mor's school the letters of the alphabet on the back of a spare tombstone that had been given to him by the church mason. The 'chip, chip' had been almost the only sound in the village. The only visitors had been the wild animals and birds made bold by hunger. All winters were a trial and a dread, the more so the older one got – and Mor was now in his early thirties – but the last one had been worse than any he could remember, and more hungry.

When he peered down the cliff of woods towards Paradise Mills, he saw a crimson pool, formed by a million buds tipping the trees with small, rich explosions. The whole wood brimming out of the gorge was struggling into life; a corpse was striving to inhale. In cups of earth below and around Horsfalls' worsted spinning mill, fulling mill, finishing houses and the latest still unoccupied building that they had heard for some time called 'the apprentice house', the litter of a sleeping season was pricked with the green stains of violet leaves, and with the first acid colour of wild garlic or bluebell fronds, curling wickedly out of the earth, preparing for their spring revolution, Mor thought. At the bottom of everything, the river, rid of her fringes and lace of ice, did her work of driving machinery and washing cloth.

Again leaving the road, Mor walked home along the top edge of Mr Horsfall's woodlands. These embraced most of the valley; ash, beech, birch, hazel and a sprinkling of old oak trees. The silver boughs still sang of winter in the bitter, razored wind that had discovered them; a dancing mesh of light, locked behind a high, new stone wall. 'Blood Wood', that wilderness named after an ancient forgotten battle, where for centuries people had gathered firewood or nuts, cut bracken for animal bedding, fished and snared birds, or simply stared at the trees, had recently been enclosed. Its wild character was trimmed, neat green drives ran through it and it was now guarded by a force of gamekeepers. There were new notices poking out like sentries:

BLOOD WOOD ESTATE. PRIVATE. SPRING GUNS AND STEEL TRAPS SET HERE.

Be damned to the Horsfalls. Damn. Damn. Damn . . .
>The law arrests the man or woman
>Who steals the goose from off the common,
>But leaves the greater rascal loose
>Who steals the common from the goose.

Throughout the day, manufacturers had been meeting in Huddersfield. Luddites, machine-breakers, had raided their homes for arms, as well as breaking into their mills. A waggonload of new machinery had been ambushed and smashed with hammers. A cloth mill, uninsured against acts of 'riot and civil commotion', had been burned down. Nothing was left but smoke-blackened stones and charred timbers hissing in the falling snow, which even the followers of King Ludd could not hold back, though in every other way they held command of the country-side. One mill-master, who had skimped and saved to buy a twelve horse-power steam engine, had been afraid to leave his house whilst he listened to it being broken to bits. Another had been called from his bed to comfort daughters frightened by the sounds of Luddites drilling on the moorland and of orders barked in the fearsome local dialect. They had further problems, due to the wars. The Government's 'orders in council' forbade exports, and one million pounds' worth of their cloth was rotting in warehouses. They were loud, blunt-speaking – and frightened.

Only Mr Nicholas Horsfall of Paradise Mills, son of Nicholas Horsfall, the founder, was unflurried. He treated his colleagues with contempt, and stood aloof. He was tall, lean, ready for anything. His confederates appeared to him mostly fat and stubborn, puffing themselves out as robins do to survive the cold. They were self-made men, but he himself, he believed, belonged to the 'true gentry', those who had owned land before they owned machines. The others were frightened because the military authorities were unsympathetic and would or could do nothing about the elusive Luddite bands. But Mr Horsfall was an army man himself. He quartered senior officers in his house, offered them fishing and provided whores. As a magistrate he overlooked the existence of brothels for the soldiers. If there were to be a raid on Paradise Mills, he was sure that *he* would not have any trouble with it.

They talked, talked, talked, and he calmly fingered a rose in his buttonhole. The rose, so unnaturally displayed in March, showed that he owned a hothouse. While the magistrate, Mr Joseph Radcliffe, complained yet again that the Home Office was doing nothing to help, Nicholas Horsfall, with an unwitting display of sensuality, buried his nose and sniffed the aroma of petals. Nicholas took the flower from his coat. Holding the bloom in perfect awareness of its fragility, as one might hold a bird or a small child, he proceeded to shred it, petal by petal, dropping the pieces and finally throwing the denuded stamen away.

The chairman of the meeting (who also happened to be named Horsfall) dictated an appeal to be published in *The Leeds Mercury*.

'It appears to this meeting that a violent and determined spirit of insubordination has gained ground amongst the workmen. The Committee hereby offers a reward of one hundred guineas for information . . .'

But as the manufacturers left the inn that day they found Mor Greave's note left for them in the lobby of the hotel.

Gentlemen, you have opressed us beyond endurance, and have no notion of what you do, but you idle and dance whilst we labour. We asert our right to LIVE by our employment. Pull down your obnoxius machines. Pay fare wages to the weavers, their wives and children. Otherwise, sooner than see our numerus families of children cry and starve for bread we will pay with our lives to reduce your property to ashes.

Yr obedient servant, KING LUDD.

After the manufacturers' meeting, a spy, known as 'B', was sent upon the trail at once. What so alarmed them about Mor's letter was not its contents, which they were used to, but that it was literate. An educated man could turn into a leader.

'B' tracked Mor a little way in the Outlane direction, finding a militiaman, a maidservant, an old woman carrying a warp upon her back, who had noticed hurrying by one who might be described as 'a working man with gentleman's manners'.

'B' was a man recruited in a debtors' prison and paid by Mr Radcliffe according to his information. In his pocket he carried several of the more usual Luddite letters:

You Damned Dogs! It is nown to us you has masheens. If you dont destroi them we will do it arselves. We will cut orf yur Organs we sware by Almity God . . . Yours in haste. King Ludd.

General Ludd hereby orders you to take down yur mashines. Damn yur soles it shall be blud for blud in a very short time!

The spy, a bankrupt manufacturer and a connoisseur of these plebeian epistles, was now pursuing someone who left out the letter 'o' at the ends of such words as 'obnoxious' and 'numerous'.

'B' reached the pothouse at which Mor had called.

'He spoke educated,' the maid told him. ''E used a lot of words, like a parson. "I think of my children's legs," he said. "After a day's work they can 'ardly bend 'em . . ."'

March 14th

Mor, working at home, was hungry. He knew that his wife and children would return from the factory to find little but oatmeal and bread and a little preserve. There was no meat, and no fish at the end of winter. In his mind was stuck an obstinate picture of a place by the river in the park where he knew that there were trout; you cannot expect a fox not to be a fox, nor blame him for it. On Saturday, in the afternoon following a hard day on his piece, Mor left his loom. Avoiding the drilling militia, he made his way down to the bridge. Waiting for passers-by to disappear up the hill, he examined the water's colour, depth, density and speed. The new banks of weed, that would soon flow in the current, were beginning to prick the mud. He took final, quick, fearful glances in every direction, climbed a wall and darted for cover.

He knew the eddies of the stream, and where there would be fish; whenever one was caught, there was always another greedy to take its place. Going downstream, feeling with his feet and trying to look every way at once, searching for the edge of a mantrap or the lead of a spring-gun prised to blow his head off, he made an arc through the woodlands, returning to the bank at a point where he would be hidden.

A slow, curving shine of water lay before him. A clear brown colour, it caught and rippled over stones, glided over gravel, and sulked in deep pools. He worked his way back upstream. There a trout rose. After a quick, quiet, excited plop up to the surface, she abandoned the glitter of her sides upon the water, and sank down again. There another one tipped a nose to the river, leaving circles.

But Mor wanted a fish near to the bank and he knew where to go. This was the spot he had been savouring at his loom. It was a deep place carved out of the bank by the swirling water. The trout was concentrating on the other direction, upstream, that brought her food. Mor saw her lips touch and break the tight drumskin of the surface, sending shivers of silver, swept away on the current's flow.

He watched her gently pluck the surface of the pool a few times.

When she had sunk down again, Mor crept forward. He felt his way with the balls of his feet, so as not to crack a twig nor tinkle a stone. Nor did he throw his shadow over the river. His awareness of everything around sent through him rhythms of joy. The river's music was like a sweet gathering of fiddles. He listened for the approach of keepers. Alert in every organ, this was how an animal lived, his life concentrated in each second, and living in this moment only.

A foot behind the trout's tail he knelt, still keeping his shadow clear. His hands felt through the cold water. He was wearing the same hat as two days before and a snowdrop fell drifting on the flow. He had forgotten the flowers. His face lay so close, lipping the water, inhaling the cold breath, the faint fog lingering over the pool, that he could see the petals' denting of the river's skin. He wondered if the trout would rise to them or if she would be alarmed and plunge to the depths. She was not disturbed. He kept his fingers moving like pale weeds played by the current and once or twice he touched the trout's sides. He felt the impulses of contained energy, from her who was so still. He relaxed his fingers gently around her. He gripped her tightly under the gills.

The trout, ten inches long, in a sudden flurry was in his grasp, her tail swinging trying to swipe at him, her speckled head gaping and gasping, her many little teeth glittering, her beautiful vermilion spots dimpling her flashing sides. It was like trying to hold oil. The more tightly he gripped her, the more she slipped, thrashed and squirmed. For a moment she lay still, her eye regarding him without reproach, as fishes will, and as if she understood the value to him of her plump body. Then she tried to leap again. There was a throbbing in his palms. Gold and silver necklaces of water fell all about her. She was disrobing for sacrifice.

He banged her head quickly on a stone and the thick muscle that had been a fish became limp. Already her gleam was drying and fading into a mist of grey scales. He thrust her into one of his deep pockets.

Travelling upstream and hungrily taking a chance close to the bridge from which he might have been seen, he caught a second trout. Finally, there was a third one.

Three brook trout, although small, composed a feast, so that Mor could be satisfied. The father of a hungry family had roamed from his work, but he now had something with which to return home.

As he went back, a sunset bled upon the countryside. Liquid drops like red communion wine fell upon the trees and thickened in the river. The night when it fell was restless, as it often was these days. From across the bogs, or amongst boulders, Mor heard rounds of shot fired. These were from small gangs drilling, sure of their escape routes across the hills or through networks of tracks unfamiliar to the soldiers. Mor heard a song softly following him out of an alley-way:

'You heroes of England who wish for a trade
Be true to each other and be not afraid.
Though the bayonet is fixed they can do no good
As long as we keep to the rules of King Ludd.'

Exposed on a hillcrest he glimpsed Lydia Horsfall, the manufacturer's wife, taking one of her frequent lonely walks. Always she avoided people. In her loose, dark velvet clothes she was like a black, soft-feathered owl, haunting the banks and woodsides.

Why did she ramble so much, especially in the dark? What restlessness pursued her? What dissatisfaction, that she could not bear to stay in her own home? Everyone in Lady Well wondered about it. It was known that she carried two pistols and in The Old Tup they said that she went out to hunt Luddites. 'Nonsense', others answered. But what reasons could they think of for a woman who had wealth and every comfort to walk so restlessly at night? What conceivable reason could there be?

As Mor came close to Lady Well the taint of smoke in the air steadily thickened, but tonight it was not only the smoke of household fires. Mor saw, amongst the dim, grey shapes of stretched cloth, that the wool on some tenter frames had been burned. Its embers were still smouldering. A soldier, an anxious private of the local militia who did not like performing such a duty, was guarding the ashen rows.

Mor, climbing the hill, arrived in the street where was his home. The roof and window lines of the terrace of houses were horizontal but the road rose steeply: consequently the houses gradually decreased in size uphill. The cellar-room of the lowest cottage was large enough to be divided off into a separate dwelling, whereas the final house on the hilltop possessed hardly any cellar at all. Mor's cottage was in the centre of the block, with a tiny room at its foot suitable only for storage. Across its little window a low flight of stone steps led up to his front door, before which a suspended paving-stone made a mid-air platform. An unused gravestone formed one side. Iron railings were on the other, and down the steps. Mor had once tried to grow a rose here from a cutting given to him out of the hothouse by one of Mr Horsfall's gardeners. He trailed its branches over the gravestone and railings, but it had shrivelled in the keen winds and the ceramic pot that held it had cracked open in the frost. Mor stood in the street for a while. The shutters were not drawn. He watched the candlelight and firelight flickering in his home, afraid of something in there that might kill off what he had experienced out here, drowning it with cares. What he had felt so strongly was fragile when brought into the human world.

He closed the wooden shutters over the windows, with a squeak of hinges, and a bang. His family hardly looked up as dark wings closed over the glass. They knew who it was. At last he climbed his steps and entered. To seal in the warmth he pulled the door shut behind him. With his heel he secured the rag that was laid along the bottom of the door to keep out the draughts. There was a smell of smoke, human staleness, the oil of wool and machines. The cottage had a stone-flagged floor; furthest from the fire it was a dark colour from rising damp; close to the hearth it was a dry, sandy yellow. There were three stools, a chair with arms to comfort the man of the house, a table so scrubbed that it showed ridges of harder wood where the soft parts had been worn away, two brass candlesticks, and a cupboard ranged with wooden bowls and platters but containing also, behind doors, Mor's violin. There was a lidded barrel with a tin scoop, for oatmeal. A large brown jug for water stood on the floor. There were a couple of stoneware ornaments, loved by Phoebe. One was a spotted dog, the other a huntsman. A geranium, at this time of year no more than a dead stick, stood on the windowsill. Behind one door a flight of stairs, without space for a landing, climbed to the two upper rooms. Beyond another door was the old scullery, cut out of the bank, very damp and used as Mor's school. The room in which he stood would have been damp, too, but for the big stone fireplace on his left. Crowded over the flames were a smoke-blackened stewpot, a pan for water, and a flat iron dish for heating oatcakes. A rack draped with cakes had been hauled by Phoebe up to the ceiling, to warm above the fire. This had been allowed to sink low, in reproach, he thought, at his lateness . . . people went to bed at dusk to save the cost of candles.

He had left the greater part of himself outside, and he was slapped by the strangeness of what lay before him. His family of three, all still in their factory clothes, were close to the fire. When he entered, Phoebe hovered over the pot and guiltily pushed under it some sticks from the pile of kindling kept to dry on the hearth.

Mor believed that his wife was still strong, but past thirty she was, as was to be expected, grey. She was a small woman, so thin that on his few opportunities to hold her, he felt all her bones, and it was frightening. She might break under the gentlest touch. He still found her light movements sensual, especially if he could make her laugh. More often, though, she jerked erratically, like a person long-unsatisfied.

'So you've come back,' she said, in a voice prickly with hurt. 'You left your piece unfinished, just like on Thursday.'

'I've done enough this week. I wanted to think out some lessons for t'school. Commit a few points to memory.'

'Hmm!'

'Me feyther's back,' Edwin said, tired but smiling through his mill-dirt. Mor's younger son, nine years of age, his latest born still-living child, 'My last and dearest 'ope,' squatted on the hearth itself, polishing the stones with his bum, where he had been determinedly trying to count, using the cinders – a method his father had taught him. He also had rows of roughly made and painted wooden soldiers, French and English.

Pain and guilt typified Edwin's elder brother Gideon, who was fifteen. He did not greet his father, nor look up. Mor and Phoebe's 'love child', for whom they had married, sat upon a stool, rubbing his knees through which pain shuttled like a hundred frozen needles. It attacked him most in the evening, after work. He had a candlestick, to light his Bible, and had probably, thought Mor, taken the opportunity of his sceptical father's absence to read aloud to his mother. She, who could hardly read herself, enjoyed listening to it.

At length Gideon raised his eyes.

'King Ludd set his men to fire cloth, whilst you were out. He asked why you were not there, and says to tell you, he recorded the fact. He says you're not going on the raid against Horsfall's shearing machines, neither.'

'No, I'm not. Crawshaw's a fool. It's one thing to prepare for a revolution, another to follow a blustering blackguard like Arthur Crawshaw, probably into a trap.'

'He's our King Ludd . . .'

'A raid in our own village, too. Anyone who spots us'll know us.'

Behind the door Mor hung up his belt, his hat and coat, leaving the fishes in his pockets, and thrust himself to the fire. He came smelling of earth and river, making convivial gestures, and rubbing his hands in appreciation of the fire, which was beginning to flare from Phoebe's sticks. Mor did not lift the pot himself. That was for the woman to do.

'We'll blacken our faces,' Gideon said.

'Blacken your faces! Put on women's dresses! We've armed soldiers to face and a government looking for someone to hang, lad. It's all right for Crawshaw, 'e's from another town and a bachelor. But I've you folk to think about. Does 'e know what defences are planned for the mill? What soldiers'll be about? He couldn't organise a Sunday School picnic, let alone summat that risks the lives of father of children. All 'e wants is to play the 'ero. A man sent in from another place, to "organise" us. He knows nowt about Lady Well.'

Mor stood with his back to the fire, warming his hands behind him; the master. Edwin was at his feet, seeming to concentrate on his ordered rows of cinders and soldiers, but listening.

'Well, Wrigley is to be asked to take your place . . . you with your bold messages! They'll say you're a coward,' Gideon added.

'And he's superstitious, your "King Ludd" – wanting twelve men for his raid!'

Arthur Crawshaw, like some others, believed that twelve men were necessary because that, excluding Judas, had been the company of Jesus.

Mor changed and changed his hands behind his back, over the flames, with his eye on Phoebe, who cooked his food.

'He's read the works of Machiavelli, his *Advice to Princes*, and Tom Paine and so on, your Crawshaw, or so 'e says. 'E's been sworn in by the great John Baines in Halifax, but 'e's a superstitious fool still. All those magical-Methodist "radicals", believing in superstitions. The times are plagued with 'em. They're our ruin, not our salvation. Antinomians waiting for the end o't'world, waiting for Christ to come again . . . !'

'There mi't be some truth in it,' Phoebe quietly interrupted.

Mor took no notice of the woman.

'Opening the Bible at random for guidance, like John Wesley . . . 'e calls that being a leader o' men! I've no time for t'chap. No time at all. He'll 'ave us all up before an 'anging judge before 'e's done.'

Gideon's disapproval of his father for being more keen on writing

20

tracts and his autobiography than on such things as burning cloth on tenter-frames was, in the manner of an adolescent, exaggerated into hatred. Added to this was the arrogance of a first-born child.

'We'll be seeing some 'anging before we've done,' Phoebe sighingly agreed. 'The Lord knows who it'll be to suffer. I fear the day. Young ones, old ones . . . There'll be no . . .' She could not think of the word she wanted. When she had found it, 'Redemption,' she continued, like a parson.

She gave a dry little cough, as was her habit.

'Wrigley's got himself wed at last,' Mor, to change the subject, told Phoebe, with a smile. 'He's married Nancy Stott. He was drunk when she got 'im to the church.' He put on a haughty voice. '"What do you mean by bringing him to the altar in this here state?" asks the parson.' Mor's voice altered again. '"Well, Mester," she replies, "'E will no' come when he's sober."'

Gideon did not think that it was funny.

Phoebe laughed. She brushed by Mor, careful not to touch him. She threw a nervous glance under the lid of the pot, then went to busy herself taking a wooden platter and spoon from the dresser for him. When a husband comes home, no matter where or what from, he is hungry. He must be satisfied. Her mother had taught her that.

Her husband had looked to her as ridiculous as a drunken mummer, with the last of the snowdrops falling from his hat, and the wet earth stains on his clothes, but she did not think that he had been mumming. He had been poaching. Quick as a hungry animal, she had noticed something heavy pulling at the sides of Mor's coat. For what was her family's diet? Apart from poachings, all she was ever able to put upon the table was oatmeal, eaten as a porridge if they could afford milk, with treacle as an occasional luxury, or with dock leaves, nettles or blood added and baked into a cake; sometimes potatoes, without greens, except maybe in summer; wild blackberries or whinberries; a little salted meat once in a while; and, as another rare luxury, a fruit preserve pie. They were now forbidden by Horsfall even to gather nuts from the woodlands. So Phoebe had hoped all evening for Mor, when he arrived, to laugh and pull an animal, game bird or fish out of his trousers; hoped and yet longed also not to see such a thing, for who knew whether the gamekeeper followed, and after him the hangman? Hunger conflicting with such fear anticipated a very mixed happiness.

Mor rubbed his palm upon Edwin's head. He could smell what Phoebe lifted the lid from, in the pot. The gift that he had hidden from them made him smile to himself.

'What's four times five?' he asked Edwin.

'Twenty.'

'What's six times six?'

'Thirty-five.'

'Thirty-six, thou gobslutch, what's your 'ead for? Is it for nothing better than carrying your 'at? Thou'll not change the world without you can do sums.' Mor laughed and shook the head out of which he hoped for so much.

Edwin, looking up from the cinders, caught sight of the platter and spoon placed on the table for his father.

'Have you brought us anything?' Edwin asked.

'What could I bring?" Mor answered, laughing.

'So, as I said,' interrupted Gideon, continuing for his mother's and Edwin's sakes a story concerning Joshua Slaughter, the mill engineer, and Nathaniel Gledhill, the workers' overseer, 'Slaughter told Gled'ill that a gentleman from the West Country 'ad patented a method of raising water by means of fire. "Eh?" says fat Nathaniel, "'Ow's that? 'Ow's that come about? You can't raise water wi' fire. It would put it out." "Be means o' steam, you mophead," answers Joshua Slaughter, sharp as a ferret. "Be means of steam be means of fire?" says Gled'ill, "'Ow . . ?"'

Mor's own fun died on the air. He was a stranger to his family. Working alone and at home as he did all of the week, he saw little of them, but they were together at the manufactory or in its vicinity; Tiplady's cropping shop where Gideon was employed was only a few yards down river. It was in order to be with them a little that Mor often accompanied them in the mornings to Horsfalls', before he returned home to his loom. His very house was filled with the smell of the oil of the machines amongst which they, but not he himself, worked; it had a rank vegetable odour, being concocted out of the seeds of rape. As soap was something they could afford to use only lightly, every few days, their clothes, their skins, and by now most things in the house reeked of it. Mor was separated by this, too, for he was fated to his own individual smell; of the natural oils of wool, and with something of the country where he roamed.

Phoebe, seeing Mor turning impatiently to the pot, recalled her wifely duty and again brushed past to reach it before he did. This time their hands met, accidentally, above the hearth. She pulled away as if she had been burned. She was instantly sorry for her retreat, but this did not show.

She recovered quickly. Mor remained shocked for some time. He moved from the fire to his oak chair. He loved it; the ten bulbous spindles at the back, the shaped uprights, the legs that had been shortened for a man who was not tall. It gave him comfort and warmth merely to look at it. Phoebe filled his plate. She saw that his hands were shaking, as he gripped the chair arms.

Gideon had observed the incident. He had smiled as he watched his mother pull away.

'Go on wi't'story,' Edwin said, laughing. 'Tell us what 'appened to fat old Gled'ill.'

'"'Ow?" says Slaughter. "Be means of an engine, that's 'ow. So tell 'Orsfall about it." "What sort of an engine?" asks Gled'ill, scratching 'is 'ead. "A steam engine driven by coal fires." "How can that be?" Gled'ill says. He couldn't believe it, tha sees.'

Gideon was good at telling stories. His mother was laughing.

Mor, supping at his broth of turnips and bits of vegetables that had come their way, felt the weight of his marriage. He longed to touch and be touched by Phoebe but she had convinced him that he was a man with an unhealthy desire for contact. As Mor brought the spoon up to his mouth he glanced with a husband's possessiveness at Phoebe, whose laughter had ceased. Sometimes their eyes met; hers so large, in a drawn face.

He looked over his spoon at Gideon. With one palm, the youth was rubbing his painful knee, and with the other he was again searching through the Bible. His hands were big and still growing larger. His wrists were powerful and so would his whole frame have been had he not been underfed.

Mor took a loud sucking of his food and looked again at Phoebe. When she had been a girl she had been like a weasel, lithe and alert, he remembered.

Made nervous by Mor's watchful eyes, Phoebe busied herself around the room. She never felt short of something to do. She did everything that she could to make her home clean, neat and comfortable, showing a pathetic desire to please Mor especially, through being as good a mother as she could be.

When she looked at him, she saw that he was staring at his hand which had touched her, and was still trembling.

Gideon found what he was searching for.

'"In the sweat of thy face shalt thou eat bread, till thou return into the ground." We're nowt but the children of Israel, Edwin . . .'

Phoebe was at her happiest when listening to him. Their son, she often said, would make a good non-conformist preacher, if he was able to stand in the pulpit.

Whenever Phoebe thought of the six-year-old child whom she had taken for his first day, calming his fears, to the manufactory, her eyes dampened.

'That boy was once a proverb for straightness,' she said.

She was blaming Mor, even though she knew it was not his fault. When Mor had realised how Gideon's knees were growing, he had wheedled and begged to break the boy's contract at Horsfalls' and had got him apprenticed in his friend's cropping shop.

Edwin was staring at the flowers of the fire, the petals of the flames, the dark textures of the cinders and the burnt stones of the grate, where his crude wooden soldiers were ranged, the English in neat rows, nearly all the French lying on their sides. Like his father he took pleasure in looking at things, which seemed to many such a curious pleasure. He had his father's love of learning and of wandering. By using sandy banks, dried puddles, or the ashes of fires, Edwin drew maps of Lady Well or of what were to him mythical places, Africa, America, Greece and the Indian Ocean. There remained a chance that Edwin might be able to go exploring, for his legs were still sturdy. But, as for all the children of Lady Well, it was most likely that his bones would be crippled from standing at the machines, walking or crawling under them for twenty miles a day.

When he heard his mother declare that Gideon had been 'a proverb for straightness', he slowly, quietly, not wanting to be noticed, stretched first one leg and then the other to test whether his, too, ached. They did indeed contain that typical freezing pain. A promise of suffering was sealed in them, like an embryo demon trapped in a block of ice.

There'll be no Africa, America nor India for me . . .

Often Edwin had cried, just as Gideon before him had wept at the beginning of each day, thinking of the hours awaiting him at the mill. He had cried, with some frustration as he saw that his mother too had damp eyes when she pulled him from his bed, cuddling him and then having to slap him to keep him awake. But by now, at the age of nine, he had given up his trust in tears. He would have liked to have gone poaching on the moors today with his father. He would like to do as Gideon had done and get out of the mills into some less oppressive employment. He did not cry about it. He knocked over another Frenchman, and pounded him into the cinders with his fist.

His parents were afraid that Edwin might one day, through tiredness or childish carelessness, fall into the spinning-frames, as had happened to Mor and Phoebe's third-born child, their daughter Esther, when she was nine. She had dropped amongst the whirling steel rods, and had been pulled out, her bones mangled, miraculously still alive, but only just. They had spent a shilling or two on a surgeon, but could not afford a good one, nor one for long. For a week Esther had tried to hold her bones together herself, as she lay in bed, before she died. The parents could never bring themselves to speak of this memory, but they longed for Edwin to reach an age when he would be safe from childish play and inattentiveness.

Their second child, who had died before she could be given a name, had been born one year after Gideon, her misfortune having been to come forth in the winter. Phoebe had no milk so Mor had begged at the back doors of farms, at the vicarage, at Mr Horsfall's mansion, for butter and eggs to feed the mother, but humbling himself and promising to have no more dealings with 'radicals' had proved useless. So when, two years after Edwin, a further son had been born, again in the winter, a child who, had he lived, would have been their fifth, Mor had said to himself, with the grim realism of suffering, 'Christmas baby, then go back to Christ.' He had decided that it wasn't worth humbling his soul and telling lies to try and save a baby doomed anyway by the season in which it was born. 'A child gone back is a poor man's blessing,' Mor said.

Phoebe began to resent Mor for his pride. She would try, however helplessly, to feed their children, which God, if not joy, had given to them. Hunger, labour, and the knowledge that she could not make a world fit for her children, whose very conceptions were terrifying, troubled her.

Ironically here now was Mor's eldest son resenting him for lacking pride and fight.

Once, when Esther was five and Edwin nearly three years old, when there was a recession in weaving and the schoolteaching that supplemented Mor's work had dried up too, Mor had gone to the Lady Well Famine Relief Committee, who had told him that they could give him nothing so long as he 'kept at home' an infant who could be employed in Mr Horsfall's manufactory. Gideon by now already worked there and it was Esther who was wanted. Mr Horsfall was chairman, so his interest was evident. Horsfall, who dressed his own infants, especially his little daughter, like two dolls, banged the table and shouted, 'Don't look so savage, sir!' (Though it was the millowner who looked angry.) 'I know that you operatives indulge yourselves with idleness and vice upon the backs of your infants' labour. For what other reasons do you breed so many brats, but to squander their wages in public drinking houses? Or is it on fiddle music, eh?'

As if the last implied something worse than drunkenness; sedition, perhaps.

And so Mor's children, with the others of Lady Well, had been put under contracts to labour at Horsfalls'. They had been lifted from their beds, in the dark for most seasons of the year, and were dragged or carried off, as Mor put it, 'Same as blind helpless nestlings, or baby rabbits I might pluck out of hedgerows and tufts of grass.'

To break the contract for his children made their father liable to punishment in the House of Correction.

Mor had finished his turnip broth. He licked the spoon. Phoebe was hovering near, wanting to play the housewife, the weaver's wife, not a mere spinning-woman, and she cleared away his plate.

'And now . . .' Mor announced.

At last he went to his coat and produced the first of the trout, dangling the spirit of water by its tail. It was a drab sight now, stained, limp, patchily bald of its scales, smelling, and its eyes glazed over, yet the room was transformed by it. He brought out the others and laid them upon the table, side by side, as reverently as if they were his own dead relatives.

Edwin ran from the fire to see them. His face, reaching over the edge of the table, came eye to eye with the fish. He stared hard, excitement on his face. Resentful of his brother's sullenness, he was glad of proof of his father's care. Yet Gideon too showed a restrained interest and, although not leaving his stool, he peered in the trout's direction. From Phoebe it was sufficient that she smiled. The trout, in the dim light, had turned into religious objects, sacrifices borne to their altar. They were the tiny focuses of all their hopes and joys.

'There!' More said. 'Three beauties.'

Mor was the proud father now, an animal who despite mill-owner and the 'rest of them' was able to care for his young.

With Edwin peering, Mor gutted a trout into a bucket. The two others he placed on the floor. Candlelight glittered on the scales and eyes. The mouths had fallen stiffly open, showing rows of grimacing, tiny teeth.

Edwin, with a smile, nervous and fascinated, put forth a little finger. He hesitated, then pushed it forward determinedly towards one of the mouths. He kept it between the teeth, looking up into his father's face.

'Why is its mouth open?'

'The muscles go slack when it dies.'

'It's got a tongue.'

'Fish 'aven't got tongues, you gobslutch,' Gideon said, irritably.

'So it 'as,' Mor said. 'Fancy you noticing that.'

With a frown for Gideon, Mor carved a slit under the belly from the gills to the tail. He scraped away blood and tissue down to the bone, carefully removing the chain of congealed, black, bitter-tasting blood along the spine, handling the knife dexterously so that he did not lift the hair-like bones through the flesh.

'You 'ave a go at it.'

Mor put the knife in Edwin's hand and stood behind his shoulders, his arms around him, helping him to gut the next fish.

'Why don't we eat that?' Edwin asked as the offal slipped into the bucket.

'Stop asking questions,' Gideon said. 'Thou'll get a thick ear for it. Give him one, Feyther.'

'If you tasted a bit, you'd know why. It's bitter, like poison.'

'Don't crows eat it?'

'The crows'll peck at it, yes.'

'Crows'll peck your eyes out,' Gideon offered. 'When you die.'

He talks of death like a preacher, thought his father.

Mor went to the door and descended the steps, Edwin following. Thin spears of light from the cracks in the shutters burst across the road. The dark folds of the valleys, like the rich velvet of funeral clothes, rolled dimly before them. They were illuminated by a new moon, thin as a nail paring; a bright yellow line. The constellations of Orion and the Plough were visible in gaps of cloud.

'Orion, Edwin! There's the Plough. Do you remember the comet last year, eh? You remember?'

27

Edwin remembered. He had been told that it forecast revolution.

Mor crossed the road and swilled the bucket of fish offal over the wall. They could hear lambs.

'Look!' Edwin said.

They themselves were watched. From out of the dark fields sloping down to the noisy river two sharp eyes, inches above the ground, were filled with starlike flickerings. A spy out of the animal world, on the fringes of which Mor and Edwin waited, had sprung up for the fish offal. Man, boy, and animal hypnotised one another for a while, then the two lights were extinguished in a dark ripple.

'It's a polecat,' Mor whispered.

It was a species almost extinct, with the fear of this expressed in its furtiveness, and in its eyes. It was frightened of the territory it had once owned. And yet, sniffing the air so carefully, in danger, it was alive, as, say, the cared-for, productive, but captive sheep dozing in the meadow were not.

They returned indoors. Edwin and Mor wrapped the trout in dock leaves and hid them under a bedroom floorboard until tomorrow. The children, the wife, and the father all went to bed happy at last, thinking of fish.

All happy except that, while Mor was out, Phoebe secretly spat a little blood into a rag.

Mor and his wife did not normally lie awake for long. They removed only their outer clothes through the winter, so there was little to see or touch. Unhappiness left a smell upon their bodies; the one smell that they had in common, and it made them unpleasant to one another. The rough bedding did not induce love-making. Phoebe coughed a little, with her dry little cough about which she would not speak. Then she fell asleep.

Mor lay awake longer, wrestling with a temptation, listening to the river. He tried to keep his hands to his sides or folded harmlessly across his chest. At last, with stealthy delicate motions, he moved his fingers towards Phoebe's garment. He was controlling his hands from touching himself, for in 'self-abuse' lay, he believed, the tumble into madness. At first he was timid, then he gripped her dress tightly and desperately, like a drowning man trying to save himself by grabbing a frail clump of grass on the river's bank.

Comforted, he began to doze and lapse into a dream. The words of a sermon of his youth that had lashed him from a high pulpit – flails descending from the sky – returned to him, with the image of the parson, black arms waving. He held a tiny leather collar fitted internally with spikes, to be worn over the penis in case of an improper erection disturbing sleep.

Frightened, Mor jolted awake, hearing once or twice the sounds of gunshots across the countryside, clutching the edge of a woman's cotton garment, and thinking.

Sunday morning brought leisure, for they rose late and they stayed away from church, daring a visit from the vicar.

That's not likely. If we work in a factory he thinks we're too much like animals, for him to give attention to . . .

Mor and his sons spent an hour bringing buckets of water from the pump at the end of the terrace and heating them over the fire. After using up much of their soap, they changed into clean clothes. Mor had a shirt often-darned by Phoebe's patient hands. She wore a flower-patterned dress, almost bleached from washing, which Mor had bought for her after taking his piece to market and selling it for a good price, five years before. Gideon and Edwin were in clean breeks and stockings. All were feeling chilly without the protection of their work-dirt.

Mor, slipping a glove on his hand, went outside, at the back of the cottage, where the land rose against the wall of the chapel. He could look down on his own roof. A cock blackbird landed on it. Impelled by its flight, it ran a few feet, lifted its head and chest to brake against the air, and tried the chill day with a song. Since the earliest spring days before other birds were singing, Mor had listened as its tune grew daily, from the merest wobble, feebly challenging the rain and wind, to full melody. He might be sentimental, but the chains of sound brought tears to his eyes.

He plucked some young nettles. A spring scent rose as his feet crushed the grass and plants. It arose from the smear on his gloves from the nettles.

When he returned, Phoebe was scraping and washing the trout again, unnecessarily except as a way of giving herself to the fish that had given up its flesh to her. She sprinkled them with dried thyme before grilling them. The stewpot into which, all through the week, were thrown cabbage leaves, a swede dropped from a cart, a mutton bone, was put aside, like their working clothes. Mor ordered Phoebe to boil the nettles, and some old potatoes. He was as confident as if he had in fact possessed her. He burst into song:

'As I went out on a May morning,
On a May morning right earl-ay-ee.'

Phoebe smiled. They were as happy as a pair who had made love all night. Gideon was absorbed in his Bible. Edwin helped with the fish, getting under his parents' feet. He held a sprig of thyme to his nose and sniffed, lingeringly.

'Our cock blackbird's been singing out there, Edwin. God bless 'im. Spring's coming.'

Mor touched his wife's dress, hoping for it to seem accidental. She stiffened and automatically leaped back.

He turned the fish over. He loved the trout for the creature it was, living only in the clearest running water that was full of air. It seemed to be not a water but an air spirit.

Phoebe, ruffled, fidgeted about, keeping away from Mor, trying to forget that he had touched her, and that she had instinctively leaped away. She tried to please him by tidying the house, rubbing at the pottery ornaments, turning the geranium round to the light. To be still, made her ashamed and guilty. When Mor announced that the fish were ready, she took them to the table, with potatoes and nettles in a steaming bowl.

They all sat down. Mor did not approve of saying Grace. 'The God who starves and cripples children for other men's profits needn't be thanked,' he declared. Phoebe had been taught that not to Give Thanks before meat and fish put one on the level of animals, 'that do nothing but grunt over their food'. Gideon and she muttered together, 'For what we are about to receive may the Lord make us truly thankful', while Mor filleted the trout.

They would have liked to drag this meal out, but were famished. Phoebe would have enjoyed a display, with table-cloths and china instead of wooden platters. That they were eating potatoes was enough to make it a special occasion. Mor would have taken his meal slowly and with dignity, but was forced to behave like a constable, coping with two quarrelling boys and having to share three fish between four people.

'Thee two are as bad as the English and French,' he remarked.

30

'I'm the English!' Edwin shouted.

'Tha's a Frenchie,' Gideon taunted. 'Thou'd eat frogs!'

'I'm not!'

'Y'are, though . . .'

Mor carved the fish sensitively, avoiding Phoebe's eyes because they made him feel ashamed of his hands, so clearly afraid was she of them touching her. But they could be as delicate as a woman's. He fed the tastiest bits of the fish into Edwin's mouth. When they had all finished, Edwin asked for the skeletons.

'What does thou want them for? There's not enough meat on 'em for a cat,' Gideon jeered.

'I only want to look at 'em. I want to play wi'em.'

'You can't 'ave 'em. I'm chucking 'em on to t'fire.'

He had already thrown one spitting onto the flames. Edwin, too proud to shed a tear at Horsfalls', was crying, screaming, in a flare of temper kicking Gideon's shins and clawing his sleeve, because he held the remaining skeletons aloft over the fire.

'I'm not a Frenchie! I'm not! I'm not! I'm not!'

'Thou'rt a Frenchie, 'cos thou collects old bones.'

'I'm not. Gi'em to me!'

Mor got between.

'Give them to the child.'

'The kid doesn't want 'em. 'E's only going to play wi'em. They'll stink on the hearth, and me mother's been cleaning. She 'as enough to do.'

'Give them to Edwin.'

'Shall no', *Judas*!'

'You call me "Judas"! Why, you . . .'

'I want 'em! I want 'em!'

'What for?' Gideon leered. 'What do you want them nasty things for?'

'My collection. My anat . . . anat . . . anatocomical collection.'

'Anatocomical! Anatocomical! Gobslutch!'

'Anatomical,' Mor corrected. 'Gideon . . .'

Mor's hand was raised. *Judas*. How it smarted. Gideon dropped the skeletons from a height onto the hearthstones. One of them snapped.

Mor's blow fell across Gideon's ear. The boy kept smiling, with stupid fixity, maintaining his challenge of his father. He wanted to show that all this was beneath his contempt.

31

Edwin pounced. 'Thanks!'

He laid the unbroken skeleton out neatly upon the stone at his usual place on the hearth, then tried to piece the other one together. Slender, delicate, pale-as-pearl bones. Edwin forgot tears and quarrels in the instant that they were laid out before him.

Mor was flushed and his heart was thudding. This was not what Sunday should be. Phoebe was awkwardly keeping her eyes turned away. In the room they were silent, subdued by Gideon's hate.

To calm the quarrel, Mor took his fiddle from where it rested, safe from children's hands and domestic carelessness, at the back of the cupboard. He lifted it out of its case and ran his fingers, trembling, several times up and down the strings to clean them, like a man caressing the spine and shoulders of his mistress to excite her.

Edwin held a skeleton horizontally, his hands at its head and tail.

'Swish, swish,' he said, and made it swim.

'Why 'as it two rows o' bones at the top and one at the bottom?' Edwin asked.

'The curved ones are at t'top to guard the organs of the body. The row at the bottom is stiff to make a keel to balance it upright in the water.'

'Why . . .'

'Stop asking questions,' Gideon interrupted, trying to ignore his burning ear. 'It's nought but God's Universe, as He created it. Curiosity killed the cat. Thou deserves a thrashing, asking questions.'

Mor tucked his instrument under his chin. They all fell silent, with attentiveness now, instead of with anger. The schoolmaster had brought up his children to be respectful before music.

From the moment he bent his cheek upon it, the head of the man and the delicate body of the violin, light as a bird, versatile as a swimming trout, were one. The tune running up from the sounding board, amok through his head, drove him crazy with delight.

If he raised his face he would see Gideon's distaste. The boy sat with his hand over his ear, humiliated, and ashamed of the mark. Mor was hiding his tears at having had to chastise a boy who already had so much to contend with.

Mor could feel, too, Gideon's dislike, or pretended dislike, of fiddle music. The reason, though he will never admit it, is that it brings pleasure to me. Who is there who can admit, even to themselves, that they are being selfish?

32

Mor looked at his eldest boy.

'Nothing is so frail and light as a fiddle. A child can smash it. I've seen a parson stamp 'is foot through one because 'e did not like the music. Any brute can put 'is foot through a fiddle, yet the music survives. Like the snowdrops are strong, that come in the earliest days of spring. They look so frail, they bend, but they push through the frozen earth and flower in the cold.'

Gideon sniggered. Mor continued playing.

The music stirred Phoebe. Mor recognised in her eyes another light to that of a couple of hours before.

From outside came some bars of a hymn tune being tried out on the chapel's harmonium.

'Are you going to the Methodists this afternoon, Gideon?' Mor asked. 'Mr Whitehead from Halifax's taking the class. You'll not want to miss 'im.'

Though addressing Gideon, Mor was smiling at Phoebe. On Sunday afternoons, Lady Well packed its children off to the Sunday School. It was the only time men had to lie with their wives when not exhausted. Sunday Schools were therefore very popular and most children had been conceived while their elder brothers and sisters were blessing the Lord's name.

'Can I go down to the river?' Edwin asked.

'Keep out of the wood, then. Don't go in the wood, don't go in there.'

'No, I won't.'

'Promise me.'

'I promise.'

'You can go down to the bridge. Who are you going with?'

'My friends.'

'Tell them the same, to keep out of Horsfall's game copses.'

Edwin was already setting off.

Mor bedded his violin and put it away in that cupboard which his children had been brought up to regard as sacred. He was tense and his hands were still shaking.

Phoebe was quivering, too, but with alarm at that tender side of herself which had shown itself to her husband.

Edwin was already going out of the door – a martin, a swallow, off to enjoy his Sunday.

Mor took hold of Phoebe's hand, at first meekly and then gripping it as he felt a reluctance. With Phoebe, the most tender hold felt like a

33

violation. The light bird-like bones, ivory coloured through her blood-less skin, were quaking.

Gideon was watching. His hands, too, were shaking as he tied a kerchief around his neck for chapel. He was trembling with anger at the threatened violation of his mother. He hesitated, unwilling to leave the house, and then he left suddenly.

Mor had not let go of Phoebe. He avoided her eyes, but understood the meaning of her reluctant hand.

'What is it, Phoebe?'

I know I won't get an answer.

'Nothing.'

Her head was bowed. She frowned with irritation.

'What is it?' he repeated, as so often in the past. He felt annoyed at her refusal to talk, and as usual he struggled not to show it. And, as always, she answered, again, 'Nothing.'

Sixteen years before when they were courting and he had walked her home after church or fair, out of the dark or the summer dusk brimming with noises of lovers, she would sigh. Her heart was breaking. 'What is it, Phoebe?' 'Nothing,' she answered. 'Nothing, think nowt of it.' So through the weeks, the months, and the years of their marriage she had answered him, 'Nothing.'

This Sunday afternoon, however, she allowed him to pluck her away, like a plant from a hedgerow, a snowdrop from a bank. There was no weight to her body. He opened the door at the foot of the stairs and led her up. She coughed nervously, and he, one step above her, clutching her hand, turned momentarily. She looked guilty even about her own cough.

Their bedroom was at the front of the house. One wall was filled with a row of slender windows, not for the view but to light that huge ancient inherited loom, on which Mor had learned his trade. His half-finished piece, abandoned the previous day, hung accusingly upon it. On the struts and nearby, Mor had pinned lists of wild herbs and flowers, their common names matched with their Latin ones. There was a tiny library of books, Plato, Rousseau, Tom Paine, a Latin Grammar, and Goldsmith's *History of the Earth and Animated Nature*. Always one was propped open for him to read a page and digest it as he worked. The room was quiet, dusty, brightened with shafts of light breaking among the loom strings and piercing the whitewashed corners. This whole area, the major part of the room, was

34

an emblem of his nature. He felt there like a scholar in his quiet study, or a monk in his cell, or like one of the Old Testament prophets, working out his thoughts in a cave in the wilderness.

The bed for Phoebe and himself was forced into a corner. Near to it on a rough table Phoebe's bridal things were displayed. Clean and undisturbed, preserved under a shining and polished glass bell jar that had been given to her by the apothecary as a wedding present, this was *her* emblem of herself. She enjoyed the preserved fact that she was married more than the acts of marriage themselves, meagre and rare though they were.

Phoebe was out of breath and it was not merely from climbing a flight of stairs. She was terrified because her marriage had brought a baby every two years and she was due to conceive now. Despite the fear, Phoebe, like all other women, had helplessly conceived, thinking as little of it as possible, because it was what everybody did. Pregnancy at least was a period when she could rely on her husband not touching her. She feared that another birth would kill her. With child two years before, she had 'sent it back', using the abortionist, Rose Gledhill, the wife of Nathaniel Gledhill, the overseer of Horsfalls'. Mor believed she had miscarried.

She spat quietly into a rag. It was a nervous habit. Also by habit she began to tidy the room, until Mor grew impatient.

Finally resigning herself, for the sake of her husband whom she did, after all, love, Phoebe collapsed onto the bed, without disrobing herself. She had no wish to display her skin that was so coarse, her limbs marked with the scars of mill accidents, and her stomach ploughed with stretch-marks from childbearing: the working man's wife, on the working man's bed stained with tears, menstrual blood, sweat and semen.

There was a commotion and shouts in the street. Mor had to see what it was. Before he reached the window, he heard the noise of a stone striking a door. He expected soldiers, perhaps an arrest. It could be that they had come for him.

There were no soldiers in view. He saw a procession of strange, frightened, silenced children. They were those whom he had met a few days before being brought in a cart, and now in the charge of that same Nathaniel Gledhill, husband of the abortionist, overseer of the Sunday School, as well as of the mill. Mor's neighbours were throwing stones and laughing at the children.

35

He remembered how, when he was a child, they had chased the strange witch-woman Anne Wylde through the streets.

Why did we do it? I joined in myself. I had to be like the other children. But I tried to miss. Afterwards I'd go running to shelter in a woman's apron, ashamed. Crying. 'What are you crying about, mardy?' I couldn't tell her, because I didn't know myself. In those days I joined in when they burned effigies of Tom Paine. I ran after 'em when they were clattering pots and banging drums outside the window of some poor old woman who they said was 'conspicuous'. Next thing I'd be crying about it. I still feel too ashamed to tell anyone, even now. Even though I did nothing. 'Man's inhumanity to man', as Burns the ploughman put it. There they are, still throwing stones at their fellow sufferers. How can they enjoy mocking them? If instead we formed a revolutionary contract, declared our brotherhood, the rights of man, stayed together, let none get between us, and kept to our highest not our lowest aspirations, the earth would be ours, no one could oppose or oppress us.

Mor was relieved to see that the apprentices were at least fairly clean and well-dressed. He tried to convince himself that things were not as bad as he had feared. The girls were in new, blue pauper's uniforms for the Lord's Day and the boys were in breeches which were also new, intended for Sunday only, and, like the prayer books which they carried but could not read, objects resentfully provided by contract from the Hackney Workhouse. Gledhill marched in front swinging his notorious briony stick with its sharp-eared devil carved out of the knob. He never glanced at his rear but took it for granted that all was obedient and orderly behind.

Mor turned away from this sight that he could do nothing about and glanced at Phoebe. He caught her in her moment of relief that he had, for the time being, abandoned her. When she met her husband's eye, her expression changed. She showed her usual torment, of wanting to give love, yet dreading the touch of hands.

He walked towards her along the flank of windows which gave him, above the heads of the procession, such sweet, soft, watery-green views of Yorkshire. He went slowly so as not to seem to attack her, then he realised that his slowness might make him more menacing.

Not saying anything about the noises outside, he stripped to his underclothes. He settled against her side. As, like other working-women, Phoebe did not wear drawers, she protected herself by keeping her legs together. Gently, with one finger, he stroked her thigh, at first over, and then under, his favourite, flower-patterned, bleached dress.

How much he longed for hands, female hands, and how vulnerable he was to them. Having been an orphan, a baby found on the workhouse steps with nothing but the name 'Greave' stitched on his shift to identify him, he, especially, had suffered from the lack of being touched that all boys suffered. Girls were fondled by their relatives but boys were not, lest it 'spoil' them, and he had grown up knowing that his only hope must come from a wife. Hence his lack of judgement. The need for caressing hands had overcome other considerations, hence his ill-judged, over-eager devotion in courting unrewarding Phoebe. In his rush for hands, he had been enslaved by the first ones to touch him . . . they were hers. Her failure to satisfy him had increased his desperation and his eagerness to marry, ironically and tragically, this one person least likely to satisfy him. He had never dared admit even to himself what he most wanted. He became ashamed of it. Oh, to be caressed, held, stroked, fondled, stroked, held . . .

He was torn in the jaws of a trap. One set of teeth rending his flesh was his desire for touch, touch, touch. The other jaw was his guilty conscience telling him to evade and deny it – anything to stop his wicked desires surfacing.

'I'm tired,' Phoebe said, frightened. 'I'm so tired, Mor. Do we need to . . .'

Because of those five births and the abortion, the use of her vagina caused her pain. She had sores and scabs where the apothecary had cauterised infections. She had wounds caused by the burning chemicals that had been sold to her by him, or by itinerant barbers and pedlars, to use as post-coital contraceptives. Heaven only knew what compounds they were, and because she never saw many of the itinerants again, she could not ask them. They pained her, the wanderers, if not through the medicaments they sold, then with the interested look in their eyes. Some pedlars were also preachers, holding forth, under an ash tree, or by a cross-roads, with wonderful ideas that she had never thought of, before they described Hell and Redemption, in such vivid pictures.

Mor fumbled hurriedly in her dress. It was either that or madness. Slack as they were, he lifted her nipples, to arouse them. Even now she was most concerned to occupy her hands with straightening her dress and with tidying bed-clothes. She desperately put her hands out sideways to them, as though she was pinned down and drowning. She had once heard a ballad about a maiden chained to a rock as the tide came in. That was how she felt. She choked under his mouth.

Then, when that cruel horrible business she dared not think about grew inevitable, she felt some pleasure . . . she dared not think of it . . . how could she dare tell him . .? from the submission. Without going so far as to make her legs welcoming, she ceased to clamp them so tightly together. She felt sorry for her husband. She started to moan, restlessly turning her face away. She closed her legs one minute, and in the next moment she was clutching him, feeling at the curls upon his neck, suffering the bristles of his chin and the saliva of his half-parted hopeful mouth, as she desperately embraced that which she could not avoid. She did what she believed all women did . . . she pretended to be happy. As friends had said, 'It won't last long. It won't hurt much. You might feel something . . . a tickling, but pretend you're enjoying it. They like that and it keeps 'em quiet later. They go to work wi' their minds rested.'

Mor heard her muttering. At first he could not tell what fragments of articulation were escaping from her. Then he picked out, scattered amongst other words, 'pray', 'altar', and 'soul'. She was confusing love with church-going.

He entered her. Usually the greater part of the animal pleasure was taken from him, because he dared not forget himself. He knew that he must pull out fast, or have a child. By this method they had unintentionally conceived six times during their marriage. He hung tormented on the edge of forgetfulness, thinking:

Coitus interruptus, at least I know the Latin for it. I'm not *ignorant.*

They were his last thoughts before oblivion. He had waited for such a long time and today it was not to be taken from him.

'My gown,' she muttered. 'My gown.'

She felt Mor's semen in her womb; a river loosed into the sea. The tide was coming. She was terrified. Tears were upon her eyes.

Mor fell heavy and slack beside her. He felt desolate. It was a desolation that might now be filled with another unwanted child.

He thought that perhaps Phoebe would rather have been in chapel, or with the followers of the prophetess Joanna Southcott in Bradford. If only she could love him for himself, and not for some Christ-Saviour that she was looking for, through him. Nothing has happened.

The sense of something, someone, being absent, was like confinement within a prison. The entire world was a prison. The universe was a confinement. It was something he could not escape. Oh, to be with the love whom he could imagine! Oh, yes, he had imagined her, imagined it. He would rather clutch a stone, than have nothing more than this. Yet if the beloved had existed, a single squalid room would have seemed bigger than the universe and all the spaces of the stars.

Singing burst from the children in the chapel. He slipped his arm under Phoebe's dress beneath her shoulder blades.

'Did you like it?' she asked.

'Yes.'

'You feel spent now?'

'Yes.'

'Men need to spend themselves or they'd be tempted . . .'

'Yes. Thank you.'

'It's all right. You need it. I know what men are. You can do it if . . .'

'Thank you.'

She placed her face upon his chest, at last with some acceptance of love-making, now that it didn't threaten her.

Mor slept. A membrane was stretched between his inner and outer worlds. Shadows were cast on the membrane. Dreams.

He had a dream that had come to him several times before. A female, without precise lineaments yet he was sure she was the same woman each time, held a dark red flower out to him. She beckoned him to take it, but when he put his hand out, he woke up. Always he would lie for a long time, just as he did tonight, wondering about the significance of the woman, the flower, and the redness of it. He would think of it during the daytime, when he struggled to recall the woman's features. Always she remained faceless, though the flow of her shape was clear to him, and it was always the same shape. Each time, he thought she had said something, but he could not recall what it was. He could not quite remember what the flower was, either, although he was a botanist. He was certain only of its redness. He knew that dreams mattered, because of what happened in the Bible. Joseph, though in captivity, through interpreting dreams saved the land of Egypt, and made himself rich. Mor felt sure that the flower, whatever it was the symbol of, was something that he must search for and grasp. Or it would find him, some day.

(3)

April 16th

Every weekday morning between five and half past the bell rang on the tower of Horsfalls' spinning mill to call the women and children. Families hurried through the town or down from the hills, across wastelands, between enclosures, and by the sides of the woods.

A month had passed, but it was still dark in the mornings. Their lamps formed over the countryside a huge star, or a quivering crocus-coloured flower, reflected on a late frost. The lamps were necessary mostly under the trees, for the clearest of moons hung above. It had a wide blue circle around it, clear as a baby's eye, further encircled by a rainbow.

All the doors in the Greaves's terrace had opened, or lamps were moving behind shutter-chinks. There was the noise of clogs, and the crying of children.

'Look . . . !' Mor exclaimed, as he stepped out of doors.

'Aye, it's cold,' Gideon said.

'No . . . the moon . . . Edwin, look! Clear as a babby's eye. Don't you like to see the moon, Gideon?'

'No. It's cold. My leg aches.'

'Y'ave to look upwards sometimes.'

'Not if it makes you stumble ont'ground, you don't. No one else's doing it.'

'No.'

'I am,' Edwin answered.

'You're always gawping at summat,' Gideon said. 'Curiosity killed the cat.'

Phoebe and her sons, like other families, carried, as well as lamps, their 'baggin', their food for the day. Phoebe had a basket, Gideon and Edwin had bags made of rabbit skins. The food was usually oatcakes and ale. This morning Edwin's baggin held a leg of rabbit, filched from his father's poachings. It was a secret – like his bottle of ale already hidden in a basket of wool-waste in the mill.

Gideon limped along, his pale, clenched features still turned towards the spillings of lamplight on the ground.

The few women who still span at home, on their small jennies, were raking their morning fires. They hardly spoke to the mill-women, as if they belonged to a different sect of church or chapel. Phoebe still felt guilty before their eyes. The first women to go into the mill, when it was new, had their windows broken.

The 'bang bang' of hand-looms was beginning through the town. Soldiers quartered in the Adam and Eve public house were hanging around the door, where the moonlight shone off buckles, weapons and tunics.

'They say in t'cropping shed that they brought down wages year by year 'cos Mr Pitt come up with an income tax for t'masters to pay,' Gideon said. '"If you cannot pay t'taxes and adult wages, then tak' children to th'work," Mr Pitt told 'em. We're going to change all that. Beginning wi't'raid we'll rise up. All will be together. The day is drawing nigh.'

They passed the church. Beggars sat in the porch, each without either a leg, or an arm, or both, from the Wars. There was a younger boy, from a hill-farm, who had been crippled in a factory accident and, not being able to help with the family's livelihood, had been turned away from home.

The crowd went downhill by the vicarage. The children ran to the young eagle which had been captured by the parson when, during the winter, it had strayed out of the hills in search of food. She had stooped upon the parson's pigeon-cote and he had wounded her with his blunderbuss, staking her with a four foot rope in his garden. A crow has captured an eagle, Mor had thought. As she crouched on beaten, fouled earth where her prey, the domestic hens and pigeons, no longer feared to come close, she was like an old, dying vulture or kite. Her unkempt feathers, in the light of the moon and the lamps, were grey as dirty, neglected pewter. When first fastened up, the great bird was unable to believe that she could not fly. Each magnificent, confident, stately rush had been stopped by a shot of pain. She had crumpled into an undignified bundle of feathers like a burst pillow-case in the snow. The parson laughed and his daughter cried. Eventually the eagle gave up, merely condescending sometimes to peck without relish at the charity of mice thrown to her. She stared balefully at Lady Well, through her yellow, unflinching eyes. Birds do not weep.

'Anything that starts wi' foolish talk in t'cropping shed will be shot and pinioned as easy as yonder brave, young eagle. There's your symbol for revolution. If we show we've got wings and brains and ideas, that's how they'll serve us,' Mor said.

He glanced at the litter of mice thrown at the eagle, which she would not touch.

'When we're defeated and cowed, instead of giving us our rights they'll relieve us wi' charity. They'll 'ave collections for us. Subscriptions to save us from starving. Charity'll taste very nice to them that give it. To us it'll taste like poison. They won't understand why we don't thank 'em. They'll smile when they give it. But if we show that we expect bread as a right, for the work we do, by going and taking it, they'll hang us for it.'

The children had run to throw stones, spit and laugh at the great bird, because she was weak and tethered. Edwin was uncertain, at the back of the group. Then they were disturbed by the arrival of the night-soil cart, collecting buckets of urine for bleaching the cloth in the mill.

They climbed down the long flights of stone stairs through the woods. The bell was still clanging. Ewes, giving birth in the folds, were crying across the valleys. The first lambs shivered on long, wide-spread tottering legs, their tails twisting in circles, as they pulled at the teat.

The moon, on the blue-lit frost, transformed some banks into pale and ghostly wings. Sometimes you can feel all the weight of the moon, and see that it is no more than a cold rock heavily rolling around. But when shining high, round and bright, as it was this morning, it is like a tunnel revealing a glimpse into a brilliant universe beyond.

Phoebe hurried along, her wiry arms moving briskly. Even from a distance, from the back, you could tell she was a troubled person, by the stoop of her shoulders, the sharp edges of the bones thrusting through her shawl, and from the dangle of her arms.

With Edwin at her side she was holding her lamp close to the ground to search for primroses, their petals shut against the dark.

Mor and Gideon caught up with the other two. Phoebe turned upon Mor her face of suffering and forbearance.

It gives a man an impulse to hit her, he thought.

Edwin asked his father at what time the flowers would open.

'When the sun comes up. If you slip out o'doors then, it's like entering the gates of Heaven.'

'Go out o't'mill?' It was impossible!

Mor laughed.

42

'I'll come with you! We'll all run away.'

Edwin was thoughtful.

'Which way is America?'

He had asked this question often, but still loved to hear the answer. Mor pointed.

Edwin turned his back on the part of the night sky that promised a rising sun, and stared towards the barrier of hills.

'How far is it?'

'Thousands and thousands of miles.'

'How long on a ship?'

'Months. A year if it gets lost.'

'Where do y'ave to go first, to catch ship t'America?'

Edwin knew the answer to this question too. *Liverpool*; his tongue licked the corner of his lips, where lingered the taste of the sweet, exotic word.

His father merely smiled, letting the boy answer for himself.

'They sail from Liverpool, don't they? Have you been t'America?'

'No, my son, I've not been to America.'

Just as he had answered many times before.

'Why not?'

To Edwin, a place so out of reach that his father had not been there was the most fabulous of all travellers' goals.

'I suppose it'll be only full of strife and trouble, same as everywhere else. They call it "the land of promise", though. Perhaps I'm wrong.'

They had sunk further down the walled stairway, by the trees. Bursting out at the foot of the wood, into the louder clang of the bell, they were in a clearing of moonlit land by the river, near to a block of new large houses built for the overseer, the engineer, and the clerk, where they could watch over the mills and tenter-frames. The workers threaded between the lines of cloth.

'What did you join t'Volunteers for, Bandy Legs? Didst tha want to learn the use of a gun t'elp us win t'Revolution?' a skinny, wild-eyed girl shrieked at the guard.

It was *she* who had the crooked legs. She envied and longed for the straight-limbed young soldier.

He had no answer. He had joined the militia to escape his village, and poverty, and to fight Napoleon, and he was trying not to hate the work that he had been given. He tried to keep in mind what he had been told: that Yorkshire, too, was a frontier.

43

'That's tomorrow, Sally,' her friend joked. 'Tomorrow, as never comes. Gi'o'er teasing t'poor recruit. He'll be missing his mammy.'

The friend, though speaking to Sally, was looking at the recruit, to make him blush.

'I'm not teasing 'im! Some o't'lads do join up for that, don't they, soldier? Just to find out how to use a gun.'

Mor was laughing. He saw an awkward youth, armed, but unable to defend himself against a couple of spinning girls, who made him blush.

The laughing females passed on. A crowd had collected off the hillsides. They poured through the narrow passageway between the mills and the wall at the foot of the garden in front of Mr Horsfall's house. The mansion, with its yellow stone blackening slowly, was raised up into the steep bank of the woods so that the master could hawk over what went on below his rose gardens. A broad-shouldered groom was posted to try to stop the work-people waking Mr Horsfall and his family. There was also a couple of militiamen. Nevertheless the women and children did what they usually did to make their presences felt. They began a rhythmic, frightening banging on the cobblestones with their boots and clogs, and looked up.

It was not for the master, nor his wife and children, that they searched. It was for the face, high up and remote in the house, of one imprisoned who could not sleep, locked away because of his ugliness. In the light of lamp or candle, a corroded, terrifying face would waver for a second behind the glass, frightened of being seen, yet not able to resist looking.

'There's the ghostie, there's the boggart, there's the ghost, there! There! There!'

The wages of sin. The fear of Hell, thought Phoebe. The wounds, the tortures, the burning scalding pains, that the preacher selling treacle for a cough told me about.

Phoebe too was trying to glimpse that body which the members of its own family would not go near. Food was taken in by a servant with a scarf drawn across her face for the stench, and to hide her revulsion. The skin of its face was drawn back in tight furrows, leaving a thinly covered skull. The eyes were dead pools. In one, a little yellow twilight still lingered, to take in dim impressions of the Yorkshire it had once commanded. The nose was eaten away, flesh and bones, leaving no more than a volcanic scar. The lips were drawn back and had almost vanished, the gums were rotting, the few remaining teeth were standing proud. Its throat and tongue were corroded, so that it could not scream. It could hardly breathe and it moved slowly.

The vision faded back from the window, the glass clouded with a breath that fortunately the spectators could not smell. The spectral, still-living body, rotting from syphilis, of Nicholas Horsfall, Senior.

The workers turned to their right, in between large gateposts. These separated the narrow end of the main, three-storeyed spinning mill, which was at right angles to the river, from the counting house and a row of cloth-finishing sheds. The gates of Paradise Mills were made of iron and brass, with a grinning yellow sun, the Horsfalls' family insignia. Overhead was the motto, *Labor Omnia Vincit*. ('A corrupt form of "*Amor Vincit Omnia*,"' Mor had explained.) The pillars were decorated with the carved figures of Adam and Eve – an Hebraic myth depicted anachronistically in the style of Greek sculpture, bigger than life-size, and naked except for fig leaves. Facing out towards the woods the pair were shown in Paradise, under vines. Adam was grasping his spade, whilst the sensual Eve dallied with the snake, which nibbled at her lips, kissing her. On the inner flanks of the posts, our forefathers slunk into exile – into the mill.

The women and children entering saw, ahead of them, that new house for 'apprentices' built on the river bank. On their left was the spinning mill, its furthest end against the stream for the sake of the water-wheel. On their right, across the yard, was the old fulling mill built half a century before by the clothier Benjamin Greave. This was also at right angles to the stream, because of a more old-fashioned wheel. The fourth side of this square was made up of a row of finishing sheds. In these the woollen pieces, brought in by the hand-loom weavers, had their nap raised in a gig-mill, then were clipped smooth by Horsfall's own croppers, using shearing machines, and finally passed on to the dye-house.

Paradise Mills were the grandest in the district. Their finishing shops meant that Horsfall did not have to depend upon Tiplady's, nor on sending woollens elsewhere in vulnerable cartloads to be finished.

A reservoir, or 'lodge', held water to drive the wheel. Except for the locked opening by which the engineer passed from the water-wheel housing onto the bank of the lodge, all doors faced into the mill yard. The windows were barred. The main gate was locked after the workers entered and only unfastened for the passage of carts. The place was, in fact, a fortress.

45

Gideon passed on, by the mill wall, and downstream fifty yards to Tiplady's.

Mor called at the office, to see about obtaining credit from Horsfalls' to purchase a warp from them, then he retraced his way through the trees to his home and to his solitary loom.

All over the high parts of the countryside cocks were crowing, although it was still not daylight in the valley and merely a yellow tinting was to be seen by the birds on the hills. Only seconds after the first cock had alarmed the hillcrest village at Heights, like the bursting of a clock-spring suddenly they were all calling, on and on, through Yorkshire and Lancashire, the land ringing with them before the day began further below.

For the women and children, the doors of the spinning mill were ready open. Within was a shadowy cave where rows upon rows of candles were still lit.

What'll 'e do all day? wondered Phoebe, turning her back upon her husband as he climbed into the sun. 'E'll not get on wi'is piece. I know 'im. Books! Staring out o't'window. Going down to t'river.

Nathaniel Gledhill, with his briony stick, was waiting at the entrance, behind his reading-desk, beneath the notice:

RULES TO BE OBSERVED BY HANDS EMPLOYED IN THIS MILL
Fines shall be administered as follows.
For waste on the floor, 1d
For any oil wasted or spilled on the floor, 2d each offence, besides paying for the value of the oil. Any person neglecting to oil at the proper time shall be fined 2d.
For every oath or insolent language 3d for the first offence and if repeated, shall be dismissed.
All persons in our employ shall serve Four Weeks' notice before leaving but N. Horsfall shall and will turn any person off without notice being given.
Any person wilfully damaging this notice will be dismissed.

Whoever'd deface it? Mr Gled'ill 'as written it 'imself. In real grammar, I was told.

As usual, he smiled, to welcome Phoebe and her boy to twelve hours amongst the machines and the fine sifting choking dust. A man appears more fearsome if he can beam upon misery, and when his face did cloud with anger, Gledhill seemed the more terrible.

46

Edwin hated the blinding plunge into the dark; the cloying smell, the sizes of rooms, men and machines. It's like one of 'is pictures of 'Ell, that he shows us in t'Sunday School . . .

Gledhill took out a large handkerchief. He brought it out so often and proudly, it might have been the British flag.

'It's 'ot,' he declared, smiling at Edwin.

Edwin did not know whether he was expected to answer.

'Isn't it?' insisted Gledhill, threateningly.

'Yes, sir.'

'Oh no, it isn't. It isn't 'ot yet. Not as 'ot as it will be. Is it?'

'No, sir.'

''E's a good boy,' Phoebe said. 'He does try 'ard . . .'

'No, sir! It 'orrors me to think 'ow 'ot it'll be when the frames begin.' Gledhill looked at his watch. 'In five minutes' time.'

The overseer, smelling of tobacco, breathed heavily above the boy. The machines had not yet started, the door was open, the sun had risen a little more and they could hear the cocks all over the countryside.

'But not, mark you, as 'ot as it is in 'Ell. Mark my words, it'll not be that 'ot.'

'No, Mr Gledhill, we can be sure o' that.' Phoebe laughed. 'Though we can't be sure who's going, can we? Who shall be called. Some shall.'

They say 'e was in India. A sergeant in the army. They say 'e could do what 'e liked with *anyone* there. Well, *my* bobbins are clean.

'Read that,' Gledhill commanded Edwin.

The overseer stood behind a reading desk which sloped towards the workers. There was a large Bible, with a fresh passage exposed daily. To reach up and read it, Edwin had to bounce on his toes. Gledhill made a hobby of scouring the woodlands with a tin vasculum for botanical specimens, so he had chosen to exhibit –

'Sermon on th'Mount! Consider the lilies o' the field 'ow they grow they toil not neither do they spin . . .'

Edwin took in another deep breath, and flew over commas and pauses to get it over with.

'And yet I say unter you that even Solomon in all 'is glory was not arrayed like one of these wherefore if God so clothe the grass o' the field which today is and tomorrow is cast into th'oven . . .'

Gledhill slammed his palm on the desk.

'Enough! Thou's not much style about thee! This is an affecting passage o't'Bewk, it needs some expression putting into it.'

47

'Stop now, Edwin, that's enough,' Phoebe told him. 'Mill's waiting. Time and tide wait for no man.'

'Where did you learn to read like that?'

'Me feyther.'

He speaks like his father, too, Phoebe thought. Short wi' folk. It can be taken wrong.

'His father teaches 'im, sir. It could 'elp 'im advance.'

'I 'ope so, Mrs Greave. Too much schooling isn't always a good thing. Some go wrong just because of it. I've done all right for myself, wi'out schooling. The army taught me all I need to know.'

Suddenly there was, except for the hard clatter of feet, a quiet like a hole in the universe. The factory bell had ceased to clang. It was half past five precisely, as registered by the clock on the tower and the watch that Gledhill portentously held upon his palm.

'Time to close the gates of Paradise!' some joker said.

Some joker always said this, and someone always laughed, though it was not funny anymore.

Phoebe went straight to her spinning frame. Hers was one of the tidiest, cleanest in the factory, yet she was amongst the first to reach her work. She picked up her feather duster and started to tease out bits of fluff that had settled out of the laden air during the night. It was a feminine task, which she enjoyed performing. The other women were idling to their work. Who was Phoebe trying to please? Nathaniel Gledhill was not yet in sight. It must have been God.

The younger girls, under the overseer's supervision, in a room with the small boys present, were stripping and dressing themselves in their factory smocks, which they called 'bishops'.

Gledhill lifted the hem of a girl's skirt.

'Come on, let's see thy legs! Let's see how Mother Nature has endowed thee!'

'The more moral a girl is, the more she suffers in this Christian place . . .' Edwin remembered his father's words, as he hid under his shirt the leg of rabbit out of his baggin.

He was just in time, for Gledhill next turned his attention to the boys, who had to put their baggin and clogs into a cupboard. The overseer banged his stick on the floor for silence.

'Praised be the Lord and God save the King!'

They all chanted after him, 'Praised be the Lord and God save the King!'

From the dust, from the heat, the children's voices were as harsh as a choir of crows.

The overseer exchanged his staff for a three foot length of leather belting, and the bare-footed children were ushered onto the acre-sized floor, into the heady fumes of the rape oil which bathed the drive-shafts and the gears. The timing was synchronised with the moment when Paradise Mills shook and shuddered into life.

Joshua Slaughter, the engineer, was on the lodge bank. The setting moon was a great tired dewdrop close to the hills, swelling as it neared the horizon. In another part of the sky the sun had risen, igniting the songs of blackbirds, thrushes and robins. A pied wagtail, in smart, new spring feathers, was scurrying and bowing along the top of the bank that separated the reservoir from the stream.

The world had been cold blue but the sun cast over the perspectives of frosty fields and slopes an orange light. For a short while everywhere was caught in a mixture of lights from opposite ends of the spectrum, a brilliance that faded quickly, as the frost on southern slopes was warmed into breath and mist. The sun drew threads upright off the dark, still waters of the reservoir. The higher they rose, the thinner they became and the faster they vanished. They were, fancied the engineer, being wound upwards onto invisible bobbins on the spinning frames of Heaven.

Joshua was a childless widower, having lost his wife in childbirth, and in his work too he was a loner, but he contemplated this day with satisfaction and pleasure. He loved his machines, and in the evening he was going to Bradford to spend an hour or two praying, debating and looking forward to the Millennium with a group of the followers of Joanna Southcott.

The engineer cranked up the sluice-gate. An edge of water creased, folded, sucked leaves off the surface of the reservoir, twisted in braids of silver and fell with a swift, silent glitter into the mill. A snake of water entered the factory, as secretly and quietly as a spy to do its work. Having fallen out of sight onto the bottom of its stone hole, it thundered onto the blades of the wheel.

He slipped back into the wheel-housing, locking his private door behind him. The wheel, twenty-five feet in diameter, six feet wide across the blades, catching the flow at the top and on the downstream side, was turning so rapidly that you could hardly catch sight of it under its cloak of rapid silver. The rough-fitting wooden axle groaned. The raging wheel was a god in its watery element, powering a great mill with its cargo of lives. Most of the stream fell away with a roar at the bottom of the turn but some clung and dropped later, screaming at the wheel's rise, in a glitter of rainbows, like those which had recently clung around the moon. They snapped into small pieces, joined in trembling circles, broke again and darted in fragments —bright dragonflies round the turning god.

Once the wheel was in motion such a great force of water wasn't necessary to keep it running and the engineer diverted most of it. Wasted it, he couldn't help thinking, although everywhere in the world it ran downhill anyway, and God Himself was wasteful. He did not appear to realise what can be done with the sleeping powers He has created. How can a man understand that? Joshua wondered.

He listened, his ear cocked, discriminating amongst the orchestra of sounds from the wheel-housing and reaching him from inside the mill. They all had a meaning to him. On hearing one that was not quite right, or out of his excruciating love imagining it so – like a mother with a spoiled child always thinking it sickly – Joshua threaded between the gears and wheels to make an adjustment. He was a slender, lithe, not very tall man, 'handy for worming and diving amongst my engines,' he said. After he had made his adjustment Joshua heard with satisfaction the whole universe change its tune.

With all the time in the world he stared, listening and marvelling at the gears and at this rage of energy which through the night had lain dormant and harmless in the lodge until he fed it into the manufactory. Slaughter was one of the few at Horsfalls' who 'laboured in his vineyard', as he put it, alone, at his own pace, and had time to contemplate such things. He was in charge of the machines, rather than they mastering him. Oh, what an emblem of the powerful body of God is a manufactory for spinning worsted woollens! He himself felt like God. He found time to compose 'instructive similes' comparing, for instance, a manufactory for mechanical weaving to the greater dynamo of the world and its stars. He made up verses on such subjects as 'The Mechanical Hoist', or 'The Railway To Heaven Arrived At Through Teetotalism And Methodism', or 'The Railway To Hell Reached Downwards Through Drunkenness'.

The only initiate into the mystery of machinery, he was a priest and a king. He would not allow anyone else into his wheel-room, his powerhouse. Good engineers being rare and essential, he could even keep out Mr Horsfall.

Slaughter put the wheel into gear and it ran more quietly. He went into the main building, where a man was snuffing out candles, and the hands were at their stations. All over the room coils of light, the spun threads, were unwinding down to the spindles. It was beams of light that they were spinning, not wool.

He saw something which, no matter how long he was familiar with it, touched his heart. Some machines, that he loved in every other respect, were designed to the scale of a child, with the lowest rows of bobbins only two or three feet above the floor. They were called 'throstles', or thrushes, for their sweet singing sound. Those machine-makers, thought Slaughter, Mr Smith of Keighley, Mr Platt of Dob Cross, must have hard hearts! They might as well be forging slave-shackles.

Slaughter felt for the women and children. He and Gledhill were now hardly on speaking terms, although they lived next door to one another. Yet Slaughter was not a Luddite, a machine-breaker. In his view, if society was to be improved, things must not be destroyed but, on the contrary, must be better made. For him it was a case of society needing to be better engineered.

At the far end of the mill he caught sight of Phoebe Greave. 'Winsome Phoebe,' he whispered, aloud, with no one to listen. He admired her for the way she looked after her frame. She herself was as neat and gleaming a woman as you could expect to meet in such circumstances, and how she kept herself so clean, he did not know.

But he must not dwell on that tantalising sight; others might notice him. He turned to contemplate the satisfying movements of the rows of machines, where there was no grief nor despair, but only the possibility of infinite improvement. Sadly, he felt that the operatives showed little appreciation for what they operated. 'Just like women', they only noticed when they broke down. Even Phoebe Greave did not seem to grasp the refinement of scientific principle involved, though he had stolen the opportunities to talk to her on this subject.

For the widower was drawn by unsatisfied love and desire, just as his great wheel suffered the torment of water.

Edwin's work was to be servant to the impatient demands of the spinning frames which brought delight to their master, Joshua Slaughter. Edwin was a 'piecer'. He had to guide the threads through the eyelets and the metal channels. When threads snapped, he must join them up again. He retrieved waste wool and put it in a basket. He had also to keep his mechanical mistress supplied with raw wool, either by fetching it himself or by bullying one of the gangs of apprentice girls, whose first job was to fetch and carry.

The manufactory ran upon bullying as much as it did upon water power. The grand-bully of all was the overseer, for Gledhill was paid according to productivity. As he walked the aisles he banged his strap upon the frames, hummed, sang a hymn or made jokes. Children would smile sycophantically.

'Wake up from your dreams, you sluggards, your vain idle dreams!' he would shout, genially. He might even let them mimic him behind his back. But if he actually caught them daydreaming, 'Idleness! Debauchery! Sluggards!' he would yell. 'Thou'd fall asleep over thy work, wouldst thou? Cheating your master of wages! When I was apprentice I'd never dare sleep in my master's time. I'll give you something to droop your 'eads for, I will!'

The nails of his thumb and forefinger were long and curved as hawks' beaks. With these he pinched their ears, until his nails tore the flesh. He would dip his victims head-first into a tank of cold water, or he would 'leather' them, when imprisoned in one of the big wheeled baskets.

The spinning machines were unprotected. Where the infants scrambled beneath the frames were the drive-shafts, oily and unguarded. The floor was slippery with oil. It took only a moment's forgetfulness for the frames to grab their loose gowns and ragged trousers.

'Look, Gledhill,' Nicholas Horsfall said. 'It's wasteful having children maimed, their fingers ripped off. A great loss of money, so keep 'em awake. How do we fight Bonaparte if we can't keep our factories running? And if an accident occurs, make sure they're buried a long way away, outside the parish. These damned morbid factory inspectors with their philanthropy will fall heavily on you as well as me, you know.'

When eight o'clock arrived, a board was turned to inform everyone that they had ten minutes in which to clean their machines. Mr Gledhill swung a handbell. The children lined up, in groups of different sexes, to be led out to satisfy their natural requirements. It wasted time, but the product eked out the night-soil used for bleaching cloth.

The overseer never missed a chance, in chapel or mill, to castigate.

'Varmints! Vagrants!' he shouted.

Children fidgeted, afraid to show that they needed the yard.

'What a rabble! If Mr 'Orsfall knew one 'alf the trouble I 'as 'e'd send you right back to the workhouse, or set you loose to starve upon the moors.' The overseer described the wastes with a sweep of his arm. 'How would you like that, eh? Think of the snow and ice that'd lie on your poor forgotten graves, with no one to say a prayer for you. Why should our good and respected Mr 'Orsfall 'ave to put up with illegitimate scum of wastrel parents, Godless thieves, liars and beggars, eh?'

No one had the answer, so he plucked heads and prodded backs.

'Admit it!' he yelled.

'Yes, sir! Yes, sir!'

'Yes, sir! Nothing can redeem you but the productive labour in which you are so fortunately employed and even to that you have to be driven!'

The overseer and his wife, Rose, who couldn't think why she had married such a man, led them out, boys in one group and girls in another. The abortionist wondered what her husband would make of it if he knew that she sometimes cheated him of victims. They went under the blue sky of a clear day that had arisen without them. A lark rose into it, singing. It became a speck and vanished high up, like something thrown into a fire or a lamp. A blackbird, squawking, crossed the cobbles. Godforgi'me, why does everything scream at us?, one little girl wondered. They wouldn't receive their indentures until the age of twenty-one. How well they'd know these few yards of light by then; which stone sets had been cut by the iron tyres of waggons, which were smooth; groundsel and chickweed in corners; purple and yellow steam from the dye-house; the swearing and cursing; the dull thud of wooden hammers and the tang of urine from the fulling shed; the sunlit glow of freedom through the big gates, and the square of changeable sky.

There was, however, one little freedom that could be practised after they had visited the 'necessaries', when they were all for a short while thrown together in the yard.

Edwin had formed a friendship with that girl who had just asked herself why the world could only scream at her. She was dark with dirt and grease, thin from ill-treatment and hunger, her hair was brutally cropped for working amongst the machines, and so that it wouldn't harbour lice. She looked the same age as himself, but was so starved who could tell? Her eyes were luminous, inquisitive and extremely pale. She had reminded Edwin of his dead sister Esther who, until she broke her bones, had been like a mother to him, because Phoebe had always been at her work. It was Esther who, as early as the age of four, had dragged the infant Edwin around the cottage in her arms.

When the apprentice and Edwin had first met he had been gnawing a piece of dry oatcake.

'What's 'at?' the girl had demanded. 'Gi'it me.'

'What's your name?' Edwin asked.

'Gi'me that!' she answered.

He gave her half, and waited for her to finish gobbling. 'Go on, tell us what your name is,' he repeated.

'Gi' me more,' she said.

He asked her, a third time, 'Go on, tell us your name.'

The girl, though no bigger than Edwin, seemed much older. Although in some ways more frightened, vulnerable and confused, she looked and talked like a shrivelled old woman. He gave her more food.

'They call me Numbskull and th'Ackney Cow and Little Bitch and 'Prentice and You There and anything that comes into their 'eads. I forgot what name they wrote in a book.'

'I'm going to call you Margaret.'

It was the name of a beautiful saint on a flag in the Sunday School.

The girl was drawn to the boy who teasingly, gently, gave her oatcake and a name, and she trusted him . . . almost. She repeated, 'Morgarit, Morgarit,' in a queer mixture of accents, from the north, the midlands and the south, which intrigued him. She spoke rapidly and fluently, used to the fight for survival, to constantly adapting herself and her speech. After only a few weeks in Yorkshire, she was practising shortening the definite article before the noun with a glottal stop.

They had begun to give their minds to devising ways of meeting. Today in the yard, Edwin pushed forward the leg of rabbit.

'What's 'at?' she demanded, grabbing it before he could answer. He explained what it was for and she obediently hid it under her bishop.

The children were re-assembled into groups, this time of mixed sexes, but divided into apprentices and local children. Rose Gledhill led her batch to the apprentice house for their breakfast porridge, and Nathaniel took the others to a corner of the spinning mill to devour the baggin they had brought for themselves. At half past eight they were all back at work.

Margaret was a doffer. She and her gang of girls had to climb the machines when the bobbins were full, replace them with empty ones and put the loaded reels into a wheeled basket. When the skip was full they pushed it out into the yard near to the water-wheel, or if they worked on an upper floor, to a platform above a hoist. Then they brought back the empty skip. Edwin and Margaret had discovered that by bribing her companions she could stay hidden in the yard until the other children came with the next load, or even until the one after that.

For Edwin, who was without an excuse for going outside, it was difficult to dodge the law of the frames, yet if Margaret tipped him that she had placed her bribe, he could not help himself from following, to snuggle with her in a nest amongst old baskets, timber, bits of masonry and machinery. Sneaking between the machines felt like going poaching with his father.

At eleven o'clock Margaret came by, one of four pushing a skip. By now, Mor's piece of rabbit had been passed on and hidden in another's bishop, soon to be concealed under a hairy, unclean blanket in the apprentice house, to soothe some unknown hungry sobbing misery in the dark.

The Gledhills and Joshua Slaughter were out of sight and so was the under-engineer who supervised the oiling. Edwin drew forth the flask of ale that he'd hidden in some waste wool, thrust it among her bobbins and told her, 'Don't give that to anyone! That's for us.'

Eventually Edwin had to go rooting for what had dropped on the undersides of the frames. Instead of returning with a bag of scavenged wool, he peeped out of the far side to make sure that Gledhill was not in sight and escaped to look for Margaret where she was hidden in the yard at the foot of the hoist. She crept out from a mass of new, oily leather belting and machinery piled against the wall of the wheel-housing; new spinning frames, and also cropping machines. She dutifully clutched the beer.

'I've found out 'ow to sneak in by the water-wheel,' Edwin told her.

'Godforgi'me, 'ow?'

Her eyes were wide and hopeful. Their paleness almost sparkled.

'In a minute yon engineer'll go in there to check. I know 'is times and 'e leaves the door unlocked 'til 'e comes out again. So we slips in behind 'im, and stays there after 'e's left.'

'We'll be locked in.'

'Huh! Slaughter comes back in an hour. So then we sneaks out back to our work.'

'Cor. What if 'e sees us?'

'Huh! I know 'ow to 'ide. Me feyther showed me 'ow to 'ide from gamekeepers. Most important thing is to stay still. Remember not to move an inch, especially if 'e looks right at you.'

Hidden in the corner of the yard, they listened for the engineer. Joshua made a lot of noise, clattering his iron-tipped boots on the cobblestones and singing a hymn:

> 'Give me the faith that can remove
> The mountain to the plain . . .'

Why's he want to remove it? Edwin wondered. In one hand clutching the beer, and with the other holding Margaret's hand, Edwin led her towards the wheel-house. All seemed safe. He tugged the terrified girl towards the shadowy, roaring wheel, in its glitter of water. There was a bright opening of sky where it fell out of the lodge. He pulled her in after himself. He never thought of looking ahead. Unable to see, they both stood, holding their breath. Fortunately the engineer was out of sight. They grew used to the dark and saw that no one was in it. Edwin's confidence grew, and having a frail, trusting female companion made him decisive. He led her, blindly, but pretending to know the way, climbing up between the pouring wheel and the wall, onto the windowsill.

The sun illuminated and warmed the golden stone. It was like new-baked bread. He sat on one side and she trustfully squatted at the other. He stared through the bars and so she did the same. Looking up the valley between the trees they could see the light on the slopes, where gangs were building walls. Long walls were thrown like ropes over the horizon. In an enclosure filled with ewes and lambs, all the lambs together were scampering from wall to wall, running races. They turned, their noses raised, some leaping in the air, waiting for one to decide, and then they set off again. Nearby, little triangles of glassy light were dancing upon the water. Margaret wanted to scoop them up into a heap of jewels.

But it was merely dark and noisy water that poured close by, down into a murky, thundering hole, the bottom of which they could not see. They were drenched by handfuls of water from the wheel. They crouched by a storm of liquid shining, of darkness, low rumblings, rainbows and soakings. Edwin, and Margaret when she had been taken to Sunday School, had noticed how the water raged, and had shuddered at the fear of dropping into it.

They heard the engineer enter and move around, mumbling, far below, and sometimes they caught sight of him.

''E talks to himself.' Edwin stifled a giggle. 'Can you see what 'e's saying?'

He wondered if Margaret had learned to lipread yet, like the other workers amongst noisy machines.

'Yes, if . . .'

She caught her breath, afraid of being heard. But, as Edwin expected, Joshua did not look up. They watched him run his finger meditatively through the oil that smeared the gears. He put his thumb and forefinger together to feel the viscosity, then he *tasted* it. At last the engineer left, locking them in.

Edwin uncorked the stoneware bottle of beer. He swigged it, then passed it to Margaret. She was tugging at the stubble of her shorn hair.

'I wish it was long,' she said.

'What's it like in the 'prentice 'ouse? What does Gledhill get up to?'

'What's 'e get up to? Ph . . . e . . . ew!'

Margaret tried to whistle, pursing her lips as boys did, but no sound came. Edwin whistled, to show her.

'They say 'e does nasty abominable sins. Me feyther thinks 'e's practising for 'Ell, and that's why 'e talks about it so much in chapel.'

'If 'e doesn't like a gal 'e spits 'is tobacco on th'floor and mak's 'er lick it up. Sometoimes 'e mak's y'open yer mouth and 'e spits into it. I've 'ad that done to me, plenty o'toimes.'

'Huh! All the girls 'ave 'ad that. T'other operatives get round and watch. I've seen 'em.'

''E mak's us eat dirty bits o'candle. 'E says nasty things. 'E comes up from behind and screws 'is fingers in yer ears. 'E goes toighter and toighter inside of you. 'E watches and asks if you've wetted yourself, and doesn't stop until you tell 'im you 'ave. Every night I 'ear different ones crying themselves to sleep in th'prentice 'ouse.' She paused. 'They miss their mothers, I suppose.'

She paused again, and added, 'My mother's still in London. I'd like to go and foind 'er. I thought I'd see 'er when they sent me to 'Ackney

57

again from Derbyshire, but I was only a few months back before they sent me up 'ere, so I never met 'er.'

'You were in Derbyshire?'

'I was apprentice there for two years, then the summer come dry. There was no water for the wheel, they said, and they couldn't feed us with no work to do, so they sent us back. That place was worse than this one. We didn't even get out to Sunday School there. Mrs Gledhill's kind, but that Mrs Newton down Monsall Dale . . . !

'The night before we went up there, I'd been crying. My eyes were red. They won't take anyone with sore eyes, 'cos they get like that from the fluff and they don't want no trouble. I was froightened they wouldn't take me. I wanted to get out of 'Ackney and said I was eleven. I was noine, I think. I don't know 'ow old I am. I'd been put in the workhouse 'cos my mother was ill and I only ever saw 'er sometoimes on Sunday. We was took off in the middle of the night and my mother never found out where I was for a year, but Jimmy Dawson's mother kept on at the workhouse master. My mother walked to Derbyshire to find me, and 'er ill. She ate grass on the road. She pushed 'andfuls of straw in 'er mouth to stop 'erself feeling 'ungry. She was crying and I got all wet from 'er kissing me. Mrs Newton washed me and give me a clean pinafore before she sent me in to 'er. I don't know what Mother would 'ave said if she'd seen me normal. She wanted to take me away but Mrs Newton said I couldn't go 'cos I was indet . . .'

'Indentured.'

Margaret remembered the paper that she could not understand, but which had imprisoned her; the black gothic letters, the coat of arms wrapping the first letter, the bright red seal, the smell of hot wax, and the words that meant nothing when some were read out. No one had the patience to read much, nor to explain.

'I touched a red 'orse on the bit o' paper and made an "X" where they said, and they paid me a shilling. I never saw me mother after. 'Er last words were to tell me not to steal, but I couldn't 'elp it. I was 'ungry. She went away all stooped up and didn't look back. I was expecting to see 'er again in 'Ackney. She was ill. Do you think she's . . . she's . . . ?'

'She'll be all right.'

Edwin hurriedly pointed over the reservoir, above the trees, to unenclosed moors dark with wintry heather.

'Me feyther takes me up there when we go trapping hares and fishing.'

'You go fishing and trapping?'

'Mr Horsfall lets us,' he lied, and swigged more beer, wondering if he had said too much.

'Mr Horsfall does?'

Mr Horsfall was God, and she did not believe that God could be kind or generous. Only, sometimes, it was said, Mr Horsfall had pretty girls into his house. Mr Gledhill took them there.

'There's streams all over th'moors, just like under the mill, only th'water's not black, it's all white and brown and shining.'

Edwin looked down into the murky growling unfathomable pit that was what became of the streams after converging from the little valleys of the moorland. He swigged more beer.

'Do you think me mother's still aloive?' Margaret whispered.

'Don't worry. She'll be somewhere.'

'I saw two girls die in Cressbrook Mill in Monsall Dale. Sarah Goodling was knocked down by Mr Birch. He asked why 'er frame was stopped and she said she didn't know. "I'll learn ye to know," 'e said and when she tried to get up 'e kicked 'er down again. She was twelve. They said we 'ad to work 'ard to 'elp fight the war. She was carried up to the 'prentice 'ouse. Mr Birch said "nothing ailed 'er but idleness". The master ordered camomile tea and 'er to go to bed, but when 'er that shared with 'er went up she found 'er dead . . .

'There was another girl was swinging 'er can with 'er food in it, and it 'it the doorpost. Mr Newton kicked 'er where 'e shouldn't and she wasted away. She was always sleepy, 'til she wore away and died.

'I don't know what's going to 'appen to us all at 'Orsfalls'. I wish it wasn't so long. I want to finish and 'ave done.'

'That'll be ten years.'

Edwin swigged some more beer. It was having its effect. Dreamily, he looked at the sunlit hills beyond the bars.

'Sitting 'ere's like being on t'moors,' he said. 'Let's pretend it's Sunday.'

Margaret quickly bent her head.

'Our father which ort in 'Eaven, 'allowed be Thy name . . .'

'Huh! We never go to church!'

'Why not?'

'My brother Gideon likes going to chapel. When it's wet I get sent, if Feyther's feeling tired and wants to go to bed. Rest o't'time we go on t'moors and roll our trousers up in t'sun.'

'It's not always sunny.'

Margaret was envious. She watched him. To imitate, she lifted her pinafore and stretched her bare, skinny legs into the sun. They were oily and scarred. Yet today she liked displaying her body. From being in crowds of children, her preoccupation had been to hide, but Edwin's company made her feel different. She imagined that the windowsill was the bank of one of those streams. She would love to see one, but it was remote from her; truly in Paradise, and not in a place which merely stole its name.

Edwin, staring at her legs, almost knocked over his ale flask. As he made a grab for it he nearly followed it into the mill-race. Margaret caught and saved it. She returned it with gratitude at being able to do something for him. The effort had pulled her skirt up over her thighs, which were also battered, bruised and scarred. She slowly, luxuriously, rubbed one foot against her calf.

Edwin took a manly swig at the ale.

'Boys 'ave got something you 'aven't got.'

'What?'

She accepted that boys had lots of things not possessed by girls, but she wanted to know what particular thing was on his mind.

'It's a secret.'

'Godforgi'me,' she exclaimed, imitating the carter who had brought her here. 'We've got a secret, too!'

'What's that?'

'You can't know until you're married.'

'Huh! Girls 'aven't got anything at all. That's their secret. You've got no willies.'

'Yes, we 'ave!' She blushed at her easy lie, and added quickly, 'If we get married you can be told my secret, 'cos no lady ever tells before she's wed 'er secret place for putting things.'

'Can you 'ide your ale in it?'

'It's for babies! Y'ave to go to church first, though.'

'I'm not going to church.' Edwin boldly turned his face to the moorlands. 'Never.'

He lay back, sleepily basking in the sunlight, with his eyes closed.

'You only 'ave t'ave a ring. If you give me a ring, I'll show you what I've got.'

Edwin opened one eye and swigged the beer.

'I can get you a ring. Just you wait.'

He swung off the windowsill and rode down, clinging to a spoke of the wheel; a black sprite in a cascade of water, his hair and clothes clinging like the shiny skin of an otter. He leapt off and clambered amongst the gears, from which a greased shaft ran through a hole in the wall to the spinning frames. She thought he was going to throw the lever that would stop the machines, but he swung back up to her, nimble as a tomtit on a branch and holding a scrap of brass pipe.

'You're putting it on the wrong finger!' It fitted.

She had begun this day happy, she had smiled and now she even laughed. She poked the correct finger at him and he roughly, with embarrassment, slipped on the ring of brass.

Margaret lifted her skirt completely.

'Now put your finger inside there and you'll make a baby.'

'I don't believe yer.'

'It's true.'

Edwin had never been timid before, but now he could not touch her faintly rosy flesh.

'Gledhill filed a girl's front teeth 'cos she went without 'er clothes on with some boys,' Margaret whispered. ''E told 'er it would sharpen 'em for eating 'er Sunday dinner. You don't get Sunday dinners in the 'prentice 'ouse. That's why 'e thought it was so funny, and we all 'ad to laugh. We 'eard 'er screaming.'

Edwin was still hesitating.

'Don't be froightened. Go on.' Disappointment crept into her voice. 'I know that's 'ow you do it. It's magic. I know 'cos I saw a turnkey from Newgate do it to my mother when she was ill, and 'e laughed and told me that's where I'd come from. My mother said it was true. 'E said 'e was my father, but I know that was a lie. Go on! Don't be afraid. We'll make a baby and call 'im Edwin. But y'ave to wait nine months.'

'What for?'

Margaret did not know how to answer.

What would his mother have called her? A forward little 'ussy, no doubt. He wasn't sure what that meant, it was always said in such a hushed way, but he didn't feel anything dreadful about Margaret. He might have touched her; but he had to lean, tottering over the edge of the sill, and stream into the darkness. He looked down and saw Mr Gledhill staring up at them, shaking the knob of his stick and unable to shout, choking with anger.

Margaret followed Edwin's gaze. A picture of a giant in a story book, brought into the workhouse by a parson, shot through her mind.

She pulled down her skirt and pressed so hard into the wall that it rasped her back. The Devil's head on the stick was swinging wildly to deliver blows to the children's feet and ankles.

Edwin, after a flush of fear, hated. He tried to loosen a stone to smash into the overseer's face. He'd kill him, though he'd be hung for it. The boy grew tired and, with Margaret, crouched against the bars. She was whimpering. Though tears stung Edwin's eyes, he would not cry.

Gledhill, out of breath, ceased to swing his stick. He rested his clenched fists on his waist, and said nothing, very threateningly. He simply waited for them to come down.

Edwin went first, with Margaret close behind. As if he could protect her! They were approaching an alligator, a mad dog. The long claw nail gripped Margaret's neck and almost went through the skin. When he slapped her face hard she stopped screaming, went limp and quivered.

'Open ya mouth,' he commanded.

Margaret clamped her lips together. Her face tightened. It shrank and was like a little old woman's.

'Open thee gob, I telled ye!'

Quivering, she opened. All of her body was rigid, except her lips and cheeks which were trembling. Gledhill was sweating and excited. Lather trickled on his face. He pursed his lips and formed a bead of spittle in his cheeks. He was taking aim, fascinated by her trembling, moist orifice.

She closed her eyes. Something white and sticky landed and clung vilely on teeth and tongue. She did not know whether to swallow it or spit it out. Some was trickling from her lips. Afraid of rejecting it, she swallowed, and felt sick.

Gledhill was beaming, relieved, relaxed and satisfied. He let go of Edwin, who flew at the overseer with pummelling fists, which hardly did any more damage than his bare feet did, kicking. The ineffectiveness of the child made Gledhill smile for a moment, before he delivered a punch that sent Edwin head-first through the open door, to sprawl on the floor of the spinning mill. Margaret was roughly dragged after him.

Before Edwin could pick himself up, Gledhill had him by the neck again. Like two dead, half-plucked hens, the wet, bedraggled children were dragged along between the rows of machines, their feet sometimes touching, sometimes lifted off the ground.

'What are't doing, 'iding in corners? Are't' spies for t'machine-wreckers, and Bony-Part?' The yelling overseer threatened to skewer them, drown them, tear them to pieces and have the bits spun into yarn. 'Thou's been absent from parade too often!' More realistically, he said he would tie weights to their ears and hang them down their backs. He promised his favourite torture which he called 'knock and bang'. They would each hold a stick at arm's length, at the same time balancing on one leg on an iron drum in front of a spinning frame. Each time the machine swung outwards it would knock them from their perches, so that they would fall, in danger of being minced by the machine; then back onto the drum.

He tied them by their wrists and biceps, crucified upon a cross beam above a moving spinning frame. The children had to keep lifting their legs clear of the machine's inward and outward drift, peering down into that chasm of needles and rolling metal that could slice off their feet. If they slipped out of the ropes . . .

Gledhill sauntered away. Women worked on with their heads sunk, hiding from the sight of something that they could not prevent nor soothe.

'We'll run away,' Edwin mouthed, over the noise. 'I'll get us out.'

'Where to? 'Ow?'

'Liverpool. We'll catch a boat t'America.'

'I'd like to find me mother,' Margaret cried, softly to herself.

Phoebe, from a far part of the mill, saw her son and the other child crucified upon the beam. She shrieked and, letting her spinning frame shift for itself and ravel its threads, she ran, her exclamations catching with gobs of blood in her throat, the singing of throstles drowning her cries. The rushing and her nervousness made her breathless. She began to cough. Clutching to her mouth her red-soaked piece of cloth, she dashed in panic round the spinning frame that she could not stop, and no one dared to help her. Running in circles and spitting blood, she was as desperate and ineffective as a mother bird around its chicks in a trap. She caught Edwin's eyes and saw an expression of suffering and impotence like that of Christ's when hung upon the tree. She lost her desperation and knelt upon the oil-soaked stone. She prayed, but no one could hear her because of the noise of the machines.

In John Tiplady's cropping shop they worked without an overseer and at their own pace. Although the work was hard, Gideon might sit down during the day, rest his legs, drink ale, and gossip. The croppers were an aristocracy, better paid than weavers. How manly Gideon felt, growing dreamy from the beer, and being taken seriously by the men who were about to change England.

But what happened to women and girls in the spinning mill was creating a hell of guilt for him. The worst disgrace was his mother having to go in there. Had she too suffered all these things, when she was a girl? She would not speak about it. He wondered why not, when other mill-women were so coarse. He did not press her, being proud of his mother's modesty. He hated his father most for not being able to keep her at home.

What could he make of Gledhill, who attended chapel, was a good religious man, and yet who did such things? He did not know.

He knew that he did not know very much. Only God knew everything.

The croppers would stroll over to the open door, look out, and turn over in their minds the human condition; upstream was the spinning mill. At midday, Arthur Crawshaw leaned on the doorpost, tugging angrily at his pipe. Against the wall was the tombstone which Tiplady had through the winter painstakingly been carving with an alphabet for Mor Greave's school. He had reached the letter R. Though not a mason, Tiplady had struggled to do it with neat serifs. 'Thou'll want it in Roman, for a school,' he had said. Even the tombstone made Crawshaw angry.

'R for Revolution!' he muttered over his shoulder. 'There's a joke! It's a bit of 'ealthy violence that we need. We should be making guillotines, not school alphabets.'

He had come outside because he was fuming indoors. Tall and thin, he stared, like a tattered heron or a bittern eyeing a snake's egg that is about to hatch, at Paradise Mills where the new finishing shop held a set of mechanical shears, a cropping frame. Over a month ago the croppers had seen it brought on a cart past their workshop from the forge of the blacksmith who made man traps for the woodlands, and spinning machines with bobbin-racks a child's height from the floor. The cropping frame consisted of no more than hand-shears attached to a wheel to draw them over the cloth, but with it, one unskilled man could do the work previously done by three or four skilled ones. Crawshaw felt bullied, by Progress, by what he had often heard called the Inevitable Future, by Improvement, and he loathed bullying more

64

than anything. He had suffered from it early, when apprenticed to 'a tyrannous wool cropper and his equally insensitive wife', as he always described them. Later he discovered that the great parliaments and rulers of the world were from the same mould as his village master and mistress.

Because of the trouble that his tongue landed him in, he was a wanderer and a bachelor, carrying off with him little more than his tools each time he was sacked for arguing with his master. On his travels he met Wesleyans, Presbyterians, Quakers, and mad preachers with religions of their own, raising recruits by speaking to scattered congregations. Just as they went from chapel to chapel, so he went between the public houses, speaking of his cause.

Today Crawshaw wore an armband of white crêpe. So did John Tiplady and when Gideon had arrived that morning he too had been given one. It was in memory of the Halifax cropper, Samuel Hartley, killed in a Luddite raid on Mr Cartwright's mill at Rawfolds, Liversedge, near Huddersfield, five days before and whose burial had taken place on the previous day. The funeral had been chaotic after the efforts by Mr Jabez Bunting, the local Methodist superintendent, to prevent Hartley's being buried in a Methodist graveyard. 'Methodism hates democracy as much as sin,' Mr Bunting had announced on refusing to conduct a service, and the gates of the chapel had been shut.

Crawshaw's mission was to inspire a raid on Paradise Mills, planned over a month since, on the heels of the Rawfolds defeat, when some had been shot, and others chased until they found cover or died of their injuries in the hedgerows.

Behind King Ludd's back, John Tiplady put down his shears. They weighed thirty pounds and stood four feet high. Although they had deformed him with that horny swelling of muscle, the 'cropper's hoof' on his wrist, Tiplady would not let anyone else touch them. The cloth that he had cut, neatly folded back and forth by Gideon, lay at the end of a long table.

Like all who worked with woollens it was Tiplady's habit to feel the surface of any cloth and he hardly realised that he could be picked out for his trade because he could not resist putting forth his hand, whether to curtains in a room, or the material of a lady's dress; just as a carpenter cannot help himself running his hands over furniture nor a mason keep from fondling stone. So, in the silence hanging over the shop, Tiplady stroked the product of the morning's work.

Crawshaw had told them that, after the soldiers had killed two Luddites, maiming others, they should use firearms themselves and not confine themselves to sticks and stones.

Tiplady's hefty wrist had trembled. 'So we too are to sink to shooting our own countrymen!'

'We should burn all 'Orsfalls' down, 'ouse and mill and everything! Burn down everything in sight and start afresh. Nothing short of a fresh start will do us any good,' Crawshaw argued.

'And all the pictures?' Tiplady said. 'All the fine things?'

'Killing folk·never did anyone no good,' answered Samuel Wrigley, with a smile.

He was thinking of Nancy Stott, who was pregnant when she led him to the altar. He believed now in the living. Wrigley was a young man incapable of treating life as other than a joke. He was joining the Luddites because to upset the masters appealed to his sense of humour. He loved life, and he loved himself, not in a vain way but as part of his delight in everything. While he spoke he had been tightening the biceps of his right arm, and caressing it with the forefinger of his left hand.

When Arthur Crawshaw was more or less calmed, he put away his pipe, returned and faced the others. He was so tall that he had to unwind himself from under the lintel.

He looked at Gideon, who relaxed on a bench against the window, resting his legs and supping the ale which Tiplady's wife had brought into the shop. Crawshaw and Gideon formed one group, Wrigley and Tiplady made up another.

'What's your father doing today, Gideon Greave? Reading bewks and thinking nobody'll take away 'is loom?'

Crawshaw's Adam's apple rose and sank in his scrawny throat. Even that seemed angry.

Gideon, although he agreed, out of loyalty to his father could do no more than scowl.

'We need our messengers and scribes too, perhaps more than we need murderers,' Tiplady commented.

The master was a broad, proud, steady man who controlled both his sorrow and his anger. He would take a grip of himself by biting hard into the stem of his pipe.

King Ludd gave an angry kick at the leg of a table.

'Authors! Poets!' he exclaimed, bitter and contemptuous. He took his ale and sat next to Gideon.

'Poets,' repeated Wrigley, humorously. Over the lip of his tankard he looked at Tiplady. These two leaned against the tables.

'Poets,' echoed Tiplady, respectfully.

Wrigley smiled back at him.

Crawshaw angrily touched the band of white crêpe on his sleeve. ''Ave we forgotten about 'Artley? This is no time for larking.'

He turned to Gideon for agreement.

'Bible says . . .' Gideon began.

'Bible says everything under the sun, and contradicts itself,' Tiplady interrupted. 'It's time we stopped looking there so much, and making ourselves confused.' He was annoyed at the cutting off of the flow of humour, upon which the good work of his shop depended. 'You're not the only one to mourn 'Artley, but maybe we don't all want to remember 'im by piling up dead bodies.'

It was Tiplady's turn to take his ale to the door, cooling his temper, losing himself in the sight of the swelling buds lighting the tips of the trees, the sunlight leaping between the tree trunks, and in listening to a chaffinch. Tiplady read Wordsworth and, through his past courtship of a Horsfalls' maid, had trespassed in the mansion, where he had been enthralled by the paintings by Constable and Turner.

He set his ale on the ground and lit his pipe. The smell of the smoke peacefully rising brought him great satisfaction.

'Our Government,' Crawshaw pronounced behind his back, 'keeps us in a poverty-stricken, out-of-work condition so as we'll submit to being dressed up like fairground dolls and sent off to fight Frenchmen or Spaniards and to enslave negroes. In a time like this we don't need bewk-authors nor dreamers and yonderly folk, staring at the flowers. We need the Revolution to start. I know from travelling about the countryside that thousands are ready, and Rawfolds shall ignite the flame. There isn't a village in the north not ready to act as one man.'

Wrigley took no notice. Crawshaw turned to Gideon.

'You'd better go and talk to your father. Teach him sense. The time to act is whilst men are angry, and the Government still doesn't understand what we've got prepared for 'em. This is the moment to take our courage in our 'ands. Before they send more army. If we don't, then you, my lad, will be thrown out amongst the rubbish.'

Tiplady came back and put down his empty jug, thus suggesting that they all began work again.

King Ludd stood up, grabbed Tiplady's wrist as he was about to pick up his shears, and dramatically held his cropper's hoof in the air.

'What's the price of that? 'Orsfall and his like care nothing for it, so we must look after ourselves. And any who are not with us is against us. We'll know what to do with those who should be our brethren, after.'

'After what?' Tiplady asked, retrieving his wrist and annoyed. 'The 'angings?'

'I've always said we should smash yon finishing shop,' Gideon muttered.

'That's because you fancy going at night with your face blackened and carrying a pistol,' Tiplady told him. 'Playing at being a brave but desperate man.'

'It's time yonder fellow learned the price of a cropper's 'oof.'

Crawshaw spoke with such bitterness . . . the price was that of excruciating pain, learning to work those great iron shears which some could hardly lift, let alone operate. The mechanical cropping frame would do away with their suffering, yet for the light of the brief comet of revolution Gideon would put up with pain, and the revolution that he and King Ludd envisaged would get rid of masters, but preserve traditional ways, no matter what deformity they caused.

'What are we going to do for our friends from Rawfolds?' Crawshaw continued. 'This is a time for 'eroes. Either we let Mellor and Thorpe and our brave and glorious brothers be flushed out and strung up like rabbits or we fight 'til we have altered the constitution of England.'

He paused, and added weightily, 'Because of what 'as 'appened, we are called to assemble tonight and do our part by going ahead with smashing yon finishing shop.'

'Who'll be defending the mill? What do we know of the forces 'Orsfall can muster?' Tiplady wanted to know.

'I have my own spies amongst the militia,' Crawshaw answered. 'There'll be no soldiers, not that we can't deal with, anymore than on any other raid.'

'Rawfolds?'

'That was defeated because some men didn't stand true.'

'Orsfall 'as the military under 'is thumb,' Tiplady said.

Crawshaw took no notice.

'Wrigley,' he said, 'Gideon Greave's father 'as deserted and we're a man short. Will t'join with us on this raid?'

'I'll do anything tha likes.'

'The age of King Ludd is coming!' Gideon shouted. Lopping off heads and making a revolution looked to him as easy as clipping the nap off a piece of cloth was to a skilled cropper. He had already, one night a month before, burned cloth upon a tenter-frame and he had once taken part in an ambush to smash a load of shears that were being taken to be sharpened. By now the threat of the hangman's noose merely excited him. 'If Mr Perceval wants us 'anged he must come and get us!'

'If you don't stop blabbering, 'e will,' Tiplady told him.

'I 'aven't said nothing, yet! We're all supposed to be democrats 'ere. 'Ow *can* we be, if I mayn't open my mouth?'

Crawshaw gave Gideon a look that showed he, also, thought him a fool. Gideon blushed, stammered and then he too went to look out through the door.

Upstream, through the trees, he saw a boy's head rising out of the torrent that poured from the lodge into the wheel-housing.

It was his brother Edwin. As soon as Margaret and he had been cut down from above the spinning-frame he had once more led her into the wheel-housing, this time not even considering the engineer, so tenaciously was he thinking, where water can get in, we can get out.

The child knelt on the bank and reached down to help a little girl. Both were completely drenched, their hair and clothes plastered to them. They had been nearly drowned in struggling against the tiger of that powerful sluice. They ran towards the shelter of the woods.

Sauntering along the bank came Nathaniel Gledhill, using his midday hour to collect ferns. Suspended from his neck was his tin vasculum. With the metal box banging against his side, its lid open and trailing its specimens, he gave chase.

He caught up with Edwin at the wall. Margaret had already been pushed over, but twenty yards into the trees, she had no heart to go on alone and she returned. In terror she climbed the wall back to her friend and her prison. For the second time Gledhill dragged them, fluttering weakly like two butterflies that had fallen into the water, to be punished in the manufactory.

Tiplady came over to find out what Gideon was staring at so fixedly.

He said nothing, but slammed his pipe down on a table and walked out.

Crawshaw showed the stem of the pipe to Gideon: the deep set of angry teethmarks.

'Now go and talk to your Judas father,' Crawshaw hissed.

April 16th

Phoebe, like her husband, had been brought up where her mother span at home, her father wove and supervised the labour of his family. Their fire burned peat and coals which they dug out of the moor. Their squatter's farm was a sooty, grey place, being near the coal-shaft, but to Phoebe it was a lovely spot. Nowadays she remembered the poultry hesitating around the open door, in a wedge of sunlight gilding the stones. Beyond, in that high, lonely place, was the ripple of distant hills. Although their room was simple – crude table, chairs, cupboard, a mere ladder to the bedroom, a linen chest, a small oak box for her father's lexicon and other volumes, a framework of pulleys to raise oatcakes above the fire – it was not bare or cheerless. Her mother had been a servant at a clothier's and she had brought away, for her dowry, gifts of lace mats, a set of fine crockery, knives, forks, and a Bible, which she herself could not read. They possessed no clock. They watched the movement of light, of regular travellers on the Blackstone Edge road far below, and of birds, to register the time. Her parents worked as they willed or thought best. The sight of travellers hurrying brought them peace and contentment with their own lot. If it was fine they were in their garden, or their two enclosures, in one of which they grew oats, and in the other grass for the pony; or they were on the open moorland, cutting rushes, peat and coal. On cold, wet days they operated loom and spinning wheel indoors or took their cloth to Benjamin Greave's fulling mill and finishing shop. The children had leisure to play in the stream that ran close to the door. They dabbled in the water-trough. They played at hide and seek under the sheets of white, new weaving hung out to dry. They never thought that the manufactories being built along the valley bottom would transform their lives.

Phoebe, 'the sun', had an elder sister whom their father had named Selene, the moon, and who died at the age of eighteen, after four years of a hard lump growing in her breast.

When Phoebe was six and Selene was thirteen, they were plucking watercress out of the stream, when the elder sister said with an enigmatic smile, 'Wait till you play hide and seek with feyther.'

She would tell Phoebe no more; but all through that summer she continued to suggest 'things'.

'What things?'

'You will see.'

Their father became for Phoebe a pending mystery, a dark cave of immeasurable size and content she must some day go into, even though at present she, like Selene, played in the sunlight.

Their father had been both an angry and a loving man, to extremes. It was not until Phoebe grew to womanhood that she realised he was not the big man she had always thought him. The realisation had come upon her in a single moment of insight: it occurred to her one day that when she looked at him, she looked him in the eye. Awesomely dependant upon his changeable moods, finding him so mysterious after Selene's suggestions, from childhood onwards she used to fix her riveted attention upon the way his face creased when he smiled, and on the two furrows vertically above his nose when he was angry.

One day her father suggested that Phoebe stay at home, while her mother and sister took to market a basket of whinberries, on which they had spent a whole day, crouching to pick them from the undersides of low bushes on the moors.

Selene, as so often, wore upon her face that enigmatic smile which Phoebe associated with plucking watercress and with semi-revelations during games under the tenter-frames.

As soon as they had gone, Phoebe's father complained of being tired and he went to bed, as he sometimes did during the day, with one of his Greek volumes. Half an hour later he called to Phoebe.

'Come closer, by the bedside.' He touched her hair. His hands played tenderly. There was a smile on his lips, but the rest of his expression was angry and florid. It made her shiver.

'Don't be frightened. You're not frightened, are you?'

'No.'

'Get into bed with me, then.'

She was terrified.

'Phoebe, me loved 'un!"

He rippled his fingers through her dress and petticoat. She did not know what it was that he put between her legs and thrust into her. She

72

thought it was his foot. He sweated, grunted and closed his eyes. He seemed to forget about her. He bounced up and down, so that hurt too. He fell asleep and let go of her. She crept away with stickiness between her legs. She could not walk properly and was very weak.

Although her mother on her return was perversely blind to all this, Selene took it all in, especially Phoebe's painful bow-legged walk, and she smiled.

Her father began regularly to feel 'tired' whenever Phoebe's mother and sister were visiting relatives, or away with baskets of eggs, whinberries and other moorland produce. Phoebe grew to dread it. When she knew that her mother and Selene were going on an errand she could think of nothing else but what was bound to happen. On the days beforehand he would give her a sweet biscuit, and wink, telling her to keep it a secret. He told Phoebe that she was his favourite daughter. She could think only of the coming pain. He alternated sweetness with bullying. He was resentful of anything that she did wrong, so she grew weak, and nervous. The more frightened she was of him, the more cruel he became. She watched his face set as he pushed her to the limit of fear.

Half an hour after he had climbed the ladder to the bedroom he would call, 'Phoebe.' It was no use her pretending not to hear for he would simply shout louder, then become quiet and tender again to suit his purpose. He would smile at her frightened appearance, and whisper, 'Phoebe,' running his fingers inside her dress and legs.

'Do you like it?'

'Yes.'

She whispered because he whispered, without knowing why. She did not know whether she liked it or not, nor what it was she liked, or didn't like.

'Get into bed with me, then. It's lovely and warm.'

She was hypnotised. His bulk swelled over her. He dominated and kept her in fear. Her weakness and timidity were his pleasure.

One day her mother and Selene came home unexpectedly early.

Selene now was often in pain. She was thin, yellow-skinned, and had a wistful look because she understood mortality. By habit she clutched herself under her breast, and they had ceased to take notice of it when she gasped. She grew easily tired, which was perhaps why they had returned so early – perhaps. They stood listening at the foot of the ladder. When her mother could stand no more, she coughed.

73

Phoebe's father hissed at her to leave. He pretended to fall asleep, his face pushed into the mattress. Phoebe climbed shamefully down the ladder, flushed and frightened, hardly able to move, her legs when she reached the ground spread with the pain. Her mother banged the pots and angrily spoke one word.

'Whore!'

Phoebe had no idea what it meant, but she was certain that she had done something wrong and that the pain was a punishment.

'Whore, whore, whore!' her mother repeated, holding back her tears, unable to think of anything else to say, wringing her hands with a terrible savage clasping and unclasping of her fingers.

'Will I go to Hell?' Phoebe asked.

The words stuck to her teeth and tongue, like sticky bread clinging to an oven.

'Yes!' her mother hissed. 'Yes! Yes! Yes!'

She was gladly condemning her daughter. Then she saw Phoebe's look of stricken, helpless horror, but could not take back her words. She slammed out of the house with a bucket of scraps for the hens. Phoebe listened to the poultry squawking away from her angry feet. They were sounds from another planet.

She sat by the fire. She did not know what to do with her hands. She could not look at her sister. Side by side they were staring into the burning coals, feeling the weight of heat upon their eyes. Selene, trying to breathe lightly to save herself from sharp stabs through her breast, was exhausted with life, so she behaved as if she understood everything. Everyone knew that one who wasted away, died in a few years. They told her that she was going to Heaven. She, who also had been enjoyed by her father, knew that she would go to Hell.

Selene threw a stick into the fire. It burst into flames.

'Look at it burning. Imagine burning like that for ever in Hell.'

Selene repeated, slowly, 'For ever.'

'Is your mother there?' her father timidly cried, at last.

Phoebe realised that, although he made such a show of strength and anger, he was afraid of her mother.

Phoebe did not answer him, making him shout louder. Even she could give just a little pain, and enjoy doing so, sometimes. Her hands were wrapping and unwrapping themselves in her apron.

'Is your mother down there..? *Is your mother there?*' he bawled, exasperated and afraid.

74

'No,' she grunted, eventually. She wanted to answer, 'Yes,' but to tell a lie would fan the eternal flames.

'You won't go to Hell,' he comforted.

But, unlike her mother's voice, his was without authority.

'You will,' Selene whispered. 'I have seen God, and I know.'

There *were* people who had seen God. Such awful prophecies came from those on the edge of the grave. Selene could say that she had seen God, as another might say they had visited Mr Horsfall. She claimed to have looked into the pit and to know what was waiting for everyone.

Phoebe felt that she had already descended too far down the shaft of Hell to be recalled.

Outside, she heard shed doors angrily slammed. Her mother tripped on a balk of timber. She cursed and loudly blamed her husband for leaving it there. For him to overhear, she lamented to the blank walls about his failings; a roof not mended, money wasted at markets, and 'time lost in reading books'.

She returned indoors after half an hour. She at first said nothing, though noisy enough with crockery and furniture. Then: 'You'll burn for ever in Hell, you little whore,' she hissed.

'You'll burn in Hell, Phoebe,' spitefully repeated Selene, who had seen the parting of the golden gates and been given glimpses of the pastures of Heaven. It did not occur to Phoebe that Selene was reassuring *herself*, not wanting to descend into Hell alone.

All that day her father dared not leave his bed. He was too frightened to make a sound. He did without food. Nobody went to see him. Nobody mentioned him. He was dead. Phoebe decided never, never to marry a coward.

Eventually the girls went to their beds, and whispered conspiratorially. They waited for their mother to come up. That must have happened very late, for both the daughters had fallen asleep, despite themselves. They were woken by the row. Mother was screaming abuse, and father merely grunted his defence. It was a clear, quiet night. The horse neighed in fright from the stable, the hens were awakened to chortle and peck one another on their perches. The nearest neighbour, a quarter of a mile across the moor, came to her door with a lantern. It was all cut deep in Phoebe's memory.

Her father never touched Phoebe again, and she missed it. Although filled with horror, yet she wanted his affectionate touching, his fingering of the tabooed parts that were the cursed gift of Satan; the petals shamefully hid like evil fungi from the light. Her father's reserve, as extensive as the love he had once shown, was terrible. What had she done?

Her sister never relented in her spite, her mother in her coldness and suspicion. Years later, she was still giving her husband and Phoebe lingering suspicious glances when she found them together for a moment.

One day, Phoebe burned a pan of porridge.

'Oh, you ungrateful . . . you ungrateful *thief*,' Phoebe's mother shrieked, unexpectedly.

'I'm sorry, mother.'

Phoebe did not understand. She looked into her mother's face. Envy and hate were written there.

'I'm sorry,' Phoebe repeated and lowered her eyes.

Her mother banged the pot. She clasped and unclasped her fingers, as she had done on that day when *it* had happened.

'You should be. You should be. Stealing him from me like that.'

'I'm sorry.'

Phoebe couldn't think of anything better to say.

'You're young, you've got your life before you, but me, I've only got him . . . and my own daughter steals him . . . *We've no oats left*,' her mother howled.

Phoebe, her eyes still cast down, watched her mother's fingers. She was tearing at them as if she was trying to pull out the nails. She was plucking, out of her finger ends, all the tension and pain in her body.

'I'm sorry.'

Especially after this, Phoebe made recompense by frantically desiring to please. She grew up trying and trying to be 'all that a daughter should be'. She made unburnt porridge, tended the garden and animals, shovelled and dug for coals, cleaned and cooked with passion. She did everything she could to look chaste. She wore the dullest clothes. She kept herself buttoned at neck and wrist, showing that she was willingly imprisoning her guilty body. As her mother never relented, and her father was now afraid of showing affection, Phoebe struggled harder and yet harder to please, not realising that she was doing so, until it became a habit.

'Phoebe's a *good* girl, a Godly daughter,' it was said.

She did all that she could to nurse the burdensome sister who would not let anyone sleep, with her nightly howls, delusions and visions.

When Phoebe was eleven, Selene died. She took her secret with her, wherever it was that she went. As there was now no need of an extra hand at home to take care of her, Phoebe was sent to earn her living in a spinning shed, where fifteen other girls were employed.

She now took the greatest pains to please the overseer. It was his turn to play with her. He did so more than with the other girls, because she was the most biddable in the shed.

Because of his attentions, her work was spoiled, and, as he knew, Phoebe was terrified of returning to her parents with her wages cut for having been 'a bad girl'. He kept the frightened little creature behind. He placed his blunt, stained, repulsive fingers down the back of her neck. He promised to say nothing about her spinning, if she would submit.

As she spiralled down the hellhole of submission, his face shone more and more with pleasure.

She, without realising, and out of an instinct of self-defence, acquired the deceptions of a whore. She pretended to give in, but wanted to kill him.

When the overseer saw, with surprise, her hatred for him after she had submitted, 'Women are all fakes and liars. They're born to it. Never trust 'em', he bitterly concluded.

Phoebe grew obsessed by terror and guilt. These most significant events of her life she never spoke of, yet her distracted mind was always turning them over. She became virtually a mute.

She did not realise that she had become one. She froze whenever a lad came near her, and she remembered the pain given by men with that look in their eyes. Whenever Mor approached, it terrified her. She could not help recalling her father.

There were, indeed, some brilliantly happy moments. When Mor Laverock Greave spoke with authority of classical things and gave Latin names to flowers, she was reminded of the powerful, comforting side of her father. When in her teens she watched Mor playing 'knorr and spell', knocking the wooden ball with such boldness and force, determined to burst a hole into Heaven, she was happy. Also, when he walked her home through the dusk; yet she knew that, from her deep silences, he concluded that she was unhappy. It was agony not to be able to explain how she felt, and even worse when he touched her and she could not tell him how much she feared it. She could never tell him anything.

She began to believe in fantasies. She remembered Selene's sense of security, and what she described as 'glory' that she felt 'in Jesus'. Through the dark's muttering and love-fumbling, Phoebe began to think that if only it were Jesus Christ who entered her, then she could give herself, and be 'justified', as Selene had put it. To remove the stiffness from her limbs, Phoebe would close her eyes and imagine that her Saviour was entering her with His 'spirit'. It was in this panic and fake ecstasy that she had conceived Gideon before she was married, Edwin and other children later.

Although Phoebe could not talk, she could pray, at the foot of the frame, the children dangling above it. Careless of the oily floor, recklessly bringing her petticoat and apron close to the machinery, she prayed for Edwin.

Who was that other child? She knew nothing of Margaret. The person she saw was her own daughter, Esther, dropped amongst the steel rods, dragged forth and laid out with her leg and arm broken, hideous, askew.

Phoebe looked up and saw Nathaniel Gledhill. Gledhill felt the eyes of one who would murder him. Because he thought so well of Phoebe for being the tidiest, most scrupulous and obedient woman at Paradise Mills, he couldn't understand why she disliked him. But it flattered him. In these days any who paid their taxes and spoke up for the King must expect to be shot at.

At last it dawned upon him that one of the children was Phoebe's. He smiled. She coughed, nervously, and bent her head, displaying her neck, vulnerable as if for an execution. She was in his hands.

He passed on, smiling.

It was Joshua Slaughter who ran up and stopped the frame. He climbed and cut down the children, carrying Margaret first to the ground. They would have run like frightened rabbits off among the forest of machines, but Phoebe nestled them both for a while under her bony arms.

Joshua stood looking at her. He wanted to say . . .

Joshua had once put out his hand to her. She had told him not to and it had stopped him. It had actually stopped him. Another man would have carried on trying to seduce her, but he had merely looked at her with soft, brown, devoted eyes. She had felt safe, and grateful.

Now he wanted to say . . .

For the rest of the morning Phoebe could not concentrate. Edwin was sure to get into more trouble, she thought. He'd do something else. He'd think of something. He wouldn't be stopped . . . not him. She saw him passing by her frame, and no matter who was watching she went to soothe his arms and shoulders. He would hardly answer her. He seemed unable to bear his own mother's face. He was brooding.

Shortly before the noon sit, Phoebe went to find Joshua Slaughter in the water-wheel housing. He turned upon her those faithful eyes.

My weasel.

'That damned Gledhill . . .' he began.

She did not respond.

'We are going to Bradford tonight,' he continued, hopefully. 'A group of us. We've 'ired a cart. Art 'coming?'

'Bradford?'

Only ten miles away but it was as if she had never heard of the place. She could not think what he was talking about.

'Bradford. They are awaiting the Millennium, when Christ will return to us. We know it will be soon. In the darkest hour of the night, that is when the dawn light breaks, Phoebe Greave. They know all about that.'

'Who?'

She knew perfectly well who, but could not think, having nothing else on her mind but where she might obtain ointments. Her only light at the moment was through that door to which Slaughter had the key, onto the lodge bank.

'Followers of Joanna Southcott. Joanna 'as seen all in dreams. She knows when the light will break. "I have been led on by types, shadows, dreams and visions since 1792 to the present day." We 'ave it from 'er own mouth, Phoebe. Because people will not believe, she 'as to lock 'er prophecies in boxes, to be opened when it 'as been proved they are true.'

Phoebe only wanted to get out of the mill. With teasing and shifting, with smiles that were so provocative because they were rare, she reminded Slaughter of his enslavement to her. She made movements and gestures of a kind that Mor would not have believed she was capable.

Slaughter came forwards, in the twilight. Was he going to touch her?

'Come with us all to Bradford.'

'Let me *free*,' she pleaded.

He lifted his hands.

79

'Yes! Yes! Joanna sets all her people free.'

His fingers were brushing her apron.

'No! Let me free. Let me out. Let me out!'

'She will let us *all* out of our darkness.'

'Open the door.'

'The door is open, for all who seek it.'

'Onto the lodge.'

'To the lodge?'

Baffled, he stopped pawing her. Was she suggesting that he went out there with her?

'I must go to think.'

'Think about it, and pray, yes, yes!' He was turning the big key smoothly, in the oily lock. 'Spend an hour or two in nature's bosom, think and pray. A change of heart. Miracles can 'appen.'

Without looking at him any further, she slipped out into sudden light, and the brightness reflected off the sheet of water. She did not look around there, either. She was dazzled and frightened. Like a fox or an owl, her instinct was to dart for cover again.

Her instinct was not wrong. There was Gledhill strolling on the lodge bank. She ducked round the rear of the mill. This was shortly before the two children also went, for a second time, into the wheel-housing, climbed the sluice and ran for it.

Circling the mills, Phoebe went along the yard between Horsfall's house and the finishing sheds, then past the tenter-fields. She knew that Gledhill never left the region of the mill during his midday break, and she safely went to his house, knocking at the back door.

The servant girl, a thirteen-year-old who slept in an outhouse, felt that she was nonetheless better off than a female who had to work in a factory, and she was aloof.

'Master's notat'ome.'

But it was Rose Gledhill whom Phoebe wanted.

Rose, seeing Phoebe at this hour, with a white, sick face and footsteps tottering, concluded that the factory woman was with child. Mrs Gledhill, who had something of a fine manner, dismissed her girl, invited Phoebe to sit down, and set about boiling a pan of water.

Phoebe buried her face in her apron, just as she had earlier turned it towards the turf, not able to speak out her errand. She was quivering like a puppy or kitten pulled out of a litter. Unable to speak, she was kneading one hand with the other, as her mother had done. She was overcome with envy and a sense of unfairness. Rose's cottage was comfortable, warm and dry. She had the time to keep it tidy, and a servant. On a sideboard were pies, some of them only half-consumed, showing that the Gledhill children were not hungry. The place smelled of comfort and cleanliness. With the pies on the sideboard was a glass case containing the eggs of wild birds, laid in artificial nests. At last Phoebe began her story, and then she could not stop.

'Well, I don't know what to say, Mrs Greave . . . Phoebe. I don't know what to say. To think *I* married him . . .'

As the story unfolded, Rose was quietly placing bread and slices of preserve pie by Phoebe's side. She took away the large pan that she had set on the flames and in its place swung the kettle on its hook.

Phoebe sank down, muttering into the clutches of her apron.

'Go on . . . go on, Mrs Greave . . . I don't know what to say . . . *My* husband . . . I can't say I'm surprised though. To think that I, of all people, of all people, should have married such a one. I'm most particular . . . I'm ashamed.'

Phoebe's words faded into sobs.

'I can't say I'm surprised,' Mrs Gledhill repeated. 'To think I once liked him to throw his weight about! But that was with men of his own size, in the public house, not amongst women and children in the factory. In those days I thought it was big to do things with a lot of noise. My brave soldier indeed! It's all my fault. Yes, it is – for encouraging him. Don't we learn! Don't we learn, Mrs Greave. But your man . . .'

Phoebe raised her head.

'I don't know what to do wi'im, Mrs Gledhill. He's yonderly, as everyone knows. It's 'armless, but 'e *does* nothing. He does *nothing*. A bit o' weaving, nowt with an eye to what anybody wants, and 'e's satisfied to be off combing the moors.'

'Doesn't he bring anything back?' Rose cautiously suggested.

'Well . . . maybe.' Phoebe changed the subject. 'Everything's in 'is mind, Mrs Gledhill. Reading books, that's what 'e does best. It's all in 'is mind.'

'He keeps a school? He runs an academy?'

'*That* brings us nowt, only a bill for coal. Half of 'em don't pay for their schooling. 'Is teaching'll get him in trouble, too. Though he wouldn't hurt a fly. It's so unfair. *It's so unfair.*'

Brewing and drinking the overseer's expensive tea, the two working women consoled one another over the ways of the world, that is over the ways of men. Mrs Gledhill enjoyed the feeling of doing good. Phoebe enviously looked around the room, with its furniture polished, and Mr Gledhill's botanical specimens, dried, pressed, mounted, framed for ever, on the walls.

'Such nice things,' Phoebe said. 'All those flowers. And eggs. How does 'e make such lovely settings? The nests are like the hair of babbies.'

'It's the 'prentices' hair. After they 'ave to be cut. They're all just children, are men, when it comes down to it, collecting birds' eggs. We go up to the altar with a man, so we think . . . then we learn. We learn we have to treat them like children, telling them only what's good for them to know.'

'Mor Greave doesn't know I sent a child back two years since,' Phoebe said, sly and pleased.

Rose slapped Phoebe's knee.

'Don't tell him. We can take care of ourselves, can't we? We can, Phoebe Greave, we can.'

Rose got up and began to fill a basket with ointments and the pickings of her larder.

'I have more than I want,' she said. 'Gledhill flatters me that I'm a good housekeeper. He doesn't know where the money comes from. He doesn't know I make it by stopping children coming into his world to slave in his mill. Half of those I sends back are his own, too, the beast. You could say, he's eating his own children!'

Rose began to laugh. So did Phoebe.

Once started, Phoebe could not stop. She doubled up, gripping her thigh, playing with her apron, tears running from her eyes.

'The filthy beast,' Rose said, dabbing at her eyes. 'He eats his own children! Oh, dear, I can't stop myself, it aches!'

Phoebe's mouth, too, ached with laughter. She could not understand why she was doing it.

'Oh, the dirty pig!' Phoebe spluttered.

'Oh, the pig . . .' Rose echoed.

Phoebe stopped laughing as suddenly as she had begun. She was her usual self again, worried and ashamed.

'Don't hurry with the basket. Return it any time you're passing,' Rose said.

When Phoebe left, she had no intention of returning to the mill. They could dock her wages for it, she didn't care. Climbing the stone stairway up to Lady Well, she had from time to time to brush away tears that were now less of sorrow, than of amazement at the world's kindness.

God is kind . . .

She had never travelled this way before without it being crowded. When she had risen to some height, she was breathless, and set down her basket. She even smiled momentarily at it. God is kind.

Inspired by her memory of Rose, she looked bravely across the hills. She lifted her eyes high above the roofs of Horsfalls', to where small, light clouds were dancing over the skyline, and light beams were splintering upwards, bursting out of the clouds. Then, once more, she felt guilty at having laughed so much. Her face set with purpose. She climbed onwards and reached the village. Phlegmy blood and breath-lessness gagged in her throat. She must rest once more, but where could she safely linger? On the streets, other women would ask questions. People were suspicious of a factory woman, her grimy look showing where she had come from. They would think she had been sacked. She went into the churchyard.

It was not to visit Horsfall's newly built church. What consolation could a woman find amongst its cold marble monuments to what her husband called, 'Colonels and captains memorialised for spreading oppressions at home and abroad'? That was no place for women's thoughts. The last time she was in it, newly hung over the nave was a blood soaked flag brought back in tatters from Spain and she had thought, not of glory, but of murdered sons. In her pocket she, too, had a rag soaked in blood. Phoebe turned to the ruins of the old church, burnt to the ground by a previous incumbent, the mad pyromaniac, Parson Doubtfire. Roofless and unvisited, except when a farmer turned sheep or geese to graze and shelter there, it had wild flowers growing from the stones of its blackening arches, and between the packed graves. She put down her heavy basket, sat and watched the sheep gnawing at the bright pencillings of grass between the stones and graves. She recalled how sheep had gathered in the angles of the walls beneath her window 'at home', dripping milk from their udders sometimes, and delivering an orchestra of cries. Occasionally they hit a precise, heart-rending, human note.

She looked at some fragments of mildewed paintings clinging to the remaining plaster. One depicted a woman hanging upside down, long dull-red hair cascading out of her head. Her limbs were gaunt, broken, tortured, pulled out of joint, yet her features transcended pain. She was Saint Uncumber, patron saint of distressed women. Women once used to pray to the Saint, placing a sacrifice of oats before her. Nowadays they had no food to offer. Phoebe did however put a little of Rose's bread there. The birds, at least, would eat it.

She reached home well before her boys. The only consolation she could offer Edwin was to have, for once, a table spread with food, ironically provided by his tormentor's wife. All this while she had been thinking of the things that she would clean at home, now that she had the time.

Mor, working his loom alone before his window, watched the cycle of light and shade across hills and valleys. He daydreamed. He thereby discovered a keyhole in the black prison of his life and although he had no key, he could still peep through the dream, to see how vast and golden it was beyond: a dream is a rent in eternity.

Wearing his weaver's faded, coarse-blue apron, he pulled the string to drive the shuttle from left to right, he pressed down with his right foot to change the lines of the warp, he pulled back the drawer-bar with his right hand, and depressed his left foot. Clack, clack, all day. Clack, clack. The sound of any working day in Lady Well. God bless Kay, who invented the flying shuttle. Because of him Mor did not have to employ a boy to stand at the side pushing back the shuttle . . . in other words, have someone to disturb his thoughts: not all inventions starve and break the working man.

On the other hand, in the old days his assistant would have been Edwin. Whilst the child was with him, he could have taught him. Clack, clack. Bang, bang.

Across the warp, his shuttle threaded the colours of a sunrise. A broad band of saffron yellow that faded into red. The call was for sombre cloths, but he was symbolising revolution. True to his symbol, everything around it was dark and shadowy, both the room, and the country beyond, out of the roots and stems of which his promising rose-and-yellow, unsaleable tints had been distilled.

Clack, clack, bang bang. He sat all day like a crow perched in a forest of strings and bits of wood. Mor's worries over things he could do nothing about built up the tension of a coiled spring in his chest. He could never catch up with his work. Horsfall, like other masters, had doubled the standard of length for a piece of cloth, and had cut the payment to half of what it had been, so that in effect he was paying quarter wages. 'I've a warehouse full of the stuff because of the Wars. Until they remove their Orders in Council and we can export again, it'd suit me best to take none at all,' his manager declared, in his office with its roaring fire, leather armchair, step-ladder resting against racks of ledgers and order books, water-colours of 'scenery', a portrait of Mr Horsfall, Senior, in his younger days, and brass scales for weighing money and letters.

There Mor, seated on a wooden bench, was kept waiting like a naughty schoolboy. He had no choice but to deal on Mr Horsfall's terms because it was Horsfall who supplied the warps, on credit.

Mor never stopped looking for some small opportunity for food or money. If he went out, he was poaching. If he caught nothing, he was thinking up lessons for his school – a man has to think. At home he was weaving. He could only weave what he was able. What he felt good about. Phoebe thought that his life was without humiliation. Someday I'll tell her. Stop being so soft-spoken. Tell her what's really on my mind.

Mor would pause to write down some of the things that drifted through his brain. His own loom being silenced, he became aware of the loneliness of the Lady Well afternoon into which his thoughts fell. Other looms were banging in the town, but they accentuated his loneliness. He soon rushed back to his work, in hope of its noise driving away his thoughts. But his mind continued to rage. He was a boiler full of steam.

He returned again to his book, which he had entitled *A Beggar's Complaint*:

The ~~suferings~~ sufferings of the Poor are not the efects of Divine dispensation. They are the offspring of wicked men and notorious systems.

The slaves of the West Indies have but little reason to envy the Poor of Great Britain.

~~Phesants,~~ Pheasants, Hares, Partridges, Snipes, Woodcocks, Moorhens and Trouts, being protected by Laws and Gamekeepers, are a PRIVELEGED ORDER compared with the Poor of this Realm.

THERE IS NO MORAL OR POLITICAL EVIL IN THE WORLD WHICH MEN MAY NOT REMEDY IF THEY CHOOSE.

Beneath his window he saw the pretty Horsfall children, a boy and a girl, walking through Lady Well with Lydia Horsfall. Flounces and frills decorated the little daughter, who was like a doll bought fresh from a London store. There was an open lightness about her dress and about Mrs Horsfall's fashionable clothes that anticipated the spring, which they were so at liberty to enjoy. The boy was in a velvet suit; it would never come near machine oil. Loaded baskets on their arms, they were entering houses, with smiles upon their faces. They accepted thanks and curtsies from all around, because they were distributing charity. The little girl was the best performer as Lady Bountiful. The boy was sullen. He'd be just as happy to bayonet everybody, Mor thought.

Mor saw that Lydia Horsfall was on her dignity, behaving formally, shutting out the town which clearly horrified her. It angered Mor that she appeased Lady Well with gifts. Who does she think we are? A colony of Africans, to quell with guns one minute, pacify with gifts the next? Cold as charity, as they say . . . Mor hated it, and never regretted rejecting it, after the death of the baby who would have been his fifth child.

Though he'd have appreciated a slice of beef or pie, he flashed down the stairs and slid the bolts to. He was back upstairs again by the time they tried the door, expecting all in Lady Well to be open for them. They knocked but were still not received.

As Mor peeped and watched them go away he thought of Gideon and Edwin. The confident footsteps, erect carriages, clean skins and most of all the straight legs and other limbs of the Horsfall children over-whelmed him.

Why? Why? Why? Why should it be so?

He watched them out of sight. Before she disappeared, Mrs Horsfall turned, with an expression that he did not expect to see, and that she did not think was observed. It was the yearning, inward, poignant look of an exile.

Then she faced her daughter, with a relaxed smile; a happiness that she was preserving, just as Mor preserved something, against the outer barbarity. She looked at her son with a different expression. It seemed there'd been a quarrel between them, Mor guessed because the boy was without pity.

Soon Phoebe was hammering at the door which she, too, was amazed to find locked. Not to trust one's neighbours was unheard of in Lady Well. Mor heard her shout. He was consumed with the fear that there had been an accident. His boots clattered so fast and heavily down the steep and narrow stone stairs that he almost fell and injured his back. His face beamed its full lantern into her eyes, asking her, 'Why?', even before he got out a word. Her arms were full of amazing gifts.

'You met them?' he asked.

'Who?'

It was still an effort for Phoebe to collect her thoughts.

'You met the Horsfalls and you let them give you all those?'

She could see how angry he was. His anger, that he put into talk and books, was more important to him than what happened to her every day in the mill.

'Nay, I 'ave no' met them. I've been to Mrs Gledhill's.'

'Gledhill's! Of all people, her. Mutton dressed as lamb. You take her charity!'

'Horsfalls 'ave been 'ere and you 'ave turned them away,' Phoebe said, coldly. 'You starve us for no reason. You, who . . . you . . . It was Mr Slaughter who 'elped me in the end. Not you. Mr Slaughter! Where were you? . . . you don't know what I 'ave to put up with.'

They faced one another, both brittle with anger.

'I don't know? Oh, yes I do. You've been telling me all your life. What about me? What I 'ave to put up with . . ?'

'Books,' she said, contemptuously.

'What's Slaughter done? Why are you back at this time? Slaughter! You . . . with 'im. I'll kill 'im . . .'

She flushed. She hadn't thought he could take it that way. She was angry that he could think her capable of such a thing. She was pleased, also, to have the power to make him jealous.

'The things I have to do to get us food,' she said.

'What 'ave you done?'

He, too, became flushed and tense, at the thought of what she might have done, behind a wall, as other mill women did.

'What 'ave I done? What do you think I've 'ad to do all day? And then you won't take food when it's given you.'

He was ready to strike her.

'What 'ave you done? What? Tell me. No, not you! What?'

'Have you done your piece, husband? I know . . . writing books . . .'

She leaned upon him. She was crying.

He was sorry.

People in Lady Well paused in their work to watch Mor dashing through the town, not speaking to anyone and hardly seeing them. His face was crimson with anger. Slipping twice on the downward flight of stones, brushing his face against a punishment of twigs, he rushed to the mill. All that he felt was his anger, needing to be spent. He had no plan beyond the sullen, hammering determination: No longer will a child of mine slave in a manufactory. We'll do without bread altogether first. I'll go to the House of Correction first.

In sight of the bastion of the grey mill, with jets of livid yellow steam bursting out of chinks in the dye-houses, and the water-wheel clanking through its waters – Moloch the child-eater – he realised that there was nothing he could do. They would all starve if he did not send his children to labour. Edwin's pennies filled the tiny gap between starvation and subsistence.

Phoebe thought that he did nothing. Well, it was true. Not anything that was any use. Mor's helplessness rotted his soul. What authority could he appeal to? Upon what or whom could he revenge himself? Impotence and breathlessness turned his raging face to ash-grey. His legs were quivering. Coming to a standstill in the field of tenter-frames he stared at the mill, clenching and unclenching his fists with one thought in his mind: Smash it, smash it. Join that raid on the mill tonight, after all.

Why, in truth, had he withdrawn? Perhaps his objections to Crawshaw had in fact been an excuse to avoid learning what sort of man he, Mor Laverock Greave, was, for whether one was a hero or a coward could not be known until tested. Maybe he feared self-knowledge.

Maybe it was always this fear, or modesty, that kept people impotent. Crawshaw, who hated bullying so much because he himself was innately a bully, was at least a man of action.

The first trickle of workers was coming through the gates. Those who knew Mor saw at once that this was no time to greet him. He himself noticed hardly anyone.

When Mor found his child, dragging his feet, his empty bag dangling from his shoulder, he wordlessly scooped him up in his arms, put him on his shoulders and carried him up the hill.

Edwin was crying into Mor's neck. At last the child cried. Mor said nothing. Does Edwin think I'm a coward? he wondered. He knew that silence was turning his soul into a rotten quagmire, but it would

88

not last. He would soon be doing something. But he would not tell the child.

Jerked about on his father's back, if Edwin shifted his position to ease one pain another rose elsewhere, clamouring for attention as if it was envious.

After Gledhill had found Edwin trying to run away, he had given him a further beating. Edwin remembered how the overseer had struck him, walked away, and turned. The sight of the boy helpless in his pain had roused the overseer into a fury. Edwin cried, squirmed and begged, which made Gledhill even worse . . . So on, time and time again.

Mor, in his impatience to get home, hardly looked at his child until he set him down in the house. One of the boy's eyes was closed and his mouth so swollen that he could barely speak. He was soaked and cold. Again Mor wondered, Does he blame me because I can do nothing?

By now Phoebe had cleaned the room and laid a table. On seeing her son, she was once more in tears.

The worst is that we're helpless before God. Leave the mill to get balm, and what happens? I'm away whilst Edwin's punished again.

How could she bear the agony of a mother who has been separated from her child in pain? There was nothing any of them could do, but endure their suffering.

Neither my husband nor anyone else in Lady Well, this cursed town, will ever do anything about it, no matter how they talk.

There will be no outcome until Heaven, if Heaven is deserved, and who knows that?

Preachers had confused her. She would like to ask, to say . . . I don't know what to say. They never ask women.

If she went to the kind of church where women had tongues, a peculiar church, she could ask and speak. But she could not think of any words.

Here is this man, nothing but words . . . though it's God that disposes, in the end, ne'er mind all his talk.

She would have liked to talk to her husband, now, in the fire of suffering, about God. But Mor was clenched in a silence. She felt that his waves of anger were directed against herself. She wanted to say, It's not my fault. Don't 'urt me. I 'aven't done anything wrong. Not with Joshua nor anyone. Or something like that. But, afraid of making him angry and provoking him to recklessness, she kept silent. She feared that Mor was brooding over the revenge he would take on Gledhill and

89

which would get him imprisoned or transported. Then she would be husbandless and utterly defenceless. Oh, what a thought.

Before they ate, Phoebe took water from the pump outside and heated it on the fire. She used up the last of the soap. She put ointment on the cuts, bruises and marks of lashings. She examined that eye.

Edwin tightened his jaw, determined not to wince. Edwin, like Gideon, was learning to endure through means of righteous anger. It was in silence today, but the hour for justice would come. Despite his pain, his glance strayed to the colours and the movement of the firelight and he forgot much of his hurt in his sudden joy. The beauty of things was his consolation, and this he shared with no one.

Mor sat at the head of the table, his arms on the wings of the chair. The children were on stools at either side. Phoebe was on one at the foot, reaching out and fidgeting with the platters, getting up to put something to rights – her ornaments, the spotted dog, the huntsman. Mor could see that she was angry, from the way she gripped and banged things down, but said nothing.

At the first mouthful of food Edwin turned white, his lips lost their colour and he was sick. Phoebe enfolded the child, pressing his tearful face into her apron. Neither father nor mother spoke.

Gideon pointed his spoon at Edwin.

'What do you say to that?' he demanded of his father.

Mor answered nothing.

'What do *you* think we should do, Mother?'

Gideon spoke angrily, and clearly contemptuous of his father. Phoebe was crying. She brushed it away. She could not say what they should do. She could only mumble excuses for her tears.

'It's nothing . . .' she said. 'It isn't anything . . .'

Phoebe had a hundred ways of saying 'nothing'. Sometimes tense or angry, and sometimes, as on this occasion, there emerged a quiet sound that just managed to rise out of the well of misery.

Gideon, still smarting under the tongues of Crawshaw and Tiplady, turned on his mother.

'Nothing! Thou never says nowt but "nothing". Look what doing nothing got for us. I'd rather be 'anged than go on doing nothing.'

'Don't speak like that to your mother.'

'Don't . . . !'

'No, don't.'

'We're slaves in Egypt and thou does nowt about it, neither. Nowt!

90

Thou does nowt about owt. Nowt at all. What mother 'as to submit to . . . Doing nothing'll get us starved, even if we're not 'ung.'

Goaded too far, Mor, rather than strike his son, rose, almost breaking his chair, and left.

'I'll be there on your raid.'

He whispered so quietly that he could hardly be heard. He banged the door and went into the next room.

Phoebe heard him, though. She turned white. Her hands were shaking.

If they catch him, they'll hang him, because he's the clever one. He can write and read boks. He has a school.

'What did 'e say?' Gideon demanded. 'What did 'e say?'

'I don't know,' Phoebe answered. 'Nothing. I couldn't 'ear.'

Edwin lifted his eyes.

'Me feyther's not angry with me, is 'e?' he asked.

In his little schoolroom, for ten years Mor had berthed the ark of his learning. The walls were hung with charts showing the Latin names of flowers, with maps of Greece, Rome and the Biblical lands, and with an alphabet. The windowsills were filled with pebbles, the skulls and skeletons of birds and animals, and with flowers, twigs, or birds' eggs, according to the season. The room was damp and cold because it had been dug out of the bank at the back of the house. On the wall over the shelf holding a few tattered books, Mor had written in bold characters:

I HAVE MADE A CONQUEST GREATER THAN CAESAR OR THE DUKE OF WELLINGTON BECAUSE I HAVE CONQUERED A NEW MIND.

He had heard his dozen pupils, of all ages but all of them male, noisily gathering for the past half hour. They were not the poorest children, the ones he would have liked to raise up because they most needed it; these were too occupied in getting scraps of food, and would probably therefore always be poor. They accepted that they would live the lives of donkeys and this belief would not change no matter what lamps he strung along the dark tunnel in which they mined their existence. The saddest thing about the poor is the poverty of their hopes.

Mostly the children were the sons of uppish artisans, who wanted to get on and become little Horsfalls themselves. They paid Mor an erratic and stingy penny per week, or sometimes instead a bag of corn, a gamebird or a fish. They did this in order to have imparted to their offspring the basic skills of reading, writing and arithmetic, not the subjects that Mor loved most, political philosophy, history and literary composition. A minority of clever students were hungry for learning, but they wanted first to try out their fledgling gifts for argument against Mor himself, who ironically had trained them to question and argue.

From the gossip of the village they already knew what had happened to Edwin and, as so often happens, with their cleverness went a lack of compassion.

'They say t'bottom's gone out o't'and-weaving trade, Mr Greave,' one cheeky twelve-year-old suggested. *He* did not look hungry and dispirited: his father was a pawnbroker. 'Is it 'cos o't'machines, d'yer think?'

'It's because o'the way machines are brought in, my boy, regardless of people. Not because of the machines themselves.'

'My feyther says the Luddites want to smash all t'steam looms.'

'I believe that the philosophy of many who follow King Ludd is not that machines are in themselves obnoxious, but that attacking frames and other articles of the masters' property is the only way of drawing attention to their plight.'

This was too elaborate and subtle. They wanted the fun of hearing him damn the King or utter some other outright sedition. They fidgeted. They put their tongues out at one another. They swore, under their breath. They threw pellets of dirt at one another.

They despised someone who had to teach *them* for a living.

Mor's anger flared at their supercilious mocking. He had his raised dais, his wobbly desk with his schoolmaster's cane hung upon it, all his symbols and means of authority, but he did not use these. He burned his boats in one glorious fire of sedition. He invited the hangman. He waved his arms and pointed them towards the small, grey, cloudy windows. His limbs were wild, and his face angry.

'How many of you 'ave ever seen butcher's meat? Your fathers 'ave told you the price of grain. One hundred and fifty shilling the bushel, and still rising. Farmers and landowners, keeping it back, are profiting mightily out o't'scarcity. Last year's bad harvest and the ports of Europe closed to our exports of Yorkshire wool is of the greatest advantage to them . . .'

'They're t'clever uns, then . . .'

'I'm not staying 'ere. I'm going to be a farmer . . .'

Mor refused to be diverted.

'So why must we allow ourselves to starve? Some folk can 'ardly afford the poorest quality of flour at eight shilling per stone that dribbles from the oven when they bake it. Is it any wonder our famished populations are threatening Government, King and aristocracy? They 'ave undertaken a weary war to crush freedom in France and force a king upon that liberal nation that has rejected it. They suppose we're too ignorant to realise we must starve so that our betters may wage such a "great and glorious war". It is supposed we are ignorant barbarians, who do not realise it is our duty to lie down and die, not to stand up and shout for justice.'

The room had gone silent.

'But what we are capable of seeing is that our hearths are cold, our wives and children crying pitifully for bread.'

While Mor was roaring in his schoolroom and Phoebe had gone to the pump again, Gideon winked at Edwin and said, 'Come with us tonight, lad. We'll do some work that'll make you feel better.'

'What work?'

Edwin drew the back of his palm across his damp cheeks, as if it would wipe away his pain.

'Summat, that's what. Summat!'

'Are you going to set fire to the mill?'

His fear for Margaret, locked into the apprentice house, made Edwin's heart leap like a young rabbit in his chest. There was no escape from the apprentice house.

Gideon did not answer.

'Is our feyther going with us?'

He believed that in that case they would not fire the building.

'Maybe. You never know with 'im. Our feyther changes his mind, doesn't 'e? He's as inconstant as the wind. No faith. "Faith that can remove/The mountain to the plain"'.

'I'll go if me feyther's coming.'

'First of all thou must be twisted in.'

'What's that?'

'Summat, I tell thee!'

Edwin winced from being shouted at.

'Don't be frightened. Being twisted in is only an oath that you must take not to betray the Brotherhood.'

93

Gideon picked up a scrap of thread dropped from Mor's weaving. He held it before Edwin's eyes and gave brief sharp tugs at its ends.

'Watch now. Watch carefully. This is strong because all the fibres is twisted together into one bond. Thus we are strengthened through belonging together. Don't forget it. Twisted in with one another, we will smash the machines in Horsfalls' mill, to start the Revolution in England.'

'Combinations and all that sort of work's an 'anging matter.'

'How did you learn that?'

'I've 'eard 'em talking, 'aven't I?'

'Nobody knows proper what's an 'anging matter and what isn't. Only judges and them sort o' folks knows about that, and they won't 'ang us, because there'll be fresh judges in England after next May Day.'

'You're not going to fire the mill! There's children in there that can't get out.'

Gideon looked at his brother with contempt. He ought to understand that if there is to be a revolution, some must be sacrificed.

When Phoebe entered, Gideon told her, 'Mother, we've serious business to attend to tonight and we're taking Edwin.'

She was weary. She put down her pail.

'You can't take Edwin.'

'He must come with us, to grow up. Women can't interfere with men's work when it comes to politics.'

He looked at his mother as men do look at women: kindly, but firm.

'After that business today! . . . No . . . He's too young.'

'You can't grow up too soon in the times we're living through.'

'They'll not stop short at 'anging children, if they want to.'

But Phoebe in the end knew that you must not argue with men and she said no more.

Mor was standing at the door.

'I'll come along on the raid with you, but we're not taking Edwin. It's not for children.'

'He can be twisted in. Samuel Wrigley's to be twisted in by King Ludd tonight.'

'I want to go!' Edwin cried.

'He's not going to be twisted in and he's not coming with us. There's no question of it. Twisting in children! Is this what Crawshaw's been telling you? Your mother's right. They'll not stop short at 'anging kids.'

'I want to go to the mill!' Edwin repeated. 'I want to get my own back on 'em.'

'Thou's not going,' Mor repeated once again.

'You'll not be setting fire to it . . ?' Edwin asked.

'We're not going to fire it,' Mor answered.

'Some have been fired,' Edwin insisted. 'Mr Crawshaw'd fire it, to make 'imself famous.'

He could not be consoled.

After dark, when the 'Watch and Ward' patrol might arrest suspects in the streets, Mor shoved a book in his pocket and slipped out with Gideon, first of all going to Samuel Wrigley's house. Mor gave a Luddite rap upon the door, one sharp knock followed by two slow ones, and Samuel opened it a crack. He was already half-way into his coat, and smiling as if he was going, not to start a new parliament, but to a picnic.

'The Loyal Georgian Society, and the Lord protect us,' Gideon grimly announced.

Wrigley turned to his new wife. 'Your oatcakes are burning,' he told her, to get her out of the room.

'Who's that at the door?' she asked, peering, peeping; not that she cared, it was merely to show that she was not stupid.

'The schoolmaster,' Samuel answered, carelessly.

Satisfied now to do as she was bid, to be taken for a fool, and pretending she did not know that they were trying to get rid of her, nor why, she went to haul a rack of oatcakes down from the ceiling in a back room, her hands and apron dusty with flour.

'Repeat the password,' Gideon demanded.

'Give over!' Wrigley teased. 'You know who I am.'

Mor was laughing.

'Answer!' Gideon hissed. 'Say, "The Lord protect us."'

Wrigley, also, was laughing. Leaving the others standing on the step, he retreated into his house for a moment. He shouted to his wife, 'I'll be out for a while. Then I'll be back.' He was on the street with them. He was game for anything, healthy, rakish, and strong.

''Ow's married life suit thee, Samuel Wrigley?' Mor asked.

'I didn't know I was married until I woke up and found myself i'bed. It's better than doing everything for meself . . .'

Wrigley turned to Gideon. 'Thou's in a bit of a state, my young comrade. 'Appen it's because our King Ludd and John Tiplady give you a rough time this afternoon?'

'That's nothing to do with it,' Gideon snarled.

'Isn't it?'

'No.'

'Well, thou shouldn't take any notice o'Crawshaw. He's too fond of his own voice, that one. It's nothing more than that.'

Skirting the Adam and Eve because of the soldiers billeted in it, they came to the back door of the Radical's pub, The Old Tup. It was on the edge of town and there seemed no sign of life. The shutters were drawn and showed no chinks of light; they were well-made, of good boards, recently renovated by a Luddite joiner. Here the party stopped.

Edwin lurked fifty yards away. Because he was following a Luddite band, all his aches seemed worth bearing. He prepared himself for a wait. He rubbed at his wrists, which were almost pulled out of joint. He made one fanciful plan after another. From time to time he attended to his kicked shins, or his eye. He banged his clogs on the road.

Gideon knocked at the door of The Old Tup; the same rapping that had been delivered upon Wrigley's.

'Who's there?' answered Arthur Crawshaw's voice. You would not have dreamed that there was a soul in the building.

'The Lord protect us!' Gideon called out.

Wooden bolts were slid back, opening into a primitive cave-like room, with a stone floor, and the ceiling made of great stone pavings, too. Shadows and light were shaken over the scarred, whitewashed walls. There was a large, brilliant fire in the grate. These working men, nearly all of them croppers and weavers, knew where to get the best coal, just as they could rely upon joiners to repair their shutters. A large pot of rabbit stew was cooking for a celebration after the raid. Other poached contributions were recklessly laid out on a sideboard. There was illegally brewed whisky and there was ale, all for after the attack. By the light of the hearth and of ignited ropes dipped in pitch, the kitchen showed the men already loosely gathered around a Bible and a hammer, placed in the centre of the room. There were also firearms. One gun was fitted with a bayonet.

'You've been on a raid already, then,' Mor remarked.

'And you were not with us,' Crawshaw replied tartly.

'Well, there wasn't much to that,' Tiplady added. 'We'd only to climb through a stable window at back o't'Adam and Eve. There wasn't a guard in sight. You wouldn't know about that, Mr Crawshaw. You were at t'front door.'

96

'Nonetheless, Greave wasn't with us. Now he wants to be one of us.'

Crawshaw looked around for his audience. 'So then there'll be thirteen on the raid. Is someone else to drop out, or what?'

'I don't mind not going,' Wrigley answered. 'It's all the same to me whether I join in the fun or not.'

'It won't be no fun,' Crawshaw told him.

'They'll call you a coward, Samuel,' Tiplady warned.

'Nobody'll ever call me a coward, not if I come to hear of it.'

'We know why you have decided at last to join us, Mor Greave,' Crawshaw said. 'You 'ad no intention of it until something happened to your own child in the factory. You've come for personal reasons and not for the greater cause that inspires the rest of us. You have proved too often a back-slider before, Mor Greave.'

'Tha says that to me! Thou does! You! . . .'

'Steady on,' Tiplady warned.

'You, Crawshaw! You're the one looking out for thyself, for a bit o' private glory.'

'Let's get through wi'out quarrels, for God's sake.'

Tiplady filled his pipe.

'*Thou*! The pot calling the kettle black . . .' Mor, angry, would not be stopped.

'We're all going,' Tiplady interrupted, taking command of the fireplace, with more authority than King Ludd himself, touching long tapers to the flames and sucking at his pipe. 'We need every man we have, and who in the future would want to admit that 'e'd been left behind?'

'That'll be thirteen,' Crawshaw said.

Tiplady looked at Crawshaw without blinking.

'Yes,' he answered, 'it's time to break wi' superstitions.'

So Wrigley allowed himself to be sworn in, his hands upon the Bible and repeating after Crawshaw the Luddite oath, with careful enunciation:

'I, Samuel Wrigley, of my own free voluntary will, do declare and solemnly swear that I will never reveal to any person or persons under the Canopy of Heaven the names of the persons who comprise the secret committee, their proceedings, meetings, places of abode, dress, features, complexion, under the penalty of being sent out of the world by the first brother who shall meet me. And further do I swear to use my best endeavours to punish by death any traitor or traitors should any rise up among us, wherever I can find him or them and though he should fly to the verge of nature I will pursue him with unceasing vengeance. So help me God and bless me, to keep this my oath inviolate.'

'You're twisted in now, Samuel Wrigley. You're one with us, and you cannot break it without breaking with us all,' Crawshaw announced. He addressed the whole company: 'Since the last week of February our brothers in Huddersfield have attacked the dressing shop of Joseph Hurst there and destroyed an obnoxious cropping machine. They've 'ad a go at James Balderson's on Crossland Moor, and they've done for all t'machinery that was put in at William Hinchcliffe's on Ley Moor. They've broke into John Garner's of Honley and Clement Dyson's at Dungeon. We've smashed shearing frames at Linthwaite, Slaithwaite, Golcar, Honley, and Holmfirth. In the days since Rawfolds, Lady Ludd has raised the banner of 'er food riots in Sheffield and Rotherham. So our defeat at Rawfolds 'as not been a defeat, it 'as inspired us. It is sent by God, not to crush us but to refresh our justified anger, like water from 'Eaven upon the spring grass. Are we going to let women show us the way . . . ?'

Before the speech was finished, the machine-breakers were disguising themselves and smudging lamp-black over their features. The large hammer was given to Wrigley, in honour of his strength and his skill. As well as the firearms, picks and iron bars were distributed. Crawshaw tucked a pistol into his belt. Tiplady took the gun with the bayonet. Others rummaged in a cupboard that was filled with women's clothes and they dressed themselves in petticoats, cotton dresses and bonnets. Sad amateurs of conspiracy and revolution, the men in female dress crossed back and forth through the shadows and the firelight like weird priests. Tiplady started singing:

> 'Ye weavers of England, give ear to my song,
> When I sing of tyrants I seldom do wrong,
> For if they transport me t'America's wild shore
> I then shall have freedom, when I have sailed o'er;
> > Freedom from slavery,
> > Fetters and knavery,
> Never tormented with tyrants no more!'

Mor had composed it, words and tune. Tiplady emphasised the last line with the steps of a mummers' dance, banging his iron-tipped shoes heavily on the stones.

All except Crawshaw welcomed Mor. They broke into the ale and toasted him back into the fold. He warmed in the glow of companion-ship.

'We need actions, not songs and poems,' Crawshaw muttered, blackening his face, impatient to get out and cut throats.

Tiplady coloured himself with care and deliberation, just as he would tackle cloth with his shears.

'I hope your informers in t'militia 'ave done their work. I wouldn't be surprised to find Horsfalls' guarded with a whole troop of dragoons. His mill is not like the others. Him and the cavalry officers . . . they all piss in the same pot, you might say. And with the moon tonight, they'll see us coming for miles.'

'There's no spies amongst us,' Crawshaw declared. 'Nobody knows what we've planned.'

Nonetheless, King Ludd was tucking pistols into his belt.

He briskly divided his men into two parties, the youngest and strongest to enter and smash the cropping frame, the eldest and weakest to keep watch. He drilled them for a few minutes. The manoeuvres were difficult for men dressed to the ankles in tattered women's frocks, who were making do with a farm-rake, a collier's pick, and a poker for weapons. Several got carried away, clapping their hands in imitation gunshots.

Tiplady shook the ashes out of the bowl of his pipe.

'Are we to stay here drilling like toy soldiers until the moon rises and the countryside is alive wi' soldiers?' he said. 'Well, you are the captain, not I!'

At last King Ludd was satisfied. Boots rang to attention for the last time on the stone floor. Through the door they took a quick look up and down, and stepped out on their mission. It was a cool, light night, faintly grey and silver, the moon not yet up. One man was sent ahead to look for soldiers and for the Watch and Ward patrol. He was to give a signal at each corner. Apart from that, as they knew that no neighbour would betray them, the band showed little caution. It was almost impossible to recruit a Watch and Ward patrol in Lady Well, anyway. Crawshaw was at the front, muttering but making his peace with Tiplady. Samuel Wrigley strode at the rear, carrying the hammer easily upon his shoulder. The others, in between, were trying to save their skirts from tangling with their heavy boots. A hundred yards to the rear Edwin followed, not able to recognise which one of these weird shadowy figures was his father.

When they reached the top of the stairway that dropped down to the mill, the moon rose. With its leering, steadily brightening face it transformed the whole of Yorkshire. Hill was folded upon hill, like grey soft cloth folded in the cropping shop. It was so bright that the tightly shut daisies opened and turned towards it.

To hide from the light, and also because there might be a guard on the stairway, the machine-breakers climbed the wall and cut through the wood.

Edwin followed, tingling with fear of man traps. In the damp under the trees, the scents were so powerful that he felt he could reach out and touch them. Solid trees and rocks were changed into lights and shadows. On the other hand, trunks of beech and ash became shafts of light. The boughs of the hazels were flecked with a rain of pollen-heavy catkins.

Someone pounced, and grabbed him by the scruff of his neck.

'What's your name, son?'

Edwin would not answer. He was asked several times and cuffed around the ears.

'Ow, it 'urts there!'

'Greave, isn't it? And your father is twisted in, if I'm not mistaken?'

The man was still not given a reply. He pulled Edwin along in the wake of the machine-breakers.

'A schoolmaster. *Educated*,' he said menacingly. 'One that's fond of catching the master's hares and trouts, I believe. Isn't that so?'

'I'm not a fool . . . Ow!'

Edwin's cries might alert other Luddites, so the man did not hurt him anymore.

'You're a clever young fellow, I can see that. But you can speak free and easy with me, you know. You're fortunate, because I've been twisted in too. Why aren't you marching openly with your father and the rest?'

Edwin was pulled along by the curls at the back of his neck, which were still machine-greasy. The stranger took hold of him by his hardly more pleasant collar.

'Come on, speak up! There's no secrets kept between us in the Combination. To evade the laws so wickedly passed against us, we call ourselves Loyal Georgians.' The man laughed at the title. 'Did you know that?'

'No.'

'You're a tight one, I must say. O'course you know! Your father invented the name, didn't he? Own up, it's nought to be ashamed of. A proper little Luddite, you are. You must come along wi' the rest of us to raid Mr Horsfall's property. I'm sure you'll conduct yourself bravely in the fray. How do you spell the word "obnoxious"?'

'I don't know 'ow to spell.'

'Your father's the schoolmaster, isn't he? I thought you'd be having a try at Latin grammar by now. Your father, I've heard, is a very knowledgeable lettered man. You must often have heard from him the phrase, "obnoxious frames"? Or from others, maybe, as epithet for the new cropping machines? So how do you spell it?'

'I've heard it but I don't know 'ow to spell . . . ouch!'

'Liars burn in Hell! What about "ignominious"?'

He stopped speaking, because ahead of them Crawshaw hissed for silence. The band, carefully following a drive through the trees, had broken out of the wood. A sheet of bright moonlight lay like silver-grey icy water upon the mill's tenter-field. A guard was sitting by a fire with his musket on his knees, looking out not for Luddites but for rabbits. His attention was fixed on one at the end of a row of cloth.

So all hovered for a while, wondering what to do next. There was a rabbit, nibbling in the cold dew, ignorant of muskets and revolution; a soldier who thought that perhaps revolution was not going to occur this night after all; a King Ludd who was biting his lip so tightly that he tasted blood on his teeth; an apprentice cropper, Gideon Greave, whose knees were hurting and who imitated Arthur Crawshaw's anger; armed men with smudged black faces or dressed in ladies' ribboned bonnets, their hairy ankles protruding from the bottoms of dresses and petticoats, who were in terror of the guns in their own hands that might lead to their being transported; and a small boy held some distance away in the shadows.

Eventually, King Ludd felt that he could lead his men on, as the soldier was absorbed in watching the rabbit. The Luddites had little fear of the houses of the overseer and the engineer on the bank top, for these people put their trust in the soldiers, and slept in peace.

Crawshaw led to the wall of the apprentices' building. This was the simplest place from which to break in. It was the furthest from Mr Horsfall's house, and most difficult to patrol because of the tangled wood nearby, and the river. The noise of water would also cover the sounds of the picks, and this spot was the most unlikely, therefore the least suspected, way in. It was remarkably easy; mill-owners and soldiers were such fools.

The Luddites posted their guards and big Samuel Wrigley started to swing at the mortar below a windowsill. This led into the girls' dormitory, where the shrieking children were already out of their beds, watching the trembling of the bars.

'Be quiet!' Crawshaw ordered, frightened. 'Be quiet!'

Gold dust from the tip of Wrigley's pick sifted downwards through the moonlight. Mor and others inserted crowbars and eased out the sill. Samuel climbed a tree, in order to hack at the lintel. For a moment, sill and bars were dangling from a lintel, ready to fall, floating in air. 'Eh up!' Crawshaw shouted. As they leapt out of the way, sill, bars, and bits of masonry dropped in a cloud of dust, then with a soft thud, onto the river bank. The larger stones toppled heavily into the water. The raiders were ready to go into the mill, demolish it, and change the world.

Like a nestful of happy starlings the ragged little girls were putting their squeaking heads through the hole in their prison wall, out into the cloud of dust.

'Those of you as wants to be gone, be gone!' Crawshaw yelled. 'England is still a great free country, though you're maybe only free to starve in it. But don't block the window. Don't block the way or t'soldiers'll be coming. Let us get inside!'

Crawshaw, the fool, shouting out so loud!

Mor also heard his eldest son, mumbling quotes from the Bible. 'Oh, children of Israel! And they made their lives bitter with hard bondage, in mortar and in brick . . .'

What silly useless amateurs we are at this game.

The girls who had longed so much for freedom were afraid to take it. They were too used to their confinement, and only a couple dared clamber through the gap. The others ran into the darkest corner of their prison, huddling together.

Most of the raiders did not feel that they had time to spare for persuading them. Tiplady lifted out in turn the two little girls who were brave enough. With a smile, he put his hand in his pocket and gave them two pence each. Not even pausing to look at this amazing gift, they ran off into the darkness.

Margaret was not one of them. Edwin, some yards away, held back by his captor, painfully watched. The man's grip was a loose one, revolted by a dirty evil-smelling factory child. At last Edwin was away like a fish, tearing off to that window through which King Ludd's men had now been swallowed.

'Margaret! Margaret!'

Soon her head was peeping through.

'Margaret, take my hand. Let's away!'

'I can't . . .'

He pulled her out. She slithered down the wall with a scream of pain.

'I can't do it, I so hurt!'

But she was out of the mill now, crouching against the wall, frightened both of going with Edwin, and of returning.

'O-ow! Oh! . . .'

Her flesh was burning wherever it was touched. Her hand, which Edwin grasped, was in pain. In the creamy light of the moon now high in the sky, he made her run, leap, stumble and crawl, careless of man-traps, ditches, brambles and branches.

'I hurt,' she repeated, but she still kept going. 'My feet. I can't go so fast.'

They heard the manufactory bell tolling. They listened to shots fired, and thought that they were hunted. They struggled on, on, out of sound and sight of Luddites, soldiers, factory bells, apprentice houses and spinning machines, looking for London and Margaret's mother, for Liverpool and America.

Mor, by himself, stumbled from the mill, crashing into bogs and tangles of bramble. He had not been wounded when they had come across soldiers hiding among the frames, and when Crawshaw had fired off his pistol, killing a private. He did not know what had happened to his comrades, even to his own son, though.

Hungry, tired, afraid, not daring to return to the appetising rabbit stew at The Old Tup, he came by a place known as Lower Laithes. It was a derelict group of buildings, with much of its stone removed to build the Horsfalls' mansion. Mor paused there, as he often did, full of curiosity about a place that had once belonged to the Greave family.

He felt compelled to enter under the precarious archway, into the eerie courtyard. It might be a place to rest in and hide, in case he was pursued to his home.

He was overcome with awe. It kept him moving forward. He found himself walking among the tumbled stones, dilapidated barns, holes that had once been the cellars of buildings, doors hanging from hinges, collapsed floors, suspended lintels, old carts and stone troughs, broken chunks of classical carvings and hunks of plaster daubed with fragmentary depiction of the 'muses', all the fashionable rubbish of a previous age, with an unseen hand guiding him. Though he possessed a poacher's skill of not making noisy stumbles in the darkness, even so the ease with which he moved round these death-traps was extraordinary. He surely would not have collided with anything even if he had behaved carelessly. He was searching for something, though he did not know for what. He was desperate. He was mad. Yet in one instantaneous flood, the sense of beauty overrode the bestiality, the cruelty, the smoky ugliness and the poverty that soured the spirit and the flesh in Yorkshire.

It was very dark between the buildings, and Mor pulled his head back, looking for stars. The whole of the heavens were re-arranged in a symmetrical pattern of great loveliness. The stars had formed themselves into a wheel, the hub of which was over this courtyard. Some incredible crown was fixed over this place. Yet it seemed quite a normal event.

Moving on, he found himself in a covered passageway, a tunnel into the buildings, and at the other end a garden door which, feeling in the pitch dark, he discovered was locked. He was compelled to turn back. At the mouth of the starlit courtyard he was unable to stir. His feet were locked into the ground, his hands fastened to the walls where he reached out to steady himself. The empty courtyard had the potent feeling of a stage upon which the curtain has risen yet it is still empty of characters; when the gentlemen and ladies have become motionless and silent in their boxes and all are waiting for the great tragic actress.

Mor began to shake violently. He quivered in waves from his head down to his feet. A cry took possession of him, and gripped his throat. It was not his own cry for he had no control over it and it was not even his own voice. It was an inhumanly savage call torn out of some unsuspected deep well within him. It began quietly but with each successive wave grew louder. At each attack he felt he could bear no more, yet still they came. His throat was strained, yet though he was longing for peace, he shook the universe with his cries. His body was being rattled to pieces. He did not know which frightened him most – the uncontrollable yells that tore him, or the appalling silences that followed each spasm; his violent shaking or his feet being locked into the ground.

Then something compelled him to move. Like the voice, it was regardless of his personal desires, and he had no more control of his motions than he had possessed over his rootedness. His usual limp was suddenly, miraculously, eased. He began to dash about the courtyard at great speed, with some invisible force pushing or pulling him; the marvellous coronet of stars above, his only light.

He found himself banging pitifully on the long-abandoned doors, and he had no idea why he had chosen them. Heaven knew what ghosts were summoning him. He begged, begged, to be let in and freed of the exhausting, frightening exhilaration. Then he was off again, dashing about the courtyard.

He was shrieking and screaming. What control he kept of himself he used for a terrified pleading to be released from the awful suffering, especially in his throat, and from the tearing pain at his inner organs. He was being skewered in pain, possessed by a frightful purpose, clinging to a driftwood of hope that he could survive. Yet before he completed his pleas that rival cry was tearing out of him, that seemed not his own.

He was confronted by a small ash tree growing in a crack of masonry, and found himself pulling branches from it. The first twigs to hand did not satisfy his occupying spirit, which made him tear desperately at others. He crushed the branches and leaves onto his head until he was soaked in their cool moistness.

Now calm and happiness possessed him. He was laughing. Holding the branches aloft he began to pace up and down the yard. He lifted his head back and laughed at the marvellous, transformed sky. He was overflowing with ecstasy, he was roaring with delight because he knew that he had survived. He was certain that something wonderful was about to happen.

Tiredness overcame him and he sank upon the cobblestones, still crushing the branches to his head. Leaves hung over his temples, down his neck, over his shoulders and breast. He was silent now, exhausted and trembling.

Out of the darkness a stone came forward and he found himself gripping it tight. It was not heavy, but required both hands to hold it comfortably and preciously as it demanded. It was as smooth as a bird's egg, a perfect oval, untypical of any local stones, even those shaped by streams; these split into shale or were eroded into twisted and complicated forms. He clutched it to his breast, and it anchored him to the world, which now resumed its motions. Mor returned to his consciousness of it. He was exhausted, but he was illuminated. He was glowing like a hot coal.

The moment that he thought of rising he became stiff with the fear of the objects amongst which he had been dashing. The yard was littered with the torn branches of his madness as well as with stones and pits. Whereabouts was the well? It must be waiting somewhere to swallow him up.

At last, stumbling tentatively, he made his way to the yard's exit. All the stars had disappeared and the darkness made his head spin.

Lydia Horsfall was disturbed in the dark. She was not sure whether the gunshots, the shouts and the tolling bell were part of a nightmare full of men, but the bell continued to ring after she awoke. Men were running and yelling outside the house. At last it has come; a Luddite raid. Inside the house she heard a scream and a curse, more urgent than normal in the games between the officers billeted upon them and the whores. She also heard something that was quite usual in the nighttime – the panicked cry of a child, not one of her own children – and she shuddered. If there had been a raid, it had not made Horsfall change his plans for his night's pleasures.

Mrs Horsfall, as her husband did not want her and she did not desire him, slept alone. She chose a remote room so as to be away from such calls in the night. Her bedroom was, however, beneath the even more distant room where was kept the elder Nicholas Horsfall. Every now and then she heard him above her ceiling. Each dawn he was inspired, like some form of slime life, to respond to the light. She supposed that at such a time he could not but feel some hope. His noises as he scratched at the window were not loud, for he had neither breath nor energy for it, but were frighteningly inhuman, as if he had been changed into a reptile or a toad.

The mill-owner's wife awoke, as usual, to her hatred for this house, with its whores, its frightened, bleeding children, its drunken officers, and its terrible spectre, the barely fleshed ghost of a syphilitic old man. These were the horrors that drove her out, night or day, whenever she could find excuses and the weather was not impossibly inclement. On each return Lydia had to pause before re-entering. She chose the same spot at a hundred yards' distance to breathe deeply, and recreate the composure she must feel and the features she must bear to go into this abominable building.

How many of the finest houses in England were haunted by a syphilitic old man in an attic, a daughter languishing more poetically from consumption in the drawing room? A great many, Lydia knew that. There were far more revolting creatures in the remote rooms and attics than were admitted to.

She tried to think that she should not be so sorry for herself, but she had additional afflictions. Her husband's trips to London and Brussels . . . she knew, all right, what he went for. Reasoning to herself that his deflowering of twelve-year-olds in a brothel was because of his terror of catching from an older woman the disease that rotted his father, did not make it easier for her to hide (as for society's sake she must) her revulsion and disgust. She also had the problem of being a woman from the south having to put up with 'the barbaric north'. She looked over a crowded industrial valley, on the edge of the growing town of Lady Well, yet it was to her a place where 'nobody' lived, that is no one of her own class. There were only those for whom she felt charity, and deep sorrow. She never went 'in there', that is into the factory, and the nearest she got to her husband's employees was in church or when distributing charity in the village, where the people kept a respectful distance. At second hand, she made it her business to know a great deal about them, though; their names, trades and misfortunes. She had gifts delivered secretly to 'the most deserving cases' – some money to be picked up on the doorstep, a pie supposedly sent by a distant relative. People who received manna from Heaven were easily persuaded not to ask questions or gossip; if they had done so, her husband would have prevented her from 'spoiling' the workpeople.

Though she had little direct contact, she heard them, all right. Every morning, for much of the year in the dark, they tramped down that long gulley, the yard at the bottom of her garden, with a savage noise like that of insubordinate prisoners. She was sure that it was on purpose to awaken her. If she dared to look out, she would see them jeering and pointing, it seemed in her direction – actually, at the monster in the room above.

The daylight was seeping, grey. She felt the tiredness forming creases around her eyes and across her forehead to make her ugly, even before the day that would exhaust her with its emptiness had commenced. What, what was she doing here? At the age of thirty, a cast-up, rejected woman, young enough to count herself still beautiful, yet too old to satisfy her husband's passions. A woman without friends, or a purpose, at any rate one that it was possible for her to fulfil.

She heard the old man scraping and wheezing above. She remembered the stages of his disease. A handsome, confident man, like his son today, he had formed a habit of picking his nose. Though people remarked upon it, he could not help himself, even in company. There had formed an incrustation inside his nostril, and a little pus mixed with blood began to run. His mouth and throat were sore.

One day, she overhead from behind a closed door the kind of conversation a lady was not supposed to hear.

'Pray, sir, what is the matter with me?' Horsfall asked the surgeon.

'The matter? Why, sir, you are poxed up to the eyes.'

In any case Lydia would have soon guessed the diagnosis, because of the cure. He was treated with the notorious 'blue pills', a combination of mercury with a quarter of a grain of opium, taken in a concoction of sarsaparilla. It was a long while before a gossiping servant dropped hints about the ulcer on his penis, but the ones in his mouth, his throat, and the purple or yellow spots over the remainder of his body, could not be hidden from her. Eventually it was tacitly assumed she knew what the disease was, without the words 'pox' and 'syphilis' ever having been mentioned in her presence.

The 'blue pills' did not improve things, so mercury was applied as an ointment. Horsfall's cheeks became covered with a yellow crust and the pimples on his face gave a watery discharge. He had difficulty in breathing and they tried steaming his nostrils over a bowl of hot water. That gave him some relief, yet the decay still continued. Because of his appearance and the embarrassment of his foul breath, he gave up going into society altogether and abandoned his business.

Instead he spent his time studying the Bible, not in search of a philosophy that would transcend suffering, but for a means of ennobling his disease through its association with the great and holy. He saw that his affliction was that same 'leprosy' that was the curse of Job, Herod and King David. He turned over in his mind Psalm 38, 'Neither is there any rest in my bones because of my sin', 'my wounds stink and are corrupt because of my foolishness', 'my loins are filled with a loathsome disease', 'my lovers and my friends stand aloof from my sore; and my kinsmen stand afar off', 'as for the light of mine eyes, it also is gone from me.'

His eyes became enflamed. 'Wouldn't it be better to have a darkened room of your own and rest your eyes?' suggested his son, not able to bear the sight nor smell of his father.

His family finally locked the wreckage of a man away. The miasma of his breath made it impossible for them and their servants to hide their disgust.

A yellowing of the light grew in Lydia's room. She watched it tinting the painting by her father's protégé Thomas Gould: a misty morning evaporating over fields. She did not know whether she loved the picture more in the first blue light, or in the later yellow one. In her room were several other paintings, including her portrait, by the same artists. If there were not something beautiful in my life, she thought, I could not bear it.

Her maid came in, distraught. Her apron was awry and bits of hair were escaping from her cap. Lydia was brought with a jolt back to the realities of this house. She reprimanded the girl, who could hardly hear for her panic, as she curtsied around the bed, her eyes full of tears.

'They 'as tried to break down the mill, ma'am, but the soldiers was there waiting. A man was shot. A soldier. Three children have run away, ma'am, Mr Gledhill says. He says they're spies for Luddites fearful of being appreyended for telling secrets to the French.'

'Nonsense.'

'Please, ma'am, didn't y'ear the bell ringing all night? We all, the servants I mean, couldn't sleep for it.'

'I heard the bell, yes, and the soldiers.'

Lydia spoke slowly, with authority, emphasising the personal pronoun. It helped her to feel that she was the centre of the universe, which was how Mrs Horsfall should feel.

A roar of pain rose out of the depths of the house.

'I take it that these desperate persons did not succeed in breaking down our mill?'

'Thanks be to God, ma'am! Two of the men is injured and crying for a surgeon downstairs but Mr Horsfall will not give them any help.'

'Why not?'

'Until they tell on their comrades.'

The girl's eyes filled again. The mistress was now vertical in her bed.

'Which men are they?'

'Wrigley, ma'am, and John Tiplady.'

'Help me to dress and I will go to see.'

As she was being dressed before her mirror, she studied her face, which was fattening through unhappiness, or rather through her consolatory addiction to rice pudding made with cream. Attired in sable slippers and Chinese silk gown, Lydia suppressed her own thoughts and sent Mrs Horsfall forth, to do her female duty of quelling disputatious men.

In the great passageway, the width of a carriage drive, that reached for the whole length of the house, a knot of servants was preparing cleaning equipment, ready to enter a room as if to make a military invasion. Halfway along she spied a stranger, a messenger or suitor in outdoor clothes, hovering with his hat in his hands. Nearby, girls were polishing stair rails, door knobs, the wood and tiles of the floor. A boy in a green apron was bringing in coals. These were perfectly usual sights, when the servants returned, with the normal light, after cockcrow, from their wings of the house; but although their brisk attitude when she made her appearance had always shown that they had no greater wish than to spend the whole of eternity in polishing her floors and bringing her coals, sly and shifty looks met her this morning. The girl at the banister rail looked boldly at her mistress, making no effort to hide her face and her squalid apron, as she had been trained to do. The messenger from industry twisted his hat in his hands as if they were around the throat of a despot. The boy with the coals banged them down outside the library door and stared at her.

Further along the passageway, Lydia met the last of the night's whores, making a show of refusing to be dismissed. Lydia knew who she was. She was called 'Mary The Scar', for something she always kept hidden under powder on her cheeks; a night creature, a pale moth, confused and absurd when caught in the morning light. Her thickly whitened face with its circular rouged patches, under red hair, was designed for candlelight and it looked garish in the day. She was a striking woman, tall, dressed in green boots and a loose dress falling from where it was pulled tight under her breasts. It was in an out-moded 'Grecian' style, and even this betrayed a sympathy with the French Revolution that had favoured it. The looseness suggested freedom.

'That's your aristocracy for yer! They offer you a bed and then throws you out in the middle of the night because someone tries t'assassinate 'em. I think I'll satisfy myself with common soldiers from now on. What do you think, ma'am?'

The whore spoke to Lydia as if she were another prostitute and it made the servants laugh.

Lydia turned to ice.

'Get out of my house.'

'Someone 'as to keep your 'usband's bed warm, my dear. But it isn't me, neither, what does that. I'm 'ere only for his friends.'

Lydia was still angry from this encounter when she went into her husband's study. Moaning upon stretchers on the floor were John Tiplady and Samuel Wrigley. A whimpering servant girl was trying to soothe them. Nearby was a captain, a sergeant, two privates, Nathaniel Gledhill with a bottle in his hand, Mor Greave and a gentleman whom Lydia did not recognise.

Nicholas Horsfall, as if patiently awaiting an outcome, was staring through the window. The early morning light fell upon his conservatory, its frame made not like the spinning mill of inflammable wood, but of cast iron. Its pillars were cast into the forms of leaves, ionic column heads, bunches of grapes and flowers. There he indulged his more respectable hobby, growing roses. In the room they were all waiting for Horsfall to give them a lead, but he was baffled to understand why artisans should want to destroy his mill and machinery, when it was through these that he provided them with their bread.

'What is happening? Revolution?' Lydia demanded. 'The servants stare at me like Jacobins at Marie Antoinette.'

'My dear Lydia, do leave us. This isn't a place for a woman.'

He realised, wearily, that she would not go away. She could be a most determined woman.

Lydia peered down at the bodies.

'I wouldn't get too close,' warned the captain.

Lydia was able to see so deeply into the wound at Tiplady's shoulder that she perceived pieces of bone floating in blood. She pulled back, turned white and sickened, but managed to hold back the vomit in her throat.

Men, for Lydia, were normally cruel, perverse, obscene beings. They ruled and crushed. They rotted vilely in hidden rooms for their sins. If they were of a lower class they might murder one in one's bed . . . so she had been told, and told, and told. But here she saw a being equal to herself, vulnerable, weak, and feeling pain. She had seen, not a Luddite, but a man . . . one for whom she felt sorrow; sorrow for the grey hairs curling on Tiplady's neck, for his freckled hand, for the pale, harrowed features and the torn shoulder, for the eyes closing and opening in pain like the gills of a desperate fish dragged out of water, taking in only veiled shaky glimpses of the books, the people and the paintings.

'Stop this cruelty. Stop it, for the love of charity,' she said, in such a firm, strange voice that they thought it was someone else speaking.

'Lydia, don't you think it would be better to return upstairs?'

Nicholas Horsfall turned back to the window, to the distance, thinking, Damn! The bitch is mad. What can one do with her? I know what to do. I will have her put away, this time I *will*.

'It isn't charity we want, Mrs Horsfall,' said Mor Greave. 'It's our rights. We need beef and pie as a right for the work we do, not as a gift to those that suit you. We want our work and fair payment for it, and if you intend changing things, we want to be consulted.'

She stared at him, trying to comprehend.

'"Needs", "wants", what all this?' Horsfall joined in again. 'You are members of a Combination. That is the truth of it. We must face up to the facts. Are you also in Napoleon's pay?'

'For God's sake shoot me now and put me out of misery.'

'May I bring some warm milk for Mr Tiplady, ma'am? Look at 'im . . .'

The maid was struggling with rag and bucket to prevent blood from reaching the carpet.

'Of course. Bring some brandy,' Lydia rapped out sharply, to cope with her tears.

'Lydia, my dear, are you well? I should go upstairs,' Nicholas said with menace.

The bitch! She'll ruin everything.

The servant left before the order was countermanded.

'They are the traitorous followers of King Ludd, Mrs Horsfall,' patiently explained the stranger. 'They are armed, and shot a man. Fortunately we foiled their plans in advance.'

They knew about a raid, yet Nicholas continued his revels!

'Who is this person?' Lydia asked with contempt.

'A spy,' Mor as contemptuously told her.

'I was guarding the woods for Mr Horsfall at the time I met the rebels. They drilled like soldiers and were armed against the King. 'Tis certain they will not stop, but are aiming to overthrow their betters.'

112

'We drill so's not to be th'rabble you describe us,' Tiplady whispered.

'You drill to overthrow your country!' Gledhill knelt at his side, to administer something. 'You shot a man.'

Tiplady screamed. Gledhill had put aqua-fortis on the wound.

'Damn you, damn you . . .' Mor could think of no other expression. 'Damn you . . .'

Wrigley tried to swing a blow. A gentle pluck by the maid, returned with the milk, restrained him. Lydia winced and pushed her sleeve in her mouth.

'What do you know of Luddites?' Horsfall demanded of Mor.

Crawshaw, who had killed the soldier, had disappeared. Only these three had been arrested, though God only knew who had been recognised. Mor wondered where Gideon was. He himself had been stopped on the edge of Lady Well, for being abroad in boots caked with mud 'at an unreasonable hour'. As Gledhill, the Watch and Ward captain, had remarked, 'If he has not been at the mill, then he's been poaching.' It was as he was being brought to Horsfalls' that he had put his hand in his pocket and realised he had lost his *Rights of Man*. The chances were that it was in or near the mill, and his name was written on the flyleaf.

'Nowt,' Mor answered, 'I know nowt about Luddites.'

'You have associated with murderers. You're a schoolmaster and, they tell me, an educated man. You should know better.'

'I know what Socrates knew. That he was the wisest of men because he knew that he knew nowt.'

Horsfall was impatient of philosophy.

'Tell us who King Ludd is, and it might earn you a pardon from transportation.'

'Tis fair wages that will cure this illness, not magistrates. If there's right wages, King Ludd will die.'

'We shall return England to the green and pleasant land of King Arthur's day,' Tiplady contributed. 'To the constitution of Old England.'

'It never was a "green and pleasant land", John. It always was ruled by scoundrels who exploited their fellow man. Isn't that so, Mr Horsfall? What you say is nothing but a foolish myth, John.'

When Lydia looked through the window she saw, beyond the glass conservatory flecked with rose blooms like spots of blood, the dark hills parting from the valleys like the lids from eyes, the streams running out of their corners like tears along ducts gouged with weeping. 'Go away, go away,' they said. The place had finished with her, and she had done with it. Houses and mills were blackening with the soot of steam engines. She felt a pain behind her eyes. In this room of her own house, wounded upon the carpet was John Tiplady, a thoughtful, honest craftsman with a quiet, philosophical turn of mind, and Wrigley, a cheerful, lusty young man who had recently married. There, threatened with hanging or transportation, was the village schoolmaster. On the other hand, two of the worst men she had ever known, her husband and the awful Gledhill, with the help of that slimy spy, evidently some kind of decayed gentleman, triumphed over them.

'You seem faint, Lydia. *I think you should leave us.*'

Lydia looked in turn at each figure in the room, absorbing a new understanding, from the very ways in which they held themselves, from what they had said, and what they hadn't said. She saw them, not so much in a new light, but as she had always really seen them, only more vividly, so that at last she realised what they were.

The world was upside down, and she knew that she could bear no more of this place. Greave's words were like Tiplady's wound. Gaping with pain, yet they opened new worlds of understanding and feeling.

While Mor was held by the sergeant, Gledhill waved the aqua-fortis bottle under his nose.

'You are the King's prisoner. A poacher, a writer of sedition, a traitor, too.'

Mor aimed a kick at the overseer's leg, which landed home.

Gledhill was about to return the blow.

'Stop that, Gledhill! What sort of man are you?'

Nicholas had never known her speak in this unladylike fashion before the lower orders. Everyone was looking not at Lydia but at him. Like himself, they thought that Mrs Horsfall, who wandered the moors at night, was a lunatic. Mor Greave, only, stared at her with a different expression. He realised what she was thinking. She saw this as her husband, smiling, put an arm around her shoulders, dug his nails into the base of her neck and pinched tightly as he repeated, 'My dear, I think you ought to leave us.'

He was diverted from expelling her by the scuffle taking place between Mor, Gledhill and the sergeant who restrained him. It was clear that the soldier liked fair play, and didn't like the overseer.

114

'He'll be swinging on the gallows tomorrow, sir. Let justice take its course.'

''Anging's too good for seditious Painites,' Gledhill spat out. 'Do you know that he teaches sedition in that cellar? They're the ones we 'ave to catch. Catch them that do the reading and writing and the filling minds wi' sedition, and you'll kill stone dead the fear of revolution.'

'I 'aven't done anything except take a walk in the moonlight.'

'Very poetical, I'm sure,' sneered Horsfall.

'A great deal may be perceived by the light of the moon,' Lydia remarked. 'Unfortunately. Around this house. And I'm not leaving. Not yet.'

She knew that in the last resort she could defy her husband because of what she knew about him.

'Is your wife all right, sir?' the captain asked.

Rubbing his shin, Gledhill knelt by Samuel Wrigley.

'Tell us who King Ludd is.'

John Tiplady part-turned to his friend.

'Can you keep a secret?'

'Yes,' whispered Wrigley.

Tiplady motioned to Horsfall.

'Can you keep a secret?'

There was no politeness in the dying man's address.

'Yes.'

'Come closer.'

Horsfall, though he hated to come close to malodorous working people, bent down.

'Closer.'

Close enough for Tiplady to observe the twitching of a man who could not help but show his repulsion.

'So can I,' Tiplady whispered and then he died.

Lydia went to her room. She had seen too much, and her husband grasped that she had grown into an enemy. Because of what she knew, she could destroy him. She realised what he would do. He had already threatened to have her certified as a lunatic for her moonlight strolls and for 'morbid philanthrophy, encouraging the dissolute and feckless'.

Women, from the poorest to the richest, led double, deceitful lives. When Lydia secretly gave away her possessions, she felt that she herself had been filled with a gift. The opportunity to ease suffering was a privilege. Until she had realised this, she had felt starved and discontented. Incapable of celebrating the joy of others, as well as of experiencing their pain, though she was spoilt with the best things, she had felt only fear of losing them.

Her father, distrusting 'the Horsfall tribe', before her marriage had placed her money inherited from her mother in trust. Therefore she was the only woman in Lady Well who could act for herself and leave. Her first act was to write to her father that she wished to endow an 'improved' hospital as an annexe to the workhouse. 'Lady Well will be the better for at least one Horsfall,' she wrote. Next she composed a letter to Thomas Gould.

'Home has been for too long the theatre of my exploits and the boundary of my view and prospects. All my affections have been for too long hidden inside my nature. I am leaving and bringing my daughter with me. My son I will leave behind. He is too like his father for me to bear it. May we escape our disgrace by flying to the Continent? You have often said that we could.'

Finally she advised the Factory Commission to visit Paradise Mills, suggesting that the inspectors hold interviews without witnesses.

She would not trust her letters to a servant but, at around ten o'clock in the morning, took them herself to the post office. On the way she wondered about the fate of her pictures, not only Gould's but also those she purchased with his advice – Constable's and Turner's. Her husband would burn them or send them to the sale room.

She met the weaver, Mor Greave, in a hurry, with a roll of cloth under his arm.

'There's no one'll buy your piece today, Mr Greave. All business is stopped. The office is closed.'

He had a smile for her, because of what he had heard her say earlier.

'Can I see it?' she asked.

He unrolled the piece over the coping of the roadside wall, and stood back, a mixture of diffidence and pride. The smoke-blackened stones heightened the bright colours, as the dark leading of a cathedral's window intensifies the stained glass.

'It's dyed-in-the-wool,' he said, proudly.

His eyes were looking anxiously up the street or over the hills.

'But everyone else is weaving soldiers' cloth!'

'That's what my wife says, Mrs Horsfall. That no one'll buy it. I know it's not any use, but I wanted to . . .'

She was opening her purse. She was taking out sovereigns.

'I don't want any charity, Mrs Horsfall.'

'It's not charity. I'll buy it from you.'

'I haven't change for a sovereign.'

'Will you sell it to me?'

'Yes. But I've no change, and I need the money now. Today.'

'I know you do. I know.' They looked at one another and each knew that the other was leaving. 'I want it to remind me of Lady Well.'

'I thought you didn't like us much, Mrs Horsfall.'

'Does your piece mean anything?'

'Mean anything?'

'Hope, perhaps . . .'

'No, it doesn't mean anything,' he answered cautiously. 'Why should it?'

'Does two sovereigns seem a fair price?'

'Two sovereigns!' He laughed and then grew annoyed. 'I don't want charity.' He stared across the valley. 'I don't want charity, Mrs Horsfall.'

'It's not charity. It's worth all of that to me.'

'Do you know what a weaver's paid for his cloth, Mrs Horsfall? I'd do well to get ten shilling for it: I dunna want you to think I've made a fool of you.'

'I know the value of things. It's worth two sovereigns to me.'

He was hesitating. She took his hand, prised apart his thick stubborn fingers, and pressed in the two coins. He looked away from her, as he brushed his cheek with the back of his hand, clutching the sovereigns.

'Bless you.'

'Will you carry it to the post office for me?'

He walked behind her, humbly, and also because he could not keep up with her, being both laden and crippled. She stayed ahead, in the embarrassment of not being able to communicate with a weaver. He took it inside for her. She let him go. In front of the postmaster, they could not exchange any more words.

Because she was leaving Lady Well, Lydia shook the postmaster's hand after she had given him her letters. Before, her handshake had been a mere limp extension of her arm, indicating that she had no need to put herself out for anybody. Today, out of a new determined self, she warmly pumped his hand.

'Lady Hell,' she muttered as she returned for the time being to Horsfall's house, 'Lady Hell, Lady Hell . . .'

In a few weeks' time, depending on the post, she would be able to leave.

April 17th

Edwin knew which way to run, where lay east and west, because he had drawn all those maps, asked so many questions, taken notice of where the carts came from and where they went to.

In contrast to his purposefulness it had never occurred to Margaret to consider that there was a direction in which to search for what one wanted. She had never been allowed to decide; she had always been taken, or she had been confined. It was other things that were active with purpose. Men. Birds. Swallows, swifts and a stray gull or lark that she had watched, although she did not know the name of one from another. 'Godforgi'me, they're all sparrers,' she would say. They occupied the rectangles of sky above her various prison yards, in Hackney, in Derbyshire, in Yorkshire, and the stopping places in between. The birds were going for something, therefore they were looking, she supposed, for happiness, but from their chaotic wheeling, screeching, happy circling, she had not realised that there was any particular way in which to go to Heaven. Heaven for her was a magical ring all around, outside her, above her, beyond her walls and out of reach.

Now Edwin dragged her by the hand in such a definite way along the course of the brook through Blood Wood to a point a couple of miles upstream where the main hill-route crossed it. Again she was being taken, just as she had been led to the workhouse, and as the carters had taken her to and from London.

She had appealed to the carter, looking in awe at his strength, and even, when she got the chance, rubbing herself pathetically against him, as if he might be her father. 'Godforgi'me . . .' he had responded, almost affectionately. But he had taken her to the apprentice house.

Now Edwin was leading her; bewilderingly, not towards another misery, she was sure, but towards happiness; something for her associated with nothing else but the feel and smell of, once upon a time, comforting folds of motherly flesh, though she could hardly remember . . .

She complained about her bare feet being hurt on stones or brambles (it was all right for him, he had shoes), and then for a long while neither of them spoke. They were breathless and they were overawed by their own daring. Being out in the nighttime was like being in a church; they felt they had to stay quiet. Despite her sore hand, Margaret felt happy when Edwin gripped it, and anxious when he released it. This he had frequently to do, leaping across the current to lead her first along one bank and then the other as the terrain required. She was anxious even though he was never more than a foot or so away from her, visible as a shadow wavering amongst the black and silver dappling of water and moonlit trees.

How can he so ignore his pain?

She did not realise that he, too, felt that there was not a square inch of his body which was not on fire, but that he was hiding it from her.

They heard more gunshots. They listened to the mill-bell ringing through the darkness. In hillside farms and cottages, lights appeared, hanging on immense walls of darkness. This must mean that people were hunting for them, but Margaret did not dwell on this thought. She was like a shipwrecked voyager whose attention is not on the engulfing ocean but on some small and solid point of the shore. No matter what her suffering, she must cling to her floating spar of hope. Her exclusive worry was to save herself from drifting away from that other child's hand. It was wrinkled, bony, and like her own soaked deep in the oil of wool and machines — although his surface dirt had been recently washed away, making it strange. As they clambered onto the bridge and scrambled up the hill towards the moor-line, Edwin let go of her. She quickly took his hand again.

The bare slope exposed them in the full light of the moon. They were upon the great east-west route, which was so busy during the day, but was now empty. A parallel line of moon-blue paving stones, long grooves worn in them by cart wheels, the edges chipped and scratched by slipping hooves, stretched upwards. Here were cuts in the wall where a runaway cart had crashed against it, over there tiny clouds of wool had been left clinging to thorns and brambles.

They heard the jingle of military harness and the children leapt over a wall. The soldiers were in a hurry. Margaret, crouching against Edwin, felt his heart beating as heavily as her own. That they were cavalry meant . . .

Edwin saw that she was biting her lip, and that she was silently saying, We ought to go back!

'Huh!' he said and pulled himself away from her. But she had crept close to him out of tenderness, not to accuse him.

He realised that she had noticed the quick beating of his heart.

'I've done this climb lots of times with my feyther and never got puffed at it before. I don't know what's up wi' me today.'

To save any more explaining, he leapt back onto the road. Therefore she must join him. As she mounted the wall, he saw her, dressed in nothing more than her shift, wavering like a tallow candle in the moonlight.

'What's *your* feyther like?' he asked.

She did not answer.

Some boys turned upon misery like that, but Edwin did not feel like a child. 'What was your mother like, then?' he added, sidestepping in a gentle, adult way.

Margaret took some time before answering, pretending to save her breath to climb the last bit of the hill. She made a display of puffing and panting.

'She 'as long fair 'air all the way down 'er back, wi' curls at the end an' ribbons. You'll see what she's loike when we meet 'er. She 'as dresses of silk to the ground and lives in London where the King lives. He's going mad. He 'as to be strapped in a chair loike in Bedlam.'

'Your 'air isn't fair. It's black.'

He hated lies.

'It wasn't, till I come 'ere. It's only black because it's dirty.'

'The King is called George.'

'Yes,' she answered, matter-of-fact.

'Who told you 'e's mad?'

'Everyone in the workhouse knows.'

They walked on a few more yards.

'I saw a girl in Derbyshire go mad. Caroline Thompson at Cressbrook was so beat she went out of 'er mind. They could do nothing with 'er and sent for 'er mother in London. Her mother got some paper signed and Mrs Newton give Caroline back to 'er. But when she got to London she 'ad to 'ave the strait-jacket on, and she died so.'

'Me feyther says that England is a country all gone mad, wi' desperation and lust. P'r'aps it's because something's driving the King mad, who's at the top of it.'

'What's lust?'

'Ssh!' commanded Edwin; as he didn't, in fact, know.

They had breasted the hill and were in Height. Normally it was silent and dark as a grave at this hour, except at the inn where the carters stayed. Tonight people carrying lanterns through passageways and gardens were arguing. Some said they knew why the mill-bell was ringing and cavalry chasing around the countryside, some pretended they knew, and others were enquiring. The children still believed that this attention was all for themselves; yet here they were slinking down the main highway with no one to stop them.

Margaret would not be quiet. 'Betsy Witnough threw away some bread that was bad. Mrs Newton saw it. She said if no one'd own up we'd all 'ave our 'eads shaved. We all 'ated 'aving our 'air cut, let alone shaved. So Betsy was found out and Mr Newton brought to beat 'er. 'E did it 'til she couldn't see out of 'er eyes, they were so swelled up. 'E swore 'e'd make 'er work, though. One day she went creeping out to get some water. There was a big fish pond at Cressbrook and she fell in 'cos she couldn't see what she was doing. She was wrapped up and put on an 'ot bake-stone and 'ad 'ot liquor poured into 'er, they were so scared, but she was dead sure enough.'

A tall dark woman in a blue cloak, green boots peeping out from under it, was suddenly in front of them.

'God 'elp me! Children! Where are you going to? You should be in your beds. Watch out Mr Horsfall doesn't catch you, my girl.'

The woman carried a lamp and by it they glimpsed her red hair and her whitened face. To Margaret she looked as clean as a princess. She was as she believed she herself might be if she could live differently. Edwin was aware of a feminine aura, largely composed of her scent.

She was in a hurry. She disappeared, her lamp swaying through the night.

Beyond Height they found a ridge of level, bare moorland with two cavernous valleys tilting off its edges at either side. After being dipped into depths of shadow, the vales arose luminous. Further valleys and bars of slate blue hills creased the distance. The strips seemed transparent in the moonlight. A road long, straight and level, stretched along the hill-crest before them. It was peaceful here. Sometimes there came the sound of water falling out of a bank, through a broken or unfinished wall, down a gulley, or into a trough erected for a weaver's horse, or for him to wash his cloth in. The noises drew one like the voices of friends, that then passed by and faded, often without having been seen. Other disturbed creatures besides themselves called. Sheep and lambs were crying with clear, clear voices all over the distance, as well as near at hand. There was the plaintive repeated squeak of an unseen, mysterious nightbird.

As they were passing through a long shadow near to a quarry they were frightened by the snorting of a horse that burst directly into Edwin's ear. The monster was leaning over close enough for him to smell the odours of its mouth. He saw no more than its breath rising in a small, tight cloud around a dark and bulky shape. He jumped, bumping Margaret's shoulder.

'Tripped on a stone,' he explained.

After that leap of fear in his chest the boy wondered if they oughtn't to take their rest for the night.

'These roads 'ereabouts are the very devil to walk on, 'specially in the dark,' he said, 'They're not the same as them London roads, built for nowt more than a mad king to walk on. These are ruined wit't'traffic. We ought to rest somewhere afore tackling Blackstone Edge tomorrow.'

'Where'll we stay?'

'Huh! Ne'er you mind that.'

Edwin boldly climbed the wall fencing the quarry. He did not bother to look behind but assumed that Margaret would follow. Nor, carried away by a need for a brave gesture, did he consider what might lie ahead.

All that happened was that he banged his ankle on some abandoned implements and stung himself on the fresh nettles springing amongst them; mild injuries, which he ignored, turning instead to help Margaret.

She made a bold and unconsidered leap. It was a good job that he held her hand and kept tight hold of it. Thereby she was enabled to stumble immediately back a few feet, all her breath knocked out of her by what she had glimpsed below. They had landed on a strip of grass and loose rock only four feet wide at the edge of the quarry, which dropped in a sheer face through the darkness.

Edwin flushed. He was hot all over, but especially down his back, where he felt the cold sweat trickling.

'Thou must look before thou leaps,' he chastised her.

'Yes, Edwin,' she answered mildly and as if it were her fault.

He scouted for dock leaves to cure his stung legs and found them close by. Nature always offered a balance: a leap into darkness with a limb-breaking drop into Hell, yes, but also a hand to pull one back again; both stinging nettles and soothing dock leaves growing in reach of one another.

Also, ten yards away was a shed with its door open. Because Edwin was rubbing at his legs, Margaret was the first to go forwards and step into the dark opening, stretching out her arms and fingers. The fear of what she might stumble upon made a yard feel like a mile. But all that she found was the smell of a pony that must normally live there.

Edwin came after her and pushed past.

'Sense things wi'thee feet!' he ordered, annoyed that he had lost his leadership. 'That's what we do when we go poaching, to be sure we don't make a noise by tripping up.'

'You go poaching?' she whispered. 'Cor! You'll get 'ung for it.'

''Angin's nowt. We all 'as to die sometime.'

'I've been in prison . . .'

'Ssh!' he commanded, for he was concentrating.

They felt their way to separate corners of the shed and it was Margaret who found − yes! − a pile of straw. Edwin heard her flopping down happily upon it.

Looking back from her joyful bed Margaret surveyed the peaceful triangle of moonlight framed by the door, with a piece of moorland, a thin strip of wall, and a bit of the quarry.

Edwin came to lie beside her. He, too, stared out, entranced. She watched him removing his clogs. He saw her expression, and gave her his jacket.

'You've been in prison?'

She felt ashamed and did not answer. She could not see his delighted face. For the people with whom Edwin, his father and his brother mixed, prison was associated not with villains but with heroes.

'You've been in the low gaol!' he repeated softly, and whistled.

'Only 'cos the man who said he was my father took me,' she answered indignantly. 'He said the sights I'd see'd teach me a lesson to be good that I'd never forget. He said that my mother was a whore, that means a bad woman and that was why she was ill, but I don't believe a word 'e said to me. He wasn't my father. I know it 'cos . . .'

'What did you see there?'

Before she could answer, he was asleep. And a moment later Margaret, still thinking of entertaining him with accounts of the hangings she had witnessed, also fell asleep.

They awoke to chrome yellow sunlight pouring into their shed, lending its strong colour to the old bleached straw of the pony's bedding. They lay in a bed of gold. Neither had ever known what it was to sleep so late. Margaret had never been given the opportunity and Edwin, though granted his Sundays, had always risen early to enjoy them. The sun had inched across the floor until it was full upon their faces. Because of it they opened their eyes at the same moment, suffering vertigo, having spent their previous hours in such deep restful stupor that they did not know where they were nor how much time had passed.

Covering their night-broadened irises from the fierce light, they heard the clatter of hammers rising from the quarry, and a fall of stone. Edwin, the first to stand up, noticed a leather bag on the floor. A quarryman, in the dark of the early morning, had left it, and had been too uninterested in his working day to notice anything, even two children sleeping. Edwin opened the bag and pulled out cheese . . . bread . . .

'Gi'it me!' Margaret was at his side. 'Gi'me some.'

She was cramming cheese between her teeth. Edwin ate some too. When Margaret grabbed for more, he put it inside his shirt and folded his arms.

'Save that for later,' he said.

'We'll sell the bag.'

'No.'

He left the bag on the ground, open to make it look as though rats had got at it.

'We must 'ide our trail,' he explained.

'Would they 'ang us?' she asked.

He saw the speeding soldiers, the prison, a boy and a girl dangling upon a gibbet.

He saw his mother, his bed at home, the kitchen fire. He smelled drying oatcakes. Almost his mother's last words were about their 'not stopping at hanging children'.

'Nobody'll 'ang us,' he answered bravely.

'Not after what we've gone and done?'

'We'll be all right. I'll . . . .'

He choked on his words, and turned away from her, to put on his clogs. He led her out to the shelf of land. She was still wearing his jacket. Below them they could see men with the pony, which must have spent the night grazing the moor. It was hauling a laden sledge across the face of the quarry. Above the wall were the heads of carters and horses, the hats of merchants, the rims of carts and the tops of high loads of wool travelling the road. There was a line of packhorses, led by one magnificent swaying animal, its harness decorated with brass studs and badges, its head bearing a plume and on its shoulders the elaborate arch of a collar with a bell at its peak, like the flagship of an armada.

Edwin ducked down and Margaret followed his example. They scrambled, crouching, regardless of the grey nettles, spring-new yet already coated with stone-dust, along the foot of the wall, to where it turned at right angles, marking the boundary between the moor and the quarry. They climbed over the wall, and ran up to the crest of the hill. The small bright flowers of cropped commonland, the thyme and turf that had knitted itself into a tight pile an inch deep, sheared by geese and sheep, were sliding beneath them. 'Chit . . . chit . . . chit . . .' went a nondescript bird, twirling in a gorse bush.

'That's a twite,' Edwin said. 'It's called "the fool of the moor".'

So he knows the names of the birds.

As they climbed steeply higher, the vegetation changed to sparser clumps of heather, old and burnt, with sharp new spears thrusting brightly up amongst it. There were more and more stones, then followed utterly barren peat and dark sour pools of lifeless water.

'All the 'ills are black,' Margaret remarked.

'Well?'

He had never thought they could be any other colour.

'In Derbyshire they were great white rocks. You could never get past 'em. We were put away at the end of a long valley, so nobody came near us.'

Edwin looked for a hidden but sunny place where they could eat the remainder of their breakfast. He made for a great purple-black boulder; a swollen, pregnant belly, glittering with silica. There were lots of such huge stones in a line along the moortop. This one hid them from the busy road, yet from its other side it gave them a view of the countryside, and it was warmed by the sun. He knew what he was doing, all right. He was as sure of himself as if he had spent his life, not in a manufactory, but upon the moors. Even though he had been up here only on Sundays, evidently it was Edwin's element.

In the shelter of the stones, he pulled the bread and cheese out of his shirt. They sat side by side and stuffed food into their mouths. Margaret's face was so clogged with dirt that she could hardly see.

But, through their greedy gobbling, they did see. The panorama of moorlands, commons and woods, was a vast hall filled with spectacle. Lady Well was now only a grey mark on the horizon and did not matter anymore.

Larks hung with their tails fanned to the limits and their wings buzzing so fast that they became invisible, except as small clouds around their throbbing bodies.

First Edwin and then Margaret lay back in the sun that poured upon the rock, closed their eyes and listened. A crow bawled harshly across the valley. A man in an enclosure far, far away, was angry with a horse.

A blackbird startled them through coming close by into a rowan tree, where it called mellow and loud.

'What's that?'

'Blackbird,' Edwin lazily answered.

'It sounds like a rich king has come with a trumpet.'

'Huh!'

Life before had not offered either of them much peace in which to be contemplative. They were drugged by it. With eyes closed, they felt themselves float through the vast space.

A smile upon her face, Margaret opened her eyes, turned, plucked a stalk of grass, tickled Edwin's cheek and asked, 'What we going t'eat next?'

He kept his eyes closed and did not answer. He was in ecstasy, but could not tell her, because he did not know the word, 'ecstasy'.

'You said you was a poacher, so are you going t'unt deer for us?'

No reply.

'And fish? And 'ares? And where are we going to sleep tonight, since you're so clever?'

For answer he rolled over, put his arm around her neck, as he would if playing with a boy but more gently, and pushed her face, which had contemplated the sky for the first time in her life, into the vegetation and the earth. She gave in willingly, because she had never been happy like this before.

Their faces were pressed into tiny blossoms, too small to notice when standing. Some were star-shaped and multi-petalled; some had only two or three petals, one perhaps forming a drooping lip; others offered up waxy, half-transparent tunnels. Tickling their skins were the fibres of intricately knit stalks and roots which gave off a dusty aroma when Edwin stirred them with his nail. Insects stumbled amongst them, just as the packhorses, carters and traders struggled along the east-west route. Edwin tried to imagine beetles, earwigs and the millions of ants with their loads, toiling unnoticed over the vast moorland. Did they also go into manufactories and carry cloth? He laughed at the fancy.

A large bee came bumpily over the thyme and everywhere else was so quiet that its noise filled the universe. Margaret turned her head to watch it burying its head into a flower, like a baby snuggling at a breast and pulling at the tit. Its rear legs were kicking with happy abandonment in the air while the head tugged and sucked its nectar.

'Which way is the Blackstone Edge road?'

Edwin, dozing in the scent of thyme, again did not answer. He opened one eye and noticed that she was still wearing the ring of brass that he had placed upon her finger.

'Does the road go to Liverpool?'

'Yes.'

'My mother's in London,' Margaret said, wistfully, foreseeing the inevitable parting from Edwin. Do ships go from Liverpool to London? she wondered. Once, travelling by in a cart, she had seen the thousands of masts stretched along the wharfs from Greenwich, and she must believe that at least some of them came from Liverpool.

Edwin got to his feet and set off, in the measured, positive fashion of a workman who knows his skill and the value of it and who enjoys being watched. As Margaret followed, her attention was caught by a track shining upon the far slope and busy with figures. In between was a deep valley.

'Is that the Blackstone Edge road?'

'Yes. My mother lived over there,' he said.

Girls were always asking questions. Edwin decided that it was time he asked her something.

'What was it like in th'workhouse down London?'

They were descending into the valley, which was deep and wide. To hide themselves, they passed down dry gulleys and kept behind walls or at the sides of hillocks from which no habitation was in view. They were making for a point below, where Edwin had marked that the route crossed another river. He reckoned that after they passed over the bridge and started the ascent to the Edge, which was the high dark boundary between Yorkshire and Lancashire, they would finally be out of reach of Mr Horsfall and of Lady Well, and no one, other than the occasional village constable, would be interested in two travelling children.

'We couldn't leave the 'Ackney workhouse, no more'n Cressbrook nor 'Orsfalls' mill. The windows was barred, the same. I saw beggar girls standing outside and wanted to change places, though they was in the rain with nowhere to go. Every now and then someone'd come to pick us out. We'd be glad to go to anything, except for chimney sweeps. They always picked boys for that. A lady came every year from an agency and chose the best of us for servants. We stood in a line and she'd feel us and look at our teeth. She squeezed our arms and looked in our eyes and made us take deep breaths. Sometimes I used to be sick because I was so sad. I thought I'd never get out of 'Ackney. Then they came from Cressbrook. They said that in the north we'd be given silver watches and fed every day on roast beef, that we'd be able to ride 'orses, and be paid money.'

They were descending into a net of small lanes that threaded the enclosures. Hand-loom weavers' cottages were scattered over the slopes. They were bleak little places of dark stone and mostly without trees, unless they had a token ash or rowan planted by a spring. Tenter-frames radiated in star-shaped lines from every cottage's walls.

'Why are the 'ouses all over the place?' she asked.

'They 'ave to be like that to 'ave their own springs.'

'Why?'

'For t'weavers to wash their cloth and such.'

They came to a roadside trough and knelt by it, peacefully.

'I loike Yorkshire.'

Margaret drank with gorgeous pleasure. Edwin cupped the water in his hands.

'Drink to liberty!' he commanded.

'What d'yer mean?'

'You drink, and then say "To liberty".'

'Who's that?'

'To freedom, then. It's a spell to make it 'appen.'

'To freedom!' Margaret shouted at the top of her voice. Meanwhile her handful drained away. Edwin's palms were full again.

'To the downfall of tyranny!'
'To the downfall of tyranny!'
She swallowed her drink quickly enough not to lose it.
'What's tyranny?'
'It's what 'appens in Lady Well.'
The water streaked Margaret's grimy cheeks, so that she looked as if she had been daubed with paint. Edwin, too, was beginning to look as dirty as he had been before his mother washed him on the previous day.
'There's going to be a revolution,' Edwin announced.
'A revolution?'
'It means there'll be a change in t'Government and nobody'll want to catch us for running away. There was a comet last autumn, did you see it?'
'No. What's a comet?'
'It's a sign of revolution. A great blaze right across the sky. Everyone in Lady Well went out to look at it and we all said there'd be a change.'
Edwin lay on the grass at the side of the overflowing trough of clear water, wiped his nearly-closed purple eye, and smeared the dirt from around his mouth with the back of his hand. She did likewise, as she rested by him. They closed their eyes against the sun. How delicious it was to walk, rest, walk, rest, and not be driven by a machine.
'Go on about th'workhouse, then.'
'The first toime when we set off from 'Ackney it was loike we was going on a picnic, all of us laughing. They washed us and gave us new clothes and some ginger bread. We were eight days on th'road, locked in. No. Five days – I forget 'ow long, 'cos I was sick. We was all sick, wi' that yellow stuff that comes when you've 'ad nothing to eat. It smelled. The carter 'ardly spoke to us except when he let us out every now and then to – you're not supposed to say it. 'E used to wink at us. I didn't like it 'cos I didn't know what 'e meant. We never 'ad a wash, but we were given soup at public 'ouses. A lady brought us soup when we were sitting again' a wall while the boys swilled the waggon and changed the straw. When two died they didn't make a sound, and no one knew until we was all turned out and two didn't come. They was buried in t'dark on the top of an 'ill and the carter got drunk with the sexton. We was scared. We didn't know what 'e'd do when 'e was drunk. 'E came back to where we was in the cart, banging the sides and laughing. He called us "animals".

'When we got to Lady Well, the people came to watch us unloaded.

That Mr Gledhill took us in. I could see straight away we were going to be shut insoide. From then on the girls was separated from the boys. It was cold. There wasn't any fires, and I didn't ever see any in Derbyshire, neither winter nor summer. Mr Newton and Mr Gledhill said we'd set fire to t'mill. We didn't get no beef, we were given porridge and some sticky bread. We 'ad to eat in silence. Then we went to bed. Two of us 'ad to share. We didn't say prayers loike in the workhouse, so I prayed under my breath and asked to be with my mother . . .'

She closed her eyes. She felt the press of the hot sun on her face and her lids. Inside her head yellow circles spread rapidly outwards, as when a stone is thrown into a pool. She opened her eyes, rubbed at her tears.

Edwin was squatting over a patch of gravelly sand in which he was absorbedly drawing with a stick.

'What's 'at?'

He did not answer.

'It's a fish!'

He leapt up and ran down the hill. Lower down the lane he waited for her and, panting, they happily descended into the village by the bridge.

They need not have passed through Ripponden, but it was the easiest way to travel and they thought they would be safe now. Finding, indeed, that no one took notice of them, they loitered on the bridge where old men were smiling at the water, the rising fish and the passers-by. Edwin got Margaret to fetch him stones. Each time she ran up with one he aimed it first at a certain clump of reeds, that is, he claimed this had been his target after he had hit it, and next at some ducks, which he kept missing.

Margaret thought he was wonderful. By now she thought Edwin was wonderful at everything. The old men cheered him on and laughed at the way he had got the girl carrying for him. 'She's a good 'un,' they said. And laughed. And laughed. 'The sight o'them two little lovers is better than a physic,' they said. The children could not see what it was that appeared so funny, or joyful, about themselves.

'Whatever 'ave ye done, to be in such a state?' the old men asked.

'Fell over.'

Edwin threw at some small, greenish-white flowers that grew in clumps on the river bank, some full-blown, some shrivelled.

'What's 'em?' Margaret asked.

'Snowdrops. *Galanthus nivalis*, in Latin. Why?'

'I've seen 'em before. When we were coming into Lady Well a man stopped the cart and put 'is 'ead in. 'E 'ad them in 'is 'at. 'E said the same as you. 'E gi' me one. Some o' the boys trampled on it.'

They passed on down the street. Their good fortune continued, for they met a kindly old man, a cobbler, sitting outside his shop, repairing shoes and offering his bald head to the gentle spring sun. He stopped, with his hammer poised, and a shining smile for them.

'God bless you, you look tired. Where 'ave you two darlings come from? What's 'appened to your eye, young man?'

They could not answer such questions, but fortunately he did not insist. 'Martha! Martha!' he shouted, as joyfully as the Prodigal's father whose own son had come home.

Martha came running, used to obeying. She did not look pleased – until she saw the children. She was a gaunt woman with the deep-set features of one who has survived much misery. She reminded Edwin of his mother.

'Would you like a bite t'eat?' she asked.

'Gi'us food, ma'am!'

Margaret thrust forward, on her toes, clutching, as always, at any half-kind offer.

The peacefulness of the afternoon, of the hamlet, and their present tide of good fortune, lulled both the children into not suspecting offered food. The woman retreated into her house and could be heard drawing from a barrel. She was at the door again, smiling still, with ale in a deep jug, and with two hunks of cheese.

The children gobbled without speaking.

'I thought thou was 'ungry,' remarked the cobbler. 'If you'll not say where you're from, will you tell me where you're going?'

'Over Blackstone Edge,' Edwin answered.

He took a swig at the cool ale.

'What – now? At this time of day?'

'Huh! It's nothing.'

But Margaret would rather have had a bed.

'Nothing!' The cobbler touched his fingers together prayerfully, and his wife, clearly used to imitating him, did likewise. 'I pray to the Lord for all the lost sheep of this desperate countryside. You look as though you 'ave 'ad a few accidents already. We can't let you go yonder at this hour.'

'I think nowt on it.'

'Brave words! Then will you step inside and have some decent repast before you go on?'

'Aye. Thank you,' answered Edwin, but still proud.

'And maybe my good lady'll wash you. You're factory children, I can see that.'

Edwin gave a start.

'What of it?'

The cobbler stood up and put his kindly arms around them, hugging them so closely that they could smell his greasy leather apron. He compelled them gently into the shadowy house.

'Nothing of it, young man, nothing of it. You're a bold one, I must say. Has no one taught you to walk 'umbly before God? 'Appen it's true what they say about the Godlessness in public mills? Poor children, denied the wisdom of the 'Oly Book.'

The home of the cobbler and his wife was that of a pious, modest couple. The musty smell, coming from ancient leather, and the shadows, were those of a church. Saint Jerome was upon one wall, in an immaculate steel-engraving. He had a venerable, bald crown like the cobbler himself, and perhaps that was why the picture had been chosen. Christ sagged from his cross on another wall. There were half a dozen hand-stitched texts. A large black Bible with gold clasps was placed to catch the light from the window. Buckles, leather straps, laces, pincers and shears hung from beams or over the edges of a bench, with a sacrosanct air, as if they were the holy preserved instruments that had been used for torturing Christ. The earthenware jugs for water and ale, the wooden platters for bread and cheese, seemed objects on an altar-table. They were so carefully placed, it was as if they could only be removed by order of a spiritual council. The couple put down every object with deliberation, and they performed their little duties for one another with the slow, mournful self-consciousness of officiating priests. Even the sense of the sparse clean room having received few visitors suggested, not that the couple were shunned by their neighbours, but that they had chosen to be holy hermits.

It was Edwin who noticed the chapel-like atmosphere. Margaret's eyes were darting to see a loaf of bread on the sideboard, some coins on a mantelpiece, and into a cupboard where the door had been left open a crack. The cobbler's wife began working the pump in the back room. Soon she was beckoning them.

Edwin, as he went forward, held Margaret's hand again. She wanted never, never to let go of it. But she must do so, being chosen as the first to be washed, because she was by far the dirtiest. With haste, suggesting that there would have been an indecency in lingering, the woman stripped her.

'My goodness, you've had a fall! Or maybe it was a beating somewhere?' she inquired. Neither of the children answered.

Edwin, though he had seen nakedness often enough, felt ashamed before Margaret stripped, and he had to look away. Only after a while dared he watch the strong, deliberate movements of the woman rubbing and washing the naked girl.

'But you, young man, look as if you might 'ave a mother,' remarked the cobbler's wife, because Edwin was not quite so dirty. 'But your eye . . .'

Stripped, for Margaret in her turn to see the dangling little button that distinguished him, he hid his embarrassment by splashing the water about the kitchen.

'You both look as though you've come from where they believe, "spare the rod, spoil the child." Can't say I blame your mothers, neither, the way you carry on. You young devil, stand still.'

But the woman was smiling. Edwin winked and grimaced at Margaret. Despite the fact that every touch hurt them, they were happy.

Martha tried rigging them up in the cast-offs of a cobbler and his wife. The effect was ludicrous, and the children had to climb back into their own dirty clothes. Edwin retrieved his jacket.

Dressed once more, they sat on a bench in the workroom, where the cobbler read aloud passages from Proverbs while his wife prepared a meal.

'The name of the Lord is a strong tower: the righteous runneth into it, and is safe . . .'

Beef-steak and potatoes! Before they had finished dining with this God-sent couple Margaret and Edwin fell asleep at the table, both almost at the same moment. They had to be carried up the stairs. There Martha prepared two cots. She had to awaken the children to strip them of their clothes, before setting them into her clean bedding.

Through the window they could see the sun biting into Blackstone Edge. They were asleep again almost before their guardian angel had left the room, being just able to register the fact that the woman locked the door upon them.

Downstairs, the cobbler went outside again to enjoy the very last of the sun. He took with him a heavy volume, in which with his tongue curled out of the corner of his mouth, he wrote:

A fare Day tho will no doubt turn out less Gude tomorrow. Planted tatties in the small Inclosure. Went to here Mr Saville preach in Halifax on Isaiah XXXII, 'let the Hills and mountanes rejoice.' Sat outside my Shop an hour mynding my own busyness when comes by two children evident run from a Public Mill. Will return the runaways to their Ritefull gude master, Mr Horsfall I'm sure it is tomorrow, and pay the shilling Mr Gledhill gives into our Chapel fund. So ends a gude day with some gude work done on the Lord's gude Busyness.

He carried on writing until in the last light of the day he saw another stranger, with a pack and a fiddle upon his back, coming down the road from the Lady Well direction. The man, who had a slight limp, was small, and dark. He carried his hat in his hand, so that you could see his long, greasy locks reaching to his shoulders.

April 17th

Mor had always nurtured dreams of escape. Were they being fulfilled now that he was on the run? There was no point in becoming part of a chain-gang to the colonies, nor in letting himself be hung. At the moment they were hunting for Crawshaw. He had a day, at least, before they searched the factory and found his book.

When he had reached home he had found that Edwin was not, as he supposed, tucked up in bed, but had sneaked out of the house and not come back. Mor guessed that the boy had followed the Luddite band, thought he had been recognised by soldiers, and had fled. He remembered the two children whom John Tiplady had helped out of the apprentice house. Was one of them Edwin's little friend? That would explain it all.

Mor had to find his youngest son. He convinced himself that he had only to stay away until May 1st, when the revolution would commence. From the combing shops, public houses, meeting places of Combinations and illegal debating societies of Yorkshire, Cheshire, Lancashire and Nottinghamshire, would flow a mighty river southwards to 'o'ertopple t'Guvernment'. Then he would be able to return to Phoebe, to home, home, home, having found Edwin, bringing him back to enjoy a new England. Phoebe, Gideon, Edwin and himself would all be different then, when they were not crushed, after the English Bastille Day. 'Liberté, Egalité, Fraternité' would bring about not only a fair distribution of property and goods but would also solve the disputes in the hearts of men. So thought many, and so hoped Mor. How else could he achieve peace of mind?

Perhaps he, like other men, was given to believing in such things, that were contrary to his reason, because circumstances gave him no other choice, nor hope. 'You'll never sell that piece,' Phoebe had told him, bitterly. 'You're wasting your time. No one'll want that. Revolution, indeed!'

This morning Mor, after meeting Lydia Horsfall, had been to get his shoes re-soled and rotted stitching replaced. The cobbler, Abraham

Binns, was a rotund, happy man, who had a wooden leg, from the Wars. He would not charge Mor, because he had educated the cobbler's son.

Mor stood, as Binns sat at the door of the shop, looking across the valley. They talked about what had happened during the night, with Wrigley captured and John Tiplady dead. The cropping shop was closed. How could his widow run it? What manufacturers would now take their trade there? The alphabet that John had lovingly and hopefully set himself to carve for Mor's school would never be completed. It was stuck ironically at the letter R. The school itself was closed.

'There's still a cold wind about,' Mor said, brushing his cheek.

Mor wept for the memory of John's spacious style, when the two of them, on many summer evenings, had strolled side by side to enjoy a peaceful hour on the hills. Their seeing things together was a way of embracing. 'You can feel eternity on the hills. It's better than a thousand sermons,' John would say.

The cobbler drooped his head towards his last. He banged the nails in with tight, hard, angry strokes. When nearly finished he looked up and again stared across the valley.

'It's grand across there today,' he mused. 'Grand! I don't think you could find a nicer spot than this, no matter where you travel. And the best water i' Yorkshire, 'ere. I'll swear to it. Look at the light dancing there, see it?' He paused, then repeated, 'Grand!'

After another pause, Binns asked, 'Do you think you'll return to us? Do you believe in this "revolution"?'

'"One who suffers, hopes, and one who hopes, believes", as the saying has it, Mr Binns.'

Abraham had finished the boots.

'Don't worry, old friend! Thou'll not be a wanderer all thy days, wilt thou?' he asked, uncertainly, looking Mor straight in the face. 'You'll come back to us?'

'I'll come back.'

Mor completed his third errand. He collected the Lower Laithes' stone from where he had dropped it when he was arrested by the Watch and Ward patrol.

Then he returned home to press one of Mrs Horsfall's sovereigns into Phoebe's hand. He did not explain. He wanted to see her delight.

She did not ask him where he had sold his cloth. She said not a word, but merely gasped. Who could tell what she was thinking? Did she think perhaps that her husband was a thief, a dyed-in-the-wool thief, and was she shrugging her shoulders to it? Even as she locked the coin in a drawer, she was bitter, and hurtfully saying nothing.

She doesn't want to be pleased, not by anything, anymore. Mor saw it.

He too has stooped to begging for charity at last, Phoebe thought.

'So why must you go?' she asked.

Although she spoke harshly, she was already preparing food for him to take. When he had been dashing round Lady Well trying to sell his piece, she had been collecting together preserves, oat bread and a flask of whisky. She had been to neighbours, who had sacrificed, one cooked meats, another a cheese for Mor's flight.

'Edwin'll come back when he's tired of th'ills. Why must you go?' she asked.

He stood with his back to the fire. She had her shoulders to him, and he could see neither her tears nor the way in which she occupied her hands. He would have been surprised to see the thoughtful, delicate way in which she cut and wrapped the food.

'He's not the only one who's run off. That girl 'e likes, the one 'e calls "Margaret", she's gone too. Another pair got away, but they've been caught. Edwin'll not come back without he's fetched, wife. Besides . . . I've dropped my book somewhere. My *Rights Of Man*. I think I left it in the factory. My name's inside. They'll want to 'ang someone for killing the soldier. It'll either be Crawshaw, or me, 'cos I keep a school and can read. Gledhill told 'em I was teaching sedition. They'll not be looking until tomorrow, though. I've time.'

''Appen Mr Gledhill's right . . .'

Then Phoebe was silent.

Gledhill *right*!

What Mor wanted at a time like this was affection. He didn't want to hear her justifying Gledhill. Where were her arms and lips? It struck Mor, like an epiphany, that he hated her.

He could hear the sound of the spoon as she scraped it inside a jar.

She said, slowly, quietly:

'Why did you 'ave a book in there? Why? And why did you leave it behind? Why are you so yonderly?'

He gestured desperately in the air, then returned his hands to where they had been, on and off, throughout this conversation: holding his forehead, hopelessly.

'You'll be all right,' he said. 'I've give you the sovereign. I've spoke t'our Secretary. Loyal Georgians'll pay you something each week, whatever it works out at. There was a lot o' rabbit stew we were going t'ave after t'raid, and some other stuff. Your share'll reach you. Y'ave Mrs Horsfall's sovereign.'

'Mrs Horsfall?'

'She gi' it me . . .'

I might have guessed. He'll beg when he thinks he can't get away from me without it.

'You would be reading a book, wouldn't you? You would be reading a book, that's what you would do, read a book. When Edwin was . . . you 'ad your nose in a book. I know you. My God, I know you by now. All sins are known in th'end. You're a bas . . . you're a Greave, all right . . . What am I doing? I can't think . . .'

She abandoned the cloth with which she was wrapping cheese, and out of her dress she took a different rag. She held it to her mouth, trying not to cough. He could hear only a little of what she muttered, as she let her thoughts run like pus out of a wound.

'You're a true bastard of that Oliver Greave all right. You know y'are. God knows who your mother was, 'appen some whore, but it's clear who your father was. Gideon mi't 'a' been a bastard too if I 'adn't . . . oh, I've seen too much! Begging for food, I am, and *you* turn it away, when it's for your children. Today though you're begging for yourself . . . I hate you, I hate you . . .'

'What did you say?'

She took the rag away from her mouth, and sighed.

'Nothing. Nothing at all. Nothing that matters.'

Again she turned her back, so that he could not see her wrapping food. He was glad that she had not taken up his challenge. As little as he had heard made him realise that he could not bear it.

'I know what you said,' he could not help telling her. 'I heard.'

Gideon burst into the house. He threw himself into his father's chair, vigorously rubbing his knees, sheepishly looking away from his parents.

'Where've you been?' Mor demanded.

'What were you doing?' Phoebe asked, and added, 'That's your father's chair.'

'On Black Hill. I was thinking. No one saw me. I've decided . . . We'll not let ourselves be defeated. If Crawshaw's gone, they'll need another to tak' 'is place.'

'You!' Mor was bitter and sarcastic.

'Why not? Someone must show determination. If the place is vacant at the table why should I not fill it? King Ludd will not be put down. We'll go and fire the place properly and 'ave done wi'it and show 'em what we're made of. They'll not expect us to come again so soon. Tak' 'em by suprise.'

In the wild unheeding agony of his determination, Mor saw once again the fervour of a preacher.

'Lead a raid! Thou can't even walk, lad. You're made o' nowt but wind and air. For God's sake rest at 'ome for a while. *For God's sake!* Thou's welcome to my chair.'

Mor spoke more with pity than sarcasm, but it was the sarcasm that bit. Gideon's hands, shoulders, face were twitching and shaking. He turned white. He picked up a wooden platter from the table before him, gripping it tightly with both hands as if he would tear lumps out of it. He threw it across the room. Bang, against the meal-barrel.

Mor simply stared. He seemed calmed by it; in fact he was chilled. His face, too, was white. Phoebe turned her back, showing those humped shoulders that made one want to hit her.

Perhaps they had that effect upon her son. He stood up. His body still shaking, he picked up the next thing within reach. Phoebe's Staffordshire-ware huntsman.

'King Ludd'll not be crushed! He'll not!'

He smashed the ornament into the room's corner.

Phoebe whipped round, with her apron to her face.

'Oh, God! Oh, God!'

She was kneeling amongst the pieces, cupping the smallest fragments within the bigger ones, hunting with screwed-up eyes for the smallest bits, exhibiting those tempting humble shoulders and bowed back.

Gideon slammed an earthenware pot containing ale down on the table. The ale bounced high enough to make a brown stain on the underside of the ceiling-boards. By the time that Mor had wrapped his arms, from behind, around the boy's shoulders, Gideon had collapsed, weak as a trembling puppy, and sobbing. His mother was still fumbling with the pieces.

'Oh my God, my 'untsman . . . my 'untsman . . .'

'Sorry . . . I'm sorry, mother. Sorry. Mother, what a pass!'

He caught sight of her face.'

'Mother!'

'It's not your fault,' Mor soothed. He let go of Gideon. 'It's not any of our faults.'

'Oh my little 'untsman, so 'andsome 'e was. My gentleman so 'andsome. Gideon! Gideon!'

'Dunna blame yourself,' Mor repeated. If the boy went over and held her it would help. Surely she'd let him. 'It'll mend,' he said, going to help Phoebe with the bits on the table.

'No, it won't!' she howled. 'Nothing'll mend. Nothing. Nothing. Nothing'll mend.'

'It will. It will.'

'It won't. Nothing'll mend, ever!'

Though it was a fine spring morning, Mor left home wearing his thick leather jerkin belted tightly. Already he had a tramp's way of shutting out the expected worst, no matter what the weather at the present time. Under it he had a double layer of woollens. It was a dress such as one would wear for poaching game on a freezing night. Because of the warmth, he walked holding his hat in his hand. Otherwise, like a tramp or a pedlar he carried all his possessions upon his back. One way over his shoulder went his fiddle and crossing to hang upon his other hip was a leather bag holding a change of shirt, his unfinished manuscript, the stone from Lower Laithes which had anchored him in his madness, and the food which Phoebe had packed for him.

Phoebe walked with him a little of the way.

'I'll be back soon,' he said.

'Where'll you go to now? Oh where, where'll you go?'

'I'll be back. I 'ave to go. You must see there's nowt else for it. You'd not ever get over the disgrace of an 'anged man for 'usband, would you? You must see, Phoebe . . . you must see it. I'll be back. I will.'

'What'll I do?'

Mor said nothing.

As usual, he has no answer that really helps, she thought.

'The 'untsman,' she said, and started to cry again.

At the edge of Lady Well, before the road in the London direction dropped into the gorge of boulders, tangled trees and the white torrent frothing out of the mill, was an ash tree that was famous in many corners of the world. It was imprinted upon the memories of soldiers, seamen, of men and women being transported or imprisoned, and those more hopefully leaving to seek their fortunes elsewhere, for it was the last point from which it was possible to wave and still be seen from the town. The place was imprinted on the imaginations of all children at an early age. There were few families which had not received their last sight of at least one relative there. It was old, gnarled, sacred and dreaded. A fearful spirit soaked in memories lived within it. The earth was bare under the tree, from people standing there.

Phoebe, her own turn come round at last, accompanied Mor thus far.

'You called me *wife*,' she said. 'This morning.'

He kissed her, moved a few yards, and turned, for the brief moment which was all that those passing into exile could allow themselves, if they were to keep their resolve. Phoebe took away the handkerchief that she had been clutching to her mouth as she walked. With it in her hand she pointed at the sky and screamed:

'There is One above Who sees it all!'

Mor turned away, cowering from the accusing scream as from a hail of stones. He hurried, stumbling, down the hill, hearing her sobs for a long way. No more words followed. When he was out of reach of her cries, he carried on a little further to be sure, and turned again. He waved at the distant figure of the woman who was standing quite still except for the stained bloody rag fluttering to her face.

He knew what she would do now. She would hurry home, staring down at the street. (Would Gideon have stayed in the house?) She would slam the door and, to save herself from sitting there in tears, knowing that she would find it hard to rise again, she would make herself busy tidying, cleaning, struggling to forget her huntsman, to forget that for some absurd reason when he was leaving he had called her 'wife' for the first time in years (*why* did I do that?), trying to get that stain off the ceiling, thinking all the time that it would please and placate him, Mor, who had left. Taking this chance of the mill being closed to clean her house would be a spell to bring him back. Eventually she would lean against something, faintly brushing strings of hair from her eyes, and, if Gideon was not present, crying, imagining her husband sitting on his chair, grumbling about lacking peace because he wanted to study Goldsmith's *Animated Nature*, or some old volume.

His own words, 'I'll be back soon,' rang in his ears. He believed that he would be back. Everywhere the loosed children were playing, amazed and excited because the mill was closed. A group of young women, though dressed in their work clothes and aprons, had found a sunny bank to lie upon and were laughing.

Well, if the Luddites had managed to close the mills for even a day, that was something.

Mor turned, not in the direction of the London turnpike but towards the cover offered by the moorlands which was also, he guessed, the way Edwin had gone, heading towards Liverpool.

Mor reached the bridge. He still did not dare look back at Lady Well. He stared at the water. It was so quiet today, spinning delicate white threads amongst the stones. During the recent fine weather it had cleared itself from a dark brown peaty colour to a light transparent chestnut, glazing the weeds that had started to rise from the bottom. Where the river covered them they were bright green and swaying in the current. Where the diminished river had sunk below the level of the weeds, islands of them silvered, drying in the sun. It was no use looking for trout today, in such clear low water.

Downstream, outside the mill, he could hear the soldiers busy. All Mor's sensitivities, his awareness of life, were alerted now. He remembered the polecat that had peered at him out of the darkness when he had gone out with Edwin to get rid of the fish offal. Fearful and hunted in the territory it had owned for centuries, yet because of its exile, because it was dispossessed, it had sniffed the air and sensed with the full faculty of being alive.

Before he climbed over the hill's crest beyond Height, Mor leaned upon a wall top, resting his hat out of respect there. He finally could not resist taking his last melancholy look back, as a person will do, even if leaving a prison. In honour of the view he plucked a white saxifrage flower from the bank and placed it upon the wall as a fleeting memorial of his thoughts – of alleyways full of memories, the sweet water running from the springs and troughs below the church, his little school, Gideon . . . Phoe . . . Tipl . . .

A swallow flipped over the top of the wall. Scissoring its wings to duck under a current of air, it skimmed the road surface, flashed a dot of warm orange-brown, a sheet of blue, and with excited cries, as if it had just been born to discovery and delight, it shot over the other side of the road. It had disappeared and Mor had plodded three or four paces forwards before he realised that he had seen the first swallow of the summer.

From Height he walked where Edwin and Margaret had previously gone along the level moortop. He was entering into the sky, the earlier blue and rose of which had changed to a midday silver . . .

He continued to brood. Mor now found everything arduous. It was that final looking-back at Lady Well that had depressed him. Until then he had stayed on course, but the realisation of what he was losing brought a hollowness worse than hunger.

He dared not think of it. He was existing now in the constant hope that some relief would by miracle appear, that some understanding, or a decision about a proper course of action, would arise, if not from some source outside himself, then perhaps an inspiration from within, as a bubble of light and air rises from the mud at the bottom of a well.

How, suddenly, he hated the hills. Nature, he realised, is beautiful only when she harmonises with creative thoughts, and at other times her majestic aloofness is terrifying. The hills standing around were silent oppressors.

He could not bring himself to pass the time of day with anyone, especially as so many of those he met, such as a young man enjoying the spring lanes with his arm stealing towards the breast of a girl from Horsfalls' mill, were happy with their holiday, hardly knowing and not much caring that he who hobbled past them on the road had so much to do with bringing about their unexpected freedom. His misery showed in his dumb detachment from every human, beast, bird and flower. For a few moments he watched a twite pecking and flitting above the heather and felt that he could not understand that light, tiny fragment of life. What was it so happy about? Only that it lived in the present moment. Only that it did not remember the shadow of the hawk passing over the sun. But Mor felt shadows. He walked onwards feeling a cavern inside himself. It was in place of a cry that might tear the universe.

I'll be back. I'll be back. I'll not ever leave Lady Well. No one, nothing, will drive me away.

The day wore onwards. Evening came with yellowing light and spring bird song, bubbling up out of the valleys, overflowing from a pot. Every day, steadily now, the twilight bird song was growing louder and longer.

Mor descended to Ripponden, which also seemed busy with happy and active young people. Perhaps this struck him because of the contrast to his own mood, for they were actually doing no more than going about their business. His worries made him feel old. He thought he might not reach the end of the street before his spine became dust. He turned his face away because they would see something ugly and disgraceful – features in process of decay. Young men offended him with their brusqueness and with the thoughtless expressions of their energies, swinging their shoulders. Girls with beautiful skins and expectant eyes, one gutting fish upon a bank, others as they went to the well or gathered around a pedlar selling almanacs, filled him with envy. He was too poor for them to look at him and he blamed them for it. Having turned thirty, an age when it is possible to feel both premonitions of death and the flushings of still-lingering youth, as an autumn day can belong to both summer and winter at once, he saw that age was not dignified, but was furtive and shameful. It seemed a disgrace not to have energy and clear resolute thoughts.

The only one with whom he passed the time of day was a sober cobbler, sitting outside his shop in the last light of the evening and smoking his pipe. At his feet was a large volume like a ledger in which he had evidently been writing, for the ink pot and quill were balanced on it. The shoemender was one of those people who wait for travellers, placing themselves to weigh them up from a distance, their lips already half-parted in a greeting. One would find it nearly impossible to pass him by without speaking. In any case Mor was attracted by that evidence of literary interests.

'A fair day, thanks be to God!' announced the cobbler. 'Though it'll no doubt turn out less good tomorrow. It generally does.'

'It's a fine day,' Mor agreed.

'One to make the hills and mountains rejoice.'

Mor settled himself nearby, opening his bag to partake of his bread and cheese.

'Have you seen a child, a stranger, running this way?'

'A factory child?'

'Yes.' Mor was alert with hope. 'Or maybe two children together?'

'You're not an officer from a manufactory, are you?'

'I'm a weaver. I've come from Lady Well. One of them's my own child.'

'I thought you were not a manufacturer's gentleman, by your boots. Those have been mended recently for walking some distance, I'd say. Factory children do come this way, sir, when they run away. This is the road a few have taken from different mills. I haven't seen any from Mr Horsfall's. I don't like to see the poor sad runaways. I think we should all persevere in the duty to which God calls us, instead of running away.'

'Yet God calls some to some very unpleasant duties.'

'I do not believe it is for us to question what God does, if that is His wisdom. Mr Saville told us in Halifax today that Mr Wesley rejected Swedenborg's description of Hell because it was not filled with everlasting fire but only with red-hot ashes. Such is the eternal fate of those who evade their duty to God. You said you were from Lady Well. From what I was told in Halifax you have seen there the damage that is done by those who evade their duty to God. Machinery destroyed and a man shot dead in Mr Horsfall's mills, I'm told. Much alarms. Poor Mr Horsfall.'

Mor now discovered more of the food which he had not known Phoebe had put into his bag. He felt her presence lingering in the way she had wrapped a stoneware jar of preserved blackberries, and cheese, in scraps of waste cotton. He felt in them the love which she had been prevented from giving to her home and to him. Each neat fold of the cotton was speaking for her.

'Are you a disciple of Mr Wesley, sir?' the cobbler continued.

Not merely Gledhill, but every factotum of Mr Horsfall was a Wesleyan Methodist, deliberately chosen because they could be relied upon for their loyalty and for what they themselves called 'regularity'; arriving on time, coming to the mills every day, and keeping proper accounts.

Mor shook his head, and drooped it, trying to hide the shame that religious people can make you feel, even when you don't believe in their religion.

'No, I didn't think you looked as though you would be,' said the cobbler disapprovingly.

A deep red sun was throbbing and biting a slice out of the crest of Blackstone Edge. The evening bird song had finished. The air was filling with the coolness that suggests to bird, animal and human instincts that it is time to find shelter. Anyone without it feels anxious and sad at this hour.

'Is there an inn at which I could stay in Ripponden?'

'We have several houses.' The cobbler thoughtfully sucked his pipe. 'There is yonder splendid inn that you can see by the bridge. It has meat, vegetables, tea and coffee for respectable travellers, and some splendid oak stabling for your horse, if you happen to have one.'

The cobbler fixed his expert eye suspiciously on Mor's boots.

'Pardon my saying so, but I doubt your being made welcome there, amongst the merchants, you being shod for travelling a good way on foot, I see. Such attire doesn't make you welcome amongst gentlemen. I don't mean to insult you, sir, but maybe you hasn't the means. I have never set foot inside there myself, except by the back gate for custom, repairing boots for gentlemen, ladies, and their servants.'

The cobbler looked Mor unflinchingly in the eye.

'You yourself said that you have come from Lady Well. In any case, they would suspect that a man shod for a walk is a fugitive from justice, unless he has a trade to follow. We are living through dreadful times. There is so much sedition abroad. We need a gibbet at every crossroads, these days.'

From a room only a few feet above Mor's head, so that he could have leapt up to the glass, there came the cry of a child, awakened it seemed from a dream.

'You have a granddaughter?' Mor interrupted, looking for some safer subject of conversation.

'A granddaughter, yes, sir . . .

'Then we have an inn of the second rank,' the cobbler continued hurriedly. 'That one is mostly used by packhorse drivers, for though it has no stabling, it has some rough pasture fit for mules. Then there is also . . .'

Mor next heard the cry of a small boy.

'Martha!' the cobbler shouted.

His wife came out as soon as she was called. She was thin and bony, like Phoebe. Mor already felt envious of this domestic scene; the biddable wife and the home.

'We haven't seen any factory children running this way, have we?' the cobbler asked her. 'This gentlemen is from Lady Well . . . nothing to do, he assures me, with the trouble there.' The cobbler nevertheless lifted his eyebrows in an expression full of suspicion. 'He says he is looking for a factory child.'

'You've lost an apprentice?' Martha asked.

'No – it is my own child.'

'Your own child! Was it a boy or a girl, sir?'

'A boy, answering to the name of Edwin. There might 'ave been a girl with 'im, called Margaret.'

'No, we haven't seen any. None have passed this way. Generally this is the way the varmints run, sir, but there haven't been any at all. It's a sad loss for the masters when they lose one, isn't it, sir, after they have gone to the expense of clothing them and teaching them their trades? You must have seen some terrible sights when those murderers attacked the mill in Lady Well last night. We heard about it.'

'Stop your chattering, now. Go down to Mrs Rawdon's inn, Martha, and say to her, I have a respectable gentleman looking for accommodation for a night. I'd put you up myself, sir, but my room is filled. Go to Mrs Rawdon, Martha, and say to her that I "have a suitable occupant for her accommodation".'

'That's kind of you, sir.'

'Think nothing of it, sir,' replied the cobbler.

Martha disappeared over the bridge. It had grown quite dark. Her dress was caught every now and again in the lights of lanterns.

'My wife will only be a moment away. She is a good woman. Have you heard Mr Saville preach?'

'I don't go in much for listening to preachers.'

'That must be sad for you, sir, to be so preoccupied with worldly matters that you have no time to listen to a preacher. Myself, I found the time to walk to Halifax today for Mr Saville. I would willingly walk a hundred miles to hear a good preacher.'

'I don't like the lack of debate at religious meetings.'

'I have a mind to think that you would soon be terrified for your immortal soul if you listened to Mr Saville, for he has such a strong line in dreadful sermons, though he has such difficulties to overcome in life – he is a cripple. I am fair sobered for a week by hearing him, he has such a way with him. He can depict the fiery pit better than most men could describe their own hearths. Through the words of the Lord.'

'I do not accept any lords.'

'Not accept any lords! Every man and dog must have a master.'

Mor rose from the ground, which in any case had grown uncomfortable, and lost himself in the darkness on the river bank. He stared restlessly for a while at the water. He did not like this conversation. For some reason he did not even trust his pack and fiddle with the pious cobbler, but took them with him.

Martha returned breathlessly from over the bridge. In her hurry she brushed by Mor without noticing him. He followed her.

''Tis all right, husband, Mrs Rawdon says she has accommodation for a suitable occupant.'

Mor was relieved. 'Well, thank you, sir, for your help.'

The cobbler waved his hand dismissively.

'I would think it a disgrace, sir, to accept thanks for so small a service. Mrs Rawdon is a good woman, though she has been only a short time amongst us, coming from London. I believe she often attended chapel there. They call her the "Abbess". I do not like the Popery of it, but they say she has earned the title for her good works. She is well thought of.'

He gave Mor directions, too elaborate for him to be able to follow them all. After asking his way several times, the inn turned out to be an unsigned dwelling in a back alley. It was a rambling decayed edifice, with many outbuildings, where Mrs Rawdon, 'an unhappy widow', so Mor was told, 'come into the north to drown her grief', brewed ale, and ran a slaughter-house in the back yard.

The crowded smoky room into which Mor burst was filled by a surprising company of men and women to be recommended by a Wesleyan cobbler, unless he had been inspired by his master's description of Yorkshire, 'that place suits me best where so many are groaning for redemption'. The majority were soldiers of the lowest rank, not cavalry, but militiamen from another county, under the command of an aggressive sergeant. The rest was that flotsam of life which gathers in a hamlet near a bridge, just as the rubbish carried by a river ravels about the bridge's piers. They were an exotic crowd of teasel-collectors, leech-gatherers, weed-pickers, stone-wallers, moor-guides, and 'broggers' who scavenged bits of wool from fences and out of the litter of markets. Some fiddlers were already there before Mor. There was a dirty looking apothecary, his table spread with pills and cosmetics that he sold to the women in the room. He had white lead, used to blanch cheeks and make a lady look as if she did not have to labour outdoors, and mercuric sulphide to redden lips and heighten the cheeks. The white lead caused first an irritation of the skin, and then paralysis. The mercury brought tremors of the limbs, and madness eventually, but he did not advertise these facts.

Nothing could have kept this crowd in order but the fierce presidency of Mrs Rawdon. She turned out to be a narrow-lipped, severe woman, the only one there you might have said would meet with the cobbler's approval. She was dressed in black. Her overdone but quality mourning was both exotic and authoritarian. The lace was plentiful and expensive, the cloth heavily starched. Supervising her servant girl who ferried ale from a back room in which it was brewed, she was ostentatiously busy, yet doing nothing with her own hands, except that from time to time she showed off her privilege of poking the fire. Some of her customers called her 'Abbess', others addressed her as 'Mother' or 'Mother Superior'.

'So you is the "suitable occupant for accommodation"?'

She was one whom you would never expect to laugh, yet there was mockery in her eyes, which she hid from time to time behind a black fan.

When he had answered her, 'Sit you down and you'll be attended to,' she commanded. 'I 'ear you have come walking on your feet from Lady Well?' She did not wait for an answer, but rustled off through the crowd.

Her knowing already where he came from gave Mor a shock. Aware of being conspicuously isolated, he settled in a modest corner, tucked his bag and fiddle safe from thieves under his feet, and placed his hat on the bench beside him. Nowhere in the inn was comfortable. It was reduced to its permanent surfaces of wood and stone, for anything more fragile would have been demolished by the customers. The room was permeated with a smell of urine. Sitting next to Mor was a dirty fellow whose proximity did nothing to make the ale-house feel pleasant; neither did the malodorous lady at his side.

Mor watched Mrs Rawdon. By her gestures, and the movements of her eyes when she pulled her fan away, it was clear that she was talking about him. Alarmed that news could travel so fast, he thought he should get up and leave. On the other hand, that would attract more suspicion, and there was nowhere for him to go to.

It was equally obvious what kind of woman Mrs Rawdon was speaking to, for ever since the beginning of time the one advantage to the common man of a town full of soldiers has been the availability of Our Lady of the Shadows; of doxies, drabs and prostitutes. Several were gathered around the table of the one-time member of the Society of Apothecaries (who probably had been cast out for the poisonous potions that he sold), or they were dancing with the soldiers. Chapel-goer or not, pining widow or not, Mrs Rawdon had come from London to run an interesting and lively business.

Mor, unused to anything but sober company in Lady Well, to his Loyal Georgians, dismissed his first prudishness, recalling that he was away, also, on an adventure. Even a poor schoolmaster weaver might not find it impossible to have, not merely a bed, but one warmed with animal comfort . . .

For there she soon was: a tall whore walking towards him as direct as fate, and smiling. She wore a fine, white cotton dress with a high waist-line tight under her breasts. It was in the French-Revolutionary, classical style, with many clinging folds which displayed the lines of her body in a fashion now shunned in anti-Gallic society. With one hand she kept the hem clear of the mud and spilled beer, thus displaying her neat green boots. Her hair was red, bundled in curls and ringlets. She wore glass earrings. Her face, covered with white-lead cosmetic, reflected the darting lights, orange and yellow, of the inn's fires and candles. Her lips were drawn bright red with the apothecary's mercuric sulphide. Her right arm was hampered by her 'indispensable' – her embroidered handbag – when she was not making gestures with her shawl, which she carried more to hide and reveal teasing glimpses of her shoulders and breasts, than to cover or warm them. A most impractical and purposeless dress, except for a whore, but she carried off her display with sedateness.

She was such a strange flower to discover blooming out of the earth of Yorkshire. It made him think of how the rich colours of his weaving were distilled from local sombre heathers, roots and berries. From far off, as she appeared and disappeared through the crowd, her smile so strong that it seemed to advance in front of her, Mor knew that she had marked him out. He caught and held her eye and felt that something was inevitable. She got tangled in a dance around a fiddler, and she stopped for a moment to take a drag at a soldier's pipe, yet Mor had no doubt that she was making her way purposefully towards him. Her long legs made watery folds of her garment. Her stride was sure and happy enough to take in the whole world and never tire or lose confidence. She could doubtless keep on walking forever and in fact, in her trade of soldiers' whore, would probably do so.

She mouthed something to him from only a few yards away, and which he could not hear because of the music and laughter. He had only just left home and wife, yet he could not help himself, when the woman disappeared briefly behind the backs of a sergeant and his companions, trying to catch her eye again. He could not understand himself, for he had so recently been moved by the presents lovingly wrapped by Phoebe.

She reappeared, her face intent upon the space next to Mor, which was almost the only vacant seat in the room. His face, too, opened in a smile. They might have been old acquaintances. Some strangers can make you feel that you have known them all your life.

He found himself removing his hat from the seat and putting it under the bench, so that she could sit down. Casually and inevitably she took her place next to him.

'Soldiers! I've 'ad enough of *them*!'

She pouted, blowing a wisp of hair from her very dark eyes, over her sharp nose. She looked straight ahead, except that once or twice she took quick sideways glances at him, and twitched her shawl. Whether she had come north with Mrs Rawdon or not, he could tell as soon as she spoke that she was originally a local girl.

She spread her legs and inelegantly plonked her indispensable in her lap. Perhaps she had only been trained to walk and not to sit. She scratched at her white face. Her left hand had found its way into a slit hidden in the folds of her dress. Mor was aware of the cleanliness of her bare arm under his nose. Covering a few inches of her shoulder was a small puffed sleeve made of transparent muslin. Her shawl had slipped away, and poised beneath Mor's face was a scented shoulder.

'More and more soldiers are coming into the north every day,' he said.

'You're telling me! I'm tired out.'

If I tell him I don't like soldiers, he'll seize the chance to pick me up. I must get on with this business fast. If General Maitland isn't satisfied . . . I know him . . .

'I often marvel at all this distress we are put under,' he returned, his controlled tone out of keeping with what he felt.

'Distress? Is that what you call it? They've . . .'

They've wore me out!

'Do you know that all this trouble began in Nottinghamshire, from no better cause than that stockings 'ave gone out of fashion amongst the gentry? The artisans and makers of Nottinghamshire cannot deal with the lack of demand and neither can the Government, though they are appointed to know better. They only know 'ow to throw men out of work and recruit them as soldiers. So from a little thing like that we are led to the destruction of machinery throughout the land. On top of that comes Orders in Council, blocking foreign trade for our cloth, bringing a tenfold drop in our exports . . .'

'Eh?'

She had not ceased to survey, admiringly, the soldiers she'd 'had enough of'. She also continued to watch the movements of her colleagues. But when she realised that she did not understand a word of what he said, she removed her hand from her face, turned and stared at him.

'You're a strange one,' she said.

She had expected him to make crude fun of her and treat her with contempt in order to save his face with a prostitute. It was an attitude that she was heartily sick of but she expected no other.

'Myself, I like a stocking,' she continued. 'It makes the commonest fellow a gentleman of refinement, like the way they talk does for some and the way they're generous with money does for others. Why don't you shout for some ale for yourself, weaver, and for me a drop of gin? They make good ale 'ere, for it's good water in the brewhouse. There's iron in the hillside, that makes it special, though it turns the beer darker brown than anywhere else, except that at Upper Spout which is all right and good for physic, so they say. I've known all the places 'ereabouts since I was a child.'

Her knees were lightly touching his, yet she spoke straight ahead, waving and smiling at the apothecary, who was basking before his pile of money. She still had smiles for soldiers around the room. Her voice was hoarse, not necessarily from smoking, but maybe from smoky atmospheres. Stirring in its rough throat it made him think of a rich, dark bird ruffling its soft feathers in a nest of brittle thorns and twigs.

The fellow at Mor's left side put onto the table a stoneware jar filled with slimy water and leeches. He drew up his trouser-leg.

'Look at that, sir! The leeches 'ave tore off my skin with their sucking, look at it. But we must be glad of the spring when we can work, sir . . .'

Mor heard only the whispering of the whore's clean, slender arm against the battered leather of his own coat.

'How do you know that I'm a weaver?'

'Oh, I can tell every sort of man.'

The ignored leech-gatherer returned his attention to his own lady. She held in her lap a basket of wool-scraps gathered from fences, and had bits of wool stuck over her dress and hair.

The whore restlessly tapped the table with her finger-ends. They marked her as either a lady or a prostitute because they were unbroken and clean. With the other hand she again scratched nervously at her cheek.

'There's oil and fluff on you, even though you do give it out like a schoolmaster. And do you play the fiddle as well, dear? They say you come from Lady Well where they attacked a mill last night.'

Mor jumped. He glanced at the leech-gatherer, who was however still occupied with his own companion.

'You don't have to tell me. I don't care what you are. Not many tells the truth to a whore. They said over there you was a – never mind. You're a strange one. I'd describe you as innocent, sitting 'ere as if nothing could 'arm you. What about that gin, master?'

She moved her knees an inch away. He could see that there'd be no more touching until her gin was on the table.

Mor went to the kitchen door where the 'Abbess' confronted him as if this shyest of her customers was the most troublesome.

'Well, my young cock?' she asked truculently.

'Ale for me and a gin for the lady.'

Not caring that she insulted him, Mrs Rawdon held her palm out for money before she would serve him. He put some coins in her palm and she snapped her fingers together like the jaws of a rat trap.

'Sit you down with the lady, and my girl will bring you what you want.'

When he returned, the woman, making a display, opened the silver clasp of her indispensable to produce an orange-scented perfume which she daubed upon her neck. Her manner was the ostentatious one of a pedlar displaying wares. The aroma pushed back the fug of smoke, the smell of ale, tobacco and urine, and made the two people intimate, wrapping them in their own invisible cloud.

'I'll tell you something for nothing, shall I? When you was over there with Mrs Rawdon, I was thinking, "I've never met a gentleman like that one before." No, truly. I expect you think that's what I always say, but I don't. Usually I have to take 'em down a peg or two. But you . . . I wish I knew what it was.'

But she knew what it was. It was the seriousness with which he had treated her, as if she were any other woman.

'You're very innocent, sir. You want to be more careful than what you are.'

Her voice had become tender and motherly.

'Haven't you come my way before?'

He didn't answer her.

'No, I don't suppose you could have done or you'd 'ave remembered me. They don't forget me. I just 'ave a feeling that I know you. Do you think we might 'ave met in a previous life? Do you take an interest in things like that?'

'I've never thought about it.'

'You ought to. It can be an entertaining 'luminating subject.'

Mor, making a first physical gesture, took the edge of her shawl between two fingers and carefully felt it, just as he was always tempted to feel at woollens.

'And you think no one can't tell you're a weaver of wool! I wonder what else you are, master.'

'That's fine wool, is that, very fine, smooth as silk,' he mumbled, embarrassed. 'And nice cotton, too.'

'Glad you like it. It was a present from an aristocratic gentleman, my shawl . . . From one of my "*eros*tocrats", as I sometimes call 'em. A gentleman made up that word for 'em. Tell me about yourself. Left 'ome, 'ave you? How long 'ave you been away? You look tired. Been awake all night? You're not the only one, neither. I was at . . . never mind that. Tell me about yourself.'

He did not answer.

'I could tell you lots of things about yourself, now, master, that I'd bet even you don't know. Just from looking at you. Just from the way you sits and walks across the room and holds your face. You don't need to say anything to me. You can trust me, darling, but there's no need to say a word you don't want to. Not even your name. I'll wager you're an interesting gentleman. Oh, I mean it, my love. I'd wager an 'ouse and lands. I could tell at a glance you're something out of the usual.'

He's a shy one. This one's going to be hard work. I don't like this spying and poking, and working for the general's silver. Sedition's an unpleasant business. They say 'e writes letters. Maybe I should take meself off where they can't find me, take my little 'Arriet from them, then they can't do nothing . . . Go down to Bristol, find me a proper 'ouse in White Ladies' Road settled up with Thomas or some other slaver or a tobacco merchant.

She waved and laughed to some acquaintances, who quickly looked away. The leech-gatherer and his woman had now turned their backs, too. The apothecary was packing up his stall.

She knows everyone here. It made him feel insecure. He himself knew no one. Yorkshire nowadays was full of strangers.

Mor realised that he and the prostitute were locked in a transaction. The room of turned backs was telling him that he was in business and he'd better go through with what he had begun. Common sense cautioned him not to be carried into indiscretions with a whore, yet she excited him to feel more trust and affection than he had ever felt with Phoebe.

The ale and the gin were brought by the skivvy. Their knees were touching again. The whore was no longer glancing around the room whilst they spoke. He was foolish with sudden, forgetful happiness.

'Tell me your name,' she demanded.

'Mor Greave.'

'Mor Greave? More Grief? I like that!' Dressed up as she was, she slapped her thigh and laughed. 'That should have been my name! I've come across every name there is, but not that one. Do you know 'ow many Georges there are? More than there are stars in the 'eavens. And I've counted the stars, I can tell you, for I've 'ad to lay out many a time with a weight of sadness on my chest. I'm sick of Georges. I'll throw up if another man tells me 'is name is George, so you can thank your God, if you 'as one, that yours isn't, I can tell you. And Thomas. I used to know a good one o' them in Bristol, said 'e was a sea captain but they all say that. I wonder where 'e is now. Probably manning a slaver to America. William's another name that's sown like stars in the 'eavens. But More Grief – I like that. I'm called Mary. Mary Wylde.' She looked at him. 'I've always been called Mary, 'onest that's my name! You can believe it. Without the word of a lie, it's true.'

'I believe you. Why shouldn't I?'

'Mary, Mother of Jesus, Mother of the Immaculate Birth. I've seen a few girls 'ave those, not a father in sight when it came to it. But I've never 'ad a babe myself, except for one, that's managed to live for long. Thank goodness, in my profession.'

'A child gone back is a poor man's blessing, so they say.'

'No man knows 'ow it breaks a woman's heart, More Grief. I'll tell you a secret, shall I? I do 'ave one daughter adopted by a gentleman that's rearing 'er to something more than I've managed to become. Her name's 'Arriet . . . You see 'ow you can trust me? 'Ere I am telling you all about myself. You can tell me all about yourself, deary love, don't bother about it, 'onest . . . I'm . . .'

She paused, with a moment's powerful, unexpected emotion. 'I'm going to see her soon, over the hills. I've no time to waste. I'm warning you. I'll be off soon, over the hills.'

Mor wondered how old the prostitute was. The cosmetic, intended to make her seem gay and young, made her appear sad and old. He wondered why she applied it so thickly and kept scratching it. She looked nearly as old as himself, but then a prostitute would wear out quickly. He felt she was tired and at the end of her career.

Perhaps, he thought, she is looking for love.

He liked her. He told himself to be cautious.

They had finished the ale and the gin. This time the maid-servant was hovering near, looking him over. He carefully fingered the sovereign and the few other coins in his pocket.

'Aren't we getting sad!' Mary said, because they had fallen awkwardly silent when the servant had left. 'Now go on, tell me about yourself, you promised you would. Who was your mother? Tell me about your mother. Who was she? Pretty, was she? Affectionate? Loving? Do you miss 'er?'

Mor laughed.

'Why should I tell you about my mother? I didn't promise anything.'

She pressed her knees tighter against his.

'Aven't we got a slow one 'ere. But I like 'im.

She brushed her face upon his shoulder.

What man is there doesn't start off by telling me about 'is mother, 'ow 'e's lost 'er, 'ow 'e wants to find 'er again? That's a fact of nature, I could tell you, but I won't. One what even the French 'aven't put in their encyclopaedia yet, so that scholar of Oxford said, coming to me regular so he can wear his dead mother's dresses in bed. Wants nothing else except to spend the night by my side in 'is mother's nightgown.

'I don't have a mother.'

'There's one thing all men 'as is a mother, More Grief. If you miss her, it's my speciality. I can be a gentleman's nanny, too, Master Mor. Would you like that?'

'I mean, I never knew mine. I was orphaned early.'

'Then I'm sure you're still looking for 'er. A lot of them are. Wanting to know 'ow she looked, 'ow she behaved, whether she was like this woman what you meet or like that one. What she smelled of. Roses, mimosa, kitchen wells. What she wore. Thinking of 'er in silk maybe? Do you like silk? The feel of it?'

Not getting an answer, she said impatiently,

'You can tell *me*. A lot of men are of that category of 'uman nature.'

'I'll tell you then!' He was full of reckless confession. 'My mother left me in the church porch at Lady Well. All I 'ad was my name "Greave" stitched to my shirt. She must 'ave done that because my father, it's said, was Oliver Greave.'

My Gawd, *Oliver* Greave!

'He used to be an important man in these parts before he went bankrupt,' Mor continued. 'He was of "a wayward disposition", they say, fathering children here and there. It was our present Mr Horsfall's father that cheated 'im of his inheritance, they say. So perhaps what Horsfall 'as, should be mine. So now I've told you the truth . . . Are you all right?'

'Yes, I'm all right, my love. Thanks for asking. Stranger things 'ave 'appened, More Grief. You don't know who your mother was, then?'

'No.'

'No memories at all? Don't you remember . . . the colour of 'er 'air? Was it black?'

'I don't know.'

'How old are you?'

He looked sad, even shamefaced.

'I'm . . . turned thirty.'

'I'm always being told some sad tale like yours by my gentlemen. I 'eard about them Greaveses when I was a child. Peculiar things 'appen . . . There are so many interesting categories of 'uman nature, aren't there? Are you interested in anything special, dear?'

'Goldsmith's *History of Animated Nature* was my constant companion at my loom.'

'My Gawd!'

She laughed, and sighed. 'Well, then. It's not your mother, your interest? That's a pity, I'm good at that. What is it then?' She put forth her toe. 'Do you like my boots?'

Still carrying on my business, out of 'abit. I'll have to go on with it. They'll smell a rat otherwise. So will 'e. Know something's wrong and run.

He didn't answer.

'They're green.'

'I can see.'

158

'Are you slow or something?' She laughed at him. 'You can say anything you like to me, you know, my dear, I've already told you. Tell me anything you're interested in. You won't be able to tell me anything new, you know. I know everything. If I can't satisfy you myself, someone else 'ere will. You interested in widows and funerals? You seem on the melancholic side. That's Mrs Rawdon's line . . .'

He wasn't answering.

'What *do* you like?'

'A short while ago I was reading Goldsmith on *The Origin of Rivers . . .*'

'My Gawd!'

She slapped her hand to her cheek and screamed with laughter.

Once again ale and gin were on the table, and Mary winked at the servant.

Mor found himself easily getting drunk. He was very tired and he didn't often take alcohol.

He also drank faster because he didn't like the feeling of being out-talked by a woman.

She gently stroked the back of his neck.

'Have you been a *bad* boy, by any chance? Is there anything you think *nanny* should do for you? There, there . . .'

But he did not respond to that either. What a game!

She quickened her voice, as if she were losing interest in this performance and wanted to get it over.

'Then tell me what was that about "stockings out of fashion" and "destruction of machinery" and "distress we are put under"? That's what you said. Tell me about that. I'm a very patient listener.'

But it was her *im*patience that stung him. He foolishly raised his voice.

'I'll tell you, all right! By God, I'll tell you a story, if you want one. In York I saw a judge in solemn pomp put on 'is cap to pass sentence of death on a dozen wretches, telling them they should be 'ung by the neck and their bodies given to surgeons. One had stolen a pair of old shoes that 'ad been left to be mended and 'e put them on 'is own feet because 'e needed them. So they could 'ang 'im, they were valued at one shilling. I saw those shoes and thought they were not worth fourpence. The shoemaker at first said they were not worth three-pence, then someone 'igh up told 'im to say otherwise. What a cursed world, where little knaves are 'anged or transported if our judges can do it, but great ones swim in wealth and pleasure and are flattered with titles and dignities.'

'Don't shout so loud. For Gawd's sake, don't shout so loud, More Grief!'

It was her turn to cast worried glances around the room, and at the leech-gatherer, who was busy with one hand inside his lady's bosom. Nonetheless he had picked up what Mor had said.

'That's right, sir, that's right! They allus 'ang the wrong 'uns. You tell the lady.'

The drink and the encouragement were affecting Mor. He shouted even louder. Perhaps the whore with her 'warnings' was egging him on: a woman encouraging a man, as a little girl will encourage a boy to climb a tree by telling him that he mustn't do it.

'Pheasants, hares, trouts, partridges are privileged compared wi' the poor and distressed like us.' He waved his hand towards the smiling leech-gatherer. 'They are protected by gamekeepers and laws and fed without stint to make 'em fat. Truly, Mary, you are not to be blamed for what 'as 'appened to you.'

'Thanks very much. You talk like an educated aristocrat, More Grief, only they don't usually shout out their business loud. I can't puzzle you out.'

'I keep a school.'

'*You* . . . keep a school? Teaching writin' and Latin? Never! You don't know nothing about life. Say some Latin to me, then.'

'*Sic transit gloria mundi.*'

'Gawd help me, just like a parson. What's a weaver doing keeping a school?'

'If I don't teach my neighbours what I've learned from going short . . . short . . .'

'Your speech is slurred.'

He pulled himself together.

'Short-sighted by candlelight, they'll be taught something else by the vicar, in the Grammar School.'

'Goodnight, sir, goodnight,' said the leech-gatherer, and led his cheerful woman away. They had left a puddle of spilled ale and a pool of dirty river-water on the table and the floor.

'God bless 'em, I 'ope they 'ave a roof,' Mary said.

Mor looked fully at her. She returned his look. There was something between them that, like her perfume, pushed the smoke and smell of the room into the background.

'You're sorry for people like that?' he asked.

'Oh, More Grief . . .'

She appeared to him quite differently now. Her restless glances and movements had ceased. An essence of closeness, of familiarity, surrounded them.

'Our vicar in Lady Well says our life is an 'eroic labour in darkness and ignorance, to earn an eternity of bliss and ease. That's just putting things off. He never talks about what should be a parson's concerns, love and duty to our neighbours, and forgiveness. Instead he tells us we mi't be snatched away into eternal fire between this sermon and the next, if we don't keep our noses to the grindstone. So I've stopped going to the church. People only listen because they like to watch his Adam's apple going up and down in the pulpit.'

'Don't talk so loud, More Grief! . . . Please.'

Mor did not know that whores could cry so easily.

'Tell me about yourself,' he said, softly. 'How did you come to . . .'

'To be a whore?'

'Yes.'

She smiled again. 'I don't mind my profession. We are what we make of what 'as been done to us, I say. I've made the best of my fate. What I was born with is just something to make a living with. It's only men that think women 'ave got a temple between their legs. None of us females gives a pig's fart for it. Not even ladies. Especially them, in fact. They'll drop their drawers in a wink for the sake of a fortune and a marriage and a chance to pretend to 'ave 'eadaches whenever they like.'

She gave a different glance around the room now . . . spying out danger?

She understands something that I know nothing about. I mustn't get rattled. They'll not 'ave found my book yet. If my nerve goes, I'll never survive.

'I'll tell you what happened, if you really want to know, More Grief. When I was fourteen I was turned out by my father for going behind 'is 'aystack with a lad, and that's 'ow I came to follow my trade. 'E wasn't my real father. I was adopted, like you. A black boy took me as a babe in secret and not even my own mother was supposed to have known I'd live. I know why they adopted me. They wanted a slave, but they'd picked the wrong one. They thought I'd be afraid to raise my 'ead because of a mark . . .

'I was thrown out with nothing but my trunk. I wasn't sorry to leave. He once nearly kicked my eye out with the tip of 'is boot 'cos 'is dinner was cold. Called me a "bastard" and said even my natural mother couldn't bear the sight of me, 'cos I shouldn't 'ave been born. Yet one day 'er, as I called my mother, sent him to the well for water and off 'e went, meek and mild, like a woman. I knew then that something 'appens in bed that's 'idden from the light of day and I made up my mind I'd find out all about it . . .

'So there I was, thrown out o' the farm, which I didn't mind at all, for I've never been in love with pig sheds and rainy weather. Then along comes a young man and picks me up, just the same as you've done today, but 'e was younger and in them days I was more worth 'aving . . . Whoops a'daisy! I shouldn't be telling you that, should I? Mrs Rawdon wouldn't be pleased. "'Ullo", I thinks, "'Ere's me fortune coming." I wasn't no green fruit, I can tell you, that could find a Mother Superior easy. I'd lost my virgo intacta behind that 'aystack, which was foolish because if I'd gone whole I'd 'ave been worth twenty pounds and that would 'ave bought me a bride's trousseau for an aristocrat, wouldn't it? He took me in his phaeton to an 'ostelry, no expense to myself, just like in a novel. We stayed a week, as I'd nowhere to go. 'E said 'e was a lord and I believed 'im, for 'e behaved like one. I was waiting for 'im to take me to 'is family or introduce me to a lady who'd employ me as 'er maid. He talked about "love" and "I wish you were mine". Then he stuck me in a whore 'ouse. 'E said it was to pay off my bill for gin. I finished up in London. Just listen to us talking. What about you? You told me as far as being left in the church porch. When was that? Where'd your mother live? . . . Oh, my Gawd!'

'What is it?'

'Oh, nothing. Just the sergeant there . . . Mad Dick. I 'ave to watch 'im. Go on with your story. Your father was Oliver Greave, you said?'

'Yes. I was put in the workhouse, then I was sent out to a weaver and 'is wife. They brought me up well. I was lucky. "He shall grow up imbued with bewk knowledge, as well as practical, especially that which 'as a theological bent, and 'e shall be learned to write a good 'and."'

Mor began to mimic the weaver's high pitched voice. He had not made fun like this since the days when he had courted Phoebe.

'He taught me the principles of science. He said the verses of Mr Wesley was better than Shakespeare's. He taught me the miraculous varieties of nature, through Oliver Goldsmith's book.'

They were interrupted by the drunken sergeant stumbling against their table. He was a huge, wild fellow, with a Tyneside accent.

'You're talking deep, Mary The Scar! Let's play games. 'Ow about you, sir? Let's go upstairs . . .'

'Fuck off,' Mary answered. 'Go on, Mad Dick! Fuck off. I don't want yer, Sergeant Chadwick.'

'What's up with yers?'

The soldier spread his arms, lost his balance and reeled backwards into his companions, who, having nothing to fear from his size because of his drunkenness, pushed him back to the whore's table, as if he was a sack of wheat.

'For Gawd's sake, why don't the King take you lot off to fight Napoleon and stop you pestering 'onest English whores?' Mary yelled.

All her frantic manner had returned.

'I'll tell you what . . .' stuttered the soldier and addressing Mor, 'I 'ate Napoleon. Don't think I'm not a democrat, I 'ate Napoleon, 'cos o' this: 'e's spilt more blood to find crowns for 'is own brothers than the Revolution in France spilt to instit . . . to instit . . . to institute the liberty of man. Isn't that so, friend?'

'Don't answer him,' Mary commanded fiercely.

But Mor had to nod his agreement.

'Now there's an 'onest gentleman,' the soldier smirked. 'Are you the one that our friend, "B", is talking about? You don't look the type. You look an 'onest gentleman. Tell me what you think.'

'For Gawd's sake keep your mouth shut! You're a fool, More Grief, you're a babe in arms.'

The sentimental sergeant turned as vicious towards Mary as previously he had been soft.

'That's a democratic sentiment that wouldn't be un'stood by whore, Mary The Scar! When I was in the pit . . . when I was in the Newcastle coal pit . . . ah, what's the use? There's nothing that the common man can do, is there, sir? You know what 'appens in 'Is Majesty's armies when you dare to complain? Ah, what's the use? No wonder the army's on the edge of revolt. Tell you what, Mary The Scar, come and play wi' me, 'tis better, I'm sure, than thrusting on this kind genalman 'ere your ugly face. Do you know, sir, what she's 'iding under that . . . that . . ?'

Mary threw her gin at the soldier. She amazed Mor with her quickness to defend herself. Mad Dick collapsed and staggered away. Mary was only a little flustered, as if she were used to this kind of scene with the sergeant.

'You've dropped your bag,' Mor said.

He picked it up and put it into her lap, taking the opportunity to brush her lower leg and thigh.

The sergeant, restored to his companions, was meek again. 'I love her. I love her . . ."' He was in tears. But he did not come back.

'You never know with 'im,' Mary said. 'One moment 'e's crying on my shoulder, the next 'e's . . . 'e's a brute.'

'We suffer from what Byron in the House termed "a double affliction of an idle military and a starving population".'

'No peace for the wicked, you might say. 'Oo's Byron?'

'The owner of coal pits near Rochdale and a grand 'ouse in Nottingham. But he speaks for us in Parliament. A good man, though a Lord.'

'Oh, my Gawd, an aristocrat! There's one or two of them come to me regular to have their bottoms smacked. 'Appen he's one of them, they generally don't give their proper names.

'I'll tell you something else about the respectable classes, More Grief. They all marries unhappy, and that's because they can afford to. The poor 'as to select with greater sense and make the most of what they gets.'

Mor gulped.

''Ave you ever 'eard of a poet called the Earl of Rochester?' she asked suddenly.

'No.'

'I can't read a book nor anything writ down myself, but a gentleman of mine reads his verses to me out from a book. 'Ave you really never 'eard of 'im?'

'No,' repeated Mor, irritated at having a gap in his learning discovered.

'I'm surprised at you. He was profligate. What does "profligate" mean?'

'It means he threw his money around.'

'I wish I'd met 'im. I was taught one of 'is poems by 'eart. There was nothing else to do in bed with my friend. Get us another gin, sweetheart.'

While Mor was away, he thought of what he would tell her when he got back.

The ale and the gin slopped out of the pots. He set them down, leaned comfortably next to her, and said,

'I'm looking for a red flower. I saw it in a dream.'

She touched his arm and left her fingers lingering.

'What sort of red flower, More Grief?'

He closed his eyes.

'A splendid deep red rose, like nothing on earth.'

'I can see it! I can just see it! I can bring a man a flower, redder than any sunsets . . .'

Watch it, Mary, she told herself. Not with this one. Habit of a lifetime.

'Do you believe that Christ will come again?' she asked.

He wouldn't answer.

'There's lots do. There must be a reason for it. Miracles 'appen. You'd be surprised at what 'appens.'

She removed her gaze from him and stared at the floor. His violin poked from under the seat.

'If a fiddler plays right you can feel Christ is in the room with you,' she said.

When she looked up she saw that several more soldiers had gathered round the sergeant and 'B'.

'Oh, my Gawd, come on upstairs now!'

Mary was already standing. Mor felt in his pocket.

'Never mind your money!'

She had hold of his hand, as she looked in different directions.

She tugged him to his feet. Drunk as he was, he remembered to pick up his bag and his fiddle. In her haste, dragging him off, she abandoned the elegant holding of her dress.

'You don't know how your fortune's changed, because I've changed my mind about you!' she shouted over her shoulder.

Phoebe might have been in another country; Phoebe who kept her bridal gear under a bell jar. Laughter followed the tall whore and the crippled weaver as she dragged him towards a battered oak door, which looked as though it led to a coal cellar or a place for animals rather than to the pleasure chamber of a lady. It opened to a dirty staircase.

'You 'aven't any idea 'ow to look after yourself, 'ave you, More Grief?'

It was so steep that as they climbed the hem of her dress dangled above his eyes. Halfway up, on a tiny landing, they had to press themselves against the wall for the skivvy carrying a bucket of coals to pass by. Mary gave the girl some money and Mor turned away. Through the window he saw the moon beaming upon stagnant blood and piss in the yard. He could hear low slaughter-house moans, and from the head of the stairs, the similar cries of a whore-house.

They were climbing again. They arrived on a landing which reached deep into the house. The cries and moans were increased. A woman in a bridal dress and veil opened a door. For no perceivable reason, she was crying. As she ran on light feet, she seemed to swim down the long artery of the corridor. Mor heard a man's scream. A woman passed by wearing a small eye-mask, immense artificial cats' whiskers attached to it, and holding a black fan. A huge-breasted, angry-seeming woman, carrying a whip, crossed the corridor after her. There followed an old man in the tunic of a Roman slave. He had a distant expression on his face, until he almost collided with Mary.

'Sorry, Nanny . . . The Paphian revels . . .'

'I don't know, Doctor,' Mary answered. 'Now go away, that's a good boy. Nanny's busy.'

She opened a door a short distance along the landing. They went in and she shot the wooden bolt.

Her room, in contrast to the barren stoniness downstairs, was a warm red colour. It was invitingly lit by a newly stoked fire. As Mor expected of a whore's room, the double bed was the most striking thing; an antiquated four-poster of black oak, with curtains, and carvings of fruit and flowers. There was a chaise-longue, which to Mor looked a valuable piece of furniture, although it was scratched and kicked. There were mirrors – more than he had ever seen before, except at Mr Horsfall's. There were large cupboards and wardrobes, so cavernous that for a moment he feared a spy hidden in them, then he dismissed this as ridiculous. Most of the furniture appeared as unloved as the depersonalised items of a coaching-inn and was evidently not Mary's own. It contrasted with some casual-looking hangings; some pieces of lace, a blue cloak flung over a chair, and a silk scarf dropped as if casually, to transform the effect of a large and very battered, leather trunk stiffened with a framework of brass and iron. A blue Chinese vase for biscuits decorated the windowsill. There was a ewer of water and a bowl with forget-me-nots painted on the rim.

'Never let yourself be brought here again led by the nose with "a suitable occupant for accommodation".'

'Why not?'

'Gawd, you're a child, you're a babe in arms. You need me to take care of you. Didn't you notice the way it was said, solemn like in a church? It's what they always say, meaning you're suspected as a fugitive, that's why. They know you're from Lady Well 'cos you told them yourself. They sent me across to find out about you because they 'ope to get out of you what you've done, for a reward. What *have* you done? "B" thinks you might 'ave been in Huddersfield . . . My Gawd, don't start telling me. I don't want to know.'

Mor put his bag and fiddle down carefully, removed his scratched, greasy leather jacket and ran his fingers around his neck where he had sweated with fear. Mary placed her indispensable and shawl upon the chest. The adventure had not put *her* out.

He fumbled in his pocket. He had never been with a prostitute and did not know whether to pay her before or after. He felt that a sovereign was too much, but his small change amounted to too little. He did not know where his sovereign would be safe, or whether he could really trust her, though trust, indeed, was what he felt.

'I don't want no money,' she said. 'No, don't, I don't want none. Anyway, you'll 'ave to stay, now you're 'ere. There's nowhere else for you. You can choose your own side of the bed. Look at whatever side of me you want. I don't always do that, because there's some Georges and Thomases I don't like. You're gentle, but they don't know how to treat a lady and so I doesn't give them privileges. Anyway, I expect you'll sleep.'

She seemed quite sober. She sat on the edge of the bed and lifted the hem of her dress to give him his first erotic glimpse of her ankles, above her boot-tops that were laced across a part-open front. They were outdoor boots, dirty and much travelled in; ones which would not normally be worn with an evening gown and so were either a practicality for this foul inn or a 'whorish device'.

'Tell me about your wife.'

He did not answer.

'Go on, tell me about her. You can do. I won't be jealous. You promised to tell me.'

'I didn't promise!'

'Tell me, anyway. Please.'

167

'Nothing.'

'What do you mean, "Nothing"?'

'Phoebe – that's what she always said to me – "Nothing." Even when we were courting. I'd walk 'er 'ome through the dusk and she'd sigh. "What are you sighing about?" "Nothing", she'd say. "Nothing". When I left, she said – nothing.'

'Poor dear! I wager she 'ad 'er problems.'

Mary lifted her dress higher. She wore a petticoat which was also white. An absurd thought of it as virginal and bridal crossed Mor's mind. After all, she was virginal and bridal to him. Certainly she was without shame.

She had another little bag hung from a cord around her waist. She rolled petticoat and dress higher. Her stocking-tops were gripped and gartered by what, as she raised her outer clothes still further, he realised was a man's pair of woollen drawers, worn back to front. Thus she could easily get at the strings of the waist, normally worn at the rear.

She untied the strings and peered.

'Damn!' she said, loudly. 'I'm unclean, More Grief. The blood's come. I've got the flowers.'

His disappointment thudded like a lead cudgel.

'I felt something, downstairs. I thought it was . . .' She laughed.

She untied the string that held her pocket and slid that under her pillow. She slipped off the bed and stood erect, so that her clothes fell into place again, her white dress all around her, a crumpled flower. She turned her back to him, and bent her neck. She was expecting him to unfasten the strings and buttons at the rear, but he was unused to such delights.

'Are you going to do it, or must I call the servant girl?'

He didn't know how to. He fumbled and eventually succeeded. She hobbled with her legs apart towards her commode. She looked so awkward that he went to help there, too. He could hardly believe that he was doing such a thing. It was dreamlike. He removed her boots and moved to the garter at her knee, while she was pulling down her drawers.

'Careful,' she warned.

Some solid objects were caught above the knee. A silver watch and a spoon.

'What's this?'

'What's what?'

168

'This . . . these . . .'

'One's for telling the time, the other's for dipping in your dinner, if you 'as one. A lady 'as nowhere to keep nothing, but I expect you've never realised. It's a problem, being a lady. I'm sure you must be glad not to be a member of our unfortunate society.'

She took the watch and spoon to her trunk. The blood was dripping.

'No need for you to wear a sheep's bladder tonight. But I'd wager an 'ouse and lands on it you'll sleep. Anyway, we ought to behave, you and I. I'm not very religious but still . . .'

He was looking at her in amazement.

'You don't know what I'm talking about, do you?'

'No.'

She spent some time burying the spoon and the watch amongst her clothing. She took out some rags, washed but lightly stained, and positioned them. She put on a nightgown and slipped into bed, sitting half-upright. Her finger scratched at her face. She did not seem to realise that she was doing it. She was thoughtful.

Peeling off his layers of coarse woollens, from which the oil had not been washed, so that they would repel the rain, Mor felt rough and unpleasant. He reached his shirt, then his canvas underclothes. He was more conscious of his body than he had been in years.

'If I am marked and deformed, it is by the 'istory of my class.'

'I would have guessed before long you was a schoolmaster, you know. I'd have known.'

Mor made use of her chamber-pot in a hearty gush.

'Don't be surprised that I know gentlemen, More Grief. There's types from every level of the land comes after me. I can talk to 'em all, bishops and dukes and Members of Parliament and military officers, 'cos I've learned their way of speaking. You must have noticed. The aristocracy of England 'as been my downfall, More Grief.'

'Mine, too.'

'Come and lie down, love.'

She spoke softly.

'Why do you like me?' he asked.

'Oh, if you knew what I've seen and put up with . . ! Oh dear . . .'

He did not care about any more of an answer. Lying next to him, *him*, Mor Laverock Greave, on a clean and sheeted bed, was the flesh of a woman, smelling of a jungle of perfumes. He kissed her shoulder. Avoiding her lips and cheeks because of the paint, he kissed her neck.

Her flesh tasted not of rank machine oils but of tingling, erotic essences. He was longing to try the olfactory excitements of her body; to do what he had never done but only imagined; to bury his nose between her breasts, under her armpits, in her cunt; to kiss her toes. He had never in his life lain with any woman except Phoebe. He was amazed, charmed, by the variegated red streaks of her hair, by her still wearing her glass earrings in bed, by her perfumed cleanliness which made him feel ashamed of his own dirt.

'Do you believe that Christ will come again?' she repeated.

'No.'

Not another Phoebe! Are they *all* waiting for Jesus?

'I do,' she said. 'He promised, and Christ is one who'd never break a promise. He's the only one who'd never do that.'

He could not continue the conversation. For the first time in two days he was able to relax. When she felt how tired he was, she with one spread hand pressed the back of his head onto her breast.

What Mary most wanted was for promises to be kept. When, during girlhood, she had seen cottagers, with their battered carts and tattered baggage, coming from where they had been cleared off newly enclosed lands, hoping to make new homes on the moorlands, she had thought: They were promised homes to live in peace and have been given nothing. All earthly people, she had found, broke their promises in the end. All lovers had failed her. She preferred to be a whore, following the rules of brief fantasies, with contracts that had only to be kept for a night. In fantasies she could play Goddess in her own Garden of Eden, where there were no promises to be broken.

Once in Halifax, when she was a girl, she had heard Joanna Southcott speaking to a large crowd, fifteen thousand people, before the Cock Inn. Christ had promised to come again, Joanna said, bringing a thousand years of continuous days of rest of the poor, starting at the Millennium, which would be 'soon'. Mary heard this message not from a parson, but from a woman like herself. He-who-would-keep-his-promise would be born, as before, to some humble earthly woman, Mary was told.

An immaculate conception. No men. Save a lot of trouble.

His mouth was sticky and would hardly open. The whore-house was still noisy with distant clatterings. He heard a male shout, not quite a scream.

More than anything else he would have liked a glass of water. His head was thick and buzzing. The fire had died and the moon patterned the floor with light so substantial that he felt he could pick it up and give pieces of blue silk to the woman at his side. He looked upon her sleeping face as at an awesome miracle.

His staring so intently woke her. Her eyes were wide and still.

'Won't you go inside me, More Grief?' she whispered. 'Never mind the flowers.'

Before he climbed onto her she removed her protective cloth, dropping it to the floor outside the bed. He thought of Phoebe's blood-stained rags, after she had held them to her mouth; she never let him see the other kind of rags, hiding them as if they were obscene.

Mor came quickly, excited by long abstinence and the expert manner in which Mary entwined her arms around his neck, violently yet also tenderly, and by the way she stroked his shoulders. Her white painted face, with the heightened red patches of lips and cheeks as if they had been stung, had the tranced look of a death mask, or of that death-mask look that the unknown artist had given to the painting of Saint Uncumber on the wall of the old church in Lady Well. Perhaps it was only in moments of death and love that character was so extinguished.

'Kiss me on the mouth,' she asked softly. 'Kiss me.'

He brushed and lingered over the lips, which had a strange bitter taste like poison. He did not want to say that he did not like it. She opened her mouth and he inserted his tongue. They searched one another. She would offer him all the entrances of her body. They felt together the influx of the most revolutionary feeling in the world, the force that breaks up everything else, and reconstitutes it about itself . . . He did not dare mention love, lest something so insecurely planted should vanish. They felt that they had both tumbled into a conspiracy.

'I'll tell you something about whores, More Grief. We all keep one place that none of our clients can touch. For some it's the breast, for some the pit of the neck, and with one girl I know it's 'er feet. That place is for their true love's sake and is so that they has something special for them only. It's to keep love pure. With me it's the lips. They can all go into me 'ole down there, anyone that pays for it, but you're the only one that's kissed me on the lips for years. No one else'll be doing it, I can promise you.'

The moonlight showed the wateriness of her eyes.

The one place she wants to be kissed is where the poison lies, thought Mor.

'I can't stay around 'ere much longer, More Grief. I've got to go somewhere, over the 'ills. Tell me before I go . . . tell me . . . Tell me, can you promise to love a whore, More Grief?'

PART 2

April–May 1812

April 18th

Mor awoke in that terror, akin to vertigo, of a deep sleeper in a strange place who takes minutes to recall where he is. Mary was still asleep beside him; red hair tangled out of control, the earring nearest to him white and broken into glassy fractures as it caught the morning light, tossed like a buoy in the henna-red sea. Her sleeping face too was beyond her control. She had a defenceless, naive look which made her seem young. He was stained with the blood in which he had slept, and could remember little of the rolling about which had spread it upon his stomach and arms. It was on the pillow . . . no, that was dye from her hair.

He remembered a dream about water. He thought it was a river which he had been anxious to cross.

Rosy dawn was over. The whitened light showed him that it was late into the morning. This felt like the days of his youth, before the factories, when a man could rise as early or as late as he chose, if he would pay the price of it. He had slept as unconsciously trusting as a baby. Several times she had called him 'baby', he remembered. They had twice made love, despite the blood.

'You might say we're blood relatives,'' she whispered.

After the second time, he had fallen gently asleep with his penis resting inside her, her arm around his shoulder.

Though awake, he had not moved his limbs. The mere stirring of his eyelids seemed to awaken her; she was as responsive as that to his body. She awoke later than he because during much of the night she had not slept, from protecting this babe in her arms, realising how much he needed sleep.

They both had a desperate need for the chamberpot and the call reminded Mor of last night's drinking. So did his longing for water. His head was sore and his mouth was coated.

He tried to feel guilty, but was unable to do so, though he turned over thoughts of Phoebe, of the children, and of Lady Well. He was on the run, having to learn the new skills of watching his back all the time, yet paradoxically it was now that he was at last his own man, free. The coiled spring of anxiety that had always been in his chest had vanished.

Mary, in her nightgown, used the pot after him, unfastened the window and emptied it into a space blasted by the smell and the moaning of cattle. The wild colours of her face in laughter met the light. Slowly scratching her cheek, she shouted to some men in the yard.

She turned her face, smeared with spoiled rouge but still lit with pleasure, towards Mor. He was lifted on a pang of love, just from seeing her like that. He went to join her at the window and looped his arm around her waist.

'Kiss me.'

He obliged.

It promised to be a stormy day. Strong fleet sunlight fell momentarily upon Ripponden, yet above the hills, heavy clouds, of that most-threatening greenish tinge, gathered and the slopes were shadowed with rain. They could see a street busy with sober men, and workshops or manufactories along a rapidly flowing stream that was glittering like a suddenly opened drawer of cutlery.

There was a large mill with a beam engine now rocking with gigantic leisurely strength upon its horizontal shaft. It put forth steam, smoke, and a dirty smell of coal.

'*Dies irae, dies illa/Solvet saclum in favilla.* Gawd, I don't like the morning.'

'You're a Catholic?'

'I pick up bits of knowledge, like you do. "Day of anger, day of mourning". It's their Mass. "When to ashes all is burning." You're not the only one with a bit of Latin.'

He closed the window and Mary replaced the pot under the bed. She used a fresh clean rag, and then dressed as she had done yesterday. Mor noticed that the slits on either side of her petticoat were lined up with two further slits cleverly hidden in the folds of her outer dress at the hips, so that she could get at both the purse hung around her waist, and into the gap at the front of her drawers.

She slipped into her boots. She lifted out of her trunk a small wooden cabinet and, taking it near to the table that held the ewer of water, she opened the lid of the box. Within a padded red silk lining were small bottles, sable brushes, a piece of sponge, small porcelain palettes, a bar of palm-soap and a silver-backed mirror. She washed and dried her arms, the tops of her breasts, her neck and some of her face.

'I 'ave a gentleman says that cleanliness is the virtue against which is to be tried all of his associates, and any deviation is sufficient reason for the declining hov social hintercourse. No one trusts a lady no more what isn't clean. You should use the ewer, too.'

Mor felt that he himself was one who liked to be clean, yet this interest in, he presumed, daily washing amazed him. She renewed her old layer of cosmetic, mixing some white lead and using the sponge to apply it to her face from chin to hair-line. She heightened her cheeks with fresh rouge. She tugged at her eyebrows, before she used one of the brushes to paint them. With mercuric sulphide rouge, she also coloured her lips. Her face made him think of the hectic colours of autumn when the leaves are dying.

She realised how fascinated he was to watch her.

'I wager you can't tell I was brought up on a farm,' she said.

She turned back to her trunk for the silver-backed hairbrush, and worked at her hair. All this took a long while and he continued happy to watch. Like a married man, he thought.

'More Grief, why don't you wash yourself, too, before I throw the water away?'

He had been considering that very thing. He washed himself and dressed at last.

'We should get you some shirts . . .'

She let this unintended hint that there was a future for them both together, a time for buying his shirts, hang in the air. She returned to her trunk, replaced her cosmetic box, producing napkins and a teapot. She pulled the wooden bolt back from the door. She took the pot downstairs, saying she was going to order a breakfast.

'I'd like a jug of water,' he said.

She was some time away. She returned without the pot, but with Mor's hat and some drinking water.

After a short while, the breakfast was served in her room. The servant girl was peering everywhere and especially at Mor. She was not pleased, possibly wanting a tip.

'Be careful with my teapote, instead of puttin' your nose into a lady's business. That was a present from an aristocrat, that was,' Mary scolded.

When they were alone again, she held the fine willow-patterned china with her finger crooked delicately through the handle, like a lady but probably even more showily.

'He said he was a lord of some place that I found out later never existed.'

'Who?'

'The one who gave me the china, o'course. Who d'yer think I was talking about? Saint Paul? That was a one, I can tell you. I was glad to be rid of 'im, he used to bring his dog in with him. Dirty beast.'

The white lead that was still upon her fingers left smears on her oatcakes.

Mor, who had never in his life had fine china in his hands, did not know how to hold it. He touched it gingerly, frightened of breaking it, as if it were a wild bird's egg.

'I need to get some change,' he said.

'I don't want paying. Don't insult me no more . . .'

Mor's heart jumped with fear. A man stood at the door, an open razor in his hand; a sinister fellow who smiled and said nothing. He turned to beckon someone in from the landing.

The servant girl came in, this time with a bowl of warm water and a towel. Mary, during her absence, had arranged for the services of a barber.

The girl left, her face stiff.

More sat on the trunk. He realised how jumpy he had become. The house was more or less quiet now. Against a wall he could hear the soft banging of a broom.

'They told me last night before I came over and spoke to you that you was a "desperate man",' Mary said, after the barber had left.

'Yes, I'm desperate. Magistrates think the only cure for it is a noose at the end of a rope. To what pitch 'ave we been driven, that we will so readily face the hangman or the soldiers' canon? It is not only the feckless who starve. Families in full employment, who can do no more, are also starving and they will become desperate, too.'

'You don't have to make excuses to me, More Grief. I don't care what anyone's called. Think 'ow often I must put up with being called "whore". I've never wanted to be anything but an 'onest woman. Just because I enjoy life, such as it is, they don't understand it. I judge by what I finds out for myself about a man.'

She asked him to go with her to the slaughter yard. She would not say what for. Judging by her familiarity with the place and her manner with the workmen, it was a regular errand. She collected a supply of sheep's intestines, already dried for her, cut into short lengths, knotted at one end and hung in a shed, where they were causing amusement.

'What are those for?'

'Where've you been all your life, schoolmaster? Spare my blushes. Them over there know what they're for and they don't 'ave no Latin. They're for me to 'and out for my gentlemen to wear.'

They stood in the blood and the yellow liquid staining the cobbles, surrounded by the brutal shouting of slaughtermen and the defeated lowing of cattle.

Abruptly she said, 'I don't care what we are. I mean, whore and . . . whatever . . . Will you promise never to leave me?'

It seemed the most inevitable and natural thing for her to say, and for him to answer, without a pause, 'Yes.'

They walked silently for a while, feeling stupid because they said no more about it. The world had changed. He meant what he said, but found out that he meant it only after he had spoken. Then he understood the implications, for a woman who had explained to him how heartily she believed in people keeping promises.

They found themselves walking quietly, in awe and reverence, yet every step seemed to echo and be amplified.

They returned past the lowered, tethered heads of bullocks. Their warm smell. From a barn they heard scampering slipping hooves and the heavy fall of the pole-axe.

'You said you 'ad to 'ave your daughter adopted?'

'That's right, More Grief.'

'I've lost a child, also,' he confided. 'My boy ran away two days ago from the factory.'

'Oh, my dear!'

Mor, in a rush, described Edwin. His curiosity, his desire to learn, his longing not to be crushed, his interest in distant places. Mor was finding himself, because of his love for this woman, articulate as he had never been before. He told her about Phoebe and Gideon.

'Edwin's *my* boy. Gideon's much more his mother's. He'll turn into a preacher . . . Something o' that sort.'

'Which way do you think Edwin's run?'

'Liverpool. He was always asking where Liverpool was. He will 'ave gone into Lancashire, either along the turnpike road to Oldham, or over Blackstone Edge to Rochdale.'

'I've business to attend to in Oldham,' Mary announced. 'I told you I

179

'ad to go somewhere, well, that's where it is. We'll go together and maybe find news of your child. Even if he's gone by Rochdale, I've friends could 'ave heard of him.'

'It might take a long while.'

She smiled.

'You'll be away a long time, all right. I'm told you killed a man on your raid on Horsfalls'.'

'No!' When he was startled she put a calming hand on his shoulder.

'They don't say it's you for certain, but they're looking for people that was there, right enough. You'd best all scatter and lose yourselves. There's a fellow called "B" on the trail . . .'

'I'm not going on trial! I killed no one. I'll gain nothing for anyone by getting myself transported.'

'We'll both be away lying low for a long time together.'

'What about your – your business with Mrs Rawdon?'

'I pays a nightly rent to 'er for the room and some of what I takes. I'll arrange things with our Abbess. Someone else'll use the room and properties whilst I'm gone.'

'Properties?'

'Theatrical devices what we use. You'll learn, schoolmaster! It's all pretend. Mrs Rawdon does the widow-taken-in-grief. I do Nanny. I've a friend who does the ravaged bride. You saw 'er last night. We find out what our client wants and then we make it real for them . . .

'I'm known for my wanderings, Mor Greave. It'll surprise no one that I go. There's people in 'igh places what'll cover up for me and say to Mrs Rawdon, "She 'as business to attend to, don't you worry about 'er, if you know what's good for you." I'm known for knowing what's going on all over the counties, I am. I'll pack my trunk and 'ave it sent to Oldham, charge of my friends. We'll meet it there. You with your fiddle, and me with my own instrument for playing, as you might say, we'll get by. There's a good living to be made on the roads out of the soldiers and if there's none of the officer aristocratic class to be found, there's masons and navvies with money in their pockets from building public mills.

'We might be lucky and I can introduce you to one of my aristocrats. Your Lord Byron up 'ere inspecting 'is coal pits and estates. I'll wager e'd like to meet a lady at the inn, wherever it is 'e stays. That's what I mean by knowing what's happening – I'd find out where 'e was going before 'e knew proper 'imself.

'All the girls know where everything's 'eading. You 'ave to, don't you? There's generals will talk in their sleep about what they're planning, even before they've made up their minds proper. I know General Maitland, what's to be in charge of the 'ole operation up 'ere. They've forgotten by morning what they've said. A girl's only got to prompt such as them with what she knows and they're blissful as children, thinking they've found a lover who understands their thoughts before they do themselves.'

She laughed.

'I'll introduce you. It's often republicans like you turn out best in a gentleman's service. After they've changed their minds. A general's bed-chamber'd be the best place of all to 'ide a fugitive. How'd you like to be intimate servant of General Maitland? He'll be needing one when 'e gets 'ere. You'd hear everything then, mister machine-breaker. I can't see you as a lackey, though.'

There was evidently nothing she would not do for Mor so long as she believed his promise to love her. Love, instant, total and inexplic-able as this, frightened him. It also made him feel more daringly a man. Mary could not resist the feeling that she was inspiring daring in a man.

It was soon called for. When they returned to the inn, the soldiers had been alerted to find and arrest the 'Ludd' who had been trailed from Lady Well. Under Sergeant Chadwick's direction, they wrenched open pot-cupboards, pushed their bums inelegantly into the air as they poked their noses under tables and chairs, and one even sifted through a pack of cards, apparently to find their quarry.

'Get into our room, quick.'

He made for the stairs. Mary lingered.

'No time for whores this morning,' one soldier said to her and she blew him a kiss.

'Our progress is remorseless,' Mad Dick boasted. 'The place is surrounded. Whoever he is, he's trapped.'

Before Mary went up, she spoke to the skivvy. The girl, who crept around the inn like a damp rat in a drain, followed soon after, carrying past the unobservant soldiery a bundle of her own spare clothing. Soon, a private searching the passageway outside Mary's room imagined that he heard the sounds of unspeakable morning pleasures. It was laughter from Mor being dressed by Mary in the clothes of a servant-maid; a cheap black cotton dress, a baggy apron smelling of oatmeal, and a wig from Mary's cupboard.

The true servant departed. A scrambling outside the window told them that the soldiers were combing the slaughterhouse. They had turned the cattle loose into the yard, which a sudden heavy shower of rain made slippy and miry. The frightened beasts were sliding and bellowing. Mary looked out and saw brilliant sunlight glittering on wet hides, cobblestones, soldiers' guns, tunics and leather belts.

Military attention could be heard concentrating outside the door.

'You'd better get some practice to make it convincing before they break in. 'Ere, fasten this on my leg for my business in Oldham. And don't say anything when they come in. Pretend you're dumb.'

She sat upon the bed, waiting for him to tie a scarlet garter around her thigh. It was while he was doing this that Mad Dick burst in with two privates.

'Sargint Chadwick of the Cumberland Militia!' he announced as he led his soldiers to hunt a desperate fugitive amongst Mary's clothes, scent bottles and underwear. 'You got a tall, thin one with a neck 'idden in 'ere, Mary The Scar?'

It's Crawshaw they're looking for, then . . .

'I like my little boots,' Mary said, wistfully and calmly, as she too realised that Mor was quite safe. She stared down at her feet. 'They was made for me special by a cobbler. He fitted out a cottage so I'd stay in 'is nest, but to be a cobbler's bird in a cage was never what I wanted. He wanted me to be 'is *awl* but it would never 'ave *lasted*.'

'Our orders is to find and hunt down a tall thin long one with a neck!' snapped the sergeant. 'Who may or may not spell "notorious" in a clownish fashion. You seen 'im? There's an 'andsome reward. It's gone up to five hundred guineas. That'd set you up with a decent retirement. That's what you want, so you was telling us.'

Mary turned her eyes, bovinely wide and placid upon the soldiers.

'My cobbler was a gentleman at 'eart, though, not like a common soldier.'

'Listen to me, you fucking whore!' shouted Mad Dick, who seemed to have forgotten that he had approached her with drunken endearments the night before. 'Have you opened up your sewer to a machine-breaker? If you 'as, you'd better tell us 'oo, or we'll 'ave you transported with 'im and the rest o' the mob from the Rawfolds and the Lady Well jobs.'

'Why would I do that? Who do you think I'm working for?'

'Because you might be working for them as well as us, that's why. Knowing you. Who was that with you last night? 'E'd come in from Lady Well. Where's he gone to?'

'Left. He give me the slip in the night. Went out the window, 'cos it was the wrong time of the month. You want proof? Look at that.'

She picked up the rag from the floor.

'Don't be disgusting. 'Ere, *you*,' the sergeant said to Mor. ''Ave you seen anything? What *are* you? Where've you come from all of a sudden?'

'I'll thank you not to use language before my new maid, soldier!'

Sergeant Chadwick was laughing.

'Maid, my arse. The things that go on in this whore-'ouse. They're disgusting. Well, Vicar, or Doctor, or whatever you are, tell me what you've seen.'

'She can't tell you,' Mary interrupted. ''Cos she's dumb. She's never been able to speak a word since she was a babby. A born idiot, that's what, aren't you, love? It's a good job I took you in. She's just arrived today, a gentle girl brought into service because 'er father died for 'is country in Spain. He gave up 'is life by impaling 'imself upon the spikes at the fortress so that his comrades could climb upon his back to their glorious victory, as is mentioned in the despatch of the Duke of Wellington. A general 'imself told me of the 'eroic deed. It makes me weep to think on it. But true bravery is a stranger to you scum what is only fit to hunt your own unarmed countrymen.'

'I hate Napoleon as much as any man!' Once again but more soberly protested Mad Dick, who was disappearing in and out of cupboards, tipping petticoats and dresses onto the floor and getting his boots entangled. 'I'd be as glad as any to cut off his tail in Spain, 'cos he's spilt more blood in finding crowns for his own brothers than the Revolution in France did to institute the liberty of man. Isn't that so, Vicar?'

Mor had to nod his agreement, as he had done the night before.

'I don't know anything about politics,' Mary said. 'I can't read newspapers, can I?'

Playing the lady, she lay back upon the coverlet and let Mor perform his duties. He picked up the underwear soiled by the soldiers' boots, folded and replaced it, taking his first look into one of those great cupboards. Its size, the shadows, the harnesses, buckles, belts and thongs hanging there, made it seem more like a stable and he could not think what they were all for.

The privates had dragged from the cupboard what looked like a carpenter's sawing-bench, with straps and buckles attached.

'Mind my 'orse,' Mary said.

One of the privates came to Mor to show him his tattoos. The snake wreathed around a sword upon his arm and the eagle that hovered in a sunset which might have been painted by Turner, were new and raw, and the recruit stroked his flesh admiringly, trying to pretend that it wasn't painful.

'Feel that, Vicar,' he said, putting his bicep under Mor's chin.

'You don't want to touch him,' said the other private. 'He's probably diseased.'

'Don't you speak of my lady's maid like that!' Mary interrupted.

'Sorry, miss,' laughed the private. 'I don't care nothing for anything. I've been around. I know a thing or two. Feel that.'

Mor put forward one finger as if it was into the claws of a lobster.

'I'm called Jack. Trooper Jack, for my boldness in the fray.' He turned to Mary. 'What's 'is name?'

'Lactitia. Lactitia, 'cos she likes the cream off the milk.'

'You'll get the pox off the old whore, sweet'eart, if you 'aven't contracted already. She's got a scar from being bitten by the Devil, under all her powder and paint,' Jack teased.

'Fuck off,' said Mary.

'All right then, scrape it off and show the vicar. We'll see then where the Devil bit ye. Everyone knows. Ask our sergeant. Don't they, Sergeant? He knows. She's got the Devil's 'oof on 'er cheek.'

'That's right.'

Mary was angry.

Sergeant Chadwick continued to hunt for fugitive Luddites. He even tried to smell them out, holding the prostitute's most intimate clothes under his nose.

'We'll get the bastard! Come on, let's 'ave 'em – where's your love letters?'

'Love letters to a whore? You must be joking.'

'Let's 'ave 'em! They're evidence. We're looking for a tall thin 'un that spells "notorious" in a comical fashion.'

'You couldn't read spellings if you saw it in writing, Sergeant Chadwick.'

'Yes, I can. I've written letters myself. *And* to the newspaper.'

'No, you 'aven't. You got someone else to write it down. I know you,

Mad Dick.'

'So?'

'So what's the point of you seeing my letters, then? Go out and fight your battles like a man, instead of spying in a lady's correspondence.'

The second private, a shy young man who was laughing to himself, searched quietly but more usefully through Mary's cupboards and wardrobes.

The sergeant threw Mary's cloak onto the floor, and began to dig into the chest.

'Now, just look at this!' he said, dangling the watch. 'What do you know about this, Vicar? How did you come by this, Mary The Scar? Not 'onest, I'm sure o'that.' He put it into his pocket. 'Evidence. You might get 'ung for it, we never know our luck, do we?' He dug even more excitedly into the soft masses of clothing. *''Ere, what's this?'*

'*Lookoomia*,' Mary sweetly informed him. 'Turkish Delight. If you have forgot already because of your drunken stupor what I told you the day before yesterday, it's a present to me from your own superior officer what has travelled in the Turkish peninsula of Greece. As a matter of fact he might call this morning to whisk me off to a gay party in the Manor 'Ouse, so you'd better be careful 'ow you treats 'em – and me. 'E doesn't want 'is fruit knocked about by you scum.'

''Ere, but they're disgusting!'

'Let's 'ave a look, Serge!' pleaded Trooper Jack.

'They're disgusting,' repeated the sergeant, and spat upon the floor.

'You didn't find 'em so when you were sucking on 'em the other night,' Mary said. 'They improved your passion no end, then. I saw the evidence with my own eyes.'

''Ere, I never touched 'em!' said the sergeant. 'One thing Sargint Chadwick isn't, is a sweet tooth. Ask the lads.'

'Let's have a peep, Serge!' the shy private was inspired to ask.

Mad Dick held one forth on the palm of his hand, but looked away as if he might faint from the offending sight. The cube of Turkish Delight had stamped upon it an erect penis and a set of balls, dusted with pale sugar.

'Is this what you were sucking the other night when you left us drinking, Serge?' asked Trooper Jack.

'No, it was not. I've never 'ad such a thing as a prick in my mouth in my 'ole life . . . I'd be sick.'

Sergeant Chadwick carried on searching. After a moment, in his hands he exhibited sweets crudely stamped with nude females, males, and couples glued together in all the possible and many impossible positions.

'Come on, you stinking whore, where's the moulds?'

'There aren't no moulds. I told you, they're a classical present from Greece.'

'I don't believe you, and I need to confiscate evidence in order to prosecute my case. Your mind's nothing but a farmyard drain, Mary The Scar. If you don't want to go to Van Diemen's Land, you fuckin' Devil's spawn, I must warn you it'll go better with the judge if you 'and over the evidence, and all your letters . . .'

The sergeant stopped dead. The shy private had found, hanging on the wardrobe rail, what appeared to be the leather tail of a giant mouse. He began to pull it out into the room. Sergeant Chadwick blushed and lost his words, then he began to shout. But before the private could be countermanded, he had dragged the whip, handle and all, onto the floor.

The private began to crack the whip on the furniture and Mary, laughing, rolled on the bed.

'Look at our Serge! His face is as red as his tunic!' shouted Trooper Jack.

'Attention, Company! It ain't no use looking for Luddites in a whore's room! They 'aven't enough spunk to know what to do with 'em. Out of 'ere, quick march! "Quick", I said! Quick march!'

'That was a scare,' Mor said.

'No, it wasn't. They were only clowning because they were in a whore 'ouse. If I'd told them you're a parson, they wouldn't 'ave believed me. Mad Dick wouldn't arrest anyone. He's not on that side. They 'ad to pretend to be working, with "B" in the 'ouse. 'E's the one to be careful of. Better keep out of 'is way. It's a good job 'e's looking for someone tall and thin. You'd never pass as a woman. We'd better get out of 'ere fast, though.'

Mary left him to change, while she went to Mrs Rawdon.

'So the Lady Well one give you the slip?' Mrs Rawdon said. 'Out of the window, Chadwick told me. He wasn't the thin one. But you shouldn't have let that happen. They were going to arrest him, more than once last night, only you took him off.'

'I thought I'd give 'im his last rites. He said he'd die for 'em.'

'What?'

'His rights.'

'You should have kept tight hold. He might have been in the raid. He could 'ave been anything.'

''E 'asn't got away, Mother. I've got 'im in my room now. Don't you worry about that business. I've 'ad a message. I 'ave to see a senior officer in Oldham right now. This morning. I'll take 'im with me. Hand him over on a plate. Leave it to me, Mrs Rawdon. I'll be away a while. Just send my trunk over. Make sure we leave without any trouble, so he won't suspect nothing.'

Her trunk, laden with her clothes, silk drapes and teapot, the objects that were intended to transform the temporary rooms into which she moved, and one or two of her 'theatrical instruments', were to be sent by traveller's cart. When she returned to the room, she placed her personal belongings, such as her cosmetics cabinet, hair-brush, a small leather purse for sheeps' bladders and a tiny mirror, in Mor's bag. Their sharing of one bag struck him as being very intimate, like sharing a bed.

They left the whore-house. Dashing between showers, they climbed to the moorland that divided Yorkshire from Lancashire. Mor carried the bundle and Mary took the violin, sometimes sheltering it beneath her flapping cloak. The stony road shone before them like pewter, as it crossed open stretches of heather and whinberry, under the swiftly flying sky. Here they sheltered against a boulder, there under a rowan tucked into the cleft formed by a stream. In the fair spells they dashed forwards, laughing.

After an hour or two, when they had reached the watershed between the counties, the weather changed. The storm showers were over. As they looked down a broad saddle of the hills, the meadows and enclosures of the Lancashire plain lay before them, quietly sunlit. Peaceful unharassed farmers were examining the grass. One could even say that it was hot, where the slopes were at right angles to the sun. Yet the hill peaks had become, in the last hours, touched with snow.

He wondered where, in that plain, Edwin might be. If Mor had but the eyes that could penetrate, the boy could probably be seen, down some lane or hedgerow, or somewhere amongst those newly built mills and scatterings of raw, new houses around Hollingworth, Rochdale or Oldham.

Here he was, thinking selfishly of his own Edwin, and not noticing that Mary was troubled. He thought it was because she did not like daylight and fresh air. Challenging it with her competitive white-and-red self-created face and her coiffure, she looked very out of place.

But that wasn't it, he decided. There was something on Mary's mind, to do with her business in Oldham.

'What about that watch Sergeant Chadwick found?' he suggested.

'Well, what about it?'

'He said you could be arrested.'

'Poof! They'll not arrest me. That matter won't get no further, 'cos Chadwick'll want to sell it 'imself. I know Chadwick.'

He asked her one or two other questions, but she did not answer. She threw dreamy glances into the landscape, or she nervously adjusted her garter. Was that the key to the puzzle?

He wanted to make love to her again. Mary glanced into his face and began to wiggle her behind like an actress on a stage.

'My sweet Lactitia, let us rest,' she teased.

They went towards some rocks that edged the hill. They descended perilously a few feet down a small cliff-face, then along a narrow shelf of grit and sand; a slender beach, half-moon shaped, its edges not washed by sea but by air and the great green-yellow-grey sea of valleys. They scrambled up into a crevice and sat in a wedge of sunlight, on dry warm gravel. Mary got rid of her cloak and placed it to dry, as well as it would, in the full sun. She stroked the back of his neck, then gently bent him into a supine position. She raised her dress and removed her menstrual cloths.

In response to her first caresses upon his neck, Mor fingered that delicious spot, the nape of her neck, then her shoulders. His other hand followed her leg inside her dress.

She fell upon him. 'Oh, my dear . . . Kiss me . . . Kiss me!'

For the first time since Gideon was conceived, Mor made love in the open air; seeing, before he lost consciousness, the jackdaws waft and startle across the face of the stones, hearing from villages, farms and fields below the sounds of spring. Once again he came into blood. It settled upon him like a cooling skin.

'What do you think of when you kiss me?' she asked.

He opened his eyes, to see above him her eyes, wide and expressionless as moons. She had given herself in such a wholehearted fashion that her features had become blank in their entrancement. She had emptied herself into him, thrown herself into a well, lost her personality.

He could not think how to answer her. He could not say that he did not like the taste.

'You do love me, don't you?' she said.

'Yes.'

'I want to tell you about my child,' she whispered. 'Not 'Arriet. Another one. It didn't die natural. I 'ad to bury it in a well, for it was born without eyes, as well as without a father. Without any eyes at all, just a skin. It could never have survived, 'specially in my way of life. Poor thing just screamed, so I 'ad to put earth in its mouth to stop it. What else could I do, More Grief? I was going mad with it. What do you think I could do? Oh, my Gawd . . . it was a girl as well. Couldn't 'ave been born with less fortune.

'So now you know my story that could get me 'ung. I 'ad to tell you about it. We can't betray one another now. We're like brother and sister . . . aren't we? It's a pact.'

She took some clean rags out of Mor's bag, adjusted her dress, and was eager to be away. As if she had not said anything at all. The two struggled, like twins being born, out from between the lips of the rocks. Threatened, like new-born babies come for the first time into daylight, by the great bright space and by the currents of air, they hung perilously for a few moments against the huge wrinkled flank of rock. She walked across to a stream to wash her bloodied rags. The brook was a rich chestnut-brown colour from peat, white bubbles frothing on it, after the storms. Her cloths made it redder. She spread them to dry on a sunny rock. They lay side by side on their backs in the dusty heather. Larks were rising, singing, and falling.

'There's no bird builds so low, flies so high, and sings so sweetly,' Mor said.

'Eh?'

'As a lark. My middle name's after them, "Laverock". The workhouse master called me that, because I loved to lie in the grass and heather watching them.'

'That's what we are, More Grief. Building in the muck, but we can fly high and sing about it, can't we?

'"There's something that draws us upwards,
There's something drags us down,

189

And that is what always keeps us
Between muck and a golden crown.'''

'Laverocklaverocklaverocklaverock . . .' Mor trilled, imitating the
bird. 'Onomatopoeic.'

'I don't think I need to, More Grief.'

'A lark can save its own young threatened in the nest by carrying
them to safety in its claws. I've seen it 'appen. Imagine if I could do that,
for mine.'

They packed the damp rags, too, into the bag. Soon, smiling both to
themselves and to one another, in possession of each other's secrets,
they were descending to the village of Denshaw, which lay in a valley
before Oldham. They took food and ale at the inn near the church. The
first dandelions of the year were in flower; not *dents*-de-lions, but
powerful manes of lions; gold yellow suns. Here they shared the last of
the salted beef and pickle that Phoebe had sacrificed.

The oat bread which Phoebe had shaped on the kitchen table, and
which bore the impress of her hands, stunned him into silence. He tore
off her handprints and pushed them into his throat. Piece by piece, he
was swallowing his marriage.

'What's wrong?' Mary asked.

He paused.

'How did you bury a child in a well? Did you drown it?'

'That would have polluted the water and they'd 'ave found me
out . . . Oh, don't *ask* me, I can't bear to think. I choked it with earth
first, then in the night I climbed down a ladder and hid it in a cavity in
the wall. A mason that had repaired the well 'ad left the space on
purpose for 'iding secrets. He was a clever fellow and wanted a secret
or two 'e could blackmail us whores with in return of our services. 'E
knew that every now and then one or other of us'd want to be rid of a
babby. Oh, 'e ruled the roost, all right. Cock o' the yard with it. Slimy.
It was a decent burial, though. I did bury 'er decent, Mor, 'onest I did!
Six feet below the earth, but no signs to show. Worse things happen.'

Mary's damp and glistening eyes.

They climbed one last hill, to Grain's Bar. Mor could taste the smoke
in the air. To reach Oldham they dropped through Greenacres, where
the land was being enclosed for building mills. Unfinished threads of
walls were being fed upwards onto the moorland. Groups of men
worked at their furthest ends.

Spread below Mor and Mary was a dirty landscape spotted with cotton-spinning mills, made of brick. They were driven mostly by steam engines, and had tall slender chimneys, which even on Saturday afternoon were spouting little twists of smoke. The beam engines 'tump-tumped' like so many frogs. Collieries and grey ash banks were scattered amongst them. The old grey-stone church and the brick or stone buildings of the old town rose in the midst, with Oldham Edge behind.

They passed safely enough through the toll gate at Water Sheddings. By the time the pair reached Mumps, the great brick mills of Oldham were towering over them. The smoke was now bitter and scouring in their throats.

'That's Mr Lee's mill,' Mary said. 'Over there, that's Mr Hilton's.'

She knew the owners of all the factories and entertained him, not with information about their beam-engines, but about their mistresses.

They climbed up Yorkshire Street, towards the church. At the side of the churchyard was a three-storeyed inn, The George. Today was market day, the market taking place a hundred yards further on, where Yorkshire Street became High Street. The traders' brightly tented stalls, cream-coloured or striped, spilled down the cramped road, up to the door of The George, like a flotilla of small sailing-craft around a mother vessel.

It was now four o'clock in the afternoon and the market had reached its hour of ripeness. The earliest carts, the first pedlars and cottagers bringing their baskets and bundles, their one spare chicken in a box to sell at the roadside, their pieces of weaving rolled upon their heads, had been there since dawn. By now a pleasant spring afternoon helped those who had enjoyed a good day's trading to feel pleased with themselves. They offered generous beaming countenances from sunny doorways, or from the benches outside the public houses: The Eagle at the corner of Domingo Street, The Roe Buck and The Weavers' Arms. Those who had not done well were packing up early and going home, or were thinking of visiting a different fair, or of making things better or worse in the ale house, or they were hesitating over these things in the gentle collapse of the fair.

Mary led Mor into The George, through the grand doors of the kind of coaching inn which only a day previously he had assumed would spurn him. Under the fanlight, with a red symbolic 'rose of Lancashire' etched on it, they entered a lobby full of merchants, dressed in tall hats, in finest quality woollen suits, and in shining top boots. The yard, visible through a large polished window to the rear, was busy with grooms, well-brushed horses, and shining equipages.

'Why, there's Mr Sam Lees!' Mary exclaimed. 'He turned the old corn mill at Water'ead into a cotton mill, 'cos it already had a drop of water to drive a wheel. He's made a proper fortune out of it. The way 'e spends it! Oh, deary me!'

Mor was worried that they might be thrown out. Mary was no more upset by her exotic appearance than an actress would have been on braving the candlelight of a stage. Things altered when she came into a room. People left one group and went to another. They changed their conversations to take account of her, struggling for anchorages in an unexpected storm.

'Most of 'em are doing nothing but chase around the countryside for water-power,' she said. 'For sheds to rent, to put a bit o'machinery in. For some place 'idden up a wild valley, where they can ill-treat children until they kill 'em, and nobody'll know nor care, 'cos the local magistrate'll turn a blind eye to anything so long as it brings in trade and money. There's nothing to respect about 'em.'

They had no sooner left their hand-luggage with the porter, before a gentleman made his way towards them. He was small, and plump from a lifetime of feeding on beef, Mor thought enviously. The gentleman was himself like a rarely-done steak, red, juicy, and tender as a baby's bottom. Everything about him was baby-like; his gurgling laugh, and his glances of apprehensive dependence, like a child with an unreliable mother or nanny, towards Mary. For no reason that Mor could understand he was in a nervous sweat, which glistened upon him like warm grease. His forehead and cheeks were beaded with sweat. His dark thinning hair, and his palms when he waved them excitedly, shone with perspiration. His eyes were continually shifting, not only over the whore but also about the whole room, in a hungry fashion, with an appetite, whatever it was for, that never could be satisfied. His eyes seemed shaped by this nervous habit – they were narrow but elongated, as though the pupils from so much swivelling from side to side had elongated their sockets.

'Nibbles!' Mary exclaimed.

Unable to wait a moment for her gratification, it seemed, she held her arms out in willingness to clasp and hug him. He rolled into her embrace. In the press of the crowd, she bent his head to her bosom.

From where he was already lost, in the dark wool valleys of her cloak, between her breast and the pit of her arm, he mumbled:

'We're in luck, my dear . . .'

She choked his words, pressing his face into the cloth.

'My naughty little boy! What *have* you been up to?'

So this then was her business in Oldham: nothing more than a vulgar assignation with a factory owner! Mor felt he had been deceived and betrayed with lies. It had taken her only a second to throw herself into his arms. Mor had never seen a woman behave so passionately. Her whole mind and body were absorbed. She shut Mor out completely, as she gave away the riveted attention of her eyes and the swaying of her hips. Her long arms wrapped around the man's body. For a moment she seemed even to be offering the possibility of her pursed lips. He remembered what she had said in bed about being kissed on the mouth.

The man was struggling to be free, lest he choke, lest he look too undignified before his colleagues.

'Look, Mary . . .'

'My child, my babe in arms! . . . There, there . . .'

These were the very words she had used to Mor. He felt himself thrown into a horrible pit. This was what it meant to associate with a whore; inconstancy, betrayal, and lies. He had not allowed for this and he could not bear it. He hated this stranger. He loathed him.

Now Nibbles had recovered his head from the folds of Mary's clothes and was caressing her shoulder, first with his light, podgy, butterfly of a hand, then with his lips, possessively and familiarly. Yet his eyes were drawn towards her thighs and ankles. He pulled away, to look down at her feet. Then he returned with his lips pursed, aiming at Mary's mouth.

'Nibbles, this is Oliver,' she introduced Mor. 'Call him Oli.'

Both Nibbles and Mor gave Mary a surprised look.

'But we've urgent matters to talk about,' Nibbles said. 'We must be private.'

'It's all right. Oli's my brother. You can trust 'im same as me, no different. Oliver Wylde. Oli's in trading. 'E's taking his piece to sell in Manchester 'cos there's no business left in Yorkshire. It's the fault o' them Luddites. Oli, this is my friend, Mr Emanuel Burton.'

Mor offered his hand, but Nibbles wasn't interested.

'Are we to take tea?' Mary asked lightly.

Frustrated of his kiss, Nibbles led them towards a table, one that was neither too public nor too private to attract attention. He bounced ahead like an infant in front of its mother or nanny, adventurous but staying within reach of protective arms, every now and again looking back for approval. They became seated. Nibbles must have felt more secure now. Changing from being an infant, he put on a display of being a worldly man, calling the servant.

'We'll have our tea, and then we must retire privately to talk business,' he said, briskly.

'Nibbles,' she softly answered.

Smells like a pox-doctor's clerk, she thought.

'Oliver, Mr Burton is a most heminent cotton goods manufacturer of Middleton, what 'as at last installed ingenious steam machinery to drive his looms despite the opposition of obstinate workmen. That takes bravery, p'raps more bravery than dying useless in the Duke of Wellington's wars, Oli!'

'Oh, I hardly think so.'

Nibbles was blushing.

'Don't be modest.'

Mary spoke mock-sharply, but was stroking Mr Burton's thigh, his arms, and lingering on his hand. She braved his cheek now and again, though it made him quite irritable, in front of his colleagues and her 'brother'. By turns he was baby-soft in her arms, then he played the stern captain of industry. Mor was choking, but as the brother of a prostitute, he could hardly be possessive.

When the servant girl had left, Mary confidently poured the tea and said, 'I'll tell you something, Oli, about Mr Burton if it won't make him blush. 'E's the best boy, I mean the best man, I ever 'ad. 'Onest, Oli, he was the one learned me what love can mean. I don't know 'ow he does it.'

'Oh, come, Mary. You can't really say . . . I always thought . . .'

Mr Burton's shifting eyes, Mor noticed with pain, drifted constantly towards Mary's legs, which she was displaying beyond the edge of the table.

'Ah, but it's your feelings what a lady appreciates, Nibbles. You're so sensitive. Wouldn't I be the one to know? You're not a brute like some and it does charm a lady into a swoon.' Her voice turned gentle. 'Oh, the words you say! I don't know where you were learned 'em all. You're a poet.'

Mary talked loudly again – too loudly, at least for Mr Burton, already embarrassed by Mor's presence. She could be heard at the next table.

'Oli, this is the gentleman what I told you could read out the Earl of Rochester's poems, reciting 'em beautiful. Beautiful!'

'You're interested in verses, sir?' Mor asked.

Mr Burton failed to get a word in.

'You see 'ow I have to talk about you, Nibbles? . . . Do you like my new boots? They're green.'

She was smiling at them, while he gurgled.

'And I've a new garter . . .'

She was lifting her hem.

'You can kiss it later,' she whispered, as if not wanting Mor to overhear. 'And me green boots. They could do with a *clean* from someone. A special privilege for you, Nibbles, if you're good. Oh, my breast 'eaves for you. My poor maternal 'eart's too soft and I can't help myself, but maybe that's not too bad a failing. Feel it! Put your 'and there, Nibbles. You're my favourite of all my naughty boys, as I always said. It's because you're a poet yourself, I always said so. You say things lovely and it shows in the way you treat a lady and make her feel. And the things you can do with your hands . . . Oh my! Maybe I'm the one that appreciates it more than anyone, that's why I say a soft 'eart's not too monstrous a failing, is it? Nibbles, shouldn't I be the one to know?'

'Yes, you should, but . . .'

'Well, then . . . such a sensitive, brave boy!'

Mary cooed, with doting eyes, apparently amazed by him.

'You can't mean it?'

'Oh, I do, I do!'

Mr Burton's blush deepened.

'So 'ow's 'Arriet then?' Mary asked sharply.

'Harriet?'

'Now then, Nibbles, you naughty boy, I'll 'ave to smack your bottom, and choose someone else to clean me boots. Me daughter, 'Arriet.'

'Yes, of course! Your daughter.'

He continued to blush, trying to escape the role she cast him into, yet finding himself, for all his struggles, locked in the trap of his own secret nature.

'How is she? Still getting good reports for her 'arpsichord, is she? . . . Ooh, are we 'aving cakes an' all? Sweetmeats! That's what I call a tea.'

Mary started gobbling and Mor followed suit. Mr Burton waited for the servant to leave.

'Her studies are expensive, you know, and my fortune is not so great as all that.'

Mary had not seen her daughter for eight years and in her mind rose a picture of a slender angelic creature in a pretty frock with bright eyes and washed curls. She spluttered cake over the table.

'Now'n'Nibbles!'

'My father and I have so many problems. The operatives object mightily to steam looms and spinning machinery, which I am quite at a loss to understand. I have wagered a thousand guineas, *a thousand guineas*, think how far that would go in your purse, that with the aid of steam I am able to spin out a hundred and sixty miles of thread from a mere one pound weight of raw cotton. I love a sporting offer. But what happens the moment I am about to find a taker? I am forced to withdraw, by insubordinate operatives who would smash my machinery.'

'We can't allow ourselves to be 'indered by the malicious opponents of progress, can we, Nibbles? Look at Oli and me. I told you 'e's in the weaving business, trading. Fleeing from those same insibord'nat' op'ratives, them desperate men, what 'ave destroyed the trade in Yorkshire. Shame! We 'ave walked all over them moors to see you, for nothing'd stop us in *our* purpose. My boots could do with a *very special* cleaning and polishing later, after the effort we 'ave made. If I was you I'd get the soldiers to bayonet them insibordinat' op'ratives. Where's my brave boy, then? "*Bang bang bang*", them naughty boys is dead! A brave boy like you can do anything he wants. It's poor Nanny what's helpless. 'Elpless before rude nature. But a big boy like you . . .' She paused. 'I'm thinking of taking 'Arriet away with me to Bristol . . .

'*Bristol*,' she repeated.

His face collapsed again.

'An education's expensive . . .'

'To *Bristol*. I'll come to Park Mount and get 'er. A tobacco slaver who lives on White Ladies Row wants me. I'm sorry to say, it's a long way to Bristol. He won't let me come back to give Nibbles what only I can give 'im, I know that. Thomas is that kind of man. Determined. He knows 'is own mind.'

She had taken her hand off Mr Burton.

'There's no need to decide precipitately.'

'P'raps I should smack your bottom.'

Mor tried not to smirk.

'If we could wait . . . talk this matter through? At this precise moment in time, perhaps we could take a less expedient view . . .'

'My gentleman's taking ship for Africa on the spring tide, only waiting for the moon, 'e tells me. What else can I do than go with him? What chances else 'as a poor woman got? If 'Arriet and me go with 'im, 'e might decide not to bring us back to these shores again.'

'I'm sure we can arrange something.'

'I'll 'ave to come round for 'er, to Park Mount. I can't be sure when I can come, so if your wife's at 'ome . . .'

Mr Burton was sweating.

'I think at this moment in time we should . . .'

''Ow's 'er French?'

'Capital, I believe . . .'

'I think nothing's more important than French and the 'arpsichord for seeing a lady through life. It'll open all doors. Shouldn't I know?'

Mr Burton found himself once more enjoying Mary's hands. Perhaps he was forgiven. But, also, because of her silence he did not know if he was forgiven . . .

Mary left with Mr Burton for another part of the inn.

'I'll only be an hour. You take a look at the market if you get bored. I'll find you there. Don't worry.'

How could Mor not worry? He was suddenly alone with his thoughts, his bewilderment at where to look for Edwin, and his fear of what might be the outcome of his running away. He was worried about what he took to be suspicious eyes from all over the inn.

Fancy her thinking of calling me her 'brother'! he was thinking.

On a table nearby were newspapers and, before he left for the market, Mor grasped the opportunity to read his favourite newssheet, *The Leeds Mercury*.

He first of all opened the April 11th issue, which reported the execution of nine food-rioters at Caen, Normandy, with a comment that it demonstrated 'the leniency shown under the British Constitution towards food rioters and machine-breakers, compared with the sanguinary courts of France'. In the current edition, Mor read of riots in Manchester where a baker's shop was raided; in Barnsley against the high price of potatoes; in Sheffield where workmen 'came in a body' to the corn market and attacked the potato-dealers before destroying 'fire-locks, drums, uniforms and banners at the local militia's armaments-depository'; in Stockport where machinery for making calico shirting was destroyed and the manufacturer's house set on fire; in the market at Carlisle where a pregnant young woman 'was shot dead on the spot' by the soldiers; in Cornwall where the miners at Truro had 'risen' and compelled the market-traders to sign an agreement to sell wheat at no more than 30 shillings per bushel; and in Ireland where in County Cork three thousand people assembled to burn down a starch factory because it made use of potatoes that they, who were starving, could have eaten.

So Crawshaw, hearing the mood of cropping shops and inns, carrying inspiration from one group to another, had been right in this at least – twenty or thirty places in the north had risen in the week since the Rawfolds raid, which had ignited the Revolution. Mor felt no doubt about it. Where was there not a state of riot? Before he returned to Lady Well, it would have happened. He would go back to his home on a triumphal cart. He read in *The Mercury* that the reward for the capture of machine-breakers had risen since March from one hundred to a thousand guineas. But it would be ministers, generals and judges who would be hung. Somewhere, sometime, in the next few days, Mor would look through a window, down a street, or from the top of a hill, and see the revolutionary people of England *moving*. Who would be their leader? Never mind for now. Sir Francis Burdett, perhaps? George Mellor, the cropper from Huddersfield? Henry Brougham? Someone would appear. Some King Ludd. Mor was inwardly shaking with excitement. He could hardly believe that such momentous information could be conveyed on a newssheet, on the same pages as 'Wanted to rent, a cotton mill, with or without machinery', an advertisement for 'Elliots' lozenges for destroying worms and purifying the body after measles', and another announcing 'Mrs Pearce respectfully requests to acquaint the nobility and gentry of her arrival at Mrs Jackson's, shoemaker, with her celebrated and highly distinguished stays . . .'

Mor felt eyes piercing the newssheet. He looked up to find a soldier, glassy-eyed, motionless, staring at him as if he had been doing so for quite a while.

'What are you reading about?' the soldier asked, in the blunt manner of one who, because of the blood he had shed, had earned the right to say what he liked to anyone, and who regarded reading as a weakness.

Before Mor could answer, 'I cannot read,' the soldier boasted. 'I don't need to 'cos I expect it's all about riots and machine-breakers and I can see with my own two eyes what's going on with them, long afore the newspapers is appre'ended of the matter. You see that mud what's on my boots? Do you see it?'

The soldier was determined that Mor should take a good look at his boots.

'You look as though you've been . . .'

'That's splashings from my ride hot-foot from Huddersfield today, bringing intelligence to some senior officers, consulting in a room of this very inn. I was on duty at the court martial of the soldier, I cannot name him "comrade", who refused to defend the Rawfold's mill. The coward refused to use his musket, "Because I might hit some of my brothers," says the miserable traitor. I ask you! He 'ad been tampered with by the Ludds, o' course – a common weakness of our soldiery, so it has to be punished 'eavy, don't it? A deadly silence fell on the court as the sentence was pronounced. Three 'undred lashes! He won't survive the 'alf of it; which is as well, for the sentence is to be carried out in public at the scene of the crime itself, Tuesday next, because of the disgrace. Scum of the earth is Ludds and revolutionaries, ain't they? What do you think? They did a raid at Lady Well on Thursday night. That's before it gets in your newspaper. Did you know about that?'

'I didn't know, sir, no. I'm not interested in politics.'

'Not interested in politics but you're reading a newspaper . . . ? You look scared, sir. If you're fearful at what we do to them Ludds, you should learn of 'ow we treated 'em in Spain!'

The more ignorant people are, the more they talk like the newspapers, whether they read them or not, Mor thought. How do they pick up the phrases? The soldier shouted more loudly because he saw that the people of the inn, especially the ladies, gave him indulgent smiles. The inn-servant was laughing, nodding, and showing her willingness to attend one of our 'brave defenders'.

'I'm freshly posted back from Spain. I've travelled, I can tell you, seen all sorts. They're just like Ludds over there, them diegos – nothing but a load of scum. We call 'em diegos 'cos that's what they all say, when you ask them their name. "Diego, Diego!" That's all they say. I've seen how they live. O' course, we soldiers dwell in mud 'alf the time, but that's different. We're building an empire. But them diegos! Them Jimmies! Well! I tell you what, me and my colleagues strung one up on a tree, one of them "olives", and without anything over his face, so you could see it swell and the eyes of 'im pop out of his head. I sat down and scratched my noddle and calmly started thinking. I thought, "That's war, my fine fellow, and it's a shame for you, as you're another human being same as myself, but you should 'ave told us where your brothers was 'id. We'll find them in any case, in the end. We 'as to string you up before we can have a Christian empire, and that's a benefit, surely, to the 'ole of human kind, even if you, swinging up there, my fine Papist, cannot see it."'

Discoursing now to the whole appreciative company, he continued, 'I've seen 'em garrotting priests for being Papists. That's when you twist a rope round their neck so tight that their eyes pop out. They ain't Christians, that lot, are they? Ugh! Barbarians, with their incense smelling. So they deserve it. I've seen more than once the corpses of an 'ole village piled on the ground. They paint the 'ouses white down there, and the blood was splashed red as roses on the walls. It's what they should do to these Luddites.'

One of the gentlemen who had been listening strolled towards them, leaving the smiling company of ladies who had encouraged him to it.

'I admire your sentiments, sir! I heard all you had to say upon the subject of our distressed unhappy land, and if you are not a reader of the newspapers, you have certainly acquired a happy turn of phrase . . .'

'Just listening, sir, just listening to others, 'ow they speak.'

'And a laugh so unshadowed it's a tonic to the heart. Clearly the blood of true Englishmen still courses through the veins of our soldiery. And I hope you receive promotion for it.'

'Thank you, sir. I am but a poor corporal freshly posted home from Spain and looking to settle in England, 'aving serious intentions. Perhaps take a little farm and find me a strong wife to look after the poultry and the dairy. Someone quiet. I'm not particular 'bout 'aving to break 'er in for myself. One that's p'raps been a lady's servant and knows about the finer things in life that 'ave escaped my attention in my rough soldier's life. That wouldn't be a bad fate for a maid, would it? . . .'

Mor was hurriedly getting up and leaving.

''Ere, where're you going to? Where're you going? I thought we'd 'ave a conversation. No need to be like that!' The soldier turned to the gentleman. 'This is a funny one! A comical turn . . . reads *newspapers* and 'as nothing to say for *himself*.'

But Mor had left.

⑧

April 18th–20th

After Mor had last seen Mary, she had been led by Mr Burton down a passageway guarded by two privates with muskets, and into a wing of the inn that was entirely occupied by soldiers. He took her into a room as bare and unloved as a cell, with no more than a scratched table, several rickety chairs, a pack of cards on the windowsill and the soldiers' much-used counters for gambling. Tobacco smoke staled the atmosphere. In its bareness, it felt ominous.

'Why did you bring your brother with you?'

'I told you, 'e's going to Manchester with 'is cloth.'

'He hardly said a word.'

'Quiet. I'm the noisy one in our family.'

'Mm. You get up to some strange business, Mary.'

'Am I the only one? What's this new thing you've brought me to Oldham for, Nibbles? A friend of yours to be initiated into the Mysteries? I'm not interested. I want to know 'ow 'Arriet is.'

'There's to be a meeting of radicals and machine-breakers at Dean Moor near Manchester tomorrow.'

'You mean they're not going to church? I'm surprised at 'em.'

'I'd like you to be present at that meeting.'

'And report to you what's going on? It'd be more than my life's worth.'

'I already know what's "going on", as you so felicitously express it.'

'Eh?'

'They'll be discussing their plans to destroy my mills and steam machinery, and if they should succeed in doing so I would not be insured against the loss, it being an act of "riot and civil commotion". I'd be reduced to beggary, Mary. Think what would happen to Harriet then – not to mention all your little presents. I want to take no chances. I want you firstly to discover what their plans are, but, much more important than that, I want you to use your fullest charms on the general who is to be in charge of the operation in the north. General Maitland has arrived to make a secret reconnoitre before he takes up his posting. Don't say anything about his being here, but use your charms on him, this evening if possible and certainly not later than tomorrow after the Dean Moor meeting, and persuade him to take aggressive steps to forestall attacks upon my mills.'

'General Maitland? Oh, no, I couldn't go before him! Who is 'e? Where's my indispensable? I'm going. That's more than I dare . . .' She paused, examining him. 'What's it worth?'

'It's worth, to you, thirty pounds.'

She shivered.

'This is a cold shop, this place. It gives me the shivers. Fifty, Nibbles. Not a penny less than fifty. It's a dirty business and I don't know as I'd enjoy this General Maitland's speciality, what's 'e like? 'E might want to do something that'll end me in the Rochdale Canal, and I've my daughter to think of.'

'I'll give you thirty pounds now and twenty when the military effectively forestalls any risks to my mills and machinery. There's no need to be afraid. The general has already expressed his interest in meeting you.'

'What's this general like?'

'I can assure you there's nothing unusual . . .'

'Come on, you can't fool me, an aristocratic officer wouldn't be looking for an old scarred hag like me unless I satisfied 'is speciality. He'd 'ave a virgin girl. What's 'e want?'

'Nothing you can't satisfy. You'll soften him, I'm sure. He's a stern man, regarded by his colleagues as eccentric, but if you do as he wishes I know he'll treat you kindly.'

'And if I don't I'll end up in a sack at the bottom of the canal. And maybe also if I do. I know 'is sort, the "eccentric" kind. Give me the thirty pounds now, then.'

Mr Burton was opening his wallet.

'If I end up in the canal, I'll go down shouting lots of things about you, Nibbles, so you be careful, too. And I'll need my coiffure attended.'

'How did you guess?' asked Mr Burton, surprised.

She didn't answer that.

'I'm too cheap with my prices, that's my trouble,' she said.

He had closed his wallet and the money lay on the table. At least with him she did not need to count it, and she scooped it away.

Apparently Mr Burton was prepared for a hairdresser. He went to the door and called out, whereupon one, judging by his manner, accustomed to lady clients, appeared in minutes with his equipment. He busied himself, hastily in the repugnant room. Mary and Mr Burton argued; he wanted her hair one way, she insisted it be raised under a head-band, to display curls at the nape of her neck.

'I know what I'm talking about, Nibbles.'

She was very insistent and Mr Burton, growing sweaty again as he anticipated his interview with the general, gave way.

A cavalry sergeant interrupted them.

'You ready for King Tom, sir?'

He conducted them up a flight of stairs, along further corridors, towards a room on a remote top floor.

'Oh, I don't think I can face up to a general, Nibbles. That's a very superior officer. Oh no . . . Do you think the fierce general will like me? I'm only a poor timid woman. I'm scared. If 'e's new 'ere, who knows what he'll be like? I'd got used to old Chippendale, I could manage 'im.'

'Don't worry, my dear . . .'

'Don't worry, don't worry,' she mimicked. 'They've been telling me, "Don't worry," since I was born. They'll be saying it when I mount the scaffold.'

''E's a character is King Tom Maitland,' interrupted the sergeant. 'Full of surprises. After the French Revolution 'e led a secret expedition for the Royalists what somehow ended up in America and the West Indies. He was in San Domingo and surrendered Port-au-Prince to the black slave leader Toussaint L'Ouverture. Don't remind 'im of that, by the way. A sore spot. Served on both sides of the world 'as King Tom. Calcutta and Madras, Commander of Ceylon, then in the West Indies.'

The sergeant clicked to attention and swung open a door, himself waiting outside, with very nearly a smile.

The room was one designed for male activities of the officer or merchant class; board meetings, smoking, or sophisticated cards. Thick wood-panels and a layer of green baize on the door ominously sealed off the noises of the inn. It was lavish in materials, but bare of ornament. The only thing on the walls was a mirror, opposite the leather armchair in which General Maitland awaited.

Even during interviews and meetings, he liked to observe his similarity to the Duke of Wellington. There was around his jaw the same relaxed droop of flesh, like the haunches of a contented bull in a field – the Taurean features of a commander who has occupied his territory. Also similar, in his upper face was the contrary expression of big, dark, alert eyes, raised eyebrows and a brisk haircut, signifying the other half of a soldier's nature; the readiness to be up and off, to take advantage and use initiative.

The whore could see that the course of the interview had been fixed before they came in. Mr Burton collapsed into the only chair available, mopping his scarlet brow, leaving the prostitute standing where she could be surveyed and embarrassed in centre stage.

Like a pig brought into a ring, Mary thought.

Burton stared at the bowed head of the general, willing him to take approving notice of the prize he had brought.

Maitland paid no attention, neither to Mr Burton nor to the whore. He was one who made tactical use of remaining mute. When speech might be expected of him, he would maintain a silence of such unnerving power that people looked at him as if he had in fact spoken and said something profound, or alarming. Through awesome silence he communicated what was deeper than words: something threatening.

The whore stood, not daring to speak and slowly, not realising that she was doing it, scratching her face. Emanuel mopped his brow, even afraid to pant and blow in his usual manner. He was disturbed by the feeling, often conveyed by military men, that they are the cream of life, with a right to the best of everything. After all, real power, the command of men, was at the general's elbow.

They could hear from outside the calls of the market, the cries that in this situation seemed absurd: obscenities they dared not take notice of, and jokes at which they were afraid to laugh.

The general at last looked up.

'Have a brandy,' he snapped at Mr Burton.

He stared at Mr Burton's soft hands around the glass.

'I'll have one, too.'

He next stared at Mary. He did not return her smile. She was still scratching herself.

'You should have that face of yours attended to by an apothecary.'

'It's nothing, sir. It's an itch that all the ladies get. Nothing but an itch, sir.'

'It'll land you in the surgeon's hands, you mark my words. You use lead, don't you?'

'Yes, sir.'

'Come here.'

She stepped forward.

'Open your mouth.'

She did so. With his fingers he pushed back her lips.

'There's a blue line on your gum. You know what that means, don't you? Do you know what lead poisoning does to you?'

'No, sir.'

'Paralysis. Can't digest. Bowels closed. Your skin'll go grey. You'll die a terrible death. And do you know what comes of that mercury rouge that you use?'

'No, sir. We can't afford to care, sir . . .'

'Stomatitis. No one'll go near you because of your bad breath, and that'll be a blessing for my men, won't it? Madness. Every woman who uses mercuric sulphide goes a bit strange – it's the coming madness. Like the hatters ensconced in this drab and lunatic town. It's the mercury they use in their trade. You're a bit of a strange case already, aren't you? You'll get the tremors. Your hands are shaking now.'

'No, sir, that's because I'm . . .'

'You women would be well advised to pay a visit to a Bethlehem before you commence your business. Why don't you use natural cosmetics? That's what the ladies of London and Edinburgh are turning to these days. Sour milk or horse-radish makes a fair skin, I believe. Lemon is good too. You could use chalk as a whitener instead of lead, and cochineal for a rouge. That's what a lady should do.'

'They're expensive. We can't get them. We don't think they're as good as the old way, sir.'

'The only cure for you now, madam, is to drink sulphuric acid, two and a half ounces to a gallon of water, like they give to the lead-miners of Derbyshire. Otherwise you can count yourself a dead woman.

'You see what I have to concern myself with, Burton? I have to be a whore doctor, otherwise my men are riddled with diseases. Sedition is as rife amongst them as a disease, already.

'Which brings us to the subject of your letter, doesn't it? Our men are, as you say, "singularly ineffective in arresting the troublemakers" in your mills. Something is going wrong, as you say. What is it, then? Now I'm here, or all but here, in a manner of speaking, and bringing another seven thousand men along with me, what shall I do? Do you think we might become more effective through erecting communal barracks for the soldiers, instead of quartering them around the inns of the countryside? In barracks they would be safely away from the attention of disaffected radicals and whores. Perhaps Mr Pitt, in not giving Oldham a barracks, made a mistake.'

Mary smiled, but dared not laugh openly.

'Lodged in public houses, my soldiers come into daily contact with the corrupting populace. Are you aware of what happened recently in the defence of Mr Cartwright's Mill at Rawfolds in Huddersfield? A disaffected private refused to "fire upon my fellow countrymen", as he put it, and he has perforce to be delivered up to an exemplary sentence, to a vicious flogging. None of us wants to hand out that sort of punishment anymore, but one has to put this business to an end. It is most distasteful, Burton, firing at one's own countrymen when there are enemies abroad to be shot at.'

'It seems to me, General, that rather than putting ourselves to the expense of erecting permanent buildings for a temporary force . . .'

'Temporary force!' The general slapped his palm upon the table. 'I wish it was, but it seems to me that as usual in these circumstances we bring in a few soldiers for a week or two but are soon compelled to pour in more and more troops and establish a garrison for a lifetime. Look what we have to do in Ireland. In India. In the West Indies. As if you don't know we've a war to fight overseas. What will happen to your Lancashire if we lose our battles against Napoleon? You are sapping our strength.'

'We are threatened with *Revolution*, General. There will be no point in fighting Napoleon, if we are to have a Bastille day at home.'

'I'm most annoyed with you, Burton. You and all your kind. But never mind! Never mind!' The impatient general clapped his hands, and it sounded like gunshots. 'Tell me more about your proposal, here. It sounds most interesting. You suggest that this woman informs us about the forthcoming meeting at Dean Moor.'

'Dean Moor is near Manchester . . .'

'I know where Dean Moor is,' General Maitland answered, testily.

Mr Burton screwed up his courage.

'I'd like to learn the scale and date of the planned attack, an estimate of how much military assistance will therefore be necessary, and how much can be counted on, to support my own tiny band of sixteen bold defenders of my mill. Chippendale, our Captain of Militia, suggested I put it to you.'

After the effort of this bold speech, the manufacturer slumped in his chair.

'Ah, yes, you yourself at least are trying. I'll give you credit for that, instead of always shouting out for cavalry – you who have never seen what a cavalry charge does to its victims. Someone ought to show you mill-masters over the ground after a battle. Show you what you propose we do to your own countrymen. And you want this woman to apprise herself of the situation and persuade me to take the action you would like to see taken? Because I am fresh to Lancashire, you intend to be the first of the mill-owning brethren to come to me with your complaints? To influence me?'

'I'll tell you what the root of this matter is, Mr Burton. The price of food has trebled, whilst wages have fallen in the same ratio to that in which provisions have risen. What would you expect the weaver to do for his starving children? Lie down and die? Pay decent wages, Burton, you can afford it, and your devil, King Ludd, will be dead tomorrow. What you have done by bringing us into the northern counties is to leave us with the fear of an army rebellion on our hands, dammit! When my new force arrives there will be twelve thousand regular soldiers in the north. Plus militia. Wellington took only ten thousand to Spain. Yet what arrests do we make? The villagers are tight, they will tell us nothing. Children spit at the cavalry. We offer large rewards to starving people, but no one collects them. Pay proper wages, Burton, and you'll have no need of soldiery. It doesn't need a philosopher to see that. I speak only as a man of practical affairs, not as a democrat. For, by God, if I have to put a revolution down, I will.'

'In cases of civil commotion we have no insurance for our properties, that is why we need defence . . . cavalry.'

'You don't take in a thing that I say. Why don't you steady yourself with a drink at the bar, Burton? Whilst I talk to the woman.'

Mary wanted to cheer.

General Maitland paused.

'What are you waiting for?'

The general behaved as if the lowly man of commerce had already left and he concentrated upon pouring, for himself only, another glass of brandy.

When Burton had gone from the room, the general put his hands behind his head, restfully, and smiled at Mary.

'He's not much of a man, is he, that Burton?' she said, smiling back. 'Give us a drink. I've walked it all the way.'

'A wet and dismal journey too, I'll be bound. This is a dreary country. I'm used to hot places. I'd die of rheumatism if I stayed here long, so I intend it to be a short posting. You mark my words, we'll be hanging them for Christmas. Where's the nearest spa?'

'That at Upper Spout's quite good . . .'

'Where?'

'I don't suppose it'll do for you. It's just a sulphur spring coming out o' the ground.'

'That they decorate with flowers on May Day. And cast spells?'

'Yes.'

'This is a barbaric part of England. I want somewhere where I can . . . dance. Where there are ladies. Decent young *men*, too. It'll be Buxton or Harrogate, I suppose. I'll start off my headquarters in Manchester. If this business takes more than a month, I'll move to Buxton. I'll be damned if I'm staying in this wild, wet place. It'd kill me.'

Mary helped herself to a drink, using Mr Burton's emptied glass. She went round the table and sat upon the general's knee, carefully giving him the opportunity to fondle the curls at the base of her neck. He liked that, she knew.

'King Tom!' she murmured.

'How's Mrs Rawdon? Has she brought all of her establishment northwards with her?'

'Only some of it. A few of the girls. Not all our implements. Imagine *them* dropping off a cart.'

King Tom laughed.

'Not 'er 'arpsichord neither. I remember how you used to play Clem . . . Clem . . .'

'Clementi? Mozart?'

'When you came to us in London.'

'Delightful pieces, some of 'em.'

'All the girls loved it. We all remember.'

King Tom smiled at himself in the mirror. Mary filled his glass, while he hung onto her curls. He sipped and relaxed, from time to time looking at his reflection.

'I'm glad you sent us up 'ere. Back 'ome,' she said.

'My force will be here soon for you. Have you found anything out for us, yet?'

'I've only 'ad a few weeks, General! I 'eard that someone 'ad damned the King. The Ludds threw a corporal in the Rochdale Canal, 'cos 'e wouldn't join with machine-breakers. I don't think 'e 'ad any more of a mind to join 'em when 'e came out, than when they threw 'im in.'

'You have reported the matter?'

'I think 'is officer already knew.'

'These Luddites travel. Our intelligence is that a great deal of trouble spreads outwards from Yorkshire. That's why you're based there. You should have found out something.'

'I'm trying.'

'Well, you can forget about going to Dean Moor to satisfy Burton. I don't want you there, attracting attention, Mary The Scar. I've my own men amongst the rebels to play their part in their decision-making. I want from you something that I know you're good at. You are to provoke a few scenes when they raid Burton's Mill. They'll probably decide to go there on Monday. It'll certainly be next week. No matter what Burton thinks or expects, there won't be any soldiers to defend it, but we'll turn up afterwards. These damned machine-breakers have had it their own way for six months now, it's worth sacrificing Burton's to catch them. If they put it out of commission, we might even find the working folk themselves turning against the machine-wreckers, for taking away their employment. We'll come afterwards and have an excuse to hang a few of the ringleaders. Then we may all go home. My commission will be over before it's properly started. That's my plan. Your business is to provoke 'em to as much damage as you can make 'em do. Make sure they do enough damage . . .'

'Or I'll end up in a sack in the canal.'

'We could hang you.'

When she didn't laugh, but looked frightened, 'Forgive me my humour,' he added. 'But I *shall* have my own way, Mary, and quickly. You know that. As well as a report on you from a mason about a child buried in a well, there's cutlery, watches, and clothing you've stolen over the years. You'll go too far with it one of these days, you lunatic woman. The civil authorities will catch you, and it'll be too much for us to save you. You'll be swinging outside Lancaster Castle, and not even have the good fortune to die of paralysis and insanity in a bed in the Bethlehem Hospital. Mrs Rawdon's not expecting you back, is she?'

'I've cleared it with 'er already. I knew you'd want me for something. But I need a safe and secret place to live in hereabouts, General. With my brother. I can't be a "Luddite" and live in a soldiers' whore-house, can I? I need a place, and my things delivered there tonight. They're with the porter at the moment. Also I'll be 'aving a trunk 'ere soon, I'd be obliged if you'll send it on with a big strong lad.'

'Leave your face alone, madam! I tell you, that face of yours will land you on a surgeon's dissecting table. According to our reports, you're twenty-four years of age. You look thirty.'

She left off scratching her cheek and looked at the general with moist serious eyes.

'Please promise me 'e'll be safe.'

'Who?'

'My brother.'

'Why? What side of the law is your brother on? Thief? Pimp? Poacher? Murderer?'

'It's not that. We need to stay together. He's ill, and needs me. The surgeon says he 'asn't long to live. His 'eart is suffering. We can't be parted. Promise me we'll be left safely together.'

She knelt and rested her cheek against his thigh.

'Promise me!'

The general carefully filled Mary's glass to the brim.

'Bottoms up,' he said and watched her raise the glass, amused to observe whether or not her hand was shaking.

'I promise. We're not interested in him, but in how you behave yourself. We'll find you a hovel to hide in.'

Her hand was steady.

His thick fingers were raking through her curls. They began to reach into her clothing.

'Mmm . . .'

'You're a *man*, King Tom. So when are you wanting me to come to you again?'

'After the raid. Make sure you keep in touch. We don't want any of your disappearing tricks. You keep going at your business. Make sure you sleep with as many as you can. Non-commissioned officers especially. Or rather, make sure you *don't* sleep.' The general chuckled. 'This is an important time coming now. Do you understand me? We'll pay you next time we see you.'

'Promise me another thing,' she said.

'Something else?'

'If your soldiers find a child, a boy of nine, wandering the hills and places, saying he's looking for Liverpool, will you tell me? Name of Edwin Greave. From Lady Well.'

Mor wandered around the market for a while, until he was brought up suddenly. Twenty yards away, head and shoulders above the crowd, was Mary, alone, her back to him as she strolled amongst the stalls, baskets and litter of the dishevelled market. She emanated such a huge personal calm that it made him think of a big quiet wave, moving through a sea of choppy little ones.

The sun was setting at the end of each alley-way and street, through a sky of soap and roses. It was an artificial-looking gaudiness, against which Mary's exotic appearance was not out of place. He saw that her hair had been newly fashioned in a high pile of ringlets. For him? Gratitude and joy made him want to rush up and kiss her.

He saw her take an apple from a stall and, as calmly as she did everything, without paying for it she slipped it into her dress. His impulse to kiss her vanished and his panicking eyes darted from her to the stall-holder.

Fortunately, this person was staring, with simple-minded engrossment and pleasure, her hands lapped comfortably under her apron, at a scene on the other side of the street. A mare was being sold by a gypsy and a rich farmer in a blue cut-away jacket and top-boots had drawn open its mouth to examine its teeth.

Mor secretively, with fear and shame, followed ten yards behind. The next stall at which Mary paused was one selling lace. Mats and handkerchiefs were strung under an awning and displayed on tables. The stall-owner was occupied in packing away his goods. Mary took a lace mat and slipped this, too, into her clothes. It was only Mor who looked anxiously towards the stall-holder – Mary did not bother to glance at him.

Further on she collected a pair of shoes.

She also surveyed the passing men, showing a bold interest in the bulges of their trousers. A habit? Surely, after what she had said about love, it must be no more than that. Some of them gave her a brief touch, as they went by. They continued to laugh and make jokes about the whore as they passed Mor.

In fear and panic he ran towards her, wanting to say so much, and yet speechless, his mouth stopped by the vision of the pair of them swinging on a gallows. When he caught up with her, she smiled and gave him an apple. He could not eat it. He felt that it would choke him. She did not seem to notice.

'I found a room,' she told him sweetly.

'Stolen?' he said viciously. 'Or is it a gift from Mr Burton?'

Her manner changed completely, to that of one who has been needlessly hurt.

'People owe me favours. Stolen from no one. I'm not a . . .'

She was drowning, struggling to explain the inexplicable, with tears in her eyes . . .

'Filthy Luddite.'

It was too late to bite off her tongue.

It numbed him. He even lost interest in looking out for pursuers.

'I thought you believed in our cause,' he croaked.

She tossed her head of new curls. They walked in silence. She had hardened herself with a shell of self-righteousness. She had that cutting, confident smile of a woman who is used to getting the better of men, with her sharp tongue and the situations that she creates.

Excited noisy deals were taking place on either hand. Pigs were squealing, hens squawking, people laughing, yet Mor's and Mary's seemed the only lonely steps in an emptied universe. He longed to take a leap off this sterile, cold planet that they now inhabited, and join those others, but their argument stuck to them like a shipwright's glue.

She longed to remove the stain of her words. She tried to placate him.

''Tis a nice little room in a cellar. It belongs to a cobbler who must leave it, if you must know, because he 'as been spying for His Majesty's forces and 'as now been found out by some radicals who will send 'im to 'is Maker when they catch 'im. It 'asn't anything to do with Mr Burton, More Grief. It 'as entrances on different streets, so we'll be safe, and not get trapped.'

He wondered how he could ever disentangle her lies from the truth.

She stopped in her tracks so suddenly that a boy with a tray of loaves ran into her.

'I believe you're jealous!' She felt suddenly hotter. 'You can't be jealous with a whore!'

She pulled a sheet of paper from the caverns of her underclothes.

'*Read it*. Go on, it's a letter from Emanuel Burton to myself.'

He read. 'I dream of when I shall draw your shift from the snowy mounds of your breasts! – Your skin softer than the down of swans and scented like the spices of India! – Your eyes that dart a million piercing

213

arrows! – I think of you as a being of another order! – As a goddess! – I worship you with every breath! – As the living sun!'

He could read no further.

'That's what Mr Burton thinks of me.'

'You said you couldn't read.'

'I didn't need to. He sat on my bed and read it aloud to me, 'bout half a dozen times, then 'e give it me to keep. It means nothing, nothing at all. Listen! 'E carries everywhere a pocket guide to the pleasure gardens and gin palaces of London. It 'as a French letter tucked into the fly-leaf and a chapter of precautions 'ow to avoid syphilis and paralysis of the insane. But that means nothing either. Why? 'Cos he never comes anywhere near me. He can't get it up! 'E can't do nothing at all, except with 'is tongue. And that ain't no fun for me, not the way 'e does it. He told me that the reason was, when 'e was a child he used to have a nursemaid what sucked him to send him to sleep and ever since then an erect cock makes 'im feel dozy. I don't believe a word of it myself, it's just excuses. However, the point is, you've nothing to fear from *him*. But if you don't like using 'is money, of which 'e's got too much and, as you said yourself, has taken it from the sweat of the poor, then you can fuck off and get yourself hung instead. You should be grateful for what I does for you.'

Tears were in her eyes.

'I want a man with some boldness in his nature. It's a pity you was never a soldier.'

After all that she had said about the military! He looked at her in amazement.

'All right! But I was watching you at the farmer's stall – what about that?'

'Have a bite of apple, sweetheart,' she said, softly.

'I don't want it.'

'Why not?'

'It would . . .'

It would choke me.

'Why not?' she repeated in a maddening, victorious tone.

He wanted to believe that she was not a thief. What a misfortune it would be if he had accused her wrongly! He wavered.

'Why were you 'iding it?'

'I wasn't 'iding it.'

'Then why was it inside your clothes?'

214

'It wasn't in my clothes.'

'Then where've I seen you bring it out from, then?' he shouted.

His exasperation had the effect of calming her.

'A lady 'as to put her things somewhere, don't she?'

'You've a lace mat in there as well, and a pair of shoes.'

'What nonsense you talk, just because you're a poet.'

'Well, show me and prove your case.'

'Don't talk to me like a judge accusing a common whore.'

'I don't think you're a common whore!'

'That's how you behaves towards me.'

'No, I don't!'

He realised that she was talking much faster than he was so that he would not be able to keep up with her.

'Everyone treats me like a common whore,' she complained.

She was trying to sulk, but it wasn't natural or easy for her.

Her grip of her gown loosened and a pair of shoes fell upon the market ground. She snatched them up and slipped them under the arm that was away from him.

'Where are those from?'

'Where's what from?'

'Those shoes.'

'I 'aven't no shoes. Is it any business of yours what I does with my earnings? I'm nothing but a common whore anyway, why do you care?'

She was crying, but he didn't know whether to believe in her tears or not.

'You stole them,' he said grimly.

'I'm not a thief!'

'Can't you see how you're risking bringing us before the justices and deliberately courting the gallows?'

'Leave me to my whoring, then, if you don't have no stomach for nothing.'

He remembered that in the afternoon they had loved one another on a shelf of sunlight.

'You stole those shoes.'

'I didn't.'

'You did.'

'I didn't.'

'You did.'

'And you told me you was going to catch hares and trouts for us. So what's the difference? Left to you, I think we'll starve.'

'The difference is, to be secretive, not ask for the hangman to come and fetch you.'

A pause.

'I don't want the fucking shoes anyway. I don't need them. I've plenty of money!'

A pair of new shoes, whorish in design, flashed their over-statement of buckles and the fresh bright-yellow of their unsullied leather soles through the last light of the afternoon, as Mary flung them high across the market, anywhere so that they'd be away from her, over the heads of the crowd.

Why did she steal, if she was not short of money? He could not understand.

One shoe hit the base of a pyramid of turnips, which tumbled and destroyed some carefully built piles of potatoes, carrots, onions and leeks. The other shoe struck a fishmonger upon the shoulder.

'It's a riot! Lady Ludd's coming. It's a food riot!'

To the women who had been arguing with the store-holders about their prices, to the poor and hungry females who likely enough would be beaten by their husbands if they came home empty-handed, the flying shoes were the signal to commence battle. A housewife with the physical mould of an Irish navvy flung one of the fallen turnips. It struck the fishmonger again, this time upon the forehead. Frightened, he crouched behind his stall.

His cowardice inspired the women. Mary, grasping hold of this diversion, sprang to the head of the 'mob', leading them to tip offal and a barrel of salted herrings onto the fishmonger. None of the other stall-holders helped their comrade, in case it drew the fury of the women upon themselves. But, as with the fishmonger, cowardice did not help them. When one tried to sneak away to rouse the authorities, the women up-tipped him into his barrel of oats and nearly drowned him.

More and more women joined in the havoc. Mary and Mor in the lead, they advanced between the stalls. Cottons and calicoes were ripped into shreds. The women filled their baskets. One stuffed a couple of fish into her bosom. To add to the chaos, Mary let a crate of hens loose. She released some geese and sent them flapping through the fair. Finally she unfastened the cages of wild birds, letting surprised goldfinches and larks escape towards Oldham Edge and the moors, their wings, as they rose above the house-tops, glittering like glass.

At last a sniggering band of Oldham Volunteers arrived. But not even their captain could take the fighting of a market-full of women seriously. The soldiers were smiling, blowing kisses, and wishing that their own women would start riots and get vegetables, meat and fish, instead of 'robbing' their pay to feed themselves and bring up babies. Eventually they were inspired to make a brisk but good-humoured charge. 'Whoops!' 'Ooh!' 'Ooh, dear!' the soldiers yelled, trying to frighten but not harm nor arrest anyone.

'Don't worry,' Mary found the breath to say, as they all ran away.

Out of the dispersing crowd she led him uphill, through the back ways where the hand-looms clattered on the north side of the market, to a Baptist chapel on Oldham Edge. The front, facing south across the valley, was grandiose with columns, and had two entrances for the sexes. The rear was set without dignity into the bank. Mary went to the back where was a narrow yard between the chapel and the high wall holding the field. It was the site of the spring that filled the Baptists' tank; a spring at which Mor and Mary could refresh themselves. It was a hidden place, and indeed somewhere to be ashamed of, dark, greasy and filled with rubbish. It was shortly before nightfall and already darkness had gathered here, amongst the dripping ferns.

'I'm sorry for what I said about... about... I can't say it again... about the Luddites, More Grief.'

They embraced, as they washed themselves and drank the baptismal water. Her hair was falling out of its band. He noticed that where the henna was wearing away it showed black patches.

The spring also filled a trough for a row of cottages lower down. Going right round the building, they descended to them. Following a set of stone stairs, they sank even further through darkness to the cellars, built deeper into the wet bank.

They met a patched door that had a piece of rope dangling through a hole, to raise the latch. The cellar, like the rear of the chapel, smelled of moistness and wet cinders. Their eyes were compulsively drawn to the window at the far side, through which in the last silver light of evening was still distinguishable a more open view of a lane. Eventually they were able to pick out a bed, holding straw and rough blankets; a few chairs; a fireplace with an untidy litter of damp, abandoned kindling and logs beside it. The floor, and the ceiling too, was made of large millstone-grit flagstones, whilst the walls were constructed of brick.

There Mor saw his fiddle and his bundle waiting for him.

'But how . . ?'

'I told you, I can arrange things, More Grief, I can, if you'll trust me, if you'll only trust me – and I'll find your child. Forget what I said, *please*, More Grief. Promise me you can love a whore, promise me! I'm sorry about the market, and I've no need to thieve. I'll not do it no more. It was out of habit, I'll stop now, I promise. I couldn't admit the truth then because you confused me.'

'*I* confused *you?*'

She seemed unaware of the lies she told about himself, the confusion about what she was really doing with Mr Burton, the lie which was her whole appearance. What, for instance, was really the colour of her hair?

'Yes, I was thrown off me balance. But I've found us a home, 'aven't I? People owes me debts. Don't you worry about it, and the next thing my friends'll find is your Edwin.'

What was the point of worrying? What choices did he have?

He moved as cheerfully as he could towards the cold ashes and set about relighting a fire with the kindling, taking tinder and flint from his bag. Of course she wouldn't find Edwin.

'What *is* it you've got with Mr Burton?' he asked.

''E's useful to me, that's all. I've got 'im where I want 'im. 'E's frightened of me turning up at 'ome and trying to claim 'Arriet. O' course, I wouldn't do such a thing. 'Ow could she be better off with me, than where she is? But 'e's scared of my turning up, 'cos his wife 'as adopted 'Arriet, and he thinks I don't know. What a row there'd be if his Lisette found a whore trying to claim her daughter! He's scared stiff of his wife, is Burton. The funny thing is, Burton thinks 'e 'as an 'old on *me*. You shouldn't inquire into these things.'

'What colour is your hair?' he asked.

'Red. Why?'

'Oh, nothing.'

'Why do you ask?'

'It doesn't matter. It's nothing . . . Nothing at all.'

The flames played upon the black chimney, over the fireplace, full of pattern and life upon the crumbling, blistered, cracked walls, whilst darkness settled outside.

Out of his bag Mor put the stone on the hearth. The oval pebble glittered with small stars which changed as it moved. It was like the twinkling of a whole universe at night.

'What's that?'

'Something I like to carry with me.'

'You're mad.'

Once again, they both fell asleep instantly upon reaching the damp bed.

During the night Mor awoke abruptly to the delight of finding, not the leaden thoughts of wrong, injustice and misery that usually called him, but the presence of a naked woman.

His wakefulness awoke her. Her hands and her legs gently explored him. They cuddled, she placing her head in the nest of his shoulders, then he putting his in hers. They kissed, mouth to mouth, and called one another 'love'. To be happy was . . .

'A flower growing on a dung heap,' he whispered.

'What's that, More Grief?'

'We've grown a flower upon a dung heap.'

'I'd like to be with you, all the time, anywhere, oh anywhere on earth, just to touch you from time to time, to be with you. How's this 'appened? 'Ow on earth's it 'appened?'

He comes into me so shy, thinks he's no right to a woman. I'll cure that. It's charming. I'm grateful. But . . .

She was determined that there would be more.

'Forget all about it's me here. I'm just a woman. I'm just your woman. Think of yourself, only yourself. Forget me. Forget me.'

It made him even more self-conscious. His penis, already well within her, retreated.

'Kiss me!'

He felt all her body opening to him. It was moving in a dance, which shifted his penis from side to side. She was showing him not simply to thrust, but to explore inside her.

For the first time, he discovered his own body. He'd possessed neither thighs, nor chest, nor buttocks, nor groin before. He'd never had a penis, simply the affliction of an embarrassing stick, the sooner it was over the better; and then it was that the guilt and worry started.

Her movements drowned him. Touching one place, she was nonetheless all over him at the same time, a light net of surprises, showing him fresh things, leaping at him with little bites, digging her nails into his shoulder blades. She was searching for him – for anything she could find that he had not yet expressed. Things which she sprang upon him as her own caprices were responses to gratify what he had shown her about himself, unknowingly. Tempting words flew by, randomly, like migrating birds.

Safe because of her menstruation, he forgot all about his coitus interruptus. At the first ejaculation, she buckled with him in orgasm. He found himself calling out to her from the deepest most inaccessible part of his voice, from the pit of his throat. He had never done such a thing before. It was a sound he had never made before. He let out several such calls, hardly knowing that he was doing it, each progressively louder. Lifting his head back, he was an ecstatic animal baying.

Mary felt he was calling her to orgasm. No client had ever done this to her. When they had finished, he curled over her back, as she lay on her side, humming with contentment. Inside her, she felt a warm bath of semen. The heat ran all through her body, right up to her heart, as they fell asleep again.

They awoke quite soon. Apart from kissing one another, her tongue feeling inside his mouth, they did not make love this time.

He knew that her body belonged to him. He had filled her flesh.

He had never known until now a woman's contentment ooze through every touch.

The ashes had ceased to glow in the grate. A single huge star bejewelled the window, and as Mor stirred his head, the metallic blue planet changed its shape in the twisted glass, ran quick as mercury, then twisted off in the other direction.

At their next awakening it had slipped down to the corner of the window-frame.

In half-conscious seconds before their fourth awakening he called out, 'Phoebe.' The two whispered syllables sounded like the weak calls of a small bird in a hedge at twilight or dawn, so that he hoped that she had not heard him, or had even mistaken what he said for 'Mary'. He felt ashamed. She did not reply.

At the fifth wakening the dampness had caused an ache in his back. He turned on one side to ease it and felt Mary's limbs. He ran his fingers over a thigh as smoothly-cold as marble and he tried to warm her legs between his own; worried about her; but she kept on sleeping. Or half-sleeping. She was muttering something, out of a dream, before she disappeared again into it.

It was still dark and starless, yet he heard a cock crowing, on a roof or a hill-top where it caught the rising light. Then a robin was singing and people were stirring.

The sun hit the street. Shadows were passing by the window. Boots and clogs, some tipped with iron, rang upon the stones, not with that clockwork sound of work-people forcing themselves to the factory, but with the more haphazard noises of people in the enjoyable hours before they had to go to church. 'It is Sunday, it is Sunday,' the clogs were saying.

Mor rose, shivering. He wiped a patch of dirt from the window and took a look. They were going forth for a jug of milk, to relieve their bladders after last night's drinking, or to release their poultry and collect the eggs from the little crofts that still survived amongst the mills and collieries. They walked through stripes of bright yellow light cast by a low sun. Pleasure was expressed in the way that they dawdled against walls. A man stood shaking off the final drops, without a care in the world.

The family that lived above the cellar was making a happy noise, too. A man was clattering bits of wood. Cheerful and unsabbatical, he was presumably knocking together something for his family, on his holiday.

Mor returned to the bed and the lovers dozed once more, back to back but at peace. Yet somehow they awoke in one another's arms, not to make love, but to enjoy the feeling of being fulfilled.

Mary knew what he was thinking.

'What colour are his eyes?' she asked.

Mor smiled.

'Blue.'

'I'll tell all my friends, don't worry. The soldiers'll find him.'

'*Soldiers!*'

'There's nothing to be frightened of. I pretended it was me 'ad lost a child making for Liverpool, not you. A mother'd know what colour 'er son's eyes are, wouldn't she? So I'll tell them, they're as blue as a thrush's egg.'

'No, they're blue-green, more like a blackbird's. Not a piercing colour, more thoughtful, grey-blue.'

'I'll tell them all that. What I can understand of it. I can talk most poetical when I choose, you must have noticed?'

He kissed her.

'You don't believe me, I can see,' she challenged him, laughing.

'I *do*. I must find him and take him home.'

They slept again, their mouths lightly together.

When at last Mor arose, leaving Mary still dozing, it was late into the morning and to the sound of church bells. Outside, shadowy figures, like wind-blown leaves, were weaving their own familiar patterns, to which the refugees were strangers. It made Mor feel bound more closely to Mary.

'There's a chaffinch singing,' he said, when she awoke. He pointed it out as he would have done for Edwin, or anyone else he was fond of.

'The bird, you mean?'

She turned to sleep again.

'No, listen. Listen to it. Listen! It's music. More coarse than the willow-warbler, but similar, and still beautiful, in a different way.'

'I thought it was just a bird.'

But she listened; and also to the crackle of Mor's newly lit fire.

'When I was a boy, I used to wander the moors on Sunday, listening to the bells in the valleys. All the people were down below, bowing and whining in church, and 'ere I was, picking whinberries, catching trout, reading a book if I 'ad one. I used to lie in hollows where no one could see me. I feel just the same now. I've escaped! Though Monday'll come, I know. I'll 'ave to go back.'

'*How* do you know?'

'You always end up back at your work.'

There was a stone sink and a bucket of water, brackish but it would do for washing. Using Mary's soap, he cleaned his face and, in a pang of cold, his genitals.

When he looked at her again he felt that she was sulking. He had forgotten what he had just said.

'What's wrong?'

'Nothing.'

As he could not guess, he ignored it.

Outside, people were going to their various churches. Girls in their best dresses were in hope of making passes at the lads. The boys were eager for the girls they only saw on Sundays. Old ladies thought of meeting a sister from over the hill, and men of a deal to make en route to the church porch. But they were isolated in their sects. Methodists would not speak to Baptists, who would not murmur a word to

Anglicans, who would impale or burn 'Papists' if they could. The members of one denomination would not so much as pass the time of day with another, even if they lived next door. They moved through a place that was filling with mills and chimneys; this was transforming their lives, yet they were most interested in the trivial points of doctrine that divided them.

Mary rose at last, shaking herself like a bird in a dust bath. She hunted through Mor's bag for her belongings. It was an entrance into his privacy which, far from offending him, warmed him, because she was taking their intimacy for granted. She lifted out her cosmetic box, her brush and hand-mirror. She renewed her appearance, smearing on the white paint with her sponge, touching up her cheeks and her lips with a sable brush dipped in a porcelain bowl of red cinnabar. She plucked out strands of her hair. She saw him watching her, and was annoyed.

'You always end up back at your work – as you said.'

She took the bucket of rose-coloured water in which they had both washed and, as self-assured as a housewife in her own home, she left through the entrance by which they had last night entered, ascending the steps near the chapel. She flung the water down the street, narrowly avoiding the chapel-goers, who were already disgusted because she was emptying her slops on a Sunday, and because of her appearance. But she went to the same spring as they, and filled her bucket. She heard them singing hymns.

'Me, I live for the day,' she said to Mor, back in the cellar. She spoke harshly and bitterly.

He still hadn't realised what he had said to anger her. The sight of the water from the well of baptism, its mercurial surface glittering as it slid about in the bucket, made him happy. Just that, made him happy.

Mary, from the other well of her clothes, produced ham, beef, eggs, a rabbit that would make a stew for further meals, and a loaf of bread, all saved from the market. She hunted through the cupboards and found cooking pots to set over the fire. Here for the first time in her life she was creating, not that display of illusions, a whore's studio, but a home, a shelter for a man, though frugal and temporary. The birds and animals at this season were doing the same thing; the chaffinch at the window paused in its song to pick up a straw in its beak.

Mary was herself building a nest, in which to lay an egg of happiness. This was the only way to keep him close to her. She would warm the egg until a new life chipped its way through the shell and flourished. No matter what she had said earlier, she would pay with any amount of thieving, lying, spying; any degree of compromise with the circumstances that were thrust upon her; and keep all that unshared in her heart, for the sake of the peace and happiness of a lover who had promised to love her for ever; who had promised to keep his promise.

They had eaten. They leaned against one another, staring at the fire.

'Gawd, this is peaceful,' she said. 'I'm happy. Gawd, I'm happy.'

Mor got up and was pacing about restlessly.

'I wish I could look for Edwin.'

She smiled.

'Just sit here with me. Do you think you'll find him? All you'll do is get yourself arrested. The soldiers're looking for the boy. They'll do much better than you, and they'll tell me when they've found 'im. Stay by the fire.'

'I don't know what I think of having soldiers looking for him. What *are* you up to?'

'If it wasn't for me you'd be in custody by now.'

He became restless again.

'What are you doing?' she asked.

From the bottom of his bag Mor produced his notebook and an ink bottle, as if it was the most natural thing in the world. He sharpened a quill, tipped the bottle on its side because it was nearly empty, and began to write with the notebook upon his knee.

'Writing.'

'*Writing?*'

'Writing. What else should I do? I don't often get the peace for it.'

'What are you writing?'

'My thoughts, as they come to me.'

'You know 'ow to write down in words and letters?'

She stood up to survey his busy handwriting in *The Beggar's Complaint*. It reminded her of rows of black trees on a distant horizon, or of the shapes of enclosure hedgerows racing across the landscape, as she had seen them when travelling with the girls from London in that big old-fashioned coach. She watched the quill entering the bottle, leaving it and touching the paper, hardly able to believe the sight. The people whom she had seen writing had been magistrates, clerks, clergymen and majors, who made a great display of it and who were mostly copying formulas; but that a handloom weaver should fill a book, line after line, gracefully, *inventing* sentences, without any fuss . . .

She moved around the room in silence. She was in a holy building. Her footsteps were softened. She kept looking at him and biting her lip.

'Read me what you've written, then.'

'These poor creatures whom God made and Christ redeemed were sent in multitudes to Spain and Portugal. Why is it, oh why is it, that all this slaughter should go on and no-one put on the bowels of compassion for his fellow creatures, taken in their youth, led away in their simplicity and inexperience to be slaughtered with more cruelty than ever practised by butchers in a slaughter house . . .'

'For Gawd's sake stop! Is that what you've written? It'll get us 'ung. Do you know 'ow little you can get yourself 'ung for? And you worry about an apple from a market. You don't know nothing, More Grief. I would 'ave 'andled any soldiers that 'ad come along, but if that gets into the 'ands of a magistrate . . .'

'It's no more than people are saying, all the time, everywhere.'

'They don't write it down! They can get away with things in an ale house. Look at it from a general's point of view. What they're scared of is of anyone taking any *notice*. But suppose thousands of people get to read that? Suppose when they're all gathered together someone reads it out to them?'

'There'd be a revolution.'

He smiled.

'And you've got it all written down in words as evidence! You're a child, a babe in arms.'

After thinking for a moment, 'It sounds like a sermon,' she added. 'If you make it sound enough like a sermon, you could say you was practising for a Methodist preacher.'

'You don't understand. My thoughts are only for myself, for the time being. This manuscript is what I want to leave behind. It's all that I will be able to leave. Can you understand that, Mary?'

'At any rate we'll be saved the worst when you run out of ink. You 'aven't much left, 'ave you?'

He went back to his work. He felt refreshed by his writing. It was like dipping into a river on a hot day. Mary crept out of the building. There was no place for her in it. It was full of silent thoughts.

All the mill chimneys were still. The street was nearly empty, except

225

for two soldiers pinning a notice on a tree, to which were tethered their horses; a couple of nags requisitioned from a farmer.

Oh my Gawd . . . Mad Dick!

'So what can we do for you, now you've turned up in Oldham again, my fair maid? Private, this is Mary The Scar. She's someone every recruit has to meet before he can call himself a soldier.'

Unintentionally she roused the sergeant, walking towards him like the bearer of a secret.

'I want a bottle of ink, Mad Dick. Where did you steal your old nags from? The field of some poor weaver? They're true infantry nags, is them. You'd 'ave to walk all the way with 'em.'

The sergeant showed off in front of his comrade.

'They're first class cavalry 'orses, just a bit short in the leg for me, and not 'ad enough oats to liven 'em up. They brought us from Manchester, anyway. What do you want ink fer, my hinny? You canna write.'

'Maybe I know someone who can.'

'Is he another clergyman, or a fucking aristocrat again, Mary The Scar? Tell the private 'ere. Who's your latest fucking aristocrat?'

''E's an aristocrat amongst men, with more refinement of feeling in 'is little finger than you lot will ever know. Fucking militia! You can't even read what you're pinning on a tree. You're animals. Nothing but animals.'

'Oh yes, I can read. And I can write, too. What's your fancy man going to write for you? Love letters? A complaint on your behalf to a Member of Parliament?'

'The chapel'll 'ave some ink, Serge,' the private said, quietly, frightened of Mad Dick's size and truculence. To encourage the sergeant to give his permission, Mary gave a glance at his trouser-bulge. She felt sickened with her profession.

'You can do some mighty things through a bottle of ink, so I'm told,' the sergeant said at last – looking at the whore, not at the private. 'Write down all sorts of acts of Parliament. Go and see what you can find, then.'

The soldier set off, running in order to appear breathless at the Baptists' door, to convince them of the military emergency necessitating the requisitioning of a bottle of ink.

After he had left, the sergeant squatted against the base of the tree, in the sun. He unfastened his tunic, a fine display being better than words.

But Mary was staring over his head, reading the notice.

'You can't read it,' the sergeant challenged. 'What are you looking at?'

'What's it say, then?'

'It's about some poor runaway Ludd they're going to 'ang, poor sod. Now what're you going to do for me in exchange for a bottle of ink, hinny?'

'I 'aven't seen no ink, yet.'

'You should be careful of bottles of ink. They're like gunpowder. I ran away from the Newcastle pits and landed in the Cumberland militia because of a bottle of ink I'd dipped my pen in to write to the paper about the slavery of the pit men under contract to the mine owners.'

'You've already told me all about it. You didn't write it, neither. You bullied someone else into setting it down for you. He's the one got transported, you said. Because he could write, they had to deal with him severe, you said, let that be a warning. I remember it all.'

'I 'aven't told you I've been playing my bagpipes most nights at The Eagle Inn at the corner of Manchester Street. You should come along.'

The Baptists were glad to help the military, and the private was now returning with a little stoneware jar. He pressed it upon Mary as if it were a valentine.

'Have you got any more of them notices, Mad Dick?' Mary asked. 'I've some errands to perform around Oldham today. If you give them to me I'll pin them up around town for you, and you can go to the public 'ouse. I bet I know better than you the sort of place where a Ludd'd be 'iding.'

The sergeant looked at the private, and winked.

'Where're you going to put them up for us?'

'I'll put you one against Mr Lees' Mill, for I knows 'im, and one by the Unitarians' chapel and . . .'

'Aint we got something better to do on a Sunday than hunting poor Ludds?' the sergeant interrupted. 'We could be going to church.'

'Give 'em to 'er, Serge.'

'Might as well be 'ung for giving the King's messages away to a whore, as for anything else. A kiss on the cheek for 'em, then.'

He gave her a bundle of half a dozen notices and she kissed the sergeant on the cheek.

'"Oh, I am slain by the darts of a fair, cruel maid", as the song goes. Give the private one too, for his trouble.'

Mary re-entered the cellar on tiptoe, the notices hidden in her clothes. She hovered, hardly breathing, and in awe of Mor's writing. She put the ink beside him. He made a sound of surprise and pleasure, then carried on writing.

She could hardly bear this desert of silence into which he had flung her. And he had said he would go back to Lady Well. She stood behind him, leaning over so that he felt her chin on his head, and she locked her arms around his shoulders. He carried on writing. She hummed quietly, swaying her body to make him dance with her, as she read what he had written:

'England has been in friendship and notorius enmity, at war and peace with Spain several times in the past twenty years. If we were to see one man hit another and spit in his face, then caress him and hug him and kiss him and call him dearly beloved brother, and then again pick his pocket and kick him and brake his head and spit in his face, and then again embrace him and call him nobel friend and the bravest and best of men and so forth, we shuld see the relatif picture of England and Spain.'

'What do you get from reading and writing books?'
'I survive my pain because of it.'

228

She did not understand what he was talking about. If he had drunk the ink, she might have understood just as well.

'I know a street, Holywell Street in London, where you can buy and sell all sorts of books of descriptions, in plain covers. Murders. The infidelities of the Prince Regent with ladies of pleasure. Mind you, you can be mistook. A gentleman paid a guinea for Mr Wesley's sermons because they was wrapped inside a plain envelope. Those who can write them make a good living from it. Novels I mean, not sermons. There's some take them round selling them to the servants at the back doors of 'ouses. Why don't you write a novel, instead of sedition, and make us some money? My friends'll publish it for you in Holywell Street.'

Because of her chatter he had to give up at last. In any case, he was cramped from sitting. Putting his manuscript on the floor by the bed, he got up to stretch his limbs, walking around the room, and ending up by the window.

Mary had gone to the fire, stooping over the flames.

'If you're short of ideas, More Grief, I can give you a few. I can talk for hours the way men like to 'ear. "She was wide open waiting for 'im" (the Turk, that is) "Wide open waitin' for 'im to fill 'er with his thrust, fill 'er with his seed and she was powerless like she was no more than an 'ole in the earth waiting to be planted. 'Oh no,' she said, no she whimpered, they like that best, 'Oh yes,' she whimpered, 'Oh, oh, just fill me up and plunge me deeper.'" If I say it for you, you could write it down. It comes to me as easy as spitting.'

'What's that you're putting into the fire?'

'Nothing . . . just some bits of paper.'

'It's my . . .'

He had hold of her wrist, tightly.

'No! *No!* It isn't . . . Let go.'

'You're lying! Thief and liar, you've burnt my . . .'

'You're hurting me!'

She stood up, her arm twisted in his grasp. His grip was tighter than he realised. Eye to wide-open eye, they were glaring at one another from a few inches' distance. He could have been looking into the burning fire itself. He was staring into her eyes without caring what anger he showed. He did not care about anything but his lost manuscript. She had burnt *The Beggar's Complaint*. That meant that all trust, that *everything*, was gone. He could not stay a moment longer

229

with her, because not for a second ever again would he feel secure. There would be nothing at all to show for his life if his manuscript was destroyed. He let go of her and tried to rescue the charred bits of paper.

A fledgling had once dropped from a swallow's nest under his eaves. Picking up off the street the smear of tissue and blood that might have looped and twisted in flight, he had felt as he did now.

'Look, *look*, it's all there,' she said.

Of course it was; all there, on the floor, by the bed. He hadn't even looked.

'You've hurt me!'

She rubbed her wrist. She sat on a chair with her back to him, her head in her hands. Her shoulders were heaving. She looked old and frail. He remembered seeing Phoebe with her shoulder blades poking through her dress like that.

Outside, shadows were returning from the churches. A few faces glanced in through the window.

'What was it, then, that you were burning?'

'Filth. Just some filth.'

'Filth? Like you've just been describing and wanting me to write down?'

'Filth, yes, *filth*! Ordure, vile muck, shit, fucking filth. I hate it I hate it I hate it! Don't you think a whore hates filth and muck more than a clergyman, More Grief? Haven't you ever thought of that? I only do it because *men* like it, not for myself. Why do they blame me? Judges? Parsons? How I hate their . . . Do you think I like their . . . After I've been . . . After they've been . . . . *I've* been the one that's 'ad to climb down a well-shaft in the dark alone burying my own baby that I've been forced to murder and soldiers looking to 'ang me when I come out. That's what I've done for someone's moment of pleasure . . .

'Oh, More Grief, don't let anything happen to you . . . please . . . I'm sick . . . sick . . . sick . . . of . . .' She ended in a howl. '*The . . . e . . . e . . . mmmm!*'.

Early on Monday morning they heard the footsteps of yet another band of men and women. The lovers still in bed caught the words of a song:

> 'How gloomy and dark is the day
> When men have to fight for their bread . . .'

They glimpsed colliers carrying their picks like weapons upon their shoulders. Four or five passed by, and, following a gap, some more.

There came other trades, bearing their implements with a threatening swing. Masons or builders with hammers, carpenters with heavy steel foot rules, and a fishmonger with a knife. There were flurries of white as bands of women passed. It was snowing aprons. The women were carrying heavy rolling pins. Another group was singing 'The Oldham Weaver':

> 'I'm a poor cotton weaver, as many a one knows,
> I've nowt t'ate in th'ouse and I've wore out me clothes,
> You'd hardly give sixpence for all I've got on,
> My clogs are worn out, and stockings I've none:
> You'd think it were hard to be sent into'th'world
> To starve and do't'best as you can . . .'

'They are going to Middleton to destroy Mr Burton's mill,' Mary announced, calm as an oracle.

'How do you know that?'

'Why do you think I wouldn't know? 'Cos I'm a woman, or something? I know the secrets of generals. I've seen all of Mr Burton's letters from 'is angry workmen, when 'e thought they'd fill in the boredom of a night and 'e read them to me. Though I was yawning, I got the drift, denouncing vengeance against looms. 'E's trained sixteen of 'is own men in firearms to defend 'is steam-looms. That's no secret to anyone. 'E boasts about it as loud as he can, to frighten people. They 'ear 'em drilling inside the mill. Poor devils, them traitors, says I, when the mob turns up. 'Ow do I know? 'Cos whilst you were writing yesterday, I was on the street asking questions. There'll be thousands'll turn up today, from all over the north.'

Mor took little in of the coincidence that this whore he was sleeping with knew what he himself, a Luddite, did not know. He was too hastily pulling on his boots and throwing his woollens and jerkin over himself, hardly listening or trying to make sense of it yet. One word lit up his brain – REVOLUTION – one which somehow would resolve both his new love for Mary and his more dutiful regard for Phoebe. Edwin would return from hiding, Gideon receive a straightening of his limbs, and the fish leap out of the streams into the hands of the common man. He would no longer have to run for his life, and machine-breakers would be regarded as heroes. Tomorrow.

In a moment he was outside, where the light of a bright spring morning yellowed his face. He knew that riots were occurring in towns, villages and cities everywhere in the north of England. Across a valley from a wood crowded with birds came their singing.

A few dozen people had gone down the street. Others were still coming. The first thing he noticed was that the crowd consisted largely of youths, boys and young men. 'The Oldham Weaver' normally had a melancholy cadence, to console an impotent people. They were now giving it out in remorseless hammer-blows.

Then someone broke into the 'Marseillaise'.

'Allons, enfants de la patrie,
Le jour de gloire est arrivé . . .'

The young fellow had no more French, but what he knew rose clear as larksong over a meadow, and others were soon humming or whistling it. No misery in *this*, to keep people down. Soldiers were not around, otherwise the young man would have been arrested as a traitor. People could sing as many gloomy songs as they liked; it kept them gloomy, and doing nothing about it. But the 'Marseillaise' inspired the young men and made them dangerous.

Now they were blowing kisses at the women and girls, who formed an aisle of flickering white cotton for them. Young colliers, weavers, blacksmiths, farriers, joiners and were hammering on doors.

'Come on and join us, old man. I climbed up t'chimney to get out o't'prentices' dormitory this morning.'

One weaver, ashamed of himself, shoved some money through his door, which he opened a crack, and slammed again. But others came forth with the clubbed sticks which they used on the moors for clouting rabbits, or with scythes and sickles, which as it happened had already been fetched from store and sharpened because the fine spring weather might find them with some work cutting grass for the farmers, thus taking them out of doors.

'We're going to smash the mill! We're going to smash the mill!'

The wife from the house above the cellar, who possessed or rather was possessed by a large family, descended her long flight of stairs into the road. She leaned against the wall with her two smallest children, who one minute buried their faces and the next peeped out of her apron.

'I've sent *Him* to join them.' She shouted to Mor above the noise of the crowd, and pointed her thumb towards the upper window, seemingly associating her husband most with the bedroom.

Curious about her new neighbour, she came closer, her clutching children dragged after.

'These young fellows'll need the steadying hand of an older man, won't they? My master's too old for jumping through hoops, so I hope they don't bring out the soldiers. I'd go myself if it wasn't for the children, and the next one on his way. If they bring out the soldiers, I don't know what I'll do. Well, we'll have to see. Some say the soldiers'll be on our side. They was kind enough in the market on Saturday. Did you see what happened in the market?'

'No. What happened?'

'I've never 'ad so much food come my way in my life before. Lady Ludd appeared. You know Lady Ludd? She come by. Nobody knows where she comes from but she comes, and finds food for us all. Them farmers from Cheshire, the devils, could do nothing and 'ad for once to take a fair price. If women can do that, perhaps men can do even better, when they try. We 'ad beef and cheese I 'aven't seen for years. The soldiers just stood by laughing and playing games. Where did you two come from?'

'We came from over . . .'

Mor struggled to invent an excuse, but she saved him the trouble by asking him a further question, 'Are you a father?'

Mor, now that he had discovered how to avoid answering, merely grunted.

'After finding 'ow Lady Ludd set-to in the market, the men held a meeting at The Eagle public 'ouse, and now they're after Burton's Mill in Middleton. But they are coming from all over, today. So there must be leaders somewhere, even if we don't see 'em. There's that man in the Parliament . . . what's his name? . . . Burdett. That's who He says it is. It is for the children's sake we must do it, He says. "Perhaps they would like us not to have any," He says, "but as we 'ave to, being 'uman, then we 'as to make sure they doesn't steal us bread from us," He says. My 'usband's a joiner. We don't live as bad as some do, from that. What's your trade, mister?'

'I'm a weaver.'

Mor smiled and made comical faces at her infants. He could not help his face overflowing with smiles.

'It seems they are to see history made,' he remarked. 'A day for them to remember always.'

He looked up from the child to the crowds. 'Allons enfants . . .' That was who revolutions were for – for children to make, and be rewarded by and be killed in. Not for old ones like himself. *Was* there a leader? Was Sir Francis Burdett or Major John Cartwright or William Cobbett really waiting to stand at the head, ready to set up a new Parliament? Some said they were, and some that they weren't. Or was there, in truth, nothing better than a lot of Crawshaws scurrying about, with no substance to them? *Was* the army ready to revolt? Or, as many others said, had all the radical spirits been sent already to the front lines against Napoleon? These youngsters, behaving with such certainty, knew no answers to these questions. Mor thought of how many countless times through the ages young men must have set off down this and all the other streets of the world, to wars and revolutions, singing with joy, and had returned, if they had returned at all, with maimed limbs.

'We're going to smash the mill!' they were yelling. 'We're going to change the world.'

Mor went indoors.

'We're going to the mill!' Mary echoed the shout of the street, and laughed.

'This is the moment, is it?'

'They're coming from all over the north.'

'Why?'

'What do you mean, why?'

'Who's told 'em to?'

''Ow do I know that? Somebody must 'ave done. I thought this was the day you've been waiting for.'

'Maybe. Maybe not. I thought so, even half an hour ago. But just look at 'em.'

'What do you mean? There's some lovely young men there.'

'*Children*. Just look at 'em. If they stay together, perhaps the army will join in. And if they scatter over the countryside, they'll be hunted down. If the army and the people stay together, perhaps they'll march to London. If someone'll lead them. Perhaps Sir Francis Burdett's on his way now. If he's not, then, a hangman's waiting.'

'"If," "Perhaps." You said you'd march with us. You promised.'

She stopped laughing. She tossed her head and sulked.

'*I* said I would?'

'Yes. You said you would love me forever.' She put her head down and said, quietly to the paving stones of the cellar, 'I don't want to think of you as a coward.'

'No, I'm not a coward!'

Well, why not go? Some fool of a Crawshaw steps to the head and gets the glory for himself and the rest of us killed, and the innocent young steps into the trap, just like a thousand times before, but why not go and have a try? There isn't any wisdom in this love for her, neither. One foolhardy adventure or another is what lies before us, or we die anyway. Allons, enfants!

Mary sealed her victory by the simple means of assuming that she had already won it.

'Burton's the guardian of me daughter, 'Arriet. I must go to see what 'appens. Just in case.'

She carefully tied up her hair again, opened her cosmetic box to take another look at herself, then gathered up her cloak, ready for going outside.

April 20th–21st

It had been an incongruously peaceful Sunday at Park Mount, the mansion in Middleton of Emanuel Burton: a man proud to see brought together in his huge steam-powered beam-engine, for the first time in history, the four elements of earth, water, fire and air, as defined six centuries before Christ by the Greek philosophers from Ionia. The earth was in the iron and steel of the mechanism, the water was in the boiler, where it was converted through the agency of fire into powerful air, that is, steam.

So Emanuel explained to the vicar, entertained for lunch as compensation for not having had his sermon listened to. Yesterday Burton had taken tea with a whore upon whom classical allusions would have been wasted. Today, the description should appeal to a man with an education. But the vicar returned the Burtons' neglect of his Sunday-morning endeavours with an equivalent lack of interest in steam-looms.

The dozy hour of three in the afternoon arrived. The meal was demolished to a filthy chaos of carcasses, fatty bones and the inedible slime of greens. The servants melted away with it to distant kitchens. The ladies retired to one room, the gentlemen to another. Although the clergyman had been sufficiently compensated, yet irritatingly he was making no move to return to his parsonage. Emanuel's father, Daniel, a bombastic gentleman whose main pleasures were to drink brandy, bully people and tell smutty stories, was going a little too far with them, as a way of getting the clergyman to make for the door.

Emanuel Burton's swivelling eyes passed over velvet drapes, rosily firelit mahogany furniture, and the ankles of the maid who brought in a silver pot filled with Jamaican coffee.

Mary The Scar's green boots.

He took the clergyman by the arm and led him to the window. He pointed out, below the slope of the garden, and standing at the foot of Wood Street near the market at the centre of the town, the 'famously-progressive' mill of Messrs Daniel Burton and Son.

I will buy her some red ones.

It being Sunday, all was quiet except for the movements of the workmen trained to defend the place. The fabulous engine had stood against the end of the building for some time, but the Parish incumbent had so far not found it necessary nor educative to 'come into contact' with it. However, the classical point of view led the vicar to look with just a little curiosity.

He was able from Park Mount to peer over the top of the recently built wall that surrounded the manufactory. The engine stood at the end of the mill, like a huge horse before a cart, its big awkward limbs awry, as if it were taking a rest in the shafts. The horizontal pine-beam, fifteen feet long, was pivoted at an angle, with the pistons at either extremity. One piston was a vertical pillar of steel, shining like a silver fall of water, the other at the lower end of the beam was sunk into its iron casing. The three brass balls of the governors, that whirled through the air when the machine was in motion, now hung quiet and still, like shining baubles for the amusement of children. So *that*, a soulless contraption of the four material elements, was the cause of all the late troubles in the parish, in the town, and in the whole of Lancashire!

Looking from a warm comfortable room, through polished windows, over sheltered lawns and shrubberies to the carefully constructed vista of the manufactory, itself artistically dressed to appear like a gentleman's country residence, it was more natural and easy to dwell upon loftier matters of the soul. Nature displayed a majestic prospect in a circle all around, and Park Mount on its smooth hillock was the axle of God's creation.

Spread for them to view were six or seven miles of wooded dells, tucked into the folds of smooth, green enclosures. Here was a small peaceful town or village made of red brick, and there a church tower, a spire, or an occasional manufactory in the same delightful style of architecture as Messrs Burtons'. The whole was contained in the magnificent semi-circular wall of the Yorkshire moors, as within a huge garden.

By peeping around the other side of Park Mount might be seen an older residence, Alkrington Hall, and the plain spreading mistily towards Manchester and Liverpool. This was, it had to be admitted, a less tidy view, which was why Park Mount faced the other way, yet it was still impossible to imagine that only a few miles in that direction, on this same Sabbath Day, were being discussed, planned, and already betrayed (so Mr Burton had informed him) the working-men's meeting at Grange Moor.

Before dawn on Monday morning Burton's Mill came into life, with three rows of lights glowing along its flanks, like a great house lit for a ball. Or it was a huge ship, anchored in the waves of dark vales.

Emanuel Burton was up early. As he could see through his bedroom window, the beam of the engine rocked majestically up, down, up, down, on its pivot, 'cch! . . . bump . . . cch! . . . . bump . . . bump!' in the fierce light of the furnace that heated the boilers. It was a savage idol dancing in the flames, its metal gleaming, obscured sometimes in veils or billows of rosy steam. On the ground floor it worked frames for spinning cotton, on the second and third floors the Reverend Edmund Cartwright's design of mechanical looms, of the type that had been destroyed already by working people.

Only a very few of the operatives who entered at half past five thought of the romantic associations – those workmen who stayed up all night reading books. Most regarded the steam-engine only as a dimly perceived symbol of their oppressions. Cch! . . . bump . . . bump . . . cch! . . . bump . . . bump . . .

Today, despite what was rumoured and threatened, the work-force was only slightly diminished and, Mr Burton noticed, it was peaceful. They must have heard something of what had been said at Dean Moor, but evidently most in Middleton were more concerned to keep, rather than to destroy, their means of employment.

They treated the cannon in the yard with impertinent familiarity. Burton's overseer not being a harsh man, the children used to play on it and young men sat cockily astride, pretending to fire at the girls. As Emanuel knew, most of the trouble was engendered not by his own work-people but by artisans scattered around the town and country-side; the employees and owners of small craftshops, the home-workers in the villages, who were the ones to suffer from competition with power looms; and from Lancashire's cells of literate Jacobins and Republicans.

The morning progressed in its usual fashion. The lack of restiveness, and the fact that there were no soldiers present in Middleton, soothed everyone into believing that there was nothing to fear.

Soon daylight crept through the building and the smelly lamps were extinguished. There were few signs that anything unusual or revolutionary would happen. The overlookers went about with an unusually brisk, martial air, making a fuss with their firearms and cannon; Mr Burton was a little irritable and nervous, leaving work unfinished to bolt out of his office and scurry around his machines and the yard, at times nearly blind with fear, then returning to stare at his bills and papers, or to snap at his clerk.

But at two o'clock in the afternoon a report came that several thousand armed young men, and women too, were 'converging from every point of the compass'. They were marching down the roads from Bolton, Bury, Rochdale, Oldham and Manchester.

The hungry men were breaking into provision stores, helping themselves to bread, cheese, bacon, sugar and other groceries. After they had fed themselves they were wilfully wrecking the shops of unpopular tradesmen.

A crowd swept Mor and Mary through Oldham. It filtered along the alleyways to the market place, whence West Street flowed into the Middleton road. More and more groups were joining in, and the march filled the width of the street. Those behind were pushing forward those in front. There was no sign of timidity or nervousness. They went past the residences of Mr A. Clegg, Mr J. Clegg, old Mrs Clegg's house and Mr W. Clegg's mansion at Westwood, shaking their fists at the deliberately blind windows of the factory-owner's family. Beyond Westwood, they broke into the countryside, with roadside cottages, and the occasional colliery visible. In every house, the looms were silent.

It was gently rolling country, sinking and rising through marshy little valleys, that seemed flat to Mor after West Yorkshire. Yet though he loved Pennine ruggedness, for a change the sweetness of this place delighted him. The villages were of brick, or black and white timbered houses. The enclosures, made from hawthorn hedges, were a bright green, for here spring was more advanced than on the hills.

Spring had finally come on an irresistible wave rising from the south. The plants and trees, that had waited for so long, were responding as lovers to caresses. The trees of Chadderton Park were brushed at their tips with opening buds. Chestnut trees were coming into leaf; the clusters of great leaves hanging down with weariness, it seemed, at the effort of being born. Struggling in his limping fashion to keep up with the fast youthful crowd, Mor the naturalist observed the spears and buttons of plants thrusting through the dross of dead grass, twigs and wrinkled leaves. By the time they reached Chadderton, Mor had seen or heard several summer migrant birds – a willow warbler, a chiff chaff, a swallow, and a whitethroat. If those delicate creatures had come a week before, they would have been caught in a frost. Revolutionary crowds themselves, they were brought on a warm front drifting northwards from the Mediterranean.

Mor plucked a violet. For a hundred yards, a hedge-bottom was thick with them, their colour suggesting distant misty valleys down in the thorns and grass. Their blue filled him with vertigo.

For the purpose of changing the world, Mor had to turn his eyes from such sights, and keep up with the others. Were his bookish concerns, his guilt, his desire for change, merely because he was not big enough to take into his soul a hedge-bottom dense with violets, larks skating across gaps of blue in a spring day, or the song of a whitethroat?

He pulled another violet and gave it to a comrade, who crushed it roughly through his button-hole.

There should be either a bright sun or a fierce thunderstorm to herald a revolution. Today the sun was behind a gauze. Now and again, here and there, it gleamed lemon-coloured and cheese-textured. It even broke into small patches of blue, but never became more than a soft delicious promise of itself. It was not strong enough to evaporate the fecund sweat that bloomed from the trees and plants. This was one of those misty spring days when even the hills turn into light clouds. Within that foetal sac of mist was a sleepy promise of growth and of summer. If anyone was to die today, it would be especially cruel.

But in the midst of these jolly young men, singing their songs and ballads, showing no more concern for bayonet and gunshot than they did for larks and violets, you would not guess that anyone could possibly be killed. Women with trays slung around their necks were selling red paper roses, the symbol of Lancashire. On other roads, no doubt, the white roses of Yorkshire were being sold, to celebrate a victory.

It was for his chirpy singing of the 'Marseillaise', his hat pushed to the back of his head so that he could look up for bright gaps in the sky, that David Knott, a twenty-year-old glazier, was given a loaf of bread by a servant girl out of Chadderton Hall.

She was a maid who found consolation in her attic room by telling herself stories. She missed evenings at home, sitting at the hearth with brothers and sisters, listening to the yarns of her grandparents, and she imagined doing the same as they, some day, for her own children and grandchildren. Hearing of the young men coming, she had boldly crossed the park, the turf and the avenues, with the loaf. She was no kitchen slattern, but neat in starched white pinafore. She reminded David, a grubby and desperately hungry young man, of a white immaculate dove, come to the door of its dove-cote.

Though brave enough to outface eyes watching from the house and park, and full of determination to make a gift to these heroes even if dismissed from her post for it, yet the girl was shy when she confronted the tattered young men sweeping by along the road. She became self-conscious, blushing and sweeping back strands of hair. She could not decide who to choose. She spotted the young glazier and made up her mind, although to reach him she had to elbow her way through a crowd, getting smutty, greasy stains on her apron.

After a moment's attention to the girl's shining face, he turned to the loaf that she was pushing forward. He was much more hungry for that, than for embraces. By the time that he had got over staring at the bread, he had passed her by. 'I'll be back later,' David shouted, laughing over his shoulder.

The crowd dragged her a few yards in its wake until discarding her at the end of the park wall. When David turned, in order to share his food but also to take another look, and note where she lived so that he might call on his victorious return, he saw her wave promisingly and smile. He lost her in the crowd pouring in at the junction with the Chadderton road, just before the bridge over the Rochdale Canal.

Thus this river of people was gathering tributaries at every junction. The Hollinwood colliers had come with their picks, from the south by way of Cow Hill and Warcock Hill. From Royton they had poured west, to rouse the villagers in Chadderton. On the canal bridge there were handshakes, embraces, and hats thrown into the air. Orators termed the murky little canal 'the Rubicon'. They spoke of Cicero and Roman republics. It was declared that a 'ring of people was tightening around Middleton'.

The more they closed in, the more they were emboldened by numbers to raid the shops. At first it was only food stores, then every shopkeeper notorious for meanness, unwillingness to give credit, or cheating. Lizzie Chadwick, known for resting her finger upon the pan of the scales, diverting attention with her slander; Mr Wrigley, whose packets of tea and sugar contained short measure; Fry the draper, who was for ever creeping off to tell tales to the vicar or the magistrate.

All the while the crowd was getting larger – the most destructive joining last of all. More of the women who lived along the route thought that they 'might as well be hung for a sheep as a lamb'. It was better to raid a shop than be beaten by a husband for having no food in the house. After they had filled their bellies and had helped themselves to clothes and fancy goods, the crowd would finally smash up the place. Shopkeepers ahead were boarding their premises. There was Fry, standing at the door of his shuttered store with money in his hands, smiling upon the onslaught.

Eventually, two or three thousand halted in Middleton market square, excited, ravenously devouring their thievings, perhaps saving some for their families. They stood or squatted on their heels, as their orators, mostly the older men, discoursed. Kings Ludd, Harry, Arthur, and 'the Constitution of England' were evoked; Greece, Rome and France; and those emotive words, 'bread', 'corn', and 'obnoxious frames'. 'Nature and time destroy the vain opinions of the day, but soon comes justice fleet of foot!' declared Joseph Jackson, a sixteen-year-old baker's apprentice, practising his rhetoric because he wished to become a preacher . . .

An empty stall ignored in the market tempted Mor. A few men were sitting on its edges, laughing as they ate their stolen apples. One had some crockery, another a clock, to take home to his wife. When Mor's eyes alighted upon the still-empty space, he felt that only he could see it. It loomed forward. He left Mary's side and scrambled up. He did not choose to do so; he was compelled.

'Friends . . . friends . . .' he began.

His mouth went dry and he believed it would refuse to give up another word. His throat tightened. He felt himself the loneliest man on earth. His heart pounded. One of those on the edge of the planks at his feet turned and laughed, spitting out apple pips, waving the core at him, telling him to shut up.

'Confederates in the fight for bread and justice . . .' he began again.

He had never made a public speech before. Instinct told him to struggle for the attention of a few eyes, and persevere, over disregard, laughter or insult.

'Less that twenty years ago, a meeting was held amongst Oldham weavers to petition King George the Third for a reform of Parliament. It led to nothing better'n fighting amongst the spectators. Or were they government agents provoking trouble? The meeting was broke up . . . .

'All of us 'ave seen, in every village, ignorant Church-and-King mobs burning effigies of that light to liberty, Tom Paine, so as to crush our few hard won freedoms . . .'

He found himself harvesting interested eyes. One or two, then three or four, five or six attentive faces were blooming in the crowd. His words filled out with pride and confidence. Silence spread outwards through the people. Someone, quietly, placed a quart of ale at his feet.

'On Christmas Day, only five years ago, on Oldham Edge, was held a meeting of those who wanted a truce with France, to open up some trade for the weavers. Four years ago we was on strike when Parliament rejected our petition and, then as now, soldiers were brought in. The masters have continued to increase, even to treble, the lengths of our pieces, without paying more for our weaving. Two years ago there was a strike affecting thirty thousand workers, reaching from Preston to Stockport, and at the end of it we was starved back to work with a fifty per cent *cut* in wages. Is it any wonder that by now we 'ave reached breaking point? And are we going to be defeated this time, also?

'What will save us is that, now we are here, *we stay together*. Refuse to be scattered, friends, no matter what. If the army cannot pick us off one by one, the disaffected amongst them will join us. If a few come, the many will follow. *If the army is with us, we will win over the whole of England.* All the working people will follow. This time we can march on London and secure the Parliament . . .'

He was gathering the largest audience in the market. They were drifting away from others to listen.

Just as most of them had drifted to Middleton, sent from their villages by some local Crawshaw. One had gone from Stockport to tell them in Bolton of the 'preparations'; another had walked from Bolton to Ashton; and so forth. All said that the whole of the north was ready for this march. The crowds had come because they were hungry and angry, because their friends had joined, because they did not wish their womenfolk and children to think them cowardly, and because 'there was nothing else to be done'.

243

And now what was to be done? They had been swept by minor currents into the body of a river, but it had flowed into a half-stagnant lake, swirling, unsure. The speechmaking and the conflicting calls to action occurred because, with the mill before them, the crowd realised how impregnable it was. Break into those great stone walls, demolish machinery, change the course of history! Before the arrival of soldiers! Impossible!

On the other hand they had not come to Middleton to listen to people spouting as if it were a Methodist gathering. All over the market were other commanders. They had not been elected. Some had used their size to overbear their colleagues, some had been in the army and learned to command, but most had simply said, 'Do this', 'Do that', only they had been in the right places at the right moments, and it had seemed at the time to make sense. With every one lost and desperate for leadership, an individual had only to possess the confidence actually to advance, and not merely make pretty speeches, in order to find himself obeyed.

But still, with their conflicting orders, they were not leading their followers to dare the mill. They were procrastinating, collecting armories of brick and cobblestones. A few were lobbing missiles in the direction of Burton's, without reaching it. Before the walls of the factory, the march had drifted into anti-climax. It was then that Mary got upon some boxes, pointed her arms and shrieked the obvious.

'There is the mill!'

Her shout was simple and dramatic, and they thought it a great laugh to listen to a woman, especially such a 'conspicuous artful doxy', with her red hair, her red and white cheeks.

It was not her intention to be seen at the gates by Mr Burton, but she had now awoken the crowd, and Mary arrived hanging behind an armed party. Once again they stood helplessly, seeping around the building like water eddying before a dam, undecided and confused. Through the barred windows were poked guns and the faces of the sixteen defenders. Men were around the cannon in the yard. These were the only workmen left inside. Emanuel Burton had dismissed the others. Some joined the marchers. Not many, though, for they had well-paid jobs.

The defenders were afraid of the weapons in their own hands. They had now discovered that both they and their fellow workers in the street had been tempted into the same trap, which could be sprung by their guns. They understood that they had been placed, unwittingly, on opposite sides in a battle.

Desultorily the crowd broke the ground-floor windows, to create panic with the sound of breaking glass. A fat little man, who had strutted all the way from Oldham with a pistol in his hand, loaded it, pointed it at an out-of-range rook, and fired a signal. The pistol shot, the smashing of glass, the missiles and the shout, 'We're smashing Burton's Mill', caused panic in the building. A blaze shot out of the mouth of the cannon. There was an acrid smell and a blackbird's alarm call in a garden. A thin blue column of smoke was rising in the still air of the yard, to drift away gently when it reached the roof-line. Most expected to find themselves dead. Some women screamed.

When they saw that there had been no casualties, someone shouted, 'They're firing nobbut powder! They daren't use bullets!' The crowd thought that victory was theirs, and a hail of stones poured into the upper windows. They hacked at the stonework. They prised the hinges and padlock off the gates.

Then the first real shots were fired. Mor saw Joseph Jackson, the baker's lad with a gift for oratory, receive a ball in the groin. A look of incredulity swept over his features. He let go of the chisel with which he had been stabbing at the mortar and he cried out to God; but it was to his companions that he turned, with an unforgettable look of surprise, that lingered on his chalk-white face. Minutes before he died, he had passed beyond pain. His friend threw a coat over his mangled groin, hoping Joseph would not realise what had happened to it.

David Knott, the glazier, was smashing windows at the rear of the building. 'We came to Middleton to find bread and work, and by God, there will be plenty for glaziers when this day is done!' he shouted. He stared at the slippery tangle of his intestines spilling over his hands, as if it was not part of his own body but an alien creature, an animal with a life of its own. He tried to bundle the snaking mess back into his stomach. Then he fainted.

The crowd, especially the workers from Burton's, could not believe that their own fellow-workers had fired upon them. Surely, they thought, such a thing had never happened before in the whole history of mankind. They began to disperse.

'No, no! Stay with it! Don't go! . . .' Mor shouted.

They finally fled in panic when they heard that a troop of the cavalry of the Scots Greys was approaching from Manchester.

In the late afternoon, a servant maid in Chadderton left her work and crossed the park to stand in the road for a clear view towards Middleton. She met impatient angry men, without songs on their lips, who could tell her only that four had been killed, whilst the 'obnoxious steam-looms' had remained invincible. She tried not to be impatient while the crowd kept coming, until it thinned into a trickle. Perhaps the young glazier was returning along a different route and would come by Chadderton Hall on another day? The bird song of a spring evening simmered in the woods and bushes of the park, at first so quietly that it wasn't noticed. She waited until the songs of blackbirds, robins and thrushes pierced the last light with their clamour, and there was no one left on the road.

George Albinson, a nineteen-year-old weaver, bled to death two miles from Middleton, which was as far as his wounds would allow him to go. With his last scraps of breath he urged his companions to return on the following day and burn to the ground Burton's mansion and the houses of the mill's defenders.

It was George's last wish. He could not travel another yard without the help of a surgeon, and there were none who would help machine-breakers. His friends, soaked in his sticky blood, could do no more than lay him in a roadside copse and promise to fulfil his last wish, vowing curses upon themselves if they failed. 'We'll 'ave us a revolution. Don't worry, lad, us'll 'ave it. Dawn will break, dunna fear.'

George had imagined that his life would be an obscure one, measured out in the ale that he drank in The Eagle or The Roe Buck Inn; a life without a thought of immortality. He had come along because of his friends and did not care whether he 'weaved by steam' or not. He would marry that Sarah who worked in a dairy and rear a family. It was his being shot at 'as if on a foreign battlefield' that turned him into a revengeful beast.

That evening at a meeting in The Eagle they decided to return to Middleton to fulfil Albinson's wishes on the morrow. If anyone wondered why neither militia nor cavalry had appeared in Oldham, they did not raise the matter. Such was their hubris that nobody considered it extraordinary. They believed that the soldiers were intimidated by their numbers. At any rate, the Forfarshire militia, stationed in the town, and the Oldham Volunteers were lying low.

The only soldier around was Mad Dick. The sergeant of the Cumberland militia had deserted from Manchester. His tunic was unbuttoned and stained with ale as he talked of 'cutting the throats of bastard officers and mill-owners'. He seemed eager to be rid of his money, and was aflame to seek martyrdom.

'The army will follow my example,' he swore, tottering with drink. 'There's not a man content. I've seen recruits crying with hunger. If you step out of line they flog you. They're terrified of us coming over to revolution. If the army deserts, they know they've lost the day. Well, I tell you, they *have* lost the day. The army's had enough.'

The army was breached! To Mor, as to the others, Mad Dick's defection was the most exciting news, the real victory of the day.

Mor and Mary did not sleep in their cellar that night. In the yard they helped make a six-foot-high figure out of sacks stuffed with straw and pinned to its chest a card saying, KING LUDD. The ostler provided wheat-straw, the landlady gave a swede for its head, and an old weaver who lived in bachelor retirement at the inn, haunting the tap room with memories of France during the Revolution, contributed a pair of his white corduroy trousers and his most precious memento, his blue cap-of-liberty. Mary cheered on the work by kissing the weaver on his bald crown, and by miming obscenities to the growing figure. With a large carrot for a penis, she made him truly a king. Dressed and ready, King Ludd was set up on the landlady's donkey-cart.

At ten in the evening, Mor slipped out, going down Domingo Street past the Methodist chapel, crossing West Street and up Cheapside at the corner of the market to retrieve his violin from the cellar. The army is deserting! he kept saying to himself. Meetings like the one at The Eagle were taking place all over town. He called in at several and told them the good news. The kind of people whose greatest pleasure is to run from door to door with tales, were scurrying around Oldham, in effect keeping these public-house and cellar meetings united.

Mor returned to The Eagle. It was crowded with people come to ogle the deserter. Mor played his fiddle, Mad Dick blew his Northumbrian bagpipes and the others danced and sang. Who cared about anything tonight? The whore, without actually offering her body, moved around appearing willing to give herself to the bravest. Under the influence of music, dancing, alcohol and the baleful King of Straw, so frightening in the light of swaying lamps, curses were uttered against mill-owners, machine-makers, Combination Laws, deer parks, enclosures, the King, and finally against God, 'the greatest manufacturer and most murderous king of all', declared Mor Greave.

At around midnight, Mad Dick led a raiding party to the armoury of the Volunteers. The sergeant was so drunk that it could only have been the luck that cares for fools and babies that brought him success. Yet he returned with guns, swords and bayonets that had been stored at the rear of the factory owned by their colonel, John Lees. There was a light in Mad Dick's features that caused others to grow silent, give way, almost to bow before him. He was treated with awe; a primitive king feted and worshipped on the eve of being dismembered and fed to the earth. He again played his pipes, swaying upon the cart with his arms around King Ludd, pausing to kiss the figure that through the effects of drink and the unsteady lights seemed to be stirring with life.

It was four in the morning before most were asleep. Only half the revellers reached their homes or the bedrooms of the inn. The others collapsed in the angles of the yard, the stable or the woodshed. Mor found a corner, lined it with straw from the stable, and dozed peacefully, waiting for Mary.

When Mad Dick saw his chance, he pinned Mary against a wall.

'Who's the one with the fiddle – your "brother"? 'E ain't your brother, is 'e? I can tell the way you look at 'im. And you were touching 'im, when you thought no one'd see. What sort o' rascal's 'e, that you're 'iding?'

She tussled and pushed him away.

'Don't think you can make a fool of me,' Mad Dick said. 'I've seen 'im before. 'E was with you at Mrs Rawdon's, wasn't he? I remember 'im. He comes from Lady Well. You're a one, Mary The Scar. They call *me* Mad. 'E's the one you wanted the ink for, then? Isn't 'e?'

She was still struggling to get away, and he took it for a game.

'I'sn't 'e? 'E's the one doing the *writing*?'

Thinking she wanted to be overcome, he thrust harder against her.

''E's the one we were pinning a notice up about, isn't 'e? Mor Laverock Greave? Kept a school? Wrote a fair hand?'

She pulled even harder away from him, but he easily held her.

'Absconded from 'is family, the bastard. You choose 'im, and you could 'ave a *man*. Show us your cunt, my pretty, show us your cunt!'

Their faces were inches away from one another. Mary looked ready to spit.

'Why did you run away from the army, Mad Dick?'

'For love of my fellow man, my fellow soldier.'

'What have you done? Fucked one? . . . Ow! You're 'urting!'

'Don't say that to me. I'm not *unnatural*. I wrote a letter on behalf of my fellow soldiers.'

'Not that again! *You can't fucking write*. And you're jealous of Mor Greave, because 'e can. 'E can do a proper 'and . . .'

'All right, then! All right! Someone put it down, but I was the brains. I can be a scholar too, but it's all in my 'ead. I composed it. It was to the newspaper, about flogging in the army.'

'I'd 'ave thought you'd enjoy that, Mad Dick – OW!'

He hit her so hard, she was quivering, and spitting out her hate.

'But you were both drunk when you sent it, Mad Dick, and when you come to, sober, you realised they'd tear the army apart to find out who sent such a stupid letter, and when they found 'im they'd flog 'im to death, slowly in disgrace in front of 'is comrades. So you thought you'd do best to join a revolution instead. I know you!'

'Yes,' he said, simply. 'That's it. I'm like you, then. I'm 'ere looking after myself. So we should stick tight together, shouldn't we? Really tight. As tight as two people can be . . .'

'No, Mad Dick. No! So fuck off.'

She bit him, and fled.

'I'll get you!' he shouted. 'In the end. The pair of ye.'

Mor, feeling the soft rub of her flesh, opened his arms, noticing that she was breathless but otherwise realising nothing.

At around eight o'clock the word got around to muster in the yard. The chill and strength of a spring morning as sharp as a lemon awoke them. They straightened and remembered all that they had promised and threatened on the previous night. Minute by minute, bird call by bird call, the brassy music of an army of trumpeters, they remembered.

Mad Dick thought the day would end in a cavalry charge. He knew that most of the others, dozily rubbing their eyes, stroking their aching heads, dousing themselves at the pump, could not imagine what that would be like. He was not going to tell them, or they'd turn tail and run. The cavalry wouldn't hack limbs off all of them. The important thing, as far as he could see, was to get a huge crowd confronting the militiamen, who were more pliable than cavalry. They would be persuaded to desert, and he then would be the leader of a gang of desperados, not an isolated, hunted fugitive.

The sun rose sufficiently to smash the roofs into glassy splinters of light. It skidded and poured over the tiles, down to the yard. They fingered their weapons, afraid of the pieces sprung into their un-soldierly hands; the heavy gleaming metal, tough bolts and springs, and careful filigree chased upon weighty wooden stocks. To be in possession of them was probably sufficient to get one hung. Fortunately there were not enough to go round and most, though they pretended otherwise, were glad to find sabres and muskets snatched from them by those who had been in the army and knew how to use them.

Mad Dick, the only skilled soldier, took command. He was an awesome sight in his tattered uniform of a non-commissioned officer of the King. He showed a lust for blood, pure as an animal's.

They set off again along the road to Middleton. The crowd was joined from streets all over the town. They poured out of The Roe Buck Inn, a hundred yards down King Street, beyond the now-deserted Iron Foundry where mill machinery was made, and out of a dozen other public houses. Along West Street, for a second time they passed the Cleggs' houses, even more defiantly singing Luddite songs and shaking their fists at windows which the occupants dared not unshutter.

'Come cropper lads of high renown
Who love to drink good ale that's brown
And strike each haughty tyrant down
With hatchet, pike and gun . . .'

As on the previous day, groups from surrounding villages joined at every junction. The decision to return to Middleton had swept across the countryside, from public house to public house, like a fire through a warehouse of woollens. Mary, their mascot, was given the red flag to carry. Mor and Mary were at the head of the Oldham contingent, with King Ludd on his cart, and Mad Dick.

At midday, when they arrived, a silence fell. The Cumberland militia were camped inside the yard waiting for them. They had been sent from Manchester late on the previous evening, after Mad Dick deserted, and were now roasting meat over a camp-fire. The smell of food, and of oily wood scavenged from the back of the mill, hung in the air. Few of the mob had enjoyed a breakfast, other than a handful of currants or a piece of bread given to them along the way, or something

250

stolen from a shop. The hungry and the fed do not belong to the same species.

As the crowd, keeping out of range of gunfire behind the walls, set King Ludd up near the gates, adjusted the lettered board and set to rights the awry cap-of-liberty on his head, a militiaman shouted, 'My God, it's Mad Dick!'

'We'll be along to watch ye swinging, Sergeant Chadwick,' yelled another.

The deserter put himself boldly in view.

'Come and join the Revolution! Here's your chance to change the army. Either that or come out and fight your battle like men.'

'Not likely. We're safe 'ere. We'll leave you lot to the cavalry. Thou'll run fast enough then.'

'*Come out, damn ye . . .!*'

Mad Dick knew that the militiamen would not abandon the safety of the mill, except to desert.

'Divide yourselves into three forces,' he roared to his own men. 'You, and you – you're officers, one for each group. You watch me, 'ow to do it. All them on this side o' the post, line up! Form ranks, damn you! Right? See 'ow it's done? Now you two, choose your men.'

Mad Dick's section shuffled into something like lines, the others into loose groups.

'Now then,' Mad Dick continued. 'Your lot can stay 'ere to keep the militia busy. Say what you like to them, they won't do nothing about it. I know them. Country bumpkins all of 'em, never seen nothing but the back of an 'orse and plough. My section's off to the 'omes o' them damned blacklegs that fired on our comrades yesterday. They're not going to get away with that. You others get off to Burton's house.'

'Oh no, not that! Not there!' Mary shouted.

'Why not that, Mary The Scar? You've been keen enough on the battle so far.'

'My daughter, Mad Dick. Mad Dick, my daughter's in there.'

'Your daughter, eh? So what sort of a mother are *you*, talking about your daughter?'

'Eh up,' Mor said, threateningly. 'Stop that.'

Mad Dick laughed at him.

'What do you think you can do, runt?'

'You can't, Mad Dick. You mustn't . . .' Mary appealed.

'Mustn't I, Mary The Scar? I don't think I know the meaning of "mustn't". I'll do as I like. Don't worry – you think Burtons'll stay in there? They'll be gone before anyone gets near.'

He turned to the troop. 'What were you lot before you joined a rebel army? Asleep every day in a public 'ouse? Quick, march! Off you go to Burton's 'ouse.'

'We'll go with them,' Mor said. 'Come on.'

Mary's red flag was set in the crook of King Ludd's arm before the factory gate, and off they went.

Mr Burton, his French wife Lisette and the servants who were loyal watched from the elevation of Park Mount. They believed that the factory was safely in the hands of the Cumberland militia, with the cavalry on the way to back them up. They saw the mob converge and gather at the foot of the park, before the mill gates, yet none of the militia opened fire. Mr Burton glimpsed, outside the gates, the rebel sergeant.

'The army's revolted. That's why there's no one to defend the mill. They're the last loyal remnants. We're doomed! We're destroyed! Revolution! In England, Lisette!'

His lips were dry. He ran his tongue over them and they felt like cracked, rough stone.

'There are *women* amongst them,' he added, in bewilderment.

And then he saw Mary The Scar. Was that her brother with her? He saw workmen with picks, shovels, fourteen-pound hammers, and axes, set off towards the residences built for the mill's most trusted artisans, for the clerks, managers and engineers, in a suitably superior block at Back o't'Brow, clear of the smoke of the mill engine. They had gardens, with flowers at the front and vegetables at the rear; bow windows, alabaster fireplaces, and in their back yards, rows of brick kennels where the poorest, most unfortunate breed of maid-servant lived in proximity to wash-houses and sculleries. The Burtons, from a distance, watched the destruction of these eternal, secure, civilised amenities. These crumbled under blows from the expert hands of men who had built them. Dainty rows of peas and other sprouting vegetables were being trampled. The mob set fire to the mill-engineer's shed, where he experimented with steam-boilers and turned bits of brass on a lathe. They threw all his brass-turnings onto a tip. From four of the houses, they pulled out the furniture and made a bonfire. Men and women were fleeing and screaming.

It was, for Mr Burton, the end of civilisation. As a child he had travelled around the countryside on horseback with his father, looking for streams and rivers, patiently making measurements of the falls of water, staying at cheap inns and, in wet, lonely woods down gloomy valleys, drawing diagrams of the contours, thinking of possible reservoirs. They were looking for a site for a cotton mill, before finally settling on – of all places – Middleton, a flat district with little water power.

They were philanthropists. Emanuel burned with the injustice of it. They had come here to give employment to women and children in their factory, but had also thoughtfully considered that hereabouts was plenty of hand-loom weaving for the men. They had been prepared to pay a price for their considerateness. Elsewhere they could have used God's free agency, here they had to buy a Boulton and Watt's engine and purchase coals. They had hoped thereby to deflate any trouble with revolution. Look what it had come to. Why should it be Burton's Mill? Why did they not set fire to the property of Mr Horsfall in Lady Well, who never did anything for anybody?

Burton spotted the party that was making its way towards his mansion, and realised that his family must either be burned up themselves, or flee.

Lisette, fussing noisily all over the house, like a canary in a panic at the loss of its familiar cage, was creating chaos. The servants, who should have been ordered to saddle horses, were being sent to check upon a Chinese powder-box, or a candlestick, the whole family history of which had first to be retold to them. Lisette behaved in the same distracting fashion as she did when they were going to a ball or a party; only this time, at the foot of the park, there pressed a rebel army, one so violent that twenty yards of iron railings collapsed beneath them.

'There are *women* amongst them,' Mr Burton repeated.

The crowd was swarming over the low foundation wall and their boots were churning up the splendid lawn.

At last the Burtons got into a carriage drawn up under the portico. Emanuel grew impatient with Lisette, who was now fussing over their adopted child Harriet, a pudding-faced creature, slow, stupid, bovine, ugly and always waiting for something to be done for her. As a matter of fact, he hated her, but he had to provide his wife with a child from somewhere. He had thought he could bribe the whore into silence by

253

taking the girl under his wing – kill two birds with one stone. That enterprise hadn't worked.

Lisette's personal possessions still obsessed her. She could not spare a thought for the mill, and the danger of revolution. Emanuel did not know whether it was her egoism or her bravery, but she was next delaying because she did not like the shoes that she was wearing. She was leaning out of the window and, against the murderous howling of the workmen pouring across the park, was instructing the coachman to look for another pair in the trunk.

Emanuel Burton leaned out of the other carriage window. Some of their servants were scattering across the park, some were welcoming the mob.

'Drive on!'

'Darling, you will catch a cold,' Lisette screamed at her husband, as usual with such intensity that it was as if the mothering instincts of a lifetime were being released. Nothing irritated Emanuel more than such cosseting, when it happened to come from his *wife*.

'Coachman, drive on!' he yelled.

'Dar-ling, the shoes, in the basket!'

'Drive on! Drive on!'

The wildest of the band flooded under the colonnaded porch and boldly in at the front doors, not caring whether or not anyone was within. The milder attackers entered, as they thought proper to their station, through the kitchens. Mor and Mary, hanging behind the others, hoping not to be seen by the Burtons, went however to the front, when the carriage was out of sight.

On the steps Mor came eye to eye with Crawshaw, who had arrived with a group from Rochdale, Littleborough and Todmorden. He had a white paper rose of Yorkshire in his lapel.

'Dragging your feet again, poet? Last to arrive, as usual.'

Crawshaw vanished into the house.

The crowd was also divided into those who evoked the storming of the Bastille, and those determined to find something to eat. The ones with a penchant for oratory made straight for the drawing rooms. They paused before the cut-glass mirrors. Contemptuous of art and frippery, they studied their poses nonetheless, as they prepared to make their victory speeches. They had been savouring this moment of revenge. In heavy boots they clambered upon exquisite tables as if they were apple crates.

When they looked around for an audience, few were there to listen. All the way from Oldham or Rochdale most had imagined, not the pleasure of smashing drawing rooms and making speeches, but those of gorging on the food stores in the cellars. They visualised preserve jars full of plums and raspberries, joints of cold meat, finely matured cheese, and bottles of spirits.

Never at Park Mount had food been swallowed with such gusto. What was not eaten was spoiled, from the excitement of being surrounded by plenty. Heaps of cheeses were knocked to the floor, scrambled over and abandoned. Joints of meat were flooded with spilled wine.

They then returned upstairs, to satisfy their appetites for destruction. In the main withdrawing room they found gleaming mahogany and what seemed like acres of glass, windows on one wall, mirrors on three others.

Mor would have expected to number himself with the orators, but when it came to the point, he saw how useless that was. He went for something to eat. He stole only one thing apart from food – a length of fishing line.

His next impulse was to smash something. He remembered how Edwin had looked when brought from Horsfalls' Mill. But the impulse passed. With amazement, he watched others smashing furniture, mirrors, crockery, and could see no point to it. Then he again came across Crawshaw, with his maddening smile as if to say, 'Well, poet, I'm all right. What about you?' How Mor blamed this 'King Ludd', for the fates of Tiplady and Wrigley, the flight of his son, and himself a fugitive . . . The elegant room temptingly waited to be smashed, like a still pool asking for a stone. Mor, without knowing whether it was Burton or Crawshaw whom he was attacking, and taking no notice of the strutting orators who were boasting, as orators have always done, that 'today is born a new age of justice, equality and fraternity', picked up a jelly-mould and threw it at a window.

Around him, sober carpenters were taking pleasure in prising apart the elaborate joints of furniture which they themselves might have made and been proud of, and in kicking through door panels. These were all proper young men who went to church or chapel and obeyed their mothers, but now other characters had invaded their skins. What would have horrified and filled them with incomprehension to have merely heard of yesterday, thrilled them today.

The orgy came to a climax when one pissed and another shat on the carpet. They did it with such naturalness in the midst of a crowd that no one at first took any notice. Looking down at a man crouching at their feet, the others thought that he must be injured; then they saw that he was leering or laughing, and they realised what he had done. At the same moment, a woman was pissing into the fireplace. Elsewhere a man sprayed the pedestal that had been assumed by a tubby little orator with the light of a glorious future in his eyes.

When the destruction of the drawing room was complete, some women drifted upstairs into the bedrooms. There it was demonstrated that the sex excommunicated from politics could be the most savage in revolt. The women were the first to go into the Burtons' bedrooms, tittering as they sniffed at fine linen sheets before they tore them from the beds and ripped them asunder. They howled with laughter as they held before their bodies the dresses, suits and hats, then cast them aside. One poured the contents of a chamber-pot over a mattress.

They grew tired of this orgy as rapidly as it had arisen. When most of the house had been wrecked, the destruction took on a weary, commonplace cast. Trampling ashamed through a mass of broken furniture, they drifted, like people come to the end of a genteel party, onto the terraces and lawns.

Mary ate little of the food, except a few delicacies that she grabbed as she was rushing by. She hunted in panic through room after room in case Harriet had been left. No one takes care of an orphan like their own. Perhaps they'd even be glad to forget 'er.

She was still hunting attics and remote corners after everyone else had left. When she was satisfied, she tore down one of the curtains, twisting it into a taper, lit it at the embers of the fire left in the grate, and thrust it under a sofa. This set alight the remaining curtain, and the fire soon spread to the whole house.

It was a conflagration that would surely satisfy the general. She ran out into the garden, where everyone, stunned into silence, was watching the blaze lick through the orifices of the mansion.

Not to be outdone by a woman, a party of young fellows went to Mr Burton's adjacent farm and set fire to a haystack. They released the beasts from the barn and burnt that. Across the valley, they could see the furniture of the overseer, the engineer and mill-mason burning.

For fires it was a perfect day, blue and green with a slight breeze. In the distance the ring of Yorkshire hills was brushed by shadows soft as blue feathers. Wonderful banners of smoke stretched across the sky. The fire they had lit might spread across the whole town, the whole country, maybe even the world, and everything be born again from ashes.

(10)

April 17th–23rd

After Mor had left home, every time that Phoebe tried to say something, she merely cried. On her way back from the ash tree she met her neighbour and, hiding her problems, she tried to speak about the weather, but at the first syllable she burst into tears. Had there been no one in the house she might have been able to get on with cleaning it, as Mor had imagined, but when Gideon greeted her with the angry words, 'What are we to do, Mother?' she looked up at the stain he had made on the ceiling, and she burst into tears.

'What are we to do?' All of Lady Well was asking this question – of its preachers. The famous locals, Jabez Bunting and Jonathan Saville, and the obscure, came in, obeying the 'call' of distress at Lady Well, where the radical leaders, Tiplady, Crawshaw and Greave, were dead, fled or vanished. Methodists in one house, Congregationalists in a second, Baptists in a third, grovelled for mercy.

It made the cynical soldiers smile. They came to Phoebe's home on the first afternoon, after they had found Mor's *Rights of Man*. They had the cursed book, that had ruined her life, in their hands. Detachments of troops in the streets or near to the mill she had seen usually as genial presences, but in her house they turned into shocking, angry, violent men, crashing contemptuously into the furniture and cupboards. Two of them were larger than any other men she had ever seen within her walls. She imagined how easily they could violate her, if they wished. Giving in to what could not be prevented might be a release from her burden. The thought of rape scorched her; a terrible thrill, a lightning that shocked her brain. The soldiers only violated her house, however, taking away the works of Plutarch, Shakespeare and Herodotus, saying that they were seditious works. Phoebe did not know any differently.

'Tak' 'em! Gladly! They've been no good to me. They do nowt but make folk idle, and make weavers think gentlemen of themselves.'

The soldiers missed only Goldsmith's *Animated Nature* and some other books of botanical and bird illustrations. Also, thank goodness, they did not find the sovereign she had hidden, where Mor used to hide his poachings and Gideon had put some seditious broadsheets, under a floorboard. She had been on tenterhooks about that. They told Phoebe that because of her husband's disgrace, she would no longer be wanted at Horsfalls'. Gideon was out of work because Tiplady's was closed down. 'You ain't even fit to sign on as a soldier, are you, young man?' one said, studying Gideon's lame walk. The family would therefore, said the sergeant, have to seek charity, unless her husband was found. If he was innocent then he could 'clear himself like a man before the courts, and they could live honestly again by 'andloom weaving and decent employment'.

The soldiers addressed Gideon, for when they spoke to Phoebe she burst into tears yet again. Her howling pained her and she spat blood. The soldiers left hurriedly then. 'Ma'am, you should seek the infirmary,' were their last words.

Phoebe felt that only death, choking in tears and blood, awaited her; except that she had Gideon, and Edwin if he returned home, to think of. Mor, she thought angrily, had left her with nothing but the past; his loom, his damned books, his chair, his bed and his cottage. He had taken the future for himself, and had left her with ashes and memories.

This shell of her body, this house, were lifeless husks without a husband. She hardly thought it worthwhile maintaining such a poor thing as herself. She felt too ashamed to go to the churchwardens. Probably they would say she was mad with grief and put her in the workhouse, where they had terrifying facilities for 'lunatics and refractory paupers'. She knew how easily, once within the walls, she could become one or other of those. More lunatics and refractory paupers died there, than ever entered the building. She had heard their screams.

She kept her surviving ornament, the spotted dog that Gideon had not broken. She took the Goldsmith and the other natural-history books to the bookseller in Halifax. Mr Slaughter arranged a lift in a cart. Because the mill was shut, there were many people on the streets, and Lady Well was listless with defeat. People determined to be silent when questioned by soldiers, were practising by being moody with one another. Only tutting and muttering followed her. They weighed her down with their sympathy, just as they did Tiplady's widow, and Mrs Wrigley, whose husband would be transported. The books Phoebe held made her burn with shame. She was glad that none of the Horsfalls were about. She would have felt even more ashamed before her superiors, rather than feeling wronged by them.

She was glad to get clear of her home town, on to the hills. In the finer streets of Halifax, you would hardly guess there was so much trouble in smaller places. She tipped the volumes onto the bookseller's desk like someone ejecting poison.

'Books 'ave never done me any good,' she said. 'I don't suppose they're much use to anybody else, either.'

Until she spoke, he had been thinking of offering her a guinea.

He murmured over the headings. '"*Division of Spinous Fishes, The Frog and its Varieties, Origin of Rivers, Varieties in the Human Race, Turbinated Shell-Fish of the Snail Kind.*"' He fingered the engravings of hares, larks, fishes, and snakes. 'Much defaced with notes,' he mumbled. 'The scribbling's unfortunate. And encylopaedias aren't fashionable at the moment anyway. Too French.' He looked at her over his spectacles. 'We've seen of late what a little learning does for the working man, haven't we? If they'd been of a theological bent I could have done better . . . Five shillings.'

'No, they can't be worth so much, master! You're making a mistake.'

'I should never have been in trade,' he sighed. 'But I'd like to help you.'

'Well, that's very kind of you. Five shillings!'

She came away laughing. She could sell Mor's loom, too.

By the time she had walked home she had begun to think that the comforts to be bought this way would not last long. She put the five shillings away with her sovereign – clenched under the floorboards.

After dithering for a further day, she went to Joshua Slaughter to offer her services as a housekeeper. From within several houses as she passed by she heard the murmurs of prayer meetings, where neighbours were gathered around one person's fire; a second contributed bread, a third ale, and so forth. Occasionally the voices rose into a hymn. 'O thou who hast for sinners given/Thine own beloved Son to die.' It was sung like an animal's yelp of pain.

She had never before been indecent enough to enter, alone, the home of a man known to be her admirer. Hurt by the reputation of factory women, Phoebe was more prudish than most. She slunk to the place, trying not to be seen from Gledhill's, next door – though the overseer was very busy, elsewhere.

From the habit of a lifetime, Phoebe knocked at the back door. The kitchen was clearly that of a bachelor, without frills. It was not dirty, because an irreproachable widow used to come in occasionally, but there were oily rags on shelves and in food cupboards. On a sideboard, instead of Staffordshire ware and ornaments, was a small wheel-cutting machine for making brass gears. The main touch of homeliness was given by several clocks, dominated by one large one upon the wall, that ticked in harmony like crickets in a summer meadow.

Joshua sat at the table, not doing anything, just looking thoughtful. The mill was closed, his life was empty. She noticed upon the table a bowl, with a hen's egg in it.

'Josh . . .' Phoebe began, but before she got as far as 'I'm an 'onest woman, I've been too much put upon', she was crying again. She had been thinking what to say all the way there, and had believed that she had control of what felt like a bloody rag stuffed into her throat.

Joshua looked at her with the burning eyes of a hawk ready to swoop. He thought from Phoebe's face that Mor had been arrested. For several minutes he stared at her, but when she was not capable of saying anything, he declared, 'Let us pray,' in the grand, quiet, fatherly voice of one who understands everything. His chair scraped back from the table and he knelt on the flagstones, putting his hands together, his slender engineer's fingers touching the tip of his nose. He waited for her to kneel beside him, just as if miracles happened every day.

When the whole town was at it, why had she not thought nor dared to pray before now? She who had always been unable to speak to humans about her troubles. It was Mor who had stifled her prayers.

She knelt, an unseen hand forcing her shoulders. The chill of the stones touched her like baptismal waters. She slid lubriciously into another world. She was thrilled with silent confession, thinking of Jesus.

Lord, Lord, how weak are thy servants . . . For the first time in her life Phoebe allowed her thoughts to rise at least as far as her throat, though she still dared not let them hit the air. None, save Jesus, knows me. I have done wicked things.

Several minutes passed.

'Joshua . . .'

'I *know*. There's no need to say anything at all. I *know*.'

They were silent, the ticking of clocks harmonising like a summer wood full of birds. The engineer and she at last met, in this mutual silence. There was love in the air, without there being any scandalous touching, no compromising and suggestive words. There was an unspoken complicity. Yes, a miracle was about to appear in the humble kitchen.

Phoebe's eyes were closed. She saw Jesus with his slender pale beautiful suffering limbs descend from the cross. With the same power as the soldiers, he smothered and filled her, ploughing her like the earth. She even felt the moistness and the touch.

Her praying hands had lain flat, gently covering her face. Joshua saw her make fists of them and screw them into her eyes.

'Do you feel anything?'

He spoke in awe, quietly. He knew that she had seen something.

'It is the breath of the Holy Spirit,' he continued. 'I have seen God. I know.'

In surprise, Phoebe opened her eyes. She recalled Selene; not only the words were identical, but also the tone. When someone spoke like that it was impossible to say that you doubted them. She expected him to tell her that she was redeemed.

Putting his hand upon her bowed shoulder, he stared through the window, penetrating the silver mid-afternoon light. She expected him to say, 'All is forgiven you.' She continued to scrutinise the stones. The mill was closed and silent and she could feel his sorrow, conducted to her through his hand. The only noise was from children, who knew no better, laughing somewhere; a breeze was weaving in and out of the sound, dispersing it. She could feel that Joshua was ready to talk to her, even though she could not see his lips.

They were half-parted and trembling. With grandeur and certainty, in words as dead as polished monumental granite meant to hold down a corpse, he began. He had spoken to God in Bradford. While other men were scrambling in the mud and dark on a futile raid, Joshua had joined a group of followers of Joanna Southcott.

He took the egg from the table and delicately put it into Phoebe's hand. It was light and had been blown. She was just capable of reading what was written on it, with uncertain flourishes, in royal-purple ink.

CRIST IS RISEN.

'Mary Bateman's egg.'

Phoebe did not understand.

'Mary Bateman. Her hens laid them with that already written on them. Nature's own miracle, announcing the coming of the Messiah. Only the spelling's bad. Jesus was an 'Ebrew, you see. Not one of us.'

262

Nonetheless, He had His way of helping a poor old woman survive in starving times, by providing her with the kind of eggs she could sell at double the price in Bradford market. It was but one of the ways He would help men gain an increase in wages, if they had faith in Him. There was the egg, cool, perfect in Phoebe's hand, and her hope was strong despite her weakness.

'Do you believe in th'egg?' Joshua asked.

'One who suffers, hopes. And one who hopes, believes,' she answered, mechanically.

Mary Bateman, a follower of Joanna Southcott, had been hanged in York four years before as a poisoner. Joshua said that, like Jesus, she had been accused and pilloried, although innocent. She was in fact a simple honest woman – one such as Phoebe, who had been chosen by Christ.

A servant in a great mansion thinks more of himself than one in a small house, though in either case he does no more than scrub floors. Joshua had authority like no other man she had ever met, since he had become the servant of Christ.

'Have faith that out of the mud of despair flowers the rose of joy. 'Ere, in my 'umble kitchen, you see the bud. You have only to shine upon it with the sun of faith.'

She could believe that, too. It was only faith in an inscrutable all-powerful will, the kind that could write its consolations upon eggs, that could redeem joy out of misery. A moment ago Phoebe had been the unhappiest of creatures, but now that she had discovered prayer, hope and faith, she enjoyed the happiness of one at the beginning of a new life.

She *believed*.

Trust in God; everything happened for the best. The coincidence of the change in Joshua, with her husband leaving home, was surely intended – dare she think of such a thing? – to bring them together.

'Margaret.' Edwin awoke in the dark. 'Margaret. Are you awake?'

Her cot was at the other side of the cobbler's room. After a long while, 'Yes,' she answered.

There wasn't another sound. She was lying quite still.

'So am I.'

'I know.'

After another pause, 'She locked us in,' he said.

263

'Yes. Why?'

Edwin waited a couple of minutes.

'I don't know,' he answered.

He got up, clasping his arms around him because of the cold, and went to the door.

'Where are you going?'

She sat up in bed.

'Trying the door.' He shook it gently. 'It's locked. They want to catch us. They'll send us back to 'Orsfalls'.'

Both their voices were sinking lower. They listened, and all the house was quiet. They could only hear the stream outside.

'I 'ad a dream,' Edwin said. 'I 'eard me feyther. Clear as a pikestaff. I 'eard 'im. I think 'e was outside.'

He turned and looked Margaret in the eyes, as they picked up the light of the clouded moon.

'Do you want to go 'ome?' she asked. 'To your mother?'

'No,' he lied.

'Don't you miss your mother? I miss mine.'

'I think we should get out of 'ere,' he said hurriedly, hiding his face.

'Now?'

'Yes. I don't trust yon cobbler. 'E'll turn us in.'

Margaret climbed out of bed. She went to the window and tried the latch.

'We'll break the latch,' Edwin said.

'There's no need.'

She had already swung it open. A cool breeze brought in a smell of moorland.

'What if she 'adn't left us our clothes?' Edwin said. 'We'd be stuck.'

'There were some girl's shoes down there,' Margaret said wistfully, as Edwin was putting on his clothes. 'I could 'ave got 'em.'

'No, you couldn't. It'd've been stealing.'

'Everyone steals,' she answered.

He left his jacket for her. When he was dressed, he put his foot over the sill, onto the stone of a lean-to. Stone scales, silver in the moonlight.

'I'm scared,' Margaret said, also getting dressed. 'Wait for me.' She clambered out after him, wearing his coat.

'Be careful where it's mossy,' he told her. 'Walk where it's dry.'

'Godforgi'me, how do we . . .'

'Keep away from the edge. You'll be all right.'

He had climbed onto a neighbouring roof and was standing upright, by the chimney. She did not dare to rise from all fours. She climbed cautiously. When she had joined him, the moonlight showed her that the roof on that side went nearly down to the grass. She watched him walk sideways down the slope, and disappear. She heard him land in the dry stalks of grasses, then his head popped up.

'Come on.'

She followed. She jumped. He caught her.

The moonlight shone on the church clock.

'What time does it say?' Margaret asked.

'Half past six. Can't you tell?'

'Never been shown.'

The town was almost deserted. Two drunken soldiers were shouting in a porch.

'Huh! Militiamen!' Edwin spat.

The children went, not in the Oldham direction, but along the other side of the great moor, over Blackstone Edge, towards Littleborough, Rochdale, Middleton and Manchester. As soon as they climbed above the town, a stormy dawn arose, with shuttles of rain hissing around them. The clouds were violated by patches of brilliant light, followed by more darkness piled upon the moorline, dispersed in thickets of steel needles. It reminded Margaret of being surrounded by the spinning machines. Like Mor and Mary later on that same Saturday, the children had to dash between the showers, pausing for shelter. Edwin pressed forwards so manfully that Margaret felt guilty. She, every few minutes, could not help sneaking a backwards look for pursuers. Behind them, two horns of dark hillside were closing in on the view of farms and enclosures.

The track grew so busy that they were at risk of being thrust from it by packhorses and drivers who were hurrying, bent and swaying, to get out of the weather. Ten or fifteen feet below the ledge of the path was a stream, with pools that peat and mineral ore curdled to the colour of old blood. It hastened off the moors with relief, and in song.

Margaret and Edwin reached the head of the valley. No musical falls anymore. The stream divided into veins of slush and dampness, oozing over the peat bog. Finally the view levelled into smooth wings of moorland, scattered with rocks, sinewed with gulleys. Distant hills, misty in the rain showers, floated like grey rafts. Upon the highest projections settled flickerings of snow.

'This track's been in use since olden times,' Edwin, with a touch of the schoolmaster, informed her.

''Ow d'yer know?'

Though she was now ready to believe anything he told her.

'From me feyther. That trough in t'middle used to be filled with sticks and heather to make a brake for th'horses pulling the chariots.'

At the crest, Edwin started running. Like a young animal escaped at a market, he dodged amongst the legs of cursing travellers. Margaret saw the rounded tip of a dark stone post, gradually and dramatically rising out of the ground.

'Th'Aiggin Stone!' he shouted.

'What's 'at?'

'The Edging Stone, then,' he translated impatiently. 'We call it "th'Aiggin Stone". It marks the edge. We've made it! Lancashire!'

Ahead of them, far below, tentacles of light were slithering over the plain after a rain shower. It shone with the mirrors of wet fields, roads and new canals. Towns and villages bristled with the tall chimneys of new and half-completed manufactories.

It took their breath away. Yet none of the merchants and artisans took any notice of it.

Down below was a heartshaped sheet of water.

'What's that?' it was Edwin's turn to query, though not expecting Margaret to be able to tell him.

'A lake,' she answered, simply.

It was incredible to her that she should know something that he did not, and that it should be something so ordinary. But he had never before seen a lake.

The distant edge of this view, where round-nosed headlands nudged forward like great, grey animals feeding at a trough, was blurred by another shower. The spectacle was snatched away by a storm that rushed upon them with the huge wings of a god. All ran for the shelter of some boulders, some distance away, scattered at right angles to the road. The piled stones were struggling free of the moor, biting their way cumbersomely out of dark rushes and peat, with a grudge against the land that enslaved them. Monumental ruins, they rose into high and crazy towers; the forms of spectacular monsters; of huge stomachs on slender stems; of gigantic snakes, beasts, phalluses and heads. Some leaned over into the abyss of tormented sky.

A beggar with a stick and a bag stumbled out of the rain and wind. His clothing, in tattered banners, clung like remnants of skin to a skeleton. He fumbled around the edges of the boulders, the ribs and deep chimneys. Whenever he found himself out of shelter, he screwed up his face against the rain. His stick was clamped between his thumb and forefinger, to leave his other fingers free. He put his stick down and knelt, in danger of being torn away and flung across the moor. He bent over. Was he praying? The stones were pitted with basins which were as perfectly formed as birds' nests, filled with water, and he began to splash his eyes. He was so close that they could see his long fingers, ivory coloured, light and transparent like the quills of feathers. When he'd had enough, he turned his face towards the silver plain, the nudging hills and the newly soaked, brilliantly green enclosures. The sunlight was again swimming fast across the landscape, and he gave it what seemed to be a long and thoughtful stare. But he was picking up little more than shadows and the warmth of the light, for one eye was but a gaping, empty socket, the other was a sea-grey orb with little sight in it.

'The water in the stones is supposed to cure blindness,' Edwin whispered. 'Lots of old fellows and batty women believe in that.'

The beggar's hearing was keen.

'Will you help me down, children?'

He lifted his stick. He cautiously sniffed the air several times, and moved towards them.

'Factory children,' he said, when he had picked up the smell of vegetable oil and grease soaked into their clothes and skin, and had surveyed them as well as he could, with his one dim eye. 'Runaways, I'll be bound.'

They were frightened, thinking he might intend returning them to Lady Well. But before they could escape he had grasped hold of Margaret. He held her shoulder firmly with one crab-like set of fingers, and with the other he gently felt her skull and bones, his stick grasped under his armpit, his smelly bag swinging loose to the front.

Margaret and Edwin appealed to that inexpressive, gaping, damp and not very clean hole, and to the one watery eye.

'I can hear, thou knows, what I cannot see, and I've heard the children taken in dirty carts to be slaves in manufactories.'

267

He felt the trembling in Margaret's shoulder.

'Bless thee, I'd never send you back. I've come by many a runaway that's been happier taking to the roads – think of that!'

He let go.

'If thou'll not tell me where you're from, will t'inform me where you're bound?'

'America,' Edwin answered.

'London,' Margaret said.

'America and London. Well, well. Does thou know the way?' He struck his stick upon the rock before pointing it across the valley. 'Is it that way?' He stabbed the air. 'Or is it that a-way?' He pointed into the flank of the moor, a smile upon his leathery lips.

'That way,' Edwin indicated, ignoring the fact that the beggar was nearly blind.

'Is it, now? And where, then, is the great met-ro-po-lis of London?'

There came only the hiss of the wind in the wet grass.

'You doesn't know, poor lambs. But I'll tell you what; you can trust Abe Fuller to show you the way. I may not be sure of where to put one foot in front of the other, being near blinded from what 'appened to me in a lime kiln when some rough-'eads from a public 'ouse pushed me in. The lime made me blind as a scholar. But I can find my way all around the roads and by-ways of this little old faithful country of ours. Funny thing that, ain't it? I can 'ardly see my way from this rock to the next one but I can feel wi' my stick and my good nose, picking up one sign or another, from Chatham Barracks where I've lately been talking to the soldiers, to London, over the plain of Salisbury, across the ancient ways left by the Romans to Lincoln, and then to Liverpool, which is where I might be going now if you would join me. I don't know about London, though. I'm not intending going there for a long while. We'll 'ave to think about that.

'I'll tell you something about old Abraham Fuller. He's 'ad a lot of misfortune in his life. He was once taught by a parson and liked to stay up at night reading books, could 'ave been learned, then this 'appened. 'E's never cheated nobody, 'asn't Abe Fuller, but there's lots that steal from 'im along the road, because 'e can't take care of his bits of bags and stuff. He needs someone to go with 'im and keep a sharp eye out. Could you two children do that for me and in return I'll show you the way to Liverpool first and maybe, who knows, London after? Now there's a bargain for ye. Ye'll never strike a bargain better than that at

Appleby 'Orse Fair, I'll be bound. We can be useful to each other. We can be friends. Strike a bargain.'

Abraham Fuller awaited their answer but they did not give one.

'Look at it this way, then. What are you going to eat tonight?'

Silence.

'Where are you going to sleep? Amongst the stones? You two'll be worse than the poor sheep at that. They only dies in the winter time, but you'll go to your Maker by the next spring morning. But come along wi' me and we'll all be snug in the 'Ollingworth Workhouse. Do you know where the workhouse is?'

'No,' admitted Margaret.

'I do,' Edwin said.

'Where is it then? Point my stick.'

Edwin could do nothing. He who hated lies had not been telling the truth.

'Can you see a lake down there?' Abraham Fuller asked.

'Yes,' Edwin answered.

'That's not a natural lake. It's a new lodge t'old water for the Rochdale Canal, a wonder of man in his conquest of nature. Do you see some trees at one end of it?'

'Yes,' the children said together.

'And in them trees a roof o'grey stones wi' a chimney the size of a blacksmith's furnace. Under that roof's the 'Ollingworth Workhouse. In that workhouse is porridge and tatties and warm beds for all us three. Tell me 'ow we does it? They won't take anyone in, you know. They 'as enough trouble with their own poor, wi' some of 'em screaming all night and banging at the doors. They're supposed not to let anyone in unless they 'as a magistrate's pass from their original place of residence to go through the country to where they might receive relief for their poverty, and they say there's fifty thousand travelling the country at public expense. But the only original place of residence Abraham Fuller knows where 'e might get relief is the Garden of Eden, and they didn't 'ave magistrates there. They only 'ad God, who was the same as the common man, and couldn't write.'

'He wrote on the tablets for Moses,' Edwin said.

'God bless me, so he did. You do know a lot of things. Is your father a scholar?'

'Yes.'

'Tell me, then, as your father's a scholar and probably a parson too, how he gets through the doors of the 'Ollingworth Workhouse?'

To impress them with their own ignorance, Fuller waited for some minutes. Then he smiled, spat on his right palm and held it out.

'Spit on your palms, strike a bargain, shake my 'and and come along wi' me. Go on. Make a deal. We three'll swear to be friends, and nothing can come amiss to us. You'll not last long upon the roads without me, I can promise you that, and I can use a couple o' children to get me out o' many a nook and corner of trouble. Maybe I'll return again, who knows, to London town, though I've many enemies there.'

He tried to touch Margaret again, but she leapt away.

'First you 'as bad fortune, my friends, falling into a lime pit, then you 'as good, the Lord sends you two children. That's the way of the world, as is stated in the Book of Job. I used to read that. We'll dress you up pathetic, whilst I pretend to be an old and discharged soldier whose wife dishonourably left 'im after 'e 'ad sacrificed 'is 'ealth and constitution upon the altar of patriotism and glory in the Peninsular War. That'll break any lady's or gentleman's 'eart. We'll soon learn you to impersonate a variety of affecting characters as well as if you was actors upon the stage in London or York. Spit on your palms, then, to make it real abiding that we'll always be friends.'

Abraham once more spat into his hand and held it forth. Edwin first, then Margaret, spat and clasped it. The mixture of phlegm and bones was like putting one's hand inside a rotten chicken.

'Now we're brothers, you might say. So now you leads me to the road again and then to the resyvoiyer. Then I'll get you through the door of the workhouse.'

Together they went back to the busy packhorse road. The way was all downhill now, first steeply and then gently.

They went by Windy Bank, into Littleborough. Abe Fuller collected a few pennies from people by the church.

'I was training to be a parson myself, sir, ma'am, when misfortune struck me, and wi' two small children . . .'

To get to Hollingworth, they turned off the main route. A sulphurous smell, and the noise of a string of ponies bringing rattling panniers down from the hills, prompted Fuller to say, 'Can you see coal pits around you, children?'

'Yes,' they answered. The coal workings were like an acne over the grass.

'It's a melancholy sight, I'll be bound. At one time Blackstone Edge shone in the evening light. It was, so the antiquated scholars tell us, named after the ancient Anglo-Saxon "blacan" meaning "to shine". The pits that blacken it now belong to my Lord Byron. Have you 'eard of 'im? He speaks for Luddites and Liberty in the 'Ouse, but does nought to ease the lot of his own colliers. They have his agent, Mr Dearden, the solicitor of Littleborough, on their backs. He's a man you must look out for. He'll whip you through the town as soon as look at you. But his Lordship never seems satisfied with his revenues.'

They tramped on a little further.

'If twenty rogues want to get in the workhouse and there's only say five places, what do we do? That's where what I calls art comes in. Once, I met at the door a fine upstanding young fellow. "You're a fine upstanding young fellow," says I. "What tragedy 'as brought you to this unhappy pass?" My 'eart was sinking in my boots as I surveys him, thinking I could not fight such a one in order to get my foot inside. "I'm without my loom because o't'doings o' them Frenchmen and Spaniards yonder," moans he. "They 'ave taken away my trade through their fighting, and so I 'ad to pawn the loom to buy bread. But soon, I 'ad neither bread *nor* loom, and 'ave to tak' to the road and beg. All because of yon French." "Instead of begging along the 'ighway," answers I, "why don't you go off and fight yon Frenchmen and yon Spaniards?" "I would if I knew where to find them," answers he. "I'm afraid of no man." "Where are you from?" I asks, though it was clear enough that 'e'd never in his life travelled more than a mile from his mother's breast. "From Milnrow," he answers. "If you carry on your way as far as Rochdale, which is not above another five miles, you'll find the French there, waiting for you," I tells him. "I believe they're asking for a rare battle this very night." "If they're asking for it, then they'll get it!" he answers me, his face gone red as a turkey cock with impatience to slaughter Frenchmen. "Thank you, kind sir, for telling me, and please do me one more service. Tell me which is the road to Rochdale." And that's how I got rid of 'im and was able to take his seat in the 'Ollingworth Work'ouse. You've got to be artful.'

By this time they were not alone on the road, for other vagabonds were converging from all directions. Fuller heard them coughing. Clutching his bag, he said to the children loud enough for the dim forms around him to overhear, 'There's always a bed or two to spare in 'Ollingworth, on account of the funerals. The pauper in charge of medicines cannot read, and makes mistakes with the instructions. All 'as to take a spoonful of physic every night, no matter whether they've got something wrong with them or not. 'E poisons half of them with it.'

Three of the company now decided to take their chances in the lee of a wall. The remainder arrived at the great, chained iron gate. From within came the howls of an 'imbecile', and Fuller told everyone that it was the noise of the Hollingworth 'boggart', a ghost which haunted the building. This rid him of some more competitors.

Thus they waited for five o'clock when the master let them in. The stones of the workhouse were colder than a church, but the children were allowed to sleep before the ashes of the kitchen fire. Abe Fuller had to share a box-bed with the 'indecent imbecile'. These words, which apart from his mother's name on her tombstone were the only ones he could read, were stitched upon his coat. He groaned and expectorated through the night.

The following morning appetites were satisfied with oat bread and oatmeal porridge, taken with water and just enough milk to cloud it. To express their gratitude, the paupers and beggars had to labour in the garden. The sounds of church bells, the curses of the workhouse master and his lady fell upon them, but ill words and a stick broken upon their backs did not upset them, for they were used to contrariness in human nature.

In fact Fuller talked the master into allowing them to stay for another night, in return for a full day's gardening. It was a fine, pleasant afternoon for spending thus.

On Monday morning they were turned once more upon the high-road. But they now had food in their bellies and warmth in their bones. If there was no money in their pockets, why, soon enough, two hundred yards ahead of them were those who had. A family making a tour of the north had driven up for the picturesque sight afforded by the 'lake', and by a cotton-spinning mill that made use of the water. They had come out of their way also to avoid some 'terrible disturbances', in Rochdale and in other towns.

Husband, wife and daughter stared at the noisy stream tumbling through the mill-race, at the fortress walls and barred windows from behind which came such a racketing and humming, at the furnace fire which leapt right out of its tall chimney into the quiet sky, and at the lurid colours of the dyes which curdled the stream, with such romantic passion that it rendered them speechless and awestruck; and there was not a single rebellious factory worker nor an orphan-apprentice in sight to spoil the view.

But, alas – ''Tis no Killarney nor Mr Wordsworth's Derwentwater, sir, but at least it is our own,' Fuller whined, putting on an accent suitable for a parson. 'One of the wonders of man is that lake, a monument to his conquest of Mother Nature to feed the Rochdale Canal. Controlling the flow of her breast, you might say, begging your pardon, ma'am. Ninety-two locks, six bridges, eight aqueducts and a tunnel seventy yards long costing half of one million pounds, raised by the shareholders who have, I believe, great hopes of financial gain. Ah, if only, for my poor children's sake, I had but a penny or two of it! To help educate them and bring them up. I know the benefits of education and was on my way to Oxford myself . . . thank you, sir. I'm sure you can never know what it is to be without a penny, and pray God you never will. I had a career as a scholar before me until I was nearly blinded. Just another penny would satisfy me – Oh, thank you kindly, sir, I'm obliged.'

The daughter had brought out of the carriage a small box. Stooping in the grass, she opened it. Edwin saw the little tubes of paint, small brushes of sable, and a china palette the size of a teacup saucer, delicately laid out like a display of perfumes or jewellery. She picked up a wooden rectangle screwed upon a stick and put it to her eye, in order to frame the view of the manufactory and its reflection in the water. She took up a sketching pad and drew hesitatingly, with indeterminate, knitted lines. She looked mostly not at the mill, but at her paper, being, in the manner of delightful young ladies, more interested in the effects she could achieve, than in the object of her studies. Everything about her was clean. Her tresses cascading, ribboned to her shoulders, filled Edwin with desire.

'It's 'orrible dirty in there,' he remarked, timidly.

'And what do you know about industry, child?' the mother demanded, fiercely. She was annoyed with her husband for being such a fool as to throw his money before a mendacious beggar.

'Nothing, ma'am,' Edwin answered, frightened.

'Shirkers, my dear, shirkers! The idle good-for-nothing poor, who I'm afraid are always with us,' her husband said, good-humouredly.

His wife was not to be put off.

'How would the Duke of Wellington fare if he was possessed of your mean spirit, young man?'

'I don't know, ma'am.'

'Do you know the Duke of Wellington?'

'I know who 'e is, ma'am. But I don't know 'im.'

'Impertinent, also! These people will not be satisfied until they are chopping off heads.'

Edwin noticed the lovely daughter blushing with embarrassment over her sketch.

'Forgive my poor children's manners, ma'am,' Fuller interrupted. 'It is only because they have no mother. If anyone knows the brave duke, I do, for I am a soldier discharged having lost an eye, honourably, I hope, fighting with Sir John Moore before he was buried, in haste but with all the dignity we soldiers could muster in the circumstances, at Corunna in the year 1808. For I was one of those that dug his grave by moonlight, with their bayonets.'

'The battle of Corunna was in 1809, not 1808. I'm surprised you could forget such a date,' the father said.

'So it was, sir, so it was! What a thing it is to be educated, just what I'd like for my own children. But, alas, after sacrificing my health and constitution upon the altar of patriotism and glory I came home to find that my wife had dishonourably left me with two children to make shift for as best I can. It is my last and dearest wish to educate them to the beauties of nature, which is why we are romantically tramping the roads. Though I can see nothing of it myself, I'll die satisfied if their hearts can be subdued by the sight of Whittaker Moor, bathed in colours an artist might give his eyes to catch; by the moorlands of Wardle where light and shade play their strange antics, and the champagne country that rolls from Middleton to Manchester . . . I see the artistic young lady appreciates such things. I perceive I am upsetting you, my dear young lady.'

'It's so sad!'

She was sobbing and shaking her purse.

'It's such a sad story!' she howled, as she tipped her purse into Margaret's quickly opened hands. The mother was trying to restrain her.

'Oh, it's so sad! Just look at them. Can't you see them, mother? Oh, I've never seen children like that before, just look at them, mother. Can't we take the children home with us? Oh, it's so sad. They look so sad.'

'Pull yourself together, Celia, of course we can't,' her mother answered quickly.

But Fuller hurried the children away with their winnings, just in case Celia, crying as if her heart would break, should eventually persuade her parents, and land all three of them, dressed-up like fairground monkeys, imprisoned in a gentleman's house.

At Crow Shaw, near Rochdale, the churn of a farmer who charged too much for his milk had been overturned at the roadside. A soldier was on guard, presumably against cats, as nothing else could have licked it up.

'Shame on the rebels,' Fuller remarked to the soldier. 'I 'ope you'll 'ang the culprits. You generally does, innocent or guilty no matter.'

The private appreciated the joke and would without doubt, they realised, have given them the milk if he could.

As soon as they hit the main Rochdale road again, they found themselves amongst crowds coming from Littleborough and York-shire. Young men carrying sticks, hammers and other tools said they were going to Middleton, to 'see to Mr Burton's mill'. Some had white paper roses in their lapels.

In Rochdale they were met by morris dancers dressed in coloured breeches and waistcoats. Fuller paused and sniffed, his stick driven tight into the damp road.

'Tatties!'

Yes, the smell of good potatoes, sound from their store except for a few patches blackened with frost, and still scented with earth. As Margaret hurried to gather them, a grey powder clung to her fingers, darkening as it soaked up the machine grease that, days after she had left the mill, still oozed out of her hands. Edwin helped her to pick up the food and stuff it into Fuller's bag.

When they reached the market, fish, vegetables and meat were scattered everywhere. The stall-holders had been driven off. What the crowd could neither swallow nor take away, it was laughingly feeding to stray dogs, to abandoned pigs and poultry, or was tipping at the roadside. Between the tumbled stalls, over the crushed fruit, vegeta-bles, empty baskets and broken pottery, came a procession of women, laughing, savage, yelling obscenities, setting pigs squealing and hens squawking, throwing stones at the shuttered windows of the inn and the grander houses where the traders were hiding. At their head came Lady Ludd, carrying a loaf of bread, soaked in blood, stuck onto the end of a tall pole.

The beggar turned his palm this way and that. A woman broke a goose's egg into it, and laughed. Fuller cursed and wiped it on his tattered worsted breeches.

Troops had arrived to read the Riot Act. They arrested a few, and drove everyone else home. The blind beggar and the children were requisitioned to help clean up the mess. They were given a penny by a smiling sergeant, who thought the whole day a great joke. They spent the night amongst the stalls.

There being so much scrap food still available, and some more pennies to be earned by cleaning up, they stayed all of the next day also.

On Wednesday morning they set off to pass through Middleton to Manchester. White blossoms of blackthorn fountained out of the hedgerows. Flowers of cow-parsley, great white dishes of them, poured out of the banks. Edwin brushed them with his hands. He pulled one and smelled it. He crushed one, and sniffed. He took a stem of cow-parsley and smacked at the other plants; a milk leaked onto his hands. He found a stiff old stem and made a pipe. He put a pebble inside and blew it at Margaret.

'Godforgi'me, what was that?'

Edwin stared innocently aside into the hedgerow. He was drawn again into the heart of the flowers.

'You threw something at me!'

The two children smiled at one another.

Middleton was a place of dreary quiet. Edwin spoke to the white fat cloud of a woman enveloped in a big apron, as she stood guarding the door of a grocer's.

'Ma'am, 'as the Revolution begun? We saw a loaf soaked in the King's blood on a stick in Rochdale.'

Edwin's answer was a cuff around the ears. Margaret turned again and laughed at him. Edwin, blushing, ran at her and swung a kick, but she skipped out of the way.

'Children!' Fuller said. 'Dunna be such children, now!'

In the town they met a fellow sitting on a doorstep, eating currants out of his palm. He gave Edwin some.

'Them was taken from a corpse,' he said.

'What corpse, master?'

'A corpse shot in Alkrington 'all. They said 'e was escaping from the Scots Greys, after the raid on Burton's. They left him on t'bankside, the corpse. None of us sacrifices 'as got us nowhere, I don't think.'

Edwin ran to catch up with Abe Fuller and Margaret. He showed the currants.

'Got them off a corpse.'

'A corpse – where?' Margaret asked. She would believe anything he said.

'Just down there.'

In the town centre, there was a smell of damp ashes.

'What can you see, children?'

When you ask children what they can see, they can seldom describe anything, even though they are always watching; but Margaret answered, 'There's a big 'ouse burnt to the ground. It isn't there anymore.' She spoke in doubt, wondering if this was what he wanted to hear.

'Ah! I could smell it.'

Bolted to the railings of Burton's Mill was a notice, painted on wood and varnished. Sign-painting was, apparently, the last trade enacted there. Edwin could almost read it by himself. He asked some bystanders to help him out – not that they could read, but they knew by heart what it said:

NOTICE

D. Burton and Son have determined NOT to work their looms anymore. Dated April 11, 1812.

'Ah!' said Fuller. 'A bad place. We must get away from here.'

Following the roads to Manchester, they passed rows of deserted cottages. Hundreds of workers who had lost their employment had left the town. Loaded carts were on the road. Doorsteps were crowded with people discussing it. They did not talk about revolution. They talked about how would they manage? Who were the culprits? The need for law and order; who was going to pay? . . .

'When we get to Manchester, my girl, you must board the stage coach to London, unless you wants to walk,' Fuller said. 'I'd suggest you bides your time 'til Sunday and begs outside the great church there. Tell them you want to visit your mother sick in the Bethlehem. We've got some onions from Rochdale. You must sniff one first, broke in two.

'Or maybe, on second thoughts, not that tale for folks going to church. They're saving up their feelings to weep over Christ's wounds inside and are 'ard on beggars making the church steps untidy. No, that tale's one to tell at a kitchen door, when you've time to describe artful.

When they're rushing in to praise the King of Beggars you'd do best to say you want to visit a servants' registry and obtain 'onest employment with the broom, to take you off the roads. They'd say that was moral.

'And you, young man, will 'ave to part company with your little lady, to take ship from Liverpool. You stick with me and let 'er go. I'll walk to Liverpool with ye. Once we get into the marshes of Chat Moss west of Manchester, the pools are full of pikes and eels, roach and perch. There's wild ducks to decoy. There's plenty to eat there, if you're a friend of the people. And if you're not, you'll never find a firm road across the marshes. There's many a fine gentleman the people misleads and drowns, for the gold watch in 'is pocket, or maybe because 'e's gone there as an improver to drain the waters. None of them that lives on Chat Moss *approves* of that, I can assure you. Only the newspaper folk, and the gentlemen with profits to be made, who rules the Parliament, approves of drainage and enclosures . . .'

Edwin did not know how to put a stop to Fuller's speech, but keeping pace with them was the constable of Blakeley. He carried a truncheon with a gold coat of arms painted upon it and he was very anxious to arrest Jacobins from Middleton. In the end it was not Edwin but Fuller himself who remarked, 'There is a gentleman walking at our side, children.'

'I was interested in your remarks upon Chat Moss, sir,' the constable said. 'Do you also know the marshes of Carrington?'

'We're not going to Carrington, *Constable*!' Edwin shouted, in order to warn Fuller. The beggar stiffened.

'Never heard of it, sir. I was spinning a yarn for my two poor children to pass the time on the road. It's a sad truth that the more roguish the tales you make up for the young scoundrels, the more they like it. I've tried improving tales, but got nowhere, so I have to invent ones about honest gentlemen getting lost, to point a moral.'

It didn't work. Abraham Fuller was arrested as a vagabond without means of support, nor proper affairs to attend to, and incapable of prosecuting any business.

The children were taken to Red Bank, on the edge of Manchester, and deposited in the charge of Mr Bamford at the workhouse. His principle was not to turn the key upon anyone; he did not believe that people were criminal because they were poor. In the middle of the night Edwin and Margaret therefore crept out of the place.

They stumbled upon the cathedral, where tramps muttered in their sleep amongst the buttresses. 'I'll do for him, I'll do for him . . .', 'That bastard soldier . . .' The dreams frightened the children away. They came along Mill Gate and passed the school, envious of the orphans in their dry beds. It started to rain, so they tried to find shelter amongst the warehouses along the banks of the River Irwell. They penetrated into deeper regions of the city, beginning to give up hope of finding anywhere. Every door was locked, every passage barred, and there was hardly a crevice to serve as a hiding place. All buildings were dark, except for an occasional office with a yellow light glowing where an ambitious clerk was toiling through the night. Edwin felt like a mouse in a store. The only large buildings he had been inside were Lady Well church and Horsfalls' mill. One dark warehouse following another amazed him. They seemed like huge packing cases; the streets, shelves along which he was scurrying.

They wandered along Deans Gate, until they came to the elegant houses. They turned into John Street. Wet through, they crept hopefully under any shallow arch or leaning plank, until the changeability of wind and rain drove them out again. Edwin was now the most despairing. Margaret felt at her most confident in a city, trying doors, never losing hope of finding one unlocked. At last she found . . .

'Edwin!'

He had to be the first to rush up the stairs. He paused at the top.

'Schh!' he commanded.

There was another door, and that too was unlocked. They found themselves in a big room faintly lit by a huge skylight. The place was overhung by a strange smell. Most of the floor was bare but in the middle was a gaunt wooden structure fitted with ropes, pegs and winding gear. It was encrusted with thick globules. Edwin touched one and penetrated a dark wrinkled skin, finding it red and sticky beneath.

'Blood!' he announced.

'It's a gallows,' Margaret whispered.

They must rest here, even so. Stumbling around, they came across some rolls of material, very stiff but they would do for a bed. They curled up, clutching one another. The only undressing they did was that Edwin removed his clogs. He slept immediately. Margaret lay awake for a long while, staring at the grey rainy blackness in the skylight, watching the flowering stars, before shutters of cloud were drawn over them again. As the rain sprinkled the skylight, so tears swam across her eyes. Was she to say goodbye to Edwin tomorrow? She feared that her snivelling would awake him.

After she had fallen asleep, Edwin awoke. The grey light of a bleak dawn was breaking through the skylight. It lit up row upon row of jars of pigment – cadmium red, alizarin crimson, prussian blue, chrome yellow, indigo. He leapt up, thrilled by this sight. A marble-topped table was spilled with the glowing pigment. There was a pestle and mortar, a jar stuffed with brushes, a kidney shaped mahogany board with a hole in it and colours dabbed around the rim, an oily rag, a dirty smock, and a queer black hat, such as a judge might wear before delivering the death sentence.

Edwin went up to the 'gibbet'. He turned a little brass handle, but when part of the structure started to squeal and slide noisily, it scared him, so he left it.

He turned to the palette, smelling for the first time in his life the aromas of turpentine and poppy oil. He put his finger into it, feeling the texture, the way his father fingered cloth.

He could not help himself from picking up the fattest, softest brush and dipping it into a container filled with turpentine and oil. He watched the bristles swell and droop as he brought them out. He hovered over the sunrise of colours.

Margaret awoke.

'What're you doing?'

'Nothing,' he answered, and repeated, 'Nothing.'

He loaded his brush with chrome yellow. He knelt to a primed canvas against the wall. He remembered the young eagle chained in the vicar's garden in Lady Well. He drew its great wings in flight, from one corner of the canvas to the other.

'What is it?'

'Nothing,' he said again. 'Nothing.'

(11)

April 21st–May 10th

Emanuel Burton's house was burning beyond retrieval. From the end of the Park Mount garden a crowd with scorching faces, appearing and disappearing in the smoke, watched one flaming beam after another topple through a shower of roof tiles, masonry and dust. A short distance away, a haystack was crackling and flaring. Frightened horses were rearing and cantering around a field. Across the town, at Back o't'Brow, the Hollinwood colliers with Mad Dick's inspiration were smashing the gable of the mill-manager's house.

'Our enemies, though, have escaped us!' Crawshaw at the garden end shouted against the noise of fire and the crashing building. 'The rats!' He turned this way and that, looking for a following. 'Our enemies have escaped. The bastards have gone to the father's house at Rhodes. They've gone to Rhodes. The rats. We should go and fire it while we have the chance!'

'And which of us will be 'ung for murder?' Mor shouted back.

Crawshaw tried to get away from him.

'Our enemies are at Rhodes – the father's house. Th'ole family of rats is hiding there. We can burn 'em in their hide-out like vermin.'

Mor still followed. Harriet would be at Rhodes.

'And be 'ung for murder!'

He was hoarse from shouting. He turned this way and that, following Crawshaw who was hiding from him in the smoke and coughing.

'Thou'll be 'ung for murder! All of us will!'

Crawshaw, flushed, turned on him. Already a stream of people, hornets in flight, was humming with anger towards Rhodes, obeying Crawshaw.

'Backslider! What's wrong wi'thee? Are you a coward, poet? Prove you're not a coward.'

Mor made a jump at him, into the air, and found himself hanging on to Crawshaw's lapel. He fell away, with nothing but a white paper Yorkshire rose crumpled in his fist.

'Thou'rt a coward, wi' no stomach for the future,' Crawshaw shouted. 'Short-arsed cripple,' he added, then turned and ran across the fields.

He disappeared amongst a cluster of tightly-shut cottages, where Burton's employees, women and children, were hiding, or peeping from windows. On his long legs, he soon got to the head of his followers. Mor struggled to catch up, still believing that he could explain their foolishness to blind, excited people.

Then a troop of Scots Greys was seen cantering from the Manchester direction. One detachment split off into the town, the other turned towards Rhodes, where some of the crowd had got into the grounds and yards. There was no hope of disaffection amongst these cool fellows.

The cavalry began their charge a short distance from Mor. They had no need of their swords. Mor found himself clawing, as ruthlessly as anyone else, into a soft mass of people who were scrambling away from the hooves. He did not see the tunics, the sashes, the heaving muscle of the towering horses, the clods of earth flying up. He saw only what was before his face. For a second he was thrust against the breast of a woman whose blue cotton dress was damp with milk. He had spoken to her earlier; her baby had died of starvation and cold. The crowd in its panic kicked out like the cavalry horses. Mor was the same as the rest. Cries tore by his ear. One second he was buried in flesh, smothered in the sweaty smells of fright, and the next taking in a flash of open sky.

When he was able to look around again, the Greys had passed by. Their great shifting haunches were disappearing down the wide path cleared for them, and over the brow of a hill. In the drifting smoke and confusion, there was no sign of Mary.

Mor took no interest in where the Greys had gone to, nor in what they might be doing. What he did see was that everyone was fleeing. He stood with tears in his eyes. How could they stand their ground against cavalry? They could now be picked off one by one. Grabbed on the highroads, hunted in the villages. Never mind the details. Some would be arrested. That was all. He should save his own skin. He decided to make his way alone to Oldham.

Scraps of conversation, leaves from a dismembered plant; words of bluff, or of fear, nervous advices were scattered in the air. 'Willt' cavalry chaps recognise us, d'you think? Spies are everywhere.' 'We all mun melt into t'countryside.' 'I've an aunt as bakes cakes by a mill in Meltham. Nobody'll look there.' 'We mun melt into the countryside.'

Mor knew his direction only vaguely. Like everyone else, he disregarded crops, and found himself trampling a newly sown field of oats, close to what he was told was Fox Denton Hall. Again and again he heard from nearby, 'For t'time being, we mun melt into t'countryside.' 'I've a sister in service t'a schoolmaster who writes pamphlets in Marsden. I'll go over there, I think.' 'Will they recognise us? That cavalry chap looked me straight in the eye. I don't think I'll go 'ome. He'll come looking. They'll be searching, sure enough. The women'll have to fettle without me for a while.' 'I'll go into Yorkshire. There's no village in Yorkshire that won't take us in. That's what they're like in those hill villages . . .'

Following lanes, asking his way of dribbles of people threading around hedgerows, Mor continued without touching the high road, until he saw the town and Oldham church upon the hill. He struck the Manchester Road, near Werneth Hall.

Landladies came to the doors of inns and people were lingering at farm gates. They wanted to know why so many were lugging furniture and pictures. Two men had Mr Burton's voluptuous 'Danae'. Another pair carried a mahogany cabinet. A woman, who by the look of her had no food at home, was struggling with a gilt mirror. Her desire for beauty was what meant most to her.

Mor came circumspectly into Oldham, along Manchester Street, past The Eagle Inn. He had left his fiddle in charge of the landlady, but soldiers lounged by the door. There was little sign of them elsewhere, yet Mor felt uneasy. A fellow in a fine coat, who had nothing apparent to do, was eyeing him. Mor turned left, along Cheapside, to the cellar.

Even from the outside, he knew that Mary was not at home. But why should he expect her to return? Although they had spent such a brief period in it, the sight of the building filled him with poignancy. He realised that anywhere they inhabited together became haunted with love.

Their neighbour, with her tired and tearful children, was pacing the street, up and down, catlike, stopping everyone she could. She had heard the same story time and time again, but there was no news of her husband.

'He's a joiner by trade. There's a new cradle inside he was making, not finished. He never thought he'd 'ave another at 'is age. But I'm young.'

'We know nothing of him, Mrs Johnson,' she was told. 'Seen nothing of 'im. Last we saw, 'e'd gone into the public 'ouse.'

'He's late,' she announced simply, to Mor.

From her look he knew that the woman loved her husband.

'I don't know anything about him.'

'Did you see the soldiers – the dragoons?'

'I don't think they killed or caught anyone.'

'A man was shot dead at the corner of Tonge Lane. I've heard that from several. The Scots Greys officers are not like us. They're not militia. They're gentlemen. They've no time for such as us – not if we so much as raise our heads.'

Her face came forth from behind her apron, trying to smile through red rubbed cheeks.

'The chance is only one in thousands that the one they shot's your husband.'

'Aye, 'appen so. The children are crying. You didn't see anything?'

'Nothing. We all just ran.'

'He can't run so well.'

She was stroking the head of a little girl, absentmindedly. She realised what she was doing. She wept again.

'The children . . .'

But as Mor had nothing to offer her, Mrs Johnson was already turning to others.

He found the key where he had hidden it under a stone. The cold ashes, the empty bed, the tear in the straw mattress where he had hidden *The Beggar's Complaint*, the cosmetic box, hand-mirror and hairbrush all awaited him. There was nothing to do now. They were defeated.

He sat and blubbered for half an hour. His chest ached and his throat tightened with soreness, yet the tears kept coming. He tried to recover by reading his own pages.

'The sufferings of the poor are not the effects of divine dispensations but the offspring of wicked men and bad systems . . .'

He thought of Edwin, Gideon and Phoebe. He found himself holding his breath, then a sigh would break. It grew dark. He laid and lit a fire. He lit a candle. He picked up his oval stone that he had laid by the hearth, and fondled it, deriving comfort.

He heard the door move. He turned and there was Mary. The look upon her features, one he had never seen before, took him so much by surprise that he didn't quite recognise her because of it. She was transfigured by her longing to see him, and then by finding him. Her dress was torn, her cosmetic smeared, her hair was disarrayed. His chair fell onto its side as he jumped up. Starting with lips, they were in need of four, of six, eight, ten hands, to touch every part of one another, all at once.

'Poor darling, your eyes are red! It's all right. I've found a place for us to hide. Talking to them all along the road, I found a place where we can go. In Delph,' she said.

'Delph?'

'Six miles away. Back in Yorkshire. They'll soon come looking 'ere. It's not me that I'm scared for. They'll not bother me. It's you. We're staying with a farmer named Gartside.'

'My fiddle's at The Eagle.'

'We'll go for it. My trunk'll be at The George by now. I'll think of something. We'll go for your fiddle. Take a stroll through the starlight. I'll leave a message about my trunk. Get someone to hide it.'

'And Harriet? What'll 'appen to 'er?'

'The cavalry didn't let them get near Rhodes. Burton didn't see me, so she'll be all right. She's better with 'im and never seeing 'er mother again than knowing she's . . . she's . . . Oh, I'm sick of it, More Grief! I'm sick of that life!'

The danger was not immediate, and they needed a sleep before they left Oldham. There was a lot of scurrying outside during the night. Mor picked up only a little of it, and then he slept. Mary was awake for a while.

In my life now it's either Mor or the general, this game can't go on for ever. I'm tired. I'm wore out. The men don't want me the same. I can feel they're laughing at me 'alf the time. The general doesn't understand that even a corporal can be choosy, and won't take no risks. They don't tell me no news at all anymore. To get by I 'ave to do more and more specialities. My schoolmaster-weaver 'ere couldn't stand it for five minutes, if he knew . . .

My 'alf brother! As 'is father was mine, Oliver Greave. Anne Wylde couldn't be 'is mother, as 'e's thirty. Must 'ave been from Greave's philandering before that. That's a relief, it's not the 'ole 'og. He'd be shocked, though, if 'e knew. Fancy, so I've got a family at last! That's important in life, that is. In the end, it matters. 'Blood's thicker than water', I've always said. We'll get away to the south, give the general the slip, before 'e notices. Take up a little farm somewhere, be like the Queen of France, Marie . . . what's 'er name? Otherwise I'll get picked up somewhere 'ere, and when the general's getting no information from me, 'e'll say, 'She's wore out, she is, why bother with 'er, she couldn't tell a disaffected soldier from Adam, no news from 'er for a month, chuck 'er in the canal with a stone round 'er neck.'

Or my poor brother, well me 'alf brother'll watch me swinging at Lancaster and not even know who I am.

No, thank you, not for me. I've always kept a step ahead . . .

'An-twan-ette', that's what she was called . . .

Just 'ark at 'im sleeping, blowing bubbles like a baby. Wish I could sleep like that. Gawd, though, I love 'im.

Gartside's the answer for the time being. Why didn't I think of it before Mad Dick mentioned, in 'is sneering way? 'What is it you do for Gartside, Mary The Scar, you fucking whore?' What else does he think I am but a fucking whore? It's my profession. 'He only likes men, doesn't 'e, that Gartside? What can you do for 'is unnatural practices? 'E lives up on the 'ills wi' nothing but the sheep for company, doesn't he? That's what *he* likes. "Where sheep may safely graze". Not in Delph, anyway, they can't. Shit! Why don't you run to 'im and hide? You seem to do something for 'im, I don't know what.'

If 'e knew . . .

'As a matter of fact,' I says to Mad Dick, 'that's where I *am* going – to Gartside. Gartside doesn't like men at all,' I says to Mad Dick, 'I cured 'im. 'E doesn't like nothing. 'E's one of them sort, if you want to know. Why don't you go to Gartside's yourself, Mad Dick?'

The way 'e spat then! 'Me! Near 'im! Not if I'd be 'ung for it.'

You probably will, you mad deserter. 'I think you're scared of Gartside,' I told him. 'You're scared because you can't understand 'im. You're scared because 'e's not a bully like you. Yes, you're scared when 'e turns the other cheek, and doesn't do what you expect. Like they were frightened of Jesus Christ, when it come to it. 'Cos your type what things you're men, when it comes to it, you're shit scared. You wouldn't dare do what Gartside does, who'd never hurt a fly.'

As a matter of fact, Gartside'd be perfect for me and Mor. Doesn't want anything from me, except the pleasure of doing what he's told. It's a mystery to me, too, why 'e likes being a servant. Can't be expected to understand everything, can I? There's not much I can't get to the bottom of. Bottom, ho! ho! They soon drop their drawers wi' me. But 'e comes and never touches me. Scrubs the floor, washes the privy, and pays for the privilege. Says it relaxes 'im. So long as he can watch me with a soldier sometimes. He's never jealous, he just likes me to be around giving orders. Mor'll find soon enough 'e's nothing to be jealous of, neither. Nobody'll look for us there.

I remember Gartside coming to me for the first time. The state he was in! All boastful and giggling at first, throwing his weight about, not that he has much to throw, talking about who he knew, where he'd travelled, as if I'd be impressed. I who've been everywhere.

Then it comes out. Nothing 'appened. I tried everything I knew. Nothing 'appened. Until I started getting angry. In a manner of speaking nothing 'appened then either, but 'e was overcome. Blissful.

'Oh, I see,' I said. 'I understand.' He told me he couldn't do nothing with a woman, 'ad some terrible disasters, he confessed, 'cos he felt too much like one 'imself. 'I bet I know what you like,' I said to 'im. 'Don't tell me you travel all over the place neglecting your loom, bending the ear of a Duke's footman, staymakers, hatters in business for themselves, for no reason at all.' After two or three gins he was rolling on the floor confessing to 'is Nanny. Things 'e knew I could tell someone about and they'd 'ang 'im like a dog. All his eyes were wet. Next thing he was laughing stupid, his face purple, crying 'is heart out, whimpering like a puppy, poor lamb, kissing my clothes, clutching the carpet, banging the floor. All 'e wanted was to be forgiven and then controlled. Told 'e'd been a bad boy, oh wicked, but now it was all right.

'Do you know I can do anything I like with you now you've told me all that?' I said. 'There's only me between you and the 'angman.'

And suddenly I perceived the 'ole design, I knew everything. That was just what he wanted! Me in control of things, to forgive or not to forgive. Oh, I 'ad 'im then.

You'd never 'ave believed it when he came to me. 'E was solemn as a judge, righteous as a Methodist preacher . . .

And when everything was told, it turned out that he 'adn't done any of the things 'e said, with hatters and footmen, only thought about doing them. He just wanted to be treated as though he had. The benefits of being a bad boy, without having been one.

Wonder what it's like in Delph?

And as soon as the roads are quiet, in a month, we'll sneak away to the south.

'Are you awake?'

'Yes, I'm awake, More Grief.'

'What is it?'

'Just thinking.'

'I love you.'

'It's light. We'd better be going.'

They were travelling east out of Oldham, towards Yorkshire again, but instead of going back to Ripponden, they followed the edge of Greenacre Moor at a tangent via Waterhead, Austerlands, and Scout Head to Delph. Mor's fiddle was across his back, and lying the other way was his leather bag. Other unusual travellers were on the roads. Workmen carrying their bags of tools; young men and women looking frightened. A world full of fugitives.

'You ever tried to catch a fly on a summer's day?' Mary said. 'Never settled in one place more than a second. That's how they'll never catch us. We'll melt into the countryside. They'll never find you, I promise.'

'We ought all to 'ave stayed together, in Middleton. If we'd not been dispersed, we would be undefeatable. Now it'll be sport for them to hunt us down like foxes.'

'We two will always be together. Some day soon we'll take a little farm and I'll go back to the pigs and manure. I've got some money for it. I could surprise you.'

He smiled.

'I could manage a little farm. It'll get rid of the fluff in my lungs.'

He was laughing. Of course, he didn't believe her.

'Who is Gartside?' he asked.

''E's been a friend of mine for years.'

'Oh! I thought you were tired of all that.'

'Not that sort of friend. He's different. Someone on the raid mentioned 'im as asking about me, and I thought, "That's a sign from the Almighty. That's where we go." 'E's been to me with 'is problems often enough and I've solved them. It's my turn now.'

'So what's different about 'im?'

''E's . . . 'e is different. 'E's got something special about him, this one. He's so kind, and grateful. Wouldn't 'arm a fly. I know 'ow to treat him. You don't understand. Don't worry, you've nothing to fear from 'im. I've never been to his place, it's somewhere hidden out of the way, but we'll find it. It'll be all right. When we've done with

Delph, and things 'ave gone quiet, we'll go to 'Olywell Street in London to see about printing your writing, before we takes up a farm.'

'I'm not writing that sort of thing. I write about 'istory, and 'istory's wrongs, to be its witness.'

'"A Turk In 'Is 'Areem" 's 'istory. "The Infidelities Of The Prince Regent". Anyway, it'll be 'istory soon.'

'You make it all up.'

'All 'istory's made up. How do they know what happened? When they come to write about Burton's raid, nobody'll mention us. It'll be all about "mobs" and "troops of Scots Greys". Not unless we get tried and 'ung, then our own words might get taken down. So long as we confess, and say it all started wi'not going to church on Sunday.'

Upon the road they heard more of what had happened during the previous day. A certain John Nield was shot trying to run away from the Greys near Alkrington Hall. A woman who had been watching from her window received a bullet through her arm from the Cumberland militia. A man had indeed died at the end of Tonge Lane.

'Was he a joiner?' Mor asked.

'There was an old joiner shot in the churchyard, at about six o'clock in the evening. He'd been sitting in the public house and walked out when he thought all was quiet. Mr Johnson. They say he was staring at a gravestone. 'Appen 'e 'ad something to do when no one was looking. A Cumberland militiaman decided to send a ball through his neck.'

At last they crested Wall Hill. They were facing east, with the risen sun on their faces, the road branching steeply down to Dob Cross on their right, and Delph village just hidden to their left behind Knott Hill.

'We'll have roses round the door, 'erbs in the garden,' Mary said. 'You can write in the evenings. We'll grow old together. We'll take different names. Nobody'll know that we're not married. We'll go to a different parish and be carefree as aristocrats. We'll be happy.'

They had to descend into the shadow that still flooded Delph, which hid under a great hill that was like a tombstone. Then they must climb beyond, towards Friar Mere. As they looked back, the stone roof-tiles reaching out of the shadow shone with light, flying into the sun like the glossy wings of black birds.

'I think you don't believe I could look after pigs and hens,' Mary said, 'But I was born to it.'

'Oh, I believe it. I just can't imagine that anything so sweet could happen.'

'What I've learned in life is that anything can happen. Anything at all.'

'What I've learned is that things don't change, though they seem to.'

They asked their way of a weaver who was out early in his garden, making a tilth to plant peas and broad beans. The sun drew warm smells from the crumbling earth. One would never guess that a few miles away was a disaster.

'We call 'im "Bachelor", that Gartside. Lives up there like Jesus Christ himself,' the weaver told them.

As they climbed, more and more enclosures were filled with rocks. Men, women and children were carrying them to the edges of the fields, for heightening walls or filling gaps. In the valley bottoms, walls were decently built under the instructions of masons and with foundations, but here the "moor-edgers", as they were contemptuously called, simply threw up boundaries with the cleared stones. Lifetimes were being spent in spinning a web of thousands of miles of stone walls over the Pennine Hills.

Mary knew what Mor was thinking. She cuddled up against him.

'I want a little place in the south, not here. Nothing much. Something like Marie Antwanette 'ad, the Queen of France, kept sheep, roses round the door.'

'Typhus in the kitchen.'

The road grew increasingly stony and like a stream bed, with the water overspilling from the troughs or breaking through the rough walls. They reached the moor top where the light crossed at a level angle. Sheets of sapless grass mirrored the strong dawn sun, and turned to pools of blood. The water picked up trickles and drops of light.

They passed a man heading downhill, his horse so highly laden with wool that it caught and almost toppled in the breezes which were still breathing at this height, above the windless valleys. When they asked him where Gartside lived, he smiled at them and simply pointed over his shoulder to where more jagged, dark rocks fringed the sky. Then he spoke harshly to his horse and carried on down the track. When he had descended twenty yards he turned to stare after them, either baffled or intrigued.

At last Mor and Mary arrived at their destination. It was a black little cottage with smoke torn from its chimney by the ever-present moorland breeze; at the side a small, black-stone shed. It stood with a barren air of hopelessness in a nest of unattended enclosures. No weaving was stretched on tenter-frames, which made one wonder what its inhabitant lived on. A few hens picking flies out of the bog, and an old ragged pony having a hard search to find fodder, were the only signs of husbandry. Its occupant did not appear fond of being out of doors.

It seemed an alarming spot for a hide-out, because it was so exposed. Anyone moving about would draw attention from the other side of the valley. In the sombre landscape, the bright colours that Mary wore would flash for miles. On the other hand, as they realised on second thoughts, anyone coming for them could be spotted from far off.

'Gartside is in for a surprise,' Mary said.

There was no dog tied up to frighten away visitors and this made the hovel seem even more deserted. The door was open. The cottage was probably so damp and cold as to be on most days pleasanter for air entering it from outside. It reminded Mor of Phoebe's father's place. The lintel was so low that even Mor had to duck under it. A fire was burning, and it was needed. Upon the whitewashed walls Mor saw, scrawled and corrected in a large hand:

        E
UNITY IS STRENTH
      E   E
EGALITY FRATERNITY
        E
ALL IS VANITY

Mary entered first. Beyond her shoulder Mor saw an apparently serene little man, perhaps thirty years of age, and more like a dry, little, old woman, in dark, Sunday-looking clothes, a large book on his knee. His white face was polished by firelight as he sat over the flames. A sad man, waiting for something to turn up, hopeful. His shyness, possibly, was what made him look forbidding.

'Hullo, Mr Gartside. So this is where you live, is it? We've come to see you. This is my friend, Oliver.'

'Mary The Scar!'

Mr Gartside put his book on the floor, and got up, bustling nervously.

'A remote place, sir. You live by weaving . . . ?' Mor commenced.

'Mary The Scar! Well, well . . .'

'We have walked a long way, sir . . .' Mor began again.

Gartside hardly noticed him. 'Glad to meet you, too, friend,' was all that he managed, before returning his obsessed attention to the whore. 'Mary, sit down, do. Oh, my, fancy you coming here. Who'd have thought it?'

She had already taken his seat by the fire, before he offered it. She sat calmly while Gartside was fussing around his cottage, like a woman looking for something of which to be ashamed, and tidying things away.

'Oh, yes, please . . . do warm your feet. Oh my, oh my.'

'Come and sit down, Oli. Make yourself at 'ome. Still fond of your Bible, Benjie? Ecclesiastes, is it? Miserable stuff. My friend 'ere's a radical, too, so you can trust 'im all right. Don't worry. He won't turn you in, Benjie. Come and take my boots off. Don't pull so 'ard. Oh, that's better, Benjie! Oh, my feet. Don't put them boots too near the fire. Or I'll be cross. You 'aven't changed much, 'ave you, Benjie? To be honest, we're on the run. There's been a big raid on Middleton. You 'eard of it?'

'They were in Delph a few hours ago, several of them talking . . .'

'Don't interrupt me! So you've met 'em coming this way already, then? Well, we want shelter for a while, too. We're spreading the story that Oli is my brother, so you tell that to anyone that asks. Where's your teapot? You got any good blends from your grocer's? Come on, sit down, Oli. Hanging around like a bad smell. Gartside'll do the honours.'

Benjamin Gartside swung the kettle over the fire and rooted in his cupboard for tea.

'Oh, Mary, Mary. *You!*' he muttered.

Mor sat by the hearth, not understanding what was going on yet feeling safe because of Mary's self-assurance. Like a cat, she blinked and never once averted her gaze as she watched Gartside.

'I 'ope you've got a decent room, Benjie. We don't want something where the 'ens 'ave slept before us. Now, come and 'ave some tea with us. You sit on the floor 'ere. That's nice. Now, Benjie, what's been 'appening to you? Tell us all about everything . . .'

At the end of April and the beginning of May, a warm spell blanketed the moors. Gusts of fiery wind leapt through the heat; blasts out of the door of an oven, bending and stretching the grass, creating silver waves that died off listlessly in the distance. Each morning and evening the hills were sharply defined, dancing in fire. Sky, the streams, and the bleached grass upon the moortops, became pools of red.

In the valley, early every morning, weavers and farmers took advantage of the dew to scythe their crop. The hills soon turned grey with heat. During the mid-afternoon they disappeared into a soft, cotton-grey mist. The farmers hardly looked up. They were absorbed in the orgy of getting their grass cut, dried, and into barns, lest a wet summer set in soon.

Gartside's own farm had no grass to grow. It hung, a dark little mark on the edge of the sky. Someone with arms full of grass, eyes lit with greed and all orifices filled with golden dust, with the smell of haymaking, might just be able to make him out, watching them as he leaned on his gates or walls, or by a certain rock where he went sometimes to 'pray', calling it his 'altar'.

Mor would stroll over. Side by side they would stare over Friar Mere – not a mere at all, but an expanse of bog and peat gulleys.

'"Vanity of vanities, saith the preacher, all is vanity". It's too bright to last. We'll be paying for it, you'll see. "What profit hath a man for his labour under the sun? One generation passeth away . . . the earth abideth for ever." It's a good text, that. It's looking very black over Rochdale way.'

Gartside was right. He knew a great deal about the sky above his rocks. The weather broke. The storm fastened on the grass, died and drew off, leaving the fields broken. The black cavities amongst the huge rush beds of Friar Mere filled with water.

The sun burned out again, the gullies in the moor top cracked, the farmers below re-sharpened their scythes and did their best with the wreckage.

Conversation had not at first flowed easily. Gartside was wary. When Mor tried to break the ice with, 'In my village of . . .', 'Don't tell me,' Gartside interrupted. 'Keep to yourself where you've come from and what you've done. That way you'll oblige me by never suspecting that I've told anybody. You'll find that they're all like that in these parts. They've got enough secrets of their own.'

Mor could see that the Bachelor pretended to be more of a hermit and an eccentric than he was, to inhibit questioning, and as a cover. It was guilt at his own nature that made him so pessimistic. He saw all of nature as unsatisfactory, transitory, fated, consoling himself with the gloomy enigmas and fateful questions of Ecclesiastes.

Meanwhile Mary showed herself very domestic, cooking stews of the young rabbits that Mor knocked on the back of the head when he caught them in the grass. When she'd had enough of overhearing the men, she would carve up their discussion.

'Where's my indispensable, Bachelor?'

'Over here, ma'am.'

Eventually she wanted a change of clothes and was anxious for her trunk. Presumably it was still hidden wherever a friend at The George Inn, Oldham, had put it. The authorities must not be able to track it to Delph. She sent Gartside to investigate and he came back with the news that a soldier had already collected it.

Mary refused to be upset. She was a calmer person altogether, now. This rest that Mor and Mary enjoyed was the best thing they could have. When they walked into a room and found one another, the place was flooded with one another's eyes. They touched one another constantly. They created a world between themselves that shut out others. When they wanted to be alone, the Bachelor, who had also blossomed into happiness, was glad to be got rid of.

They talked again about that dream of 'a little farm'. It could happen. They could escape. 'What profit hath he that hath laboured for the wind?' Had not Mor laboured for the wind – for a revolution that never came?

Despite Gartside seemingly holding the world at nought, every evening at six o'clock he travelled on his old pony down the hills for a newspaper. He collected from the Post Office *The Leeds Mercury*, sometimes *The Manchester Mercury*, in issues that were always a few days late, and read them aloud, for the benefit of his fellow-drinkers, over a pint or two of ale taken in his special corner of the public house. They had grown used to him there at this hour of the day. Because of his dry humour that masked a warm disposition, no one persecuted him. His iconoclastic radicalism made him popular. They did not observe that his Utopia might be different to their own, and they had ceased to mark his eccentricities.

From the newspapers, and from the fugitives passing through the remote, radical Pennine villages, Mor and Gartside learned what was happening. The travellers had come sometimes from a hundred miles away, walking via secretive routes from Nottingham, Sheffield, Manchester, Stockport, or Chester, with rumours and news from organisations or combinations, euphemistically called 'Burial Societ-ies', or 'Charity Clubs'.

They learned of the destruction of a mill holding two hundred power looms at Westhoughton near Bolton, three days after the firing of Mr Burton's establishment. At Nottingham Assizes, five boys, aged sixteen, seventeen and twenty-one, had been sentenced to be transported for from seven to fourteen years for smashing stocking frames. On May 5th, the newspaper reported, 'A woman and two men were apprehended at Middleton and safely lodged in the New Bayley prison for being concerned in the late riots there,' and 'Thirteen rioters have been committed to Lancaster castle.'

On May 9th, or rather May 10th when *The Leeds Mercury* reached them, they learned that 'the person known by the name of King Ludd is taken and committed to Chester Gaol – his name is Walker; he was a collier, and marched before the deluded mob in a large cocked hat . . .

'The deluded multitude, whose ferocious outrages threatened the most alarming results, having relinquished their measures of violence and are returning to their peaceable avocations', crowed the newspaper, as if the rebels had discovered some greater wisdom, generally called 'learning sense'; but the next paragraph gave away the real reason.

'Chester county gaol at present contains no less a number than thirty two of these unfortunate and misguided men, and some more are expected from the neighbourhood of Stockport.'

King Ludd, despite his 'arrest', remained alive and kicking.

'The tranquility of the country is only imperfectly preserved even at the point of the bayonet,' concluded *The Leeds Mercury.*

Mor and Mary were leaning together at the door. They had so far spent two weeks in the cottage, so peacefully that it was like a marriage. They were staring at the hills that had been refreshed after the storms, and were brilliantly clear. They had not known that there were so many ranges of them. Today they were cut out of glass. Mary was still wearing the white chemise which had been torn in the raid. During their earliest days in Delph, the Bachelor, producing a lady's workbox, had set about it for her, for she herself was no needlewoman.

'Who's that?' Mor said.

'Where?'

Over the crest of the field appeared the tall battered figure of Mad Dick, lopsided under the weight of Mary's trunk on his shoulder. He had brought it thus far on the pony of a weaver, who could be seen leading his beast away downhill. Mad Dick sank into a hollow, rose and, although stumbling, pushing on fast. He was filthy and tattered. He had changed his military uniform for a suit of clothes; if it could be called a suit, for it was in rags and too small for him.

Mary laughed. Mor scowled. The hens scuttled away from Mad Dick's feet. The soldier dropped the trunk into the yard. He was shaking and sweating.

'Mad Dick, you'll smash my belongings. Me china and me teapote is in there, don't you know, you madman! What's brought you here? How did you get hold of my trunk?'

'A tankard of water, for Christsake, give it to me. Water, ma'am, water! Tis 'orrible parchin'. I met one o' the general's men confiscating it from your cellar, didn't I? You owe me something for retrieving that, you do. It cost me a shilling. You can start with a glass of water. Thank you, my dear. You old whore, you, you're an angel – in disguise, o'course.'

'Who's talking about disguise? The state you're in,' Mary answered.

He gulped and spilled the water, then he looked at Mor.

'Ah, Mor Laverock Greave, if I remember right. The one that absconded. Five foot five, a runaway Ludd. Escaped our clutches once, but now . . . gotcha! Left 'is family chargeable to the town. Well, well. There's a reward for lodging you in the gaol.'

'Mad Dick, 'is name is Oli. He's my brother, Oliver Wylde. That's what everyone thinks, and don't you forget it. Or I'll turn you in.'

'We're all in the same boat now, aren't we?'

'Yes, we are,' Mary answered.

''Cos you've let Mr Burton down, and maybe the general too, so I've 'eard. I wouldn't be in your shoes. What a weight this trunk is. Try it, *Oliver*, go on, try it.'

Mor raised one end easily enough, but both ends together was a different matter. He could do it, but only just. The deserter was watching and challenging him. At last he brusquely took over. Mor did not feel in a mood for jokes and physical challenges.

'Oli, me gallows-mate, Oli. We'll both lug it inside together. I've 'ad enough of managing by meself i' the world. What do you think, weaver? You see, I remember everything. We should all work together. Democrats. Where's the one they call "The Bachelor"? I want 'im. Where's 'e 'idin? I've come for 'im.'

'I'm here,' Gartside said from within, quietly.

'Did I hear something? *Did – I – hear – something?*'

'Who wants me?'

'I do. They call me Mad Dick.'

Mary followed the two men with the trunk into the cottage.

Gartside, wearing a weaver's apron, was washing pottery.

'What do you want with me, soldier?'

Benjamin was trying to be bold, but he was frightened.

'So you're 'im, are you? You're *it*, I should say. Benjamin Robert Abr'am Gartside, late of Diggle and of Sheffield? Call yourself a man? Then stand up and listen to what I 'ave to tell you, fancy pants. I've come to arrest you. Listen to this –'

Chadwick dropped his end of the trunk. Mor obliged at the other end and Mad Dick pulled from his pocket a scrap of newsprint.

''Ere, Mr Greave, read that. Read it aloud.'

'Mr D. T. Myers late of Stamford was convicted at Peterborough last week of an unnatural crime and ordered for execution on Monday next.'

'Tell me what you think of that, Gartside. Your turn next, isn't it? Don't tell me you don't know what an unnatural crime is, you little beast, you crawling worm, that you've never 'eard of it. 'Ow many 'ave you committed?'

'None,' Mary interrupted. ''E 'asn't done nothing. 'E couldn't.'

Gartside, with shaking fingers, was lifting the corner of his apron to his white face.

'I'll tell you what 'is crimes are. There's them that 'ave 'eard 'im confessing when 'e was drunk.'

'It's not true, Chadwick.' Mary said. 'He was only talking big. Boasting. No one could witness what 'asn't 'appened.'

'Once with an 'atter in Oldham, once after being drunk on Christmas Day with a silk merchant, once with a lord's footman, so I've 'eard. He boasted of it 'imself, when 'e was drunk. I don't know what else 'e's done. Young boys too, probably. It makes me sick to think of it.'

''E's never touched no one, Mad Dick! I know, for I'm the physician. I cured 'im o' wanting it. Don't you go talking about 'im when you're drunk, either. Do you 'ear me? Do you 'ear me, Mad Dick? You've the loosest tongue in Christendom yourself when you've 'ad a drink. 'E's done nothing. 'E *can't*, and that's the sad truth of it.'

'And I know different. The truth's out now at last, ain't it, Gartside? What a bugger. If I could bear to touch you, I'd drag you off right now.

297

It needs a special sort to 'andle the likes o'you. I'm 'ere on behalf of the King who will shortly send 'is prison cart. An open cart so everyone can take a look at you, what a worm you are, see what degradation a 'uman can descend to. What you've done's worse than being a child murderer. Don't tell the judge you're not guilty. Runt! Shit! They've caught your fellow blasphemers now. There's papers on you.'

'You liar, Mad Dick,' Mary said. 'Don't be frightened of 'im, Mr Gartside, it's 'is sick 'umour. He can't arrest no one. He's a deserter. It's 'im they're going to 'ang. I'll tell you this, Chadwick. Open your mouth and I'll find you a fate worse than 'anging. I'll tell 'em about *you*. Do you want me to tell Mr Gartside to start with?'

Mad Dick laughed.

'Frightened you then, little fellar, didn't I?'

Gartside laughed nervously. Mor went to help him with the crockery.

'You can get on with your needlework now,' Mad Dick said. 'Your sewing. Your women's skivvying. I won't touch you. Not for the time being. It might make me ill. Just be careful, that's all.'

The soldier unfastened his belt and sat in Gartside's chair by the fire.

'Don't try coming near me when my back's turned, that's all. Filth! If you want to save your skin, find me a bed 'ere. A day or two. A week, a month if I like. And don't tell no one, or I'll cut your throat and nobody'll be sorry. You're worse than any pig. Call yourself a democrat? You're worse than the filthiest pig. Do you 'ear me? If you were a man you'd do something about it. I can say anything I like to you, can't I? Filth. Shit. Piss. You'll be 'anging with your friend Myers. The sooner the better. Fetch me some ale. Go on! Find me some ale. If you 'aven't none, go out and fetch it.'

'Give him his ale, Mr Gartside. Let us have some peace.'

Gartside went into the back lean-to room of his cottage. They could hear him pouring ale into a jug. He returned and humbly stooped at Mad Dick's feet. He was trembling, yet his face looked transcendent as an angel's. In this position he filled the tankard.

'Don't behave to me like you was Jesus Christ,' Mad Dick hissed. 'Don't you touch me. One thing you learn in the army is 'uman nature. It stinks.'

All four of them silently watched the ale entering the tankard. Mad Dick put his torn boot on Gartside's apron.

'Spill any, an' I'll kill you, you slave,' he said. 'Unfasten my boots, you dog. But don't touch me. Don't you dare. Ah, that's better.'

298

Gartside, leaving the jug and the tankard on the floor, stood near the back of the room, hiding his shaking hands under his apron.

'Don't threaten him, or 'e might 'ave the pleasure of seeing you swinging first, Mad Dick,' Mary said. 'We might all enjoy that. It only needs a message to General Maitland. Mr Gartside's not scared of you. Nobody is. He'll give you a bed, won't you, Mr Gartside? But only out of the kindness of 'is 'eart. Not because 'e's afraid of you, you bully, but 'cos 'e's a democrat. 'E never gets tired of 'uman nature. 'E's never met *you* before.'

Mad Dick sloppily and noisily swilled back the ale.

'Right, then. All right, then. I won't touch him if 'e's a good little girl. Where's me bed, worm? I've been sleeping amongst the stones and thorns like Jesus Christ 'imself for a fortnight. 'Ad enough.'

'You can sleep with the loom,' Mary continued.

''Ere, are you two married, or something? Who's the lady of the 'ouse, 'im or you?'

'Shut up and come with me. You're sweating with fright yourself. I can smell it.'

'No, I'm not! It's me stockings. I've been living rough.'

Mad Dick stood up quickly, grazing the ceiling, ducking suddenly.

'This is an 'ole, this is. It's like worming about in the coal pit again. You should get your wench to do some cleaning, Gartside.'

Mad Dick laughed at his joke as if it was the funniest thing on earth.

Mary led Mad Dick, in his bare feet, upstairs.

'What you going to do for me, Mary The Scar, for bringing you your fancy trunk? *I'm* a man.'

Even before they were out of the room, he tried to take hold of her. She eluded him.

'Mind your 'ead, Mad Dick.'

The deserter cracked his head on the lintel. In his bad temper he slammed the door behind him at the bottom of the stairs.

Mary was already at the top. From living in the open air, Mad Dick had grown unused to cottages, and found himself too big for one. Looking to save cracking his skull everywhere now, he followed her into a creaking room. Daylight was brilliant through a long window. Some of the panes were open, so that he could see buttercups in the grass.

'He's a coward, your unnatural friend. That's why I 'ave to make fun of him. Keep him in his place. Who's this Ludd you've made up with? What's 'e like?'

'He's a gentleman.'

'First weaver and Ludd I've met that's described as a gentleman. There's no such thing. What's he got? It's unusual for you to travel the country for two weeks with a fellow.'

'Perhaps I'm in love.'

'*In love*! A whore in love!'

'This is your room, Mad Dick.'

'Where's the bed?'

The room seemed filled with the loom, but a mattress was tucked behind it. Chadwick spotted the bed and fell onto it.

'Talking about cowards, why are you sweating so much?' she asked.

His quivering fingers ran nervously over his face; trying to rip off a mask, and not able to manage it.

'Do you know what 'appened to the private what did not perform 'is duty at Rawfolds Mill?' he said, quietly, after a long pause.

Mary sat on the window ledge, safely distant from him. 'If 'e behaved like you, I 'ope they 'anged 'im.'

'They sentenced him to three 'undred lashes.'

'You'd 'ave enjoyed it.'

Mad Dick buried his face in his hands.

'Three 'undred,' he repeated. 'Them officers are bastards.'

'Did they carry them out?'

'How could they 'ave done? 'E'd 'ave been dead long before they was finished.'

He raised his face, yet looked anywhere but at Mary. To the side of her, through the window. She could not believe it, but there were tears in his eyes.

'It's pretty up 'ere,' he said. 'No one'd find you. You could live 'ere for ever, getting that Gartside to do the work.'

'So what happened, Mad Dick? They used to give 'em a thousand. In doses. It didn't kill 'em.'

The deserter blinked.

'They gave him twenty-five, then 'ad to stop. It was the owner of the mill, Mr Cartwright 'imself, what said to put a stop to it.'

'So there you are, then. You've nothing to be afraid of, Mad Dick. Nothing you're not used to in a whore'ouse.'

'Twenty-five!'

He became angry again, pummelling his fist into his palm, the tears growing bigger and brighter.

'Twenty-five is enough to – I'm no coward! I'm norra coward, Mary! I'm not like that Gartside.'

'Leave Mr Gartside alone.'

Mad Dick smiled for a second.

''E could be useful, couldn't 'e? I could live up 'ere like an eastern potentate with 'im around to do the work. *We* could live 'ere. We could make 'im do anything. He's shitting himself with fright.'

'Leave Mr Gartside be. He's not *your* slave.'

'I'd like to stay 'ere. Take the place over. I'm norra coward, Mary, I'll take anything they 'and out to me, but do you know what it's like, twenty-five of the cat?'

'It's a long time since they whipped whores through the streets.'

'It's not fun. As soon as it touches your back you feel that you're floating. The pain goes right through your body to your toes and the ends of your fingers. It burns and freezes, at the same time. That's only the first blow. After that comes the second. After the second comes a third. Your body's broken in two. You're gasping for breath, there's a noose round your throat, you fight for air. You feel you'll never drink air again in your life. They're beating a drum, and your comrades are standing watching. That's to destroy your self respect. There's an officer standing by with a sneer on his face. And a surgeon, to see 'ow you're doing. You feel as if you're already a corpse. The fear of the next blow's worse than the pain. When it falls it cuts you in two. If they didn't tie you down you'd leap feet off the ground.

'Twenty-five times, Mary. That's just for not firing his musket at his downtrodden fellow Englishmen. After a while they bring a fresh one to carry out the sentence. They won't 'ave a tired man flogging you 'cos 'is blows weaken. That's if you're still alive. They soak the cat in water.

'They brought him to the mill to carry out the sentence, to 'umiliate 'im, and let the villagers see him flogged. Only, the crowds thought he was a hero.

'But them dragoons escorted him. Dragoons, Mary, sneering dragoons, officers, gentlemen! You can't imagine 'ow they look down at an ordinary militiaman, them dragoons, trotting around 'im. Looking down from on 'igh, sneering, like you was the scum of the earth anyway, before you'd committed any crime. Pitiless. Out of Eton and Oxford and them sort of places. That's what it turns 'em into. It makes your blood run cold. They're glad to be flogging you, because you're infantry. They say . . .' He looked at her queerly. 'They say you

301

has feelings for the one what's doing it. Not 'ealthy. Ever watched a whipped dog? Some people think you'd be angry. But when it comes to it, you're not. You feel you're both of you dancing together, and there's no one else there. No matter 'ow many are watching, crowds, soldiers on parade, there's just you and the one that's flogging you, dancing together, in rhythm. Every blow, you're sure you can't go on no more. But you go on. Your mind's not there at all. It's just your body, dancing with whoever's 'olding the whip . . .

'It's *sick*!' Mad Dick shouted. 'They tear the flesh off you for writing the truth about them to the newspaper! That's why it was done to me. And then you get creatures like that Gartside running around free. It makes you mad! There's no justice. Filth like 'im, getting up to 'is tricks, and that's what 'appens when I write a letter to a newspaper.'

'Pull yourself together, Mad Dick. You 'aven't been caught yet. And Gartside's no 'arm to anyone. He enjoys his life, and is meek as a mouse at it. Can't you live and let live? We'll find 'im very useful to take with us when we go, and it makes 'im 'appy.'

'We?'

'Me and the weaver, Oli. We're going to 'ave a little farm. Not 'ere. In the south. I've saved up the money. It's lodged with friends,' she added quickly.

He looked right through her, very strange. Murderous.

'You think you'll live for ever, don't you?' he said.

'No, I don't. Not me.'

Mary nervously scratched her face, making crimson channels in the white cosmetic. She could see no way to put some spirit into him.

'But I'll live long enough to see you 'anging, if you don't pull yourself together.'

She loathed Mad Dick's cowardice. The sea of what she thought men were had grown treacherous. She swung off the window sill, teasing him with a show of her leg.

'Ah, well, if you're satisfied with your accommodation, I'll be off to find a *man*.'

He leapt up from the mattress and pinned her against the wall.

'What do you mean by that? Don't you say that to me. Nobody's ever said that to me. What do you mean by it, you old whore? . . . and you go with Gartside!'

'Ow! Let go! . . . I told you, no one does nothing with Gartside. Now let me go.'

He was crying.

She spat into his face. He let go and she ran.

'A coward deserves a flogging!'

He did not follow. Before she reached the foot of the stairs she heard him crashing his fists into the furniture and sobbing.

How was Mor to know that Edwin hadn't returned to Lady Well? He'd come across no news. Mary had told him that she had her contacts looking for him, but still there was no news. The child was probably back with Phoebe. Mor ought to do as others did, and creep back home at night.

Thoughts of his children, of Phoebe, and his cottage in Lady Well were not spun in Mor's mind. They rose out of his stomach, like the gobs of blood that choked a consumptive. They were not mental but were in his throat, gagging on something thick and moist, which he must expel, or die choking upon the memory. Instead of caring for his family, he was hiding upon the moors with a whore.

Mary's flowers were over. One night he thought: how could he spread his seed if he had to stop the mouths of babies with earth? How could he bring himself to bury a child in a well? Or, if he did not do that, face the responsibility for the tortured, tormented lives that were conceived by working people such as himself? What kind of mother could Mary be? He had deluded himself. The truth was that this woman had made sure that he knew nothing whatever about her.

He vomited his secret unhappiness upon Mary. As they lay together, Mor saw the black colour creeping up from the roots of her hair.

'Your hair is black.'

'What? I'm trying to sleep, More Grief.'

'Your hair is black,' he repeated.

'Yes.'

She could not see the point of what he said.

'Why?' she asked.

'Nothing. It doesn't matter. I've been thinking. Edwin might have gone back to Lady Well. I ought to see if he's there.'

'Hold me,' she whispered.

'I don't . . . I can't . . . I'm afraid of . . .'

'Children,' she finished for him, and turned her back.

How can love exist without fear, guilt and horror . . . ?

The geranium in his window in Lady Well might be coming into bud; Phoebe would turn it in the sun. In the valley opposite, where he looked out between his loom and his books, skeins of lighter green would be traced across the old grass.

'Why do you scratch your face?'

She buried her hands under the blanket, safe from annoying him.

'I don't realise I'm doing it. It's a habit. You're waking me up.'

'What's underneath all that white?'

'My skin. What do you think's underneath? Buried treasure? What is this? The Inquisition? You think I'm a witch?'

'What is it you're trying to hide?'

'I'm not hiding nothing.' Only that I'm pregnant. I'm certain of it. I don't need to wait until the next flowers. I feel different. Everything smells different. I can smell More Grief all the time, wherever I go, all over me, going with me. My mind wanders. I'm not the same person. I keep forgetting where I am, what I'm doing. I'm sure I'm pregnant. Can I tell him?

'What's all this talking for?' she said, irritated. 'You're waking me up.'

'You're always hiding something. Your true appearance, your stealing . . .'

'More Grief! Don't!'

'The colour of your hair.'

'It's my profession. You know I 'ave to, More Grief. Hiding things is my profession. I couldn't survive and tell the truth. If I did I'd be at the bottom of the Rochdale Canal by now. In a sack. I'm hiding *you*.'

He wanted to bite off his tongue. But he continued.

'The lies you invent for all those men. Just so that they'll enjoy having you.'

'Quite the married couple, aren't we, tonight? Why don't you take a turn? Instead of behaving like a married man. You've woken me up. I can't sleep now.'

She spoke briskly, like a whore with a client whom she did not like. She turned angrily this way and that in the bed. He did not move nor speak.

'You've no need to be so frightened,' she said at last. 'As you're so scared of having children. I've a sheep's intestine for you. You don't need to worry. I know all there is to know about bladder-policies and machines-of-safety. That's because I've learned long since 'ow much trust I can put in a man's promises to love me and make an 'onest woman of me when he whispers in the dark. You don't want children. I know, I know! Not with a whore. Yes, that's what it is, More Grief, isn't it? Well, don't fret yourself, I don't want no babies from you, neither, not if you don't trust me. I tell you, I'd rather put my trust in a swab of vinegar, or sulphate or zinc, or iodine, or corrosive sublimate, or strychnine like some girls put inside 'em . . .'

'Strychnine! Poison?'

'Yes, strychnine. They take a chance on poison rather than run the risk of bringing babies into the world and trusting men that say they loves 'em. If I find myself with child, I know what to do, don't worry. I've learned 'ow to stop that with *bitter* experience, if you don't want it.'

Although she listed chemicals like an apothecary, she felt that they were names for the saddest thing in the world.

He turned his face into the pillow.

'Stopped with earth in its mouth,' he mumbled.

'I'll tell you this, More Grief. When it comes down to 'aving children, they all goes back to their wives in the end.'

'Don't say that . . .'

'It's true. No one wants a whore pregnant. When it comes down to it, a whore's only for enjoying life with. For the deed of darkness, when it rears its ugly 'ead. But a wife is what you need for bringing in a family, isn't it?'

'No.'

'Oh, yes, More Grief. They all go back to their wives in the end. Every whore knows it. It's the first law of the profession. Love isn't being with a whore for all you can get out of 'er, More Grief. All that kissing and falling for passions that's in novels, anybody can do it without effort, easy as picking things up in the street, with a whore. But love . . . love is the day to day living together, quarrelling but being 'appy, with children and their own old parents, grandchildren p'raps to pass on. Love's a fight and an effort with it's light 'id under a bushel. Something I've never 'ad. The men all go back to their wives for that, no matter what they've been whispering to a whore. What do you think 'appens to us when we're old? I'm dying of poison from the lead, they keep telling me.'

She was silent.

'I want you to be mine,' he said, softly.

305

'Oh, More Grief, why aren't I? There's no reason why. You sound like Mr Burton. There's no reason why I can't be your wife – in the south. We'll take a little farm in the south. Let's go, More Grief. South. To the south.'

She collapsed into tears, her body shaking. He did not trust her love. It was dark, and they were not touching.

Mary opened her eyes abruptly. Gartside was at the side of the bed. His little white hands were trembling against his knees as he bent towards her. She heard from a distance Mad Dick moaning, punctuated with brief screams.

'Benjie, what is it? What 'ave you done?'

'Mad Dick's ill.'

'Scchh! Don't wake Oli. 'E needs to sleep something off. What's wrong with Mad Dick? Have you poisoned 'im? Have you been in to 'im?'

'I daren't go in. He's dreaming. I think he might do something.'

'All right, Benjie. I'll see to him.'

She did not wish Gartside to see her breasts and she pulled her nightclothes around her as she made for the door, and into Mad Dick's room.

'My Gawd, 'e sounds as if someone's murdering 'im. Are you sure you 'aven't poisoned him, Benjie? I won't tell if you 'ave.'

'No, Mary, if he's eaten anything it's not my fault.'

She followed the cries to the back of the loom until she could see Mad Dick's body, jerking in the bed clothes – like the last spasms of an 'anging man.

'Mad Dick! Sergeant Chadwick! Wake up! Wake up, it's me, Mary The Scar. Wake up, it's only me! You're all right.'

His shoulder jumped under the bedclothes. He was like a frightened animal in a sack. She bent her face down.

'Mad Dick! It's all right, it's me, Mary . . .'

His arms were suddenly around her neck and choking her.

'*Let go* . . . !'

Though she tore at his hands they were immovable. His moans, his screams were in her ear. She dug fiercely into his ribs, and that woke him.

'Mad Dick!'

'Mary. I love you, I love you, Mary . . .'

306

'Let go, Mad Dick! Let me go!'

'I love you . . . Oh Mary, I was dreaming.'

'I know. Now let go.'

'A dwarf with iron 'ooks for 'ands had them round my neck.'

'That's what I feel like. You're hurting me. Let go, Mad Dick, let go . . .'

But his grip tightened.

Turning her face she looked for Gartside.

'Benjie! Benjie! Do something.'

But Gartside had stood for a while, watching, then had left.

'Let go, Mad Dick, let go! I'll see you 'ung! Let . . .'

He clamped his hand over her mouth, as he easily pulled her down and mounted her. She tried to bite him but his skin was too horny for her to make an impression. He was too excited for her to dare to struggle free. The first thing she'd been taught was not to struggle. Strangled and ripped apart girls were every now and then dragged out of the canal, or from the bottom of a well, murdered by some frustrated soldier with habits learned in France or Spain. Such men were all over the north country. She must put up with it until he fell asleep, then he would be peaceful as a baby. Meanwhile she concentrated on keeping his lips away from her mouth.

Mor awoke without Mary at his side. He thought she had slipped outside to relieve herself and then, horribly, he heard the moans from the other room. Not Gartside surely? Could it be Mad Dick?

He crept off after those too expressive sounds. In the dark behind the loom were the two figures on the bed.

She talks of family? Children? Love?

He went back to his room, her room, their room. For three weeks it had been their home. Mary had contrived a pathetic dressing table. First it had held her cosmetic box, hand-mirror, and hairbrush. Now added to them were the bulkier items out of her trunk. An expert traveller, she had in an hour transformed the poor dusty room, draping her silk scarf over the trunk, looping her blue cloak over the chair, scattering pieces of lace for it to look as though her maid had not yet cleared up after a visit from a dressmaker, and placing the blue china vase on the window sill, just as in Ripponden.

She lied about everything. The room was a fake. Her whole appearance was a lie. She lied about her stealing, her sources of money, her association with Mr Burton. She lied constantly about himself and, drawn into her web, he had been forced to comply. If she had saved his life, it had been to make him party to her lying and thieving.

When he looked back upon their being together, he was not able to recall anything she had told him which he could believe to be true. All that she had said about loving him must also be a lie.

He could still hear her erotic moans. He dressed in his leather jerkin. He emptied his bag of her things and filled it with his own, including the oval stone. One way over his shoulder went his bag, the other way he fastened his fiddle. He had his transportable props, too, just as she had hers, and, like their two owners' characters, they would no more mix than oil and water.

He stared for a moment at the blue china biscuit-barrel. It had a deep blue glaze, decorated with drawings, in gold, of leaves and pomegranates.

He was a tramp, who had stumbled by mistake into a brothel.

He crept down the stairs, trying not to make a sound. He put his boots on by the door. In came a cool breeze, smelling of rushes and water. The curlews had returned to Friar Mere from where they had wintered on Lancashire beaches, and one called erratically around the cottage, the loneliest of sounds, over the sweet cut grass, in the dark, bubbling out of the rush beds. The boulders bulked against the sky and stars were sweeping through fast clouds. In the middle of the night, Mor left her.

(12)

May 9th–May 12th

'To the Virgins, to make much of Time'

Gather ye Rose-buds while ye may,
Old Time is still a flying:
And this same flower that smiles today,
Tomorrow will be dying.

Robert Herrick

Margaret was in a coach, travelling away from Liverpool, where she had left Edwin. It was the second day she had spent in the coach, which was light, fast, dark with its curtains drawn, and with upholstered seats. She was not alone. There was the strange gentleman who said that his name was Pickles. This morning he spoke to her sharply, when he warned her yet again not to 'peep out and show an impertinent face'.

'Where are we going?' she asked, trying to smile. If she scowled he might beat her.

'That's none o' thy business. Tha wouldn't know, if I told thee.'

He spoke with a strong Yorkshire accent, and she did not like the stale smell of his clothes.

'I've been to London before, Mr Pickles. I'd know the way.'

'Would you then? Well, dunna you worry about it. You're safe now, my lass, and thank God for't. No more roaming th'streets, an orphan, for thee. Thou's food and bed and thou's travelling like a lady. Still thou's not satisfied. At finish o'this trip we'll 'ave a nice position for thee.'

The coach was more comfortable than any bed she had ever been in, and for most of the first day's journey, when she was brought from Liverpool to Manchester, she had slept, stretched out at full length on the seat opposite Mr Pickles. He was most interested that she should be properly rested – a concern that had never before been shown to her. From time to time she was awoken by shouting at a tollbar, a noisy market, or by the coachman cursing a herdsman for his flock of sheep or cattle.

''Ave a rest, child. Thou needs it, poor lamb, so that tha can work for

309

thy living, doesn't tha? You'll grow up to be a fine lady's maid, I can see that. P'raps to a countess. Why, anything can 'appen when we get to London.'

She had peeped out at the untidy villages, the boggy land and pools of Chat Moss. When she had travelled in the opposite direction and further south with Edwin, he had shown her the curve of the horizon. She had thought at first that it was a flat plate, and then he showed her that the world had a bulge in it. He was always pointing things out to her – 'Look at this,' 'Look at that' – and often she could find nothing remarkable about a bird, a tree, a stone. Long, brown, symmetrical lines of drainage ditches were cut in the marshes, making bright green enclosures 'testifying to th'success of the new agriculture,' Mr Pickles told her.

On the second day of her journey, though, it alarmed Margaret to be forbidden to look out. She lay back, or curled on her side, and studied the strange gentleman, small, plump, and white, who 'thee'd' and 'thou'd' her, with unpleasant politeness sometimes, and at other times addressed her brusquely as 'you'. He hid himself, covering his chin with the lapels of his coat or pulling down the brim of his hat. He hardly answered her questions. Instead he gave her a sweetmeat to fill her mouth, told her to rest, and not to worry.

He had found her cowering in a doorway in the yard of an inn in Liverpool, from which, she had been told, the stage-coach to London began.

'Where art 'oping to go to, child?' he had asked.

'To London, sir, where my mother is.'

She was both shy and stubborn, as she had been with Edwin. He had never stopped trying to persuade her to go to America. 'It's th'only thing to do. The only thing,' he repeated. 'The land of the free.' He had egged her on as far as Liverpool, but on seeing water, ships, and foreigners, rather than being excited as Edwin was, she realised that she could not trust herself to water and to hiding in the hold of a ship. She could not leave England. She said goodbye to Edwin and went to the coach-stop with the timid hope of persuading some lady or gentleman travelling to London to take her on as a servant, or loan her the fare until she obtained a 'position'. She had become so used to her dirt and her smelly rags that she did not think about it putting others off.

On reaching the inn, she had not known what to do. She did realise that she was too filthy-black to go inside. Menials were cursing her. A dog snarled. Even carts and piles of baggage bore her animosity and collided with her. A little before midday, it started to rain and she cowered in a doorway, drawn by the smell of food from the kitchen.

She had been aware of the gentleman watching her for some time before he tapped on the dining-room window, three times slowly. She could not believe it. She saw him leave his window-seat and he appeared smiling in a doorway. He looked up at the pouring sky, decided not to go under it himself and beckoned her.

From the beginning, he was hunched in his clothes. His smile glowed out of the dark cloth, through the rain, welcoming her from the door beyond which she knew there was food. She was blind to everything except that. She did not mind putting her bare feet into the puddles that were dirty with horse-manure, nor resent standing before him for some time in the rain, shivering with cold on a lower step.

'Thou'rt a lucky girl. I 'appen to run a servants' registry in London. I'm always on the look-out for such a likely article as you. How old art thou?'

'Thirteen, sir.'

She decided to stick to that.

'Thou seemed much younger. Starved, I suppose.'

He looked disappointed and in doubt.

'Have you started to . . . Do you . . . Well, never mind for now. Have you been turned out from somewhere?'

She couldn't think of an answer.

He winked.

'Well, we won't ask why you was dismissed, will we? Let's put it this way. I'll not ask questions about why you're roaming the streets of Liverpool, if you'll not ask anything of me neither. That's lucky for you, isn't it? Some employers might 'ave asked for a character. Does t'ave relatives in Liverpool?'

'No, sir.'

'That's good. We don't want anyone poking their noses into our business, do we? I must talk to you about one or two things and if everything's satisfactory I'll take thee to London. But because I've business to attend to in Manchester we'll 'ave to travel by that way first. You wouldn't mind that, would you?'

'No, sir.'

'That's a good girl. Hungry?'

'Yes.'

She smiled. He touched her head, and it made him grimace.

311

'I'm Mr Pickles. What's your name?'

'Morgarit.'

'Anything else?'

'Never 'eard of it.'

He led her in, out of the rain. Servants were now smiling at her. He passed her over to a woman who took her into a scullery where the pans were scrubbed. There were huge wood-and-coal-fired ranges and pans of steaming water. Two women scrubbed Margaret's face and neck. In half an hour she was returned to the main kitchen, where she was handed a plateful of food and a fistful of cutlery. The gentleman, who was also served with food, led her to a private table in a corner.

'I've had my troubles in the world, too. My debts to pay. But we can only descend so far and then the wheel of fortune must turn upwards.'

She struggled with the cutlery, being used only to a wooden spoon and a knife. Instead of stabbing with the fork, she tried to balance a small potato on it. It fell into the fat and gravy. She next used her knife to pierce a lump of mutton. She tore at it with her uneven, yellow, ratlike teeth. A china plate was clearing under the grease. She had never eaten from anything other than wooden bowls before.

Mr Pickles was repelled by her table manners.

'In the days when I used to dine . . .'

He forgot his disgust, as he stared at her hand.

'What's that on your finger?'

She swallowed fast.

'What's what, Mr Pickles?'

'That.'

He carried on staring. Shyly, she covered her brass ring.

'Edwin gave it me.'

'Edwin?'

'My friend. 'E gave me 'is jacket.'

'Your friend? Oh, I see. You told me you had no friends. Where is he?'

Mr Pickles stood up, eager to take away both plates. Margaret clung tightly with one hand, and with the other stabbed hurriedly with the knife.

'America,' she growled, like a dog with its teeth in a bone.

'America!'

Mr Pickles laughed.

'I thought you was too young to 'ave friends, but I was mistook, I see. I don't think this will do. We can't do business, after all.'

He was holding out his fat little hand, expecting her to politely give up her food.

'My friend's not very old.'

''Ow old is 'e, then?'

He took hold of the child's plate, his thumb disgustingly sunk in greasy gravy. She clung more tightly and gobbled faster.

'Nine,' she managed to say through the food scalding her mouth.

Mr Pickles smiled. She continued to gobble as fast as she could in case he changed yet again. He sat down.

'Let me ask you something. Something very important. Do y'ave any lady's . . . Let me put it this way. I'm only a rough man. Do y'ave any lady's problems yet?'

'Problems?'

'Problems.'

Mr Pickles was blushing.

'No.'

She had a whole hot potato in her mouth. Being used to a diet of oatmeal, she did not know how to cut it up. When she had got rid of it, ''Cos I'm not a lady,' she answered.

'Are t'sure thou knows what I mean?'

'No.'

'Do you . . . bleed?'

'Bleed? No. Where? Can I 'ave more mutton? I don't like the fat. Ugh!'

She dropped a lump of fat out of her mouth and picked it up with her fingers.

He was pointing angrily with his knife.

'Do you bleed down there? Tell me truthfully. I don't want to put it more candidly, not wanting to offend your delicacy . . . your childish . . . but I must know, thou knows. Tell me the truth. Yes or no?'

'Ugh! I swallowed that fat, Mr Pickles!'

'Do . . . you . . . bleed?'

He changed colour again. He was now white with anger.

'No.'

He was relieved, but remained white, with embarrassment.

Margaret lifted the plate and licked it.

'Are you sure? Are you telling the truth?'

She eyed him suspiciously over the rim of her plate.

'Yes. I don't think so. I don't understand what you mean, Mr Pickles. Can I 'ave some more?'

'If you don't understand me, you can't 'ave started. Some come to it late. Are you sure you're telling me the truth?'

'I don't tell lies, Mr Pickles.'

Margaret waved her empty plate at the servant and pointed. The cook mouthed something back and likewise pointed downwards at an empty plate. Edwin would have been better at lipreading.

'It's 'ot in 'ere,' Mr Pickles said. Again he stood up, ready to leave.

'I want some more food!' she shouted.

Heads were turning at other tables and smiling disapprovingly at a child with 'tantrums'. He hurried her out into the yard and into his own small coach.

'You must tak' that off.'

'What?'

'That bit o' brass pipe. Remove it. That . . . ring.'

She stared out of the window with an obstinate expression.

'Go on, tak' it off.'

He tried to grip her hand and she snatched it away.

'No! And I'm not coming with you if you make me! I'll scream!'

'Oh? Well, never mind now.' He was smirking. 'We'll see 'ow you are later, young lady.'

He took her to Manchester. After being fed again, this time with oatcakes, she was locked in the attic room of a much poorer inn, where she had no difficulty in continuing the sleep that had filled most of her afternoon.

Early on Saturday morning she was again hustled into the coach. Although still forbidden to look out, after they left Manchester she felt that they were climbing uphill, more and more steeply. Mr Pickles told her nothing, so she curled up and went over her memories of the walk to Liverpool.

Edwin and she had got lost so often, asking their way from one village to the next, that it had taken them two weeks. Leaving the artist's studio early, before anyone returned to it, they had been directed southward along Deans Gate, and advised to follow the tow path of the Duke of Bridgewater's Canal, as soon as they struck the bridge. Beyond Altrincham, where the canal made a loop (which all the bargemen cursed) around the Earl of Stamford's park at Dunham, a bargee leading a horse along the path told them that they were heading too far southwards for Liverpool, so they had ducked down an embankment, to follow a river that passed under the canal. Edwin caught trout, and that night they slept at Warburton, amongst the oak pillars and beams of the ancient church of Saint Werburgh. From here they went to Warrington, then via Speke Hall and the sands of the Mersey Estuary to Liverpool.

Mr Pickles paused once, for a brief lunch. Margaret's cheese and bread were brought to her in the coach, in which she was locked with the curtains drawn, while her guard, judging by his breath when he returned, spent the time in a public house.

After a steep drop down, the wheels squealing on the brakes, and then a climb upwards which almost rolled Margaret off her seat, they came to rest. Mr Pickles stood up, shook himself down, smiled and when he had opened the door, grabbed her hand. She could hear the horse being freed from the shafts and clomping off to its stable. Mr Pickles stepped down first. Then he handed her out, keeping a tight hold.

She could see she had been brought to the rear of a mansion. The stables, the carriage shed and the kitchen entrance were nearby. Margaret was not one who expected to be told where she was, so she did not ask. She kept her eyes down so as not to stumble and cut her feet on the cobblestones, as Mr Pickles hurried her towards the house. At the top of a flight of stone steps a door opened, without any knocking, nor anyone being visible to open it, and a woman pulled her hastily inside.

Margaret took a look around and screamed, then sank her teeth into the fleshy hand of the woman, who yelled, let go of the child, and biffed her round the ears. Mr Pickles who was behind, blocking the retreat, grabbed Margaret by the collar.

She had looked through the gates of the yard, over the roofs of wool-finishing sheds, a spinning mill, an apprentice house and an old fulling mill, to the glint of a small river and woods rising at the far side to moorlands, where the sun was setting. She was back at Lady Well, at Mr Horsfall's.

Mr Pickles dragged her in, the woman offering her unwilling help. The door was banged shut and locked, the woman removing the key and pocketing it. Lamps were lit, because the shutters were drawn. There were piles of clean, sweet-smelling washing. She had been brought to the laundry room. Her mouth, from biting the woman's hand, tasted of soap. Mr Pickles let go of her. He expected her to stand still, but off she set, flashing round the room; a small bird baffled by walls, blinded by fear. They had no idea what had got into her, for she was knocking over copper pots and piles of clean laundry. She kicked over a chair and hopped onwards holding her hurt ankle, as the woman made a grab at her. She flew at a door, but it was only to a cupboard; she wrenched at another but it was locked. Dashing away again, she knocked over a pitcher of water that was on the floor.

It was Mr Pickles who caught her. He was not smiling now. He bent Margaret's arms behind her back and clapped his other hand tight over her mouth, so that she could not bite him. He scrutinised her, puzzled.

'Whatever's come over her?' he said to the woman. 'Dashing about like a stung calf. What's she seen? She mi't'a'seen the Devil. It's a mystery. For the Lord's sake fetch some brandy! Fetch the brandy!'

The breathless woman came with a glass bottle, the stopper in her hand. They could do nothing, though, until that violent look passed out of Margaret's eyes. Mr Pickles saw that if he let go of her she would scream the place down.

'Mak' a sound and I'll beat the lights out of ye, I will. Does tha understand?'

He gave a warning kick on her shin.

'D'ye understand me? Nod your 'ead if y'understand.'

She tried to nod.

'I'm going to let go now. Mak' a sound and I'll kill ye.'

He slowly took away his hand. Standing behind her, he put it round her shoulder and pinched her nostrils, clamping her body against his own, trapping her arms and freeing his own other arm.

'Open!'

She remembered Mr Gledhill's "Open thee gob." She was back at Horsfalls'! She opened her mouth and quickly closed it. She was exhausted and could not put up a fight. She was trembling and gasping. She would say nothing.

'Fetch me a spoon,' Pickles said.

The woman, who clearly did not like her job, put down the stopper, kept hold of the brandy bottle and brought a silver spoon. Mr Pickles took it, forced the handle between Margaret's teeth to hold down her tongue and prised.

'Pour it in.'

The woman poured directly out of the bottle into Margaret's mouth, gingerly from a height, frightened of being bitten. Margaret felt it spilling off her lips, onto her chin, and a noose of liquid falling on her neck. She did not dislike the taste, although she did not like it either. With her nostrils and tongue clamped, she was forced to swallow. It made her splutter and cough. Mr Pickles allowed her to lean forward. The woman took away the bottle.

Margaret's head began to swim. They allowed her a moment, then forced her to take more brandy. There was a pain behind her eyes, clouding her head. The room was expanding and contracting. She coughed. Her legs felt even weaker. She collapsed.

When she came to she was in a smaller room, sitting naked in a china bath filled with warm, very dirty water, in a steamy, white light. Her ring was not on her finger.

The same fat woman was soaping her body and scrubbing her with a stiff brush. This was the second scrubbing Margaret had had in two days, and a really thorough one.

The woman smiled.

'There, you've had a shock. Mr Pickles doesn't mean you no 'arm. 'E's got 'is job to do. But you took your medicine like a good girl in the end, didn't you? Why did you run around like that? Like an 'eadless cockerel. Laugh! You led us a dance.'

Margaret's head was thumping. Her eyes still did not focus, things advanced and receded, but she relaxed. The woman was working on her shoulders.

'Why are you scrubbing me?'

'You're in Mr Horsfall's employ now. Mr Horsfall. You remember that name.'

'I do.'

The woman did not register the significance.

'He's master here. Mr Pickles promised you'd be found employment, didn't he? Well, you're Mr Horsfall's servant now. Nothing to be frightened of.'

'I'm not frightened.'

She was resigned. The white edges of the bath kept coming and going. So did the walls, hazy beyond the steam.

'I'm Mrs Flitcroft.'

Margaret's flesh was tingling, and had become an extraordinary pink.

'Edwin . . .'

'What did you say?'

'Nothing. I didn't say nothing. I was dreaming.'

A younger servant girl brought in a fresh ewer of hot water for the bath.

'I want to see my mother.'

'You'll meet your mother, dear. Some day. There, there.'

'Edwin went t'America.'

'Who's Edwin, then? Your brother?'

Without warning, Margaret was sick in the bath. Mrs Flitcroft patiently washed her again where it had spilled upon her little breasts.

'Never mind. It's time for outs now.'

Mrs Flitcroft helped Margaret out, stood her on a towel and dried her body, caressing her feet, calves, thighs, stomach, back, breasts, and rubbing dry her hair. It now looked very fair.

'I want to drink some water.'

'Jenny, bring a glass and water!'

The girl returned with a glass. A *glass*, for Margaret to drink out of! Anything at all could happen to her now.

'Where've you come from?' Mrs Flitcroft asked.

'I don't know . . . I . . .'

'Liverpool, I was told. They picked you up. What did you do, then, in Liverpool? Such a long way.'

Margaret didn't answer.

'Is your head bad?'

'Yes.'

She was led gently into an adjacent room, where Jenny was waiting. Amazing clothes in sunset colours were scattered upon a bed. A wardrobe door was open; it was filled with little-girls' dresses, like those upon the bed. The extraordinary new rose of Margaret's flesh was dressed by Mrs Flitcroft, first of all in loose lace-edged pantaloons, then a cotton petticoat edged also with cream lace, and over this a pale pink dress made of silk, with puffed sleeves of fine lawn, likewise ending in cream-coloured lace. There was delicate smocking on the bodice and cream lace edging the neckline. She was given white stockings and white kid slippers. A broader dark pink sash was tied around her waist, with a large bow at the back.

Meanwhile Jenny was heating crimping irons in the fire. When Mrs Flitcroft had got as far as Margaret's stockings, Jenny, with four crimping irons on a sanded tray, came forward to put curls in the child's short but thick, soft hair.

One servant at her feet, another at her head – and only yesterday Margaret had declared that she was not a lady! She brushed her hand over the silk dress; she felt at her bare scrubbed arm; things she had never experienced before. Nothing would surprise her again.

'This isn't no dress for me. Am I being adopted?'

'I could kill him,' Jenny spat out, looking away. 'I feel ashamed.'

'It's nothing to do with us,' Mrs Flitcroft said.

She placed one of Margaret's feet into a kid slipper.

'That Pickles is a worm,' Jenny declared. 'He's a slimy toad.'

'Why am I being dressed like this?'

'You might well ask,' Jenny said.

'Mr Horsfall's adopted you.'

'Mr Horsfall's adopted me?'

'He's taken a liking to you.'

'My head's sore.'

'Have you noticed 'im these days?' Jenny said smiling.

'Who?' Mrs Flitcroft asked, dealing with the other slipper.

'Horsfall. He picks his nose, just like 'is father did.'

'What are you talking about, girl? What are you inf'rin'?'

'He picks his nose, that's all, just like 'is father did, when 'e had one to pick. You just watch 'im. He doesn't know 'e's doing it, but I've watched 'im for hours when I've been serving dinner. The dirty beast.'

'You should mind your own business and respect your betters.'

Mrs Flitcroft experimented with the tightness of the sash. She fastened and unfastened the bow several times.

'There was blood on the pillow cases last week. Lucy said they was yellow with pus. Do you remember 'im staying indoors with a sore throat? How many times has that 'appened this spring? I know what's in store for 'im!'

'Has he ever seen me?' Margaret interrupted.

'He must have done, I suppose. A girl as lucky as you shouldn't ask so many questions. That goes for you, too, Jenny.'

Mrs Flitcroft had come round to the front to survey her work. There were tears in her eyes. Her hands, putting the final touches to Margaret's appearance, arranging the curls, were nervously brusque, but not unkind.

Retreating before Mrs Flitcroft's better artistic judgement, Jenny busied herself, putting away the irons and tidying dresses.

'What a picture. A work of art,' Mrs Flitcroft said.

'I don't know 'ow he could 'ave seen me. How could 'e adopt me if 'e 'asn't seen me? 'E never looked in. Was it in chapel?'

'Perhaps,' said Mrs Flitcroft.

Neither of the servants knew what she was talking about.

'Now Mr Horsfall, when you go in to see 'im, might want you to sniff something out of a cloth,' Mrs Flitcroft said. 'If I were you I'd sniff it up like a good girl. It's ether. It won't do you no 'arm. You'll probably pass out like you did before, and when you come round you'll be all right. You'll be all right, I think. Don't make a lot of noise and fight like you did before. It'll make him angry.'

'I 'aven't done anything to anyone, ever.'

'Men can be very peculiar sometimes,' Jenny said.

'I 'aven't done anything, though.'

'It'll be all right. You won't feel anything. Probably afterwards you'll be found work in the kitchens. You'd like that, wouldn't you?' said Mrs Flitcroft. 'Jenny, you'd better see to that bath. Clean it.'

'In my own time, I will. I can't do everything. I've only one pair of 'ands, you know . . . The beast!'

'When you come round, you'll probably hurt a bit.'

'Where?'

'And you might bleed, a bit.'

'Where?'

'But don't worry. You'll probably 'ave to lie down for a while afterwards, but you'll be given a comfortable bed and then you'll be all right.'

'Why?'

'Now aren't you a lucky girl?' concluded Mrs Flitcroft. 'You look an angel. A proper picture by an artist.'

Mrs Flitcroft clasped the child warmly for a moment.

'Straight out of a picture. You'd better take her in before she spoils.'

'You take 'er in,' Jenny said. 'He can tell I don't like it. I thought I was to do the bath.'

'Nobody likes doing it. We all 'ave our turn. It's the way of the world.'

'Then you take 'er.'

Margaret walked over and held Jenny's hand.

'I'll take 'er, then. Promise me you won't leave me the bath as well. Hush, you, lamb.'

But Margaret was not crying, nor saying anything.

They had to walk a long way, along corridors. They climbed several stairs. Jenny, carrying a lamp, was muttering.

'They say they've passed a law in Parliament. I don't know. Them as can read say so.'

'What?'

'Nothing, lamb. Nothing.'

They once went up, and straightaway down again. Margaret thought they were lost. Everywhere was strangely deserted. On the few occasions that a stray servant was spied ahead, Jenny pulled her into a side room and made her wait for a moment.

Margaret's guide eventually took her into a gentleman's dressing room, without first knocking on the door. It was small and gloomy, one wall filled with huge cupboards. A door was open showing trays of shirts.

Jenny knocked quietly on a further door.

'Send her in.' A man's voice, no louder than was needed.

'Go in and curtsy,' Jenny whispered. 'I'll stay here.'

When Jenny had opened the door she stood behind it, hidden.

'Good luck,' she said as Margaret stepped forwards, slowly; a stiff doll.

Margaret heard the mahogany door close comfortably into its jamb and lintel behind her. Mr Horsfall, wearing a silk dressing gown, sat by the fire. He was slowly picking his nose. What interested Margaret most was not the man, but a large painting on the wall. It depicted a little girl who looked confusingly like herself; pink silk dress, sash, pantaloons showing lace, darker pink satin bow, and curled, but longer, hair. Mr Horsfall's daughter.

He turned to look at her. She dropped the curtsy. He flushed at the sight of it.

'My rose, my perfect angel . . .'

He was overcome.

Perhaps he has found out that I am really his daughter . . .

She was aware of a thin, swooping shadow, then he was kneeling beside her, feeling her dress with delicate, unworn, man's hands.

'My angel, my rose. Oh my rose, my angel, what innocence, what innocence!'

His lips were kissing her dress, his hands feeling her thighs through it. His breath smelled of brandy – the smell of the same stuff that had been thrust into her throat.

'Your lips a perfect rosebud . . . oh my dear. Such a perfect rosebud. My heart, so sweet, my sweetest of hearts.'

He looked at her from his kneeling position.

'Your lips . . . Some bee has newly stung them, oh my sweet. Kiss me.'

She did not move. She was as frigid as the picture of which she was a replica. The sinister moth of his mouth passed back and forth lightly over hers.

'My sweetheart of sweethearts. That such a loveable creature as you should ever grow up! Such innocence – that it should be doomed to be violated by a harsh world! Alas, you know so little of the evils of this life.'

'Am I being adopted?'

'Come! Come!'

He had stopped fluttering over her dress. He stood up and led her by the hand. She had not noticed the bed before.

'Are you going to adopt me?'

'Of course I am. Yes, yes! Didn't you believe it?'

'When?'

'Afterwards. Lie down there. Let's lift you up.'

'It'll spoil my dress. Are you my father?'

'Yes.'

'*No, you're not.* I don't think so.'

She squirmed away from him as he flopped upon the bed.

'For now, I am. Lie still! Lie still, damn . . . lie still. There. You *are* a young filly.'

His voice had grown angry, then soft, as he began to have some success.

'Will there be no more Mr Gledhill?'

He was surprised.

'Gledhill? Who's he?'

'In the mill.'

'You know about him?'

'He does what you're doing to girls.'

'Does he? We'll have to report him to the inspectors, then.'

'Don't tell 'im I told you, *please*!'

'I'll deal with Gledhill, if you're a good girl. With all the Gledhills in the whole world.'

'He's your servant, isn't he?'

'Yes, he's my servant.'

She was on her back, and he was humped over her, lower down, burying his face in silk and lace as he fumbled to unbuckle his trousers, and struggled to pin her down.

'You'll spoil my dress.'

'I'll buy you a new one. Lots of them. Lots and lots and lots. Hundreds of them.'

'Shall I be a lady then?'

'Yes, you'll be a lady. And Gledhill's days are numbered, I can tell you.'

'Oh, I don't believe you.'

'It's true.'

She tried to lie on her side. His hands had reached under her dress and were playing with the laces of her pantaloons. She tried still harder to turn away, but his weight held her down.

'You're heavy.'

'Stop talking! Don't make a sound. Scchh . . . don't say a word, my rosebud, my angel.'

Remembering what had happened to her earlier, she did not shout, but she continued to wriggle, silently. Eventually she could not stay quiet.

'Oh, don't do that! I know what you're doing. You mustn't do it. Edwin'll kill you.'

'Edwin?'

He stopped abruptly.

'He'll cut your throat. He's my friend. He's in America.'

Horsfall laughed. She was angry and indignant.

'But 'e'll come back. He'll cut your throat! He told me about you.'

'Did he?'

'Yes, 'e did. Mor Greave's 'is feyther.'

'The schoolmaster? The one who kept a seditious school and deserted his family? He's a wanted man. We're going to execute him.'

'Oh no, you're not!' she shouted. 'You're a bad man!'

He put his forearm across her throat and tight under her chin, forcing her head back. She let out a choked scream, fighting for air in panic.

'Damn you, keep still!' He forced his arm tighter under her chin. 'Oh my angel, my heavenly delight. Curse . . . oh my rosebud, angel . . .'

'Nnt . . . nnt . . . nnt . . .'

The pain of what he did below forced another scream from her as soon as his concentration slackened. It was heard by Lydia Horsfall, who was used to picking up such sounds from the house.

At three in the morning Pickles took Margaret away in the same light, fast coach. A blanket was wrapped over her original tattered clothes which Mrs Flitcroft had boiled and dried. It was all that Mrs Flitcroft could do. Tomorrow, in the communal silence of prayer, she would wonder whether she was condemned for her part in what happened on nights such as this. But at the moment she was asleep.

Margaret was still drunk, weeping and giggling, with a bloody wound spreading its stain between her legs. If Pickles had not taken her she could not have walked. She could not bring her legs together and she sat awkwardly. She could hardly see him as he muttered in the dark.

'What a man. What a monster. What did 'e do to thee? I'm sorry. I'm sorry. I'm no better off than you are with 'im, me child, so dunna blame me, please. I'm sorry. There's five 'undred o' your sort walking round Piccadilly every night. You're not alone. I didn't mean you no 'arm. Oh, I'm sorry.'

It was Pickles' duty to stay awake through these nights, on hand in case of things going wrong, needing a surgeon, or for some child to be dumped on a lonely road at the border of the parish. Such had sometimes been found, wandering before dawn into strange hamlets, telling obscene 'lies'.

'Don't tell anyone. I'd be in the debtors' prison if I didn't do it.'

She wondered what would happen to her wound. Would it go bad and she'd die?

He took her to the Lady Well workhouse. No one came out to see. The master and the mistress did not want to know. Looking around to make sure no one was about, Pickles lifted her out. She was surprised that he was gentle.

She did not care overmuch where she was put. Silk dresses? Being adopted? It was all lies. Mr Pickles left her shivering and crying on the porch steps of that same workhouse where Mor Laverock Greave had been left more than thirty years before. An envelope with five guineas in it was clutched in her hand.

The coach left Lady Well that night. No one, of the few who saw it, could have known whose it was, where it came from or went to.

Horsfall did not see Margaret go. Yet, after he had shouted for Pickles to strip her and take her away and had ordered him to return later to attend to the discreet laundering of the clothing, he still stayed up and about. When Margaret departed from the rear, he was staring out of the front window. In the starlight he looked absentmindedly over the dim banks of rose beds and picked his nose. He was exhausted, but his imagination remained famished.

Pity about the child. I should have asked her name. She was supposed to be from Liverpool, so how does she know about Gledhill? If they know about Gledhill as far away as Liverpool, I'd better get rid of him. He can be sacrificed as a gesture to the magistrates and manufactory inspectors. Kill two birds with one stone.

He hoped she'd survive. Or maybe it would be better if she didn't. He felt sorry for her, but he did not allow himself to feel too much. He was a man of breeding, having a right to anything of that kind, and such feelings were unworthy of him. His search was for innocence in an ugly, corrupted world.

I'm sorry I forced her so hard. Wouldn't have done, if she hadn't said that about being 'A bad man'. And Greave. Damned Luddites. It got me angry. I think she'll be all right. Not as young as some.

The risks he took sometimes made him sweat.

He heard a carriage and realised that it had stopped, not at the rear but at the side entrance. He heard luggage being carried in and out, or something like that.

A few minutes later it swept round the front of the house and down the carriage drive. A head popped out, lit by the carriage lamp and taking a last, not regretful but interested, look at the house.

He smiled. Why did Lydia choose to leave secretly in the dead of night? He did not mind her going, if that was what she wanted. So long as she did it decently and took nothing away with her, he did not mind. It would save him the expense, trouble, and taint of disgrace in having to certify a lunatic. He didn't suppose that she would take his daughter.

He must get rid of Gledhill.

Mary left her trunk with Gartside. She wore pantaloons, stockings, two petticoats, two light dresses and her cloak. Possessions were distributed deep in her clothing. Her money was separated into two pouches so that if a thief made a grab for one he might not take the other. Those were placed, one at the bottom of her cosmetic box, under the lining, and the other inside her pantaloons. She carried her hairbrush, her cosmetic box, henna and three lace handkerchiefs in case she had to show that she was a lady. Her blue cloak hid everything. Her indispensable was the only thing visible upon her arm. In this she had a little loose change.

She was still highly conscious of all smells, most especially that on herself. Despite Mad Dick, she was scented with Mor. It flowed from where she had been impregnated; a fountain which left a veil of scent over her body.

She was still behaving oddly. She could not judge distances. Her steps were unsteady and stumbling. Working the pump handle that morning, for water to wash out the filth of Mad Dick, she had carried on, overflowing the bucket.

But she had kept her wits sufficiently to know that all these were the signs of being pregnant. She had known the moment it happened. When the smell of Mor still flowed out of her, even after her encounter with Mad Dick, she was certain who was the father. She could swear it to a Justice, though she be whipped for it, believe her who will.

Gartside thought that her odd behaviour was because Mor had left. But he had his own problems to worry about. She told him that she would be back – looking, however, not at him, but out through the open door, searching beyond the furthest visible hills, and her expression told him that she was thinking of anything but coming back.

'What about the soldier?' he asked, with frightened eyes.

''E'll be no trouble, Benjie. 'E'll leave today or tomorrow, I promise you. I told Mad Dick they knew about 'im, and would be coming for 'im tomorrow.'

'Dragoons are coming up here?'

He was more scared than ever.

'They won't turn up. They don't know nothing really. I just wanted to get rid of Mad Dick for you. He won't appear again. He 'asn't a chance. They'll easy find 'im, and 'e'll be done for. You keep the place spick an' span for when I get back, Benjie.'

She walked away through the rushes, amongst which in drier places the tiny, yellow cinquefoils were in flower.

326

Two men, in their different ways both in love, watched her go. Mad Dick, feeling imprisoned upstairs, and Gartside in his blue apron at the door, stared after a woman, a whore who was in love, but not with them.

She did not want the rapist, who was excited by fear, for she was not the slave of brutality. She was tired of playing nanny, knowing how it always turned out. The 'child' was always in actuality the circus-master, who manipulated the game. The 'dependent' flame continued to float as brightly as ever, while the oil on which it fed was consumed. She remembered how Gartside collapsed, his eyes withdrawn and his features seeming flattened in retreat, when she ordered him about. But it was for his gratification that the game was pushed further and further. She did not know if she'd be back for anything more than her trunk.

She wanted More Grief.

She was painfully sensitive to the smells of the moor, good and bad. Here it was smoke, for they were burning the old grass and heather. There she was sickened by a stagnant quagmire. In the next few yards it was a thyme, there it was a peaty smell. Odours by turn thrilled or nauseated her.

She wanted to talk about them. Mor would have talked. 'Look at this, look at that,' he would point out. 'It's only a sparrow,' she had replied. 'No, it's a chaffinch, *listen*.'

She wished that she had done so.

She followed a spidery, black sheep-track, wavering amongst the stones. She burst over the moor top, into a breeze shifting briskly in a different direction beneath the rocks.

Gartside's place sank out of sight behind her. The valley of the little River Tame, really no more than a brook, lay below, with small mills strung along its course. Horrible little dungeons. Gawd, I'd hate to be in one o'them. Little hamlets were scattered amongst the enclosures, on the slopes.

Sinking downwards, meeting the highest of the lanes that sprouted like starved pale tendrils out of the valley, she set her sights towards Ogden Edge in the east.

She was single-mindedly going in search of Mor Greave, to tell him the truth, yes, the truth, if he would believe her, about Mad Dick and the seed in her womb. She was Mor's wife, his tally wife but, nevertheless, his wife, *and* his half-sister. They must leave straight away and head south.

She must get away quickly. If soldiers picked her up and brought her before one of General Maitland's majors who had an assignment, perhaps she would prefer to hang, rather than give her body again for spying.

The thought of the gallows made her heart jump. They would not hang her while she was pregnant, and so Mor would be saving her life. A few weeks' leeway to nurse her baby and then she'd be bound for the gallows in Lancaster or York; with her in the cart, the short ladder, the rope and her own coffin. She would find that she, who knew everybody, did not have one friend in the world. Mr Burton would read about her in the newspaper, maybe read it aloud to his French wife and they would *tut* together. If she didn't find More Grief now, would he know nothing before he too learned about her in the newssheet?

She had not seen her foster parents in Soyland for years and wondered if they were still alive. She had never given them a thought, nor did they, she was sure, spare one for her. And all those men; their greasy confessions, their whispers. And what about Harriet? So long as she remained ignorant of her mother, she would be all right. But Mary, without a husband, would have no one to be interested in her fate.

She had once believed that she was no different to other women in despising 'that 'ole down there', because they all treated it as something to sell, and whether it was to the one or to the many made no difference. Now here she was thinking that she wanted no one but Mor Greave to touch her; he who did not believe her, just as no one did. Mad Dick had thought her struggle was in order to excite him and that her fight was part of the game. The more she had spat and cursed, the harder he had tried, and if she had not given in he would have torn her to pieces.

When Mary had got away from Mad Dick, Mor had already left the house. Barefooted she had rushed down the stairs and out, cutting her feet on the dark moor, lost, without bearings. She had gone back inside, to rest and think.

Now, on the following morning, she herself was leaving. Walking towards Denshaw, scratching nervously at her cheek from time to time, her clothes and belongings heavy about her, she suffered all of Mor's pain for him. She who had played the part of mother to a thousand worldly, pompous men, now truly suffered as a mother for her child.

She told herself that this pain was what she deserved for building her life on fantasies and lies, for letting fake moans of joy steam from her, her mind wandering into more entertaining thoughts, as men fucked her.

She could not move in her ever shifting, insecure world, without the support of her web of lies. She invented stories, mixtures of truths and fantasies, about public house 'cells of disaffection', and was paid according to the extremity of her tales. More often than not, it seemed to her, they acted upon her inventions but neglected the truth, and as her reward they defended her from the civil justices who would try her for murder. She stayed alive only because the army believed that she was useful to them. To the common soldiers she lied so that they would tell her their thoughts and secrets which she could pass on to their officers. When she flogged men tied to a beam or to Mrs Rawdon's famous 'horse', when she scourged them with thrilling blasphemies as they hung 'crucified' in the barn behind Mrs Rawdon's slaughterhouse, their penises dripping, they pretended to believe her.

When it came to realities, no one would believe a word that Mary said, which was why she never spoke a serious word to anyone; hardly, as yet, even to More Grief. When she had tried to, he also had not believed her.

She could not think why the colour of her hair mattered to him.

Why did he ask her so often where she had been and what she did? Surely he knew that it would torment her in her cage of lies?

In the one certain truth of her life, her love for him, she had not been believed. Mad Dick had roared outright at the thought of a whore in love.

She threaded her way, across the flanks of moors dappled with part-mown or drying grass and with cloud-broken sunlight, to reach the junction with the main turnpike at Denshaw. It was Sunday morning. Bells were clanging; single bells in small towers naked to the winds, to six sparrows and a dove – all there was room for at the little chapels. An elderly gentleman, accompanying his family stiffly dressed for Sunday, looked down at her boots. He came towards her engrossed by them, as his wife, his adult sons and daughters and his youthful grandchildren gave Mary looks of merriment or distaste. This was the kind of thing Mary always had to put up with on Sunday mornings. She had never cared about it before, finding that gaiety defeats gloom, but now she stared down at the earth that should swallow her up. Today she decided to avoid churches, chapels and their congregations. The day might be safer without them. It was confusion, her uncertainty of her bearings, and a wandering of her concentration that made her unable to face people.

She was distracted by an extraordinary happiness. She was smiling down at the ground. She could not understand herself.

What if she encountered Phoebe Greave in Lady Well? What rights had a pregnant whore over a wife, in the wife's home village? None but to be pilloried and whipped. She imagined herself, a scarred whore, not old but getting beyond the years when she could practise her profession, her red hair streaked with black, calling at the cottage of a handloom weaver, trying to tell a wife that her husband was the father of her unborn child . . .

Mary's reflections carried her the two miles to Denshaw. She began to climb the turnpike road steeply to the hills, amongst sporadic traffic. Normally able to endure long walks in all weathers, and the many hazards of the roads, today she was easily tired. Shortly before The Ram Inn, which was the last outpost high upon the moors, she did not hear the loud grinding of a cart about to overtake her and she, usually alert to everything, wobbled into its path.

The driver reined his horse aside and cursed. Seeing what she was, he smirked and offered her a lift. It was a soldiers' provision cart. An older sergeant was in charge of the horse, a younger militiaman sat with musket and fixed bayonet amongst barrels and sacks of oatmeal or wheat. Mary perched on the tailboard, huddled in her cloak, dangling her legs out of the men's sights.

'What are you doing walking the roads on a Sunday, young woman?'

'I'm a tightrope walker from a circus. I fell off my tightrope and broke myself in the fall. I can't practise no more.'

'I could tell you was something! Serge, I could tell she was something! I knew it.'

'You *are* a clever young soldier,' the driver replied. 'They should promote you, so they should.'

This was the route that Mary had originally walked in the opposite direction with Mor. Over there were the boulders amongst which they had made love.

The burning of the heather and the grass was something with which she had been familiar in the month of May since childhood, but today it was strong and choking as never before. The larks were screaming above the smoke of their burning nests.

'What got you up so early? You don't look the type,' the conscript tried again.

330

'I told you – I fell off my tightrope. I 'ad a good balancing act, 'til I fell. You can ask anyone.'

There was something about Mary which inhibited further teasing, and she was able to doze. This was a stupid thing to do on the tail of a cart from which she might tumble; or while travelling with money on her person, through desperate moorland in the company of two soldiers.

The jolting awoke her from time to time. It seemed such a long journey to Ripponden. At last the cart came to a stop. The grinning young militiaman, who thought himself very advanced in the offices of war because he had picked up a woman in a cart, pricked her bottom with his bayonet. She leapt off, less anxious for the things in her pockets, than for the precious seed that she bore.

A group of idlers were hanging around the door of the forge where they were employed on weekdays in making cropping machines and spinning frames. They were arrogant because they were well-paid, and were watching traffic converging at the junction of the two routes over the moorlands. If one waited long enough, it offered such excitements as the sight of Mary, using her hand to brush dusty oatmeal off her fancy blue cloak.

'Soldiers!' she feebly remarked.

A weak answer made them worse.

'Soldiers! Soldiers! We ain't soldiers, miss, we're just 'onest folk, we are!'

They found this hilariously funny.

'I wish I was a soldier, Sam, to guard a load like that one, I do!'

'I wouldn't mind signing on for a militiaman if I could guard summat like that through Ripponden, Joshua!'

The congregations of the chapels were brimming over their steps, contemplating Grace and considering the sins of their neighbours. A figure in black hovered nearby, spreading disapproval. He watched until his dislike had soaked through to quieten everyone's spirits.

'We could do with another Parson Grimshaw,' he announced, like a king. 'That's what these times need to put an end to your whistling and joking and your devil's fiddle music on a Sunday.'

There was not a fiddle in sight. It was near midday, Mary was hungry and she went to Mrs Rawdon's. Although the whore needed food, rest, and felt she had to get off the streets, she stayed only a little time. She had both money and appetite for a good meal, but the smell of urine and beer made her vomit. She tried to tackle the heavily salted pork and greens that were set before her but she had to dash for the door.

In any case it would not have been safe for her to linger. 'Some men from headquarters are looking for you,' Mrs Rawdon threatened.

She climbed steeply uphill, crossed a moortop, went downhill again and up. She sank down to the bridge, with one steep rise remaining up to Lady Well, and she rested, leaning on the parapet. She was tired, dizzy and still nauseated. She looked down at the water. The banks of weed now grew thick, speckled with the white flowers of water crowfoot. She watched a trout rise. There was the tiniest flash, like the spinning of a silver coin, before the fish sank again beneath its ripples and circles.

She thought of how often Mor must have leaned on this same parapet, watching the trout. She could hear, through the still air, hymn-singing and the ejaculations of the 'saved' from the top of the hill before her. Lady Well was as busy as a market. Outside the chapel, a preacher was shouting amongst the graves. Above the village, smoke was rolling off the moor. The raucous hymn singing from cottages and chapel was matched by the thinner, but more piercing singing of the larks. Who understood the voices of larks, clowning all over the sky? They sounded like the voices of joy, but at such a pitch above the burning nests, they must be the screams of distress.

Looking over the hills she wondered where all the things were that Mor had described so lovingly, so precisely, so many times. His memory had been triggered off by almost anything, in bed or on the roads, without his realising how often he repeated himself. The ash tree from which he had taken his departure. The common above the woods where boys looked for plovers' eggs.

She herself knew Lady Well from visiting Horsfalls' but, under orders to be discreet, she had never made herself known in the town. Flitting through the twilights, thrown out into the dawns, she'd had no attention to spare for trees, plovers and larks. Now she wondered — where was that bank on the curve of the river where the bubbles ran fast and there was always a trout to be found, yet you could not be observed taking it? Mor had described certain views exactly. The farm buildings were there, the walled track ran down so, the tower on the mill peeped through the trees. But although she could fully recall the moods and occasions on which he had told her, she could remember few of the details. She wanted so much to do so, it would bring her into contact with him. 'Woods and hills, the rich man's sport, may still be the poor man's place of study,' Mor had told her.

Brought up on a farm herself, it was not unnatural for her to observe the wild things and feel the seasons. It was coming back to her. Having for many years despised the daytime, the out of doors, she now loved the sunlight, the breezes, the small wild flowers, the streams. Mor had not only left his scent upon her body. She was absorbed into his attitude to things. To have him near her, she tried to see through his eyes. She hurt herself trying to see everything around Lady Well as he must have seen it. *We'll have a little farm together* . . .

There appeared upon the bridge a lone man with a gun. He seemed the more alone because from Lady Well came that noise of a fervent crowd. His dog bounded towards her. The man, a slight smile on his face, let the dog come right up, allowing it to go as far as raising the hair on its neck and growling, before calling it off.

'This is the King's public road, Mr Gamekeeper, there's no need to guard your game 'ere.'

'You're a stranger,' he accused her, bluntly.

'I'm not as strange as all that. You mind your manners, I'm acquainted with Mr Horsfall.'

'Mr Horsfall? What do you do for 'im, then?'

'Never you mind. What's all the stir in Lady Well?'

The keeper spat in contempt.

'They're mad as hatters, young lady. Don't go near 'em. First they're smashing their master's machinery and when they're caught out at that they all go religious. Not ordinary religious like everyone else, showing a respectful face at Matins, or an occasional evensong. These people 'ave to turn into screaming ranters, claiming t'world's coming to an end, but there'll be forgiveness for th'right 'uns. They call it "A Great Revival". Can you hear it? 'Appen it's the water. I'll 'ave nothing to do wi' them, myself. So long as they leave the trout alone, I mind my own business. You should do t'same. They're nothing, those people – the mob. I'd be careful they don't clap you in the stocks, whether you know Mr Horsfall or not.'

'What for?'

'Oh, it's none of my business. I've nowt to do with Lady Well folk. They 'ave their own ways. Are you all right?'

'Just tired. From walking too far. Nice to have met you, mister.'

Mary climbed onwards, hearing, louder as she came close, a shout and the burst of a hymn tune, from different parts of the town. Soon, looking through a doorway, she saw a 'hedge-preacher', kneeling in a kitchen. Others were haranguing groups along the streets. Just like a whorehouse – people who were tired of real life wanted fantasy, change, and a rest.

What was the reality? People were out of work, had run away from home, were under the suspicion of the justices, of the occupying militia, of Gledhill and other Horsfall officers. Married men slipped back from the hills at night to see their families, sleep an hour or two with their wives and change their clothes. They brought in food or money if they had some, depended upon their families if they hadn't. How many sad and secret departures took place all over the town in the early hours of the mornings!

The Lady Well crowds believed that they sang and shouted with joy. But it was an animal cry of pain and anger that she heard pouring out of the village, from every industrial wound, from every wounded sullen face. There was no peace here and there would be no forgetting. Families that had said they were starving had been ground into the dirt for daring to speak.

The hills and valleys were saying to Mary, as they had said to Lydia Horsfall, 'Go away. Go away. Get free. Get free.'

But she was looking for More Grief.

A man was standing alone. She asked him the whereabouts of the Greaves' house. He had a wooden leg, and was leaning on a stick.

'Straight on, up the hill. That's one of the houses that's taken, I believe.'

'Taken?'

'You're a stranger in these parts, I see. Taken by the Lord. They make more noise about it than any battle I've seen with the French. They tell me it serves 'im right, because 'e left home.'

'Serves 'im right?'

'That's what they say. They don't speak well of 'im.'

'Why not?' Mary continued. 'I 'eard he did lots of things for people in Lady Well, taught school, and never did 'arm to anyone.'

'You know him, then?' he asked.

'In a manner of speaking.'

He gripped her arm.

'People soon forget all such things as that, miss . . . ma'am . . .'

'Ma'am.'

Typical of a man, he did not bother to look to see if she wore a ring.

'They think differently about what's right and wrong when the Lord comes into it. As soon as folks start saying, 'There's One above who sees it all,' they mean that what they think can't be argued with. Just listen to 'em. Try getting something across to them!'

He let go of her arm.

'Who says, "There's One above what sees"?' she asked.

'Phoebe Greave does. He'll not get his house back. It's full of righteous folk. That's an easy trick to cheat anyone of their rights. Just say God's on your side, and who can argue? You can cheat a man of 'is property easy that way.'

''Is 'ouse can't be stolen from 'im, and it be right, not if it's 'is.'

She had started to walk away. She got a few yards up the road.

'Miss . . . ma'am!'

She turned and they looked at one another. He was waving his stick. He could not move quickly, because he was fat, and because of his wooden leg. But they approached one another again like old friends, long-parted. The man brushed at his face.

'I just wanted to say that I knew him too. And I knew John Tiplady. I'm Binns, the cobbler. I'd 'ave gone with them if it 'adn't been for my leg. I'm not one of *them*.'

He waved his hand at the town. 'It's all new now in Lady Well and they've forgotten what it was we fought for, a short time ago. Four weeks – it's nothing. John Tiplady dead. Ah, dear. They've lost this world and told themselves they've found The Lord instead. They've lost the present, so they tell themselves they've found the after-life. Who cares now about Mor Greave? No one. They kept expecting 'im back, the way they do expect 'em to come back in the night, after there's been trouble. But . . . no sign of him. Nothing. Now they don't even speak of 'im. I won't forget 'im, though. He was writing a book. If it's printed up, they probably won't even read it. If they read it, they'll 'ardly understand it. Not the pain that went into it. His wife knew, o'course, but she won't tell anyone about that. All she'll talk about is 'ow 'e's wronged 'er, 'ow 'e starved 'er, 'ow 'is sins kept 'er from the Lord. She's a different woman now – and to be 'onest, I never liked 'er before. I could see all this coming. She's found 'er voice and says it's the Lord's. You can't argue with that. Mor Greave's nothing but evil doings to 'er now. Bound to be true, if the Lord says so! When people get like that, they are out of their minds. They make so much noise, they cannot 'ear the truth. I'd like to . . .' He began to whisper. 'Do you have any news of 'im, then?'

''E's well, don't worry, mister. But 'e should be here, in Lady Well. He should be 'ere, mister.'

'I've not seen 'im.'

''E wouldn't make it public, would 'e?'

'Well, 'e wouldn't be welcome in his own 'ouse, not now. You might be, though.' The man laughed. 'They'd set about reforming you . . . I don't mean to insult you, ma'am.'

He raised his hat.

'Phoebe Greave's turned it into a meeting place for the Methodists so that they can rant and scream in his schoolroom. Strange the quirks of fate, isn't it? His little front room is a bedroom for visiting preachers. Gideon . . . you know about Gideon? . . . I was never too keen on 'im, neither. He reminds me of his mother's sister, Selene, as died young. The boy always took 'imself too seriously . . . 'E sleeps upstairs. He's a seven days' wonder, is Gideon.'

'He's a preacher?'

'He 'as acquired the gift of tongues, as they put it. 'Ow did you know?'

'His father always said that would happen.'

Mr Binns grasped her hand between his own.

'Where does his wife live?' she asked.

'She's moved in with Mr Slaughter, the engineer, as 'is 'ousekeeper. Nothing improper about it, you understand.'

'There wouldn't be, with 'er.'

'There wouldn't be, no. She's got born with religion, out of a fake egg . . . do you follow my meaning?'

'No.'

'You will do, when you've been up there. Eee, you're summat different to see in these parts, lass! I'm glad to talk to you, ma'am. Whoever you are, welcome. A lark in a murky day. You've made *my* day. Come round to see me sometime. I live in the last 'ouse by the church. Welcome! I live alone. I'd be glad of something 'appening to upset 'em all.'

'If I find Mor Greave, I'll come to see you.'

'My name's Abr'am. Abr'am Binns. I mended Mr Greave's boots for 'im, the day 'e left.'

She was stepping away.

'Goodday, Mr Binns.'

'Good luck, then, ma'am . . . miss.'

When she found Mor's home, there was a crowd pushing in at the door and spilling over the flight of steps.

Mor had never said it was a place of charm or comfort, but the details that he gave of a house that he loved had built a picture of something very sweet. The rose he had tried to grow, but which had failed because it was a hothouse plant from Mr Horsfall's, unable to survive in the open air; the view painfully drawn upon his memory; his books when he described exactly the order in which he had kept them, title by title along the shelf. The actual sight of it gave Mary a shock. Despite the crowd there, it appeared grey, derelict and unloved. She felt that these people, Phoebe Greave's friends, defiled it. She was horrified by the air of stale unhappiness. Whoever used what had become Phoebe Greave's chapel was refusing to live. There was a rotting body in there and an odour of stubborn unhappiness. Mary had once known a woman who, after her husband died, would not change or clean anything, letting curtains and bed clothes rot with dirt, leaving platters and knives uncleaned where he had left them at his last meal, with mice and spiders running everywhere, over a memory that was slowly rotting. Mor Greave's house had the same atmosphere. The lugubrious crowd made it even worse. It shocked Mary because, if anything characterised herself, it was her refusal to die.

The crowd was quiet at the moment, but she could hear a young, confident male voice chanting emotionally from within.

'For behold, the day cometh, that shall burn as an oven, and all the proud, yes, and all that do wickedly, shall be stubble . . .'

Mary saw that one or two were looking at her. Her ears picked up the word 'Jezebel'.

A way was made for her. When she did not move, a hand waved her irritatedly forward, like a verger angry with a late-comer. Another firmly advised 'a prayerful attitude and modesty'. A hand touched her, probably by accident, but it felt obscene. Ears were listening to the closing words of the Old Testament, eyes were searching her for a miracle.

It would happen if they wanted it. People could talk themselves into anything. She went where they forced her to go, up Mor Greave's stairs. Witholding her body from their touch, she entered through the

337

door, into the presence of eyes gleaming inquisitionally at the stranger, under the low ceiling.

'What's this . . .' she began boldly.

'Schh . . . !'

'And ye shall tread down the wicked; for they shall be ashes under the soles of your feet . . .'

'Gideon Greave's a miracle,' Joshua Slaughter whispered to her. 'Only fifteen but has been given the gift of tongues. The way he talks, the way he says it – the Bible.'

The room held a ring of darkly clad, standing figures. Within this was a herd of others kneeling. They seemed to be lapping something off the stones. By the unlit fire, a boy with an expression of pain transcended was leaning on the back of a spindled chair.

Gideon's eyes were on her who had come through the door; the blue cloak, the pile of thorny red and black hair, the red and white cheeks; but he carried on until he reached the last dot of the Old Testament:

'And he shall turn the heart of the fathers to the children, and the heart of the children to their fathers, lest I come and smite the earth with a curse.'

The room sighed with self satisfaction.

A bony, mad-looking woman sat on a stool beside Gideon. Mor had described Phoebe as 'letting folk walk over her like a doormat' but she did not look downtrodden now. Mr Slaughter's housekeeper wore a grey wool dress and new neat shoes. She had a large pocket for her handkerchiefs. She was a servant respected by all, comforted by them in her 'misfortune'. Even Mr Gledhill sat here in the cottage room with her, listening to the marvellous words that came out of the mouth of her son. Now that Mr Gledhill and she were together in the Lord, she had forgotten her hatred, her horror, at what he had done.

Phoebe looked up at Gideon with unbelieving admiration. Sometimes she coughed and hid her mouth in a handkerchief.

The sweaty smell of the crowded room made Mary want to vomit. She felt giddy, and faint.

Gideon, calm as a born preacher who feels the crowd malleable under his tongue, turned his attention to the stranger.

'Step forward, woman. Yea, even at the last moment, before the final casting down, all might be forgiven ye, daughter of Eve. Step forward into forgiveness and eternal life, or stay forever in darkness, and alone. Come, come.'

338

'Step forward, woman!' his mother shrieked. 'Step forward into eternal life!'

'No!'

Mary shrivelled in her cloak. She lifted her arm across her face.

Phoebe was pointing into the air, her stiff fingers stretched in a show of reaching up.

'There is one above who sees all!' she shrilled with her inviolable conviction. 'Do not be afraid. You can be forgiven.'

'No!'

But Mary was frightened.

'What sort of woman are you that you have no need for forgiveness?' Gideon asked. 'You who come to us a painted and gilded lily.'

Everyone could see what sort of woman Mary was.

'Come forward into eternal salvation!' Phoebe beckoned. 'All can be saved. Alleluya!'

'Alleluya!'

'It's Mary The Scar,' said Gledhill.

'Mary The Scar?' Gideon echoed. He had heard of her.

The crowd closed in on Mary.

'Jezebel!' Phoebe shrieked. 'Abomination!'

Mary fainted.

'The Lord's taken 'er! It's the power of conviction!' Joshua Slaughter said. 'It 'appened sometimes when Mr Wesley preached. Sinners in th'crowd would be struck dead, convicted of their sin, and taken safe into the bosom of the Lord at the moment of repentance, before they'd time to change their minds.'

'She's no' dead yet. Tak' 'er into th'fresh air, ne'er mind the Lord's bosom,' someone else suggested. 'She'll come round. She's hot and tired, that's all. 'Appen wi' a babby . . . Well, why not? There's something wrong with her. Who is this Mary The Scar, Nathaniel?'

Someone else laughed.

'It's Sunday,' Gideon reproved him.

'A Jezebel, like Phoebe Greave said,' Gledhill answered. 'A . . . not that I know much about 'er. But I've 'eard. She's a bad un. Mr Horsfall knows 'er. He's had to boot her out many a time, from hanging round the door, that's why I know who she is. The world'd be well rid of 'er, in my 'umble opinion.'

Phoebe Greave *said*. She had an opinion! She could even correct Mr Gledhill! She felt the confidence of one who knows she is amongst

339

friends. She had been a fool all of her life, refusing to turn to the Lord, listening instead to "'im I've 'ad to call "'usband"', but now the Lord had given her the power to speak at last. In the last weeks, in the very trough of misery, the good Jesus had borne her up. She was no longer poor nor hungry nor alone. She did not work in the factory, but in Mr Slaughter's house. She was a friend of Mr Gledhill, who treated her as an equal. Why had it taken her so long to see the light?

'Mutton dressed as lamb,' a woman hissed, as they took Mary into the open air, onto the top step of the flight of stairs. Because of her make-up it was impossible to tell whether the colour had returned to her cheeks and lips or not. Nobody was bold enough to loosen her dress; something might be made of their being so familiar. Even the women would not dare to touch such a person.

'She should be cleansed and redeemed,' Gideon said. 'Forgiven, to mark our day, our Love Feast, and brought back into the fold.'

Forgiven, he said, though from repulsion the skin shrank on his face. Tight reins pulled the corners of his mouth and narrowed his eyes. At the age of fifteen he could not understand what career had produced such a female.

'It would be a memorial to this special day of prayer if we were to cleanse the fallen woman,' Slaughter echoed. 'Let's tak' 'er to the workhouse.'

Apart from the dye houses at Paradise Mills, the workhouse was the only place that held a big stone bath. There was a row of them, to be filled with cold water for curing lunatics and hot water for washing boils.

Mary was coming round. Her eyes were open and she moved her hand to her forehead.

'Oh Gawd, what's 'appened?'

'She's speaking.'

'Nay, she's calling on God,' Slaughter said. 'What a sight.'

Someone took a grip of her shoulders and raised her to a sitting position. She was not interested in lifting her eyes above her own feet, a ring of polished shoes, black dresses, and the tails of Sunday-worsted coats. She could hear a lark singing. Did anyone else hear it? She remembered the seed in her body.

Someone was making her stand up. She could see over the iron railings at Mor's door. There was the sunlit valley. She could not search for the lark, with her head spinning. There was the awful smell of smoke.

'I can smell smoke. Mor Greave . . .'

'The smoke of Hell,' Gledhill told her.

From the neighbour's house, a family full of curiosity was peering over that spare tombstone which Mor had told her about and which bounded the stone platform suspended before his door.

'Where's Mr Greave, miss?' a boy said. 'We're wanting school.'

'Mor Greave's house,' Mary muttered.

'*My* house,' Phoebe said. '*Mine*.'

'He deserted her,' Gledhill interrupted. 'He shouldn't 'ave. He doesn't deserve the 'ouse.'

'She was killing 'im. Starving 'im. Thinking she was a good wife, she didn't know what she was doing to 'im.'

'In my own 'ouse, listen to 'er! In my 'ouse. What *evil*!'

'You know a lot, Mary The Scar,' Slaughter remarked.

They were helping her down the worn stone stairs, and pushing her up the street.

'The words of the Devil!' Phoebe said, before her own cellar door, turning her head this way and that, to whoever would listen. 'Where else 'as she learned such wickedness? Why, she's been giving 'er ear to the Devil. She's full of it. *But there's One above who sees it all*!'

She was pointing into the air. Clearly, she liked doing so.

'Please, mother,' Gideon said. ''Ave some restraint.'

'*Wickedness*!' Phoebe repeated, in a long, exclamatory breath.

'Where are you taking me?'

'To the workhouse. You called on God yourself . . . to be cleansed.'

As Gideon gingerly supported Mary's arm, he was staring fascinated into her face. Horror had begot fascination, fascination begat guilt. Guilt was as familiar as clothing warmed through by his own smell and shaped by his own body. He was fascinated to know what lay beneath the leathery cosmetic, and beneath the nickname, Mary The Scar.

My soul is a mass of putrefaction. It is a dung heap, breeding worms.

Still dizzy, faint and confused, Mary was brought to the workhouse door. How could she escape them all? She must bend with the wind.

The commotion brought the workhouse mistress to the door even before they knocked. Her name was Queen Elizabeth Farrer, or sometimes she was known as plain 'Queen Bess'. She was big, with bones rather than with fat, and plenty of muscle. She had a loud voice to match her size, severe starched clothes, hair pulled back so as to thrust her face aggressively forward, and a scrubbed look, yellow from spending her time in badly-lit, damp interiors.

'What do you want? What's this you've brought me?'

Bessy Farrer ruled the workhouse by shouting, always first, and always right.

'A Jezebel to be cleansed!' Phoebe shouted back. 'A wicked woman. Look at her! I can't tell you what she's said, *and* in my own 'ouse, telling me it's not mine. Only the Devil could 'ave said such things. You 'ave the baths, Bessy Farrer. We want 'er brought forth cleansed, meek, and 'er evil tongue cut off . . .'

'Mother . . .' Gideon interrupted.

Phoebe, to whom God had given a voice, raised her arm again to the sky.

'*There is One* . . .'

'A Jezebel,' Gledhill overbore her. 'A Mary Magdalene. Stop thy ranting, Phoebe Greave. We want her brought forth later, Mrs Farrer, prepared for conversion, ready to wash the feet of Christ.'

Phoebe imagined her washing the feet of Gideon, but did not say so.

'God's holy water, have you become dippers, all of you?'

'Not a Baptist amongst us!' answered Phoebe, insulted and shocked. 'We're all true followers and believers.'

'Then why waste God's water scrubbing the woman? All God's chickens 'ave become ducks. Leave her to me, if that's what you want. Go on, go away . . . it's not visiting day. Get on wi' your praying.'

Bessy Farrer closed the door on them. She looked over Mary The Scar, who looked back at her, boldly.

Look at 'er hands. Real strangler's 'ands are those. I'll bet she's throttled one or two, in 'er time. She'd kill her 'usband in 'er sleep, out of habit. Not even know she's doing it . . .

'What a place! Everyone's mad. I thought they were going to kill me.'

Mary, straightening her dress and hair, spoke to Mrs Farrer as if she were a fellow human being. Queen Bess did not like it.

'So we're a crazy lot in Lady Well, are we? And who are you, madam, to call folk crazy? You know where you are now, do you? I'll show *you*, madam!'

Shouting loud enough to be heard outside, beyond the thick oak door, where those who had brought Mary were wondering what to do now, Mrs Farrer let her big iron keys swing loose at her waist. She gripped Mary's arm and pushed her down a short passage, through the main room, where a dozen poor women were set to spin. It was an unnecessary business now that the manufactories did it, but the abandoned females did not mind. They would have unpicked all their work and started over again, with the same smiles, or lack of them. Life was the same meaningless disappointment in the workhouse, no matter what one did. They became silent and more brisk at their work when Mrs Farrer's voice filled the room.

'Annie Drew, you're dropping threads! Do you want a maid to clean up after ye?'

'No, Queen Bess.'

'Answer me back, you fucking cow, and I'll 'ave you scrubbing the floor after my lunatics.'

They went into another passageway. It was damp, grey and smelling of years of airlessness.

'You're a bold one, telling me to my face we're a mad lot. Do you know where you are now? Well, damn it . . . I think you're right.' Queen Bess laughed and punched Mary cruelly between the shoulder blades, so that she stumbled. 'It's ever since the raid. "They're a mad lot up Lady Well", they say, "ever since the men ran off and the Lord took over. What's up with ye all?" You're better off in 'ere with me. I 'ardly go out myself, these days. I've seen some sights, in my business, I can tell you, but I've never seen nothing like them . . . doing it all over the streets in public. Dogs! Aren't they? Dogs! You can take God too far. They can't be trusted, when you don't know where you are with them. And I'll bet you've seen a sight or two yourself, in your time?'

Mary did not take the hint to reveal her secrets. Down a side passage she heard the infirmary.

'Listen to them. I'll give 'em growling and moaning, not letting anyone sleep. Don't you try any tricks whilst you're in 'ere, neither. We know what to do about it. You're not going to be ill?'

'No, ma'am.'

She gave Mary another push.

'Keep going, then. Never mind leaning on walls, pretending to look sick. What's your name?'

'Mary Wylde.'

'I thought they said something else.'

'That's my name. Honest, that's my name.'

'Where you from, Mary Wylde?'

'From herebouts originally. I've lived in London and a lot of other places.'

Mrs Farrer touched Mary's arm, and softened her voice. 'I'm your friend. I won't let you get into their clutches, trust me, I won't.'

'Thank you, ma'am. I'm but a poor 'elpless woman, travelling in search of my brother.'

'Poor 'elpless woman, eh?' Mrs Farrer shouted again. 'No such thing, madam! If you're in 'ere, it's your own fault, you deserve what you get. We can all 'elp ourselves, can't we?'

'Yes, ma'am.'

'I'm your friend.' Queen Bess once more softened her voice. 'Tell me the truth, tell me what you've been up to, and I'll say you're sick and they can't 'ave you tonight. I'll let you out in a day or two, when they've got over it. A few of 'em stay stiff as pokers, the rest forget all about it and become 'uman again. They'll all be back at work tomorrow. They'll 'ave forgotten you. Trust me. I've seen a thing or two. The look o' you doesn't shock me at all. All I want you to do is to tell me what you've done.'

'My brother . . .'

'Never mind about your brother! I've 'eard every tale under the sun, and that one about looking for a lost brother or sister more times than you've 'ad 'ot dinners, madam. Do you know where you are? We can do anything we like to you in 'ere. Anything. If we don't like you we can chain you up with the lunatics for life. Ever 'ad a taste of the birch? So you'd better tell us the truth . . . 'Ere, you *are* sick!'

Mary, nauseated by the stench of the workhouse, had stopped, to bend over, clutching her stomach.

'Are you with a babby to get rid of? Is that what you've done?'

'It's that smell. It makes me dizzy.'

'What did you say?'

'No, ma'am!'

'Yes, ma'am! Don't take that tone with me. You're a close one! You look as though you'd 'ave an answer for anyone, but you don't say a word 'ardly. You should trust me . . . you don't want to lose a friend, do you?'

'No, ma'am.'

Bessy Farrer gave Mary another push. They were going along a corridor where paupers were whitewashing the wall.

'That's better. Is someone looking for you?'

344

'No!'

Mrs Farrer raised her arm threateningly but did not let it fall. She smiled, as Mary winced.

'Mmm. I think someone's looking for you, madam. That's why you're travelling the roads, falling foul of Methody lunies and saying nothing. You've got on the wrong side of some soldiers and they're after you. Have you robbed someone? Don't bother telling me your lies. You've robbed someone! Then you stumbled among righteous folk who'd turn you in. You thought you'd be best off pretending you've repented. Isn't that it? I'll get to the bottom of it. I always do. Suppose I do my duty and inform the magistrate? What then? Or the army officers? You don't do yourself no good, not telling me the truth. I like to know. Then I can 'elp. I'm your friend, Mary.'

Mrs Farrer, getting no response, shouted again, 'You don't say anything! You damned cow! You fucking whore, do you know what I can do to you? I've 'ad 'em all in 'ere . . . Murderers, thieves, poisoners, embezzlers. Some o' them are in and out of 'ere like a dog's dick. I know 'em all. I tell 'em when they leave, they'll be back. You'd better trust me and do as I say, if you want to stay safe.'

Mrs Farrer put on her soft voice again. 'It's only to satisfy my interest that I want to know. I won't tell anyone . . .

'You still don't say nothing! Well, it's your funeral. Go on! Get in there. Yes, down there. You fucking blind? Or is it the cockroaches scare you? You look as though you might try to be fancy.'

Mary was shoved down a short flight of steps into a semi-subterranean cellar, which had a damp stone floor, like every other lower room in the building. Barred windows high in the wall had their lower sills level with a garden, where the bare feet and ankles of paupers could be seen. She glimpsed carved faces, leering and mad, decorating the ends of the drip-stone above the window outside. From across the garden, Mary heard a burst of hymn singing. The room was filled with steam and smoke. It was mostly smoke, from a 'set-pot' – a great iron pot built into the stonework over a fire across the corner, the stone breast of a chimney curving upwards behind it. In the centre of the room was a pump. Along the wall was a row of five stone baths. A channel took the water away, from there and from the pump, out through a culvert in the end wall, which led lower down the hill. There was a big scrubbed oak table at the other end. There were no chairs, other than a regal-looking 'Windsor' with curved arms, in the corner

345

near the table, where the workhouse mistress could sit and watch through the smoke, steam, and flying specks of soot.

When Mary was brought in, an attendant in a pauper's blue uniform ceased to poke sticks under the set-pot. She knew what to do, and went to close the shutters, which were so splintered and old that they still let some light through. The other bath attendant, who had been sweeping the spilled water towards the drain, lit a lamp on the table.

Queen Elizabeth Farrer sat in her chair and took out a clay pipe. She rooted still further into her clothes to produce a tobacco pouch, tinder and flints. She packed her pipe and lit it.

'Now then, get undressed. Don't keep me waiting! 'Aven't you learned yet? Everybody 'as to 'ave a bath when they come in. Regulations.'

Mary took off her boots and cloak, then she turned to the wall to remove the remainder.

'So what are you doing in Lady Well, then?'

'Looking for my brother.'

'That story again! 'E on the run too? Escaped from prison? A Luddite?'

''E's sick. 'E's gone out of his mind. 'E left 'ome and started wandering. The surgeon diagnosed melancholy. He might fall over a cliff.'

'You're in danger of losing a friend, ma'am, if you don't tell me the truth. I'm warning you.'

'It's the truth, 'onest. I'm tired and sick from looking for 'im. 'Ave pity, ma'am.'

The sight of Mary's pantaloons made them laugh, for they themselves did not wear anything under their dresses and petticoats. Mrs Farrer slid the lamp closer.

'Looks French. Wonder what old Bony Part'd make o' that!'

She saw that Mary was wearing officer's pantaloons, worn back to front.

'Won them off a corpse?' she smirked. 'Some poor soldier kneed and elbowed on 'is way out of the public 'ouse? Telling me your lies. You're losing a good friend, do you know that?'

Mrs Farrer appeared to fall into a doze. She was one of those who, when they are not fighting, become comatose, like lions and tigers. Her pipe went out, so she took it from her mouth and sang in time to one of the hymns drifting in through the window.

Thinking that the mistress was not looking, Mary pulled forth the cosmetic box, the hairbrush, one of the purses of money, and slipped them under her cloak.

'You carry a lot of things about your person,' Queen Bess said, quietly.

'It's all my own things.'

'That your savings in the purse? And the 'airbrush? Good silver on that thing there, too. And lovely lace 'andkerchiefs you 'ave. Either you're a lady fallen on misfortune, which I don't think, or you've got friends, which I might believe. Or you're a thief.'

Mrs Farrer, being an old thief herself, knew what hanging pockets and open linings meant.

'Everything's mine, ma'am. I spent years in service to a gentleman in Manchester since I was nine at seven pounds a year to save that up. I only want to retire in peace, ma'am. The roads is full of robbers. I 'opes I'm safe now. I 'opes I'm with friends. You said I was.'

'I see! Boot's on the other foot now, isn't it? Now that we've found your thievings, you're begging. How much have you got "saved up"?'

'Fifteen pounds.'

'You must have been in an 'igh class of service to save that. What were you doing? Stealing the tea from the caddy and setting up private in the grocery business? They get up to all sorts of tricks in service to save up for their retirement.'

The workhouse mistress pointed at her with the stem of her pipe.

'You've not saved up that way, my lady. Your business is plain to see. Don't think I was born yesterday, and was carried away with all your lies. Who've you robbed whilst he was otherwise engaged, you might say? What gentleman was it? You know you could be 'ung for it. I'll tell you what I'll do . . . what's in that box?'

'Box?'

Mary in fright didn't know what to do and couldn't think.

'That little cabinet hid under your clothes, that looked so fine. What's in it? You got stolen jewels in there?'

'That's my cosmetic box. Look.' Mary pulled it forth and sprung it open. 'I 'ave to keep myself a lady, for my prof . . . please, ma'am.'

'I'll tell you what I'll do . . . Oh, I weep for you, so I do. An 'andkerchief, please.'

Mary handed over a lace handkerchief.

Queen Elizabeth Farrer dabbed her eyes, which were running because of the smoke, then tucked the lace into her own pocket.

'Fifteen pounds you've got there, you said?

'Yes.'

'There's many a starving weaver in this town could live for a year on that. Well, it's none of my business 'ow you've come by it. You've got to take your bath now, make you fit for the Good Lord. It's a great responsibility for me, looking after all that money whilst you're otherwise engaged.'

'You're very busy, I'm sure, ma'am.'

'Yes, I am, without 'aving to act as a banker as well. I've some poor lunatics coming in here in half an hour. They can get up to anything. They'd steal your money quick as monkeys. They've no morals. You couldn't complain, could you? As there's no knowing 'ow you came by it in the first place, 'ow could you raise the hue and cry? I could get myself 'ung p'raps for not turning you over to the constable.'

'Thank you, ma'am. It's very kind of you. You're a good woman, I'm sure.'

'That's right. I'm a lady. An 'andkerchief, please, my eyes are sore.'

Mary gave her the second of her three lace handkerchiefs, which like the first disappeared into Queen Elizabeth's clothes.

The hot water had been rationed into the bath. An attendant stood with hands on hips wondering what was to happen next.

'Time for your scrub,' Mrs Farrer said. 'They need you to work the pump now. Put your clothes and stuff at this end of the table. I'll try and see that the lunies don't come near it. I can't promise.'

Mary, in her comical pantaloons, went to work the pump and fill a bucket to pour into the bath into which hot water had been ladled. Trying to keep one eye on Mrs Farrer, she walked across with one bucketful after another.

'You'll have it cold,' said an attendant.

'I don't like 'ot water.'

'Make sure it's 'ot, and scrub 'er proper!' Mrs Farrer yelled. 'You arguing?'

Mary skipped away from a blow from one of the attendants. She returned to deposit her pantaloons on the table. Queen Elizabeth did not even look at her, but sat with her arms folded. Mary crept back to the inevitable bath. Both the attendants were tipping in more hot water.

Gawd, the sooner I 'ave it, the less 'ot it'll be. If I can go in slowly, it'll likely do least damage. Oh, 'ow did I get myself in 'ere? Worse than the Lancaster prison. All my life I've managed to stay free, until now.

348

No good crying over spilt milk.

She stood in the bath. Each attendant held a large scrubbing brush, of the kind used for floors, or for scouring a pig.

'Start with my feet,' Mary said. 'In the best society I believe it's always a lady's 'abit to start low down. There's a moral in that somewhere. *Ow*!'

The larger attendant, taking Mary unawares, pushed her down into a sitting position. With professional coolness, she surveyed the clownish painted face above the white and pitted body that had hardly ever been exposed. Then she started on one of Mary's thighs. She held her knee with one hand and scrubbed with the other. Her assistant did likewise on the other leg, from the far side of the bath.

'Oh, my Gawd. oh, OW! Oh Phttt . . . Oh, I can't, my breath . . . Help . . . OW! Oh! . . .'

Mary slipped about in the bath, trying to ease the stinging in her legs. Using hardly any soap, they roughly scoured her, as they would a pig. They did not speak. It was as if she was a carcass.

'No good crying over spilt milk, I'd say . . . Oh . . . no!'

They had turned her over, and were scouring her backside, the backs of her legs and her spine. She twisted about, but they knew how to hold her. They turned her over again. She was distracted. She was sick, dribbling onto her breasts. She tried to climb out. A hand pushed her down so that she slipped under the water.

''Ere, are you being difficult for us, by any chance? We know 'ow to deal with you if you are. Don't we?'

The other attendant was laughing. She had got rid of her scrubbing brush, and she had a razor in her hand. Mary's pubic parts were being scrubbed. Her stomach. Breasts. All her flesh was on fire.

What was that Mad Dick had said about being flogged? Burning and freezing, gasping for air, a noose round your throat, as though you'll never drink air again in your life. Your body cut in two . . .

'You bitch, you cow you, you fucking old whore, get down you . . . gi' me the shears! The shears, quick. Not the razor yet. The shears.'

'No!'

Mary buried her face in her breasts and tried to hug her knees. Before she realised it her hair was hacked. Handfuls were thrown onto the floor, and a few clumps dropped in the bath.

With the stump of hair that was left, her head was pulled back. The two scrubbing brushes were applied to her face.

She kept her eyes closed, until one brush ceased. Water was being splashed over her. They ducked her head, and scrubbed it.

They let go of her. She was allowed to splutter and cough. Though the water was hot, she sat shivering.

'So that's what you've been hiding! And nobody knew. Quite a Devil's hoof you've got there, miss.'

'Let me out! Let me out! Let me out!'

Mary was scrambling forth and trying to head across the room. They pushed her back.

'Oh no, madam . . . The razor! The razor!'

One attendant stood at the end of the bath and held her from behind, round the neck. The other was pushing her legs apart.

'You'd better keep still, or this'll do some damage, won't it? We don't want no lice.'

Mary lay as still as she could, her thighs quivering. The woman was tearing with a blunt razor at her pubic hair. Lumps of it floated in the scum of the bath.

'Now, let's dry you, then we can show you to the chapel folk. What will they make of what the Devil did to you, do you think?'

Mary stumbled out. While they dried her with a rough and dirty towel, she sank her head, and tried to turn it this way and that, away from them. She clasped her thighs together, ashamed of her nakedness. As soon as they released an arm, she put it up to grasp the hair that was no longer there, wanting to pull it around her face. She did not want to be seen, and she could not bear to look at them, either. She felt she was an obscenity, raped and naked, ashamed, reduced to nothing, unable to look anyone in the eye.

When they let go of her she stumbled, half-blindly, cowering, bending in shame over her own body, towards her clothes. Why was she shivering so much? Why so cold? There were goose-pimples all over her obscene flesh. Her face might be crimson, but the rest of her skin was grey. She climbed into her pantaloons, chemise and two dresses, as quickly as possible, still turning her face away.

'You're not well,' Mrs Farrer said. 'Your skin's not 'ealthy. I know what makes it that colour. Show me your gums.'

'Christ, it's cold . . . you wouldn't think there was a fire lit, would you? . . . in the month of May.'

Queen Elizabeth Farrer stood up.

'Did you hear me? Show me your gums.'

'I'm cold! I'm cold,' Mary whimpered, like a child. 'Christ, I'm so cold.'

Mrs Farrer shouted to the attendants.

'Over here! Pull back 'er mouth.'

A spasm of revulsion and shame ran through Mary's body.

''Ere, you bitch, don't show temperament in 'ere, you're not in a position for it.'

Mrs Farrer slapped her. Mary's face was burning, although the rest of her was shivering.

'We've got strait-jackets, if we need 'em. 'Aven't you learned yet that we get our own way? I want to see the state of your gums.'

Mary was still quaking.

'That's quite a mark you've got, isn't it? Someone's cursed you. What did you do to 'em? You're evil, you are.'

Mary's lips were roughly pulled back, then hurriedly dropped.

'Lead,' she said. 'How long have you been using it? How many years?'

'Always.'

'Speak up! I can't 'ear whispers.'

'*Always! Always! Always!* . . .'

The attendants and the workhouse mistress looked at one another, thinking of the strait-jacket. They let Mary continue to dress herself. She was still trying to hide her cheek, although everyone had seen it. She felt naked for the first time in her life. She was angry.

'You got a dropped wrist yet? Show me. Come on, miss, don't look as though butter wouldn't melt in your mouth, hiding your face like a blushing maid. Show me.'

Mary extended her arm. She was confronted by the fact, felt but hastily disregarded in the past, when she had waved goodbye to someone, or leaned in a doorway, or held money out in her palm, that her wrist ached.

'She's sick, this one. I'd say my prayers if I was you. The only cure is acidulated water.'

'It makes your teeth drop out. I don't want to lose no more teeth. I can't afford it. Not that as well.'

'Sulphuric acid does? I've never known acid do no 'arm, not diluted. Are you trying to tell me my business, madam? I've been 'ere in this workhouse in this village twenty years or more apart from a year or two away in York . . . where I was set up . . . I 'adn't done it . . . twenty years or more. My parents were master and mistress 'ere before me. You aren't in a position to tell anyone their business anymore, you Devil's spawn.'

'No, ma'am. But your teeth drop out with it.'

Mary received another slap.

'Don't talk to me like that! I'm mistress 'ere.'

Mrs Farrer turned to the attendants.

'You fetch the lunatics. Leave this one with me a while.'

When they were alone, Mrs Farrer brought out Mary's purse.

'Look!' she commanded. 'Go on, look at it. Never mind turning your 'ead away. You're not sixteen. Do as I tell you.'

Mary took a glance. Mrs Farrer smiled. Mary looked away again.

'One of the lunies 'as stolen your money, haven't they?'

'Ma'am?'

'I said, one of the lunatics has stolen your savings. What a shame! But you're not going to say anything to anyone, are you? Because if you do, the constable will want to know where it came from in the first place. You'd rather be in the infirmary safe for the night, in a bed, wouldn't you, than in the 'ands of that mob of praying wolves in the street? . . . Why can't you look me in the eye?'

Mary was pulling at non-existent hair. She found a few bristly pieces to tug.

'You're ashamed o' the mark of the Devil on your face, that's why. I don't like people that can't look another in the eye. It's shifty. A pity about your money, isn't it? . . . *Isn't it?*'

'Yes, ma'am.'

'As if it never existed. Why, I do believe . . . Let me look at you. Turn your face!'

Mary angrily turned to Mrs Farrer. She flushed and hunted for cover again, where there was nowhere to hide, in the cavities of her own shoulder.

'Yes, I thought so. Crocodile tears! What's there to cry about? You've got a nice infirmary bed for the night. Oh, I know your sort. Stop your snivelling, ma'am! I can't stand crying. They do so much of it.'

Mrs Farrer stood up.

'I'm going to leave you now, so don't you dare say a word, even in gossip, about that money, or I'll see you 'ung for defaming.'

Mrs Farrer had gone.

Three female 'lunatics and refractory paupers' were being brought into the cellar. Two came ahead of the other. They were mild cases, kept in chains part of every day only to remind them of what would happen if they caused trouble. Lunatics notoriously suffered from short memories. The attendants knew them well and treated them more like children than like animals. They looked forward to laughing at their antics in their weekly bath, when they threw the water all over the place, fought and argued sometimes, but did not attack anyone else. When they came in, the one who enjoyed stoking the fire rushed to it immediately. The other carefully examined the row of baths.

The third lunatic was a child, lagging behind because she could not walk properly. Margaret had been left to sleep until an hour before. She was put amongst the mad people because she persisted with her 'obscene talking that would send 'er off to 'ell.'

'Tell the truth. You've fallen on a sharp object and cut yourself badly,' Mrs Farrer had shouted. 'What was it? You've tumbled down some stone steps, 'aven't you?'

Margaret did not answer.

''*Aven't you?*'

Mrs Farrer shook her.

'Mr Horsfall did it with . . .'

'With what?'

'With . . .'

'With what, then? Did such a gentleman as 'im come for you with an axe? A knife? You've not been set upon by robbers, then?'

'No . . .'

'You realise you're telling lies about Mr 'Orsfall? Shame on you! Liars burn forever.'

'With . . . A thing.'

'What thing?'

'You mustn't say. Like Edwin's . . . Bigger.'

'I don't know what the child's babbling about. Do you know what the child's talking about? I don't.'

'Children do 'ave fancies, don't they? I used to invent all sorts. Some of them . . . strange,' the attendant said.

'Get 'er recorded as "an idiot child who does not know 'er own mind, a persistent liar who has been abandoned by 'er desperate mother",' Mrs Farrer said. 'You *are* a liar, aren't you?'

'No, ma'am.'

'Yes, you are. If she mentions Mr 'Orsfall again, beat the daylights out of 'er. And get rid of 'er when you can, as far away as possible, before she talks to anyone. She'll soon get mucky again. Nobody'll think anything. Then *get rid of 'er*.'

Margaret came into the room, still dazed, hypnotised, staring, with her legs apart, putting her feet forwards slowly to avoid chafing her thighs.

Ahead of her, the other two lunatics knew precisely what to do and how much they could get away with. One was touching the inner edges of the baths to see if they were clean and examining her finger. When she had decided, 'This one,' she said, 'I'll have this one today,' and she started to work the handle of the pump. It was without a bucket beneath it, so the water flowed over the stones into the gutter, and out through the culvert. 'The river of life!' she shrieked and thought it enormously funny. The other was packing sticks tightly into the blaze, until she was running with sweat. 'The damned!' she said. 'The damned!'

The attendants gave their attention to Margaret's bath. Her rags had already been taken away and she had been given a pauper's gown. As they undressed her, they tried not to hurt. They knew quite well what had happened, but had to pretend otherwise. When Margaret was standing in the water, she was left to herself.

Mary, left in peace for the first time, was cowering in an out-of-the-way corner, wanting only to hide. She saw the clean but frightened child, with her legs apart, a tranced look on her face, and realised what had happened. She had seen that sight too often to make a mistake about it. Mary came resolutely out of her corner, though it took some doing. Sickness, pregnancy, the baring of her scar, had robbed her of all her resourcefulness. She wondered where the old Mary The Scar had gone to.

'Can I wash 'er?' she asked.

The attendants smiled.

'I wouldn't say it was too early to lend an 'and. It'll take a few edges off you, my lady, and get you used to what 'as to be done in 'ere. You're already a bit quieter than you were.'

Mary walked through her own hair that was dropped so carelessly on the floor. They were curls of dyed red hair, though there was a fierce black stubble on her head. She went over to the child. The girl was frightened, as she was of all strangers now. Mary smiled, though she did not receive a smile in return.

It's my face.

'I won't 'urt you, chicken,' Mary said.

The attendants, occupied with the lunatics, were not looking, and Mary used plenty of soap. Margaret at last began to smile. She was white-skinned and frail as snow. Mary thought of Harriet.

'What's your name?'

'Morgarit. Why are you crying?'

'How old are you?'

'Twelve . . . eleven. I don't know. What're you crying for?'

'It was Mr Horsfall, wasn't it?'

The child was scared again.

'They hit me when I said that.'

'The beast! Someone should put strychnine in his silver spoon.'

'Tell me why you're crying.'

'I'm not.'

''Ave they 'urt you? Did they spit in your mouth? Did they stick their fingers in your ears?'

'No, lamb.'

Nothing so bad as what, so she had heard, happened in a factory. And to children. That's where this one's been, to think of things like that.

'Why're you crying then? I can see you're crying. I can see it. 'Ave you been bath'd?'

'Yes.'

'It's nice, being bath'd. But I 'urts, down there. It's bleeding.'

'Oh, my lamb! The beast, the stinking beast. Come on. Out you get, my lamb. You're shivering. Hey! A towel! Where's a towel for the mite?'

Mary realised that, for a moment, she had forgotten her new, scoured self. This was the old one shouting. One of the lunatics threw a towel. When Mary had wiped Margaret, her voice became subdued again.

'You're still bleeding. Let's put something on you to keep you warm.'

She led the child across the room. They were back at the big table, by the clothes. Mary fished out the child's-size pauper uniform from the others and dressed Margaret.

'Look. I'll show you something.'

Mary opened her box, took out her mirror and held it before Margaret's face.

Margaret touched the mirror handle, twining her own amongst Mary's fingers.

'My hair's fair, isn't it? Look at it. He didn't believe me. He'd believe me now. Why don't you look at yourself? Go on. Take a look. I've 'ad enough now.'

'I don't want to.'

'Go on, take a look. You can see what your face is like.'

Margaret turned the mirror round. Mary instinctively jumped back. Then she froze, staring at herself. For years, she had never scraped the cosmetic completely off. She had kept a flattering skin of white lead, even in those private moments when she believed she was keenly examining herself, before she covered her face again. Here now were her naked features as she had not seen them since she was a child, before a rich young man picked her up and on their second night introduced her to the cream that hid her blemish. If she should ever forget it, there was always her nickname to remind her, Mary The Scar, shouted after her by children, written down in military reports. A crimson hoof-shape, the two horns reaching to the corners of her mouth and eye, the bulk spreading down her cheek to her neck. As a matter of fact, the unblemished cheek looked the worst. It was a yellow-grey colour, pocked with black specks. Her scar was not as big or as grotesque as she remembered it. Perhaps it had faded. Perhaps she was not as sensitive as she had been, in the days when her parents had called her 'Devil's child'. Perhaps, who knows, the advisers had been wrong and the white lead had cured her. Bleached it out. Perhaps she had finished with being a clown, painting her face. Her daubed features were worse than her natural ones. But nobody could look as bad as she did today, with her scrubby hair, unhappy eyes and harrowed features. Yet what did she most need now, to survive with an unborn baby to care for and maybe no husband? Most of all she needed her pride. She needed herself.

'What's that on your face?' the child asked.

'It's something I was born with.'

'You've got some paints in your box!'

'They're for my face.'

'Why don't you put them on it, then?'

'I don't want to, anymore.'

'Why not? Can I 'ave some on my face?'

'No. It's poisonous.'

'Gi'it me. I want some. Ladies use it, don't they?'

'Just a little, then.'

Mary ground a little red pigment on her palette, and brushed it on Margaret's cheek. Margaret picked up the mirror.

'Hurry up, you two,' shouted an attendant. 'That woman knows what's 'appened to the child,' she said to her colleague. 'She's a danger. Mark my words.'

'That's what my mother looked like,' Margaret said. 'All that colour on her face. She's in London.'

Mary put the mirror back in the case.

'Would you like to go there, chicken?'

'That's what Mr Pickles told me he would do. Take me to London.'

'Pickles! You met him! Where did 'e pick you up?'

'In Liverpool.'

'Oh, my! Where did he come from, climb out of the slime at the bottom of the sea? Oh, my Gawd. Did he treat you all right?'

'Yes. But 'e brought me 'ere. I was waiting to go to London but 'e brought me 'ere. That's not fair.'

'Well, 'e would. He'd betray his own mother, Pickles would, if there was a penny to be made from it. He's not even good at it, neither. Never 'as been good at nothing, Pickles. 'E used to 'ave a business but 'is documents were in a mess. Cheating and lying, 'e got locked up. Pickles! Shit! Ptttt . . .!' She spat. 'We'll get you out of 'ere. You've had some bad experiences, meeting Pickles, and then 'Orsfall.'

'You can't 'ave 'er,' Mrs Farrer told Phoebe, Gideon, Joshua Slaughter, Gledhill, and the others of Lady Well who were melted down in the same pot of religion. 'She's sick. You couldn't take her into any clean place. She's poisoned with lead and mercury, that the Jezebels put on their faces.'

'Poison!'

'We don't want that in the 'ouse of the Righteous, the 'omes of the Redeemed. It wouldn't be right. It wouldn't do.'

'You'd never bring that one to Christ, never. The mercury makes them mad. You must have noticed she was a bit crazy.'

'Jezebel!' breathed Phoebe.

'And when I wasn't looking she painted up a child that was in here. An innocent child, that had not been in the workhouse above an hour or two, abandoned by its mother, painted up to be a Jezebel. At her age.'

'Fancy that.'

'What do you think?'

'Imagine that.'

''Er wicked tongue should be cut off! There is One above . . .'

'Let us pray,' Gideon said.

A whisper as ringing as a church bell. Upon the workhouse steps they knelt to pray for the child, and for the prostitute.

'We shall supplicate the Lord for them both, for none shall be cast out from the temple of our 'earts, none,' Joshua Slaughter said.

'How will I get to London?'

'I've got some money, my chicken. Don't tell anyone, though. I'll put you on the stage coach.'

It was Monday morning. Mary and Margaret had done two hours of chores and were eating oatmeal porridge in the main room of the workhouse. Mary had been set to do some whitewashing. Her hands were wrinkled and dry with the lime and her clothes were flecked. But she knew they would be out on the roads soon. (Mrs Farrer had given back one of her own sovereigns. 'You go as far as you can from Lady Well and take that child with you. Don't say a word to anyone about anything. You understand? Or by 'Eaven I'll make a case out that you stole my money, and they'll be very glad to 'ear that. Don't linger, neither, or I'll 'ave you in the town gaol for it.')

'Are you coming to London with me?' Margaret asked.

'No, I must stay here. There's someone I want to find.'

'What shall I do when I get to London, then?'

'Listen, my chicken. You must face it. You may not find your mother. She might be wore out by now. If she painted herself like this, she probably . . . well, you just don't last that way for long, though you 'ave a good time doing it. I'm talking to you like your own mother now, my lamb, you can trust me. What were you doing in Liverpool before Pickles picked you up?'

'Can I really tell you?'

'You can tell me. I promise. Poor thing, you've met some evil types, I can see that. But be careful who you do tell the truth to. Generally it's safer with a lie, because if they discover it, you can always invent another. But there's only one truth, and when they find that out they've got you. But you can tell me, all right. I'm like your mother.'

358

'I was 'ere in Lady Well. I was a factory apprentice and I ran away with Edwin on the night of the raid.'

'*Edwin*? Edwin Greave?'

'How did you know?'

'My Gawd! You knew 'im! So where's 'e now?'

'On a ship t'America. 'E stowed on it. He wanted me to go.'

'From Liverpool? Well! Edwin Greave. Oh, my lamb. He's all right?'

'Yes.'

'He's all right!'

'I just told you.'

'Oh my Gawd . . . I'll 'ave to . . . you don't know what you've told me. I can't believe it. You must tell me all about it. Poor lamb. What a life we 'as.'

By mid-morning, they were out in the streets. Margaret was in her rags again. It was quiet now, with most people at work. Mary being scrubbed and shorn, hardly anyone recognised her as their victim of yesterday. A few threw stones at her. Margaret wanted to fling some back.

'Don't bother, chicken. Don't take no notice,' Mary told her.

She followed the directions Mr Binns had given to his house. His door was open and she could hear him at his work. Tap, tap. The woman and child stood in the doorway.

'It's you! God bless us, what 'ave they done to you? 'Ave they all gone mad in this town?'

'I've been in the workhouse.'

'So I 'eard . . . but that they should do that to you! Oh . . . I'm glad Mor Greave 'asn't come back, to see this. 'E loved it so much 'ere. Who's the child?'

'She was in the workhouse too. Horsfall dumped her there.'

'Horsfall? Why should he do that?'

'I'll tell you what Mr Horsfall does, Mr Binns. He collects little girls from wherever he can and does what he wants with 'em. That's your big man of Lady Well for you. I think you should spread the news.'

'Horsfall! We all know 'e gets up to something in that big 'ouse, I didn't think it was that. I thought it was just . . . how do you know?'

'Because I've been in there myself. Nobody saw me go in and out because I was told not to be conspicuous. We want a cart to take us to Halifax.'

'I can find you a cart, lass. I'll send my lad to the alehouse, they've got

359

one. I don't want your money, ma'am – put it away, do. It offends me, that stuff.'

He got up from his bench and last, found his stick and went into the recesses of his house. Mary took Margaret to the wall at the far side of the road. She lifted the child up so that she could look over.

'It's beautiful,' Mary said. 'Isn't it?'

'There's the mill,' Margaret answered.

Mr Binns came back, and crossed the road to them.

'Here's a hat for you. You can't go about like that,' he said. 'Greave used to stare over that valley for hours. Rapt. "What do you find to stare at?" we used to think. Nobody ever dared ask him, he was so absorbed . . . 'E's 'appen better off with his memories. All their noise now would break 'is 'eart.'

'I'll tell you something else,' Mary said, pulling the cap tight over her skull. 'Margaret, tell Mr Binns about Edwin.'

''E's gone t'America.'

'She's talking about Edwin Greave,' Mary said to the incredulous Binns.

'I saw 'im onto the ship. We walked to Liverpool. We walked all the way.'

'Will you tell Phoebe Greave where 'er son's gone?'

'I don't like the woman, but she ought to know,' Binns said. 'She probably won't believe me . . . no, put your money away! 'Ere's your cart. No, I told yer! I don't want no money. Let me 'ave the satisfaction of doing a woman and child a good turn. I 'ave to 'ave some pleasure out o' this weekend.'

He could not take it all in. They left him confused but smiling, leaning on his stick and his wooden leg in the middle of the road.

'Where did you come from?' Margaret asked Mary when they were in the cart.

'I'm from nearby, chicken. I wasn't supposed to live, but I did do, against all the odds. I've gone on like that. Let that be a lesson to you. 'Cos o' the mark, they told my mother I was dead and buried. But I was carried off to foster parents. You ever 'eard of Anne Wylde?'

'No.'

'She was my mother.'

'I like stories.'

'When you get to London, I'll give you an address of my friend and a note to take.'

'You can write notes? You must be a lady, then.'

'I learned on the way up. If I was you I'd try to learn too, but don't ever tell anyone. It's surprising what people leave around when they don't think you can read it. And you'll meet all sorts of important people when you're in London. Keep your eyes open, 'cos anything you find out could turn out useful and maybe save your life. When you get to London go straight to my friend in 'Olywell Street. It's not far from the stage coach stop. Don't talk to any men or women on the way, because they'll be looking out for a child like you, and don't go down no back alleys. You go straight to 'er door, not looking left nor right, give 'er my note and she'll look after you. You might see some strange things going on, but don't get frightened of anything because my friend'll take you in and look after you. She'll probably make you 'er maid, so that you'll learn the ropes and you can watch what goes on without the danger of being touched for a while.'

'Touched?'

'Yes,' Mary continued hurriedly. 'There's some men like a maid demure, but my friend won't let anything 'appen to you until you're ready. You've 'ad that experience in any case. She'll teach you things that in the end'll make you a real gentleman's . . . an aristocrat's . . . 'ave you ever 'eard of Lady Hamilton?'

'No.'

'Oh, that's a story. There's love. Well, you could easily become a second Lady Hamilton. I wish I 'ad my time over again. You'll be learned to play an 'arpsichord.'

'What's that?'

'Bless you, child. You'll soon learn what an 'arpsichord is at Mrs Rawdon's London establishment, and learn to play it marvellous, too. Clementi, Mozart. You might meet a general through it. You'll even be learned to compose your own songs and perform them delightful. That's an accomplishment I never 'ad. You'll be learned to dance.'

'Dance? Me?'

'And you'll be taught to act perfect. Already you can talk well. That's a worthwhile accomplishment to start with. I don't know where you've learned it, but you're good at it. There's a gentleman to be found for every peculiarity under the sun, but what no gentleman can't stand is being bored. That's one of my secrets I'm telling you.'

They had reached the coach stop in Halifax, outside The Cock Inn, where years ago Mary had heard Joanna Southcott.

361

'Edwin was always talking.'

'That's where you've learned it, then. There's no one I can't talk to. I can take 'em all on.'

Mary paid the driver. When no one was looking she handed Margaret the sovereign that Mrs Farrer had given back. Margaret, in her rags but clean, was kissed and patted, then stowed in the coach.

Margaret was waving, waving; a little golden-haired thing laughing her head off, out of the window of the coach as it sank into the dip towards the parish church. It could be Harriet. Mary wondered if the child would cry later. The coach started to climb Beacon Hill. Mary marked its slow ascent to the gibbet on the crest of the hill; the first and the last gruesome sight for the visitor, travelling from or to London.

Mary turned away. It seemed to her that there was now not a soul around her. She was not in a deserted place, yet she felt utterly alone. Where was Mor? Not in Lady Well, evidently. Would he want her, if she found him; could she persuade him to believe her; should she go on looking for him? Would he even believe what she had to tell him about Edwin?

She was a worn out prostitute, pregnant and poisoned. With half of her money still hidden in the lining of her cosmetic box, she had enough money to last for a year, but not enough to set up her own house, like Mrs Rawdon's. She ought to spend her money on an abortion and eke out her remaining cash for as long as she could, offering herself at cheaper and cheaper rates to rougher and yet rougher soldiers and artisans, pretending to despise 'that 'ole down there', the garden she wanted to cultivate for Mor Laverock Greave. Nothing for her but lying to and lying below soldiers.

Perhaps another Mor Greave would come along, as the first did, sitting in the corner of a public house, waiting for her to walk towards him? No, there wouldn't be another one. She could still smell him over her body. She could taste him, too. The taste of his particular sweat clung to her tongue.

She had worked out her plan when lying in the workhouse infirmary bed, amongst the cockroaches. Already her steps were in the direction of Sowerby Bridge; sooner or later a soldiers', a farmer's, or a merchant's cart would turn up to take her to Delph.

She would go back to Gartside. In his care she would bear Mor Greave's baby. Gartside would be happy, serving her, washing the baby, and tending the house. He was an educated man, to bring up

Mor's child. Gartside had his own modest means of livelihood. Mary had her savings that would last for many years when sharing with Gartside. She could get Gartside to set down her memoirs for her, to sell in Holywell Street. That wouldn't be no 'Beggar's Complaint', that wouldn't. That'd be a novel worth looking at, make her famous and a lot of money. Mary had always said she'd end up with a reformed homosexual, for a quiet life. She didn't actually mind if Gartside reformed or not, of course she didn't. That was his business entirely. She'd keep a tight rein on him in other respects, the domestic especially; make him happy; and in the liberty he needed she'd provide him with a cover. That was all the 'rights of man' that she could see was necessary. He could say the baby was his own, and pretend he was a proper married man. She'd back him up in that. Most important of all: if or when Mor came looking for her again, she was certain that the place he would go to pick up her track would be where he had last seen her, at Gartside's.

She couldn't see how life might have offered her a better plan. It made her laugh to herself as she came along the roads.

Leaving Mary in Delph, Mor had walked seeing nothing but the animal-like humps of the hills and the flow of stars; hearing the creaking of his jerkin and the crunch of his boots, but listening to his own nagging thoughts. He felt anger at the very darkness, and carried the stupid hope that daylight would bring release.

By the time that the cocks were crowing that Sunday morning, Mor had got beyond Denshaw and was well on the road to Lady Well. Upon the hills he heard the calls of the cocks rising up out of the half-ring of valleys behind him. He was given a lift in a cart by a group of Methodists who, as chance would have it, were all going to Lady Well, which, they told him, had been 'awakened'.

'Many a Devil's ploughman there is cultivating the pastures of the Lord. There's come wonderful preaching being given out by the converted. Myself, I'm a tailor. You'd be surprised how my trade has flourished since I became Methody. Just out of following righteous ways. Keeping proper accounts. You don't play . . . forgive my asking, sir . . . Devil's tunes on that there fiddle instrument?'

'I play the music that belongs to Heaven.'

Mor left the cart at Ripponden, choosing to walk secretly back to his home, avoiding farms and villages, tracking over moorlands and unenclosed commons under the sweet cascades of morning lark song.

He skirted the upper fringes of the woods, and dropped to the river bank far downstream of Lady Well, tracing it upwards.

By now he was in the midst of a fulsome early summer morning that was lightly boiling with bird song. In the enclosures of a broad valley, yellow currents of buttercup flowers ran through the grass. The fields lay under a misty foam of seeds, light purple and ready for mowing. Across the meadows he could see the river in a curving, broken line. It was a slower, wider river here than the one that tumbled immediately below Lady Well. Mor ignored the notices, the messages of which he had read a thousand times before, and climbed a new-made wall to reach the river.

He had to get into Lady Well without being seen. His plan was to sneak in to Phoebe, reassure her, and escape to the hills again. Wanting to take something with him, he waded through the grass with the excitement that he never could restrain when approaching a river.

There she was, brown and white. He stared at her as she gracefully slid by, taking upon her back the buttercup petals that overflowed out of the meadows. Pale green flowers of alder and willow dripped from overhead. The swell upon the pools gleamed with scraps of blue fallen from the sky. The pools were great concave eyes, with blue irises. Sometimes the water ran too fast to catch anything, but yet was itself a sky of tiny clouds, glittering silver, as it scalloped over stones and beds of weeds.

He dug around in the meadow, until he found some grubs and worms. He took out of his bag the length of line he had stolen from Mr Burton's. With soft reverential tread, Mor went along the bank-side. Putting his fiddle and bag in the grass, he paid out his worm, in one or two places without luck. He did not really think they were good spots in which to fish, but they were where he was not in sight of farms, cottages and the road.

He stood on the outer curve of a river bend, watching the water slide in a thin glaze over a sand bank on the far side, but moving swiftly, dark brown and deep, close to him. Here was a thick swathe of weeds, and he knew it was at the edge of this where the best trout would lie. They had a channel with plenty of depth in which to manoeuvre, cover nearby, and fast water full of oxygen that brought down plenty of food.

He crept along the bank to where he could float his worm downstream, along the edge of the weeds. He had to keep eyes and ears awake in all directions – up and down the bank, on the river and across the meadows. He picked up the sound of water fluting between the stones, a lark three meadows away, and the iron-rimmed wheels of a cart grinding upon stones, hidden by trees. His own quiet alertness spread its own hush over the land. It made him feel that all of nature was attentively conspiring with him.

One end of the line he fastened tight around the first finger of his right hand, looping the remainder around his second finger. He knelt and used his left hand to thread his worm into the current of water, delicately as a woman threading the eye of a needle. The floating worm spread in a bow amongst the bubbles and was carried swiftly away, as Mor paid out the line.

Even though it was what he was hoping for, the snatch of a two-pound trout took him by surprise. With the jolt upon his hand, a thrill went through this whole body. No time for anything now except bringing in that fish. With terrific speed it leapt a foot clear of the water, curving upon its tail. A trout sometimes jumps in sheer joy of a summer's day. With the same leap, desperately fast, it expresses its anger and frustration at being caught. Making a great *bang* it plunged back into the depths. Fortunately for Mor it did not retreat into the weeds, but made a fast commanding line across the river. You could read pain and anger from the silver thread creasing the dark surface, the fish itself hidden. Back across the current; back and forth, making fierce silver cuts. As it weakened, Mor pulled it in. The trout drew away from him, making sad little coils of its body out of the water, weak desperate resistances.

Sic transit gloria mundi. A minute ago it was a king, glorying in its health and power in the river. Now it was upon the bank, trying still to resist its death, thrashing about in an element that finally it could not defeat. The chaos of a creature drowning in air, dropped off the edge of its world, had a maddening, disruptive effect on Mor, too. He, who thought that he drew in the fish, was drawn by the fish into its own chaos.

It lay still for a second, panting, hoping to recover. Its gills and mouth were throbbing, useless. For a brief moment it tried to use its tail but it was useless. Mor, gripping its fat sides, inserted his left thumb down its throat and bent its head back, to break its spine.

The trout tried to leap, to find its life again. With no water to spring from, it gave a desperate wriggle of head and tail. It had put up its last violent resistance to death. The grip of Mor's hand loosened, his thumb slipped about in its wet throat. The fish's mouth and gills filled with blood.

Its soundlessness, other than the squeak of its flesh and the crunch of still-living bone as Mor broke it, was awful. Mor, frantic to end its pain as quickly as possible, found an anchorage for his thumb again in the well of blood, and with a last effort he broke its back.

He removed the hook from its lip.

Panting, he looked quickly around. There still wafted towards him nature's sounds, conspiring with him, from the meadows. A lark, the same or another one, was singing in the distance. Another small bird was whispering peacefully amongst the alder twigs.

He wiped his bloody hands on the grass. He wrapped the fish in broad leaves of water irises and put it in his bag, with the line. He rubbed his hands together in the river, then wiped them on the grass once more. He looked about him again. He slung his bag and fiddle over his back.

He was not looking where he put his feet and the steel jaws of the man trap shut upon his lower-leg. The crash of metal startled moorhens from the reeds and sent a pair of wild duck, beyond a bend in the river, shooting into the sky. There was a frozen numbness in his calf, then a pain bolted through his thigh, his loins and his spine. The harmony of nature was shattered.

He stumbled, so that his flesh was torn further on the jaws. He fell, and tried to protect his violin. He could not rise again.

He was plunged into that same chaos, fallen over the edge of the world, that he had made for the fish. The meadows, that had conspired with him, had turned into enemy country.

His muscles quivered, his arms were covered with the goose-flesh of fear. He rid himself of his encumbrances, putting them at his side, then he heaved at the great saw-blades. He could prise them no further than a quarter of an inch. It was just enough to release the first spurts of blood, which flooded around the steel teeth, as it had flowered in the mouth of the trout. Horsfall's traps would have sharpened teeth, damn him. In a second Mor had to let go of the blades. All he had achieved was to ease them far enough to enable them to spring back deeper into his flesh. Yet, like the fish that had struggled in his hands, he must try again. In anticipation of pain, he clung to the jaws, like someone gripping the edge of a cliff. As he grew tired, the spring seemed to tighten. His arms were quivering and his back aching. His blood was fountaining around his fingers.

Here was the red flower that he had dreamed of: this blood flowering out of the wound. He tried to release the jaws gently back into his flesh, but the moment he eased the tension, they sprang back, and he fainted.

He came choking out of his faint with vomit in his throat. He was lying on his back, with a bright silver glaze of sky above him. He had to turn upon his side, or choke to death. He dribbled vomit over his clothes and onto the grass. A pain shot through his head. His leg was throbbing, but around the wound the flesh was numb.

He lay on his back again. He tried to ignore the thought of the hours, perhaps days, he might have to lie here. He might end up eating grass, insects, and raw, rotting fish. He put out his hand and drummed his fingers on the sounding board of his fiddle. Tall grass-blades hung above him, and red sorrel in shifting discs of enflamed sunlight. Absurdly normal sounds reached him. The sound of church bells and, he thought, snatches of hymn-singing from Lady Well. Above and around the nub of a hill, rooks were swarming over something in the grass.

He fainted again. He awoke to the throbbing pain. He put his hand out to his fiddle and bag. He half-dozed, or half-fainted, once more. Thus he endured through the afternoon. He was dizzy from hunger as well as from pain. The light, after it had silvered, began to yellow. He went to sleep.

When he awoke it was in moonlight and he was being lifted up at his head and feet by two men, who carried him in the honey-light of a swaying lantern, trampling through the meadow grass unheeding of the problems they were making for the mower. The one at his feet took Mor's bag, the other, his fiddle.

The jolting that awoke Mor gave him such pain that he almost swooned again. He tried to steady himself by fixing his attention, but the stars were reeling. The rocks on the crest of the hills, the trees against the sky, jumped up and down, like the teeth of the trap. He stirred as little as possible, and pretended to be still unconscious.

They were taking him to an isolated barn. They carried him in at the big cart-doors, which were already swung wide open. Half a dozen soldiers and a recruiting sergeant were inside, wearing red tunics encarnadined further by the firelight. He glimpsed several other figures, in murky clothes like his own, amongst the shadows. The shadows were many because there was no outlet for the smoke other than the open door, so it puthered around until it found the one horizontal exit. Mor was tipped onto the straw. He screamed. He fainted again.

When he came round, a sergeant held the coil of fishing line over him.

'You've been poaching Mr 'Orsfall's trout. You'll be transported.'

A surgeon knelt impatiently beside him, picking at Mor's wounds with tweezers, pulling away bits of grass and rust.

'You are a rogue, sir! Sergeant, have some hot water brought.'

'Any 'onest man 'as to be a rogue, or let the worst rule. That knocks the 'eart out. Destroys the man in you.'

'Only bruised and torn,' the surgeon murmured, feeling Mor's leg. 'But he's delirious. Listen to him.'

'He's brought his own dinner with him out of the river, though,' the sergeant said, rooting further in Mor's bag. 'Here, soldier, take this and clean it for us.'

He pulled out *The Beggar's Complaint*.

''Ere, what's this? Writing? *I* can't read it. What about you, doctor?'

'Later,' the surgeon answered. He took a glance at what the sergeant was flipping open before him. 'Sedition. The place is rife with it. Probably written by himself, from the way he talks. I think we might have an interesting customer here, sergeant.'

'Anyone 'ere can read?' the sergeant shouted through the barn. 'Anyone 'ere can read bewks?'

Hot water had been brought. The surgeon wiped Mor's wound. He shook sediment and liquid together in a blue-coloured bottle. The sergeant found someone to peruse the manuscript. He returned to his captive.

'So you're a thief,' the surgeon said. 'Are you also what is termed a "Ludd"?'

He put something on Mor's wound that made him scream.

'You tell him, doctor . . . 'ere, look at this!' the sergeant said, pulling something else from Mor's bag. 'A lace 'andkerchief. Now what lady did this belong to?'

The surgeon left. Someone, he couldn't see where, was playing Mor's fiddle. It hurt Mor because it was being strummed so badly. The sergeant was watching the expression on his face.

'You play the fiddle, then?' the sergeant asked. 'You play it well? You must do, to carry it everywhere with you, even when you go poaching. Listen, my friend. They'll hang you for stealing trout, when they know you're a Ludd. There's the doctor's evidence now. How would you like to be a soldier of the King? The doctor'll not bother about the case if you've taken the oath. You're not much good to us, but I can use a fiddler, to keep the lads quiet.'

'The King is mad.'

'It's either the mad King, or the hangman, comrade, after what you wrote. Listen to this. "The 'ole of England, the 'ole of our common lands, is turned over to the profit or the sport of a gang of naves what runs Parliament without being elected by the people." That's what you wrote, in't it? "We can 'ave any future we choose, but ours 'as been sold to the manufacturers." You Ludds 'ave 'ad it, friend. Doomed. So what, if you're right? General Maitland came to Manchester with seven thousand more men last week, to settle your business. Frightened 'em to death in Manchester, the sight of 'em. I'll give it to King Tom, 'e knows 'ow to cut a dash. 'E put two thousand of us in one camp on the edge of town. What a sight! Chill the blood. That was three regiments poised. One Catholic, one Church of Scotland, one C. of E. That's so we wouldn't get together and start a revolution in the army. I don't give a bugger myself, I'm C. of E., Buckinghamshire, a lovely village I come from, and I expect you're the same. We 'ad a fine time off-duty, fighting about the fucking Virgin Mary. They know 'ow to set us up, this "gang what runs Parliament without being elected", don't they? And we're a lot o' silly sheep, fighting about the Virgin Mary just because we like a scrap. Well, it's off to Napoleon with your fiddle and your bit o' lady's lace, old man. That's the best I can offer you, take it or leave it. You could say, your fiddle's saved your miserable life. You're lucky.'

Mor rested all day Monday on a pallet in the barn, a bloody bandage round his leg. On that day he took the King's oath and shilling.

Day after day, others were brought in from the recruiting gang's forays amongst the hill hamlets. They dragged in refugees and suspects, to bottle them up safely in the army. Many of the finest were already in the forces, and though the gang were not very pleased about their catch, it didn't matter. What was wanted was to dispose of rebels as cannon-fodder.

The smoke was making Mor's eyes sore, but at least he was excused from the drilling, because of his ankle and his leg. He watched the light changing across the door, observed what was going on in the barn, and met up with one or two old acquaintances. He had his food brought to him, and he could think. He was no longer 'his own man', that indeed had been brief, but on the other hand he liked the company, and he had more time than he had ever enjoyed for playing his fiddle.

On the day before they were all moved off to Leeds to be given uniforms and arms, Mor got hold of some paper and wrote to Phoebe. Gideon would read it to her.

'I expect to be soon transported overseas to take up arms against Bonaparte, but thanks to the truth of the things in which I have believed, I can trust that fortitude will not desert me . . .'

'You going to take that stone with you?' asked the recruiting sergeant who liked fiddle music, when Mor was well enough to sit up by the fire. 'What you going to do wi'it, fondling it all the time like it was a lady's breast? You going to throw it at Bony Part when you meet him?'

A private came running in at the door. He leapt in the air, jumped and scrambled through the barn, shouting for the sergeant.

'Perceval's been murdered, Serge! They're singing and dancing in every village through England. There's crowds mobbing Parliament. Liberty's come. There'll be reform in the army.'

He grabbed the waist of a recruit, and twirled him in a waltz.

'No more cat!'

'Between you, me, and the gatepost, who is this Perceval?' asked the sergeant. He was thinking it must be some mill-owner, magistrate or perhaps an army officer.

'The Prime Minister of England,' Mor told him.

'Don't you know, Serge? I've just 'eard from someone come on the stage coach from London. They said he was Prime Minister. They're dancing in the streets in every town between here and London, they said. Mummers are out. Bonfires lit. They're composing ballads.'

'I've always 'eard it was Castlereagh, you swine,' the sergeant growled.

'Well, it doesn't sound as though it's Perceval anymore,' Mor said.

'Friend, he died like Caesar. Fell lifeless in the lobby, cut down at the 'ands of King Ludd . . . Where's the lobby?'

'To the 'Ouse of Parliament,' Mor told him.

'I've just 'eard the 'ole account . . .'

'Be careful,' warned the sergeant.

'O'course – sedition, Sergeant, o'course, I understand. We don't want none o'that. Don't want to break rank, Serge. We're 'ere to defend the country, aren't we? Our dear Prime Minister, God bless 'im, gave up his dearly beloved soul, so I 'eard, at the 'ouse of Lord Colchester, then was taken by his tearful family to Downing Street nearby. That's where they live. There was I believe not one dry eye in the Parliament. Nor should there be. Lord Castlereagh could not give a dry utterance to 'is sentiments, they said. Instead they give fifty thousand pounds to Mr Perceval's children and two thousand a year for life to Mrs Perceval.' He laughed. 'What do you think o' that, Serge?'

'Be careful.'

'Right, Serge. I don't know 'ow the nation will recover, but we'll do it. Trust the lads.'

Deeper into the barn, 'Parlyment's been shot dead in their beds,' a recruit passed the word on, with a smile.

'That's a good idea,' his friend replied.

'It's *true.*'

The sergeant was surveying Mor. 'At the 'ands of Ludds, eh?' he said.

'Mr Perceval was about to debate an Act making the taking of Luddite oaths punishable by hanging,' the private said. 'You know how they talk first, before they go and hang someone. Stands to reason who 'sassinated 'im, don't it? And so they should – string up Ludds, I mean.'

'Then they'll be hanging his desperate fellows in these parts, even more than they intended,' the sergeant said, still looking at Mor. He pulled *The Beggar's Complaint* from his own bag. He went to the fire and burned Mor's manuscript. He turned to smile at him.

'Evidence,' he said. 'They don't like it, even in the army.'

Mor flushed with anger. My immortality. Then he remembered what Mary had said: *The only things of ours to get remembered are what we confess to, when they hang us.*

Wisdom, for such as me, lies in living for the day.

'There'll be a new Constitution for England, Serge! An end to flogging in the army. The war'll be over. We'll be friends with the French at last.'

The sergeant gave a slow wink at Mor.

'"One who suffers, hopes. And one who hopes, believes." What do you say, weaver?'

Glossary

Batty: mad, crazy.

Boggart: ghost.

Croft: a small piece of enclosed ground.

Gawping: staring.

Hinny: beloved (Northumbrian).

Mardy: lacking in toughness.

Nobbut: nothing but.

Nowt: nothing.

Owt: anything.

Puther (variation of 'pother'): smoke or cloud of dust; to billow in a cloud.

Skip: a large basket.

Summat: something.

Tenter: a frame, erected out of doors, for stretching cloth.

Yonderly: absent-minded and dreaming, staring into the distance (from 'yonder').